A CONTEMPORARY MYTHOS

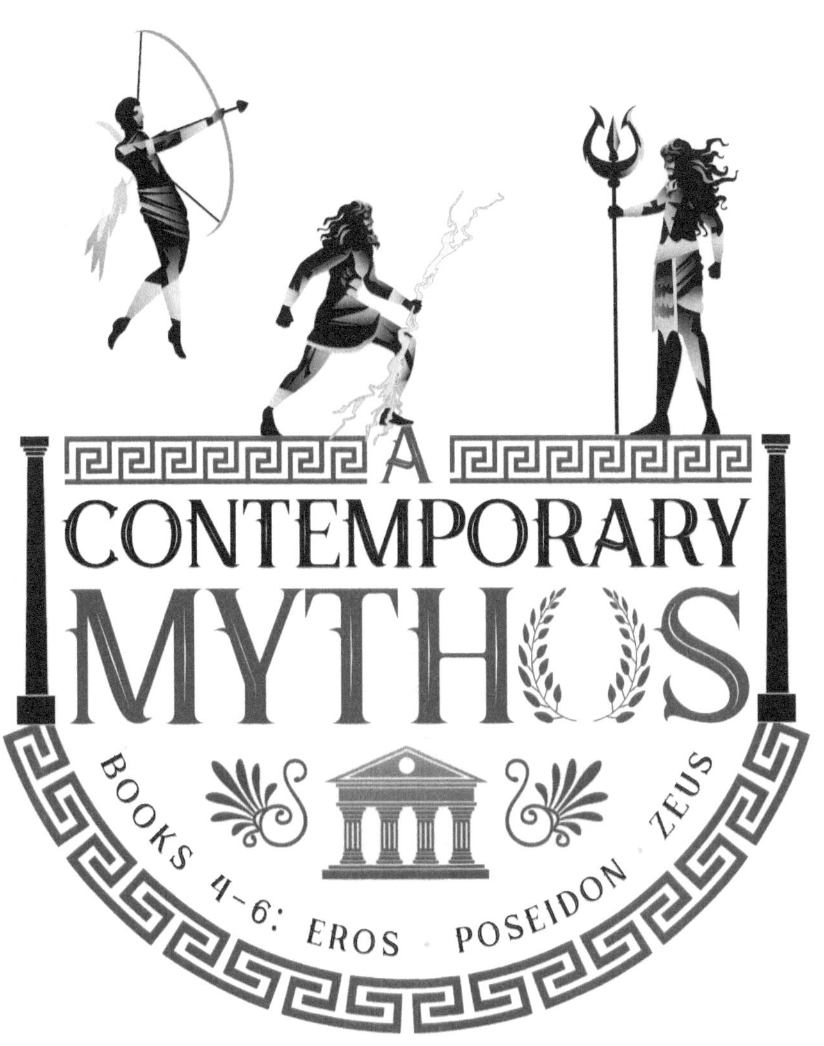

CARLY SPADE

A CONTEMPORARY MYTHOS

BOOKS 4-6: EROS • POSEIDON • ZEUS

Copyright © 2023 by Carly Spade

WWW.CARLYSPADE.COM

Published in the United States by World Tree Publishing, LLC

Cover and Interior Formatting by We Got You Covered Book Design

WWW.WEGOTYOUCOVEREDBOOKDESIGN.COM

BOOK FOUR

EROS

*There is the heat of Love, the pulsing rush of Longing, the Lover's whisper,
irresistible—magic to make the sanest man go mad.*

HOMER

ONE

MY CLIENT SAT ACROSS the desk, chatting away about something or other. The blinking purple notification light distracted me from giving her my full attention. It was either a text message or spam mail—the desire to know overshadowed Mae Stanford's exclamation of finding true love. I illuminated the screen, scratching the back of my neck in an attempt to hide the fact that yes, I *did* check my phone during a client meeting.

One text. From Dad. Not who I'd hoped yet feared it'd be.

I threw the phone in my top drawer and interlaced my fingers on a stack of papers, committing my full and undivided attention to Mae.

"I want to find my soulmate, Miss Stewart," Mae said with glistening eyes.

She was another hopeless romantic who believed in clandestine love. Every other week there'd be someone sitting in the same chair, declaring the same thing.

"Mae, as much as I wish fairy tales were true, I built this business around compatibility. Love is a chemical reaction in the brain. My algorithm pairs you with men whom you're the most likely to form a bond with for the rest of your life." Clicking through several screens, I flipped my monitor to face her, revealing a pie chart and line graph.

Mae stared at the statistics in front of her.

"The statistics don't lie, I'm afraid. The blue here in this pie chart represents married couples still married as a result of the algorithm. The red shows those who didn't follow through with the program, married, and then divorced." I winced.

Mae wasn't paying attention to the screen. Her face focused on me with an

expression bordering on pity. I clicked the pen several times, ready to continue explaining my algorithm until she leaned forward, casting an ominous shadow over my desk from the overhead light.

"Do you really see love like that? Just numbers and colored shapes on a graph? You don't believe your heart could lead you in the right direction itself?" Mae's eyebrows rose, still staring at me.

I jiggled the pen between two fingers. "Once upon a dream, maybe."

Mae sighed and sat back in her chair. "That's a shame. I feel everyone should experience love at least once in their lifetime. Even if you don't end up with the person for the rest of your life."

I tapped my pen against the shiny Elani Stewart nameplate resting near my hand. "My system isn't for everyone. I can understand why you might want to go elsewhere and would take zero offense." A weak smile tugged at my lips.

"I'll give your algorithm a chance. If the stats don't lie, as you say, there has to be something to it. And I've given up waiting for Mr. Right to waltz into the right bar at the right time." Mae smoothed out the wrinkles of her pencil skirt as she stood.

I pushed my rolling chair back with confidence, standing and jutting out my hand. "I promise you won't be disappointed."

She shook my hand with a warm smile. "I look forward to your first round of suggestions."

"You'll be happily engaged this time next year." Mentally, I shrieked at myself for making such a declaration, hoping she hadn't heard me.

Mae laughed as she exited my office. "I'm holding you to that, Miss Stewart."

Dammit.

As soon she was gone, I rolled my eyes at myself and grabbed my phone from its drawer. Knowing it'd been Dad who texted me, I opened the screen without a care in the world. My throat dried.

Another text. From Gary. The man I'd been seeing the past three months. For whatever reason, ninety days marked the hit or miss expiration with virtually every guy I dated. Not on my end—theirs. It was as if they had a secret club I didn't know about and met on Thursday nights to talk about how they'd screw with me.

Sweat collected at the base of my spine as I hit my thumb against the message. After taking a peek, I slumped my shoulders, seeing the words I dreaded most:

I'm sorry, but this isn't working.

Not having the energy to formulate a neutral, "nice" response, I closed the window and switched to my dad's text.

Dad: How's my favorite daughter?

I wasn't his only daughter, and I'd confirmed with my sister Chelsea he always used the same line on her. The man could be so sweet it made my teeth ache.

Smiling to myself, I texted him back and made my way to the hall. The neon "E-romantic" sign blazed from the main floor, casting a purple hue over the closest desks. Passing by row after row of employees feverishly working on keyboards and talking on phones, I shoved my dress jacket sleeves to my elbows, pausing in front of one desk in particular.

Alexandra Chloros. My partner in crime and the only reason I'd been able to get this business off the ground. Her dark eyes peered at me over the rim of her coffee mug—the one I bought her last year for her birthday: WARNING. Contents do not stop this Drama Queen.

"What have you been doing?" I tapped my fingernails against the metal of her cubicle wall.

She sipped her coffee, purposely making it louder than necessary. "Just adding lines to my obituary."

"Could you get any more morbid, Alex?"

Without flinching, she shrugged. "Either I write my own in the case of my untimely demise, or I'll wind up with someone who barely knew me making up things like, 'She could always put a smile on everyone's face,' or, 'She could light up a room.'"

I hung one thumb in the belt loop of my pleated pants. "What about me? Don't think I could write you a good one?"

"We'd probably end up going out together." She tapped her fingernail against the ceramic. "Thelma and Louise style, you know?"

"Ha. The first wise thing I've heard you say all week. I'm certainly heading in that direction." I slipped my phone from my pocket, scrunching my nose at Gary's text. "Number thirteen."

Alex snatched the phone from my hand, glaring at the screen.

"Alex." I reached across the desk to snag it back.

She rolled backward in the chair, thumb feverishly working the touch screen

keypad and not setting her coffee down.

"Alex, do *not* send whatever you're typing." My cheeks burned. It didn't take much to make my skin turn crimson, thanks to my Scottish heritage.

She puckered her lips as she handed the phone back. "Oops. Should've mentioned that ten seconds ago."

My heartbeat thudded in my ears as I took the phone, holding it as if it would self-destruct. "What did you type?"

Alex tossed her bangs from her eyes. "What needed to be said. The guy's been a tool since day one."

Sweet Lord in heaven.

I bit the inside of my cheek.

Gary: I'm sorry, but this isn't working.

Elani: I'm glad you said something first because my vagina was thinking the same thing.

"Alex," I shouted, leaning over her desk when several alarmed heads popped from their cubicles.

"Yes, Lani?"

"What am I supposed to say when he responds to this?"

She rested her mug on the desk and grabbed a napkin, dabbing the corners of her mouth. "He won't. Because I already blocked his number."

"You—" I glanced at my phone. "How did you do that so fast?"

She slow blinked. "This is the part where you say, 'thank you.'"

I inhaled deeply and stood straight, pulling the hem of my button-up shirt. "Thank you. I'm going to grab a snack. Would you like something?"

"A donut," she quickly answered. "And *no* rainbow sprinkles."

"Yes, yes. I wouldn't want to be on the other side of your wrath when colors suddenly entered your life." I half-smiled.

Alex had exactly three colors in her wardrobe—black, grey, and brown.

"I'll be back in a bit. You good with holding down the fort?" I tapped the rhythm of the song *Hit Me With Your Best Shot* by Pat Benatar with my pen.

"Aren't I always?"

I backpedaled and pointed at her. "One of the many reasons I like you."

"Woah, now," Alex shouted across the office as I got farther away. "Like is such

a strong word, Stewart."

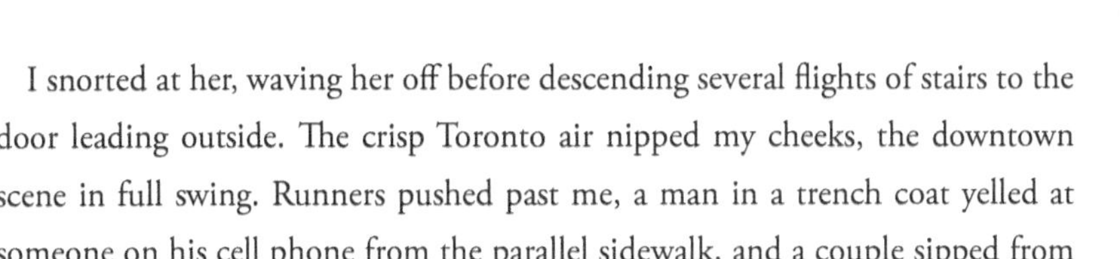

I snorted at her, waving her off before descending several flights of stairs to the door leading outside. The crisp Toronto air nipped my cheeks, the downtown scene in full swing. Runners pushed past me, a man in a trench coat yelled at someone on his cell phone from the parallel sidewalk, and a couple sipped from paper cups of steaming coffee on a bench, giving each other googly eyes. The CN Tower stood tall and proud over the rest of the buildings in the cloudless blue sky.

I pushed through the door of Cupid's Corner, my favorite coffee and pastry shop in all of eastern Canada. They had the best vanilla lattes—rich, creamy, and just the right amount of froth. Their apple fritters were also incredible, but I tried to eat them sparingly as I was sure every bite went straight to my hips. Inside looked like any other coffee shop—small tables bordering the surrounding windows and lounge chairs in the center. What made this place stand out was the décor. Hearts of every size and color were everywhere—the chairs' fabric, artwork on the walls. Even their cups had a red heart where they'd write your name. It was as if every day was Valentine's Day. As someone in the "love" business, it'd spoken to me the moment I walked past it a year and ten days ago.

Securing my hair over my ears, I bent forward, beaming at the array of baked goods on the other side of the glass. I eyed a chocolate donut with chocolate sprinkles and smiled wickedly.

"You ready to order, miss?" The young barista with orange-colored hair smiled at me from the cash register. The overhead lights glinted off his braces.

I spied his nametag. Liam. A heart replaced the dot in the "I." "Yeah. I'll have a small vanilla latte, an apple fritter, and a chocolate sprinkle donut." My stomach did a happy dance, already thinking about the fritter. Perhaps the calories would decide to detour to my butt instead this time.

He flipped a paper cup into his hand and grabbed a marker. "Sure thing. Name?"

"Elani."

He stared at me, unblinking, pleading for a lifeline.

"Spell it however you like. Get creative."

He smiled and nodded his head, scribbling over the heart on my cup.

Once he told me my total, I slid my card into the reader, waiting for the obnoxious sound to remove it.

"Dude, did you check out the *Highlander* show yet?" The other young guy with a buzzcut, making my coffee, asked Liam.

"Nah, not yet. I'm psyched to check it out, though. An immortal Scottish guy with a sword? Can't get much cooler than that."

I leaned against the counter, mildly intrigued. "Are you talking about the show from the nineties?"

Mr. Buzzcut paused the frothing machine, beaming at me over his shoulder. "Yeah. Have you seen it?"

And just like that, only in my thirties, I felt ancient.

"Duncan MacLeod of the Clan MacLeod." I laced it thick with the Scottish accent I knew best.

Mr. Buzzcut's eyes widened, his smile following. "Holy hell. Your accent is better than the guy on the show, eh."

"My dad's born and bred Scottish. I grew up hearing the accent every day of my life."

He finished frothing my coffee and popped a lid on it before handing it to me. Liam scooped my sugary baked goods into a white bag and set them on the counter. I eyed what should've been my name on the cup, only to see the word "Psyche" written over the heart.

"Psyche? That's not even the same ballpark as my name." I furrowed my brow, blowing on the hot contents from the small opening on top.

"Not 'psyche.' Psych," he shouted, doing some weird kind of gesture with both hands.

The way he'd said it confused me. Because the way he spelled it was clearly pronounced with a long "e."

"Ah. *Psych.* You two been watching a lot of nineties stuff lately, huh?" I bit back a smile.

"A lost decade if you ask me," the buzzcut one said.

I raised my coffee. "Cheers to that. Thanks, guys. See you again soon."

As I walked back to the office, I munched on the fritter, fighting the compulsion to moan. A sugary treat was like a proper kiss—the anticipation as you brought the first bite to your mouth, the surge coursing down your neck from the sweetness. Your brain succumbed to its pleasure-inducing possibilities like a reward.

I popped the last bite in my mouth as I entered the main floor. Alex's head slowly peeked over the top of her cubicle, her dark eyes squinting at the bag in my hand. Smiling, I plopped it on her desk and flicked a fritter crumb from the corner of my mouth.

She dug in and her already neutral face stayed as she yanked the donut out. "I thought I said no sprinkles?"

"No rainbow sprinkles." I tapped the tip of her nose. "Besides, those sprinkles match the color of your warm and fuzzy heart."

She bit into it with a glare. "Well played, Stewart. Well played indeed."

I turned for my office.

"Oh, hey," Alex shouted, coughing on the donut. "Mae called. Asked for you to call her back."

I gave a curt nod and slipped into my office.

Mae calling already? I hadn't even run the first report yet.

Grabbing my desk phone, I pulled up her profile on my screen and dialed the number.

"Hi, Mae? It's Elani Stewart. You called?"

"Elani, yes! Unfortunately, well, fortunately, I don't need your services anymore."

A metaphorical fist punched me in the stomach. "I'm sorry to hear that…or happy?"

"It was the craziest thing. I met up with a friend at this bar across town after our meeting. The bartender, of all people, introduced me to this guy sitting by himself in a corner booth." She spoke with several upward inflections, and her voice bordered on squeaking.

I undid the top three buttons of my shirt, fanning myself, preparing for what I knew she would say.

"I know you'll think this is crazy, but I'm pretty sure I met the love of my life today. We just clicked."

I grabbed a tissue, dabbing my clammy forehead with it. "Congratulations."

"I'm sorry, Elani. I feel terrible backing out on our agreement."

She'd signed a contract. Typically, there was a convenience fee for breaching it, but I'd feel like a complete ass holding her to it with how elated she sounded.

"Love is love, right?" I kept my tone as smooth as possible, though inside, I fumed.

"It truly is. I hope you find this for yourself one day."

I gritted my teeth, muted the phone, and let out a subdued scream.

Alex whipped open my door, twirling a set of nunchucks in her hand.

I held my palm out, letting her silently know I wasn't being murdered and scrunched my face at her weapon of choice.

Alex glanced at the nunchucks, shrugged, and ducked out.

"Well, Mae, I wish you all the happiness in the world. Can you do me one quick favor, though?"

"Of course," she squeaked.

I turned in my desk chair, facing the window and glaring down the street that led "across town." "Tell me the name of this bar."

"The Arrow."

TWO

"LANI," DAD'S VOICE BOOMED from my laptop speakers.

I jolted in my chair. "Sorry, Da. Sorry."

We were on our weekly Skype video chat due to him living in Colorado. Usually, it'd be an hour-long conversation catching each other up on our lives. My silence alerted him something was up.

"What's the matter with you, lass? You'd be talking my ear off by now about all the couples you helped this week."

I dragged a hand over my face, catching a finger on my lip. "That's precisely the problem."

Dad stared at me disapprovingly through his webcam. I concentrated on the deep grooves in his cheeks—wrinkles that'd sprouted within the past five years. Chelsea had his emerald-colored eyes, but I inherited the chocolate-colored hair with tints of auburn. His had since gone gray, but it suited him. Made him look extra distinguished even though he was the most easy-going man I knew.

"For the first time since I started E-romantic, I had a client find someone on their own in less than twenty-four hours." It sounded crazier saying it out loud.

He rubbed the stubble on his chin. "In a day? Right after signing up with you?"

"Uh-huh. They went to some bar afterward, and the bartender introduced her to the supposed love of her life."

He blinked. "The bartender."

"My reaction exactly. And seriously, who finds the love of their life in a day? Except for Disney princesses." I rolled my eyes.

"Your mum and me."

My heart sank. "Da, you got divorced." It always stung bringing up mom. Not only did I have to witness the death of true love as a kid, but then we lost her two years ago in a boating accident.

"Aye, that's true. But if we would've met at a different time, under different circumstances, perhaps things would've gone differently."

I stuck my bottom lip out. "Whose side are you on here, old man?"

"Lani." He leaned forward, filling the screen with his face, and slipped his wire-rimmed glasses from his nose. "You know I hate seeing ye like this. You can't use what happened to your mum and me as an excuse for the rest of your life."

I picked at the Intel label next to the keypad of my laptop. "It's not an excuse. It's reality."

My phone buzzed on my desktop, making a loud rattle as it bounced. I narrowed my eyes at the notification of a new e-mail.

Dear Miss Stewart,

I will no longer need your services to find a partner. As luck would have it, I found the man of my dreams in a bar. Crazy, right? I appreciate everything you've done for me these past few months and hope there aren't any hard feelings.

Sincerely,
Nicholas

"You've got to be shitting me." I dropped my phone, thankful for my thick carpets.

"What's goin' on?" Dad squinted at the camera.

It couldn't have been the same bar, right?

"Da, I've got to go. I just got yet another e-mail from a client canceling my services. I've got to stop this or risk losing half of my clientele by the end of the week."

"You're gonna confront them, aren't ye?" His bushy eyebrows furrowed.

I leaped up and grabbed my purse. After tripping over my phone, I grabbed it

and threw it in my bag. "Something like that."

"Dinna lose yer heid, Lani girl." Dad's tone dropped an octave.

I forced a smile. "I'm calm. I'm fine. Everything is *just* fine." Hovering my finger over the end call button, I waited.

Dad chuckled. "Love ye."

"Me too."

As soon as his face disappeared, my fake smile morphed into a scowl.

This bartender didn't know who they were messing with.

I breezed into the office, giving quick waves to any employees greeting me. Once I reached Alex's desk, I jutted my thumb behind me. "I need you to come with me to a bar."

Her thin eyebrows rose, and a corner of her lips quirked. "Happy Hour in the middle of the workday? Now we're talking." She maniacally grinned at me as she locked her computer and grabbed her jacket. "Which bar?"

"The Arrow." I laced my words with a dash of venom.

"Huh. This may surprise you, but I haven't been to that one."

I stopped at the doorway. "That *does* surprise me."

"Right?"

We made our way outside, and I crossed my arms in a huff when we waited at the crosswalk. "Some bartender at this place is stealing my clients."

"Ah. I knew there was an ulterior motive. You *never* drink in the middle of the day, despite my best efforts."

"Two clients, Alex." I held two fingers up and poked her in the shoulder with them. "Two have inexplicably found 'love' in the past two days thanks to this bartender."

She glared at the spot I'd poked and dusted her jacket. "Isn't that the whole point of our business? To help people find a compatible partner?"

The walk sign illuminated.

"Yes, but that's supposed to be my job. The algorithm's job. Not some whacko bartender who's giving random advice."

My stroll turned into a power walk once we reached the other side of the street.

I paused, realizing Alex wasn't beside me.

"What are you doing?" I motioned with my hand for her to hurry up.

"Calm down. The bar nor the tender are going anywhere." She caught up with me and cocked her head to one side. "Why am I coming with you again?"

"You're my backup." I started power walking again, took a deep breath, and forced myself to slow down.

"Backup? You make it sound like a breach job."

The blazing red neon sign hissed at me. I glared at the arrow flying from one side to the other, landing in a target—The Arrow.

"Oh, it's a high-stakes job, Alex. Remember, fewer clients mean less on *your* paycheck too."

The skin below her eyes wrinkled. "Valid point." She pushed her jacket sleeves up. "Let's fry the bastard. Wait. Is it a guy or a woman?"

"Does it matter?"

People laughed within the bar, a group of men yelled at the hockey game on one of seven TVs, glasses clanked, and light music played in the background. Various hockey insignia hung on the walls. There were tables on the center floor every few feet and a large mahogany bar at the back.

"Elani," Alex whispered, turning my body to face the bar. "Please tell me that's the bartender."

At first, I rolled my eyes, but a lump formed in my throat once I caught sight of him. A tall man with hair the color of a Hershey's kiss twirled bottles in his palms. He smiled at a group of women huddled on one side, ogling him, curling their hair with their fingers. The blue and green plaid shirt clung to his chest, hinting at his muscular physique. His gaze lifted, tracing on me. I yelped and jumped behind Alex, grabbing her jacket.

"What are you doing?" Alex cocked an eyebrow at me over her shoulder.

"He saw me."

"Isn't that the point? He kind of has to see you for you to rip him a new asshole, right?"

I lowered my head and peered around her elbow. The bartender poured the pink liquid into four martini glasses with a sparkling grin. He dusted his hands off and slung a towel over his shoulder, leaning onto the bar with one elbow. One of the women took the toothpick with sliced fruit from her drink and picked a

piece of pineapple off with her teeth.

"We don't know that he's the Client Thief. It's a bar. There has to be more than one bartender." I squinted one eye, scanning the area for additional workers, but aside from the two cocktail waitresses and some guy loading the kegs, he was it.

"Are you kidding? That guy looks like he could lay more pipe than a plumber."

I tugged on her jacket. "Which has nothing to do with finding the supposed love of your life."

Alex snorted. "Maybe to you."

"Screw it. I'm going in." I stood, tossed my hair back, and pulled on the hem of my shirt.

Alex was already halfway to the bar. I widened my eyes and scampered after her.

"Hi. I'm going to cut straight to the chase, slick. Do you like to play matchmaker on the side?" Alex asked the bartender, folding her hands on the bar top.

The bartender's brows pinched together, and he chuckled—deep and slightly raspy. "I'm sorry?"

I shoved past Alex, forcing her onto a stool. The bartender's gaze met mine, sending a quiver through my stomach. His eyes were like a peacock—the blue part. A wavy piece of hair hung down over his forehead like Clark Kent, and when I glanced below his lips, I had to grab the bar to keep from stumbling backward. He had it—the cleft chin.

"I uh—" I couldn't stop staring at it. Cleft chins were one of my weaknesses. And his was perfect. Prominent but not to the point of collecting water. "She uh—was talking for me."

I could feel Alex staring at the side of my face and elbowed her. She batted my arm away.

"Oh, yeah? Care to explain?" The bartender asked as he leaned forward.

A light scattering of chest hair peeked from the two undone buttons of his plaid shirt. His firm forearm muscles flexed as he gripped the edge of the mahogany.

I thinned my lips and folded my hands in front of me. "I run this dating website. You might've heard of it, E-romantic?"

He shook his head. "Nope."

"You haven't?"

Alex thwacked my stomach to continue.

"Anyway, two of my clients dropped from my program because they came to

this bar and said *you* led them to love." I poked the bar top twice.

"Well, that's great to hear."

"So, it's true?"

"Absolutely."

I could feel my heartbeat in my ears. "It's not great. You're stealing business from me."

Alex remained silent, resting her chin in her hand.

"How's it stealing if I'm getting no kind of monetary compensation for it?" He raised a brow.

I opened my mouth to respond and then snapped it shut. He was right.

"Why don't you tell me more about this site of yours? The first round is on the house."

"I'll have a wine spritzer." Alex's eyelids grew heavy.

I had no intention of having a civil conversation with him, and now Alex sealed us into a round of drinks.

"I'll have whatever. And no Sex on the Beach." I glared at him. He seemed the type to use that drink as a flirtation device.

He bit his lip. "I much prefer it in other places. Too much sand."

One of Alex's hands gripped my knee from under the concealment of the bar.

"Name's Eric, by the way."

Alex nudged her head at me. "Elani. Alex."

"Pleasure to meet you ladies. I'll be right back." He scanned my face before walking away.

"Oh. My. Zeus." Alex's grip tightened on my leg.

"What's the matter with you?"

"Are you kidding? You're a total goner. He has the chin, Lani."

I grabbed a cocktail napkin and started folding it. "I'd like to think a chin won't make me throw all scruples out the window. Besides, this guy is my competition, remember?"

"Right. Right. It makes for some of the best sex anyway."

Eric swayed a shaker in his hand—a wide masculine hand.

"Is that all you think about?"

"No. I also think about storm clouds, how many different ways to kill rodents, and muscular naked man ass."

"How in the world did we become best friends?"

She stared at me deadpan. "My electric personality."

"Here we are. One wine spritzer and—" He set a glass with a bright blue liquid in front of me, placing a lemon slice on the rim. "Sex in the Driveway."

"Ha. Ha. Clever." I slid the glass toward me, trying to ignore the way the drink made his blue eyes pop.

"I thought so." He did one quick bob with his brows.

Alex slurped on her drink, glancing between the two of us.

"So, you run a dating service. How does it work exactly?" He wiped droplets from the bar with a towel.

"They answer a questionnaire, and based on the answers, I've built a database with an algorithm that'll match them to the most likely candidate." I slipped the straw into my mouth, taking the first sip—sweet, peachy, and orangey.

"Candidate for love?"

"No. Compatibility."

He snapped his attention to Alex, who shrugged. "Please tell me she isn't one of those types who thinks love is all scientific bullshit?"

Alex sulked as her eyes roamed everywhere but him.

Eric's gaze returned to me. "You are. Oh, that's rich."

"It's not bullshit." I sat straighter. "My system is guaranteed to find them a partner for *life*, not just some euphoric feeling that's bound to end in heartbreak."

He folded his arms, accentuating his already wide frame. "Wow. The world's certainly done a number on you, eh?"

"What would you know about love anyway? I don't see a ring on your finger."

Alex slid off her stool, crouching and sidestepping toward the bathrooms.

Eric brought our faces closer. "And you're presumptuous. I don't see one on you either. Have you not used your algorithm on yourself?"

I frowned. "Of course not."

He pushed back and held his arms out at his sides. "Do you not trust your creation to find you this supposed compatible partner?"

"I prefer to do it the old-fashioned way. The system is there for those that want to use it."

He snapped his fingers. "I'll tell you what. Let's make a deal."

My heart raced.

"You run the algorithm on yourself. You have three months to find Mr. Right. If you do, I won't play matchmaker anymore."

I eyed him. "Intriguing, but what if I lose?"

A wicked grin tugged at his lips. "You let me edit your code."

I didn't want his grubby, albeit attractive man-hands meddling with my algorithm. "No way. Those fingers aren't going anywhere near my code."

"You seem pretty confident in your system, so what are you afraid of?"

Fury shot down my spine. "Fine. But when I win, you stop with the matchmaking. Not here, not from some donut shop. It stops."

"Do we have a deal then?" He extended his hand.

I stared at his palm as if scorpions crawled over it before slipping my hand into his. As our skin touched, butterflies beat at my stomach, sending a tingle down my legs. We narrowed our eyes at each other, and I snapped my hand back, clutching it to my chest.

"Do you…want another?" He pointed at my empty glass, and I continued to stare at him, absently nodding.

He rubbed his chin as he walked off to make the drink.

Alex flopped onto the stool next to me, whisking her spritzer into her hand. "You two bone yet?"

I didn't look at her, opting to glare at Eric's back instead. "We made a deal."

She choked and sputtered and ran her sleeve across her mouth. "I go to the bathroom and come back to you playing Hades? Making deals?"

Alex's Greek roots ran deep. The random drops and references to myths and gods didn't even faze me anymore.

"If I win, he won't play matchmaker anymore." I finally tore my gaze away from him.

She chugged down the rest of her drink. "Lovely, but what do you have to do?"

"Use my algorithm on me."

"Lani."

"I know, but I should have enough confidence in my system to trust it on myself."

"If you say so."

"I have three months to find him. I can do this." I splayed my hands on the bar, feeling short of breath. "Right?"

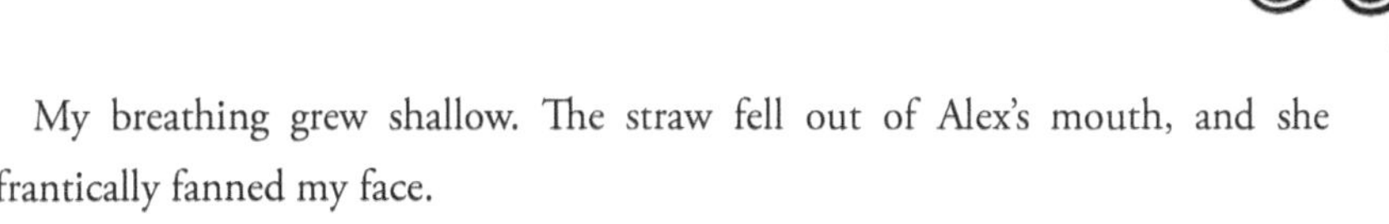

My breathing grew shallow. The straw fell out of Alex's mouth, and she frantically fanned my face.

"What happens if you don't?" Alex thinned her lips.

I cinched my brow as I looked at her. She'd helped me build this business. And here I went putting it on the line over some petty form of competition. My stomach gurgled.

"Lani?" She narrowed her eyes.

I leaned away, whimpering.

"Here we are. More Sex in the Driveway." Eric set the drink in front of me.

I slurped it so fast it gave me brain-freeze. Palming my forehead, I made a *gah* sound.

"Wow. Little antsy?" Eric asked.

Alex smacked her hand on the bar. "Let's see you in action."

"I could take that request in many ways." Eric smiled at her with a hooded gaze.

"As much as I appreciate your gutter mind—" Alex pulled on the collar of her shirt. "I'm referring to your supposed matchmaking skills. Elani told me about the bet. And I don't care if you did a blood bonding shake. I want to make sure you can do what you claim."

"You have a loyal friend here," Eric said to me, tapping his knuckle against the bar.

A lump formed in my throat. I did. I really did. All the more reason, I was the scum of the Earth.

Eric scanned the room, narrowing his eyes with each inch he took in. "Alright. Observe."

He walked to the main floor, rubbing his hands together as he approached a blonde woman sitting by herself.

"Oh. He's actually going to do it. He's serious?" We both turned in our stools to watch.

Eric smiled at the woman, bending over to whisper in her ear. His fingertips grazed her arm, and I could've sworn silver shimmers floated over it.

I blinked several times and rubbed my eyes. The shimmers were no longer there. Eric pointed across the bar to a man sulking by the jukebox. The woman slipped off her chair, smoothing her dress. Eric pressed a finger to her lower back, urging her on and off she went.

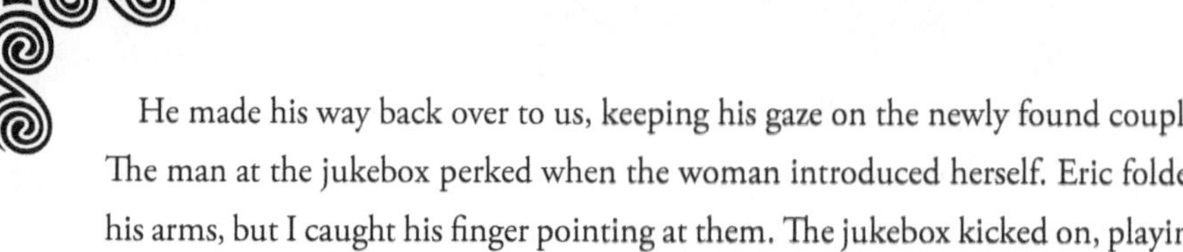

He made his way back over to us, keeping his gaze on the newly found couple. The man at the jukebox perked when the woman introduced herself. Eric folded his arms, but I caught his finger pointing at them. The jukebox kicked on, playing *These Arms of Mine* by Ottis Redding.

"This is one of my favorite songs," the woman shrieked so loudly we could hear her across the room.

Mine too.

Eric dropped his lips near my ear. "Satisfied?"

My insides folded over themselves, and I froze. "Hardly. That proved nothing. But I can't deny what you did for *two* of my clients, so the game is still very, very on."

Alex eyed Eric as he slid behind the bar, a twinkle in his eye.

"Perfect. Have your first dates here as proof you're taking part in the deal. I'll even surprise you with a different drink for each date."

"You think there's going to be that many of them?" Alex asked with a snort.

"No." He gleamed at me. "I *know* there will be."

My insides twisted all at the same time, my teeth clenched in anger. I hadn't mixed emotions like this since the finale of *Lost*.

"How much do I owe you for that second drink?" I dug out my wallet.

He shook his head. "Don't worry about it. You're metaphorically paying me back in spades. Trust me."

My chest tightened, and I grabbed Alex's arm. "Let's go, Alex."

"See you soon, Elani," Eric crooned.

I risked a glance over my shoulder. He dragged a hand through his wavy, medium-length hair, tousling it just right. A breath hitched in my throat, and I pushed Alex outside.

She forced me to face her. "Hey. Are you going to tell me what you bet?"

"The algorithm." I slapped a hand over my face. "If I lose, he gets to alter the code."

Alex's face remained blank. Her lip twitched and as she slid a hand over my shoulder, she stared me down. "Then you better win."

I'd spent most of my adult life searching for my missing half, and now I had only ninety days to find my eternal partner. The exact length as my previous failed attempts. For the love of Zeus.

THREE

COZYING ON MY FLUFFY pale pink comforter, I flipped open my laptop. While waiting for it to start up, I took a quick inventory of surrounding essentials.

"Popcorn. Red wine. And—" I tapped my phone, cueing a playlist. The song *Crystalline* by Amaranthe soothed through the room. I closed my eyes, swaying to the calming sounds of the violin intro.

Propping my elbows in front of the laptop, I took a deep breath. "I can do this. Three-hundred-sixty-five questions and I'll find my most compatible partner." The application window popped open, and I bit my cuticles.

What did I have to lose?

The entire year I took to work on the code. That's what.

Sundays were one of the only days I allowed myself a break from the office. The sun beamed through my sheer white curtains, making the whole process I was about to endure slightly less daunting. I'd opened my window a crack, letting in just enough cool breeze to keep the room fresh and airy. The surrounding ocean landscape paintings I'd hung on my bedroom walls made me wish I were there. On a beach, soaking up the rays and having only one care in the world: what would I eat for dinner.

I slapped my hands against my face. "Focus." Puffing my cheeks, I squinted at the first question. "Question one: Status of your parents? Starting with a doozy. Great."

Grimacing, I selected both "Divorced" and "Mother Deceased." I sipped my wine as I scrolled to the next question.

"Are you a spender or a saver?" I snorted. "I couldn't afford to be a spender if I wanted to."

Munching on some popcorn, I bobbed my head to *Just Haven't Met You Yet* by Michael Bublé randomly playing from the list.

"What is your favorite—" Heat flushed up my neck. "Sexual position?" Alex had to have snuck that question in there. It most certainly wasn't at the top of my list of importance.

An hour dwindled on as I answered question after question.

How do you deal when something makes you very angry?

What social cause is most important to you?

Do you think couples should be one hundred percent open about everything?

It's when I reached question three-hundred-sixty-four that my fingers froze over my keyboard.

Do you believe in soulmates?

The empty wine bottle on my nightstand didn't contain the answer. Nor did the depleted bowl of popcorn.

I selected "No." And it stung. A part of me—a tiny microscopic part of me still wanted to believe it was possible. But try as I might, the universe had given me nothing but lemons for my lemonade since I was a kid. Everyone knows authentic lemonade needs a bit of sugar.

I changed my answer to "Yes," just to see how it'd feel.

"No. No. If this is going to work, I have to be brutally honest." Punching, not pressing, I re-selected, "No," and quickly scrolled to the last question.

I'd been staring at the computer screen so long my eyes were dry. I rubbed my knuckles over them and winced before looking back at the laptop.

Did you have a happy childhood?

Yes, and no? Tears welled in my eyes, fingers hovering over the mouse. I regretted not creating a third option for the question.

The memory was as clear as if it were yesterday. It was my tenth birthday, and my dad wanted to celebrate in Scotland. My sister Chelsea had just gone off to college and couldn't come, making for a vacation with my parents and me. It was my first time there, and having the opportunity to experience a country I found mystical trumped any birthday party with ten of my friends—cake and ice cream be damned.

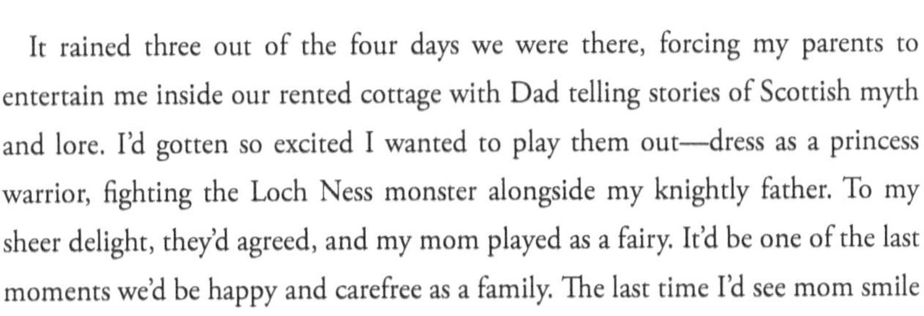

It rained three out of the four days we were there, forcing my parents to entertain me inside our rented cottage with Dad telling stories of Scottish myth and lore. I'd gotten so excited I wanted to play them out—dress as a princess warrior, fighting the Loch Ness monster alongside my knightly father. To my sheer delight, they'd agreed, and my mom played as a fairy. It'd be one of the last moments we'd be happy and carefree as a family. The last time I'd see mom smile lovingly at my dad. And more importantly, the last day I'd believe in fairy tales or true love.

As soon as we were back on American soil, they broke the news of their divorce to Chelsea and me. Devastation didn't begin to describe it. We'd seemed so happy. But looking back, I'm sure the signs were there. Expressions of love and admiration between them were more than likely over *my* happiness. I was too young to notice the anguish in their eyes—the grief of knowing what they'd have to tell me. But I'll always thank them for that final week in Scotland. A single tear rolled down my cheek as I selected, "Yes." Despite how the divorce affected me, they did the best they could.

"I wonder if my clients feel this exhausted after finishing this thing. Man-o-me." After rolling my shoulders, I hit the submit button.

Gathering my empty dishes, I hobbled off the bed, heading to the kitchen. It'd take *at least* twenty-four hours before the system would tabulate a match. I tossed the bowl into the dishwasher and froze when a chime sound echoed from my laptop speakers.

"No." I glared at the electronic notebook nestled on my bed. The HP symbol resembled a middle finger flicking me off in the distance. "No possible way."

Tripping over my area rug and teal-leather lounge chair, I fell onto my bed, staring in disbelief at a new notification on the site.

"It must be an auto-bot or something," I mumbled, clicking into it.

A match.

The name Adrian Foster stared back at me, and my heart raced.

How could the system have worked that fast?

Two more chime sounds went off, followed by another, and two more. I slapped the laptop shut with a shriek.

"Did someone hack the site? Corrupt the code?" I bit my lips together and hopped off the bed, staring at my computer like a ticking bomb.

Roughly tousling my hair, I bounced on the balls of my feet like a boxer preparing for a fight. Before I could psych myself out, I whipped the laptop open and gazed wide-eyed at the dozen matches.

This is fine. Everything is fine.

Without looking at their profiles, I sent off requests for dates to Adrian Foster and Michael Kohns, the first two matches on the list, without even bothering to look at their photos. I shut the laptop and picked it up to throw across the room but rested it on my table instead. My silent cell phone sat there, taunting me. I designed the system to connect with your phone number while keeping it anonymous. Any time now, Adrian and Mikey would be texting me to set up days and times.

I groaned and grabbed the teal paisley throw pillow from my chair, muffling a scream into it. Had I always been this competitive? Or did Eric truly know how to get under my skin?

"Are you positive you don't want me to come with you?" Alex stared at me blankly from her desk chair, swiveling.

Taking one last glance at myself in a compact mirror, I snapped it shut and tossed it in my purse. "Yes. I'd rather you not be there if it goes up in flames."

She continued to rotate back and forth in her chair, slouching far enough to rest her head on the back. "Aw, but I love fire."

"Hold down the fort. I'll see you tomorrow morning."

"Oh? Preemptively planning a nightcap?" She bounced her brow.

"You know I'm not that kind of gal."

She did one full rotation in her chair. "You could be. All it'd take is the right gentle*man*."

After a snort, I said, "Goodnight," elongating the "I."

"Do everything I would do," she shouted at my back.

I slipped my tan wool pea coat over a bright red cocktail dress. Red always seemed to bring out the auburn hidden within my darker locks—an attempt at making more of my heritage shine through. My metallic gold ballet flats clicked against the concrete as I shoved my hands in my jacket pockets and flipped up my collar from the brisk wind.

Once I reached the bar, I paused outside, staring at the blazing logo sign. The neon made faint hissing sounds that increased every time the arrow animated. I looked up at the sky, taking in the twinkling stars and crescent moon.

"To whoever is listening…please make this not be a mistake." I frowned and then gasped as a shooting star launched across the sky.

Good enough for me.

As soon as I walked in, Eric's eyes lifted from the woman he talked to at the bar. He'd been smiling, but when his gaze roamed over my attire, the smile turned sultry. He wore another plaid shirt—red and brown. It unnerved me how attractive the pattern made him look. A design I associated exclusively with lumberjacks when worn as a shirt versus a kilt.

"Well, well. I honestly expected you to back out of this." Eric flipped a glass into his hand, resting it on the bar top and filling it with ice.

"Joke's on you then. I don't break my word." I glanced at the clock hanging on the wall behind him, rhythmically tapping my fingernails.

"Nervous?"

I snapped my gaze to him and answered more abruptly than intended. "What?"

His smile warmed. "Your date?"

"Two, actually. Back-to-back."

"Wow. Already assuming the first one is going to tank?"

"Not at all. I've got quite a few matches, and I need to get through most of them to weed the right one out."

He leaned on the bar, hugging each of his biceps with his hands. "Is that common?"

"What?" I looked behind me at the door, my heart racing every time a man walked in.

"For someone to have that many matches?"

"Weren't you supposed to make me a drink?"

"Already done." He removed a cocktail glass filled with a peach-colored liquid from behind the bar.

I peered into it. "What is this? And what are the floating red balls?"

"Cranberries. This, my dear Elani, is called a Polished Princess. The main ingredient is vanilla vodka." His lips curved with extra snark.

"You're hilarious."

"I do try." His eyes lifted to the door, and his forearms tensed. "Date number one seems to have arrived."

After whipping my head over my shoulder to spy a man at the door looking absently around and rubbing his hands together, I snapped my attention back to Eric. "How do you know that's him?"

"Do you have any idea how many set up dates I see here?"

I clucked my tongue against my teeth. "Touché." Taking my drink with me, I hopped off the stool.

My date had jet-black cropped hair and terra-cotta skin, which blended well with his brown sports jacket and black pleated pants. When his gaze passed me, he squinted and pointed.

Whose idea was it to not look at their pictures at least?

I squinted back.

"Elani?" He asked, edging closer.

"You must be Adrian, judging from the confused look on your face that I'm sure is on mine too." I grinned and held out my hand.

His skin was smooth. Really smooth—so soft I questioned whether I'd put on lotion this morning. His sunken deep brown eyes warmed from my touch, and he gestured toward a table. Pulling the chair by the window out for me, I gave a light chuckle as I sat down. He took his seat across from me, the one facing *away* from the bar. I risked a glance at Eric, and he waved at me—the bastard.

"So, Adrian, what do you do for a living?" I rested my clutch on the table after slipping my jacket off and draping it over the chair.

"I'm a stockbroker." He folded his hands on the table. "And you?"

Was I so dense to think these dates wouldn't ask where I worked?

"I run a uh—a dating site." I bit the inside of my cheek. "The one that matched us."

His bushy eyebrows rose, and he sat back. "Oh."

"Is that a problem?"

His thought process melted down his face like butter. "No. No, it's not. I guess I didn't expect to hear that." He chuckled, and the corners of his eyes wrinkled.

I gave a nervous laugh. "I suppose not."

"Pardon me for saying, but your accent doesn't sound Canadian."

I took a sip of my drink and licked the taste of vodka and pumpkin spice from my lips. "I'm originally from Colorado. I moved here a few years ago to start up my business."

"Lovely." His smile hadn't faded.

"Can I get you something to drink?" Eric appeared out of nowhere with his fingers interlaced behind his back.

Adrian looked up at him, still grinning. "A vodka tonic, please, with a spritz of lime."

"You got it." Eric gave me a thumbs up with a cheeky smile as he backed away.

I glared at him, pretending the neon arrow flashing above his head plunged straight into his chest.

"Something the matter?" Adrian's face went blank.

I launched a hand across the table and placed it on his forearm. "Oh no, no, not at all. I just noticed on TV that Colorado was losing to Dallas. I'm a—big hockey fan."

Minor hockey fan. Out of all sports, it's the one I could stand to watch most.

His eyes beamed at my hand still on his arm, and I slid it back to my lap.

"Oh yeah? I'm more of a baseball fan myself. I think it's more of a nostalgic thing for me." His gaze dropped to the ground.

"How come?"

"My dad used to take me every few months when I was a kid. I lost him to cancer two years ago." He didn't look up.

"I'm so sorry. I lost my mom a couple of years ago. It still stings."

His eyes met mine, and we had a brief moment of mutual understanding.

This was good. We were connecting.

Eric returned with Adrian's drink, resting it on the table with a flourish of his hand.

"Could we get an order of buffalo wings, please? Boneless?" Adrian kept his eyes trained on me.

He didn't even ask me. For all he knew, I could've been a vegan.

"Is that what you want, miss?" Eric's gaze pulled me in, his eyes diving into my soul, searching for the answer he knew I'd bury so deep he'd need a drill.

"Yes. Buffalo wings are super."

Eric idly shook his head with a smirk before walking off.

"What kind of music do you listen to?" Adrian asked.

I circled the rim of my glass with a finger. "Oh, tons. I've got a soft spot for crooners, though."

"Get out. I love Frank Sinatra. What's your favorite song?"

I sat up straighter. "*Strangers in the Night.*"

"This is unreal. Mine too." He cleared his throat and started to sing. Though he was utterly out of tune, it was adorable.

I laughed, trying not to wince at every botched note.

"Sorry. I'm a horrible singer." His eyes gleamed.

"Oh, please. I only sound good in the shower."

My cheeks warmed. Eliciting thoughts of me in the shower at any capacity was not something I wanted to do on a first date.

His face reddened, and we both went silent.

This could work. My algorithm really might work.

"You two doing alright?" Eric aimed the question more at me than both of us.

"Splendid," I answered before Adrian could.

Eric rubbed his neck. "I'll be behind the bar if you need anything."

"Where bartenders usually *should* be. Imagine that." I widened my eyes at him, attempting a non-verbal cue of: Get the hell out of here.

Once he was gone, I turned my attention back to Adrian. He held a wing between two fingers and blew on it, his kind eyes beaming at me from across the table.

I could see myself dating a man like Adrian. I really could. He was kind, down-to-earth, had a great job, and even blushed over the idea of me naked.

Slurp.

The sound jolted me from my daydream.

Adrian chomped on a wing with his mouth open as wide as flood gates. After he swallowed, he proceeded to lick the sauce from each individual finger, sucking them dry like the elixir of life covered them.

I froze.

He did too upon noticing me staring at him. "Something wrong?"

I let out a nervous bout of chuckles. "Nope. Nope. Not at all." After finishing my drink, I shot to my feet. "Is your drink empty? Let me get us another round." Not letting him answer, I scooped his half-empty glass and power-walked to the bar.

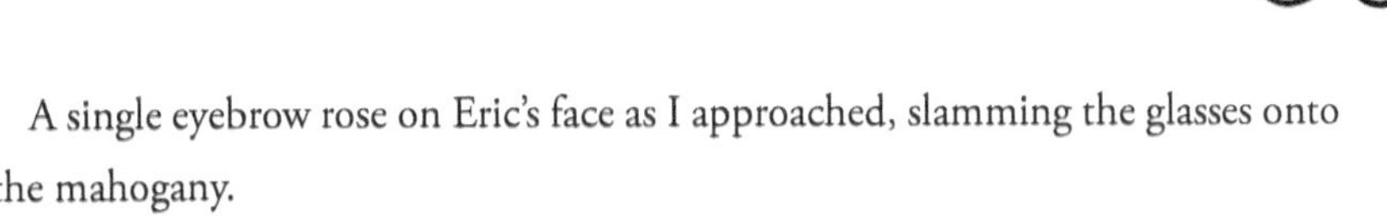

A single eyebrow rose on Eric's face as I approached, slamming the glasses onto the mahogany.

"Can I have another one of those but with a tad more, I don't know, alcohol?"

He eyed me sidelong, sliding the glasses away from me. "Things sound like they're going well."

"What gives you that impression?" My eye twitched.

He tapped his finger against the glass in his hand, waiting.

"Okay, fine. It was great until he revealed he eats like a hippo."

"Funny, I would've thought him ordering food without asking you would've been the deal-breaker."

"You enjoy this, don't you? Seeing me squirm? It's why you made a bet in the first place."

He sunk his face near mine. He smelled like fresh laundry, cinnamon, spice, and not one damn thing nice. "After this is over, you'll be able to tell *me* why I made a bet, and I won't have to say a word."

"Is this what you live for? Like, riddles?"

"Nah, I'm more about passion, honestly." He stepped back. "And I'm pretty fond of archery."

"Archery? What are you, Robin Hood?"

"Better." One of his eyes halfway winked before both fell in a blink.

"What are you doing with your eyes?"

"…winking." His gaze shifted, looking uncomfortably perplexed.

"That was definitely a blink. You closed both eyes."

"No, I didn't." He glared.

"Yes. You did." I glared back.

"Why don't you be a big girl and go call it off with Hippo?"

"Fine," I seethed, holding my head high and turning away.

The hard part wasn't breaking the news to Adrian that we weren't meant to be. It was the fact a second date would arrive in moments. In hindsight, I probably should've scheduled them further apart. Maybe even months in between. However, the worst of it was another date meant a potential repeated disaster and a reality I wasn't ready to accept.

FOUR

ADRIAN SOLIDIFIED OUR INCOMPATIBILITY when I told him it wasn't going to work out by stomping his foot like a two-year-old and announcing he wasn't paying our bill—one huge bullet dodged. Contestant number two, Michael, sat across from me, checking his black as midnight hair in the reflection of his spoon for the third time since he sat down. I'd been trying to give him the benefit of the doubt because if I looked that pretty, I'd continually check myself out too.

He lowered the spoon and grinned at me, revealing perfectly straight white teeth. If he were in a toothpaste commercial, the corner of his mouth would've sparkled. They were radiant in contrast to his golden tanned skin. "Sorry, I just want to look good for you."

I half believed him, but the way he said it made my toes curl.

"Careful now. If you looked any more delicious, I might have to eat you up." I made grabby gestures.

What in the name of Tom Cruise? Did I seriously just say that?

I peered into my drink and gave a nervous chuckle.

His smile widened, accentuating his chiseled jawline, and he leaned back in the chair, hanging one arm off the back. He shoved his thin, downward slanted nose into his glass as he took a sip.

I leaned forward, concentrating on the color of his eyes. "Are your eyes purple?" I cocked my head to one side, not thinking about how creepy I must've looked— and sounded.

He pressed his forearms to the table, bringing our faces so close the tips of our

noses almost brushed. "Would you like a better view?"

A lump formed in my throat as I stared at his eyes. They were brown, but from certain angles, took on a violet tone.

"I've never seen eyes like yours."

His smile still hadn't faded. "Apparently, I have a unique and specific amount of melanin in my irises. It makes me extra special."

"Or a mutant," Eric voiced from beside us.

I jumped and threw my hands up. "I seriously need to put a bell on you or something. How do you do that?"

Eric folded his arms. "Do what?"

"Pop up inexplicably out of nowhere."

"I flew over here. My wings are invisible." He kept his expression neutral.

Clearly bored of my verbal boxing match with the bartender, Michael picked up the spoon, checking for any rogue hairs that somehow escaped a half bottle of gel. I watched him from the corner of my eye. His lips took on a tiny pucker with every angle he turned the spoon.

"Would you look at that? There's a smudge. Let me grab you a new one, sir." Eric yanked the spoon from Michael's grasp.

Michael froze with his hands out at his sides. Those pouty, kissable man-lips curled like Elvis Presley.

Giving him no time to question or protest, Eric turned on his heel and headed back to the bar.

Already halfway off my chair, I said, "I'm going to grab another drink. You want anything?"

"Sure. A beer would be great, but Elani, I can get it. You don't have to—" He rose, and I pressed a finger to his lips.

My stomach twisted, feeling the smooth texture of his skin against mine. Alcohol-induced touching had never been in my skill set. "You don't have to stand on ceremony for me. But I appreciate the gesture."

He smiled against my finger and gave it a tiny peck. "I await your return then. Thanks."

I turned away, mouthing the words "oh my God" to myself and trying not to jump up and down. Eric leaned casually against the back counter, the spoon resting on the bar behind him.

"Listen. I really like this guy. Don't muddy it up with your antics." I rolled my shoulders back, attempting to make myself look taller.

"No, you don't." The words flowed off his tongue with the confidence of a three-time-winning spelling bee champ. "You like his face."

"Excuse me?"

He pressed his large hands against the mahogany in front of me. "You heard me. That guy is fuller of himself than the singer of Apollo's Suns."

"Who *also* has a pretty face. What's your point?"

"My point is that I took away his mirror, and he seems to have found another one."

I whipped my head around, and my face fell. Michael stood in front of the front window, turning his head from side to side, watching how the overhead lights shadowed over his jaw. He was *so* pretty, though. I whirled back around, pointing at Eric, narrowly poking him in the eye.

"You're messing with me. Trying to make me lose this bet."

He pushed his shirt sleeves up. "No. Because when I win, I want to know it had nothing to do with my interference. I'm simply making conversation."

"You give me a headache."

He bit the corner of his lip. "So, I elicit a reaction?"

"Can I get two beers, please? Molson is fine."

He yanked two bottles from the cooler, pried the caps off, and held them at arm's length. "Look. You go ahead and live in the delusional world you created for yourself. But when it happens—and it will—I get to say 'I told you so,' and the only response you get to give is a smile."

"Is this a bet within a bet?"

He slowly nodded, piercing me with his gaze and running the tip of his middle finger down the condensation collecting on one of the bottles.

"Fine." I wrapped my hands around the beers.

He dragged his finger over my knuckles, and the same twinge I'd felt before raged through me like an avalanche. I glared at him to mask the expression I wanted to give—perplexed.

"Have fun." His brow twitched.

When I got back to the table, Michael spotted me in the window's reflection and spun around with a smile.

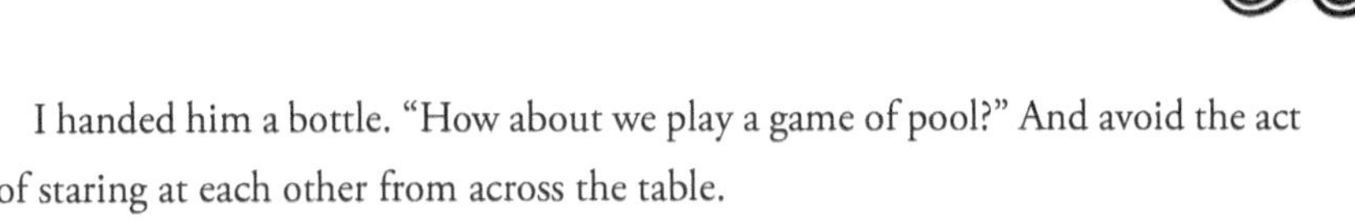

I handed him a bottle. "How about we play a game of pool?" And avoid the act of staring at each other from across the table.

"I love it. I'm sure you're a regular Black Widow, huh?"

"Ha. Not exactly. I think the last time I played was—well…"

He chuckled and delicately touched the crook of my elbow, leading us to the table. "I'd be happy to give you a few pointers."

Pointers? What was wrong with me? Here I thought doing a physical form of activity could distract me from the masterpiece that was his face, and now we'd be…close. Both bent over the table and—my hand tightened around my bottle, fumbling not to drop it.

"You want a long stick or a short one?" Michael asked, resting his bottle on the edge of the table.

I choked on my spit, biting the inside of my cheek to keep from answering what thought the question enticed. "Short. I've got arms like a t-rex."

He snickered. "Want me to break?"

I blinked.

"Launch the cue ball into the rest of them? Send them flying in all directions?" He scratched the back of his head. "Hopefully, make a couple in the pockets to impress you?"

My cheeks burned. "Break. Ha. Yes. Please. If I did it, I'd probably miss the cue ball."

He lined up the shot, striking the white ball into the rest, and sinking two striped balls.

"Look at you, Pool Shark." I sipped on my beer, snorting it through my nose when he bent over in front of me.

His pants weren't what you would call tight, but his butt was prominent enough it made quite the impression through the fabric. I chewed on the mouth opening of my bottle.

"Damn. Missed. You're up, sweetcakes. Ready?" Michael turned to look at me, grinning when he saw my eyes snap to his face.

"Yup," I squeaked, holding my stick with both hands.

"Alright. Come here. You'll be solids. What you want to do is line your stick up with your intended shot. I'd suggest going for the yellow in the back left corner. It's a clear shot." He motioned for me to join him on the opposite side of the table.

"You would know best. You tell me where to hit, and I'll smack it with my stick." Sometimes, I truly felt I'd do better to keep my mouth sealed shut. For eternity. Or at least twenty-four hours.

I bent over the table, slapping my stick onto it. He traced his callused hands over mine, adjusting them around the wood. He moved behind me, his crotch inches from my butt. The heat radiating from his chest coursed over my back, making my stomach clench.

This was a bad idea. So, so bad.

"Go ahead and line up your shot with the cue ball." His voice was soft and low in my ear like a masculine lullaby. His hands drifted over my shoulders, turning me in the right direction. "Now pull back the stick and don't force it. Let it glide through your fingers."

How I hadn't turned into a melted pile of M&M's already was astounding.

I did as he instructed, sending the stick into the cue ball with a loud *thwack*. The yellow ball flew into the pocket. I squealed, standing upright so fast my head flew into Michael's face.

He held a hand over his nose with a grimace, sniffling several times before he forced a half-smile.

"Oh my—are you okay? I'm so sorry." I lifted my hands to his face but let them drop back at my sides.

"It's all good. No blood." He pressed a finger over the bridge of his nose. "Nice shot."

I whimpered. "The pool ball or your nose?"

"Both, I suppose." His eyes beamed, despite the back of my head having plastered into them moments ago. "I'm going to use the restroom. Save the table?"

"Absolutely." I tacked on extra enthusiasm and rose to the balls of my feet as he passed by.

Rolling my eyes, I snatched my beer bottle and chugged it.

"I may be no expert in romance, but call me crazy—smacking a guy in the face doesn't seem like the right path," Eric chimed from nearby.

I lowered the bottle, holding an overflowing amount of liquid in my puffed cheeks, glaring at him, and gulping it down. "I don't know about that. Some guys find clumsiness—endearing."

If I'd broken his nose, he might have sung a different tune.

Eric held two full beer bottles with one hand. He kept my gaze, challenging me with those steely blues as he rested them on the small display near the pool table. "Remember. All you can say in response is a smile."

"Shoo before he comes back and thinks I'm flirting with the bartender."

"Maybe you are."

My neck flushed.

His brow quirked before he strolled back to the bar like a passing cloud.

Shoving my rapidly growing irritation for the man in plaid away, I plastered a genuine grin upon Michael's return.

"Ah, fresh brews. Awesome." He finished the first bottle.

"I'm really sorry about the uh—" I pointed to his face and then to my head.

"Nah." He slipped one of his large hands over my miniature one. "Don't sweat it. No harm, no foul, right?" His smile could've electrocuted me.

A squeak formed at the back of my throat as he gazed down at me, idly stroking my knuckles with a callused fingertip. Snapping my hand away, I slapped my stick onto the table. "I get another turn, correct? Cause I sunk a ball?"

His eyes fell to my hands. "Yeah. But you may want to use the right end."

I frowned, staring at the rubber end of the stick versus the felted tip. My cheeks turned crimson, and I slowly turned the stick around.

He leaned on the table, his gaze dropping to my chest as I bent forward. "You're pretty adorable."

He said it right as I hit the stick into the ball. My hand jerked, making it bounce off the side.

I idly fanned myself. "You flatter me."

Score one for Elani. He *did* find my clumsiness cute.

"That was my fault. Here." He moved closer, putting the tanned muscle of his bicep in clear view. Moving the cue ball back to its original location, he slipped the stick into my hands. "I'll let you have a do-over. And I'll help. Deal?"

My throat felt like sandpaper as I stared at his lips, only managing a nod in response. He moved behind me, pressing his hip to my side. Heat rolled from his chest onto my back, making my grip loosen on the stick. If his hands hadn't wrapped over mine, I might have dropped it. Together, we sent the cue ball flying, but no balls sunk this time. I turned my head over my shoulder. His eyes were closed, his mouth nearing my lips.

My heart thundered against my chest. I grabbed my clutch and shoved it between our faces. "I should call it a night, but can I get your number?"

His eyes fluttered open. Those crazy thick man lashes blinked in confusion. "Uh, sure. Of course."

I took a step back and handed him my phone with a new text window open. "You can text yourself." After pointing at the touch screen keyboard, I winced.

Like he's never used a cell.

He nibbled on his lip as he typed before handing it back to me. A guitar riff sound went off in his back pocket. He slipped it out and waved it at me with a twinkle in his eye. "We're all set."

"Great. I'd love to see you again." I tucked my clutch under my arm, bumping into the corner of the table as I backed up, and grabbed my jacket from a nearby holder. "I remembered I have this—an important webcam meeting with a client."

"That's right. We didn't even talk about each other's jobs."

I snapped my fingers. "Perfect. Something to talk about next time."

He chuckled to himself, and I waved, trying to walk past the bar as fast as possible, knowing Eric would have an earful to say.

"I may stand corrected. Should we pick out the wedding song? *Amazed* by Lonestar is a popular choice," Eric remarked, holding back a smile.

"Can it, Bar Boy," I said through a growl, making my way outside, impatient for the cold nip over my cheeks.

I'd mentally chastised myself the entire cab ride home. It wasn't his fault. It really wasn't. I was attracted to him and did nothing to sway the contrary, so it's no wonder he went for the kiss. The kiss was sacred ground for me. You could tell so much about a man from that one singular act. The care he took in the performance. The feeling behind it. The feeling it gave me. I'd never kissed anyone who made my stomach flutter. It was a constant setup for disappointment and standards no one should have to live up to.

I flopped face down on my bed. Michael flustered me so much that trying to recall my excuse for leaving was like wading through the hazy memories of overindulging in alcohol—which could've played a part as well. My clutch buzzed near my head, and I fished for it, narrowing my eyes at the screen saying I had a new message from a number I didn't recognize.

Michael. Ah yes. I hadn't even input his name yet.

I shut my eyes and opened the message, slowly peeking one open to survey the damage. My heart fell straight to my groin. It was a half-naked photo of Michael, posing with one hand behind his head, grinning at the camera with a heavy-lidded gaze. The shot cut off right above Michael, Jr. He included the words: A Preview.

I sighed. After the first date, a photo like that was one step away from an unsolicited "Dick Pic." And I'd never been one to appreciate them nor the type who felt compelled to reciprocate. I'm not sure what stung more—having to turn down a man masterpiece or admitting to Eric he'd been right.

FIVE

I SMILED TO MYSELF, listening to a client preen through the phone.

"He proposed, Elani. I can't believe it," Anna squealed.

"That's incredible. Where'd he do it? How?" I clicked through several screens on my work monitor, pulling up her profile. The algorithm matched her with Bryan O'Connor. They went to the same college but were never in the same courses. The fact they met through my dating service was "serendipity," as Anna called it at the time.

"Where we had our first date."

Quickly pulling up the notes, I skimmed for reminders I left for myself. It was impossible to remember the small details with so many clients through the years.

"The wharf? Wow. That must've been beautiful." I leaned back, slumping until my head pressed against the backrest.

"You have no idea. It was nighttime. Full moon. The pier had those sparkly lights hanging everywhere. It was like walking through starlit clouds."

Anna had a way of describing things—romantic enough to take your breath away at the mere thought. I closed my eyes, imagining the scene she painted. My heels clicked against the wooden dock—arms wrapped around myself from the chill in the air. Gazing up at the moon, my breath curling in the air like smoke, a man stepped up behind me, wrapping his jacket around my shoulders.

"Like a fairy tale, isn't it?" His voice rumbled against my ear—a voice I'd heard before. Recently.

I smiled to myself, turning to face him. He grinned with his dimpled chin.

Eric, the goddamned bartender.

My eyes flew open. "Get out of my daydreams," I yelled.

"Pardon me?" Anna said, still on the other line.

I pinched my lips together. "Not you, Anna. Sorry, I got lost in thought there for a second."

"Alright." She let out a fluttery chuckle. "Anyway, I know you must be busy helping out other couples, but I wanted to call and thank you personally. From the bottom of my heart, thank you."

My chest warmed. "You're very welcome, Anna. I wish nothing but eternal happiness for you both."

Silence fell over the line.

"Anna?"

"I wanted to—well, no. It'd be way too much to ask."

I shifted in my seat. "By all means, ask away."

"I want to invite you to the wedding."

My stomach gurgled. "Oh, no, no. I appreciate the thought, but you don't have to—"

"I would love for you to be there, Elani. You're the reason we're together. I know it's a lot to ask with the travel and everything, but if you can swing it, it'd mean the world to me."

It wouldn't be the first time a client invited me to their wedding. But none of them had been my client as long as Anna. She signed on before I fine-tuned the system and stuck through it until I found her "the one." Considering she was practically my guinea pig, I felt compelled to pay her back somehow.

Did it have to be this, though?

Fine.

"I'd be happy to." I forced an upward inflection in my tone. "But where exactly?"

The Caribbean? Jamaica?

"Oh, this will be amazing. We're having the ceremony in Ireland."

I shot from my chair, the phone's cord creaking in protest. "Ireland?"

"It made sense with both our ancestries. You can still come, right?"

I turned to look at my wall calendar, the cord wrapping around my torso. Dad and I would be traveling to Scotland soon to represent Clan Stewart for the yearly

Calling of the Clans festival. Ireland was a short charter airplane flight away.

How freaking convenient. Too convenient.

Dad could be my date. That wasn't *that* weird, right?

"Elani?"

I turned back to the monitor, the chord tightening over my chest. "It's perfect. I'll be there. Send over the information when you have it."

She squealed. "Alright. Take care."

Click.

I peeled the receiver away from my head, trying to put it on its cradle, the cord resisting my efforts.

Note to self: Say hello to the twenty-first century and order a cordless phone.

Grumbling, I made several circles, untangling myself from the phone's vine. An alarm went off on my cell phone, displaying the name "Jason" in all caps— another two dates tonight. It should be exciting, an adrenaline rush, but all I felt was remorse and nausea after the first two nightmares.

Making my way to the hallway, I shoved the phone in my purse. Alex sat on the edge of her desk, glaring at me.

"What have I done to deserve your stare of deathly intent?" I made sure to keep three feet between us.

"You text me in the middle of your date with Michael about how brutally hot he was and then go radio silent?" Her glare deepened.

I picked my nail against the strap of my purse. "That's because it didn't end well. I thought it did, but then he sent a half-naked photo right before I went to bed."

She pushed from the desk. "Half-naked, you say?"

"Uh-huh. We both know that was one step away from a—" I glanced around at the dozens of cubicles able to hear our conversation. "D.P."

"Double penetration?" She raised a quizzical brow.

I smacked a hand over her filthy mouth.

"D.P. And I don't mean Deadpool."

Her eyes sparkled to life, and she mumbled the words "dick pic" against my palm.

"Exactly." I dropped my hand. "And I'm not in this for Mr. Temporary."

"Understandable." She took out her cell. "Is there a reason you haven't sent that pic yet?"

"Of—" I squinted at her. "Of Michael?"

She raised her brow and looked left to right, re-emphasizing the phone in her hand.

I exaggerated pressing my thumb against my phone's screen, and the sound of rustling paper echoed, deleting it.

Alex's jaw dropped. "You witch."

I *booped* her on the nose. "See you tomorrow."

Her mouth remained open even after I turned away and headed for the elevator.

I entered the bar with about as much enthusiasm as going to the dentist. Not bothering to make eye contact, I threw my purse and jacket onto an empty stool and sat in the one next to it. Eric finished beaming at a couple of lady customers, thanking them for the generous tip. His smile brightened when he spotted me and casually slipped the cash into the register before coming over.

He leaned against the bar. "No sexy dress tonight? Still donning your business casual?"

I smiled at him with all my teeth.

His brow wrinkled. "What are you doing?"

Sighing, I pointed at my mouth, further widening my lips into a warped smile.

It took a few beats before the lightbulb lit his face—a snarky grin following. "Ah. Not work out with 'ol mutant eyes, I take it?"

"Can I talk now?" My voice muffled from still baring my fangs.

"As long as it's not about Michael, sure."

"Can I have that nightly drink you promised me?" I sulked. "Bachelor number three is due in five minutes."

"Gee. Try to tone down the excitement." He tried to wink again, doing that weird double blinkety-blink thing.

I didn't have the energy to call him out on it.

"We have this bet, yes. But don't assume you understand what I'm going through."

"Oh? You think I haven't been through the dating circles of hell?" He busied his hands behind the bar.

My gaze fell to the light peppering of chest hair peeking from the several undone buttons at the top of his plaid shirt—a red and black one tonight.

"To say no would compliment you, but fine, I have a hard time believing you couldn't nab any tail you laid your eyes on." I flicked a curled empty straw wrapper across the bar.

He snatched the wrapper with a curl of his lip and threw it in the garbage behind him. "Maybe. But that's not what you're doing here, is it? You're trying to find a partner."

I pinched my mouth shut, not answering.

He placed a shot glass in front of me with perfectly separated liquids—the top a tannish hue, bottom clear.

"We're doing shots now?" I lowered my head, eyeing it like a booby trap.

"Sounds like you could use one."

"What is it?"

He tapped his fingers on the bar with an outstretched hand, making the muscles in his forearm dance. "A Slippery Nipple. Irish cream and sambuca."

I snort-laughed with the glass close to my mouth, spilling some cream on my hand.

"Hey now. The top layer is the best part." He grabbed a towel and dragged it over my hand, grazing his finger down a knuckle.

Bubbles floated and popped in my stomach.

Ignoring it, I tilted my head back and sank the drink. I'd expected it to taste like ass for some reason but was surprised with the way the Irish crème made it smooth, silky, and inviting.

"It's like you know what you're doing back there, or something." I slammed the glass down, licking excess cream from my lips.

He caught my gaze. "It's part of my job—to know people."

"Maybe you should've been a therapist. A lot more money in that line of work."

"Mm." The sound vibrated from the back of his throat—deep and husky. "But not near as much fun." His eyes lifted to the door.

I groaned. "It's him, isn't it? Copper-colored hair? Six foot one?"

Eric rested his chin in his hand. "Uh-huh. And...a woman."

"What?" Sweat beaded at the base of my spine. "He came in with a woman?"

"An older woman."

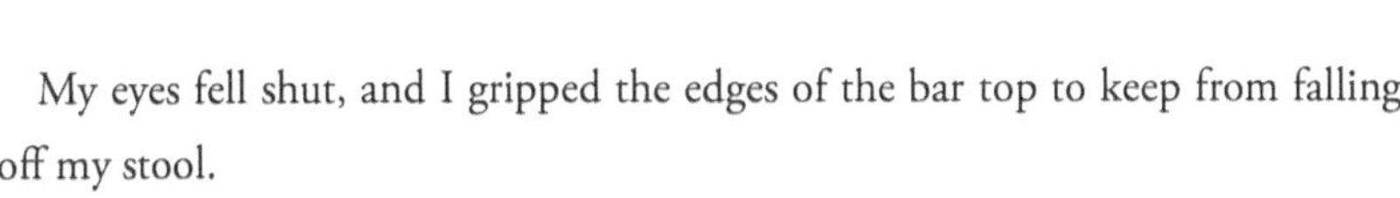

My eyes fell shut, and I gripped the edges of the bar top to keep from falling off my stool.

"Does your questionnaire have anything about being close with your mother?"

My eyes flew open. "Why?"

"Because I'm fairly certain he just called her 'mom' and pulled a seat out for her."

Whimpering, I slapped my hands to my face before leaning over the bar. "You have to help me get out of this."

"Oh, do I?" His grin turned downright slimy.

I sucked in a sharp breath. "You can't in good conscience stand there and watch this catastrophe unfold and do nothing."

"Are we upping the stakes then?"

I ground my teeth together. He stared at me, his blue eyes drowning me with questionable intent. "Fine."

"At some point in time, I get to go on a date with you. I say when and where."

My neck numbed.

No big deal. I'd already gone on plenty of horrible dates. What was one with a know-it-all bartender?

"Deal."

He grinned. "Go introduce yourself. I'll intervene at the right moment."

"The right moment? How about now? Right now?"

"What do you want me to do? Kiss you?" A fire lit in his gaze.

I pressed my knees together. "Five minutes. Intervene in five minutes."

He half-smiled and shook his head, watching me stumble off my stool.

I folded my jacket over an arm, said a silent prayer to the heavens above, and walked over.

My date's smile spread wide once he caught sight of me, and his tall frame shot from his seat. "Elani?"

"Yes. George?"

His emerald eyes brightened, and the overhead lights made the scattering of freckles on his cheeks stand out. "It's such a pleasure to meet you. Please, sit."

Zero mentions about his mom sitting with us at the table. Zilch.

I cleared my throat and sat, keeping my jacket in my lap. "I uh—wasn't expecting company on our *date*." I intentionally did *not* hide the sneer in my tone.

His mother, an older woman with violet-gray hair pulled into a bun at the

base of her skull, pursed her paper-thin lips. "I'm Fiona. His mother. Our family comes from a long line of carefully selective breeding, and we expect a certain—" Her beady black eyes fell to my chest. "Caliber."

Selective breeding? What were they, racehorses?

With as much stealth as I could manage, I lifted the jacket over my boobs.

Eric was sure taking his sweet time.

With a grimace, I pretended to stretch, stealing a glance at the bar. Eric scratched his back on the corner of a wall like a bear. He rolled his shoulders, flagged down one of the waitresses, and as soon as she was behind the bar, he sprinted to the back.

"You seem distracted," George said in a melancholy voice.

I snapped my head back, wrapping the jacket around me tighter. "Sorry. First date jitters and everything."

"Tell me, Elani, do you plan to have kids?" Fiona asked, removing a notepad and ballpoint pen from her purse.

I choked on my spit.

"Mother," George snapped.

"It is better to get these questions out of the way before you start to like her, Junior."

"I uh—hadn't really thought about it."

Fiona slapped the notepad on the table.

I jolted in my chair with widened eyes.

"Miss Stewart, this is no joking matter. Anyone who is to date my son must be a promising prospect."

Speechless. The woman made the words freeze in my throat. All I could do was stare at her and pray I'd become a gnat so I could buzz around Eric's head, wherever the hell he was.

I whipped my chin over my shoulder, glaring at the waitress still behind the bar. "I uh—understand why it'd be so important with your family line and all that jazz."

"Are you a virgin?" Fiona whispered.

My throat gurgled like a strangled frog as I slowly turned my gaze back to the ridiculous woman across from me.

George's face lit up.

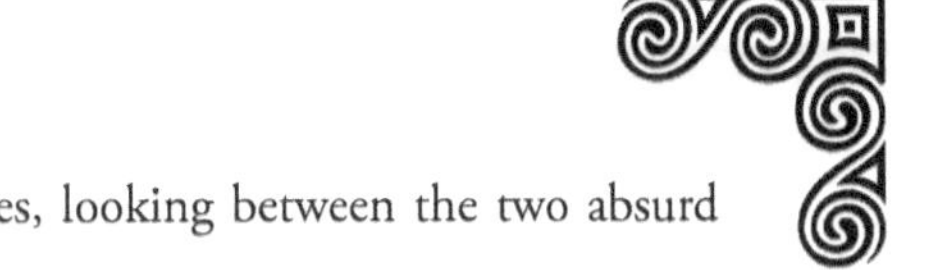

"No. Absolutely, not." I narrowed my eyes, looking between the two absurd humans.

Fiona let out a disapproving grunt and jotted on her notepad.

I tightened my grip on my jacket and fought the urge to scream into it.

"And how many sexual partners have you had?" Fiona lifted her eyes, her gaze aloof and bored.

Instead of an answer, I squeaked.

"Miss Stewart?" Eric's face appeared in front of mine, blocking my view of the two weirdos.

If at any moment I'd have felt like kissing him, it would've been now.

"Yes?" The word came out strained.

He grinned at me, and the glint in his eye made my stomach twist. "There's a call for you at the bar. Your husband."

My lips parted, my left eye twitching, but I swallowed my words. "Thank you."

His grin continued as he walked away.

George's eyes were wide—cheeks flushed.

Fiona tapped her pen against the table and then shoved it and the notepad in her purse. "You're married?"

I cocked my head to one side. "It's an open marriage. Will that be an issue?"

"Of course it is. We'll not sully our family name with a swinger." Fiona upturned her pointed nose, patting George's shoulder as she passed. "Come, Junior."

It was difficult to tell from George's expression whether he was a leashed dog with his mother or he hadn't cared about my…lifestyle. Mortification gleamed in his eyes, but his lips curved wickedly. As soon as they were out the door, I huffed over to the bar, slapping my hands on it.

"Married? Seriously? You could've come up with virtually anything else."

He shrugged, drying the inside of a glass with a towel. "It got them out of here, didn't it? Besides, you were pretty quick-witted. Nice moves, Stewart."

I groaned and fished for my phone. "I'm canceling my other date tonight. I can't take any more of this."

"Hey." Eric's hand slipped over my phone screen, and he gently pushed it down. "You have three months. It's been two days. Ye of little faith, much?"

"You're supposed to be cheering for my demise."

"I am. But watching the drive fizzle out of you that quickly is discouraging."

He slid his hand back and half-smirked, creating a tiny dimple at the corner of his cheek.

I let my forehead fall on top of my arm. "I didn't even look at this guy's picture."

"Well, a tall guy just walked in who's been glancing around the bar with his hands shoved in his finely tailored pants for the past thirty seconds."

As I lifted my head, hair fell in shambles over my face. "Is he cute?"

"Why don't you be the judge?" He reached forward, parting my hair, and curling some of it over my ear. "Go get 'em, Tiger."

I blinked and smoothed back wispy bits of hair before turning around. My next date had raven-colored hair pulled back into a low ponytail, golden tanned skin, and when his dark eyes found mine, his smile made them narrow into a sexy squint.

I sauntered to him, jutting out my hand. "Elani Stewart."

"Graeme MacFarlane," he replied with a thick Scottish accent.

And there went my head, my heart, and my loins, straight to the ground.

SIX

"A STEWART, AYE?" HIS caramel eyes sparkled with a grin just as radiant. He motioned at a nearby table, pulling out a seat for me.

"Aye. Have a problem with that, MacFarlane?"

"Impressive." He sat after slinking off his black trench coat. "Your accent is spot on."

"My da is from the motherland. I grew up hearing it."

He leaned casually in his chair. "Yeah? What's his name?"

"Don't laugh." I let my bottom lip roll past my teeth. "John."

Graeme's head tilted back as he let out a hearty chuckle. "No shite."

"Hey. I said not to laugh." I joined in with the chuckles, playfully swatting his forearm.

His gaze fell to where I'd hit him, his eyes softening before lifting to my face. "Have you been to the 'motherland' as ye call it?"

"Every year since I was ten."

He rested his chin in his hand. "A woman connected to her culture. I adore that."

The fact I felt compelled to say something as corny as "I adore *you*" made my stomach gurgle. And this time, I wasn't even tipsy.

"How long have you been in Canada?" I busied my hands, folding a paper cocktail napkin.

He counted on his fingers. "Four years, three months, and ten days. Give or take."

"What brought you here?" I rested my chin in my hand, mimicking him.

"I'm a sports agent and landed a hockey client."

"Hockey. The one sport that doesn't bore me to tears."

"Yeah? Is that what brought you here? Your accent sounds American."

"You got a sharp ear. I grew up in Colorado. Moved here to start a business."

He ran a thumb under his bottom lip, and I noted how much fuller it was then the top one. "A businesswoman too. This keeps getting better."

"You're not going to ask me what kind of business?"

He scratched the light stubble on his cheek. "I figured you'd have told me when you said you started up a business. I'm not one to pry."

My chest hummed.

"How about I get us some drinks?" I propped my chin in both hands with a brightened smile.

"A lass offering to get *me* a drink? I'm flattered."

Little did he know it was mostly because I had a deal with the bartender.

"My pleasure. What's your poison?"

"Whiskey'll do fine."

"You don't say." I winked at him before making my way to the bar, humming *Return to Me* by Dean Martin.

Eric leaned over the bar in the corner, speaking with a brunette who looked like she'd been crying. Her hands flailed around as she talked, and Eric gently wrapped them both within his massive grasp. She took two big breaths, and the red neon glint from the overhead signs made the bracelet on her wrist sparkle—their hands clasped together in a glowing, glittery embrace. Eric let go and pointed behind her. A man with a shaved head walked in from outside, one hand in his front jeans pocket, the other rubbing his neck. She gasped and leaped off her stool, nearly knocking the man over as she jumped into his arms.

Eric rubbed his temples before noticing me and smiling. He snapped the towel over his shoulder as he neared. "Judging from the glow on your face, I take it things are going well?"

I crossed my arms in a huff. "We have this bet going, and you're still playing matchmaker?"

"What do you—" He quirked a brow and caught sight of the happy couple cooing behind me. "Ah. Right." He gave a lopsided grin. "I guess I can't help

myself."

"Well, you're going to have to when I win, remember?"

"*If* you win, I'd probably end up moving."

The statement gave a peculiar feeling of disappointment, settling over my chest like an oil slick.

"Whiskey. Neat." I peeked at Graeme over my shoulder. Graeme scrolled through his phone, and we caught gazes as he, too, stole a glance at me.

"Any particular kind?"

After grinning at Graeme, I whipped my attention back to Eric. "Do you have Johnnie Walker?"

"Yes?"

"Perfect. One for me too."

He twirled a tumbler glass in his palm. "After your surprise special drink. Remember?"

"Fine."

He grabbed the Black Label bottle of scotch and tossed it over his shoulder into the opposite hand from behind him.

My insides somersaulted. "What's with the show?"

"Don't like it?"

"I didn't say that."

His teeth glinted as he poured some of the amber-colored liquid into the glass. "Occasionally, I'll bust out the moves for bigger tips and well, to show off."

"You don't need to show off to me, Eric. This—" I swept a hand in front of my body. "Is a dead end."

"I was referring to the bachelorette party that walked in." He licked the corner of his lips, following the group of women with the predatory focus of a vulture.

I snapped my head to the right, glaring at the scantily clad trio wearing penis-shaped plastic glasses, flashing penis-shaped necklaces, and Ring-Pops on all fingers. The bleach-blonde had a silver tiara with pink feathers, the word "bachelorette" arching over the top.

Rolling my eyes, I turned back to Eric. "So, where's my—"

He slid a tall hurricane glass filled with cloudy white liquid, crushed ice, and a brown powder sprinkled on top.

"Do I want to ask?" I sniffed it, taking in notes of Amaretto.

He leaned forward. "A Screaming Orgasm."

My stomach clenched, flipped, and twisted.

"Because you may as well be having one right there in the stool over Mr. MacFarlane." The corner of his mouth twisted, and he nudged the glass closer.

My eyes dropped to the cleft in his chin before snapping back to his gaze.

"Carry on, Miss Stewart. You've got eternal compatibility to find." He jutted his chin behind me and walked to the bachelorette party.

The women sat up straighter once spotting him. Two of them twirled their hair, and the bachelorette squeezed her visible cleavage together.

Growling, I snatched the drinks and walked back to Gorgeous Graeme.

"Hey, you made it back. Thought I was going to have to come over there and steal you." He beamed at me.

"Sorry, the service can be finicky in here sometimes." I handed him the scotch before taking my seat.

"Thank ye." He sipped it, and his eyes fell shut with a gratified sigh. "Walker. Prime choice."

"Glad to hear it. I love the smoky undertones it has." I stared at the golden liquid sloshing around in his glass, envious I didn't have my own instead of one of Eric's orgasms.

I made a strangled chirp sound and pinched my thighs together.

Graeme cocked a thick eyebrow. "Something wrong?"

"Dry throat."

"You…have a drink there, lass." His eyes sparkled.

I stared down at the Screaming Orgasm mocking me. "I certainly do."

I took a long sip—creamy, frothy, and disgustingly delicious. A hum tingled in my belly, a moan vibrating in the back of my throat. After a few more pulls on the straw, I opened my eyes to find Graeme staring at my empty glass wide-eyed.

I let the straw snap from my mouth, dabbing the corner of my mouth with a finger. "Guess I was thirstier than I thought."

"And she can handle her alcohol." Graeme shifted closer. "You're going to have to start having some downsides, Clan Stewart, or I might not think you're human."

My cheeks flushed.

"Ye want another?" He pointed at my glass filled with nothing but ice and

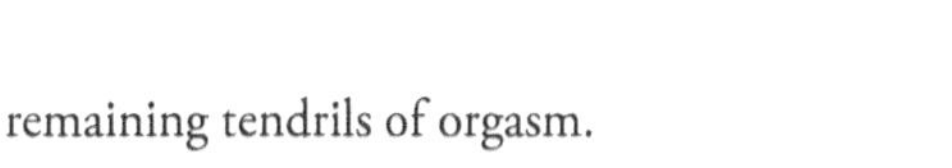

remaining tendrils of orgasm.

"Yes. But not one of these. Smelling that scotch of yours, I can't help but want one myself."

He went to grab my glass, but I wrapped a hand over his arm. "I got it."

"Ye sure? You got the last one."

I shot to my feet. "Positive. It helps me get my steps in, you know?" Wiggling my wrist with the non-existent fitness tracker on it, I power-walked back to the bar, slamming the glass down to get Eric's attention.

Eric arched a brow over his shoulder, holding a finger up at the hen harem. They all made pouty faces as he walked away.

"Is there a problem?" He folded his arms, stretching the plaid pattern of his shirt over those bulging biceps.

Focus.

"Yeah. What'd you put in this drink? It made my…stomach feel weird."

He dipped his chin. "Mm. What kind of feeling? Can you describe it to me?"

"I'd rather not." Heat shot up the back of my neck.

"Nausea?"

I shook my head.

"Tingles?"

I shrugged.

He unfolded his arms and leaned in further. "A sort of tightening twist?" The words rolled off his tongue like a delicate lick on an ice cream cone.

My stomach flew into pole vaults.

A woman squealed from behind me. "There's my beautiful boy." She jumped past me, her bright blonde hair smacking me in the face as she leaned over the bar to hug Eric.

Eric's face paled, reluctantly receiving her embrace. "What are you doing here?"

I sputtered, picking a piece of her hair from my mouth.

"I need an excuse to see my son?"

My eyebrows shot to the ceiling. Son? The woman looked my age. Maybe younger.

Eric laughed, making sideway glance gestures toward me. "Elani, this is my uh—ex-girlfriend, Ven…a." He paused, balling his fist at his mouth like he held back bile. "I used to call her uh—'*mami*,' hence the nickname." He coughed into

his fist.

Vena glared at him before turning her face at me. Her expression melted, eyes widening for a millisecond.

"Wow, Eric. T.M.I. but, nice to meet you." With a wince, I held my hand out to her.

She didn't shake it. Instead, she stepped forward until her head was inches from mine. "What did he say your name was?"

I leaned back, lifting my empty glass in front of me like a shield. "Elani?"

"How interesting." Her bright blue eyes locked onto me, and she raised one porcelain-like hand toward my cheek.

Eric grabbed her arm. "Don't even think about it, *Vena*."

I shook my head, brain fuzzy and out of sorts. Rubbing my temple, I set the glass on the bar. "Eric, could I get another scotch, please?"

He kept his gaze focused on Vena with a clenched jaw. "I'll bring it to your table."

As she tapped her pink manicured nails against the bar top, Vena's full lips slid into a Maleficent-like grin.

I looked between the two before sliding off my stool. "Right. Thanks."

They argued in hushed whispers as I hitch-stepped back to the table. Graeme had been watching the entire time, turned sideways in his chair with his legs stretched out in front of him.

"I feel like I'm at a dinner theater or something." The warmth in his eyes melted me.

I snickered, sliding into my seat with folded hands. "They're certainly entertaining."

At the bar, Vena's hands shot out at her sides. Eric sliced his hand through the air in front of her as he poured my scotch with the other.

"Hey," Graeme said, bumping his knuckle against my arm. "You okay?"

The touch was subtle but so natural for him.

"Never better." A smile pulled at my lips. A genuine grin, not forced or faked. I squeezed his knee as I brought our faces closer.

Eric reached an arm between us, resting my scotch on the table. "Another Johnnie, as requested."

Graeme leaned back, spreading his legs wide, and resting an elbow on the table.

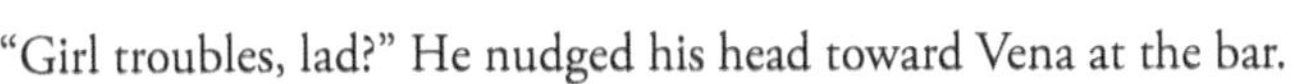

"Girl troubles, lad?" He nudged his head toward Vena at the bar.

Vena watched us with both her elbows propped up. If she could've set me on fire from her stare, I'd be a pile of ash on the floor.

"Something like that. She'll be leaving shortly, though. Apologies if it's been—distracting." Eric winced, reaching a hand over his shoulder to scratch his back.

"Not at all. Just didn't realize drinks came with a show." Graeme turned his chin just enough to wink at me.

Eric smirked, reaching his arm behind him from underneath, scratching his back again. "I try to leave the shows to the televisions." He grimaced. "You two need anything else?"

We were rivals, he and I, but watching him struggle to scratch the middle of his back unnerved me. "Need some help with that?"

Both of his hands shot up, and his nostrils flared. "No, no. Appreciated. But no. I'll check back on you in a bit."

He whisked off without so much as a sarcastic quip. Odd.

I scooped the glass of scotch into my hand, sipping it, relishing it—letting it coat my throat like smokey liquid chocolate.

"Wow," Graeme said.

I smiled at him from across the table. "What?"

"Never thought watching someone drink whiskey could be so…intoxicating." He winced. "Sorry if that offends you."

"Not at all. I tend to make an event of drinking good scotch." I dipped my finger into the caramel-colored liquid and proceeded to circle it around the rim of the glass. Lifting it, I kept his gaze as I took another sip and licked the excess from my lips.

His throat bobbed as he watched me, and he coughed, grabbing his own scotch. He held it up for us to cheers.

This guy could really work. And I know I said that before, but something about him *made* me want to flirt with him, to see him attracted to me.

Vena walked past in a huff, her red heels clacking against the wood floor. "Nice meeting you, Elani." She sneered and paused, glancing at an Eric-less bar. She held up her palm and blew a kiss at me.

An invisible force smacked me in the face, and I clapped a hand over my cheek.

After a pageant wave and a devious curl of her lip, Vena left.

I rubbed my face, turning to watch her walk outside. Blinking, I could've sworn I saw shimmers of pink following her in a spiraling trail.

"Elani," Graeme beckoned.

I bounced in my seat with my hand still on my cheek. "Yes?"

"Your phone's vibrating like crazy. Maybe it's an emergency?" He pointed at my cell resting on the table.

There were three texts from Chelsea, all of which were listing reasons why I should come to the MMA fight this time, unlike every other time I refused her. One of her female clients fought, and she could always get me in for free. I knew she just wanted to spend time with me, and not that I didn't want to see my sister, but I had about as much interest in MMA as watching paint dry.

"It's my sister. She's a public relations agent and represents Harm Makos."

Graeme's brows quirked. "Really? The women's bantam-weight champ?"

"Yeah. She always has free tickets, but I have zero interest in MMA, so I never take her up on it, though it doesn't keep her from trying." I shrugged and slid the phone into my purse without answering her.

Graeme pressed his forearms into the table. "Wait. Are you saying you can go to Makos's next fight for free?"

I blinked. "Yes?"

"You should go." He bounced in his seat. "*We* should go."

How presumptuous of him to think she gave me two tickets.

"I don't know, I mean it's in New Mexico, we'd have to do a whole day flight thing, blah, blah. I'm sure there are other things we could do."

His hand clenched into a fist. "Easy enough. I represent hockey players. Several of them have access to private jets."

He wasn't going to let this go.

"You…really want to go?"

He nodded vigorously.

"Okay. Sure. I'll let her know we're coming." I dug the phone back out.

He grinned, stood, and slapped his hands together before leaning over and kissing the top of my head. "You're a gem."

I was something, alright.

"Listen, I should go and situate our flight for tomorrow. Want to meet out front of here and ride to the airport together?" He did some form of snappy hand

gesture.

After texting Chelsea, I gave a weak smile. "Sure. Sounds great."

His smile broadened, and he kissed my cheek. "Thanks for this. We're going to have a grand time." As he left, he threw jabs in the air through each doorway.

I gathered my things to leave, glancing at the bar to say goodbye to Eric, but he hadn't returned. My shoulders slumped as I made my way outside. Something tickled my tongue, and I picked it off with my fingers.

Pink glitter. Huh.

SEVEN

IT WAS LATE MORNING, and I stood outside The Arrow, rubbing the wool jacket covering my arms because evidently, the bar didn't open that early. Go figure. Blowing into my hands to warm them, I slipped them into my pockets, bouncing on my heels as I waited for Graeme to show up.

"Wow. Miss me that much?" Eric said from behind me.

I whipped around to face him as he dug a set of keys from his pocket with a sparkling grin.

"For your information, I'm meeting Graeme so we can fly to Santa Fe in a private jet." I lifted my nose, wiggling it to ease the numbness from the cold.

"Santa Fe, huh? And what pray tell, is in Santa Fe?" He jingled the keys.

I sniffled. "A free MMA fight."

He frowned and opened the door, standing aside to let me in. "You're flying all the way there to watch a fight? I thought you said the only sport you could stand watching was hockey?"

I ran past him, feverishly rubbing my arms.

He remembered I said that?

"I did, I do—but Graeme is a big fan or something, and I mean, they're free tickets from my sister." I shrugged, covering my nose with my palm.

Eric stared down at the keys, tossing them in his hand before dropping them in his pocket. "Uh-huh, how many times did he insist on going?"

"I don't see how that's any of your concern."

"Here's a crazy idea. You could've said something like— 'no.'"

"I just met this guy, Eric. And I have a really good feeling about him. What's pretending like I'm into two women beating the crap out of each other for a couple of hours?" I ran a finger over my collarbone, remembering the way Graeme's eyes burned into me as he watched me drink scotch. "Besides, it'll give us a chance to get to know each other outside of a bar."

"What's pretending? Do you really have to ask?" He raised a brow and moved behind the bar.

"Please. Like you've *never* told little white lies or put on this front in the initial stages of a relationship." I sat on a stool, curling my jacket over my thin leggings.

He shrugged his jacket off, revealing a gray Henley hugging his chest versus the usual flannel. My stomach fluttered. "First off—" He rolled his sleeves up and turned the hot water on of the sink. "Starting things with a lie is never a good start. Trust me." The corner of his jaw tightened. He made the water soapy and proceeded to wash a shaker bottle. "Secondly, any decent guy would've sensed your apprehension and suggested doing something else."

How had he known I was apprehensive?

"Maybe he doesn't read people well."

There was something unusually sensual about watching Eric clean dishes. I pressed my palms together and slipped them between my knees.

He dried the shaker with a towel. "Or he saw it and chose to ignore it because he selfishly wants to go."

"Admit that you're worried this guy might be the winner and stop stepping on my toes, Eric." My mouth twitched. There was as good of a possibility of him being right about Graeme, but my heart wouldn't let me think otherwise. It was like some sort of hope-hardened shield all of a sudden.

His eyes lifted over my shoulder, and he bent forward, the Henley hugging his arms in all the perfect places. "Don't let anything cloud your judgment. Eyes and ears open, champ." He tapped under my chin with his knuckle, lips curving into a half-smile.

"Elani, ye ready to go?" Graeme called out from the doorway.

I traced my fingertips over my chin, still feeling the tingles Eric left behind.

Eric's gaze dropped to my mouth, and the smile faded, followed by his eyes widening as if something spooked him. He pushed away, backpedaling, and motioning toward Graeme with his head. "Your chariot awaits."

I glared at him, wondering what the hell that was all about before hopping off my stool and curling my arm with Graeme's. As we walked outside, I peeked over my shoulder. Eric paced the length of the bar, switching from rubbing his chin to the back of his neck.

You'd think during a several-hour flight, two people who'd just met would not be short of conversation. Color me surprised when we sat in near silence for the duration of the trip. Graeme spent most of the time on his phone, talking to clients and typing up e-mails. Any other free moment, he'd show me YouTube videos of Makos's fights. I was running out of fake enthusiasm.

I pulled out my phone to text Alex as we began our descent.

Me: I'm bored with Hottie MacTottie. How's that possible?

Alex: What have you guys talked about?

Me: Nothing, really. And he keeps showing me MMA vids.

Alex: You're the one that agreed to go, my dear. You made your bed now either get him to sleep in it or wash the sheets.

Me: Did you make that up?

Alex: Don't I always?

"We're here," Graeme said with a wide smile.

Me: I'll text you later.

Alex: Smack Chelsea on the ass for me.

Chuckling, I dropped my phone in my purse without answering her. "We'll need to stop at the will-call booth so I can pick up our tickets."

He wrapped his arm around my shoulders. "I can't tell you how much I appreciate this, Elani."

"Of course," I answered with a half-smile.

As the Uber carted us to the arena, I texted Chelsea.

Me: So, I'm here. In Santa Fe.

Chels: ...are you shitting with me?

I bit back a grin.

Me: Nope. I'll be at will-call in five minutes. Meet me there?

Chels: OKAY!

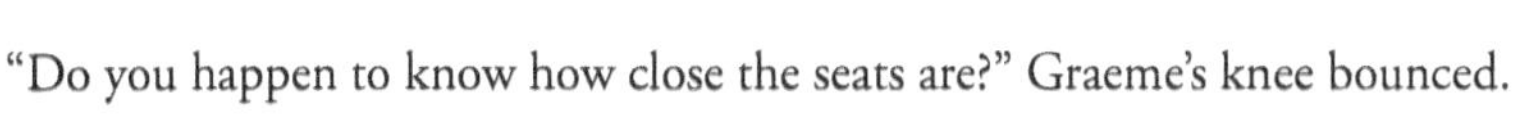

"Do you happen to know how close the seats are?" Graeme's knee bounced.

"I have no idea. I'd assume close given she has a direct connection with a fighter."

He dragged his hands down his face. "This is unreal."

I cocked my head to the side, taking in the bundle of nerves Graeme had become as we neared the arena. You'd think we were on our way to meet the King of the Gods or something.

And Alex was rubbing off on me way too much.

Chelsea was already there when we reached the ticket booth, pacing back and forth, looking through the crowds of people. Her gaze landed on me, and her entire face brightened with her smile. I grinned back, holding my arms out to receive the bear hug I knew she'd give. The waves of her fiery-red hair bounced as she ran over, somehow not tripping over the designer heels she wore.

Her arms wrapped around me. "Elani, it's been way, way too long."

"I'll try to get better about it, big sis." The familiar smell of her shampoo, honey, and apple blossom triggered memories of us as teens learning N'Sync choreography together—our escape after our parents divorced.

She leaned back, squeezing my shoulders. "And you brought a guest." Beaming at Graeme, she held out her hand.

"Chelsea, this is Graeme, Graeme, my sister Chelsea."

Graeme slapped on his charming smile, making his eyes squint as he shook her hand. "Pleasure to meet ye, and thank you for the ticket."

Chelsea's smile stretched. "No problem. And you're Scottish. Delightful." She elbowed me in the side.

We approached the ticket booth, and Chelsea asked for our passes.

"Who's Makos fighting?" A sad attempt on my part to act at least somewhat interested.

Chelsea opened her mouth to answer.

"Kelly Fitz. Makos is defending her title for the second time," Graeme interrupted, making his brow bounce.

"That's right. Big fan, huh?" Chelsea held the tickets out to me, but Graeme snatched them with a broadened smile.

"Do you need to get back to the locker room?" I watched Graeme preen over the tickets from the corner of my eye.

Chelsea folded her arms. "Yeah, unfortunately. But hey, I'll meet up with you after the fight. Can you stick around for a little bit and give your sister the time of day?"

I nudged her. "Yes, Chels."

"Good." She kissed my cheek. "Enjoy the fight."

"Oh, you know me."

"You're right." She shifted her eyes to Graeme. "I do."

After giving my arm a final squeeze, she disappeared into the crowd.

"Elani, these tickets are front row." He pointed at the seat numbers. "And center." His heels bounced in excitement.

"Nothing like getting blood and sweat in your eye, huh?" I tugged on his sleeve, leading him into the arena.

"That'd be quite the memento, aye?"

"I'd rather not have to worry about soaking my white shirt to get someone else's bloodstain off it, thanks."

"Aw, come on, lass." He whirled me to face him, brushing his hands up and down my arms. "Would ye like a pretzel? A hotdog, perhaps?"

I tapped my lips. "A hotdog."

"You got it." He handed me a ticket. "Meet ye at the seats." He gave my lips a quick peck.

I froze, hoping he didn't try to go further. When he turned away, walking toward the food stand, I let out a breath.

The seats, thankfully, were not *so* close you could get questionable bodily fluids on you. My knees bounced as I waited for Graeme, and I tapped my fingers against my thighs, peeking over my shoulder every ten seconds to spot him. The fourteenth time I glanced, Graeme walked side by side with a redhead. They smiled and laughed as if they knew each other. She squeezed his bicep before ducking into a row several behind ours.

He sat down, handing me a hot dog smothered in mustard, ketchup, and onions. Well, at least that'd play an excellent kiss deterrent—I wasn't ready for it. Would I ever be prepared for it?

"Sorry, I took so long."

"Who was that?" I motioned behind me with my head and shoved half of the hot dog in my mouth—mainly to keep myself from talking.

"An old friend. We met in Ireland years ago. Isn't it funny how two people can run into each other inexplicably from opposite ends of the globe?" His eyes twinkled.

Fate.

Talking with that much processed meat product in my mouth would've proved futile. Instead, I shrugged and smiled without teeth.

The lights dimmed as the fighter intros began. *Click Click Boom* by Saliva played for Kelly Fitz as she entered, exciting the crowds. After her opening, the familiar sounds of the *Wonder Woman* movie theme music boomed through the arena. I smiled to myself, knowing Chelsea had to be the one to pick it. The woman loved her gimmicks. Harm "Amazon" Makos worked her way through the crowd, the scowl deepening over her brow.

Chelsea had talked about Harm several times during our occasional catch-up phone calls. Most often, she used words to describe her as intense, closed-off, and confident. The woman I saw slip into the ring didn't look that way to me, however. She kept wincing, shaking her head, and furrowing her brow.

I leaned over to Graeme. "She looks distracted or something."

"Nah." He shook his head. "She's focused."

I frowned and sat back.

The fight started, and it didn't take long for Kelly to clip Harm in the side of the head.

"Oh, shite," Graeme mumbled.

Harm stared off in the distance, and her face fell blank. It was like her mind went somewhere else, leaving her body behind. Kelly hit her again, and Harm's swings turned desperate and uncalculated.

"She's going to lose," I whispered.

"No. No, she's got this. She has to," Graeme said with a snarl.

Harm stumbled backward, grasping the cage behind her. Kelly's foot slammed into the side of Harm's temple, sending her in a slump to the ground.

"I can't believe that just happened." Graeme held his face in his hands as the crowd around us booed and yelled.

Harm lay flat on her back in the ring. A man with dark hair pulled into a bun at the base of his head and equally as dark beard rushed to her side. He looked familiar. Another MMA fighter, maybe? I sighed, waiting for the inevitable text

from Chelsea. As if on cue, my phone buzzed in my purse.

Chels: Sorry little sis, I need to make sure Harm doesn't drink her way into oblivion.

Me: It's all good. We'll catch up again. Promise it won't be so long this time.

Chels: :-* Love you.

Me: Me too.

"Let's get the hell out of here. What a disappointment." Graeme shot to his feet, shaking his head and flicking his wrist at the cage like the fighters inside disgusted him. "I can't believe she lost."

"She had an off day." I followed behind him, taking one last glance behind me at Harm.

The bearded man stormed after her as she sprinted from the cage, ripping the gloves off before she even reached the locker room doors.

"She screwed up is what she did. It's hard to bounce back after a loss like that. Look at Rousey." He took my hand, interlacing our fingers.

I didn't know who he was talking about, but I found myself staring at our hands—our skin pressed against each other. No tingles. No flutters in my stomach. Not like what happened every single time with…no.

"You okay?" Graeme asked, shaking my hand.

I snapped my gaze to his face like I'd been caught staring at the lengthy impression in his pants. "Hm, what? Yeah. I'm fine, just a little tired."

"Fortunately for you, we got a semi-long flight you can sleep on." He pressed a kiss at the corner of my brow.

As we walked outside to wait on our Uber, I trailed a finger over where he kissed. Graeme was everything I needed laying out right there on paper. The algorithm chose him for a reason. And unlike the other failures, the formula matched us to our deeper-rooted characteristics. Admittedly, the Scottish portion of it was the biggest draw for me. We shared an ancient tie of culture. He even had the dark hair and eyes that always drove me wild. My gaze dropped to his chin—smooth. No cleft.

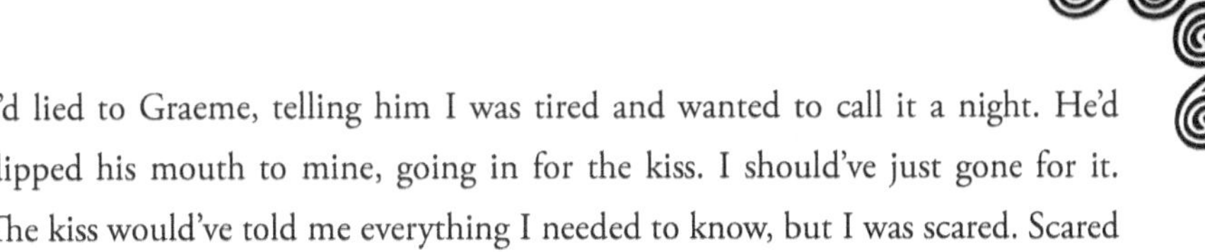

I'd lied to Graeme, telling him I was tired and wanted to call it a night. He'd dipped his mouth to mine, going in for the kiss. I should've just gone for it. The kiss would've told me everything I needed to know, but I was scared. Scared because deep down in my gut, I knew it'd tell me what I didn't want to hear. I needed to talk to Dad. He always had a way of making the world make sense. No matter how crazy it got.

I tapped my fingernail against the side of my laptop, watching the calling screen in front of me as it dialed. I glanced at the time, knowing Dad should still be up. Disappointment washed over me just as his face appeared on my screen.

I smiled. "Hey, Da."

"Elani? It hasn't even been a week since our last chat. Everything okay, lass?" His brow crinkled.

"Physically, yes."

"Lani." He leaned forward, making his green eyes fill the screen behind his glasses. "Talk to me."

"I met someone."

His face brightened. "Well, that's wonderful news. Why do you look so sad?"

"He's everything I should want. Has a great job. Charming. Funny. Handsome. He's even Scottish."

"Is he now? What clan?"

"MacFarlane."

Dad's lip bounced.

"Da." I chuckled.

"I'm kiddin'. I'm kiddin'. It sounds like your mind's made up. Do ye want to ask me what you really wanted to ask?"

I stared up at the ceiling. "I don't *feel* anything with him."

"Uh-huh. I thought you were looking for a partner for life, Lani girl. Not love."

I snapped my eyes back to him. "That's not what I meant."

"Isn't it?" His warm smile calmed me—soothed me.

Is that what I was waiting for?

No, no. Graeme and I just needed some more time. It'd click in at the opportune moment.

"I should go, Dad. I appreciate the talk."

"Lani." He leaned forward, taking off his glasses. "Don't close yourself off to the possibilities around you. Don't let what's happened to you in the past fog your chances of being happy. Eyes and ears open." He nodded once. "We'll talk again soon."

His face disappeared, replaced by a black screen. I stared at it, my heart thudding in my chest. Someone else had said nearly those exact words to me.

Eyes and ears open, champ.

EIGHT

"I CAN'T BELIEVE YOU followed me here," I said to Alex, who'd been on my heels since leaving the office.

"Given your track record lately, I don't think I can trust you with doing this alone anymore."

I bumped my hip against the door leading into The Arrow. "Do you want to date Graeme too?"

"I'd be down for a three-way." She raised one dark brow.

"Shut up, goober." I chuckled and turned my gaze to the bar.

No sign of Eric.

"Who you looking for?" Alex's chin dipped over my shoulder.

I jumped, clapping a hand over my chest. "No one."

"Liar, liar, I'm going to set your hair on fire for lying to me."

"That's not how the saying goes."

"My version does. You were looking for Eric, weren't you?"

"He's the bartender. How else am I going to get a drink? A free one, mind you?"

"I've got my eye on you, Stewart." She pointed to her eyes and then to me before sitting on a stool.

I leaned my forearms against the edge, tapping in rhythm while humming *You're Nobody 'Til Somebody Loves You* by Dean Martin.

"Dean Martin, huh?" Alex helped herself to a maraschino cherry from the other side of the bar.

"You know I love my crooners."

Eric appeared from the back room, and the sight of him made butterflies clash inside my stomach. He rubbed the back of his neck with a lop-sided grin, thanking the cocktail waitress for watching over the bar.

His blue eyes fixed on me, and a swagger formed in his step. "Ah. Brought back up this time, did you?" He grinned at Alex.

"I'm here of my own accord." Alex's face remained blank as she flipped the lid and grabbed another cherry.

"Those aren't for snacking, you know?" He snapped the lid shut.

"Then why have them so close to the customers?"

They weren't *that* close. She had to stand on the wrung of her stool to reach them.

Eric chuckled and popped the lid back open. "You know what? Knock yourself out."

He turned his attention to me, pressing his hands into the wood of the bar. The green and blue plaid of his flannel shirt reminded me of Clan Stewart hunting tartan colors.

"Did you have fun last night?" He raised his brow.

"The company was charming, yes." I folded my hands and rested them in my lap. "We have another date here tonight."

He cocked his head to the side, eyes searching my face and unabashedly scoping my chest. "You don't need to have every date here in the bar. You know that, right?"

"Sure, but I want you to bear witness to losing bit by bit." I challenged him with my stare.

He brought our faces closer, curling his bottom lip under his teeth. "How villainous."

"I'm finding my inner Maleficent."

His right eye twitched. "Funny, I'd call you more of an Ursula."

My jaw dropped, and I swatted him in the arm. The brief contact with the taut muscle hiding underneath his shirt sent a twinge from my stomach to my toes. I snapped my hand back to my lap.

He glanced down where I'd slapped him. "Well, I should whip you up another drink, eh?"

"You would be correct." I pressed my hands together so tightly under the bar

they trembled.

He tapped twice with his finger, trying to wink at me again before turning away and making my drink.

Alex's face appeared in my peripheral vision, her eyes centimeters from my head.

"Can I help you?" I leaned back, scanning her face.

"You cannot be this dense."

"Excuse me?"

She grabbed my face, squishing my cheeks, and turned my head, forcing me to look at Eric making my drink. He whistled to himself as he flipped bottles, flashing a smile now and again at the woman watching from the corner seat of the bar.

"Are you trying to make a point?" I asked with a muffled voice.

She groaned and let her hand drop. "Are you trying to tell me that you decided to come here for your date to make Eric suffer while he watched you with Graeme?"

"That's precisely why."

"Are you sure it's not because you find yourself having more fun bantering with Eric versus going places you don't like with Graeme?"

A glaring battle ensued between us. "I don't think I like what you're suggesting."

"Am I interrupting something?" Eric asked, holding a martini glass with yellowish-white liquid.

Alex glared at him and drummed her fingers. "Are you an archery enthusiast?"

"Did you see what I named my bar?" Eric pointed to the glowing red sign above us.

Her drumming turned into tapping. "You're awfully good at putting two people together. Does it run in the family?"

"You could say that." Eric narrowed his eyes.

"Alex—" I started, but she pressed a finger against my lips and kept her focus on Eric.

"You scratch your back a lot. Hiding something?"

"I've got a skin condition."

"That's disgusting."

"You asked."

My eyes darted between them like I was observing the world's strangest tennis match.

"Do any of your other names rhyme with stupid?"

Eric leaned in. "I have no idea what you're talking about, but I feel like I should be insulted somehow."

She slowly slipped off her stool. After pointing at him and then me, she pointed at her own eyes before moving to a different seat.

"That's Alex for you." I craned my head to the side. "What's this drink called?"

He squinted at Alex before shaking his head and brightening his eyes as he set the drink in front of me. "Fallen Angel."

My pulse raced.

"Does this work on women?" The words came out breathy.

"Sex on the Beach usually works fine." He grinned at me, deepening the dimple in his chin.

My gaze fell to his lips as I slid the glass across the bar. "And what's in this winged drink?"

"Gin, lime, crème de menthe – and a dash of magic."

"Magic? Wow. Did you sprinkle fairy dust in it?"

His eyes grew heavy. "Fairies ain't got nothing on me."

What was happening? Why was our dynamic changing, and more to the point…why was I going along with it?

"Sorry I'm late," Graeme said from behind me, making me jump and sputter, sending angelic liquid all over Eric's face.

I slapped a hand over my mouth, trying to hold back a laugh.

Eric had one eye closed, liquid rolling down it, and he chuckled. "Can't say I've ever had that happen before."

"I'm so sorry." I giggled as I grabbed a napkin.

Our gazes locked, my hand numbly dabbing his cheek.

"Can I get a beer, Eric?" Graeme leaned on the bar.

Eric took the napkin from my hand, making sure to graze his fingertip over my skin. The reaction was instantaneous, sending ripples of static shooting down my arm.

"Sure thing. Molson?"

"Perfect." Graeme's hand slid over my lower back, and he smiled at me as if

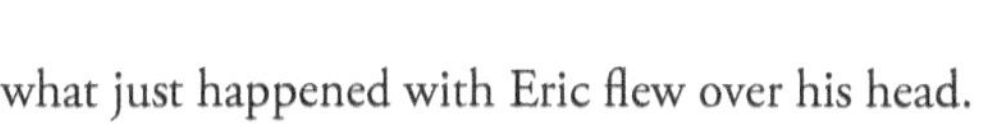

what just happened with Eric flew over his head.

I took a sip of my drink, noting the scent of mint from the leaves floating on top added to the experience.

"What drink is that?" Graeme asked, peeking at the concoction.

"A Fallen Angel."

"Prohibition classic. Very nice." He grinned as he brushed the tip of my nose with his. His eyes dropped to my lips.

I held the drink between us. "Would you like a sip?"

He squinted at me, his smile fading, and shook his head.

I could feel Alex's stare singing my hairline. She made an "o" shape with one hand and slid her finger in and out of it, motioning her chin at Eric. I waved my hands at her to stop making obscene gestures while my cheeks warmed. When I turned back to Graeme, his lips planted on mine. I tensed, splaying my hands in the air, staring at his closed eyes.

Not one single spark went off anywhere in me. No explosions behind my eyelids. Not even tingles.

He pulled away, licking at the corner of his lips. "Sorry. I've wanted to do that since the moment I saw you drinking scotch. Never thought I could be jealous of a beverage." He smirked, wiping the side of my mouth with a flick of his thumb.

"No reason to apologize. It was—" I smiled. "Nice."

A Molson bottle slammed on the bar top near us. Eric's forearms tensed as he leaned on the bar. "That'll be ten fifty."

Graeme kept his gaze on me as he fished into his back pocket, producing a wallet. My phone buzzed in my purse, and I snatched it, thankful for the reprieve—a long text from Dad.

Da: Lani, I'm feeling under the weather, and I think it's best if I skip our Scotland trip this year. I know you'll be disappointed, but take someone else with ye. Enjoy yourself. I love you.

I frowned and let the phone slip from my hand. Eric's arm shot out, catching it before it crashed to the ground.

"Everything okay?" Eric lowered his head so he could see my face.

"Sweetheart?" Graeme touched my shoulder.

I looked between the two men, my eyelashes fluttering. Words tried to come out, but only squeaks and cracks escaped. I didn't want to go to Scotland alone,

to represent Clan Stewart alone. But Graeme and I had only known each other for a matter of days. It'd be crazy to—

"Come to Scotland with me." I heard the words come out of my mouth, it was me who said them, but where they'd come from, I hadn't a clue.

Eric's eyes widened for a brief moment, and I tried my best to ignore him.

"Scotland? You're serious?" Graeme's eyes sparkled.

I nodded and whimpered at the same time.

"Well, when? How? I mean—" He blinked.

"Two days. My dad can't go this year. You can have his plane ticket. Please, Graeme?"

He chuckled. "A paid trip to Scotland? I'd be crazy to pass that up."

I jostled his shoulder. "It'll be fun. You can show me where you're from."

His eyes fell shut, and he snapped his fingers. "Two days. I have an important client meeting I can't miss."

"You can exchange the ticket? The Calling of the Clans isn't until Friday. I think I can manage alone for a night." I gave a weak smile.

"Alright. It's a date." His phone rang, and he sighed once he read the name on the screen. "I have to take this. Be right back." He pressed the cell to his ear, stood, and walked to a vacant corner.

"What are you doing, Elani?" Eric frowned.

"I'm going to Scotland with my future husband."

His brow rose. "Don't you think it's a little soon to be gallivanting across the globe?"

"You gave me three months. Nothing is too soon."

"You looked surprised when you asked him."

"You did." Alex slid onto the stool next to me. "And you sounded like a robot when you said it."

I pinched the bridge of my nose. "Will you both butt out? I have to make this work. Remember, Alex?"

She clucked her tongue against the inside of her cheek with a sigh.

"If this is about the bet, Elani, I—"

I threw a hand up. "This has gone beyond the bet. This is about Graeme and me."

There was a reason I'd never tried the algorithm on myself—an underlying

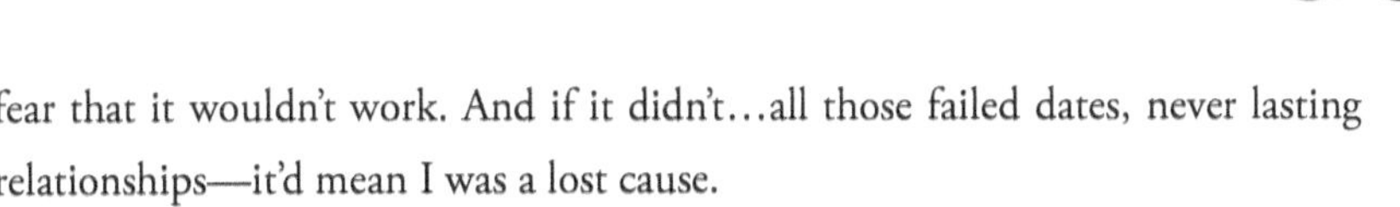

fear that it wouldn't work. And if it didn't…all those failed dates, never lasting relationships—it'd mean I was a lost cause.

My world didn't revolve around finding a guy, but the thought of living out the rest of my life alone…terrified me.

I blinked and looked at Alex. The side of her mouth twitched in her version of a warped smile.

A shadow cast over my brain, clouding my thoughts, making me wince.

"I'm going to Scotland with Graeme, and I'd appreciate it if we moved on from the subject."

Eric dragged a hand over his face and pushed away from the bar, retreating to a corner.

"One last thing, and I'll do as you ask and shut up." Alex rested her chin in her hand. "You had an open ticket for two weeks in Scotland, and instead of asking your best friend whom you've known for almost ten years, you ask a guy you've known for days. Doesn't sound like you, Stewart."

I scratched my temple. It *did* sound absurd.

She grabbed my shoulders, turning me to face her. "Honestly, I wouldn't have been so surprised if you would've picked the *other* one you've known for days, but Graeme? Is it because he's from the Motherland?"

"You said one last thing."

Alex sighed and slid from her stool. "You owe me some time tomorrow before you whisk off to the land of men going commando in kilts. Remember that."

"I wouldn't forget it for the world, Alex."

She playfully punched my shoulder and left, sticking her tongue out at Graeme as she went.

Graeme eyed her quizzically as he walked back over, slipping the phone into his pocket. "I've got to get going, Lani, but I guess the next time I see you will be in Scotland, aye?" He beamed, bending down to kiss me.

It was a brief touch of lips caressing against each other before he squeezed my forearm and whisked through the door.

Eric's face was in mine when I turned back around, making me teeter on my stool. His hand shot out, grabbing my arm, tensing to keep me from falling backward.

"Did Vena talk to you when I went to the back the other day?" His brow

furrowed, eyes unblinking and boring into my very being.

His touch rippled through me, taking my breath away.

I rubbed the skin between my eyes, trying to put together memories from that night. "All she said was goodbye."

The corners of his jaw tightened. "Anything else? Did she do anything at all, Elani?"

"Why are you interrogating me?"

He let go of my arm and balled his hands into fists. "It's important. Please?"

"She…blew me a kiss? Is that what you wanted to hear?"

His eyes closed, and a growl vibrated at the back of his throat.

"That doesn't seem that abnormal to me. I thought she was coy."

"It's—" He swiped a hand through his hair, giving the dark tendrils one firm tug. "It's hard to explain."

"You're scaring me, Eric." I curled my arms around myself, stealthily moving off the stool.

"I'm not trying to. Vena she's—she's complicated. Petty and deceitful. Do you understand?"

With baby steps, I moved toward the exit. "Sure. But what do any of those have to do with me?"

His blue eyes rippled like a strengthening current. "Everything."

I bumped into a chair.

Eric frowned and hopped over the table to stop me. He lightly grabbed my biceps and stared down at me, pleading in his gaze.

"What aren't you telling me?" I watched his anguished expression, the hard creases forming in his cheeks and forehead.

He winced and rolled his shoulders, making his jaw tighten. "Be careful in Scotland. If a thought or an action you do doesn't feel like yourself, try to fight it."

"What does that *mean*, Eric?"

He grimaced and rolled his shoulders again. "Just be careful." He grabbed my hand and scribbled something on it with a pen before curling my fingers over it. "My number. In case you want to gloat over how swimmingly your time with Graeme is going." He half-smiled but winced as if someone poked him in the side with a torch.

"I—okay. Are you alright?" I grabbed his shoulder.

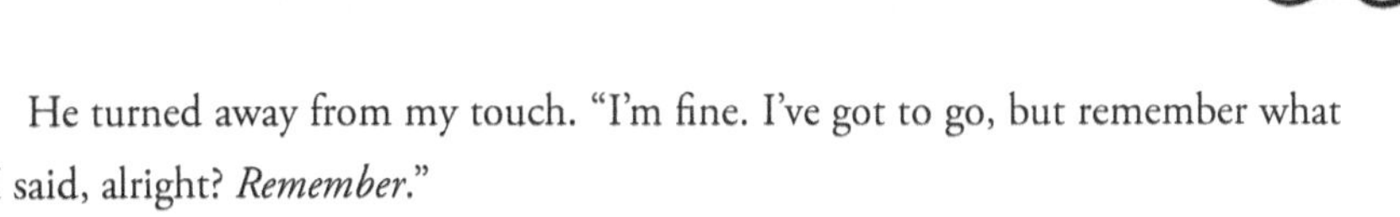

He turned away from my touch. "I'm fine. I've got to go, but remember what I said, alright? *Remember.*"

"Okay, okay."

He gave a curt nod before sprinting for the back. Either the guy had some gigantic skeletons in his closet or the world's worst case of IBS.

I opened my hand, staring down at the phone number with a tiny bow and arrow drawn on the end.

My brain told me to wash my hand, rid it of the number I didn't need. But heeding Eric's advice, I listened to my heart—a piece of me that whispered in my ear to save it.

NINE

THE NEXT DAY, I worked overtime, squaring away all my clients, given I'd be out of the country. I let out a gratifying sigh as I rested the phone headset on its cradle after the last call of the day. I pushed away from my desk, twirling twice in my rolling chair, and danced toward my office door, humming *Volaré* by Dean Martin.

Continuing my lively performance in the hallway, I belted the lyrics, using my ballpoint pen as a makeshift microphone. Alex's eyebrows rose so high it wrinkled her forehead.

"You're in an unusually chipper mood." Alex leaned back in her chair, tapping the pointy end of scissors on the corner of her keyboard.

"Why wouldn't I be chipper? I'm about to fly off to Scotland, I've got this handsome, amazing guy to go with, and I get to concentrate on finding myself a partner for once instead of matching dozens of other people." I rose on the balls of my feet and then flopped back to my heels.

"Uh-huh. I still can't believe you're going with Graeme and not Eric." She opened and closed the scissors, scraping metal against metal with each cut in the air.

I sat on the edge of her desk. "Why do you keep bringing up Eric? He isn't even on the radar."

She sat forward, flipping the scissors in her hand and pointing the handles in my face. "Are you a doppelganger? Did you switch places with my best friend?"

Delicately placing my hand on the scissors, I lowered them back to the safe

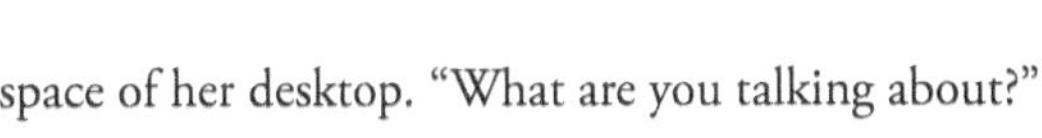

space of her desktop. "What are you talking about?"

"Elani. We've known each other for a long time. You're full of shit if you think I believe you never ever want to fall in love."

An odd sense of butterflies erupted in my stomach.

Love.

The past few days, I'd started to think of the possibilities more—open my heart to the chance of it. Graeme was that chance.

"You're right."

Alex blinked.

"I'm even singing Dean Martin songs."

She pointed the scissor handles at me again. "Ah, yes, but not Frank Sinatra."

"What does that matter? One member of the Rat Pack is the same as any other."

"Not for you." She twirled the handles on one finger like an old western cowboy with a pistol. "You only coo Frank Sinatra when you're deliriously happy. The last time I heard it was when you had that fling in Scotland with that bagpipe player whose name escapes me."

I chewed on my thumbnail. "Jamie. I blame my obsession with Outlander. I can't help that he had the same name too."

She rested the scissors in front of her. "My point is, I'm not sure you remember how to fall in love with a guy. And I have a hunch that you want Eric to remind you."

A curious irritation rumbled in my belly, and I shot to my feet. "Would you lay off on this whole Eric thing? I enjoy the banter with him, yes, but banter doesn't equate to a lasting relationship. Graeme is kind, attentive, sexy—"

Staring at me deadpan, Alex ever so slowly raised her phone as *I Want to Know What Love* is by Foreigner blared through the small speaker.

I hit the pause button.

"Come on, Lani. Let Eric bring the Frankie out of you. What have you got to lose?"

"Graeme. That's what. I like him, Alex. I really do."

At least that's what my brain told me. On the other hand, it didn't convince my heart, but my head was always my number one source of information—the "muscle" I used to make the hard decisions and lead me through life. Why would it be wrong about this?

"You know what?" She stood, sending her rolling chair flying behind her and into the back-cubicle wall. "We're going to do what I always do when I need to clear my head."

"And what's that?"

"Follow me." She brushed past me, marching as if she were a soldier on a mission.

"Ax throwing." I watched men and women of all ages hurling axes into round wooden targets at the end of each bay.

"Yes. I do this at least once a week. Sometimes more if I'm having an exceptionally shitty week." She twirled the handle of her ax in her hand.

"How did I not know about this?"

"It's not like I made an announcement every time I went."

"Throwing axes and drinking beer sounds like a horrible combination."

Glass mugs filled to the brim with frothy grainy beverages rested on the table several stalls down from ours, surrounded by a group of younger men sporting crew cuts and polos with the collars popped. Between rounds, they'd take several sips, chat, laugh, and go back to throwing.

"It's the *perfect* combination." She held the handle with two hands above her head and hurled it at the target.

Bullseye.

"Holy hell, Alex. You're good at this."

"There are few things in life that both help me relieve stress and make me giddy as a schoolgirl. Ax throwing happens to be one of them."

I cocked an eyebrow at her usual demeanor—quiet, not smiling, and heavy-lidded gaze. "This is you giddy?"

She frowned at me after taking a swig of her beer. "I'm ecstatic. You can't tell?"

"Oh, I mean yeah." I did an exaggerated nod and pointed at her mouth. "I almost see a half-smile. That's crazy."

She threw another, getting an additional bullseye. "Your turn."

Nerves prickled down my spine. "I don't know. With my track record, I'm more liable to hit the people in the next stall versus making it to the target."

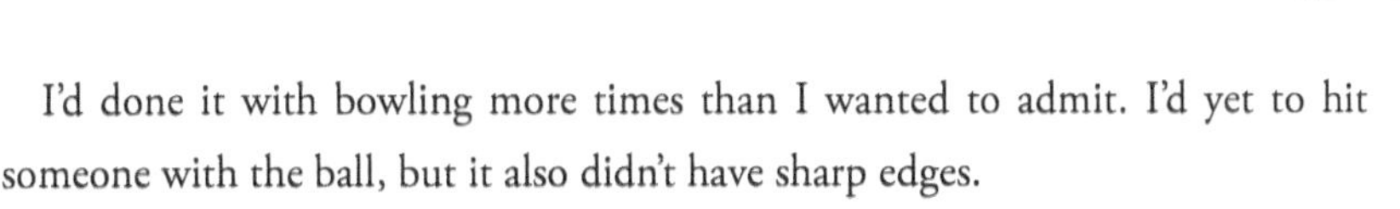

I'd done it with bowling more times than I wanted to admit. I'd yet to hit someone with the ball, but it also didn't have sharp edges.

"It's not as difficult as you're making it sound. Come on. I'll show you."

I took a decent swig of my beer, scrunching my nose at the hoppy taste curling over my tongue.

Alex held an ax out to me with a stiff arm. Begrudgingly, I took it, holding the handle with two fingers like it was a dirty diaper. Alex forced my hand to wrap around it and pulled me in front of her.

"Are we about to have a *Ghost* moment here?"

She snorted. "You'd be so lucky if I were Patrick Swayze."

Unlike most women, I'd never seen *Dirty Dancing*. Even Alex drooled at the very mention, so I didn't admit it to her. Ever.

"All you're going to do is hold the handle with both hands, lift over your head, and release." She pushed on my triceps.

Doing as instructed, I waited for her to back away before launching at the target. The hilt slammed into the side and fell to the ground in a sad slump.

"All I have to do, huh? Doesn't seem that easy," I grumbled.

Alex glared at me as she walked past to retrieve my failure. "Stop it, pity party. It was your first throw."

I traced circles on the back of my neck, thinking about that moment in The Arrow. There was a fleeting moment where Eric looked at me like I'd suddenly become the Ghost of Christmas Past. I'd been too distracted by Graeme to give it much thought until now.

"Try again, E." Alex twirled the ax and handed it to me.

Closing one eye, I lined up my shot and threw it. It not only didn't land blade side up but launched into the target sideways.

"Apparently, I was *not* a warrior in a past life. My ancestors were probably shepherds and cattle farmers."

Alex retrieved the weapon, tossing it between both palms as she returned. "Who also more than likely knew how to defend themselves."

I turned for the table of distracting elixir. "How about some beer, aye?"

"I've been thinking." Alex slammed the ax onto the table, making our pitcher of Molson slosh. "And hear me out."

"Oh, boy. Last time you started a sentence like that, you tried to convince me

Ace of Apollo's Suns was *the* Apollo."

"I still stand by that statement." She stared at me over the rim of her plastic cup as she took a sip. "And this is in the same wheelhouse."

"Here we go."

"What if Bartender Eric isn't really Eric?"

"What? You mean he's using an alias?"

"Sure." She poured more beer into her cup. "But beyond that."

I grabbed the ax. "Please don't tell me you think he too is a Greek god."

"Hey. I said to hear me out before you get all skeptical and judgmental."

I moved to the target with a deep sigh. "You're right. Talk away."

"What if Eric is the god of love?"

I snort laughed at her over my shoulder. "Eros? The god of love?"

Alex pressed a hand over her chest. "Be still, my heart. You know something about Greek mythology."

"I know more than you think." After tossing a smug grin, I turned back to the target.

"You've been holding out on me, Stewart. Anyway, think about it. He has some magical match-making ability, and women fawn over him like he's oozing with sex and charm." She rubbed one eyebrow with her pinky. "I even felt a little… tingle."

Grinding my teeth together, I hurled the ax at the target. The blade landed this time but nowhere near the bullseye. "Or maybe, he's just an attractive bartender who talks to people every day and therefore knows or *thinks* he knows how to pair people up."

"Does your brain get any oxygen?"

I yanked the blade from the packed straw. "What?"

"Your head's so thick I just wonder how it has any room to breathe."

"Ha. Ha." Sauntering back to the table, I dangled the handle of the ax between two fingers. "Besides, if he were the Greek god of love, where are his wings? Hm?"

"Grasping at straws there. You think a god couldn't, I don't know?" She flicked her wrist. "Disguise them?"

Absently swinging the ax back and forth, I stared into the distance.

Alex snatched the ax handle. "You're going to lose a toe."

The skin under my eyes wrinkled as I searched my best friend's face. For as long

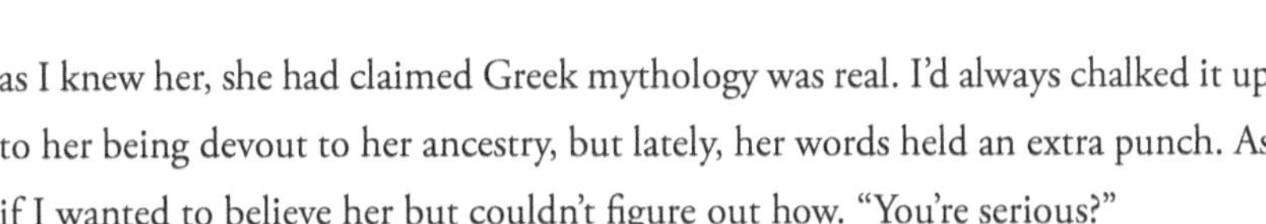

as I knew her, she had claimed Greek mythology was real. I'd always chalked it up to her being devout to her ancestry, but lately, her words held an extra punch. As if I wanted to believe her but couldn't figure out how. "You're serious?"

"Have I ever once stuttered or laughed when referencing the gods?"

"You don't really stutter or laugh when referencing *anything*."

She pointed the ax blade at me. "You're tip-toeing."

"Fine." I yanked the ax back. "If Eric suddenly sprouts wings, you'll be the first I talk to so you can scream to Mount Olympus that you told me so."

"Deal."

My shoulders tensed, I turned for the target, hurled the ax, and it slammed into the bullseye with a satisfying crunch.

"You're really worked up over this, huh?"

I turned to face her, seething. "Away and boil your head." Brushing past her, I hurried to the table, curling both hands around my cup.

"See? See? You're going all Scottish on me."

An unsteadiness gripped my spine, wringing it like a sponge.

Scottish. Scotland.

That was still happening. Very much happening without Dad and very much *with* Graeme. A part of me wanted to scream, but a larger portion pushed its way through, forcing me to preen over the thought of Graeme's sultry darkened gaze.

"Dammit, I'm going to miss you. Right when your life was getting interesting." Alex nudged me in the shoulder, which was the closest she'd ever gotten to hugging me.

"I'll be back, weirdo." I nudged her.

"Yeah. By then, Eric the Bartender AKA Eros will have already found someone else to flutter those disgustingly long male lashes at." Her nudge turned into a light punch.

A peculiar knot settled like hardened concrete in my stomach. "Good. It'll give him something more constructive to concentrate on instead of my love life."

"But—"

I held a finger up. "And don't say it's his job, Alex, or so help me."

She slow-blinked.

The digital clock hanging on the back wall read 20:45, and my shoulders slumped. "Come on. You got me for another fifteen minutes before I have to get

to bed and rise with the dead at 4:00 AM tomorrow."

Alex made a gagging gesture.

We spent the remaining dwindling minutes hurling the ax, and I didn't make another bullseye. I crawled into bed that night with a foggy brain—as if my thoughts weren't mine, and I was a stranger in my own skin. Maybe a trip to the land of my ancestors was exactly what I needed. And maybe having the first night to myself would help clear the cobwebs.

TEN

FEELING RATHER SAUCY IN the middle of the night, I slipped on the one negligee I owned—a fiery red one—and snapped a photo to send to Graeme. Highly uncharacteristic of me but I felt compelled to do it regardless. Anyone who passed up a free trip to Scotland would be a complete buffoon, but a little extra incentive couldn't hurt.

I sat in the cab the following day on the way to the airport, repeatedly refreshing my text messages. Graeme had yet to reply. Was it too forward? Did he hate red? Was my body not what he imagined with his metaphoric x-ray vision staring at my clothes in the bar?

With a grunt, I gave up and tossed my phone into my purse.

"Where you headed, miss?" The driver glanced at the rear-view mirror, his eyes hidden behind the Ray-Ban sunglasses resting on his wide-brimmed nose.

"Scotland." I rested my chin on my hand, staring out the window at people on the sidewalk, watching him from the corner of my eye.

His bushy gray eyebrows rose, deepening the wrinkles in his forehead. "Wow. What's in Scotland?"

"My family." I didn't mind small talk in cab rides but preferred to give short answers. Dad used to tell me they could be interviewing you to see if they wanted to rob you blind. I'd never been mugged, but the thought stayed in the back of my brain into adulthood.

The driver nodded, removing his blue Maple Leafs baseball cap long enough to scratch his bald head and slip it back on. "Special occasion?"

"Calling of the Clans." The air escaping my nose fogged up the window, and I drew a little heart.

The driver went silent.

I half-smiled. "Members from different clans come from all over the world to represent their own. It's a big festival. A small ceremony with mostly drinking and dancing."

"Sounds amazing. And in a land surrounded by castles, hm?" His thick mustache bristled as he grinned.

My smile widened. "It's beautiful. Even with all the rain."

The driver stayed quiet for the rest of the trip, and I checked my phone another four times with still no reply from Graeme. Once at the airport, I went through the regular humdrum routine of gate check-in, security, and two tram rides to get to my international gate. And now it was time to peruse gift shops for two hours until my departure.

Have they created teleportation yet? Ugh.

Canadian souvenirs—maple syrup, maple leaf keychains, t-shirts, and hats filled gift shop number one to the brim. All overpriced and complete junk if you asked me. As I made a beeline for the magazine rack, *The Shoop Shoop Song (It's In His Kiss)* played over the loudspeakers. It started subtly, but then the music boomed in my ears. I clapped my hands over my head in a panic, spying customers staring at me wide-eyed.

How could they not hear how loud the music had gotten?

Grimacing, I raced out of the shop. Thankfully, the music faded away, replaced by kids crying, dozens of conversations, and the faint buzz of the overhead lights. I never thought I'd be so thankful for ambient airport noises.

Another shop one gate down had nothing but books and magazines. Perfect. It was a ritual of mine to buy a new book or several magazines I'd read to entertain me on the plane ride. Though I always hoped my body would let me sleep for the duration of the flight. I dragged my fingertip over various books that caught my attention—*Blood & Promise, Famine, Divine Blood.*

My neck tensed as *This Kiss* by Faith Hill played lightly in the background. The decibel raised until yet again, it was as if the speaker blasted right next to my ear. I ground my teeth together with a growl and wanted to shout to the universe, "Shut up!"

"Excuse me?" Said a woman perusing the bookshelf next to me.

I'd said that out loud. Was I losing my mind?

"Not you. Sorry, I'm—" The word "kiss" repeated several times in the song, and the modestly-sized shop suddenly felt like a coffin.

An image of Graeme leaning forward with his lips parted and eyes closed flashed through my brain. Frantically, I shook my head with such force, my vision blurred.

I bolted out to the walkway, the coolness from the A/C vents above drafting over my face, squelching the ever-growing heat in my cheeks. Heading for my gate, I found a vacant seat in the corner surrounded on three sides by walls. After plopping down and flipping the hood of my sweatshirt over my head, letting part of it droop over my eyes, I shoved in my earbuds. I'd show whatever cataclysmic force was trying to mess with my brain who's boss. I couldn't hear music from the loudspeakers if I piped my own playlist into my head.

The familiar Italian music fluttered into my ears, and my eyes burst open. *That's Amoré* by Dean Martin. I shrieked and tore the earbuds away, throwing them into the aisle. I didn't care if someone stomped on them, stole them, or threw them away.

No more music.

Lifting my feet, I wrapped my arms around my legs and buried my face against my knees.

Was this how having a mental meltdown felt?

I ignored everyone and everything until I heard the gate agent announce we were boarding. Bring me to the land of rolling green hillsides, bagpipes, ale, and kilts. Take me away from irritating yet devilishly charming bartenders, pushy friends who made too much sense, and repeatedly failed dates. In roughly fourteen hours, I'd step off the plane, smell the dew in the air, and all problems would melt away.

ONE LAYOVER IN LONDON, FOURTEEN
HOURS, AND A TRAIN RIDE LATER...

I stepped out of the cab, taking an extra-long inhale of the fresh air. The hustle and bustle of Toronto city life never felt like this. Though the sun hid behind gray

clouds, the majestic fog sweeping over the bright green countryside all around me made up for the lack of warming light.

The driver honked as he drove away, sticking his arm out the window to give a hearty wave. A settled smile pulled over my lips, and I waved back. People always seemed more carefree in Scotland. The yearly trip was better and more effective than any therapy session.

Rolling my suitcase behind me and adjusting the duffle bag on my shoulder, I walked down the small dirt path leading to the bed and breakfast Dad and I always stayed at—a quaint cottage with only two bedrooms owned by a lovely woman named Flora. Not only was it prime walking distance from where they held the festival in Carbost, but it was right down the street from a cozy pub and a five-minute walk to the beach.

I stopped in front of the cottage, beaming at its white-washed stone walls and contrasting black shingles. A wooden sign hung over the doorway; a Celtic-designed heart carved underneath the name. *Ghaoil Cottage.*

Huh. I didn't practice my Gaelic as often as Da would like, but I didn't recall the place we'd stayed in for over a decade being called Love Cottage. In fact, I thought it was the name of some flower in Gaelic. Shrugging, I breezed through the door, pausing in the foyer that'd been transformed into a petite lobby area.

A small podium with a phone, a binder, and several sets of keys hung on pegs on the wall behind it. A note stating, "Give Us a Ring" pinned to a corner of the desk, a slightly rusted bell over it. I slapped my palm on the bell, making the chime echo.

"I'm here, I'm here," Flora's familiar voice sounded from the hallway.

A welcoming smile already stretched my face when Flora rounded the corner. Her blazing green eyes widened and then softened, arms flying out at her sides. Her salt-and-pepper-colored hair was pulled back in wavy curls to a bun in the middle of her head. The brown dress and white apron shifted from side to side as she ran forward, wrapping her arms around my shoulders in a tight hug.

"Lani, dearie. So glad to see you again," she cooed against the side of my head.

I hugged her back. My Scottish mom is how I referred to her. Whenever I was in Scotland, she took on this maternal instinct I suspected stemmed from having never been able to have any children of her own. I ate every ounce of it up.

"It's so good to see you, Flora." Not letting her go, I let the subtle smell of

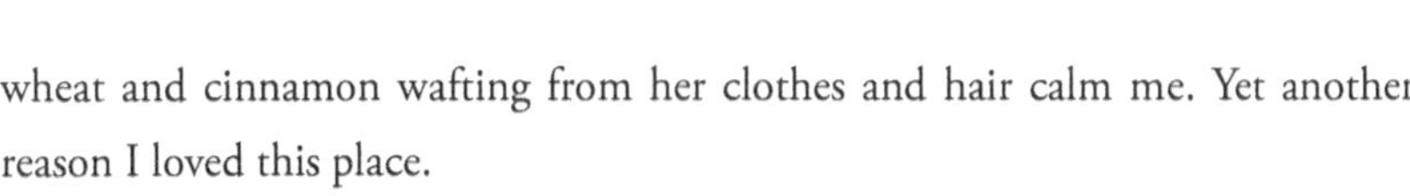

wheat and cinnamon wafting from her clothes and hair calm me. Yet another reason I loved this place.

She gasped, grasping my shoulders and pulling back. "Where's your da?"

"He couldn't make it this year. Been a bit sick and didn't want to take any chances."

She frowned and patted my arms. "That's a right shame. You've been comin' together since you were a wee bairn."

I nodded, plucking my thumbnail against the handle of my suitcase.

"You here by yourself, then?" She touched a slightly gnarled knuckle under my chin, her skin warm and smooth.

"For tonight." I half-smiled. "A man I'm seeing is coming out tomorrow for the festival."

She gave a wicked grin, making an "ooo" sound, and elbowing me. "What be his name? What does he do?"

"You have a fresh pot on?" I jutted my head toward the kitchen.

A corner of her lip lifted. "You know I always do, lass. Come, come." She frolicked into the kitchen, pulling out one of six wooden chairs surrounding a round chestnut table.

I slipped my gray peacoat off, draping it on the back of one chair before sitting. Flora hurried to the counter, whipping out two cups, sugar cubes, and a porcelain milk carton. After pouring steaming cups of rich coffee and setting everything on a tray, she returned to the table.

"Mm. The coffee is so much better here than in Canada." I wrapped my hands around the mug, letting the warm vapors moisten the tip of my nose.

After taking a seat, Flora dropped two sugar cubes into her coffee. "Oh? And why's that, you figure?"

"I haven't the foggiest." I poured a dabble of milk, followed by one cube of sugar. "The grains are more refined, maybe?"

"We didn't come in here to talk about caffeinated beverages, did we, lass?" She grinned mischievously over the rim of her mug, taking a small sip.

I tapped my fingernail against my cup. "His name is Graeme. He's Scottish. *From* Scotland. Hearty accent and all."

"In Canada? Well then. Tis a small world, aye?" She adjusted in her seat, scooting forward to rest her elbows on the table. "Handsome, I'd imagine?"

"Oh, yes. Dark hair. Dark eyes. Nice smile. He's a sports agent."

"Sounds fancy. What sport? Rugby?"

I chuckled, spitting a little bit of coffee from the corner of my mouth, and dabbed it with a napkin. "Rugby isn't exactly popular in Canada. He's a hockey agent."

"Oh, aye. Should've known that I suppose." Her smile warmed my belly more than the coffee itself.

"I missed you, Flora."

She reached across the table, patting the top of my hand. "I missed you too, lass. But what's troublin' ye?"

My eyebrows shot up. "Troubling me?"

"Mmhm. You've got this look about ye. And for invitin' a lad to Scotland, you don't look as happy about it as I'd imagine."

My stomach rumbled. "I mean—that's not to say I—"

Flora tapped my hand twice before she pulled away.

"I *am* excited, Flora. I am. It's just—my mind has been foggy lately. It's as if my brain can't process or compartmentalize my thoughts. Which, you know me, it's what I do. Hence the entire creation of my business."

She squinted one eye, making the skin at the corner form deep creases. "Do you have feelings for him?"

My heart thumped against my chest like I'd been caught in a lie. "Who?"

"What do you mean, who?" She cackled. "Graeme."

I pinched my eyes shut before bursting them open again. "Graeme. I mean— maybe? He makes me smile. He's kind, affectionate..." My voice trailed off, thoughts delving into traitorous territory with images of Eric's smile and awkward wink invading what brain space I had left.

"Aye. You're probably just nervous, Lani girl. Not every day someone goes on a romantic getaway to Scotland, hm?"

"Nervous. Yeah, you're probably right." I took a big gulp of my coffee, almost choking on it.

"Here you are drinking caffeine, and I know you must be tired."

I snickered, downing what was left in the mug. "I need a much stronger cure for sleepiness nowadays, I'm afraid."

"Sex?"

I coughed and clapped a hand over my chest. "I suppose that's uh—one way?"

"Look at you and your rosy cheeks over the word sex." Her eyes sparkled as she stared at me, sipping her coffee.

It wasn't so much the word as it was who said it. Biological mum or no, it was still awkward.

"I really should get to bed. Long day tomorrow." I took my mug to the sink, memories of the fires burning for the festival already sparking in my mind.

"Does he have a clan?"

"MacFarlane." I stared at the metal faucet. A drop of water fell every few seconds.

Flora's chair creaked against the wooden floorboards. "Is he going to stand for Stewart too?"

I frowned and spun to face her. "We didn't talk about that. I'm not sure he's ever been to a Calling of the Clans."

"Sounds like you two need to have a wee chat. Wouldn't want a MacGregor incident, would ye?" She cocked a brow and patted my cheek as she slipped past me to tidy up the sink.

The MacGregor incident. It happened nearly a decade ago, but it was hard to forget. He single-handedly made the village outlaw use of fire during the festival for several years in a row. During the processional, he zigged when he should've zagged, panicked, dropped his torch, and set fire to several buildings. It took months to rebuild.

No. I definitely did *not* want to be a MacGregor.

"Goodnight, Flora." I gave her a quick peck on the cheek and felt her lingering gaze at my back as I carted my belongings upstairs.

The sight of the two twin beds Dad and I had always used made my heart squeeze. Two simple beds with metal posting and light pink blankets. The room's smell gave away the cottage's age, but it didn't smell musty or dusty. It smelled like comfort. There wasn't much else in the room save for a small desk and chair, a window seat, and a wooden dresser painted white. Chips of the paint had started to wither away, revealing the deep brown color underneath.

Two twin beds. Oh, dear God. Graeme wasn't exactly…petite. He wouldn't fit on one like Da.

I gasped and slapped my hands over my mouth. What if he wanted to *share* a

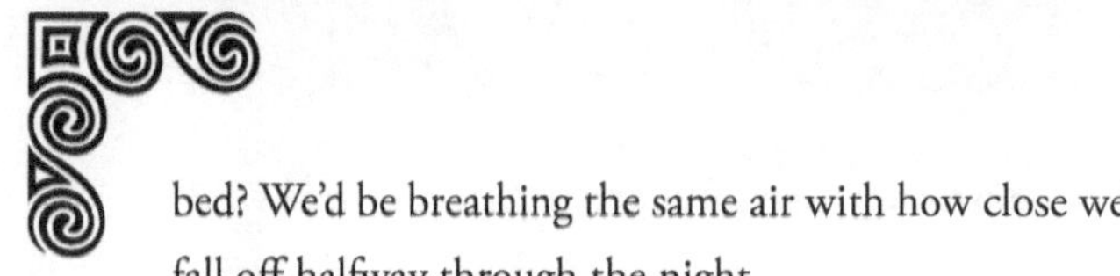

bed? We'd be breathing the same air with how close we'd have to be. I'd probably fall off halfway through the night.

Slide them together?

I pushed one bed, the metal legs scraping and groaning against the floor. Scratch marks glared back at me as it dug into the wood, and I let go with a yelp.

Great. What was supposed to be a relaxing vacation already had my anxiety skyrocketing.

I flopped my suitcase onto the bed Da usually slept in and removed my skirted kilt—white and red plaid with lines of yellow and blue. The red royal Stewart tartan was most popular, but I brought the dress colors since it was a special occasion. I carried it to the desk chair and draped it over the back to allow any wrinkles from travel to fade away.

Biting my cuticles, I snatched my phone from my purse and turned it on, waiting for it to work its magic and figure out the new location. As I stared at the text message icon, my heart galloped, hoping, expecting a response from Graeme. A solid two minutes went by, and still absolutely nothing. My throat dried.

I opened a new window and typed:

Me: I made it to Scotland in one piece! Can't wait to see you. Xoxo.

My thumb hovered over the send button, staring at the "xoxo." Rolling my bottom lip past my teeth several times, I deleted the "xoxo" and hit send. Groaning, I slapped my phone on the desk across the room and crawled into bed. I'd been traveling in the same clothes all day. What difference did it make to sleep in them too?

My mind whisked me off to dreamland, and it was full of nothing but white feathers floating around me in droves. One brushed against my lips, sending a static tingle down my spine. The same tingle I'd gotten…from Eric's touch.

ELEVEN

I'D SPENT MOST OF the next day roaming the countryside, returning every half an hour to the cottage to check for messages from Graeme. The cottage was the only place I could get a decent signal being in the middle of nowhere. The festival didn't start until sunset, but Graeme still hadn't shown, and I worried if something happened.

It was my last attempt at checking my phone before I'd give up, my heels brushing the wood floor as I breezed past Flora.

"Still no sign of him, lass?" Flora bit back a frown as she sat in front of the stone fireplace in the lobby, reading one of her Highlander romance novels.

Nerves prickled the back of my neck. "He'll show."

"Chin up if he doesn't, dearie." Her frown deepened, and she tapped her finger against the book's cover.

I lifted my head. "He will, Flora. I know it."

After slapping on as convincing a smile as I could manage, I galloped up the stairs and to the window to regain the signal. My heart raced as I watched the bars go up, staring at the tiny envelope icon on my home screen.

Nothing. Absolutely nothing.

Grimacing, I tossed the phone on the bed. It landed on a corner, bounced, and flew to the floor, dislodging the battery. I gasped and dropped to my knees, praying the expensive minicomputer still worked. After popping the battery back in, I took a deep breath and pushed the power button. Aside from the screen now appearing as cracked ice…it still worked.

I slumped on the edge of the bed.

I'd never done this without Dad. How pathetic would I look representing Clan Stewart alone? I couldn't recall the last time I'd seen *anyone* walking the torch by themselves. The sight of my kilt draped over the nearby chair made my heart swell with pride. Alone or not, I'd make Stewart's presence known and reenact the loyalty pledge from days past. Da would typically be the one to say the pledge, but being it was the twenty-first century, I didn't see one thing wrong with a woman saying it instead.

Swiping the kilt, I slipped into it, pulling the fly plaid sash over my left shoulder. I stared at the dingy full-length mirror and attached the clan brooch to the sash—a pelican feeding its young in a nest with the clan motto: *Virecit vulnere virtus.*

Courage grows strong at a wound.

My chest tightened as I ran my finger over the pelican, tears filling my eyes. Sniffling, I shook my head and pointed at my reflection.

"None of that, Lani girl. You don't need Graeme to be here. You know this festival so well you could run it blindfolded. Time for a new chapter."

There was still a tiny part of me that hoped Graeme would show up at the last possible second and sweep me off my feet. Another part of me wanted him to show up so that I could berate him for ignoring me. Wincing away the confusion plaguing my thoughts, I returned to the lobby, ready to have the time of my life with my fellow Scots.

Flora whistled as I descended the stairs, making my cheeks blush.

"Well, don't you make a bonnie representative for Stewart?" Flora's grin spread wide.

Flora was a vision in her Clan Wallace tartan—red and black plaid with thin yellow stripes. She always opted to wear the colors like a woman would've worn in the nineteenth century, wrapped around her shoulders with a muted long brown skirt.

My spirit lifted as I hugged her. "Is William standing with you?"

"Aye. He knows I'd kick him in the arse if not." She winked and held out her hand. "Our spots aren't far from each other. I'll walk with you."

Flora curled her arm with mine, and we braved the chilly nip in the air as we ascended the hills.

"Have you ever thought about movin' here?" Flora lifted her chin.

"To Scotland?"

"Nay. To this very spot here on the ground." She pointed at the grass and playfully swatted my arm. "Aye, Scotland. You always seem at peace here."

"I never gave it any thought. It's like another world here. I'd fear losing the fantasy of it all if I moved here, I suppose." The moon appeared through the clouds, casting white and blue shadows over anything the light touched.

"You want to live in a fantasy world?"

Desperately.

"I'm no child, Flora, I know a fantasy is a fantasy, but when I come here every year, I can…pretend."

The moonlight animated swirling shapes that resembled tiny sprites in my mind. They bounced from left to right, spreading the illumination like glazing sparkles.

"Here we are. Time to clan segregate, I suppose." Flora patted my hand, slipping her arm from mine, but paused, gripping my elbow. "You sure you're going to be alright?"

I snapped to attention, pulling on my long sleeves to cover most of my hands. "Absolutely. Go join William."

William stood on an adjacent hill, his white hair competing with the brightness of the moon itself. He excitedly waved for Flora.

Flora gave me a quick peck on the cheek before hiking up her skirts and trotting over to William. "Hold your horses, ye old fop."

The sound of my own breath breezing in and out of my nose quieted the low murmurs of surrounding clan members taking their spots. I forced a smile as someone handed me a lit torch. The flame flickered and popped, mesmerizing me with its unruly dance. In one swift motion, I could drop the torch and watch the fire transform anything and everything around me. Some it'd destroy, but other areas it'd touch…would be reborn.

"Clans at the ready," a man shouted, his kilt swishing with every wide stride he took through the waiting groups.

The flame blurred as tears filled my eyes. I really was doing this alone. The sound of the horn blowing, calling the clans to gather at the centerfire made my chest swell and ache simultaneously. I took one step forward, my lip trembling as

I fought back the emotions swirling through me.

A hand slid across my lower back. The long breath that escaped my lungs curled through the cool air like fog, and my eyes fell shut.

"Graeme. I knew you'd—" I whirled around, blasting my eyes open, and froze.

Eric smiled down at me, deepening his dimples. His blue eyes beamed as he trailed a hand over the royal Stewart sash adorning his chest.

"I—" The silence which held in the air stole away my words.

Eric stood before me in my clan's tartan colors—red plaid. And it wasn't just any kilt. It was a great kilt—the style they wore back in the days of Highlanders with extra fabric to fit as a cloak or used for carrying items. I said it before, and I'd say it again…the man looked *good* in plaid.

"Hi." Eric nudged his knuckle under my chin.

A single tear rolled down my cheek.

"You didn't think I'd let you go this alone, did you?" He raised his brow, tracing his thumb over my cheek, taking the tear with him.

The tears melted away, replaced with a wide grin, and I jumped, wrapping my arms around his neck.

He chuckled into my hair, returning the embrace.

"I could honestly kiss you right now," I whispered.

How did he know Graeme wouldn't be here? I couldn't ask right now. No, *not* right now.

His warm breath skirted over my neck. "I'm going to hold you to that at some point."

My body stiffened, but right then, I didn't care. I really *could* kiss him for showing up in the nick of time, saving me from the awkwardness of presenting my clan alone. I'd have done what was needed, but having someone at my side— was worth its weight in gold.

"Hey Lani girl, be careful with that torch, aye? Don't be a MacGregor." A man from the Campbell clan shouted from nearby.

I looked up at the flame flickering dangerously close to a drooping tree branch and yelped, dropping to my feet. Tilting my head over my shoulder, I held the torch up to Campbell with a sheepish grin.

"Want to explain it all to me, so I'm not a uh…MacGregor?" Eric scratched the back of his head.

I bit back a smile. "We walk the torch down the hill and wait for the 'Chieftain' to call our clan. When he does, we walk forward, announce our presence, say the clan motto, and throw the torch into the larger fire."

Holding the torch high, I watched for any other unruly tree limbs. Eric clasped his hands behind his back as we walked.

"I don't know your clan motto."

"Virescit vulnere virtus." I grinned up at him, noting how the orange glint from the fire made his eyes a pretty cerulean color. "Courage grows strong at a wound."

"Easy enough." He slipped his hands into the folded part at the front of his great kilt, taking a moment to scan dozens of other torches making their ways over the hills like giant fireflies. "This is quite the sight."

A warmth pooled in my belly. "I wouldn't miss it for the world."

"I know."

My head snapped at him. "How?"

"You say you don't believe in love, but it bursts from you. Passion for your family, for your culture, what is it if not love?" His head cocked to one side.

Tension coiled over my neck. "That's a different kind of love."

"Is it?"

I cinched my brow, forcing my focus on the embers floating from the torch. "There's also a reenactment of swearing allegiance to the Chieftain. It's a bit of a speech, so I'll say it."

"Anything I need to do?"

I appreciated he didn't press me further on the whole "love" business. "Just kneel beside me and look pretty."

His nose lingered near my ear. "You think I'm attractive?"

"You know you are." I snorted, not minding how close he was. Warmth radiated from his cheek, and I wanted to nestle into it but didn't.

"It sounds so much better coming from your lips, though."

I turned to face him, the fire from the torch casting shadows over the sharp edges of his jaw—his high cheekbones. "How did you know Graeme wouldn't be here?"

Eric frowned. "I've known plenty of men like him."

"That doesn't answer my question."

Eric sighed and took my free hand in his, grimacing from the chill on my skin. He cupped his hands over it and blew warm breath over my fingers. "Does it really matter that much to you, Elani? Can you just enjoy having someone beside you?"

The skin between my eyes creased. He was right. I focused on all the wrong things. But then—what if something terrible happened to Graeme, and that's why he couldn't answer any of my texts?

"But what if he got in a car accident or something worse?" My heart thudded at the same time my brain tried to slap me. It seemed they were in a constant battle as of late.

Eric's eyes flew to the heavens. "He didn't."

I stopped walking, turning to face him. "How do you know, Eric?"

"He came into the bar right before I left."

The world slowed around me, and my cheeks tingled as if tiny raindrops rolled down them.

"And he wasn't alone."

My bottom lip trembled.

Eric's jaw tightened, and he slid an arm around my waist, pulling me against his chest. "This is why I didn't want to tell you right now. This is supposed to be a happy moment for you."

"There has to be an explanation," I mumbled into one of his taut pecs, desperately trying not to grope it with the side of my face.

"You know, I'm surprised you're not wearing the red Stewart tartan." His deep voice echoed through his chest, pulsing against my ear.

"Why?"

He dropped his lips near my ear and whispered, "Because you look ravishing in red."

What did he—my eyes flew open, and I pushed away.

Oh. My. God. The lingerie pic.

Heat flushed up my back, spreading to my neck and face with vigorous speed.

"Clan Stewart," the "Chieftain" called out.

Mortification swarmed through me in unending waves.

Eric's fingers trailed the back of my neck, making my spine feel like warm apple pie. A snarky grin spread over my lips, and I felt tipsy—but wasn't. Not one drop

of alcohol.

"Clan Stewart, aye!" I cried out, holding the torch up while Eric yelled the same alongside me. "Virescit vulnere virtus." He said it word for word with me without hesitation.

I snuck him an appreciative smile, and he gave a botched wink. Stepping forward, I sunk to one knee, removing a small dagger from a folded pleat of my kilt. Eric knelt beside me with questioning eyes but following my lead nonetheless.

"Clan Stewart gives our fealty and pledges our loyalty. If our hand should ever raise against you, we ask this dagger find our hearts."

I spied Eric's brow lifting from the corner of my eye.

The man playing as Chieftain bowed his head with a warm smile, and I rose. He sipped from a pewter cup with two handles on each side—a Quaich filled with scotch, before handing it to me. I took a gulp and gave it to Eric. After drinking, he held the cup in his hands, drumming his fingers on the sides. I motioned with my head for him to hand it back to the Chieftain. The tradition came from long ago with the sharing of the Quaich symbolizing a bond formed.

They called the remaining clans one-by-one as we all stood around the massive centerfire. Even with its size blasting heat in all directions, a chill settled into my bones. I rubbed my arms, regretting not bringing a sweater instead of the thin fabric of my long-sleeved shirt. A red tartan curled around my shoulders, a warmth pulsing from behind me.

"You looked cold," Eric's smooth voice rolled over my neck like liquid chocolate.

My breath hitched as I rested my back against his chest. I'd imagined a moment like this since I was a little girl still believing in fairytales and warrior princes. A Highlander would wrap his great kilt around me after a long-winded battle, and we'd gaze at the rolling green meadows, relishing the quiet—the wind whipping over us the only sound.

"Thank you."

"I had all this extra wool fabric going to no use." He smiled into my hair.

"Yes, for warming me. But mostly for showing up here. It's a bigger deal than I think you realize, Eric."

"I know our relationship started with a bit of…animosity, but—"

Relationship. My toes curled inside my shoes.

"A bit of animosity?" I grinned.

"Alright, more than a bit, but I'd like to think we've moved past that."

We had. At some point in the middle of all the verbal jabs, there were genuine moments of realism. I'd dare say even…flirtation.

"I really thought Graeme was special. I'm so stupid."

His arms tightened around my shoulders. I nuzzled my nose into the warm tartan, letting the scents of fresh laundry and cinnamon sharpen my senses.

"There *is* one out there for you. You may not believe it, but I know there is. Just remember what I said before…"

My heart thumped so quickly I could feel it in my stomach. "Eyes and ears open."

"Exactly." The light bit of stubble on his cheek brushed against my forehead.

"The act we performed today has formed a bond between us all," the Chieftain announced after the last clan stepped back. "And with this also comes a promise from me to you. A promise to serve you as you promised to serve me." He pointed to the roaring fire behind him. "This fire will not be lit again until the time has come for us to go to war."

I'd seen it played out over a dozen times, but it still never failed to bring me to tears. Eric swiped his tartan over my cheeks, making them disappear as soon as they'd left my eyes.

"Thank you all for coming from far and wide to celebrate our ancestors as we do each year. I know I only play the part of a chieftain for show but I'd like to think we *have* formed a kinship." He moved his focus from one face to the next with a resounding presence. "No matter what clan we hail from, or what part of the globe we call home, we will *always* remain Scotsman and have this time to cherish."

Whistles, whoops, and clapping roared around us.

"Now for the important bit. Time to feast! And drink!" His smile widened as he threw a fist into the air.

A chuckle floated from my belly as I watched everyone scurry toward the canopy they'd set up near the fire. We were to eat until our stomachs burst and drink until we couldn't see straight.

"Did I do all of it right?" Eric asked as he slipped one half of the tartan away for us to walk side by side.

"Is this your way of getting me to say you were right about something again?" My cheeks warmed when I looked up at him.

He laughed. "Honestly, I hadn't thought about it."

"You were perfect. You don't have to stay for the party, you know?"

He pulled me tighter to his side. "Trying to get rid of me already?"

"I don't want you to feel obligated. You don't know any of these people."

"I know one person. That's all I need."

My heart pitter-pattered against my ribcage, and my mind betrayed me, dipping into thoughts about Graeme. Eric told me he saw him with another woman, and yet I still made excuses for him. I needed to stop thinking about it—about him. There was a man at my side with his arm around me, walking to a party I'd been looking forward to all year. And it *wasn't* Graeme.

TWELVE

WE'D TAKEN A CORNER table under the canopy, far enough away from the dance floor and instruments blaring we could make conversation without yelling at one another. I curled my hands around the tankard of ale, tapping my fingernails against the metal handle.

"Why didn't you text me back?" I chewed my lip.

Eric sat back, spreading his legs wide. "As much as it pains me to admit, I figured you didn't mean to text the racy photo to *me*. Didn't want to embarrass you."

"Oh? So, you decided to do it in the middle of the Calling of the Clans?" I half-smiled.

A wide grin tugged at his lips, deepening his cleft chin. "You were all flustered about Graeme. Figured it'd be the best way to pull you out of it."

Graeme. Hearing his name made me queasy but still strangely fluttery.

"You *do* look good in red."

My eyes shot to his face, his gaze sending heat up my neck. "Thank you. I don't do things like that normally."

"Take risqué photos and send them to random men, you mean?"

I swatted his arm. "Definitely not. But, no, I don't take photos like that, period."

He leaned forward with a twinkle in his eye. "The real thing is so much better anyway."

My stomach tripped over itself in a crazed bout of twists. I shoved my nose into my cup, slurping some ale into my mouth, so I didn't sit there slack-jawed.

"Are you going *true* Scotsman?" I raised a brow, dropping my eyes to his kilt.

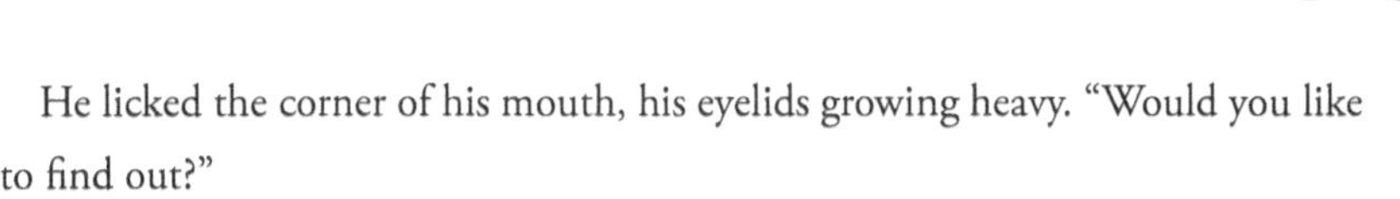

He licked the corner of his mouth, his eyelids growing heavy. "Would you like to find out?"

Yes.

I dropped my cup, clumsily catching it before it hit the ground. Thankfully, it was half empty. Otherwise, my lap would've been an ale-soaked mess.

Eric watched me with a grin, his eyes roaming from my face down to my ankles.

"What's that look for?" I set the cup on the table, not trusting myself with the simple act of holding something.

"I have a hard time understanding why a woman like you resists falling in love."

"What kind of woman am I?"

"Caring. Passionate. Adorable. Any man would be a lucky bastard to have you." He canted his head to one side with a squint.

I'd been breathing my entire life and suddenly forgot how to push the air out of my lungs. "Why are you—why are you being so nice to me?"

He rested his chin in his hand. "Elani. You can't tell me all our verbal battling was because we didn't like each other."

"I—" I snapped my mouth shut, slinking against my chair. "If you liked me from the very beginning, why try to pass me off to someone else? Why make a bet?"

"Because you're the type that needs to see the proof. Touch it. Feel it. Experience it."

My hands numbed. "Proof of what?"

"Lani girl! Come show us those Highland moves," Flora beckoned from the dancefloor.

Eric's lips curved, and he sat back. "Better not keep them waiting. Seems like a rowdy crowd."

He had no idea. I stood and walked to the dancefloor on autopilot. Physically I moved, but mentally I was caught up on Eric's words. The sudden burst of bagpipes pulsing from the band in the corner snapped me back. Flora grabbed my hand and dragged me to the center of the floor.

As a child, I loved Highland dancing. Except for the occasional urge to dance through my kitchen, I didn't do it now unless here in Scotland. Eric's eyes bored into me from across the way. He sat back in his chair with a relaxed demeanor, letting the cup of ale dangle from three fingers. His eyes glinted as he settled in

to watch me.

I threw one arm up, resting the opposite hand in a fist on my hip. Bouncing on the ball of one foot repeatedly, I pointed the other foot in front, then to my knee, and repeated on the other side. It was a constant up and down movement, switching legs, turning in a circle, raising one arm, or keeping both fists on my hips. As the bagpipes chimed, the happiness the simple dance movement gave me swirled in my stomach until I erupted into giggles.

"Lani, why's your lad all by himself in the corner?" Flora jutted her head at Eric.

I tried to avoid his gaze. There were two scenarios here: he could come to the dancefloor and change our dynamic even further, or he could stay put. Either thought had my nerves on fire.

Maybe he wasn't the type to dance?

"Laddie," Flora yelled with her hands cupped around her mouth.

Eric glanced behind him and pointed at his chest with raised brows.

"Aye, you. Get your arse up here."

Warmth pooled in my cheeks.

The world blurred around me as I watched Eric stand, adjusting the sash of the great kilt on his shoulder. He took another sip of his ale, making sure to keep his eyes on me. With a swagger only he could pull off, he made his way through groups of happily drunken guests chatting and dancing. My hands wrung around my sash.

"I believe I've been summoned?" Eric placed a palm on his chest and bowed in front of Flora and me.

Flora elbowed me in the ribs, making me squeak. "Oh, you're a looker, you are. Not a Scotsman though, aye?" Without shame, Flora cupped Eric's chin, turning his face side-to-side.

He chuckled, offering a smile warm enough to melt iron. "Afraid not. I'm… Greek."

A sizzle shot across my mind—a type of current trying to push through the fog but losing the battle.

"Ah. No matter. You wear that kilt like a true Scot. At the end of the day, that's more important, hm?" Flora beamed, and she reached for the hem of Eric's kilt.

I laughed and playfully slapped her hand, though Eric hadn't tried to stop her.

He continued to stare at me with a lazy grin.

"Flora, this is Eric. Eric, Flora."

Flora twirled her hair around a finger, shimmying her hips, all but cooing at Eric. I frowned, remembering the way Alex reacted to him.

"Who's up for The Highland Rose?" Clan Campbell shouted over the music.

The instruments died off as they readjusted, readying to switch styles.

Eric arched a brow. "Is that a type of dance?"

"Yeah. It can get a little confusing if you've never done it. We don't have to—"

He brushed a fingertip over the top of my hand. "I'm a fast learner. I didn't come out all this way to take up a seat at a table."

A hummingbird furiously beat at my ribcage. "Um. Alright. Let's be the third couple so you can see the others go first?"

Couple.

"Perfect." His lips curled into a smile that sent a delicious heat straight to my—stomach.

Eric kept an eye on everyone as I, Flora, and two other women stood in a line shoulder-to-shoulder. Eric stood across from me. I would've been far more nervous than he appeared to be, or he did a bang-up job of hiding it. I pressed my fists to each hip and bounced on the balls of my feet as the bagpipes played. The first couple went, crossing diagonally and meeting up with the opposite person.

Eric nodded once as if he already understood the dance, and two-eye winked at me. When it was our turn, we crossed in front of each other, my breast brushing against his arm. Staggered whispers clouded my ears, making me wince. The look on my face must've been anything but pleasant, judging from the cocked bushy eyebrow from my new dance partner. I forced a grin and snapped my head to Eric. He danced with Flora in his arms, spinning her around but still keeping me in his sights.

The dance continued in a crisscross pattern between couples. No matter which partner we ended up with, me and Eric couldn't take our eyes off each other. It was like a swirling wormhole, and fighting the constant pull proved useless. As the dance finished, we ended where we began, standing across from each other. I gulped as I bounced forward, slipping my arms against Eric's. His right hand curled over my left, his other arm snaking around my shoulder blades.

"How is this happening?" My eyes traveled from the Stewart clan brooch on

his sash to his cleft chin, inviting lips, and didn't stop roaming until they landed on eyes the color of sapphires.

He pressed his cheek against the side of my head. "What do you mean?"

"This." The coarse stubble brushed my skin. "I went from wanting to wipe the floor with you to keep you away from my algorithm code and prove a point to—"

He leaned back, peering down at me as he brushed a thumb along my jawline. "To what?"

The fog in my mind punched at my skull so fiercely I had to grab my head. Every time I thought I had my feelings sorted, my brain bashed me back to reality. There was a tug on my hand. I blinked—another tug.

"Come here, Elani," Eric's distant voice beckoned.

I let him lead us away from the crowds—drums and bagpipes blazing in the background. He didn't stop until we were in a vacant corner of the canopy near the roaring bonfire. He wrapped a hand over my hip, sending jolts of electricity down my legs. I moved until my back hit against one of the wooden support beams.

"Let me kiss you." His words floated like a silky whisper.

I wanted him to. So, so badly. The fog pulsed in my mind.

"What? Right here? Right now?" I risked a glance at the surrounding people. No one looked at us. They probably couldn't even see us given the shadows cast from the fire.

He didn't look away, using a gentle finger to pull my gaze back to his. "Right here. Right now."

I could tell my heart wanted to kick me in the face for not screaming, "Yes!" My nails dug into the wooden pole behind me. Not only was it keeping the canopy from toppling over us all, but it kept me from retreating.

If I could ever be thankful for an inanimate object.

"I don't know…"

His thumb swirled in circles over my hip. "I know how much a kiss means to you. The weight you put on it."

How could he possibly know that?

"But I promise you when I'm done—" Our gazes locked, and my heartbeat went into a furious gallop. "You'll be a puddle at our feet."

I stared at his lips, craving to know how they'd feel. "That's quite the declaration."

"No."

The word jarred me, my eyes darting back to his.

"It's the truth."

Who *was* this guy?

My heart lurched in my chest, and I nodded. "Alright."

He stepped closer, filling the surrounding air with faint smells of cinnamon. "There's only one rule."

"Rule?" The word cracked from my throat.

"You can't touch me." The tip of his nose brushed over my ear.

A puddle when he finished? The man hadn't even kissed me yet, and my knees felt like putty.

He dragged his cheek over mine, fingers kneading against my waist. His lips brushed one of my brows, sending a shiver through my jaw. He kissed my forehead—a light peck that kept the feel of his lips a secret. His breath skirted over my hairline as he continued his torturous tour of my face, his eyes dropping to my lips.

This was it. I was a spool of yarn unraveling. My heart raced, matching the steady beat of drums from the band.

His mouth neared mine and then moved to my nose, brushing his lips across the tip. I pinched my thighs together, the anticipation of when and if this were truly going to happen turning my insides into a Celtic knot. He pressed into me, and I suppressed a whimper at the hardness pushing against my stomach. His gaze lingered over my mouth again before gliding back to my eyes.

Like it had a will of its own, my right hand slipped over his forearm, tensing at the power exuding from the taut muscle hidden underneath his shirt.

"Hey now." He whispered into my hair. "One rule and you still broke it." A deep chuckle rumbled from his chest. He slipped his hand over mine with a gentle yet demanding touch, forcing it back to the pole.

My teeth chattered as his nose dipped to the nape of my neck, breathing me in. He gave one tiny flick of his tongue before dragging the stubble on his cheek over my skin. He lifted his head, the intensity in his stare making my insides pulse. He clamped three fingers under my chin, his gaze drifting to my mouth. My hands balled into fists, fearing I'd explode if he didn't kiss me. It was a sweet mix of torture and pure bliss that I didn't want to end.

His forefinger played over my cheek while the tip of his thumb traced under my

bottom lip. A whimper fluttered from my throat. I couldn't have held it back if I tried. Without a physical cue this time, his lips brushed mine. I pressed my back against the pole, knowing if it weren't there, I would've gone limp in his arms.

It started as feather-like touches. Pecks across my lips with the occasional lingering moment. And then he deepened the kiss, keeping his hand clamped under my chin, grounding me to the reality of what was happening. His tongue slid over the seam of my lips, coaxing me, luring me, until I opened my mouth, welcoming the swirl of his tongue with mine. He moaned, deep and masculine, pushing further against me.

As he devoured me with this mouth, he dragged a single finger over my collarbone, tracing down to the dip between my breasts. His hand slid into my hair, bunching it in his grasp. An invisible boulder had settled on my chest. I'd only now realized it existed because the unseeable force lifted—a sense of relief, freedom, coursed over my skin in waves. His tongue lapped over mine, pausing every few moments to suck on my bottom lip and dive back in. His fingers kept playing over my cheek, dragging down my throat.

The mysterious fog that'd clogged my brain for days diminished, falling from my mind into a puddle at my feet just as he'd promised. My eyelashes fluttered, the clarity of where I was and who I was with punching at my thoughts like an angry boxer.

I pulled back, staring up at him with a fresh pair of eyes. His tongue lapped over his lips, tasting me on him.

Screw his rule.

I wrapped my arms around his neck, kissing him. I'd wanted to kiss him since the moment we met. The universe tried to call out to me about him—an attempt to tell me there was the possibility of something I'd always wanted if I only gave into it. Fear was a driving force for me. But right now, at this moment, all I wanted was him.

Eric groaned and pulled from the kiss, blowing out a ragged breath. "How'd we do?" He pressed his forehead to mine.

"Are you even human?" I let out a gentle laugh.

"How do you feel?"

"I feel—" My body hummed, the bagpipes blaring in the background warming my belly. I closed my eyes with a sigh and slowly opened them. "Renewed."

Eric winced as his hand curled into a fist. "Glad I could help."

"Are you okay?" I gripped his shoulder, watching the skin between his eyes wrinkle. I'd seen him like this before…

"Never better." He rolled his shoulders and took a deep breath.

"Do you—do you need to go somewhere?"

A puff of air escaped his cheeks. "I didn't want you to think I was running away or—" He grimaced, beating his knuckles against the pole behind me.

"Eric. Go. I'll wait for you here."

He kissed my temple before sprinting away.

I tapped my fingernails against my lips, watching the direction he went. Curiosity pulled at my heart. Something repeatedly called him away—something he couldn't handle in front of everyone else. It had to be something big enough to leave after a moment like what we just had. Or maybe it wasn't as big of a deal for him as it was for me?

Time for some answers.

I pushed off the pole and followed him. The light from the fire and hanging sconces underneath the canopy weakened. My breath curled like liquid smoke from the cold air as I moved further and further from the crowds. Only the sound of the drums echoed over the hills. There was a thicket in the distance and not much of anywhere else he could've gone. I moved to the valley, spying his dark hair within the mix of trees and moonlight spilling through the leaves.

He tore his sash and shirt off, standing in the middle of the forest in only the bottom half of his kilt. After a grunt, two large white wings sprung from his shoulder blades. He tilted his head back, sighing in relief as the wings stretched, feathers rustling.

My heart punched at my ribs. "Er—Eric?" I managed to stutter.

He snapped his gaze at me over his shoulder, the look of shock no doubt matching my own.

THIRTEEN

HE TURNED TO FACE ME, palms open and raised. The wings flicked once before disappearing. Staring at me wide-eyed, he took a hesitant step forward.

I retreated. "Did I—did I see wings, Eric?"

He dragged a hand through his hair. "Yes."

My breathing went shallow, making my head dizzy. "What—what am I supposed to say right now?"

"Elani. I wanted to tell you." He took another step forward. "As you can imagine, it's hard to explain."

"Try." It came out harsher than I wanted, but the fog had lifted only to be replaced by confusion.

Eric licked his lips as he shifted his weight, making his exposed abs tighten. My legs clenched, and I forced myself to stay focused.

"Are you familiar with Greek mythology?"

The breath breezed from my lungs. Alex. She said—my blood froze. White wings. Eric. Eros. She absolutely could not have been right about Greek gods this entire time.

"Yes…"

He tilted his head back, interlacing his fingers behind his neck. "I'm the god of passion and love."

He came right out and said it. What else was I expecting? The wings gave me zero excuses not to believe.

Believe.

"You're...Eros." Alex would never let me live this down. She'd remind me every waking minute for the rest of our lives.

His face softened. "Yes. Vena. She is my uh—my mother."

I shook my head and waved my arms back and forth. "Aphrodite?"

"Mmhm."

I scanned his anguished face. "Let me see them again."

His brow bounced. "My wings?"

I nodded, unsure if I could formulate words.

He balled his hands into fists and tensed his forearms. The glorious snow-white wings flared out, the moonbeams from above giving them a shimmering glow.

I wanted to touch them, to feel the smooth feathers against my skin. No. It'd make it too real. All of this was purely unbelievable. As I turned my back to him, I could hear the rustle of his wings disappearing.

His warm soapy scent permeated the air, followed by the heat flowing from his exposed chest. The forest started spinning, my head growing fuzzy.

"Elani." He rested his fingers against my arm but didn't try to grasp me, allowing the retreat if I so desired.

What *did* I desire?

I slowly peeked my head over one shoulder, taking in the sight of his chiseled half-naked body—the great kilt fabric wrapped around his waist.

He canted his head to one side and slowly turned to show me his back. Rolling his shoulders forward, the two scarred lines on his back were undeniable. With a shaky hand, I traced my finger over one of the markings. He shuddered, making me gasp and recoil my hand.

"Sorry. It kind of tickles." He turned back to face me, eyes frantically searching my face.

My neck grew clammy, sweat beads forming at my brow. The world around me shrunk, making me stumble.

"Elani?" He reached forward, but it was too late. I faded into blackness as the tunnel vision sunk in and overtook me.

I awoke in my room at Ghaoil Cottage, the sun blazing through the curtains,

making me wince. Groaning, I sat up, rubbing my eyes. I was underneath the blanket but still in my kilt and clothes from last night.

How had I gotten back to the inn?

My mind flashed to the sight of Eric standing in the middle of the woods with his wings sprawled. My stomach gurgled.

A dream. It had to be a dream. I probably drank too much last night, and some friendly party-goer dragged me back here—simple explanation. But I *knew* I didn't drink that much.

Throwing the sheet aside, I scrambled for the door, stopping halfway down the stairs when a familiar baritone voice echoed through the hall.

"Is she up yet?" Eric asked.

"Aye. I heard her stumblin' around up there only a wee moment ago," Flora traitorously answered.

I tightened my grip on the banister, making it creak. Mustering every ounce of courage I possessed, I descended the rest of the way with my head held high. Courage quickly dipped into mortification when I spied my reflection in the hallway mirror. My hair stuck out in every possible direction, and half of my make-up smeared down my face.

"Good morning." Eric leaned to the side in an attempt to see me once I shoved my face into the nearest corner.

"Mornin'," I mumbled into the wall and peeked with one eye.

Flora raised on the balls of her feet, trying to look at me. "How much did you drink last night, lass?"

I arched a brow at her.

"You were passed out. And this one carried ye up to your room. Cradled in his arms, you were." She elbowed Eric in the side with a sparkling grin.

I groaned. If only I had drunk myself into oblivion. It'd be a better excuse as to why I saw Eric standing half-naked in the middle of the woods with wings.

Wings.

"I hoped we could…talk today?" A green and blue plaid shirt hugged Eric's arms. His dark jeans shifted as he slid forward, approaching me like I was a rabid animal.

Was he really Eros?

"Sure. Yeah. I—I just woke up." The smell of my morning breath bounced off the wall I hugged, furthering my terror.

"Oh, he can wait on ye lassie while you go freshen up." Flora whisked into the kitchen, swooping the steaming pot of coffee into her hands.

Eric chuckled and slid the brown suede jacket from his shoulders. "Absolutely."

After giving a thumbs up, I dashed up the stairs, tripping several times until I reached the safety of my room—a sanctuary I'd eventually have to leave to face reality. If what this was could even be conceived as "reality." After making myself presentable and slipping into a sweater, jeans, and boots, I took out my phone to text Alex.

Me: …you were right.

Watching the bobbing ellipses as she typed her response, my knee bounced.

Alex: I'm right about a lot of things. Care to be more specific?

Me: About Eric.

Alex: Wait. Why is Eric there? What happened to Graeme?

Graeme. My stomach lurched, and I almost dropped my phone. My God. I'd completely forgotten about him. Before yesterday I felt consumed by him, thinking about him at every waking turn, and now…I didn't care.

Me: He never showed. Eric got here right when they called Clan Stewart.

Alex: Holy. Shit. That's one of the most romantic things I've ever heard, and this is counting Morticia and Gomez.

Me: g2g. will talk more later.

Alex: Woman. You WILL explain this more.

I shoved the phone away before the temptation to type the words, "he has wings," forced my hand. She'd believe it and know I wasn't joking around. It'd give the situation a finality I wasn't ready to accept. Trudging back downstairs, I paused on the last step. I stared at my feet, nerves bubbling in my core. As my foot met with the floor, the tension building in my shoulders relaxed.

Eric and Flora sat in the foyer on one of the plush emerald green couches, sipping on cups of coffee and laughing.

"Ah, lad. You've so many stories." Flora dabbed the corners of her eyes with a knuckle, the chuckles dying down.

"Bartend long enough, and you see some fascinating people." He grinned and immediately turned his chin at me once I entered the space. He'd been smiling

before, but now his entire face came to life with a sort of…glow.

"Hi." I curled a piece of hair over my ear, my toes turning toward each other.

He tapped a finger on the top of his knee. "Hey."

Flora stood and strolled past me. "Why don't you two take a trip to Dunvegan Castle? Hm? I'll even call ye a cab."

More than an hour shoved into a confined space with him only to be followed by a romantic stroll through an ancient castle in Scotland? I'd be a glutton for punishment.

"Sounds amazing." Eric's stare could've lit my hair on fire.

I had to run my hand through it just to be sure.

"Splendid." Flora fluttered to the rotary phone, making an extra flourish with her hands as she dialed.

Eric stood, crossing one foot over the other. The time it took him to reach me felt like an eternity. My groin throbbed at the mere sight of him. Yesterday I was confused, terrified of the fact he really could be a Greek god. Now all my body could do was betray me—yearning to feel his lips and caresses.

"Are you okay?" He tapped his knuckle under my chin.

"About which part?"

He slipped his hands into his jean pockets. "All of it. Any of it."

"I'm still trying to wrap my head around it. Well, most of it."

He slid an arm around my waist, sending a ripple of need coiling to my toes. Lowering his lips to my ear, he whispered, "I won't use any of my powers or show my wings unless you ask me. Deal?"

He was serious. This was all one-hundred percent happening.

I nodded as a small squeak escaped the back of my throat.

"All set, dearies. He should be here half past ten." Flora beamed, curling her hands underneath her chin with an extra bounce in her step as she walked away.

"She cares about you a great deal." Slipping his hands into his pockets, Eric took a step back.

"She's like a second mom to me." I winced. "Well, I mean a mom in general whenever I come out here and after…" My gaze fell to the cracks in the wooden floor.

"I'm sorry."

I sniffed once. "Don't be. It happened a long time ago. Have you been to any

castles before?"

Well, if that weren't the most rhetorical question of the century.

"I may have seen most of the world at this point in my life, Elani, but I'm looking forward to seeing it through *your* eyes." He tugged my sweater sleeve, getting me to look at him. "If you need to pretend I'm not who I am, then do it. If you want to ask me anything, ask. I won't mind either way."

I wanted to fan my face, let out a deep rolling sigh, and sink to the floor. I'd only be able to go so long before blurting every question circling my brain. He was right about me. I needed proof in every way, shape, and form. As if a wingspan wider than the space we stood in wasn't good enough.

Elani Stewart: Raging Skeptic and Hopeless Romantic in Denial.

A car horn blared from outside.

"Looks like our ride is here." Eric held out his hand for me to walk first.

The driver was none other than the man from Clan Campbell, proving how small of a town this was. He stuck his arm out the window, waving at us before tugging on his cap. Eric held the back door open for me, slipping his finger over my hand as I got in. The simple fleeting touch of his skin to mine made my insides sizzle.

"Dunvegan Castle, aye?" Campbell asked, raising his grey bushy eyebrows at us in the rickety rearview mirror.

"Aye," I answered with a smile.

I curled one hand in my lap, letting the other rest on the leather seat between Eric and me. His pinky traced over mine, making me shudder. Memories of that mind-blowing kiss near the bonfire as bagpipes and drums echoed around us thundered through my brain.

Eric peered out the window, watching the rolling meadows pass. He was so calm. So serene.

"Eric?"

He snapped his attention to me, brows cinching together. "Yes, Elani?"

My name from his lips was like hearing the stars—twinkling and mesmerizing.

"Do you really have w—" I paused, my gaze shooting to Mr. Campbell drumming his fingers on the steering wheel.

Eric's glance dropped to the wing gesture I made with my hands. His eyes sparkled. "Yes."

My heart raced. "And you can—" I swooped my hands to symbolize flying.

He mimicked my gesture. "Yes."

I pressed my hands against my cheeks, staring at him as if all this would begin to make sense if I looked at him long enough.

He leaned over, resting his weight on one elbow. "And I'd gladly take you up. All you have to do is ask."

My eyes dropped to his lips, remembering how feather-like they felt grazing my chin, my brows. Pinching my knees together, I managed to nod. "I'd like that...I think."

Had I dived straight into this delusion with him?

"You two are a sight for sore eyes," Campbell said, grinning at the rearview mirror.

"Why's that?" I asked, watching Eric ogle me from my peripheral vision.

"I've not seen people so in love in well—a very long time."

I choked on my spit. "Love is...such a strong word." My cheeks flushed.

Campbell gave a knowing grin, making the gesture of zipping his lips.

"Powerful too." Eric's deep voice rumbled near my ear.

I snapped my attention to him, our faces inches apart. "What?"

"Love. It's not just a word. It's an experience."

Despite the possibility of him being a Greek god. Despite how at any moment, he could spring out wings and fly away. And even despite knowing full well that with every action and word, he reeled me in like a prized bass—I wanted to kiss him. I *wanted* to fall in love. Alex couldn't possibly be right about yet *another* thing, though, right?

Locking our gazes, I slid a trembling hand over his steady one. "Being who— you are? Can you show me?"

"I can do far more than that, Elani. But I need you to say it." He squeezed my hand, grounding it—keeping it from shaking.

"Show me," I whispered, just as the car arrived in front of the castle.

FOURTEEN

MY BREATH HITCHED AS it took in the glory that was Dunvegan Castle. I'd seen it dozens of times, but it never failed to take my breath away. Being nestled in the Isle of Skye hadn't hurt either. The rich landscapes surrounding it fluttered the land with sprouts of green from clusters of trees, surrounded by cerulean water and a view of the vast mountains on the horizon.

Eric touched the small of my back, bringing my attention to his face. He gleamed down at me, canting his head to one side. "And you say you don't remember how to love."

"It's impossible to love an inanimate object." I playfully smacked him.

"Not true." He offered his arm, and I curled mine with his. "Correct, you can't marry an inanimate object or form a relationship, but love is all about the way something or someone makes you feel. So, how does this view—this place, Elani, make you feel?"

I asked for this. I may as well dive in. Closing my eyes, I concentrated on the light wind playing through my hair and the smell of pine floating through the air. My chest tightened as I returned my gaze to the picturesque view of the castle.

"Comfort. Anticipation. Longing." The castle represented more than just a pretty sight. It was a landmark that withstood the tests of time from long ago when Highlanders roamed the countryside. "And pride."

"And when I kissed you?"

I snapped my gaze to his, my heart speeding into overdrive. "What?"

"When I kissed you." He squinted. "How did you feel?"

His lips were gliding over mine, a fingertip dragged between my breasts, his firm touch on my hip.

"I—" A gust of wind snatched my words and carried them away.

His chin tilted down. "Think about it. And when you have it figured out—tell me."

I was beginning to regret asking him to "show me." A momentary lapse in judgment.

"Do you know the history of this castle?" The chill in the air brought me closer to him, our sides pressing together.

"Honestly, no."

I gasped and halted.

He lurched backward, still hooked with my arm, and chuckled. "I assume that surprises you?"

"You've been around for what? Eons? Shouldn't you know the entire history of the known universe?"

He laughed, deep and glorious. A few sun rays peeked through the clouds, glinting off his pearly grin. "The entire universe? Wow. Can't say I've seen it all."

A whole galaxy to explore. Did the gods have the means to do it? Would they freeze as we did without the aid of a spacesuit?

Blinking the thoughts away, I led us down the path. "Dunvegan Castle has been around since the thirteenth century and preserves legends of a famous clan. One of my favorite TV shows happens to feature said clan." I quirked my brow, pausing.

He shifted his eyes. "Oh. Uh…Braveheart? Wallace?"

"Albeit an amazing piece of cinematic wonder, that's a movie, not a show."

Eric's expression morphed into the same look I had in high school while trying to learn calculus. "Outlander?"

My shoulders dropped. "Duncan MacLeod of the Clan MacLeod?"

He threw his head back and patted my hand. "Highlander. How silly of me to get my landers confused."

I bit back a smile. "You *are* silly."

"Anything else I should know about the MacLeod mansion?"

"Eh. That's probably the coolest factoid. I think the fact they renovated it enough to enjoy it for what it is versus a ruin like most of the others is impressive

in itself."

His lips suddenly brushed the corner of my mouth, sending a shockwave blasting through my core.

I traced my fingers over the spot he kissed, searching for scorch marks. "What was that for?"

"There needs to be a reason?" He two-eyed winked.

"Do you still think you know how to wink properly?"

He stopped walking, his jaw squaring off as he stared at the walkway. "Normally, I can wink fine. For some reason, it goes haywire—" He lifted his gaze, roaming it from my toes, all the way to my face. "—around you."

I clutched the neckline of my jacket, bunching it. "What does that mean?"

"I may or may not know."

"And you're not going to share?"

We paused at the main entrance, both of us craning our necks to stare at the gigantic structure.

"Nope. Right now, isn't the time."

"When is?" I turned my attention from the classic piece of architecture to the man—the Greek god standing next to me.

He patted my hand, saying nothing.

I waited for him to elaborate, to give me something—absolutely anything. But he didn't. Had he always been like this? Playing games and plotting life like a Choose Your Adventure book?

"I'm surprised there aren't more people here." He swiveled his hips, scoping the few people on the grounds—a mother with her two young boys, an older man with a pipe, and a tourist couple taking repeated selfies with their cellphone on a stick.

"You should be here in the spring. This is the off-season. On warm days, there are so many people you can barely move."

Classic décor filled the vast foyer like it'd have been ages ago. A man asked us if we wished to purchase a tour, and I politely waved him off. I was the only tour guide we needed. Not to mention I wanted privacy. There were so many questions to be asked of the god of love.

"Want me all to yourself, hm?" Eric's eyes lit up.

"Something like that." I held out my hand. "Come on. I'll show you the best

spots."

His gaze explored my body. "Of the castle—" He pulled me against him, keeping our eyes locked. "—or you?"

My chest heated. No doubt a dozen red splotches blazed my skin.

"Is that part of your power?"

"What is?" His eyes lingered on my lips.

My fingers numbed. "Things you say to me. How you say them. Your touch. It turns my insides into gelatin and confetti."

He flashed a grin—the masculine variety which suggested he knew *exactly* the effect he had on me. "I believe that's called attraction, Elani."

"No. No. It's something else. I didn't feel like this with Graeme or Michael or… hell I didn't feel like this watching Jason Momoa in *Aquaman*."

Beaming at me, he traced the freckles on my cheek with a fingertip. "Time will tell. You just have to be patient."

Were all Greek gods this cryptic? Did he have his reasons?

"Weren't you going to show me the ins and outs of this place?" He stepped back, keeping his grip on my hand.

My stomach twitched, and my grip tightened against his palm. With a villainous twist of lip, his eyes shot to my fingers like a rocket.

"Right this way, Cherub," I said through gritted teeth.

He let out a burst of roaring laughter. "Back to the verbal jibes, I see? I'm game if you are."

I smiled up at him, remembering the first time we'd met. Something had eaten at me—told me he was different. At that moment, I figured he was different in the way that someone with an inhuman IQ was, not that he was a deity.

As we ascended the winding staircase, I pointed out several paintings hanging on the walls that always caught my attention. He listened, never interrupted, and spent more time watching my lips than viewing the art.

And I didn't mind it one bit.

We paused on the top floor in front of the banister that held a view of the floor below. I pressed my forearms against the smooth wood and tapped my fingertips together.

"You're really him?" I didn't look at him, focusing more on the massive column in the center of the room.

"Yes."

I turned to face him and pressed my back against the railing. "How does it work? You don't actually shoot an arrow at someone, do you?"

Eric scanned the area with a subdued chuckle. "No. Arrows do, in fact, kill people. That achieves the opposite effect of my desire."

Desire.

"Do you throw glitter at them?"

He looked at me like I asked how to boil water. "I can achieve it one of several ways. A fleeting touch—" He traced his middle finger down my forearm, making the hair stand on end. "Eye contact." Those sapphire eyes locked with mine, pulling me into a trance for a fraction of a second. "Or I can wiggle my nose."

I'd been breathing like I was short of air until he ended it with that last sentence. "Wiggle your nose? Like Bewitched?"

His stone-cold face fell away, replaced by a wide grin, followed by laughter. "I'm kidding. I just wanted to see your reaction."

I rolled my eyes as I bumped my hip against his. "Very funny."

"In the past, I *did* shoot arrows, but they'd shimmer into magic before striking. Can't exactly get away with that in public anymore."

My brain dipped into a daydream. He stood bare-chested with an arrow notched on his bow, muscles flexed, taut and—

"Elani?" His face appeared in front of mine.

I jumped. "Have you used your powers on me?" I clutched the railing behind me.

Please say no.

The amusement disappeared from his face as soon as the words left my mouth. "No."

I stood straighter. "Not even once?"

"No." He kept my gaze.

His eyes didn't falter. No lip or brow twitch. Nothing.

"Why?"

He turned his side to me, gripping the banister, making his shoulders bulge through his jacket. "There's no fun in simply making someone love you. Nor does it last."

"You've been in love?"

A rolling sigh escaped his throat. "Once."

Psyche.

My throat tightened, and I slapped a hand over my eyes. "How could I be so stupid? You're—you're married."

"Elani." His fingers peeled my palm from my face. "We're not together anymore. Haven't been for—a long time."

"You're trying to tell me true love exists, and even the god of love himself is divorced?"

He balled one hand into a fist, beating his knuckles against the railing. "It's a long story." His knuckles turned white as his hand shook, and a grimace pulled his face tight.

My gaze immediately shot to his back, expecting to see his wings rip through his jacket. "Do you need to step away?"

"Yes." He craned his neck. "Will you be alright for a few minutes?"

"It's not a seedy gas station or something. I think I'll be fine. Go. Before someone thinks you're an angel sent from heaven or something."

He smiled, and it was quickly torn away by a scowl of pain. After squeezing my hip, he ran off.

"I'm curious where you think this is going," a woman's soft voice said nearby.

I turned to find Vena leaning against the banister with her arms crossed. Her flowing honey-blonde hair rested over a bright red dress, clinging to every curve and leaving very little to the imagination.

"The castle is about as far as we've gotten so far." I had a fair idea of what she was getting at, but knowing who she was now, I didn't want to give her any more ammunition.

She smirked, bouncing her red spiked heel against the hardwood beneath our feet. "I thought Graeme would be enough to keep you away from him, but now I see I need to resort to more—drastic measures."

She flicked her wrist, and I snatched it with a faster reflex than I'd ever seen on myself—this coming from a woman who could barely catch random items thrown at her.

She glared at my hand. The intensity—the pure rage in her eyes made my knees shake until I stared at their color. A perfect match to the radiant sky blue of Eros's. His *mother*.

"Careful. You don't know who you're dealing with." Her words flowed from her mouth like snake venom.

"I do. I know who he is. What you both are." My insides screamed bloody murder at the sudden backbone I seemed to have grown.

Her stare softened, and she yanked her hand away, rubbing the skin I touched like I'd left a bruise.

"What is this all about? And why did you try to force Graeme on me?"

She let out a deep sigh as she tossed her long locks over her shoulder, and then her entire face brightened at something behind me.

"Because she was trying to keep you away from *me*," Eric's voice boomed.

A wide grin pulled at Vena's lips, and she brushed past me, making sure to hit my shoulder with hers. She spread her arms wide, going in for a hug, but Eric batted her hands away with one quick swipe of his forearm.

She pouted. "Is that any way to greet your mother?"

Aphrodite.

The world kept reminding me that this wasn't a dream. Greek myths were real. The gods. Were. Real.

I stared wide-eyed at the young woman with a grown son who looked the same age as her.

"You meddle and expect me to be all chummy with you?" Eric crossed his burly arms, eyes forming slits as he glared down at her.

Aphrodite rolled her eyes. "I miss the days where you did anything I asked without question. It was a real sense of loyalty, commitment, respect?" She arched a thin blonde brow. "Or have you forgotten what all those words mean?"

Eric bent forward with a snarl of his lip. "That was a long time ago. And I'm not letting you interfere with my affairs ever again, nor am I your lackey. Understood?"

Tapping one of her red heels, she curled her fingers over her hips. "Are you going to denounce me as your mother now too?"

Eric leaned back as he rubbed a thumb between his eyes. "Unfortunately, there's nothing I can do about that. I'm still your son, but it doesn't mean I've forgotten all the things you've done or that the number one person in your life—is you."

Her jaw dropped, and she stomped her foot. "That is *so* not true. Even back then, everything I did was to protect you."

He didn't respond, lifting one brow in answer.

I cleared my throat. Their heads whipped in my direction simultaneously.

"Sorry to interrupt, but can someone please explain to me how and why she made me obsessed with Graeme."

"My son doesn't know what's best for him. I'm the goddess of love. I know a match when I see one, and this—" She pointed between us. "Ain't it."

"Why wouldn't you let us choose that for ourselves?" I glared at her.

Eric shook his head. "Your power has been on the fritz lately, and you know it."

Aphrodite's lips parted, and her arms stiffened at her sides. "How did you break my spell, anyway?"

Eric kept his head turned in Aphrodite's direction but did one quick shift of his eyes at me.

Aphrodite looked between us, and her eyes widened, her mouth following. "She's—"

Eric nodded.

"I can't believe—" Aphrodite traced a finger over her lips. "There really is something wrong with my power."

I'd interrogate Eric later about what the hell that exchange was all about, but for now…

"Are your powers fading because you love yourself more than anyone else?" A lump formed in my throat, not having a clue how I came to such a conclusion.

Eric's gaze fell on me, his eyes brightening.

Aphrodite folded her arms. "Alright, Smartypants. You've known we exist for what, twenty-four hours, and now think you know all there is to know about us?"

"No. It's a hunch."

"She could be right," Eric added.

Aphrodite threw her hands in the air. "Fine. Let me just jet out of here and find someone to love me. Easy, right?" She went to snap her fingers, but Eric wrapped his hand around hers.

"You have to love them in return. You know that."

Her eyes glistened like she was on the verge of tears. "I really do miss the days where you looked up at me with awe and adoration, Cupie."

Eric's eyes dropped to the floor. "Please don't interfere again. I don't need your protection. If I screw up…that's on me."

A single shimmering tear rolled down her cheek, and she cupped his chin. "I'm sorry." She disappeared in a flash of pink glitter and rose petals.

I did a quick scan of the area, hoping there hadn't been anyone around to witness it. Eric's hand was still in mid-air, and he dropped it with a deep sigh. Scooping an abandoned rose petal from the floor, I rubbed it between two fingers and elbowed Eric's arm.

"She wasn't a horrible mother, but at some point, she lost sight of her purpose. I hope she finds someone."

"Was I right?"

He took my hand and led us further into the castle. "It does make sense. But she's been so into herself, for so long, I'm skeptical it's even possible."

How *had* I known why her powers weren't working as they should?

Halting, I squeezed his hand. "Eric, how did you break her spell?"

He scratched the stubble on his chin, and I forced my gaze away from that damn charming cleft.

"When I kissed you."

The weight I'd felt lifting from my chest…

"And why did she seem surprised you were able to?"

He scratched the back of his head. "I promise I will answer this, but considering you very recently found out about me, I don't want to overwhelm you."

The skin between his eyes crinkled as he stared at me. It was a silent plea to let it go for now. Normally, I'd have felt compelled to argue with him, to demand answers, but a bubbling in my gut told me to back off…for now.

"Alright." I tugged on his sleeve. "Come on, then. There's so much more of this place to see."

He blinked twice. "You're not going to press me on it?"

"Something in my gut is telling me to wait." I led him into a room with crystal chandeliers, gold textured walls, and paintings with ornate copper-colored frames.

"That gut's been pretty damn intuitive lately."

I offered a warm smile. "Exactly why I should continue to listen to it."

Half-covered in a wide mirror, making the already vast room look even more extensive, was a gold clock on the far back wall. I'd passed by it countless times, but the two figures standing on it sparked my attention. As soon as Eric's eyes fell on the two people leaning over the clock, he stiffened—a man with wings and a beautiful maiden with her hair in a bun on top of her head.

"Is this—" I started, pointing at the winged man.

His throat bobbed. "Yes."

Eros and Psyche immortalized in gold. A clock I'd passed every year since I was a teen. Eros leaned toward Psyche with his head resting on her shoulder, holding out a heart. Cocking my head to the side, for the first time, I noticed Psyche too had wings, but not angelic ones like Eros. Hers resembled a butterfly.

Eric glowered at the clock, unmoving and unblinking.

"I'm sorry, I shouldn't have brought you over here, I—" I turned away, but his hand shot out, delicately wrapping around my arm.

"It's not bothering me. It reminds me of a time long, long ago. I had no idea this piece existed."

I pressed my back to his chest, admiring the clock with him. "It's a beautiful rendition."

He kissed my hair, and I could hear him breathing me in. "A memory of a time long past. Time to make new memories to inspire future art."

I closed my eyes, nestling into his warmth. Our bodies aligned perfectly, molding against each other like overlapping feathers of a wing. "I know the perfect place to start said memories."

FIFTEEN

WE'D TAKEN A CAB ride back toward Ghaoil Cottage, not surprisingly having Mr. Campbell as our driver again. I whispered in his ear where to drop us off, and he gave me a cheeky grin. Eros and I stood in front of a long winding dirt road, and I tugged my jacket around my chest.

"I mean, the dirt path is lovely, but this is the magical place you mentioned making memories?" Eric raised a brow.

I playfully slapped his arm. "No, silly. It's at the end of this walk, but I promise it's worth it."

"Walk? Do you have any idea how long it's been since I've walked more than a mile…anywhere?" He frowned.

I curled my arm with his. "Well, guess it's about time to get your mortal on."

"Lead the way."

It was off-season, so there weren't nearly as many tourists. I hoped we'd be the only ones when we reached my planned spot.

"Not walking. Wow. What's it like?" I moved closer, stealing the warmth that radiated from him like a sunbeam.

"Flying?"

I nodded.

"No one's asked me before, hm." His eyes closed, and he tilted his chin upward. "It's a sense of freedom. The wind caresses you, guides you, and you feel weightless. While in flight, the world ceases to exist. You can simply…be."

A sigh rolled from the pit of my stomach—deep and longing. "Sounds amazing.

I can't remember the last time I could stop and think about nothing."

"I can take you up any time you want. Remember, all you have to do is ask." His sultry gaze fluttered over my skin.

"I will. I'm just not there yet."

Mentally, I wasn't. Despite all the proof presented to me, there was still a deep-seated block in my brain that wouldn't let me fully believe it. At any moment, I'd wake up, and this would all have been a glorious dream. One I admittedly didn't want to leave.

We passed an elderly couple walking hand-in-hand down the opposite side of the path. They greeted us with brightened smiles, and the man gave his wife a quick peck on her temple.

"Mm. Those two have been together for a *very* long time. That's a walking example of true, long-lasting love."

I beamed up at him, curling his arm tighter. "Can you tell how they met?"

"Yes." The warmth of his smile made my heart swell. "She was sixteen. He was twenty-six, having just taken over his father's farm. She was a merchant's daughter, and the families were against their pairing because of the age difference, but they kept meeting each other in secret and eloped when she turned eighteen."

A tingle shot down my arm. "Love at first sight?"

"Let me guess. Complete hogwash to you, right?"

I bit my lip, desperately searching for the right words to not sound like the cynic I still thought I was. "How could someone possibly fall in love that quickly? It takes time, getting to know someone. What makes them tick, their bad habits? Can you even stand being around them for an entire day?"

A wry grin pulled at his lips, and he gripped my shoulders. "I'm here to tell you, it *does* exist, but in sporadic cases. Few will experience it but not recognize it, some will confuse it for infatuation, and even fewer will know the truth like that couple we passed."

A golf-ball-sized lump formed in my throat. The tingles I'd felt from Eric's first touch...no. Attraction. From the moment I laid eyes on him, I could readily admit he was more than easy on the eyes.

"Have you ever experienced it for yourself? Love at first sight?" I tried to meet his gaze, but remained transfixed on his chest, remembering the light scattering of hair leading down to his—my eyes shot up to his face.

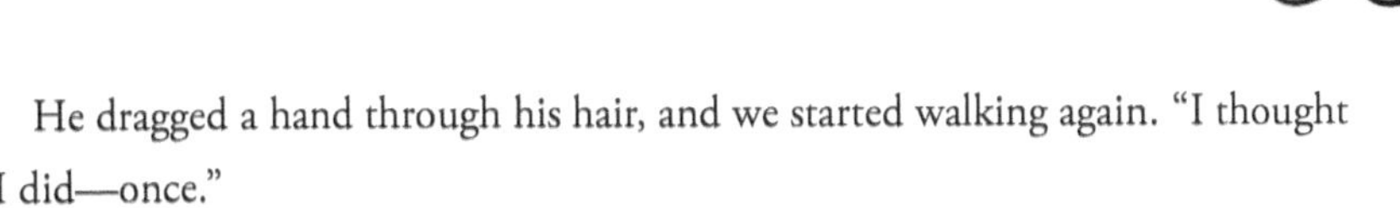

He dragged a hand through his hair, and we started walking again. "I thought I did—once."

"Her?" I wasn't even sure I should say her name out loud at this point.

He nudged me with his elbow. "You can say her name. But yes. It ended up being infatuation. And—clumsiness on my part." His nostril bounced.

A peculiar twisting knotted my stomach. A deep part of me hoped he'd have said, me—that I was his love at first sight.

We passed an older farmer pulling weeds from a nearby fence. He waved at us but then perked up, standing straight with widened eyes. Rattling off a sentence in jumbled Gaelic, he pointed at me.

My Gaelic was a little rusty, but— "I'm sorry, did you say something about marriage?"

The farmer nodded vigorously, pointing at my waist, speaking more Gaelic.

"Care to fill me in?" Eric asked, covering his mouth with his hand and leaning toward me.

"I can't be sure, but I think he wants to…marry me because of my hips."

Eric bit back a smile. "Well, why don't you? He's got land. Prospects. Wouldn't he fit into your algorithm?"

I tossed him a seething glare. "This isn't funny."

"How much would you give for her?" Eric asked, ignoring me.

Heat surged up my neck, pooling in my cheeks with such intensity, I had to peel away my jacket collar.

The farmer pointed to a dairy cow grazing in the field behind him and raised his bushy white eyebrows.

"One cow?" Eric displayed his hands over me like a male Vanna White. "Surely she's worth at least two."

"Oh my God, Eric, stop." It was my turn to bite back a grin.

The farmer tapped his lips and then sloshed over to a group of sheep. His black galoshes made funny squishing noises in the wet mud. He returned with two sheep in tow and opened his palms toward them.

"Hm." Eric rubbed his chin. "I don't know, Elani, that's a lot of money."

I thwacked him in the chest. "I truly appreciate your offer, sir. I'm flattered, but I'll have to politely decline." Yanking Eric's arm, I coaxed him to continue down the path.

The farmer frowned, his arms flopping slack at his sides. One sheep *baahed*, while the other stood motionless save for its rotating jaw, munching on grass.

"Well, now you've gone and made the guy heartbroken. You're so mean." Eric slid a sly grin across his lips.

"Were you seriously about to up and give me away to an offering of livestock from a Scottish farmer?"

He chuckled and jostled my shoulders. "Of course not. I was miffed about Graeme stealing you away. Why would I let a farmer?"

My heart raced. "You were?"

"Of course, I was." His eyes searched my face.

The familiar rock formations appeared at the corner of my eye, and I yelped. "We're almost here. I want this to be a complete surprise, so close your eyes. And no peeking."

His face brightened as he let his eyes fall shut.

"And no using your powers to see through your eyelids or something." I waved my hand in front of his face.

"I'm a god, Elani. Not Superman."

"You're saying that like I *knew* you didn't have x-ray vision or freeze breath."

"Well, I don't. Though I *can* fly." He grinned.

I moved behind him and slipped my hands over his closed eyes. "To make myself feel better."

"Whatever gets your hands on me."

"Shut up." I smiled. "Now move forward, and I'll tell you when to stop."

"I'm trusting you not to let me fall off a cliff. That's a big deal."

This man. Since day one, he never failed to make me laugh. "Okay, stop."

I peeled my hands away and let him take in the view of the serene Fairy Pools. Moss and grass-covered rocks spilled down into a lush waterfall, emptying into a pool of clear blue water.

"This is gorgeous." His eyes sparkled, and he looked genuinely in awe.

I pressed against his side. "It's one of my favorite spots in the entire world."

"Have you been many places?"

The sound of a waterfall crashing against the rocks soothed my scattered brain. "I don't have to be to know this would still be it."

Eric stepped to the edge, peering down into the crystal cerulean depths. "Have

you ever swum in it?"

"Oh, no way. It's freezing. Even more so this time of year."

"I could remedy that."

"Keep us warm somehow, you mean?"

"Yup." His brows did one quick bob." So, what do you say? Want to live a little?"

I gripped his arm as I leaned over the edge to scope how far of a drop it was and quickly retreated. "I'm not jumping."

"Never said anything about jumping." He half-smiled and took my hand. "Come on. I saw a path leading down over this way."

There wasn't another soul on the path. We were completely and utterly alone. It's what I wanted, but it made me uneasy. Time alone with Eros meant falling in an endless abyss, wishing I'd hit solid ground, but also hoping I'd float forever.

Eros. That was the first time I thought of him by his real name.

"Here, see. We can slip right in from this rock." He shrugged his jacket off, followed by his shirt.

My teeth chattered as I stared at his chiseled torso. He had a tattoo on his upper arm I didn't notice before—a hare with a helmet holding a lit torch.

"I agreed to go in. Not skinny dipping." My knees trembled from the extra chill near the water.

"I'm only going in shirtless in case my wings decide they want to make an appearance." He stepped into the water, and steam wafted from the surface. "Come on in. I can dry your clothes when we get out."

I clutched my hands under my chin, mesmerized by the handsome man—the god, standing half-naked in my favorite spot on the planet. He swirled his hands through the water, kicking up more steam before making a "come hither" gesture with his finger.

Slipping off my jacket, I folded it over a tree branch and kicked off my boots. Wincing, I slowly stepped in. The water was as warm as a hot tub.

"How in the world are you doing that?" I waded through the water until it was up to my hips.

"There's really no way to explain it. But are you comfortable?"

My heart swelled at the sight of the waterfall up close. "More than comfortable."

Ripples formed at my side as he came to stand beside me. The mist floating in

the air from the steady fall of the water made me acutely aware of his bare arm inches from mine. I scanned the light scattering of dark hair on his chest, lifted my gaze to his broad shoulders, and settled on his perfectly chiseled face. It was hard to tell what was more majestic—the waterfall or him.

"Can I see them again?" Whenever I asked, it was as if my heart had my brain in a chokehold and forced it out of my mouth.

He did a three-sixty of our surroundings and smiled at me with a dip of his chin. "Are you sure?"

I nodded, taking a step back like one of the wings would topple me over upon release.

He turned to face me, and after one roll of his shoulders, the glistening white glory of his wings appeared. The mist from the surrounding water cast a sheen over them, making them sparkle. I reached but snapped my hand back, clasping my fingers behind me.

"You can touch them if you want. I don't mind. Just uh—avoid the arches for now." He pointed behind him at the arch of one wing with a sheepish grin.

"I do—it'd be—" I swallowed my words away.

He sheathed his wings. "It would be the last stitch of realism."

I was convinced him and Alex were in cahoots. The moment was perfect. Alone with a man I was falling for but far too afraid to admit, in my favorite country, surrounded by fantastical waterfalls. With two strides, I leaped from the water, beaming inside when his arms wrapped around my waist to catch me. I pressed my lips to his, and as our mouths opened, inviting the other in, the same static shock and swirly twists I'd felt the first time we kissed rocketed through me.

I peeled back, still in his arms, blinking myself back to reality.

"Hey there." The cleft in his chin deepened with his grin.

I hummed *Strangers in the Night* by Frank Sinatra, and he twirled us through the water with the speed of a sloth. His hair had dampened, causing his locks to go slightly wavy. A curl hung over his forehead, and I ran my finger through it. His deep voice started to hum the song with me. I paused, listening to him.

He smiled. "Were you humming Frank Sinatra?"

The realization hit me like a tidal wave, and my body stiffened in his arms.

He frowned. "Elani?"

"Are you two out of your wee minds? You'll catch the death of cold in that

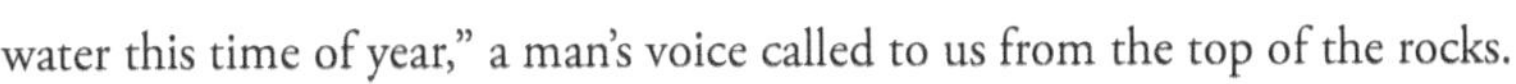

water this time of year," a man's voice called to us from the top of the rocks.

I snorted out a laugh, and Eric lowered me. We both scampered from the water to retrieve our jackets.

"We uh—we have thick skin," Eric yelled.

"Ha. And I have a thick arse. Doesn't mean it can help me not freeze to death."

I held a hand up. "Thank you for the concern."

The man waved us off as he shook his head and walked away, mumbling in Gaelic.

Eric wrapped a hand over my shoulder, and my clothes were dry. I palmed my arms and thighs with a gasp.

"You're seriously incredible." I whirled around to face him, only to be wrapped in his arms again, my chest pushing against his ribcage.

"You were doing so well and then I lost you. What happened?" He cupped one of my cheeks with his hand.

I hummed Frank Sinatra. Only one thing made me sing Frankie tunes on a whim.

"It was nothing. I'm still a little sore about the whole Graeme thing, you know? I don't like to be someone's plaything."

He brushed a thumb over my cheekbone. "That I can understand."

My gaze fell to his lips, wanting nothing more than to devour them again—to feel them in other places than only my mouth.

"We should get back." I tapped my fingers on his shoulders, resisting the temptation to explore lower.

His lip twitched. "It's been a long day." He let go and took a step back.

"Did you want to share a cab back, or—well, wait, do you even stay in hotels, or do you sleep on a cloud or something?"

He pressed both hands over his chest and bent backward in a hearty chuckle. "I don't think I've *ever* slept on a cloud, but yes, I'm in another B&B not far from yours. A shared cab would be great."

Minutes later, we sat in silence in the backseat, stealing occasional glances at each other. The driver wasn't Mr. Campbell this time, which made the stale silent air even more awkward.

"Oh, I forgot. Tomorrow I'm flying to Ireland for the night for a client's wedding." I drummed my fingers on my knees.

"Is that so?"

"Yeah. So, maybe we can catch up again the day after?" And give me time to float back to planet Earth.

His lips took a criminal turn. "Remember you owe me a date?"

My stomach gurgled. "You're still holding me to that?"

He nodded, that same smug grin plastered on his face.

"Haven't we been on several already?"

"Is that what you'd call them?"

Damn it all to hell.

"You want to call in your date favor and go to a wedding with me?"

"Why not? Being in the profession that I am—" He stole a glance at the driver. "I happen to love weddings."

"I have no idea what to expect at this thing. It could be mind-numbingly boring or one huge party scene."

"Either scenario works for me." He double-winked.

I snorted. His botched winking still managed to make me giggle. "Fine. But you'll need a tux. It's a swanky affair."

His smile deepened. "And you thought I looked good in a kilt."

My nails dug into the leather upholstery of the bench seat.

It wasn't a big deal going to a wedding with a date—what *was* a big deal was going to one with the god of love himself.

SIXTEEN

STARING AT MYSELF IN the dingy full-length mirror, I dragged my hands down the light pink silk clinging to my hips. I turned, peering over my shoulder at my exposed back, and my brain dipped into traitorous thoughts of Eric's hand touching me there.

Pull yourself together, Stewart.

I glanced at the antique clock on the nightstand—12:00 PM. Eric wouldn't be here with the cab for another fifteen minutes. Before I had a chance to talk myself out of it, I grabbed my cell and typed a quick text to Alex.

Me: What if I told you Eric was…Eros?

I hit the send button and dropped the phone on the bed as if it bit me. Turning away, I chewed my thumbnail, knowing she'd believe me. It wouldn't be some conversation of me convincing *her*. It'd be the other way around. She'd still be in the middle of the workday, so it was unlikely I'd hear back from her right away.

My cell buzzed, muffled from the thick comforter underneath it. I glared as I turned on my heel, staring wide-eyed at Alex's face and name blazing on the screen.

She wouldn't forgive me if I let it go to voicemail.

"Well, hi there. I figured you'd be, you know, working?"

"Um. You hit me with a text like that and expect me to work? Spill."

I sat on the edge of the bed, wedging my hand between my knees. "When I said you were right…that's what I was talking about."

Silence fell over the line.

"Alex?"

"Let me get this straight. Eric. Bartender Eric is the god of love?"

"You're the one who called it. Don't you remember?"

Her shriek was so high-pitched it was hard to tell if she was excited or being murdered.

"Of course, I remember, but I've never *met* one of the gods before. Now I can say I have. Oh, this is exciting."

Nausea bubbled in my stomach.

"Oh, my Zeus. Does he have wings? Please tell me has wings."

I thought back to him in the forest with the moonlight beaming over the white feathers.

"He has wings."

She let out another shrill cry.

An attempt at "girling" it out with her resulted in a simple lackluster snicker from me.

Alex groaned. "Okay, why do you sound like they canceled your favorite TV show after only two seasons?"

"Because I don't believe in myths like you, Alex. It's a lot to take in. Not to mention the fact I—" My heart thundered in my chest. "I think I might be falling for him."

She cackled. "Oh, sweetie. You've been doing that since the day your eyes fell on that butt-chin."

"Attraction isn't falling for someone."

"It usually starts that way."

I traced a fingertip over my bottom lip. "There's something else."

"Please say you banged him, and he left the wings out the entire time."

I imagined her crossing all her fingers. "No. But—he kissed me. And it was the most mind-blowing kiss of my entire life."

"Mm, it damn well better be. Can you imagine the pressure he feels being the god of passion? I'd be setting the bar pre-tty high, my friend."

Did he feel pressure? Nerves? Was he scared of anything?

"Imagine how he'd be in the sack, Elani."

My thoughts dipped into a vision of him over me, rolling his hips with godly expertise, and the wings fanned out before curling around us. My ears burned.

"I've got to go, Alex. I have my client's wedding to go to."

"A wedding? Perfect. Get all girly and romance-y, drink *a lot*, and get you some Greek god action. For me. Please."

Heat flushed my cheeks. "Goodbye, Alex."

"I'm not kidding, Stewart. Oh, and one last thing." She took an exaggerated deep breath. "I told you," she yelled, nearly busting my eardrum.

"Okay. I'm really hanging up this time, goober." I pressed the end button and let my back flop to the bedspread.

A ripple traveled across my brain, nestling within my chest and making me shiver. I sat up, searching the room as if something inside caused the odd sensation. But what was more disturbing, I knew Eric was here. As I stood, I faintly grabbed my jacket and clutch. A scowl pulled at my face, skeptical he was actually here. When I opened the door, the voice traveling up the stairs made my back slam into the nearest wall.

"I appreciate the compliment." Eric chuckled. "Thank you."

His smell. He had a very distinct scent. Everyone knew scents could trigger memories and all sorts of brain-induced reactions. I'd smelled him…from all the way upstairs and through a door.

Smoothing the front of my dress, I arrived in the lobby. My insides twisted, unsure whether the sight of Eric in a kilt or tux excited me more. I gripped the banister, trailing my eyes from the polished black shoes to the black pants, wondering what his ass looked like in them. His hair was slicked back with gel but still had a slight wave to it. He had his hands in his pockets and removed them once our gazes locked.

The intensity in his eyes could've turned my dress into pudding. I'd be standing stark naked in the middle of the lobby without a care in the world.

"Oh, Lani dear, you look—"

"Breathtaking," Eric finished for Flora.

I'd be lying if I said the desire to lick his face wasn't strong. Holding my clutch with two hands and positioning it over my braless chest, I moved in front of him.

"Dearie, you look positively flushed. Maybe you should wait outside in the chilled air, hm?" Flora wiggled her eyebrows, jutting her head at the door.

Eric flashed a smile. He held his hand out for me to walk first. It didn't take long for his fingers to graze my exposed lower back. The sensation was tenfold

from any time before. I let out a strangled gasp and grabbed for the nearest sturdy structure—his arm. I looked up at him with an expression I could only imagine looked like a lost puppy.

He brushed his lips over my ear. "Kilt or tux, hm?"

My eyes focused on the muscled chest hidden beneath the white shirt and bowtie. "You look so good I can barely concentrate on walking."

"Well. Tonight will be interesting."

Interesting? Why would it be interesting? Was he going to make a move? Would he—would he use his wings?

His smile didn't fade as he ushered us outside and wrapped my jacket over my arms since I'd apparently forgotten how to do that too.

During the hours in the cab to Glasgow Airport, we barely looked at one another but took every opportunity to graze each other's knuckles. The faint touches sent sizzles over my skin each time, and he *knew* it'd drive me far crazier than all-out hand-holding. The following short charter flight to Dublin was a blur. All I could think about was how the night would end. My core purred at the thought of having sex with him, but it would all be far too convenient. A wedding? The estrogen levels pumping through the roof, dozens of couples kissing and being lovey-dovey and cute. Far too easy. He'd need more than a sparkling smile, butt-chin, and perfect romantic scenario to make me take that dive. I was a frozen lake, ready to crack and plunge into frigid temperatures at the faintest pressure.

The church ceremony was beautiful, but even mere flower arrangements attached to every other pew were enough to be majestic. A wedding ceremony was about the people, not the glitz and glam. She could've been standing barefoot in a white nightgown with flowers in her hair in a basement. The look on her face as she connected herself for the rest of her life to the man she loved with every waking breath—there was the beauty.

If it weren't for Eric sitting beside me on the pew, I might have blubbered. But I managed to shed only a single tear that he wiped away with a toe-curling grin on his face. He told me he hadn't used his powers on me and wouldn't under any circumstance, but what he failed to realize was—I'd fallen under a completely different spell of his.

After it was over, we all shuffled next door to a recreation center for the

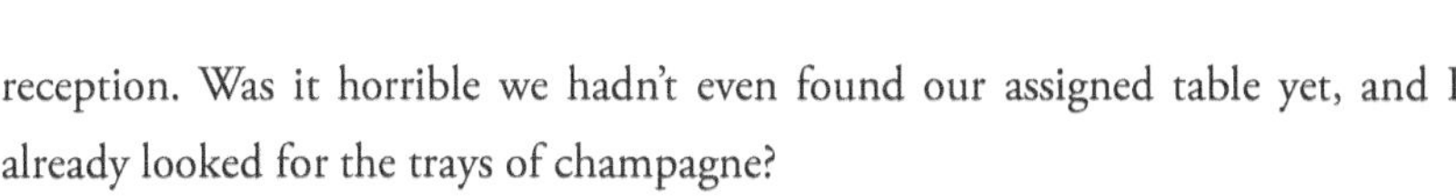

reception. Was it horrible we hadn't even found our assigned table yet, and I already looked for the trays of champagne?

"Elani, oh my gosh, you came," Anna shrieked. Her wavy brown hair bounced as she took the tiniest, fastest steps to cross the room. Her mermaid cut wedding dress was beautiful, catching the light from the hundreds of sequins and strategically stitched rhinestones.

I received the hug, ignoring the rogue leaves in her bouquet smacking my face. "You're an absolute vision, Anna."

When she peeled back, she tossed her hair and veil over her shoulder. "Thank you and—oh—" When her eyes found Eric, she instantly arched her back. "Who's this?"

Minutes ago, this woman *married* her husband, and now she looked ready to have Eric take her on the nearest surface.

"My uh—my boyfriend." I folded my arms over my stomach.

Eric's grin widened at me before turning his attention to Anna and holding out his hand. "Eric. Beautiful wedding."

She shook his hand longer than necessary and giggled. "*You're* beautiful."

I looked between the two of them.

Was I going to have to throw ice water on her?

"Have fun tonight, Anna." He trailed his fingers down my back and wrapped his arm around my waist as I started to sink toward the floor.

"Did you have to flirt with the bride?"

We reached our table, and he pulled my chair out. "I never realized introducing one's self and complimenting the bride's appearance constituted flirting."

"Do you exude sex then, or something?" I scoffed, slamming my clutch on the table.

Eric dipped his chin, giving me those squinty bedroom eyes as he took his seat. "Yes."

"Oh, come on." I played with my necklace chain. The champagne tray walked by, and I perked up, scooping one into my hand.

Sliding his chair closer, he chuckled. "It's a godly trait. But given who I am, mine's a tad more…intense."

"Now it makes sense why Alex was oogly-googly over you. She never gets like that, by the way." I took a long sip from my flute.

"You sound jealous." He turned my seat to face him, making the wooden legs groan against the floor.

I stared at him with puffed cheeks full of bubbly alcohol. Gulping it down, I ran the stem of the glass between my fingers. "I'd say more mildly irritated."

A deep chuckle escaped his throat. "So, boyfriend, huh?"

I pinched my knees together. "I panicked. I needed to put a stop to her post-haste. Could you imagine if her freshly made husband would've walked in on that? Besides, fake boyfriend tropes are all the rage."

"Elani, we've made out twice, and I *know* you've thought about more." He chewed on his bottom lip, his gaze falling to my mouth. "I'd hardly think we'd have to fake it."

My heartbeat boomed in my ears. The glass squeaked between my fingers as I held onto it for dear life. Eric's attention diverted over my shoulder with a scowl.

"What is it?" I whipped my head around.

Graeme walked in with the same redhead he ran into at the MMA match. He curled her arm with his, and both smiled like love-struck teenagers. He bent down to kiss her, further proving they were undoubtedly more than friends.

"Elani," Eric's voice called to me, smooth and tranquil.

I sucked on my top row teeth as I turned. "Hm?"

"What's going through your head?"

"How much of an idiot I am." I drained the rest of my drink, replacing the empty glass with a full one as the tray passed.

"You're not an idiot."

I tapped my fingernail. "Graeme is what happens when I let my guard down. I should've seen that he was a lying bastard, but no. He opens his mouth, a Scottish accent flows out, and I'm a goner."

"I already told you that wasn't all you. My mother put a spell on you, remember?"

I dipped my finger in the champagne and circled the rim, smiling to myself as the charming sound resonated. Pure crystal. "True. But that was *after* my insides turned to jelly from the shiny wrapping paper. I didn't bother opening it to see what was in the box. Make sense?"

He tapped his finger on the table twice. "Sure."

"He probably won't notice I'm here." I flicked my wrist in the air as I dipped my head back to drink more champagne.

"Elani?" Graeme's voice said behind me with an upward tilt.

Eric's hand balled into a fist.

I choked on my drink and turned in my seat, feigning surprise. "Graeme. What a small, small world."

"I uh—I thought you'd be in Scotland still."

The redhead on his arm squinted at me.

"As the Fates would have it, a client of mine invited me to her wedding. How serendipitous, right?" I snorted and finished my drink.

Eric's foot hooked onto a leg of my chair, bringing me closer until our seats bumped together. His arm wrapped around my shoulders.

Graeme clucked his tongue against the inside of his cheek. "You're with Eric now? Pretty quick turnaround, though I'm not surprised."

A burst of alcohol-induced confidence shot down my spine, and I jumped up. "Me?" I cocked an eyebrow at the redhead. "Why did you even bother stringing me along? For the plane ticket?"

Eric delicately pulled me back to my seat.

"Don't try to play coy, *Stewart*. You think I didn't notice the way you looked at, Eric? I was saving myself the embarrassment of what was goin' to happen. Seems I was right." The way Graeme said my clan's name made it sound like we were bitter enemies.

Eric's hand lifted beside me, and he fluttered his fingers at Graeme and his date, the faintest of silver specks flowing from Eric's skin. "Why don't you two go enjoy the festivities, hm?"

The woman wrapped her arms around Graeme's neck and sucked on his earlobe with a giggle. "Come on, Graemey. They're old news."

Graeme growled and smiled, kissing her neck as they made their way to their table. Fortunately, it was on the opposite side of the room.

I guffawed. "Wow. What a complete douche canoe." The waiter walked by with perfect timing once more, and I grabbed a full flute.

"They won't last a month," Eric grumbled, tracing his fingers over my arm.

I snapped my head at him. "Did you do something?"

"All they are to each other is a good time. I upped the aggression to get them to walk the hell away."

"Huh." I leaned an elbow on one of his legs. "So how does this love mojo sense

thing work anyway?"

"Love mojo sense?" He chuckled.

"What would you call it?"

He puckered his lips. "Love mojo sense it is."

"How does it work? Do you simply look at a couple and know their current status and future? Do you help? Interfere?"

"So many questions. I like it."

"Well, I like you." My cheeks instantly warmed, and every muscle in my body froze. "Sorry, it's the cham—"

He kissed my temple. "I like you too. To answer your question, I can tell you what everyone's story is and where it will end just by looking at them."

"That sounds exhausting. Everywhere you go, you're being flooded by this?"

He rested his cheek against the side of my head, letting the stubble rub my skin.

I kind of adored that he didn't go for the clean-cut look, even for a wedding.

"I can tune it out. And as far as helping or interfering, yes, I do. For those that deserve to find ever-lasting happiness."

I sunk against him. "Alright. Take those two, for instance."

A man with bright blonde cropped hair and a woman with bone-straight black hair down to her elbows sat at a nearby table. They were next to each other, and the woman smiled with her arms folded on the table. The man had a snarky grin with one elbow pressed on the back of his chair.

"They look pretty smitten, right?" I cocked my head to one side.

"One night stand."

I tilted my chin to look at him upside down. "What? How?"

"I don't have to use love mojo to tell you that one. Sometimes it's all about body language."

My gaze fell on the mysterious couple again. They were all smiles and suggestive eyes at each other. I didn't get it.

"See how their chairs are next to one another, but they're faced away? The man leans back in his seat rather than toward her, and his eyes keep dropping to her chest. The woman is clearly attracted given her bouncing crossed legs and the fact she keeps playing with her earring, but again she makes no move to be *near* him."

My stomach somersaulted as I dropped my eyes to Eric's arm wrapped around

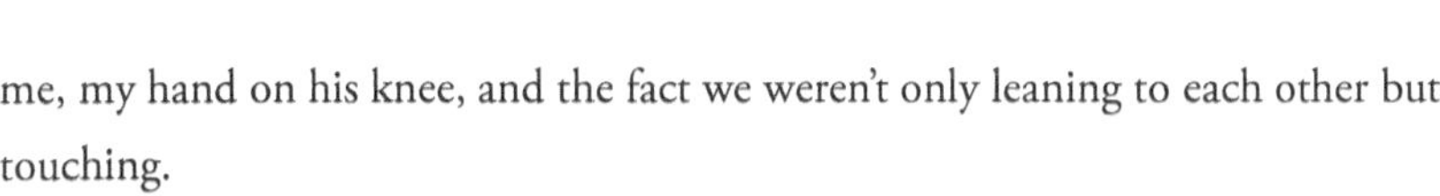

me, my hand on his knee, and the fact we weren't only leaning to each other but touching.

I sat up straight and scooped the champagne in my hand. "You're good at this."

"I certainly hope so. Otherwise, I'm in the wrong profession." His eyes brightened.

When the tray passed, this time, Eric grabbed one and held it up to me for a toast.

"To exploring passion." He kept my gaze, making my insides fizzle more than my drink.

"To…passion."

We clinked glasses and stared at one another over the rims as we sipped.

"Does alcohol affect you?" I dabbed my mouth with a cocktail napkin.

"Not the mortal variety. But I still like the bubbles on my tongue." He grinned, and then his head turned toward the dancefloor. "Would you like to dance?"

I downed my drink. "That's half the fun of weddings, isn't it?"

Being in Ireland, I'd expected a band playing jigs in the corner, but instead, there was a DJ. As soon as we stepped to the floor, the lights dimmed for a slow dance. *These Arms of Mine* by Otis Redding played.

I squinted at Eric. "Did you do this?"

"Does it matter?" He smiled and pulled me against him.

It didn't. It really, really didn't.

As we slow-motion sashayed across the squared wooden floor, I curled my arms around his neck, not looking away from him for anything. He slid one hand between my shoulder blades and trailed the other to the lowest revealed part of my back. His pinky teased the seam of my dress. I pushed closer until my breasts pressed against him. As if having a mind of their own, my fingers trailed through the thickness of his chocolate-colored hair.

His lips grazed my ear, breath caressing it, making me shudder. "Do you want me to kiss you again?"

"Yes," I said through a moan.

He didn't take long to meet my lips this time. He pressed his mouth to mine, dug one hand into my hair, and kept the other at my lower back. I groaned, standing on my tip-toes to ravenously take in more of him. When his tongue lapped over my lips, I thought I'd let out a shrill cry in front of everyone, but his

mouth silenced it.

My eyelashes fluttered against his as he pulled away. The floor seemed to disappear as he made lazy circles with his thumbs on each of my cheekbones.

"Normally in the story, the heroine would be frantically searching for her ex to make sure he'd seen this. To make him jealous." I dragged a finger over the tingle still tantalizing my lips.

"And you? How do you feel?" He cupped my chin.

"I couldn't give a rat's ass where he is, what he's thinking, or where he's looking." I beamed at Eric.

His grin was electric, and he brushed another kiss over my lips. Something strong and hard pressed against my stomach, making my heart catapult to lightspeed.

I whispered into his ear, "Come to my hotel tonight."

He let out a ragged breath into my hair. "As much as I would love that more than anything and my attraction for you is fairly obvious…" The hardness twitched. "Not yet, Elani."

I pushed back with a crinkle in my brow. "Why?"

"For one, you've had five champagnes. Call it a hunch, but I'm pretty sure you'd want to remember it."

"Fair point." I pouted.

He kissed the tip of my nose. "And two, take our first kiss and multiply it by ten."

My insides quivered.

"Elani, when you're ready to open yourself to me—" He took both my hands and squeezed them. "Truly open yourself. I'll lay the *world* at your feet."

SEVENTEEN

WE'D TAKEN THE LAST charter flight that night, and I awoke the next morning in a daze back at Ghaoil Cottage. Whatever Eric had done to Graeme and the woman made them steer clear of us the entire night. There were the occasional sidelong glances, but they kept to their side of the room, and we kept to ours. Anna thanked me over a dozen times for attending, and she became more touchy-feely the more alcohol she drank. And through it all, Eric—Eros made me feel weightless and full of life with a simple gaze or a fleeting touch.

Yawning, I grabbed my cell to check for messages—several from Alex berating me about not keeping her up to date and one from Da.

Da: Enjoying yourself, Lani girl?

A warm smile pulled at my lips, the soothing heat traveling to my chest and bringing me a sense of comfort.

Me: Very. But it's not the same without you.

Da: You needed this. :-D

I read the message three times over. It could be taken one of several ways. He responded to my message of happiness, or…he purposely sent me to Scotland by myself. Or I was utterly overthinking it, considering he had no idea Graeme never showed up.

Me: *hugs*

"Elani," Flora's voice beckoned from the other side of the door. "Are you up, lass?"

After slipping a robe over my pajamas, I opened the door.

"Oh, dear, did I wake you?"

"I was already up. Everything okay?"

She patted my cheek. "Right as rain. You have a visitor."

"A visitor? Who?"

"She didn't give her name. Dark-haired lass. Very pretty."

I bunched the robe at my neck. "Can you let her know I'll be down in a minute?"

"Of course, dearie. I'll put a pot on." She did a hitch step before fluttering downstairs.

I racked my brain but had no clue who would visit me here in Scotland of all places. Plus, who knew I was here aside from close friends and family?

After slipping into my comfy pink cashmere sweater, I headed downstairs. A woman my height with waves of mocha-colored hair down to her hips stood in the lobby, chatting and laughing with Flora. She held her coffee mug with both hands and turned her gaze on me. Emerald eyes beamed at me as she closed the distance between us.

I knew her. But didn't.

"Hello, Elani." Her petite shoulders bounced once beneath her cropped jacket.

"Hi." My feet froze to the floorboards.

"Can we go somewhere private to talk?"

I pointed up. "We can uh—go to my room?"

"Perfect." The dark skinny jeans made light brushing sounds as she moved for the stairs.

Flora handed me a steaming mug of coffee and nudged me.

I jolted to attention and led the woman to my room, closing the door behind us with an ominous click.

"Do you know who I am?" She sipped her coffee, leaving behind a light red smudge from her lipstick. She rubbed the toes of her Lita-styled boots together.

"I feel like I do, but not sure how." I squinted at her.

She tapped her glossy nails against her cup. "That's what I've come to talk to you about. My name is Psyche."

My blood froze. Inviting Eros's ex into my room suddenly seemed like a horrible idea. I backed up until my butt hit the door.

Psyche frowned. "I'm not here for what you think. Will you sit with me?" She

sat on the edge of one bed with a calm smile.

Side-stepping, I sat on the bed across from her, spine straight, and patted my palms on my thighs. I tried several times to make eye contact with her, but my gaze refused.

"Is this awkward?" She let out a nervous chuckle. "This is awkward, huh?"

"Maybe a bit. The Greek goddess who used to be with the Greek god I like is sitting on my rented bed in Scotland."

Her eyes sparkled. "You're already everything I imagined you to be."

"You're going to have to just hit me with whatever it is you need to say."

"Straight and to the point. Like an arrow." She placed her mug on the nightstand and pulled one knee to rest in front of her. "He thought—we both thought we were soulmates. Destined to eternity with each other."

The awkwardness was not improving.

"But we were wrong. The gods answered my father's prayer for a man's love, but it was fabricated."

"How so?"

Her gaze glossed over. "On Aphrodite's bidding, Eros created this love potion they were going to use on the first ugly mortal man they could find to make him fall in love with me, but when Eros saw me, he fumbled with the bottle, dropped it, and fell in love with me himself."

My jaw dropped. "I—wait a minute…"

"You heard right. The myth of Eros and Psyche was always meant to be— Eros knows it. He knows what fate has in store, and though it took us too long to realize it when certain events weren't happening according to plan, we concluded…it wasn't me."

I couldn't sit still anymore. The world was spiraling out of control, and my heart spun right along with it.

"It wasn't you because—because he accidentally fell in love with you?"

She nodded.

"So, you two parted ways on amicable terms?"

"Yes. And I'm with Anteros now."

I picked at a recently developed hangnail on my thumb. "What does this have to do with me?"

"He's destined to fall in love with a mortal. A mortal with the passion for

invoking love as a goddess."

My neck stiffened.

"You and I share a lot of similarities. My name means the soul, but yours means the *light* of the soul."

After flopping onto the bed next to her, I dug my nails into the comforter and stared at the floor.

"When I was very young, I lost my mother. And though I had dozens of suitors who found me beautiful, none of them would stay around, let alone marry me."

My knee bounced.

"My father took it upon himself to pray to the gods. A plea for a man to love me. Doesn't it all sound familiar to you?"

My sinuses stung.

"Do you understand what I'm trying to say, Elani?"

My bouncing knee turned erratic. "I'm not sure I can wrap my head around it."

She scooted closer, testing the waters with how skittish I'd be. "What do you have to fear?"

"You don't know me. I threw the idea of love off a cliff a very long time ago."

She rested a hand on my twitching knee, and it stopped. "I assure you. The concept of love didn't die at the bottom of that cliff. It clung to a rock on the way down, hoping one day you'd rescue it."

A whimper escaped my throat, and I finally looked at her. "I'm a human. He's a—"

"I was too. It's possible. You just have to *want* it." She squeezed my leg.

I rapidly shook my head and shot to my feet. "Are you saying—" Tapping my finger against my forehead, I paced. "Are you saying, Eros and me? We—" I made circling gestures in the air.

She crossed her legs and nodded. "It's very, very possible."

"How would we know for sure?"

She cocked her head to the side. "I think you already know. You're simply not ready to admit it to yourself."

I continued to tap my forehead. "No offense, Psyche, but—why are you here? Why tell me any of this?"

"Eros and I may not have worked out, but even the god of love deserves to be in love himself. And he can have it with you."

My lips numbed. "You're serious about this?"

"The myth of 'Psyche' has been yours to live all along, and Eros—is the last piece."

Heat swirled in my chest, and I wanted nothing more than to melt in Eros's arms.

Psyche rose and breezed across the room like a ghost. "I'm not asking you to make any kind of decision or come to a conclusion. All I ask is for you to believe in love again and hear what it has to say."

I stared at her, already replaying her words in my head.

She reached for my limp hand and shook it. "It was an absolute pleasure to meet you, Elani. And I hope to see you again." She turned away and opened the door.

"Psyche."

She paused, smiling at me over her shoulder.

"Thank you."

After bowing her head, she left.

I followed soon after, descending the stairs with the grace of a tortoise. Flora sat straighter when she caught sight of me.

"By heavens, ye look like you've seen a ghost."

She wasn't too far off. Gods could be considered supernatural beings, too, couldn't they?

"You don't happen to have anything stronger than coffee hidden away, do you?" I motioned at the high cabinets in the kitchen.

Her cheeks blushed, and she reached below the sink, producing an un-labeled bottle of amber-colored liquid. "A wee nip shouldn't hurt us none, hm?"

After resting two tumblers on the counter, she poured a small amount in each. We clinked our glasses and sunk them.

"Your lad has been pacing around the loch, by the way." She flashed a mischievous grin, motioning at the window with her head.

I choke-coughed on my whiskey. "Eric?"

"Who else?" She nudged my shoulder. "Go on, then."

"Now?" I scrunched my face at the older woman's spunk.

Continuing to coax me outside, she added, "Aye, now. And I don't expect you back until the wee hours of the night." She shoved a jacket into my arms.

"But I—" She'd pushed me out the door, and I turned only to have it slammed in my face.

In the distance, Eric walked the shoreline barefoot with his hands in his pockets. I slipped the jacket over my shoulders as I walked over, contemplating whether or not to tell him about Psyche. Their relationship had started with a lie, and if there were a chance for us, even a tiny one, I wouldn't want history to repeat itself.

"Hey," I said with a mouse squeak.

His gaze fixed on me, eyes sparkling as he took me in. "Hey."

"I had a fascinating conversation."

"Oh, yeah?" He picked up a rock and bounced it across the water's surface. "With who?"

"Psyche."

He'd picked up another rock, but instead of it flying, it plopped into the lake. "You…did? How'd uh—how'd that go?" His throat bobbed with an exaggerated swallow.

The god of passion *did* get nervous.

"It was…really nice." A cozy smile tugged at my lips.

His shoulders relaxed. "Good to hear. I haven't seen her in years."

"Why are you barefoot?"

"I like the feel of the soil mixed with sand between my toes." He wiggled his feet. "Is that weird?"

"For a Greek god?" I half-grinned. "Maybe."

"Listen I—" He stepped forward, and a blue swirly portal appeared behind him.

A dark-haired man with a beard and black duster jacket leaped out, landing on his booted feet with a grunt. He sniffed the air, his tanned nose twitching.

My feet cemented to the ground, and I stilled, staring as the portal shrunk away as quick as it had formed.

"I know it's here. I can smell it," he said with a cockney British accent.

"Hephaistos?" Eric quirked a brow.

The British man grimaced. "Oof. I haven't heard that bloody name in decades. It's Heph."

"God of the forge?" I finished, my jaw hanging open.

"Ah. You've heard of me. I'm flattered." He bowed before snapping his head

behind him, sniffing again.

"What are you doing here?" Eric's nose twitched.

Heph squatted at the water's edge, tapping the surface like Morse code. "Dite put out a bounty on the monster who lurks the depths."

"Nessie?" I tightened the jacket around my chest.

Please tell me, for the love of God, the Loch Ness Monster didn't *also* exist.

"Nah. She called it an elani." The tapping turned into slapping the water. "Here, Beastie, Beastie."

I shifted my eyes to Eric. "I'm Elani."

A massive green creature burst from the lake, its neck long and winding like a dinosaur. I staggered backward, craning my neck to look up at it. The long winding tail flared out, heading straight for…me. I couldn't have moved even if I wanted to, my limbs refusing to break free of the shock coursing through my veins.

"Elani," Eric boomed from somewhere nearby—his voice sounded distant as I stared up at water tendrils falling from the creature's tail looming over me.

Heph threw a squared metallic device to the ground, and a green hologram shot out, forming a translucent dome over a several-mile radius, shielding us from the outside world.

Eric's arms wrapped around me and my feet lifted from the ground. His large white wings furiously flapped as he carried me away from the lake edge. Heph's left hand splayed, and a giant golden hammer with etched Greek symbols and markings appeared.

As Eric set me on the grass behind a boulder farther away from the lake but not so far it was outside of the hologram dome, my shoulders trembled. His bare chest heaved as he looked at me, cupping my face with a palm. He'd taken his shirt off to free his wings and stood in front of me like the night I discovered the real him—half-naked in only a pair of jeans.

"Elani." He kept his voice soft, but there was a sense of urgency.

I snapped my gaze to meet his.

"Stay here, alright?"

Heph's growls and grunts followed by splashing as he fought the monster echoed off the rocks surrounding us.

I nodded numbly in response, unsure if words would've fallen away from my lips.

He kissed my forehead before flying into the air, and in a shimmer of silver, a quiver appeared on his back, followed by a shiny silver bow.

He drew an arrow and notched it on the bow, circling the beast from the air. Pulling back, he loosed the arrow into the monster's shoulder. It roared, splashing water with one of its large fins, soaking Eric from head-to-toe.

Heph ran along the edge, curling both hands around the hammer's handle. The monster zeroed in on me, my eyes locking with the large black orbs of its gaze. My jaw chattered as I gripped the rock, scraping my fingernails over its rough texture. Waiting for the beast to near the shoreline, Heph swung back and slammed the hammer into its neck. The monster writhed, hurling water at Heph. He paused, sputtering and dragging a hand down his face and beard.

"Is that all you got?" Heph yelled.

Eric swooped down, bow at the ready, and launched two arrows into its neck. The beast spun around, smacking its head into Eric's body and thwarting him into the water with a monstrous splash.

"Eric!" I popped up, my heart racing at the mere thought of something happening to him.

Heph waved his hand at me. "He's fine, love. It can't hurt—" His words were cut short as the beast's scaly tail slammed into Heph's side, making his body form a "C".

Heph let out an *oof*, and the monster coiled its tail around his torso, slamming him into the lake and dragging him underwater. The beast disappeared beneath the surface, and the world grew eerily calm. My heart raced as I walked forward, leaving the safe space of my rock. Frantically, I darted my eyes over the water, looking for a ripple or even a bubble. Nothing.

The monster exploded from the depths, sending geysers of water in every direction. Eric flapped his wings, snapping the wetness away. He had the bow secured in both hands, using it to choke the beast below the neck as it thrashed. Heph rode its back like a bull, bringing the hammer down on it repeatedly. Orange sparks flew with each stroke against the monster's scales.

"Damn it all to shite!" Heph slammed the hammer down with faster swings, but it still did nothing to hurt it.

Eric let out a ferocious yell, keeping his grip on the bow around its neck. The beast dipped and threw its head back, throwing Eric and Heph to the shoreline.

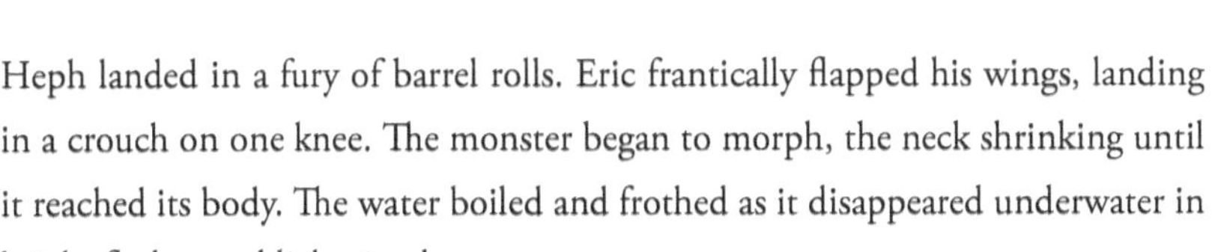

Heph landed in a fury of barrel rolls. Eric frantically flapped his wings, landing in a crouch on one knee. The monster began to morph, the neck shrinking until it reached its body. The water boiled and frothed as it disappeared underwater in bright flashes and lightning bursts.

I covered my mouth with my palm, unable to stop my curiosity from bringing me closer.

A naked man with pale skin and auburn hair crawled onto the bank. Purple bruises littered his back, and his breathing grew deep and heavy.

"What the bloody hell?" Heph picked up a stick and poked the man's shoulder.

The man batted Heph's arm away. "Christ." He lifted his blue eyes to look from Heph to Eric and then me. His jaw was square-cut, lips thin, and a light peppering of auburn hair across his chin.

"You're the—" I stuttered.

The man rose to his feet, and my eyes fell straight to *his* monster, making my cheeks flush.

"Loch Ness Monster?" He smirked, making a dimple in his cheek appear. Water dripped from his wavy semi-long hair as he shook his head. "Aye. That's what they call me."

"I'll be damned." Eric stared at him.

"Nessie is a shifter. Huh. Didn't see that comin'." Heph made a wry grin.

"I wasn't tryin' to kill her if that's what you all think." The shifter pointed at us, water dripping from his fingertip.

Eric curled his arm around my waist, easing me behind him. "Didn't look like that to me. Why attack at all?"

"I was hired to try and scare her off." He blew out a breath, making his cheeks flap.

Heph shook his head. "Lemme guess. Aphrodite?"

Eric's grip tightened on my hip.

"Aye. How'd ye know?" The shifter cocked a brow.

Heph leaned back to peer at me behind Eric. "Because she put a bounty on lil Elani, here. Why does she have it in for you?"

"She's Aphrodite. What other reason would there be?" Eric snarled. "Whatever she offered you, I'll double it if you just let her go." His gaze hardened at the shifter.

The shifter rubbed his chin and waved his hands. "Don't worry about it. It'd been so long since I re-surfaced, I should've known she had an ulterior motive." He peeked at me frozen behind Eros. "Did I scare ye, lass?"

Was that a rhetorical question? But also…no…not even a monster the size of a skyscraper was enough to frighten me away from the man standing in front of me. The man who'd fought the beast—for me. Eros.

I folded an arm over my stomach. "But you—this is so far from the Ness."

"The lochs all connect around here. Ye think I'd limit myself to one?" He raised a brow as he slowly backed away, dipping his feet into the water. "Apologies if I frightened you, Elani. And rest assured, if ye should ever find yourself near any lochs again, no one or nothin' will bother ye." He waved as he descended into the lake, leaving only a ripple behind as his head disappeared.

Eric's chest pulsed. "I need to talk with my mother."

"Now, now. I'll take care of the lovey-dovey goddess. Something tells me you have…other things to do." He nudged his head at me.

I could only imagine the look on my face reflected the mixed feelings swirling through me—terror, lust, confusion.

Eric bowed his head. "Thank you for helping."

Heph scanned Eric's wings. "You did good, kid." Heph scooped the shielding device into his palm and tossed it to Eric. "I'll let you keep that." He winked at me as the blue portal appeared, and he jumped in.

Eric tossed the device in his hand, his water-soaked wings drooping slightly.

I walked closer with my fingers interlaced in front of me. Words couldn't begin to describe what I'd seen. More importantly, what I'd seen *him* do. No denying the reality standing in front of you, Stewart. Not after that. His blue eyes lifted to meet mine, that wavy piece of hair sticking to his forehead.

With a steady hand, I reached for his wings. He stood straighter, glancing from the wing to my hand. When my fingers brushed over one of the soft feathers, the wings perked up, snapping the water coating them into mist.

My vision blurred with tears. They were beautiful—the feathers like fluffy clouds coated with silk against my fingertips.

"Take me up, Eros."

EIGHTEEN

A SPARKLING GRIN SPREAD over his lips. The wings rustled and stretched wide. He cradled me in his arms, and I stared up at those deep blue eyes, glowing now with an iridescent sheen.

"Are you ready?" Eros's wings flapped twice as if they were eager to take flight.

I pressed my fingertip against the dimple in his chin. "Yes. But what if someone sees us?"

"Reach in my back pocket."

Doing as instructed, I removed the device Heph left behind.

"Push the green button, and we'll be invisible to the world." He nuzzled my cheek with his nose.

Tracing my thumb over the button, I canted my head at him. "With all the power you have, you can't use your powers to cloak us?"

"Despite our power, we all have our burdens. It keeps us grounded." He kissed the tip of my nose.

Keeping his gaze, I pressed the button. The green hologram surrounded our bodies, clinging to us like a second skin. My heart hummed in anticipation.

"Put it back in my pocket so you can hold on." The heat radiating from his bare chest warmed my face as I reached for his pocket.

"Do I need to worry about you dropping me?"

A masculine chuckle escaped his lungs. "Never. I figured it'd make you less nervous. You could go Titanic up there if you wish."

I curled my arms around his neck, letting my fingers play through his damp,

curly waves of hair. "I'm ready, Eros."

His eyes fell shut, and a shiver vibrated his shoulders. He pressed our foreheads together, and with one push of his wings, we were airborne. I closed my eyes, fearing if I saw how high we were, I'd panic. The cold air nipped at my cheeks as he picked up speed.

"Elani," he whispered into my hair. "Open your eyes."

Tightening my arms around his neck, I opened my eyes, staring up at his serene face. He looked so relaxed.

"You're missing a hell of a view." He jutted his chin behind me.

"I don't know. I've got a pretty good one right here."

His eyes glistened as his grip on my waist tightened. "Look."

I slowly turned my head, peering down at the breath-taking aerial view of the Highlands. An airy breath pushed from my lungs. We were over the loch, our reflection invisible from the surface of the water. Men on fishing boats hurled nets or dragged them in. Cliffs and mountains covered in emerald moss rose to the sky. He steered us into a light blanket of fog and mist. I dared to raise a hand, letting the moisture collect on my fingertips.

"Let go. I got you," Eros said against my nape, his lips skirting over my earlobe.

After removing my hand from his neck, I peeled my arm away, raising both to the heavens above. A train chugged along a raised track below, curling through the thickets of trees nestled within the valley. Eros nose-dived, and I yelped, throwing my arms back around him. My heart raced, but laughter soon followed. He flew us directly above the train, its steam wrapping around us like a cloud.

I gazed up at his wings splayed to glide through the air. Every few moments, they'd flap once to keep us level. The sun peeked through the gray clouds, making the stark white feathers gleam. I pulled Eros's head down, bringing our faces closer, and kissed him. A tender brush of lips—a quick lap of my tongue. When I pulled away, the smile spread over his face could've melted an iceberg.

"What else you got?" I rolled my bottom lip past my teeth as I scratched my nails against the back of his head.

His eyelids grew heavy, and we halted in mid-air. He raised one brow, gave a mighty flap with his wings, and sent us catapulting straight up. Instead of shrieking, I giggled with delight. The wind stole away my laughter the faster he went, spiraling us and making the world spin. When he stopped, I shook

away the dizziness and gazed down at the people walking the path by a nearby waterfall plunging over a cliff. I was a giant peering through a magnifying glass at the ants below.

"Can we fly over the water?" I trailed my finger over the grooves making up his carved arm muscles.

He kissed my brow. "Wrap your legs around me."

"O—kay?" I shifted in his grasp, curling my legs around his waist and locking my feet together at the ankle. "What are you up to?"

He circled both arms around my back, and we plunged through the sky. I dipped my head back, watching the world speed by upside down. As the confidence built with each passing moment, I let go of him and stretched my arms in front of me. He grinned, did a half-barrel roll, and I was on top of him with my arms still out.

"Does it feel like you're flying?" He kneaded my lower back with his fingers.

Sea mist speckled my cheeks the closer we got to the water. The wind whipped through my hair, and I pretended those white wings peeking from behind Eros were mine.

"Yes." The word came out more like a moan.

He flipped us back around, carrying us inches from the water. I reached for it, letting my fingers drag through the clear cerulean pool. I watched the wind play through his hair, making him appear even more majestic than he already was with his bared muscular chest and radiant wings.

"Take me somewhere, Eros." It came out breathy and gravelly.

His gaze dropped to my lips, and his mouth pressed to mine. With my body underneath his and the ocean a liquid blanket beneath us, he kissed me— devoured me. I moaned, pinching each of my knees against his ribcage. Keeping one arm wrapped around my waist, he moved the other hand to clutch my hair, bunching it in his palm.

"Is there a particular type of place you had in mind?" His tone took on a new level of husk.

I bucked my hips against him, spying the setting sun spilling purple and pink hues across the sky. "Surprise me. I trust you."

He bit the corner of his lip and tossed me into his arms again, cradling my back and legs. He banked to the right, carrying us through the wind with expert aviation. A golden eagle glided beside us, its feathers varying shadows of brown

and white. It cocked its head to one side, rapidly blinking its large eyes as if it could see us.

We circled above the ruins of an old castle nestled on a bright green island. Part of the stone structure remained intact, its spires stretching to the sky. The other half held a hole as if damaged in a long-ago battle. He descended, bringing us closer to the castle.

"Here?"

He kissed the top of my head. "It's time for you to see my powers extend beyond helping people find love."

My stomach flipped, did somersaults, and dove right to my crotch.

He brought us through the small window on the top floor of the castle. I'd expected to see an abandoned dusty room of floor-to-ceiling stone. Instead, it appeared as if time hadn't so much as touched it. A roaring fire blazed in the stone-framed hearth; a brown bearskin rug sprawled on the floor in front of it. Candles and roses of every color rested in patterns on the various tables surrounding the room. He set me down. The warmth from the stone floor traveled up to my thighs.

"Did you do all of this?" I traced my fingers over a flower's petals.

The candle flames flickered from the gentle breeze pushing into the room from several open-aired windows. However, the air wasn't chilly but set to the perfect warmth—heated enough to keep my skin from sprouting goosebumps.

"Yes. Do you like it?" He stepped behind me, sliding a hand over my hip.

A shaky breath pushed from my lungs. "It's like something out of a fantasy."

"That's what you need to realize, Elani." He slowly turned me to face him, kneading my waist with his fingers. "You *can* live a fantasy. You can have it all."

Gulping, I dragged my fingers down the ripples of his abs. I followed their pattern, tracing the light scattering of hair that disappeared into his pants. "Can I start with having you first?"

His heated kiss was an answer without words. He trailed his fingers over my chin, moving them to the back of my head, tongue massaging over mine. He pulled away, peering down at me with hooded eyes. His wings disappeared, and I stifled a whimper.

"You're not going to leave them out?"

A sultry smile curved his lips. "They'll be back." His hands slid under my jacket, pushing it from my shoulders and slipping it down my arms.

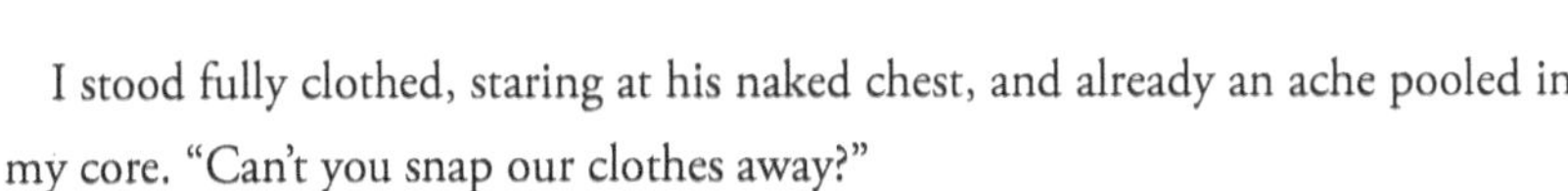

I stood fully clothed, staring at his naked chest, and already an ache pooled in my core. "Can't you snap our clothes away?"

"I could." He dragged a single finger down the line of buttons of my shirt. "But where would be the fun in that?"

I froze in front of him, letting him do his handiwork.

He kept my gaze, torturing me further with those sapphire eyes. One-by-one he undid the buttons, the skin of his knuckles occasionally brushing my skin. It was a bitter-sweet mix of anticipation and pleasure that had my knees shaking.

He peeled the shirt over my shoulders, tracing the calluses of his fingers down my arms as he slipped it away. Despite his powers making the room as warm as a bright summer day, I shivered, my nerves pouring into overdrive.

He cupped my face. "Relax, Elani."

It was debatable whether it was fear raging through my system. I was no stranger to having sex with a man, but he wasn't human.

"Is it—what's it going to be like, Eros?"

He lowered his head, grazing his nose over my forehead. "Like a man but far more—" His breath floated over my brow. "—intense."

My groin pulsed.

He used one finger to slide a bra strap off, followed by the other. Using one hand, he undid the clasp, and I let it fall down my arms, throwing it to the side once it reached my wrists. His eyes panned down to take in the sight of my bare breasts. Cupping one, kneading it, he sunk his mouth over the other, making swirls around my nipple with his tongue.

My head fell back, and I tangled my fingers in his hair. We'd only just begun, and I didn't want it to stop. Not now. Not ever. He kissed his way up my chest, over my collarbone, and paid extra attention to my nape—taking a moment to kiss, lick, and nibble.

I moaned, tightening my grip on his hair. His fingers dipped into the top of my jeans, flicking the button open and pulling the zipper down in one swift motion. He placed a hand on each of my hips, and as he slowly—torturously slow—pulled my pants down, he sunk to his knees. With each inch of exposed skin, he left a trail with his lips—outer thigh, inner thigh, the back of my knee. When the jeans were a pile at my feet, I stepped out of them and stood in only my pink lace underwear.

A masculine groan roiled from his chest as he came face to face with what remained hidden beneath a thin piece of fabric. He lapped his tongue over the satin, right on that bundle of nerves. My back arched, and I let out a sharp gasp. He smiled against my hip and stood. Taking one of my hands, he guided it to his belt, gingerly rubbing the back of my hand. I sunk my teeth into my bottom lip, making quick work of his belt, button, and zipper. His assisted strip tease had me ravenous—impatient for a meal like I'd been starved for weeks.

Warming me with his gaze, he lifted my wrists. After giving a kiss to each of my palms, he turned his back to me. Raising a brow over his shoulder, still keeping his eyes on me, watching my every reaction, he slowly slid the pants down, pulling the boxer briefs along with them. He stopped as those muscular ass cheeks poked out.

A breath hitched in my throat, and I couldn't be sure, but I may have made a hurry-up gesture with my hand.

A satisfied grin played over his lips, and he peeled the pants away entirely. The same scattering of masculine hair traveled over his toned legs. He turned to face me, giving a full view of him. All of him. I dragged my fingers over my chin and down my throat—simply staring with abandon.

"Lie down, Elani." He gestured at the bearskin rug.

As I moved past him, he followed me with his feral gaze. The soft fur brushed against my skin, sending ripples down my spine. He kneeled before me, lightly pressing a hand on my chest, guiding me to my back. My hands bunched the rug in my palms, nerves mixing with impatience making my jaw tremble. He loomed over me, supporting his weight on his forearms beside my head. He kissed me, relaxing me, teasing me with the tip of him, brushing the underwear still very, very on. My hands softened at my sides as he pulled away to give my chin a peck. His tongue dragged down my throat, over each breast, my stomach, and when he reached my underwear, he pulled them down my thighs with his teeth.

The room was silent save for the crackling fire, the wind rustling through the windows, and my uneven panting. When his tongue lapped over me, I thought I'd pass out. My back arched, and I dug my fingernails into his shoulders. He continued to lick me, occasionally stopping to suck, making my limbs shudder. A finger slid in, causing a cry to escape from my inner soul.

I traced a hand over my breast, moving it over the light sheen of sweat gathering

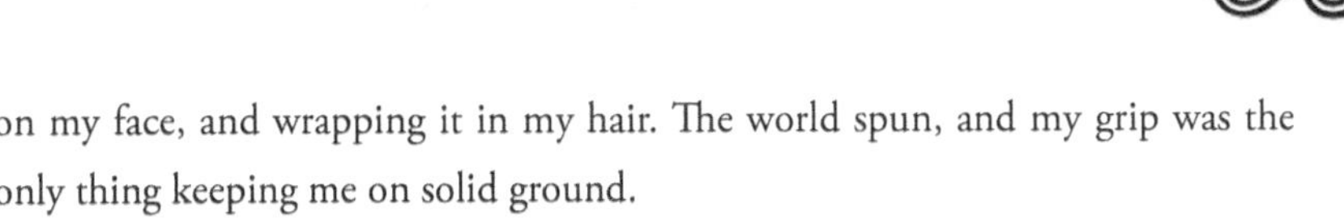

on my face, and wrapping it in my hair. The world spun, and my grip was the only thing keeping me on solid ground.

Another finger plunged in, and I called out his name—his real name. Eros. Passion. Love. Sex. It was enough to shatter me. The explosive release started in my core and traveled over every nerve like a static shock.

I could feel his smile against my folds. His fingers disappeared from inside me, and his tongue followed. As my body shook, coming down from its release, he moved over me, pressing his chest against mine.

"Elani." His voice sounded like an echoed whisper.

The need for him inside me was almost painful. No amount of water could quench the built-up thirst between my legs.

I touched his face, tracing my thumb over the cleft in his chin. "Eros…"

He gobbled my words with his mouth, kissing me. "I know."

And he *did* know. Every part I yearned to have touched, kissed, licked—he was with me every step of the way.

He sat back on his haunches, and with a flex of his arms, the wings shot out. The dim lighting emanating only from the flames around us cast wavering shadows across the white feathers. He folded them back, and as he leaned forward, I felt him nudge at my entrance. I bit down on my lip, grabbing his forearms as if I were about to plummet over a waterfall. His wings rustled with each gained inch pushed into me. When he filled me to the hilt, he paused, but only for a breath.

He pulled himself out and slowly plunged back in. I lifted my hips to meet him, deepening the connection. My heart swelled in my chest, bringing me to tears. A single one rolled down my cheek, and Eros's lips kissed it away as he started a steady roll of his hips. The carefree space I'd held in my head—my heart, before it shattered, began to chisel the stone that'd built up around it.

"Ki'taxa vathia' mess ta ma'tia sou ke I'da to me'llon mas." Eros whispered against my hair, his thrusts increasing, deepening.

He'd spoken Greek, a language I didn't understand, but still, the words dove into me, sending flashes of unexplained memories blasting through my brain like a slide show gone mad. Images overlapping—wings, a serpent-like creature, a wedding ceremony.

I looked into your eyes and saw our future.

My eyes flew open, staring up at—he was my—

"Soulmate, Elani."

My heart flew into an erratic sprint. I yanked him down to me, smothering him with a kiss I could've only ever imagined in a fable—a kiss to shake the mountains themselves. He groaned against my mouth, pulling away and sitting back. Cupping his hands on my ass, he lifted my hips and plunged into me. Swirls of golden shimmer spiraled around his arms before floating between our joined bodies—our union. A heat built in my stomach, intensifying until my heart felt like it'd erupt from my chest. Not in the painful sense but in such an overwhelming bout of serenity, my mortal shell could scarcely handle it.

"Is this your love mojo?" I whispered, staring up at him with heavy-lidded eyes.

He dipped his head long enough to drag his nose across my cheek. "I said I'd never use it on you, but I can't help showering you with passion—feeding it to you from a silver platter."

He turned us on our sides, facing the fireplace, and keeping us joined. His one arm snaked around my chest, his fingers tracing over one breast. His other hand trailed my ribs, my hip, and delved to the inside of my thigh as he pumped with slowed thrusts. One wing dipped in front of us, low enough for me to reach it but not so far to block the heat radiating from the flames.

I stroked a feather with a single finger, the wing bristling against my touch. Adding another finger, I roamed my hand over the softest parts, relishing in how they felt like a kitten's belly. As I quickly traced over the arch, he gave one quick thrust—deep and claiming, his arm tightening around me.

I curled my arm behind me, tangling my fingers in his hair, coaxing his head down to my lips. The kiss had him driving into me with more force, more passion. Every time he'd plunge forward, I'd arch my back to meet him, whimpering into his mouth. He pulled away and wrapped a hand over my shoulder, pushing me to my back. A fire lit in his gaze as he pressed his hands to each side of my head, pushing into me with such ferocity my body jerked against the bearskin rug.

The gorgeous wings fanned out, widening to their full span as he pumped faster and faster. The tingling sensation swirled inside me, churning like a typhoon until it erupted. I screamed through my release, and I'd *never* been a vocal person, but with him...with Eros, it was impossible not to let myself go—to take the time to feel *everything*.

He dropped over me again, keeping one hand on my butt, rolling, and bucking

those hips until finally he came undone. A masculine moan floated from his throat, his face burying into my hair as he shook through his release. His wings went taut, and as he blew out a shaky breath, they slowly relaxed and folded behind him.

"Anasa mou esai." He muttered against my lips.

You're my breath.

I couldn't fathom how I knew what he said, but it was the farthest of my concerns. I gently glided my lips over his, reaching behind him to trail my fingers over the arch of one wing. Both wings shivered and rustled. Eros pinched his eyes shut, and a lazy smile tugged at his mouth. I touched each arch of his wings, making the hardness resting on my thigh twitch.

"I warned you," he purred with a devilish grin and plunged into me.

For the rest of the night, he proved just how sensitive the arches of his wings were to my touch.

NINETEEN

I TRIED SEVERAL TIMES to fall asleep through the night but didn't want to miss a single moment of the living fantasy Eros built for us. Every time I'd open my eyes, he'd look at me with a smile. Did gods need sleep?

"Tell me a story," I cooed, curling against his side.

We lay naked by the fire, surrounded by a wide assortment of fluffy pillows conjured by Eros from thin air. He trailed his finger down my arm, following the "S" curve of my waist and hip.

"What kind of a story?"

I bunched a pillow under my chin, beaming up at him. "You, silly. I'm sure you have dozens of them."

"I'll be brutally honest with you, Elani. I wasn't always like this." His gaze moved to my shoulder as he drew lazy circles on it with his finger.

"You've not always been conceited, over-confident, and amazing in bed?" I bit into my smile.

He nudged my arm with a playful grin. "You haven't seemed to mind *any* of those things."

"What were you like?" I trailed my fingers through his chest hair.

"I used to toy with people. And could be easily persuaded by other gods to carry out—ridiculous requests."

"Such as?"

"Are you familiar with Jason and the Golden Fleece?"

Intrigue bubbled through me, and I sat up, resting the pillow in my lap and scooting closer to him. "Yes."

"The only reason Medea fell in love with Jason in the first place was that Hera commanded it. I'm indirectly the cause behind so many deaths." His jaw tightened, and he couldn't meet my gaze.

"What do you mean?" I rested a hand on his knee.

He turned his attention to the fire. The flames danced in his eyes, turning their blue color muddy. "My spell didn't work properly. They were supposed to be together until the end, but Jason left her for a king's daughter."

I cocked my head, watching Eros's features harden, a scowl forming in his brow.

"Medea killed the daughter, the king, and all of the children she had with Jason." His eyes lifted to me with such anguish flickering in them. "Because of me."

Lifting to my knees, I pressed a palm to his cheek. "You can't blame yourself for that. You know as well as I do, the gods' interference only goes so far. We are humans with free will. At some point, we make the decisions. We choose our path."

His face brightened. "Spoken like a true goddess."

Soulmate. He'd called me his *soulmate*.

Clearing my throat, I sat on my heels and wrapped my arms around his knee, resting my chin atop it. "The important thing is, you no longer carry out petty gods' requests and now make people genuinely fall in love."

His lips brushed my cheekbone. "Very true. Still doesn't mean I don't regret past actions."

"Don't we all?"

"Oh? What's something you regret?" He gave my mouth a peck.

It alarmed me how easy the question was to answer.

"When my parents divorced, it drove this huge wedge between my sister and me. We'd already had it rough given our ten-year age difference, but it made it worse."

He stroked my hair, letting strands fall through his fingers.

"I should've made a better effort to stay close to her, and then I moved to Canada for my business. She tries to see me all the time, and I'm always busy with this or that. Always making excuses."

"It's never too late to reignite a relationship, Elani. *Never.*"

I offered a warm smile and moved myself to his lap, straddling him. "I don't want this night to end."

The calluses on his fingertips made light scrapes up my spine. "It doesn't have to, you know. You could have this forever."

By becoming an immortal goddess.

My body stiffened, and I pressed my forehead against his to avoid him seeing the fear flushing my face. "Is it true?"

He tilted his chin up to kiss the tip of my nose. "Is what true?"

"We're—soulmates?"

With gentle care, he pushed me back, willing me to look at him. "Yes."

Tremors pulsed over my shoulders and moved into my arms. "But how do you know? How long have you known?"

He kept his touch fleeting but firm, not moving a muscle as if he knew one false move would send me spiraling. "I could tell you anyone's soulmate. My own, however, hasn't always been so easy. The universe conjured my fate the moment Aphrodite gave birth to me. I've known what it was to be and when I accidentally inhaled the vapors from my mother's potion…I thought Psyche *was* that fate." He circled my elbow with his thumb. "But I'm not wrong about you. As soon as you walked into my bar, I knew in my soul you were it, but fear crippled my power. The entire reason I made that bet, Elani, was to have the chance to spend more time with you. I never intended on actually messing with your code. I just knew you'd hate the very idea of it—knew you'd agree to the bet to prove a point."

My eyes rapidly blinked.

"And I've known with absolute certainty right before you left the bar to go to the MMA fight with Graeme."

I remembered that night. He'd looked at me with a flash of surprise and gone quiet—highly uncharacteristic of him.

"Why didn't you say anything?"

"You didn't know I was a god then, nor were you even close to believing in such a concept."

I pressed my elbows into my sides, sinking to the floor. "I—I need some fresh air."

"Hey." He curled a finger under my chin. "Just because we are what we are to each other doesn't mean I have some sort of claim over you."

I nodded and rose to my feet, wrapping my arms around my trembling limbs.

Eros frowned but quickly replaced it with a neutral expression as he stood.

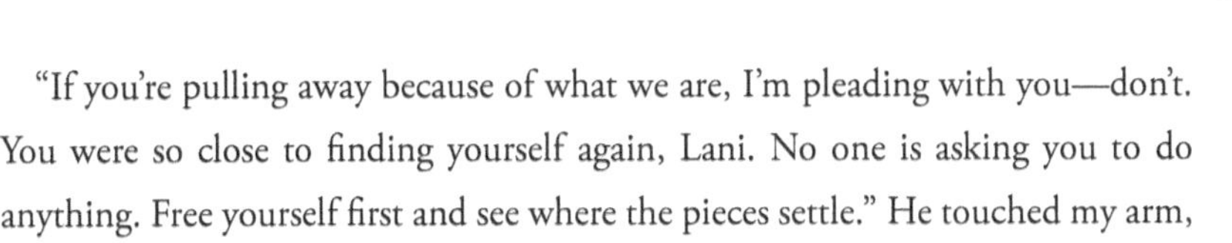

"If you're pulling away because of what we are, I'm pleading with you—don't. You were so close to finding yourself again, Lani. No one is asking you to do anything. Free yourself first and see where the pieces settle." He touched my arm, making my clothes appear as well as his own.

"I'm sorry." I held my head low.

He kissed my forehead. "You have nothing to be sorry about. I just don't want to see you getting lost in your own head again." He held out his hand with a weakened smile. "Let's go somewhere. Anywhere you want."

I slipped my hand into his. "Take me to Arthur's Seat?"

As I lay cradled in Eros's arms for the second time as he flew us across the Scottish sky, I closed my eyes and kept my ear nuzzled under his chin. Concentrating on the steady sound of his breathing, the occasional flap of his wings, and the current passing over us, I let myself relax. I'd hurt him with my sudden change in demeanor, letting the thought of having a soulmate—a true soulmate, paralyze me with fear.

"We're here," he whispered against my temple, placing a feather-light kiss on my head.

He lowered us to the grass, keeping me in his lap as we gazed over the cliff's edge. The sun partially peeked from the horizon, and my heart thrummed in anticipation, knowing the light show from this view would be majestic. It'd been ages since the volcano nestled beneath us erupted and had since gone extinct, but envisioning the molten lava claiming the hills as it flowed seemed so catastrophic yet beautiful in its own right.

As patient as he'd been since the day we met, Eros kept quiet, not pressuring me to talk about any of it. He curled his arms around me, gently rocking us back and forth, and we sat in silence, peering at the sun slowly ascending. As the orange rays spilled over the nestled buildings of Edinburgh, I pushed further against Eros's chest.

"I'm sorry," I whispered, trying desperately to keep my voice from cracking.

"You have nothing—"

I pressed a finger to his lips, silencing him and sending a tingle down my arm.

Pushing the thoughts of those same lips between my legs away, I took a deep breath. "You asked me to tell you how I felt when you first kissed me. I think I can now."

His thumb dragged down the inside of my arm.

"It started as physical. Weightless. At a loss of breath. But then—"

The sun halfway greeted us, casting shadows within the darkened alleys between buildings, painting the sky with a swirl of yellow and purple.

"I was home. It didn't make sense at the time, and it probably wouldn't have even if I'd known you were a god. But as you kissed me, everything I'd been compelled to do, everything I'd feared to explore—for that brief moment… settled and floated away."

He cupped one side of my face. "And you know deep down what that all means, Elani."

Love.

My throat numbed.

"You're going to hate me."

He hugged me tighter. "Not possible."

"I don't know if I can do this, Eros. It's all so much. A destiny? You say I'm part of yours, but what if—what if I don't go through with this?"

He turned me in his lap to face him, the colors streaking the sky above us, making his eyes gleam. "Destiny is destiny, but it isn't finality. It's seen as an irresistible force, but you wouldn't be the first to resist its pull."

The crinkle that formed between his eyes felt like a knife twisting in my gut.

"I need time."

He kissed my forehead with a light sigh. "And you'll have it. Take it all, Elani."

As the wind carried the faint sound of bagpipes over the mossy cliff, we sat in silence for the rest of the sunrise. I imagined we were simply two humans who'd met in a bar, accidentally falling head over heels for each other.

Flora hugged me tightly against her chest. "It's always so nice to see ye and worse to see ye go, Lani girl."

"I'd like to come back more often. This trip has been especially enlightening."

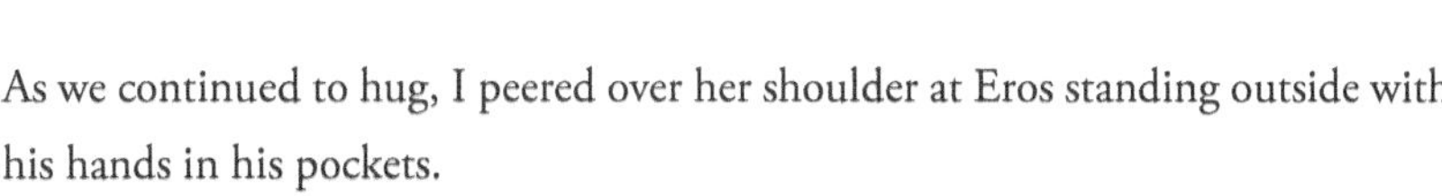

As we continued to hug, I peered over her shoulder at Eros standing outside with his hands in his pockets.

"You give your da a big kiss for me, aye?" She peeled back and squeezed my chin.

I smiled, but it didn't come as easy today. "I promise to give a peck on the cheek."

"Alright." She wiped a tear that'd rolled down her face and flicked her wrist at the door. "On with ye then before you go and miss your flight."

Giving her arm one final squeeze, I walked out, rolling my suitcase behind me.

Eros lifted his head with a half-hearted grin as I approached. "You all set?"

Dammit, Elani. You have everything you've ever wanted in front of you, and you know it.

My heart went into a battle frenzy with my brain.

"This has been amazing, Eric. Sincerely, thank you." I picked at a flaking piece of plastic on the handle of my luggage.

He winced. "Back to calling me Eric, huh?" He slid closer, letting the air escape slowly through his nose. "It *was* amazing. And I'll never forget it."

His words sounded so…final. Was this it? After our weeks of banter and play at the bar, after the magical moments here in the Highlands?

"Listen, about what I said, I—" I grabbed his forearm.

He shut me up by kissing me—a reminder of what we shared and what I had to lose. My heart fluttered, punching at my ribs, trying to wake me up.

He pulled away and swirled my cheeks with his thumbs. "Like I told you, find yourself. You know where to find me when you're ready to talk. *If* you're ever ready to talk."

Damn him for being so perfect.

I dumbly nodded, fixing my eyes on his lips, already missing their touch.

He pressed a hand between my shoulder blades, guiding me to the taxi.

After tossing my suitcase on the backseat, I paused mid-way to sitting. "Don't you need a lift back to your hotel?"

He gave a lop-sided grin as he leaned on the doorframe. "I have ways of getting where I need to go."

My cheeks blushed. "Right." I sunk to the seat, curling my purse into my lap.

He bumped his knuckle under my chin. "Have a safe flight."

Flight.

As he closed the door, all I could think about was flying with him, cradled in his arms, and watching the world zoom by like a never-ending panorama. The driver pulled out, again not Mr. Campbell this time, which disappointed me. I turned in my seat, staring at Eric through the back window. His features hardened, and he stood rigid. I slouched and slapped my hands over my face. What could be said for a mortal fool who broke the god of love's heart?

BACK IN CANADA...

I swiveled in my desk chair, staring outside at the torrential downpour that'd been plaguing Toronto for days. Funny enough, if it'd been sunny, I would've kept my blinds closed. The dark clouds, the rain falling like a giant's tears, matched my mood. Misery love's company indeed.

My door flew open, bouncing against the door jam. It could've been a burglar or a bill collector, and still, I turned my chair like a villain in a Bond movie.

"Okay, Stewart. I've given you enough time to come clean to me at your own will, but it's been three days of you moping around." Alex stormed forward, slamming her palms on my desk. "Do you realize you're wearing the same clothes as yesterday?"

I frowned and sniffed my shoulder with a shrug. "I don't smell."

"That's not the point, and you know it. And when's the last time you brushed your hair?" Alex tried to drag her fingers through my hair. They got stuck toward the middle.

I yelped and batted her away. Lifting my hand, I discovered a modest-sized bird's nest forming at my crown. "I've been locked in my office this entire time anyway. No one has to see me to find 'love.'" I did air quotes and said the word "love" like one would cringe at the word "moist."

"Okay, what the hell is going on with you? Does it have anything to do with a particular set of wings?"

My bottom lip trembled. "I broke up with him, Alex. I broke up with a Greek god! What the hell is wrong with me?"

Alex pressed her palms together in a prayer-like gesture and turned for the door. "Firstly, the door is wide open." She closed it with a calm click and sat in

the chair across from me. "Secondly, how could you have broken up if you were never officially dating? Lastly, do you want me to say what I think is wrong with you, or was that a rhetorical question?"

Groaning, I pressed my face against the desktop calendar taking up most of my desk's surface.

"I've seen you miserable before, but this is a DEFCON 1 type situation. Talk to me, woman." Alex tapped her finger near my ear.

I lifted my chin, a pen stuck to my forehead before falling and bouncing to the floor. "I had the most magical and romantic time of my life in Scotland. All because Graeme stood me up, and Eric appeared to pick up the pieces."

"Eros."

I scrunched my face.

"You keep calling him by his fake name, and you're only going to make it worse." She snapped her fingers in my face. "He's not a mortal. He's not human. He's a god with wings who obviously is so head over heels for you I almost want to vomit."

"The wings, Alex. The *wings*." I threw my arms out to my sides as if I soared through the clouds.

A devilish smile pulled at her lips. "He totally fucked you with the wings out, didn't he?"

I slapped a hand over my chest as if I had virginal ears. "Vulgar, much?

"I call it as I see it." She flicked something from under her nail. "What's the real issue here, Elani? You enjoy his company. He's clearly phenomenal in bed, he likes you…"

"My life would change. Even my relationships with everyone I know. It's a lot to ask for, to simply—become not human?"

"Careful. You're in the running for Drama Queen of the year, and I'm not ready to hand over the crown."

"I'm serious, Alex. You're trying to tell me you'd just up and say, 'Where do I sign?'"

"In a heartbeat. My life is my life. Yes, the family and friends deal would be huge, but if they're going to get pissy over something I've decided for myself, to make me happy, then they never cared about me in the first place."

I sunk in my chair until I was half falling off it.

"What does your gut say, Stewart?" She ducked her head under the desk, no longer able to keep eye-level with me otherwise.

I pouted. "I like him. A lot."

"Then what's stopping you?"

"He said we're soulmates."

"Well, duh."

My eyes formed slits.

"Your favorite coffee shop is Cupid's Corner. Part of his *name* is even in the name of your business."

I cocked an eyebrow.

She walked to the 3-D "E-romantic" logo hanging on the wall behind my desk. After running her hand over the letters "E-r-o" highlighted in teal, she snapped her gaze back to me.

Groaning, I slid to the floor like a melting snowman. "Oh. My. God."

She hoisted me up by my armpits with a grunt. "Let me guess. Because you've spent your entire life thinking such a thing doesn't exist, it terrifies you?"

"Why can't I let it all go?"

She picked up my sword-shaped letter opener. "You've built a business around the opposing force of fated love. It'll happen."

"But what if it doesn't? Or what if it does, and he wants nothing to do with me anymore?"

She twirled the sword between two fingers. "He'll live forever. Call it a hunch, but I think he'll wait."

"Well, that sounds downright selfish. Expecting him to wait around for me to stop being so stubborn?"

"Like he's *never* been selfish." She stabbed the letter opener through an empty water bottle on the edge of my desk.

I widened my eyes, shifting them from the skewered bottle to her.

"Why don't you take the rest of the day off, go home, change your clothes, and do whatever it is you do to relax. Hm?" She rubbed my shoulders, but it was more like awkward petting.

I stared at the crow charm hanging from her necklace. "She came to see me."

"Who?"

"Psyche."

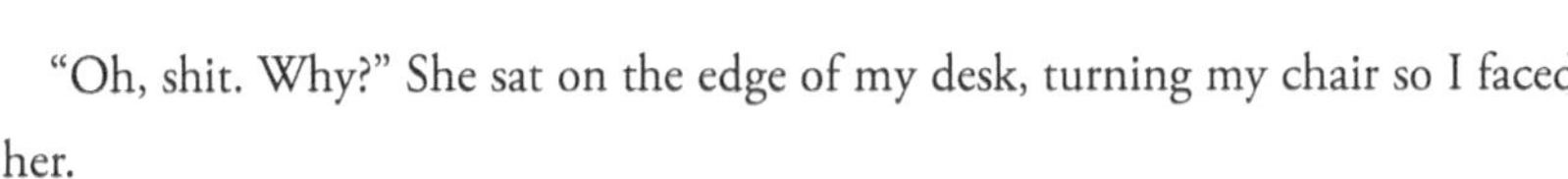

"Oh, shit. Why?" She sat on the edge of my desk, turning my chair so I faced her.

A sharp pain formed in my temple, and I pressed my fingers against it. "She told me Eros made a mistake with them. Said that she and I come from similar backgrounds."

Alex tapped her finger against her lips. "Holy hell, Elani. You do. In myth, Psyche was super close with her dad. Guys were infatuated with her, but never had one commit...and your names both mean some form of the soul."

"Yeah. That's what she said." I eyed her quizzically. "How do you know what my name means?"

She marched over and pulled me to standing. "You seriously need to get over whatever hurdle this is because, woman—" She grabbed my shoulders. "You'll be missing out on something incredibly special if you let this go."

Her expression terrified me almost as much as the idea of soulmates. She'd always been full of dry humor and sexual jokes, but right now, she was so serious her eyes bulged.

"Okay, Alex. I'll head home."

Giving one last squeeze to my arms, she stepped aside and gestured for the door. "I can hold down this fort with my eyes closed at this point, so don't worry."

I paused at the doorway, digging my nails into its wooden frame.

She really *could* handle this business. Better than I had all these years, even because she believed in all forms of love—she had an open mind. Hm.

Despite my apartment being three miles away, I opted to walk home. The crisp air stinging my cheeks kept me alert. I paused in front of my favorite coffee shop but couldn't make myself go in. Cherubs of every shape and size drowned the place. White wings hung from the ceiling, and there were more hearts than I could ever remember seeing. He didn't deserve this. He deserved someone who would give him the world in return. Someone who didn't doubt what they were feeling and fate's call.

Once home, I threw my purse and jacket on the couch, showered, and changed into a pair of comfy sweats. I'd opened the freezer, staring at the several pints of ice cream, but couldn't stoop so low to become a cliché. Instead, I heated a leftover plate of spaghetti and cued up one of my favorite movies, *How to Lose a Guy in 10 Days*. I was a glutton for punishment. Kate Hudson had just won her first game of "Bullshit" with Matthew McConaughey's family when a knock sounded at the door.

Fireflies beat against my stomach. Eros. He'd come to tell me I was an idiot—to kiss the denial straight out of me.

Without looking in the peephole, I whipped open the door with a smile that faded.

"Hi, Lani girl," Da said.

TWENTY

I FROZE WITH MY hand on the door handle.

"I assume you were expectin' someone else?" A warm smile pulled at Dad's lips.

Shaking my head, I shoved all the confusion, heartache, and shock the past days built up in my mind aside. "I'm so sorry. I *was* expecting someone else, but I'm glad to see you, Da." I hugged him. "Is there a reason for the impromptu visit?"

A deep sigh rolled from his gut, puffing into my hair. He patted my back and walked inside while rubbing his chin. "There's something I need to tell ye, and I didn't think it was right over video. I needed to talk to you about it in person."

My palms clammed up, and a tingle shot through my fingers. "You're scaring me."

"Oh, don't be scared, lass. It's not something daft like you're adopted or anything."

"What a relief."

He sat on my couch, its emerald-green coloring matching his eyes as he lifted them to me.

"I think this calls for scotch." I breezed into the kitchen, eyeing my father through the open space above the sink.

"See? Proof you *are* my daughter." He slapped his knee and drummed his fingers on his thighs, not fully sitting back.

I whisked open the liquor cabinet, pushing aside the various colored labels of Johnnie Walker, American whiskey, and a dusty bottle of tequila until I found The Macallan—a Highland twelve-year-old single malt whiskey and Da's absolute

favorite. After grabbing two tumblers, I yanked the cork from the bottle, making the satisfying *thum* sound. Walking to the couch with drinks in hand, I offered him one and took a seat in the single lounge chair.

He shoved his nose in the glass, eyes falling shut as he gave it a whiff. "Macallan. Oh, Lani girl, I didn't even know ye had any here."

"It's not easy to come by, but I stashed one away in the unlikely event you ever stopped for a visit. Or whenever I miss you terribly." I still remembered being a kid on my dad's lap as he read me a story—the faint smell of this particular scotch brand on his breath mixed with the earthy scent of his cologne.

After taking a long sip, he set the glass on the armrest. "When I told you I was too under the weather to go to Scotland, that wasn't entirely true."

I paused mid-drink and raised a brow. "Go on…"

"You get your thick head from me, and I'm entirely to blame for it. I knew you needed an opportunity to present itself, to help ye see the big picture."

The glass squeaked from my tightened grasp. "You wanted me to invite Graeme? To have alone time with him?"

Da grabbed the glass, taking another long sip. He dragged a hand over his face, disheveling his bushy eyebrows. "Not Graeme."

Nausea boiled in my stomach. "But how—how did you know he wouldn't show up? Why didn't you say anything?"

"I had to let the chips fall where they may, lass. Let you walk the path yourself, but aye, I knew Graeme wouldn't show." He leaned forward, holding the glass with one hand between his knees. "Tell me the truth. Did you think *he* was what I wanted for ye? A right Scotsman with a bang-up job?"

I downed half my drink. "A small part of me, sure. But I didn't have my head on straight with him anyway."

"A spell?"

My eyes snapped to his, suddenly feeling short of breath. "What?"

"I'm going to tell you something I've never told anyone else. Not even your mum. Though I wish I would have." He scowled at the floor. "After we had your sister, a few years went by, and your mum wanted nothing more than to have a second child. We tried everything. Even treatments. After a time, the doctors told us it'd take a miracle."

Before I dropped the glass, I made sure to finish my scotch.

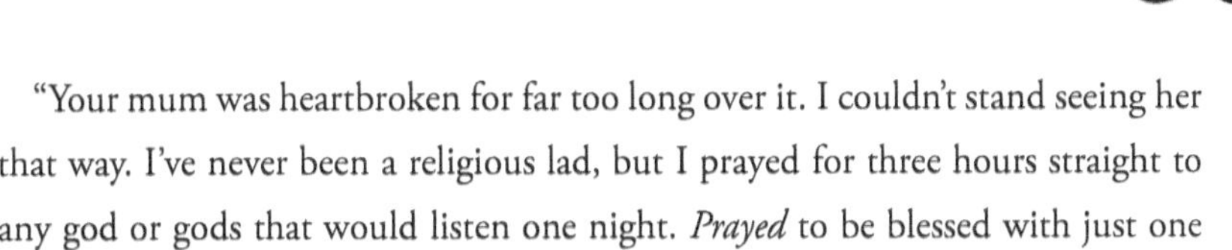

"Your mum was heartbroken for far too long over it. I couldn't stand seeing her that way. I've never been a religious lad, but I prayed for three hours straight to any god or gods that would listen one night. *Prayed* to be blessed with just one more child."

A father praying to the gods…

I uncrossed my legs and rested the glass on the coffee table between us. My knee bounced erratically, and I leaned on my forearm to stop it.

He drained the remaining contents of his drink, his gaze meeting mine. "A Greek god answered. Goddess, to be more specific."

My heart galloped as I stared at the man who raised me. It wasn't story time. This wasn't a fantasy tale. This was real.

"You've—" I had to choose my words carefully to avoid sending *myself* spiraling. "You've known they exist this entire time?"

The skin between his eyes wrinkled. "Aye."

"But why did you never say anything?"

He wiped his palms on his pants. "Oh, Lani. You should know better than anyone how daft that would've sounded."

I did know.

I wrung my hands in my lap. "Which goddess?"

"She never told me her name, but given her appearance, I think it's fairly obvious." His gaze bore into me. Eyes with years packed into them. Years of happiness, yes, but also hiding the truth. Pain.

"Go on."

"How many goddesses do you know who have an association with peacocks?"

I froze, lightly scraping my nails over my throat.

Hera.

"Wait a minute, wait a minute." I held up a palm. "Why would the Queen of the Gods care about some random middle-class Scottish family?"

He rubbed the balding spot on his head. "I don't think you're giving her enough credit. The poor woman was only ever associated with being Zeus's queen and putting up with his shite. She's a goddess of marriage—a protector of women. With all the issues within her own family, I think she made a point to make happy ones for mortals when and if she could."

Jumping to my feet, I paced the length between the couch and kitchen. "I exist

because of the Queen of the Gods. The Greek gods." I stopped and stared at my father. "You had to agree to something, didn't you?"

"There was no bargain, no. But she did tell me you would be tied to their world. You'd carry out destiny." Sorrow passed over his features. Not of the sad variety, however, it was more bittersweet melancholy.

"When I told you about Eric, did you know who he was?"

"No. But I knew Graeme was *not* the one, and with me not going to Scotland, him not showing proved it. Parents are supposed to let their children walk their own path, make mistakes. I don't regret any of it for a second." He crossed the room and pressed his hands together over mine. "You deserve happiness, and you're positively glowing, aside from the crippling fear that you've fallen in love."

I choked back tears. "Did you tell Eric to go to Scotland?"

Da shook his head and slid one of his hands to my cheek. "All of it was meant to happen, Elani. I simply removed a crater from your path to help it along."

The sobbing that followed from my dad's words couldn't be controlled. I flopped my arms around him, hugging him tight as my shoulders bounced.

His aged deep, gravelly voice began to hum. *Loch Lomond.* An eerily beautiful song about two soldiers in the Battle of Culloden. Da used to sing it to me as a child to ease me asleep and soothe away my tears. He moved into the chorus and stroked my hair. The song brought back so many memories but did nothing to stop the crying this time.

He smoothed my hair, lightly rocking us back and forth. "Why are ye cryin', daughter?"

"Because I don't know how to fix things with him. I was a complete buffoon the last time I saw him." Sniffling, I stepped back and dabbed under my eyes with a finger.

"Do you think he's going to dwell on that or be more focused on you showing up?"

I gave a playful roll of the eyes. "Do you always have to sound so damn smart?"

"You might be destined for a godly life, but I'm still your da." He winked.

"I—I'd be immortal. I lost mom. I can't bear the thought of losing you too."

He slipped a hand over my shoulder. "You're supposed to outlive me anyway. What's the difference, hm? Please stop trying to find an excuse."

"And Chelsea?"

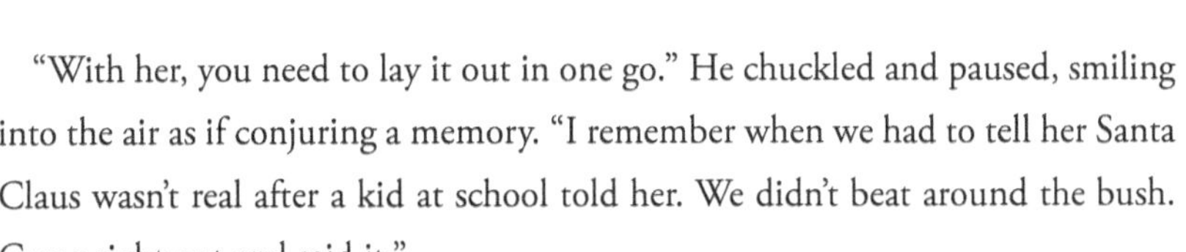

"With her, you need to lay it out in one go." He chuckled and paused, smiling into the air as if conjuring a memory. "I remember when we had to tell her Santa Claus wasn't real after a kid at school told her. We didn't beat around the bush. Came right out and said it."

Because there were so many years between my sister and me, I never knew what she was like as a kid. My heart hummed, watching my dad's expression recalling a more peaceful time in his life.

"And how'd she react?"

He laughed again, rubbing a hand over the light stubble circling his mouth. "She stared at the floor stone-cold for a solid ten seconds, her lip twitched, and then she said, 'Alright,' and went about her day."

Polar opposites. That's what Chelsea and I were.

"You honestly think she'd react the same way when I tell her, 'Hey sis, I fell for the Greek god of love, and I'm thinking about becoming his immortal goddess bride. Thoughts?'" I raised my brow, waiting for him to tell me I was right—to approach it more delicately.

"No, no."

Ah-ha.

"You'd have to tell her twice." A cheesy grin pulled at his lips, and he wiggled two fingers.

Playfully batting his hand, I pulled him in for another hug, memorizing the smell of scotch and tobacco.

"Do me a favor," he mumbled into my shoulder.

"Anything."

"Don't tell her until after you've already gone through with it."

I pushed back, slack-jawed. "What? That'd be lying to her."

"More like withholding information." He made a so-so gesture with his hand. "I only ask because if you try to muddle your way through tellin' her, you're going to go right back to square one."

"I don't know, Da."

He cupped my chin. "She won't be mad once she knows the reason. Your sister wants ye to be happy too, lass."

I rested my hand on his, trying not to focus on how brittle they felt. "Alright."

"You've got a lot to do, so I'm going to get out of your hair."

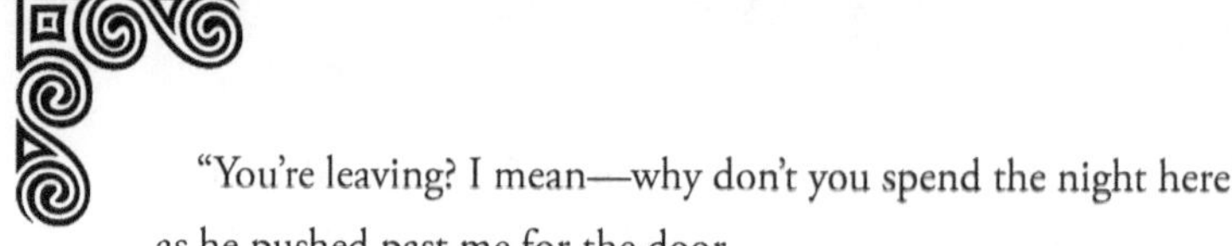

"You're leaving? I mean—why don't you spend the night here?" I stepped back as he pushed past me for the door.

"Nah, I got a hotel across town. You don't need your ole man crampin' your style if 'you know who' shows up." He offered a warm smile and kissed my cheek. "All you have to do is say the words, sweetheart. Three little words." With a bow of his head, he slipped out the door.

I bit my thumbnail and pressed my back against the closed door.

Love. *Love.*

It was easy enough to think the word, but to say it? Feel it? Acknowledge it?

Clearing my throat, I pushed off the wood with my foot and stood in the middle of my living room as if addressing a crowd. "Love." I winced. Throwing my hands in the air like a referee calling a touchdown, I yelled, "Love!"

"For the love of Olympus," Aphrodite said from behind me.

I turned on my heel, only to find the goddess of love in my kitchen, rubbing her temple.

"What uh—what are you doing here?" I adjusted my clothes and rubbed under my eyes to ensure any smudged eyeliner disappeared.

She wore light pink skinny jeans and a flowy white top that slunk over one shoulder. Tossing her cornflower-colored hair, she folded her arms with sass. "You called for me?"

"No, I didn't."

"Please. You said it at least four times." She moved her hands to her hips.

"People say the word 'love' all the time. That's all I said."

She scratched her cheek. "Seriously?" She shook her hand, making her glittery flower power glitch and pop. "My powers *are* wonky."

I pointed at her with a glare. "You tried to kill me."

"Uh, no." She couldn't make eye contact. "Heph was under strict guidelines to bring you in 'alive.' I only wanted to—scare you a little."

"How is *that* any better?"

She stomped her foot, her tan-colored heel making an impression in the carpet. "I opened that bounty *before* the whole Dunvegan Castle experience, alright? I'm sorry. Is that better?"

"The Loch Ness Monster?" My brows bobbed.

She winced as if I'd slapped her. "That could've possibly been a smidgen over the top."

I folded my arms. "What else was your fault? My inexplicable urge to send a naughty photo to Graeme?"

"I honestly don't see what the big deal was since you liked the guy…"

"Because *you* made me obsessed with him."

Aphrodite blew out a breath, blowing a stray hair from her eyes in a huff.

"The airport. The music." I narrowed my eyes. "I thought I was going crazy."

She smiled with a snort, twirling some of her hair around a finger and staring up. "Oh, yeah. That was a good one. Even for me."

A growl rumbled in the back of my throat. "Aphrodite…"

"Alright, alright." She rolled her eyes and let her arms flop at her sides. "Sincerest and utmost apologies. I'm not sure what else you want me to say. I've got some self-love to work on, clearly."

Continuing an argument with my potential mother-in-law didn't seem wise. Psyche's visit played through my mind. In myth, Aphrodite had forced her into a bout of ridiculous tests to prove her love for Eros.

"You can make it up to me by doing me a favor."

"A favor?" She arched a thin blonde brow. "I'm game. Let's hear it."

"I want you to test me."

She canted her head. "Test you? Like on algebra or something?"

"I want you to test if I—" I gulped. "If I love Eros. And *not* some ridiculous test like sorting out a huge pile of seeds or snatching a beauty ointment from Persephone in the Underworld. I mean a *real* test."

"Well, that last one would be impossible now, considering she's not there anymore," Aphrodite mumbled, flicking her wrist in the air.

I crossed my arms. "Aphrodite…"

She remained silent as if waiting for me to say I was joking. But I wasn't. My entire life, this crippling fear of loving someone and being loved back only to lose them, had controlled me long enough. It was time to get my happily ever after.

She slow-blinked. "You're serious?"

"Aye."

"Alright, Chica, but if this doesn't go the way you hoped, there are no refunds, crystal?" She splayed her hands on either side of her, awaiting my answer.

"We're clear."

She swooped her arm, sending pink glitter all over my carpet and couch. And…nothing happened. After a nervous laugh, she swirled her arm, and again, nothing happened other than making my apartment look like a strip club.

"Oh, for the love of—" She snapped her fingers, and we were in the middle of a forest.

"Are you checking my hunting abilities or something?"

She scrunched her nose. "Ew, no." She swirled her arm, and a giant toadstool appeared. After taking a seat, she leaned back on her palms and crossed her legs. "To love my son means taking everything he is and *was*. He has a bit of a rocky past. You want to prove you care for him? If at any moment I sense doubt in you…" She cut her gaze at me. "You fail."

"Doubt about wha—" I started, snapping my mouth shut once a younger Eros crawled through a nearby bush.

He walked past me as if I were a ghost. He looked the same but no stubble, thinner, and a cockier snark to his features. Another young man trailed behind him with golden hair down to his collarbone, sun-kissed skin, and bright blue eyes. The two conversed in Greek, but I couldn't understand a lick of what they were saying this time.

Slowly turning my head, I spied Aphrodite sitting there, watching the two men and shaking her head with a smirk.

"How am I supposed to know what's going on if I can't understand what they're saying?"

Aphrodite jolted in her seat. "Right." She wiggled her fingers, and the words flowed into the air as English.

"You defeat one tiny little dragon and suddenly think you're king of the bow, Apollo?" Eros folded his arms with a sneer.

Apollo. Holy shit. He looked exactly like Ace from Apollo's Suns. Alex was right.

Apollo let out a hearty chuckle. "A tiny dragon? Please, nephew. It's far more than you've done with your archery prowess. If you can even call it that."

"You can hardly compare the two. I give people everlasting happiness. You make people sick, heal them if you see fit, and any other time you're sunbathing or gallivanting around with your lute."

Apollo clucked his tongue against his teeth.

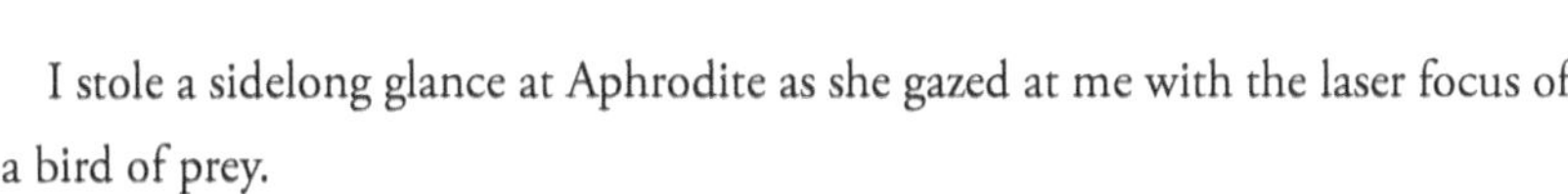

I stole a sidelong glance at Aphrodite as she gazed at me with the laser focus of a bird of prey.

"I *inspire* people. So, what? You make people fall in 'love,'" he started, making air quotations. "Half the time, you don't even decide that because you're so far wedged under your mommy's finger." He wiggled his pinky finger.

Eros's jaw tightened as a quiver appeared on his back, a silver bow materializing in his grasp.

"Watch it, Wings. You don't want to go here with me." Apollo's stance widened, and he pointed at the bow as Eros grabbed an arrow.

Eros's nostril bounced in a snarl, the sound of rustling leaves snapping Apollo's attention away.

A blonde woman strolled through the thicket, plucking flowers to rest in the basket hanging from her arm. Apollo's face fell.

"I can go wherever I damn well please, Sunshine." With a snarl, Eros fired a golden arrow at Apollo.

Before it struck him, it turned into a shimmering cascade of gold and settled over his skin. His face turned serene, suddenly enamored by the blonde woman.

Eros turned on his heel, yanking a grey arrow from his quiver, and shot it at the woman. As the silver dust rained over her, her eyes widened, and she dropped the basket. Apollo sprinted through the forest only to be met by a terrified woman who promptly ran away from him.

A villainous grin played over Eros's lips, but not the playful variety I'd been accustomed to—this grin was pure predatory satisfaction. Petty and cruel.

Aphrodite appeared beside me, her breath skirting over my cheek. "You're hard to read. But your pulse is racing."

There wasn't a doubt in my mind that Eros's actions stemmed from rage, jealousy, resentment. But Apollo hadn't been innocent in the least.

"He's changed so much. Come so far. The man I know is patient and caring. We've all done things in our pasts we regret." I caught her gaze. "But we can only improve ourselves in the here and now—the future."

Her face softened, and her eyes glistened as if tears built. She nudged a knuckle under my chin, a similar action of Eros himself, before we disappeared from the forest and reappeared in The Arrow.

Eros stood behind the bar, as usual, talking and smiling at customers.

"Is this real-time?" I touched the air in front of me, expecting to see a ripple.

"No. This is a fabricated scenario. He won't see you until you're ready."

"Ready for what?"

She jutted her chin at the door.

It was me, standing still, gripping the doorframe like it was the only thing keeping me upright.

"I don't understand."

Aphrodite hopped on a nearby table, crossing her legs. "Feelings can be complicated, but voicing them shouldn't be, Elani. Some people *show* it, some people *say* it, but you know what *you* need to do to prove it."

Say the words. It seemed so simple.

I stared at myself still clutching the door, with Eros not so much as glancing in my direction. It was as if I didn't exist in this scenario. A pain shot through my chest. I pinched my eyes shut, and when I opened them, I myself was at the door. Aphrodite disappeared, and Eros's gaze instantly met mine.

He quirked a brow, the rag in his hand dangling as he waited to see what I'd do. I'd expected him to look at me with disappointment or even anger for the way I left things. Instead, his face beamed with hope.

I sprinted and didn't stop until the bar was the only thing separating us.

"I love you." My heart hummed. For the first time in my adult life, I said the words and *meant* them.

The grin that spread over Eros's face could've lit an entire planet on fire.

I climbed onto a stool. "I love you." Crawling over the bar, I sat on the edge, pulling him between my legs. "I love you."

He dipped his head to kiss me. Every ounce of passion poured from the kiss with each graze of his lips.

"Okay. Okay. If I watch my son make out any longer, I may have to pluck my eyes out." Aphrodite waved her hand, erasing the frozen mirage with every swipe.

Eros froze in front of me with his lips puckered.

It wasn't real. I didn't actually say the words to *him*, but I'd said them. It was precisely what I needed.

"Thank you, Aphrodite."

"Don't sweat it. My kid deserves to be happy. Especially after that entire… debacle." She winced and stared at her fingernails.

Running into the bar shouting the declaration of my love wasn't enough. No. He was the Greek god of love and passion, performing miracles and leading couples to their happiness. What he needed was a grand gesture for *him*.

"Are you willing to do me one final favor?" I asked the goddess of love.

TWENTY-ONE

EROS

IT WASN'T OFTEN A mortal could surprise me, but time and again, they threw me for a whirl, and Elani was a straight tornado. So much passion in such a compact body, and she strangled it at every waking moment without even realizing it. Not to mention how she managed to make *me* feel. Me. The god of passion himself brought to his knees in far more ways than one. She had no idea the power she had over me.

I couldn't remember the last time I'd felt this antsy. Nervous? Excited? Scared? I wasn't even sure how to categorize it. The days spent waiting drove me insane, but with Elani, patience really was a damn virtue. I'd waited on the kiss even though I knew it'd break the spell, waited on sex, revealing my wings, telling her she was my soulmate. And now I'd wait for her to discover herself—or not. I'd have to deal with that too. Regardless of what happened, I'd let none of it affect her. None. She deserved that much.

"Hello? Earth to bartender?" A woman sitting at the bar screeched, leaning forward to purposely give me a bird's eye view of her cleavage.

This wouldn't be the first time as of late the customers caught me staring into space, drying an already dry glass. If any further proof needed to be said of Elani and me, a mortal able to frazzle a Greek god had to be the clincher.

"Sorry." I plastered one of my trademark grins, knowing it deepened the dimple in my cheek. "What can I get you?"

She swiveled her hips and twirled her hair, seductively biting down on her lower lip as she scanned my face, my chest.

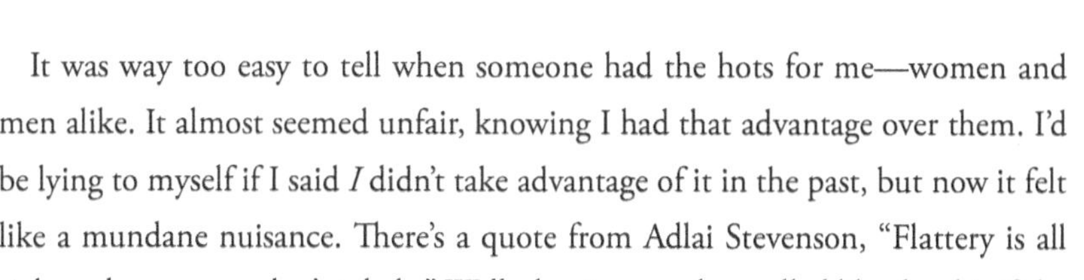

It was way too easy to tell when someone had the hots for me—women and men alike. It almost seemed unfair, knowing I had that advantage over them. I'd be lying to myself if I said *I* didn't take advantage of it in the past, but now it felt like a mundane nuisance. There's a quote from Adlai Stevenson, "Flattery is all right so long as you don't inhale." Well, the air recently smelled like dogshit if the words were coming from anywhere else but *her*.

"A mimosa and your number." She licked the corner of her glossy lips as she slid me a cocktail napkin.

I dropped my chin with a snarky smile, glancing at the napkin before lifting my gaze through hooded lids. "A mimosa I can do. And as far as phone numbers are concerned, you'd be better off getting his." I pointed behind her at a man fresh out of law school and sporting his first of many newly bought Armani suits.

They wouldn't be the others forever. They would, however, teach each other what *not* to do when they found their partners. Some people could handle meeting and marrying their first love with no one in between, while others needed molding—to gain experience.

One look at him, and her jaw hit the floor. As she stood, she primped herself, pulling at the hem of her skintight dress as if it could get longer. I went to work making her drink but had a feeling I'd be tossing it in the drain.

A woman cleared her throat behind me.

"I'll be with you in a moment."

"I really think you're going to want to hear this."

I recognized that voice. "Alex?"

"The one and only." She held an envelope and thrust it at me, violently shaking it until I took it from her.

"Do I want to ask what this is?"

She rolled her large eyes. "Just open it."

Elani's handwriting.

Sweat misted my forehead as I read the letter.

Eros,

I have something to tell you, but I thought you deserved more than just a few simple words. You've spent eons giving

"She's doing a scavenger hunt. How freaking adorable is that? And this is coming from me." Alex pointed at herself with a snort.

Alex may come off as a harsh woman with her dark humor, but she couldn't fool me. It was a defense mechanism on her part. A wall that'd take an exceptional guy to beat down with a damn Warhammer.

"The Duchess of Darkness, you mean?"

She gasped and clapped a hand to her chest. "That is probably one of the nicest things anyone has ever said to me. I think we'll keep you."

I tapped the letter on the bar top. "I should go."

"Yes, you should. But one quick question—" She motioned with her hand for me to get closer.

Obliging with a quirked brow, I leaned forward.

"Your wings when you—" She air-humped. "You know—"

Her mentioning my wings made them itch and burn at my back. The sight of Elani underneath me, staring up at them with the same affection she had when she looked at me without them. I grimaced, swallowing away the discomfort. There was no way in Tartarus I'd stop to set them free when the woman I loved was somewhere nearby, ready to spend eternity with me. At least…I hoped that was the case.

"I could put you in touch with Hermes?" He and Alex would butt heads at first but soon realize they're forged from the same mold. Cunning. Clever. Sneaky. And most of all? Smartasses.

Her mouth snapped shut. "The messenger god?"

"His wings are on his shoes, sure, but just as capable." I winked at her. A genuine wink that I couldn't perform with Elani in any proximity—a reaction

only my soulmate was capable of stirring in me.

"I—" She sat up straight, her plump lips parting.

I patted her head. "You think about it and let me know. I think you two would hit it off."

Hopping over the bar, I motioned to the backup bartender, Susie. "Cover for me, would you?"

Not waiting for an answer, I hurried outside. As I walked the two blocks she instructed, I read the letter another three times, smiling like a lovestruck teen. My heart raced. *Actually* thudded against my chest. The last time I'd felt this anxious was when I helped Bellerophon defeat the Chimera.

The red hearts and bows stood out like a beacon—Cupid's Corner. I was a part of her before either of us knew the other existed. The Fates. Those women never ceased to amaze me. I grimaced at the chubby pale-haired cherub holding a coffee mug, hovering over the word "corner." Romans. Why they'd insisted on depicting me as an eternal kid, I never got. And I wasn't even blonde.

Entering the shop, I gawked at the slew of Valentine's-themed decorations. For a woman who claimed to scoff at the concept of love, you'd think the sight of it would make her internally scream. My Elani. I shook my head as I approached the counter.

Two teenage boys flipped through their phones, leaning on the back counter. One spotted me and swatted the other in the stomach.

"Ow. What?"

I thinned my lips and gave an awkward wave as they both stared at me.

"You must be him. Eric?"

She really did have this all planned out.

"That's me."

He produced another envelope from his apron and slid it to me with a grin. "We know Elani pretty well. Comes in here almost every day."

The other kid nodded emphatically. "We're happy she found someone."

"Yeah." I unfolded the paper. "Me too."

Eros,

Isn't it crazy? I've been going to this coffee shop for years

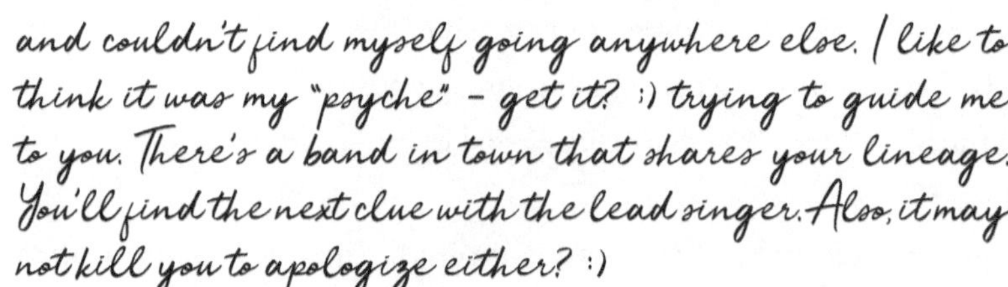

I winced. There was only one band with *one* person she could think I owed any form of an apology.

This was for her.

I'd done crazier things for my own damn mother in the past.

"Thanks, fellahs." I waved at them as I sprinted for the door.

"Make sure you kiss her," one of them yelled at my back.

The Phoenix Concert Theater came into view, and I tried not to crumple the letter in my hand at the thought of Apollo's shit-eating grin, knowing full well the ball would be entirely in his court. Given the time of day, I guessed they'd be rehearsing before the night's later performance. As soon as my palm hit the swinging door, a man the size of a hydra pressed against my chest.

"We're closed to the public currently, sir," the man's baritone voice barked.

"I know the singer. We're—" I ground my teeth. "Related."

The man slid his glasses down his nose, eyeing me over them. "You'd understand why I'd need to confirm this before letting you into the theater?"

You love her. You *love* her. You're the god of passion, godsdammit. This is nothing.

"Of course." I forced a smile. "Tell Ace, Wings is here to see him."

Knowing this asshole, he'd say he had no idea who "Eric" was, and I was already antsy making Elani wait as long as I already had.

The man gave a firm nod and disappeared. The passing minutes felt like hours as I paced a square in the red carpet, repeatedly scratching the stubble on my chin and neck. The guard's head poked out, and he motioned with his hand for me to follow.

When I rounded the corner, Apollo leaned on a nearby wall, tossing an envelope from one hand to the other. "Well, well, well. Look who it is."

Irritation roared in the back of my throat, but I mentally beat it into submission. "I'm here because of Elani, so let's not make this into any more than what it is."

"She's a keeper, that one. Funny though, I'm supposed to be all family-like over this, given your involvement in *my* past love life." He arched a brow and dangled the envelope between two fingers like a writhing worm on a hook.

"Don't be a prick, Sunshine. She's waiting for me." I held my hand out, clenching my teeth so hard my molars groaned.

Apollo snapped the letter away and wagged his finger. "She told me there are two magic words for you to say to release this clue from my vice-like grip."

I blew a puff of air from my nostrils like a bull seeing red. "I'm—" Elani's smile invaded my mind. The way she writhed underneath me when she came, crying out my name—my *true* name. "Sorry."

"Was that so hard?" He slapped the envelope into my outstretched palm.

"I still think you're a prick."

He folded his arms with a smirk. "Good. Because I still think you're a pansy. Just because we've come to a mutual understanding doesn't mean we have to like each other."

"See ya around," I said, shaking my head and turning away.

"Wings."

I cocked a brow at him over my shoulder.

"I recently went through this with Laurel. The ambrosia can be pretty intense. Be there for her." Apollo rubbed the back of his neck.

"Are you really trying to give me love advice, Sunshine?" I tapped the envelope against my knuckles with a half-grin.

Apollo smirked and waved me off. "Go get her, asshole."

As I neared the doorway, a woman's voice said to Apollo, "Who was that?" I could only assume the voice belonged to Laurel but was too focused ahead of me to turn around.

"Oh, just a Cherub on a mission," Apollo replied.

I paused for a fraction of a second with my hand on the door handle. In the past, I would've stormed back, kept talking shit with the sun god, but no. He did have *one* thing right…I was on a mission.

Once outside and alone, I read:

I chuckled to myself, imagining her bobbing around with her hands pinned at her sides.

I wanted nothing more than to *fly* to her. The modern world could be a real pain in the ass sometimes. Mainly because the idea of magic, supernatural power, immortality—nobody believed it anymore. Little did the world know how *much* of every fairytale and fable they've read existed. Keeping my wings hidden for the better part of any day, week, month—was like denying I had two legs.

As I neared the harbor, I spotted her in the distance, hugging her jacket around her as the wind whipped through her dark hair. The setting sun brought out the auburn that only showed when the light was just right. My chest tightened at the mere sight of her. I took one step forward, and she turned around as if she could sense my presence. And she could if she—believed it.

My quick steps turned into a run, and she sprinted to meet me halfway down the dock. She leaped, and I caught her, wrapping her legs around my waist.

"This is quite the surprise." I slid my hands to her ass, squeezing it.

She pressed her forehead to mine, curling her arms around my neck. "You

deserve it and so much more, Eros."

Deserve. The word hit harder than I imagined it would.

Her lips brushed mine, soft as the skin behind her knee, and with a whisper of equal softness, she said, "I love you."

A surge coursed through my body, striking every neuron on its way through. My grip tightened on her, and I winced.

She meant it.

"I love you, Elani."

Tears filled her eyes. We said the words, no more need be said, so I kissed her. Before, my kisses were meant to bring a part of her she had buried deep to the surface—to experience all I represented, all of what I had to offer. But now, the kiss was simply for her—to take it the way she wanted, the way she needed. And I'd give it all.

"I'm sorry it took me so long to realize it. I feel like an i—" She started, but I silenced her with another kiss, the taste of salt from her tears mixing over our lips.

"None of that, Lani." I ran my thumb over her bottom lip. "I'm just glad you didn't make me wait a decade." A wry grin pulled at my lips.

She smiled, making the skin below her eyes wrinkle. It didn't take divine intuition to know she wanted to say something but held back.

"What is it?" I let her body slide down mine, lowering her to the wood planks beneath our feet.

"I've spent my entire life debunking love, bashing it, constantly coming up with excuses as to why there's no possible way it existed because *my* fairytale—" She paused with a sniffle, tears filling her eyes.

I rubbed her back, not daring to interrupt her.

"My parents fell out of love." She squeezed my arms. "But I was so hung up on them losing it that I failed to remember how it started. My sister, me—we're both products of that love they shared whether it lasted or not."

Tears rolled down her cheeks, and I swiped them away with my thumbs, a lump forming in my throat that I swallowed down.

"Men have come and gone, and year after year, I kept digging myself into this hole that love simply wasn't possible."

Too long, I'd spent my godly life screwing with mortal lives, making people infatuated with each other that I knew would only end in heartbreak. A knife

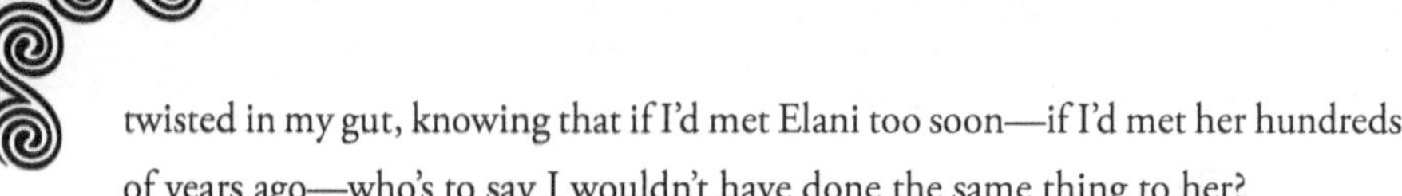

twisted in my gut, knowing that if I'd met Elani too soon—if I'd met her hundreds of years ago—who's to say I wouldn't have done the same thing to her?

I pulled her against me, resting my chin on top of her head as I stroked her hair.

"But if humans themselves could build railways across the world, create vaccines to cure deadly diseases, explore the moon—" She pressed her hands to my chest and leaned back, beaming up at me with sparkling eyes. "Learn to *fly* without wings...then how could one simple emotion be so unobtainable?"

I traced my finger from one corner of her jaw to the other.

"You're my impossible possibility, Eros. And I don't want to let go of you for anything."

My heart raced. "What are you saying?"

The water splashed near us, and a man's head slowly appeared as he ascended the ladder.

"I have one more surprise." She gave a peck to my nose.

"Poseidon?" I dumbly pointed at him.

His long dark blonde hair stuck to his soaked shirt, and he dragged a hand over his equally wet beard. "Ah. You recognize me. It's been what, three hundred years?"

"At least." I continued to point. "This isn't your mortal guise."

Elani bounced on her heels, wiggling her fingers at the sea god. "Hello again."

"I was—in the middle of something when your darling girlfriend and your mom showed up and didn't feel like changing back. Quite frankly, I miss the real me."

I blinked several times as my mind whirled. "You talked to Aphrodite?"

"Yes?" Elani clasped her hands behind her back. "You're not mad, are you?"

She made it hard to be angry with her. Hell, I couldn't even get *irritated* with her before when we'd smack talk.

"No. I'm—surprised." More on the fact my mother did something, anything, that wasn't a direct benefit to herself.

"Did you swim the whole way here?" Elani gazed at Poseidon soaked from head-to-toe.

Poseidon stretched his arms above his head. "Gotta give the fins a workout once in a while."

Elani leaned back, looking behind him as if she'd find a fishtail.

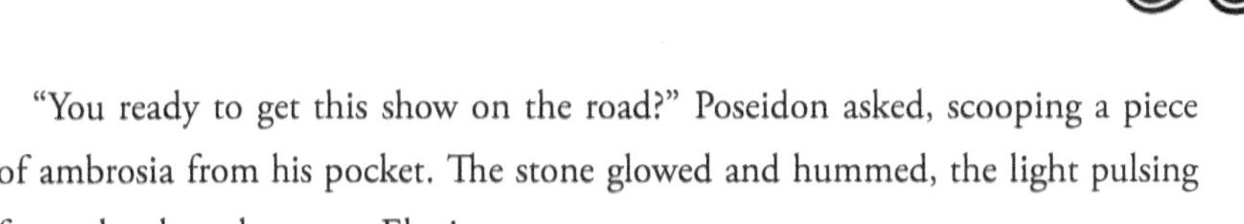

"You ready to get this show on the road?" Poseidon asked, scooping a piece of ambrosia from his pocket. The stone glowed and hummed, the light pulsing faster the closer he got to Elani.

My heart beat throttled into a gallop. "Wait. Elani, you really want to do this right now?"

She frowned, and it made my chest ache. "Why not?"

"I don't want you to feel rushed."

"Eros, I've waited my entire life for this. You've waited even longer. I'm *done* waiting. I want you. I want to share this godhood with you. And I want forever."

I'd been wrong once about my soulmate—clouded by an immature, stubborn nature that I let my own mother's magic fool me. The doubt it buried almost made me miss this too. Almost. But knowing it or not, Elani wouldn't have let it happen.

"Alright." I took her hands.

Poseidon wrapped a hand around Elani's shoulder and arched a brow. "You ready?"

"Can you give us one moment?" She held up her purse with a warm smile.

Poseidon nodded and stepped away, giving us as much privacy as a dock would allow.

Elani pulled a cup with two handles from her purse, followed by a flask.

"You need a drink to go through with this, huh?" I flashed a grin.

She elbowed me in the ribs and poured some brown liquid into the cup.

"When I was little and pretending I married the warrior prince of my dreams, it always involved a Quaich."

"I certainly hope I can live up to this warrior prince of yours."

She playfully thwacked me in the stomach. We could be together for millennia, and this dynamic would never get old—friendship, love, lust, and jokes.

She held the cup between us with both handles. "Just like the Clan festival, it symbolizes a bond formed." After taking a sip, never tearing her eyes away, she passed it to me.

I drank and kept her gaze, already imagining the passion she'd bring to the fold as a goddess of love. "We don't have to say anything?"

A satiated smile pulled at her lips as she took the cup from my grasp. "In this case, no words are needed."

Poseidon cleared his throat. "I'm sorry for butting in, but I'm going to have a furious woman on my hands if I don't get back soon." His brow shot up. "Are you ready?"

Elani gave a firm nod, keeping her gaze locked with mine and beaming.

Poseidon wrapped his hand over her shoulder. The power pulsed down his arm, swirling into her. Elani gasped, her grip tightening on my hands, and I held firm, keeping our eyes on each other. Fractals of light burst from her before disappearing and silencing. Her long eyelashes fluttered open, and she looked at me like a frightened dove.

"Was that it?"

She looked so confused, so bewildered. I couldn't help but chuckle. "Did you expect it to hurt?"

"I don't know what I was expecting, to be honest."

Her skin glowed with a radiant pink sheen. She stared at the back of her hand, turning it left to right, mesmerized.

"You look gorgeous, Elani." It was no exaggeration. She was the perfect sunset over a mountain valley.

"Don't forget this." Poseidon held out the ambrosia. "It'll make you immortal."

She held it between two fingers.

"You two good?" Poseidon beat his knuckles against his palm.

Elani smiled, balling a fist over the orange rock. "Never better."

Poseidon punched me in the shoulder. "Good seein' ya, kid."

I smirked, ignoring the brief sting he left behind. "You too. Thanks for doing this."

"Catch ya later," he said before diving back into the water.

Now that I had her, I couldn't get enough of touching her, smelling her. Pressing a hand to her lower back, I pulled her flush against me. "You set all of this up? For me?"

"You sound surprised."

"Would you believe me if I told you I'm used to giving?" I kneaded her back.

She pressed her finger into the cleft in my chin, gaining back my attention. "Well, get used to it because I'm not nearly done giving *you* as much as I can give."

As I kissed her, scents of honey and lilac tantalized my senses. She pulled away, lifting the ambrosia to her lips.

I gently snatched her wrist. "Wait."

She blinked with the speed of a jackhammer. "If you're going to tell me you're backing out on this I—"

Shutting her beautiful trap, I covered her mouth with mine, kissing her. Twisting my fingers into her hair, I ported us to her favorite spot in the entire world.

As I pulled away, waiting for her eyes to open, I kept a hand pressed to her back. Not even a flock of harpies could make me let go of her.

"We—the fairy pools?" Her hands went limp at her sides, and I took the ambrosia from her.

"If we're going to seal this deal, Elani, it seemed only fitting to do it in your favorite place."

Her eyes sparkled with tears. "Can we go in the water?"

"What*ever* you want."

I led her into the water, allowing my powers to warm it, sending steamy spirals curling through the air. She moved in front of me, trailing her fingers through the water, making it glitter and glow. I cocked my head to the side, simply watching her discover her new self.

Extending her hand, dozens of fireflies flew from her fingertips, surrounding us like an ethereal halo of witnesses.

"You're a quick learner." I dragged a knuckle under her chin.

The water rippled, the glow intensifying as she pressed herself against me. "Like I said, Eros. Home." She raised on the balls of her feet, clutching my shirt in her small hands. "You're my home."

Scooping her into my arms, I coaxed her legs around my waist and slipped the ambrosia past her lips. As her tongue brushed my skin, a growl escaped my throat, and I kissed her, keeping her tight against me with one hand while kneading the back of her neck with the other.

We continued to kiss through her transformation, sharing in the surge this time. Suddenly she pulled away, grimacing, and pushing against my chest. I let her slide back into the water, and she hunched forward, crying out in pain as she reached for her back.

It wasn't supposed to happen this way. Fear. Anger. It all swirled through my mind and body, making my vision blur as I gripped her shoulders, forcing her to

look at me. "Elani? What is it?"

"My back. Oh my—it burns so bad." She dropped to her knees, the water rising to her chest.

Panic swarmed through me, and I dropped to my knees in front of her, dragging my hands over her shoulder blades. A breath caught in my throat, feeling the familiar bumps. With a grunt, I ripped her shirt open, and two wings sprung from her back, sending the shimmering water into a sea spray around us—pale pink, angelic wings nearly as wide as my own.

Wings. Like. Mine.

"Eros." Her voice was small and distant.

"Yes?" I stared in awe. When Psyche had sprouted butterfly wings while becoming a goddess, I should've known then and there…she wasn't her.

The feathers of Elani's wings rustled as if answering me, berating me for being such a damned fool.

"Do I have wings?"

The wings flapped and went taut when she gasped.

"Yes." I bit the inside of my mouth to keep from smiling at the adorably confused face she made.

She clamped her hands over her mouth after peeking over her shoulder to see them. "I can—I can fly now?"

Tracing one of my fingers over a vein, I snapped my gaze to her face to see her reaction. She bit down on her lower lip with a moan, and the wings bristled.

"This is like having another limb."

"As much as you enjoy flying, and now you'll be able to do it yourself." I bumped a knuckle under her chin.

"Don't think you're getting off the hook." Her wings folded back as she stood, moving forward until her bare chest rested in front of my face and her arms wrapped around my neck. "There's something especially tantalizing about being in your arms amidst the clouds."

I pressed my forehead between her breasts, breathing her in, staying on my knees in front of her. "The offer to take you up will *never* go away." Lifting my gaze to meet hers, I gave one of her nipples a playful nip, smiling against her skin when she yelped. "There are also so many things we can do with *two* sets of wings, sweetheart." I kissed one breast, then the other, playing the wicked

thoughts coursing through my mind to my gaze.

She grinned down at me, pressing a hand on each side of my face and coaxing me to stand. "I've made a lot of questionable choices in my life. But this choice? No questions about it being the right one."

"You said I was your impossible possibility, but Lani, as hard as it might be for you to believe, I'd given up on finding my soulmate a hundred years ago." I kissed her forehead. "You've sparked life into an immortal. That's no small feat."

Tears filled her eyes again, and she kissed me, progressing into a frantic bout of pecks across my cheeks, over my eyes, and landing a final one on the cleft in my chin.

We'd spread love, passion, soul, and light to the masses while simultaneously *giving* it to each other. And when it was just the two of us, selfishly focusing on *only* us, we'd take to the skies and gaze on them from above.

EPILOGUE

ELANI

SOMETIME LATER...

IT TOOK SEVERAL WEEKS for me to become accustomed to my new wings—not only the flying part but the concentration it took to disguise them. It gave me a newfound appreciation for how often Eros kept his hidden when his wings were double the size of mine. There were days we'd fly side-by-side, and as thrilling as it was, there were times I wanted to be in Eros's arms with him taking the reins. He never seemed to mind. In fact, I knew it drove him wild when I asked in a breathy voice for him to "Take me up."

Though resistant at first, Alex took over the business. She developed a new algorithm and drifted the focus to love *and* compatibility—still science-based but allowing that little bit of magic inside. She *still* hadn't worked up the nerve to ask Eros about Hermes. I'd have to do something about that very, very soon. Not to mention I'd been playing matchmaker with my mother-in-law. She swore Heph drove her crazy, but every time she read a text from him, her eyes lit up. I may or may not have planted a seed between those two. Time will tell.

Just as Da predicted, Chelsea took the news far better than I expected. I didn't even have to tell her twice. Ironically, her client, Harm Makos, had recently stepped into godhood herself. Had there been some clandestine shift in the planet and stars as of late? All these mortals finding their long-lost gods?

Whatever the reason, I didn't care. All I cared about was at home, probably

ironing one of his three hundred plaid shirts.

I sat on a park bench, watching couple after couple eat at the bistro café across the street. After working my love mojo, I'd either guide their hearts in another direction or let things ride. It was yet another skill that took practice. Eros and I spent hours for weeks on end working our magic back and forth. I made a few mistakes initially, but Eros was there to correct them.

I'd taken to a particular side of love. One I'd been all too familiar with—mortals who were scorned and no longer believed in it. It'd take more than a pretty face and charming attitude to convince them, so I made it my mission to sprinkle other aspects in life to give them hope again. When you didn't believe in true love, you needed to witness the impossible. It's what brought me to Eros.

Satisfied I'd done my fair share of "spreading the love" for the day, I flew back home with the shielding device clutched in my palm. My wings flapped as I swooped through the window we'd routinely leave open when one was away and the other stayed home.

I had some exciting news to share with my love but had spent the last few days confirming my suspicions. One peek at those white feathers rustling once they sensed my presence made me even giddier to tell him.

Eros leaned back, cooking something in the kitchen that smelled heavenly. "You're back sooner than I thought, sweetheart."

I paused at the threshold, appreciating the sight of him in only a pair of boxers and those wings. By Zeus, those *wings*. I'd never get tired of them.

Flashing a bright smile, I nuzzled between his wings and slid my arms around him from behind. "Would you believe it if I said it was because I missed you?"

He chuckled, and I pressed my ear against his back, listening to the deep rumble. "I'd believe that's *part* of the reason."

I traced my finger over the arch of his wing, making my stomach flutter when he shivered against my touch. "Do you believe me more now?"

He spun around and grabbed my hips, pulling me against him. "Now I know you're *really* hiding something." He squinted at me, drumming his fingers against my skin to the beat of *Strangers in the Night*.

"Fine. It's because I couldn't wait to get home to tell you something."

He cocked a brow at me. "Oh?"

I slid a hand over my stomach, rubbing it and snapping my gaze to meet his.

He eyed my hand before the realization dawned on him, his expression slowly morphing into a radiant smile.

We were expecting a little cherub of our own. Godly pregnancies were nothing like the human variety. There'd been no warning. No morning sickness. No exhaustion. Several days ago, I'd been sitting in my favorite nook, reading *The Hobbit*, and it just…appeared. I'd have told Eros sooner but needed to confirm what I felt. Aphrodite squealed when I told her my experience, quickly insisting she *not* be called "grandma."

Eros. My god of love. My entire mortal life, I spent not believing in love, wondering, fearing that I myself was unlovable, only to realize I'd been living it since I arrived in the world. My family, my friends, even strangers, I spread the love buried deep within me without knowing it—started my divine destiny before the gods found me. The urge to develop the algorithm itself, though I thought at the time was purely based on science, was one of the most passionate elements I lent to the human world as a human myself. What Psyche said was true…Eros, the embodiment of passion, had been the final piece.

I placed his hand over my stomach, and we stood in silence, feeling the steady pulse like a drumbeat, knowing our world was about to change. A flutter tickled my insides, and I gasped.

Eros kneeled and put his ear against my belly, looking up at me with wonder in his gaze. "She's stretching her wings."

"She? How do you know?"

His eyes misted over. "The daughter I was always meant to have. I knew you were the one from the first moment I saw you, Elani, but feared I was wrong again." He cupped my face and placed a delicate kiss on my lips. "You. You…*are* my love at first sight."

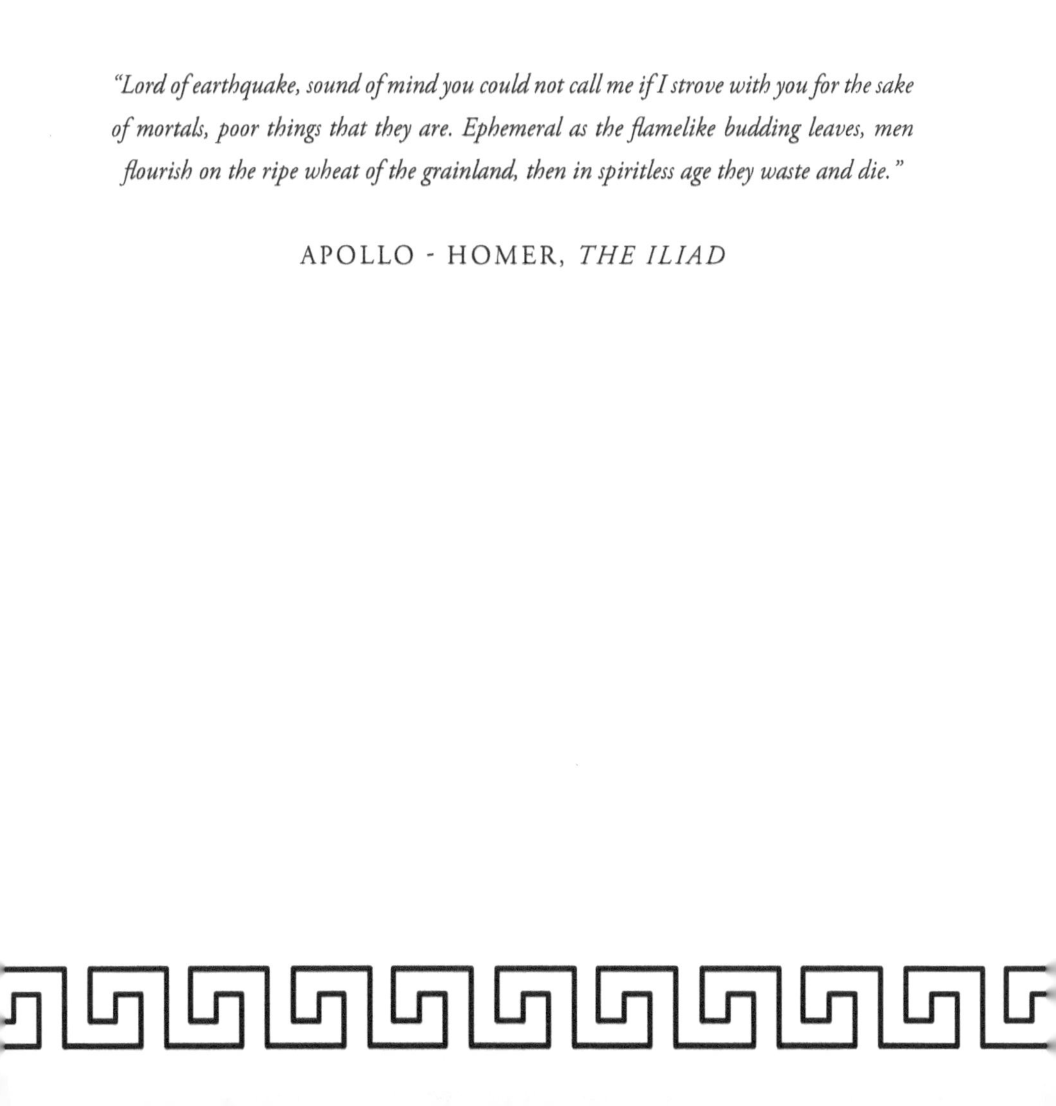

"Lord of earthquake, sound of mind you could not call me if I strove with you for the sake of mortals, poor things that they are. Ephemeral as the flamelike budding leaves, men flourish on the ripe wheat of the grainland, then in spiritless age they waste and die."

APOLLO - HOMER, *THE ILIAD*

ONE

MY THUMB FLEW FURIOUSLY across the letter-labeled buttons of my gaming controller, my index finger pressing on the trigger when my eyes aligned with their target.

"Headshots all day, boys," I said into the mic of my headset with a grin.

I'd been a gamer since I was a pre-teen. No genre disinterested me—first-person shooters, role-playing games, strategy. You name it. I played it. However, since the game *Tides of Atlantis* was released, I'd found a new calling. It was a perfect mix of both shooting and swordplay—a fantasy action game combining hints of sci-fi amidst the world of Atlantis.

During a loading screen, I glanced at the Glitch application where I was streaming my gameplay. Twenty new subscribers in a manner of minutes. Who knew you could make some extra cash by having others watch you play a video game?

One watcher commented: **SaucySiren, it's like this game was made for you.**

SaucySiren. My gamer tag and the only name any of these strangers would ever know me by.

I grinned. "Life's just better underwater, I guess." Swiveling back and forth in my gaming chair, I jolted at the time blazing at me from the corner of my monitor.

"Until tomorrow, everyone. The *real* water is calling me." I waved at the webcam before signing off and shutting everything down.

Humming the song *Beyond the Sea*, I whisked around my bedroom, gathering up needed items. My camera bag packed with underwater lenses and handles.

My duffle bag filled with a wetsuit, flippers, and mask. Pensacola, Florida had an artificial reef lurking in the waters of the Gulf, which didn't often make for the best photos. However, there were always sunken ships to explore. As a freelance photographer, I'd take photos of those ships as many times as people were willing to pay for them.

My cell phone made obnoxious buzzing noises from my nightstand. No doubt that'd be my best friend and partner in crime, Megan, calling. I scooped the phone into my hand, sliding my thumb across the screen and cradling it between my ear and shoulder.

"Hello?"

"Cordelia Pearl. You were supposed to be here ten minutes ago," Megan chastised.

I rolled my eyes and trotted over to one of the largest items in my studio apartment—my fish tank. "I know, I know. I got caught up on Glitch, but I'll be there in five minutes. Perks to living on the beach, right?"

Bright colored angelfish and platies filled the tank, swimming to the corner I stood nearby. Megan had seen them do this and called me a fish whisperer at the time. I countered with them being creatures of habit. They had one thing on their mind: Food.

"Are we still doing garbage detail after the dive? Handing out flyers and such?" Megan asked.

Sprinkling the fish food flakes on the water's surface, I grinned, watching Flounder, my blue and yellow angelfish's little mouth go to work eating it up. "I planned on it. You're not bailing on me, are you?"

Silence.

Flounder stared at me from the other side of the glass. His large eyes blinked, and I arched a brow at him.

"Meg?"

"Okay, Cory, hear me out."

I groaned and pinched the bridge of my nose. "Know what? You don't need to give an excuse. If you have something going on, that's fine. I can do it alone. I'm used to it."

"Well, now I feel guilty."

I bent forward and wiggled my finger at Flounder. He did a single twirl, flapped his flippers, and swam away.

Huh. That was new.

"Don't feel guilty. Truly. I didn't mean it to come out that way." I canted my head to the side as I watched my fish hypnotically swim through their tank.

"Have I told you lately how much I love you?"

I snickered. "You can certainly remind me in five minutes. I'm hanging up now." After pressing the big red button, I slid the phone in my back khaki shorts pocket.

Hoisting the three bags needed for one photographic dive, I waddled out the door. And as per usual, I'd forgotten to dig my keys out from my purse before loading up. To the ground, all three bags went. In a huff, I locked the door and dragged the cargo across the concrete to my yellow Jeep parked under the complex's terrace.

At five foot three, it was always an event to load the car. I raised to my tippy toes in my white Keds and slid one bag at a time into the back. Climbing into the driver's seat, I slid my sunglasses on and drove down the beach road. The sun beaming on my face and the smell of salt in the air calmed any nerves I had boiling up. Dark hair tendrils flew in my face from the wind whipping through the open compartment of the Jeep.

The view of the ocean never failed to make me smile. Many people would say the beach, the water, was like a second home. It was different for me. There was always a sense of restlessness when I was anywhere but a place I could feel the water on my skin. The moment it crashed against my feet or touched my fingertips, nothing else mattered.

Meg leaned against her car, scrolling through her phone in the parking lot near the pier. Her bags were on the ground, circling her feet. I pulled in next to her and lifted my sunglasses to rest on my head.

"Finally. Gus has, I kid you not, asked me four times when we were shoving off." Meg slipped her phone into her pocket. "I was this close to telling *him* to shove off. As if he had anything else to do on a Tuesday morning."

With a chuckle, I hopped out and grabbed my bags. "We shouldn't keep him waiting then."

"I say this in the least condescending way possible, but you look adorable every time you grab your bags." Meg bit down on her lower lip as she smiled.

At almost six feet tall, Meg made me look like a Hobbit. Given our same chocolate brown wavy hair, chestnut-colored eyes, and the Disney princess nose that curved slightly upward at the tip, we could pass as sisters if it weren't for the height difference.

I rolled my eyes and chuckled. "Shut up, Jolly Green Giant."

"Hey, I didn't resort to name-calling." Meg grabbed one of my bags before I could protest and headed for the dock.

After securing the lock on the hatch, I trotted after her to catch up. "Am I taking point this time?"

"Oh, yes. There are always creepy Hammerheads lurking around this ship. And for whatever reason, you're made of natural repellent."

"Oh, please. It's the camera." I held my hands up like I was holding the camera rig and waved my arms back and forth. "Works like a shield."

"Maybe for you," she guffawed.

"Well, it's about damn time," Gus, our resident captain snorted. His grey hair sprouted from underneath his cap, and he pressed a hand to his beer belly like he was pregnant.

I pouted. "I feel so bad you had to chill on your boat at the dock for an extra thirty minutes."

"You should feel bad. I want to be *on* the water, not staring at it from a damn plank of wood." He grumbled and removed a toothpick from his mouth, turning for the boat.

Once Gus had his back to us, Meg turned at me and made talking mock gestures of him. She held her arms out, mimicking a large stomach, and waddled down the dock like a sumo wrestler. I let out a cackle and slapped my hand over my mouth to squelch it.

Once we situated ourselves aboard the boat, Gus set sail for the sunken ship's location. I draped my forearms over the edge, staring out at the water, longing to feel its embrace. Dozens of dolphins hopped in and out, following us most of the way. Every time their heads breached the surface, they'd screech in greeting.

"You know, you've always looked at the water like a handsome man, but lately, you've been staring at it like you want to jump its bones." Meg leaned on the railing next to me.

I scrunched my nose. "Is there a reason you're personifying it like a lover?"

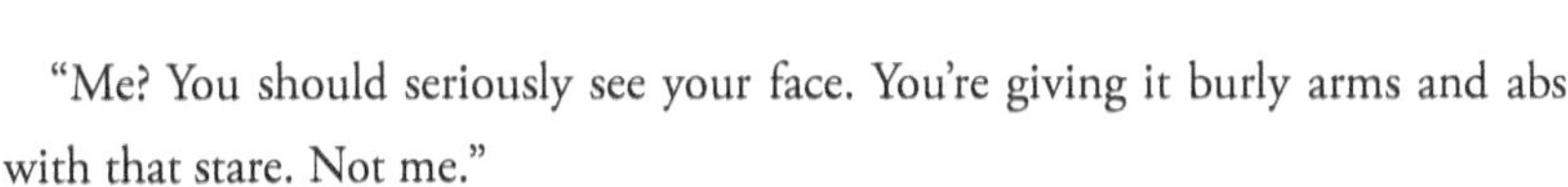

"Me? You should seriously see your face. You're giving it burly arms and abs with that stare. Not me."

"The ocean for me is like—" I tapped my finger against my lips. "Brownies drenched in hot fudge for you."

"See? The ocean *is* orgasmic to you."

"You're impossible." I laughed as I pulled my hair into a low ponytail, prepping it for the dive.

The boat slowed before coming to a complete stop.

"Here's the spot, ladies. You have thirty minutes, so make the most of it. You're on the clock starting now." Gus pointed at his wristwatch before plopping on a bench seat.

Meg unzipped her bag, pulling out a wetsuit and flippers. "Apparently, Gus' speedo is up his ass a little too far today."

"Maybe Beatrice is on him again. Remember last time? He vented to us for ten minutes about her complaining he loves the sea more than her?" I slipped into my wetsuit, zipping it up from the back.

Meg sighed and looked up. "What I wouldn't give to have someone to complain about me."

"Oh?" I sat down to slide on my flippers. "I thought you'd be hanging out with Emma. That's not the reason you're busy later?"

She frowned, absently holding her scuba mask by its strap.

"Meg?" I stood and touched her arm. "What is it?"

"Emma broke up with me."

I gasped. "What? Why?"

"Beats me. But she packed up her shit and left last night." Meg hoisted an oxygen tank on her back and secured the straps.

"Meg, why didn't you say anything? And why are you even here?"

"I need a distraction. And diving into shark-infested waters with my best friend to snap photos of a sunken pirate ship is the best damn one I can think of." She half smiled and flopped her way over to the boat's edge.

It wasn't a pirate ship, but I wasn't about to correct her now. Not after what she'd just told me. Poor Meg had been through countless girlfriends through the years we'd known each other. My theory was most of the women she'd dated were still figuring themselves out, but Emma, they'd been dating for two years. It didn't

make any sense.

"And that's why you don't want to work the shorelines afterward. Because you'd have to socialize." I offered a reassuring grin.

"Bingo. I love that as soon as I tell you a problem, you can pretty much talk it out for me." She chuckled and slid the full-face scuba mask down.

Mimicking the same actions, I sat next to her with our backs to the water.

"Can you hear me?" I asked through the mask's communication line.

She saluted. "Loud and clear, Cap."

Gripping the rigs of our cameras, we leaned back and fell into the water. Hundreds of bubbles floated around me—the water's way of welcoming me into its domain. With every flip of my fin and breath taken from my scuba tank, the water would always remind me of where I was by responding with bubbles.

"It's so clear down here today," Meg said as we made our descent.

Typically, the Gulf had fairly clear waters, but a hefty rainstorm could make it murky. It dampened that crystal blue and green color this part of the Gulf was known for.

"How many times have we done this dive now, would you say?" I asked Meg, spying the ship in the distance.

"Oh jeez. Twelve? Thirteen?" She chuckled. "Every time someone starts a new magazine here, it seems it's one of the first articles they want to feature. I'm not complaining, as it pays my rent."

"Amen to that, sister."

Meg pointed. "What did I tell you? Three hammers. Already."

"It'll be fine, Meg. Don't bother them. They won't bother you."

"Tell that to one who hasn't eaten in days," she grumbled.

"They've eaten. Trust me. It's why they explore the shipwreck. Looking for other fish hiding in it."

She stayed so close to me her bubbles impeded my vision. "How can you sound so confident?"

"I've spent a lot of time around them. Never had any close calls, so something is working, right?"

"That only happens when you're around. Before I met you, I'd almost been bitten twice." She held up two fingers at my mask.

"Almost. But not." I grinned, even though I knew she wouldn't be able to see it.

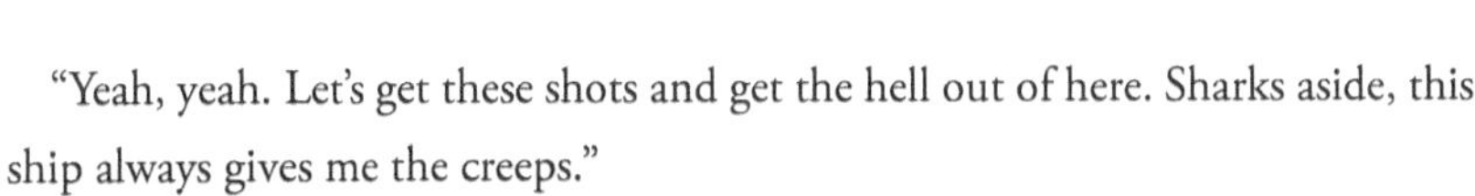

"Yeah, yeah. Let's get these shots and get the hell out of here. Sharks aside, this ship always gives me the creeps."

I spent the next twenty minutes taking photographs with Meg as my backup camerawoman. The sharks mostly kept to themselves except one who grew curious and swam into my frame. It was like he knew exactly where I aimed the camera. I could sell that one shot alone for triple any of the other shots. People went crazy for shark photos, and this one would have a sunken ship in the background with light rays bursting through the water's surface.

When we returned to the boat, Gus was asleep with his body draped over the steering wheel. It took us both nudging him with our elbows to wake him up. I sat on the bench seat during the ride back to the docks, feverishly searching through the hundred shots I took, looking for *the* shot. When it graced my camera monitor, I gasped.

"Meg, look at this." I felt for her shoulder, not daring to take my eyes away from my camera.

"What—ow, that was my eyeball," she chastised, batting my hand away. "Holy shit, Cory. That's a gorgeous shot."

"Do you think I could sell this to a gallery?"

"Are you kidding? Definitely do not sell this to the magazine. I think that's the best one I've seen from you."

The hammerhead shark was centered perfectly, the color of the water a serene blue, the ship in the background, and the rays gave it an extra touch of magic. As much as I played a videogame set in the imaginary world of Atlantis, a part of me always wondered—hoped even, it was real. And sun rays like these spilled over every square inch of it, making it sparkle. It really was the best shot I'd taken yet.

Once we were back in the parking lot and packed up our vehicles, I exchanged my wetsuit for an ocean conservation charity shirt and shorts.

"Hey, Meg, you going to be okay?" I winced, knowing it was a stupid question.

She gave a weak smile. "Not today, I won't be. But tomorrow will be better. I'll give you a call?"

"Definitely. Any time. I'm there." I hugged her before she jumped in her car and drove off.

Twirling the trash poker in one hand, a white garbage bag in the other, I was ready to start this garbage party for one. Every time I'd walked the shoreline,

picking up bottles, cans, or anything else human beings deemed worthy of tossing into the water, I got mixed reactions from beach-goers. The younger crowd would sometimes laugh as they passed, the older ones would look at me like I had scales, and the much older crowd would thank me for being so thoughtful. I didn't care what anyone thought because it was something I wanted to do—needed to do.

White sand seeped between my toes as I scooped a plastic water bottle into the bag with a gloved hand.

"Do you have a flyer or business card for the charity you work for?" A woman sunbathing on a towel asked me.

I grinned and pulled a card from my front pocket. "We're localized to the Gulf coast. Donated money helps rid the Gulf of garbage, and every year, we donate to an animal rescue and rehabilitation center."

"Wow. That's amazing. I'll look it up when I get home."

I smiled even wider. "Well, thank you very much, ma'am."

The afternoon wore on as I made my way down the shoreline where tourists and locals frequented. I'd almost made it to the end when a thin man, no more than twenty-five, tossed his empty Gatorade bottle in the sand at his feet. Inside, I fumed, eyeing the garbage can five feet away from him. They had a can every thirty feet for people to throw stuff out, but most couldn't bother to make the pilgrimage.

Grabbing the bottle with a grunt, I held it in the air and yelled, "You're welcome!"

When the young man turned around with an arched brow, I made an exaggerated gesture of throwing the bottle into the trash can. He smirked and shook his head.

Whatever. It made *me* feel better.

I bent down to grab the last bit of remaining garbage—candy bar wrappers and a plastic straw. Ugh, those were the worst.

"Excuse me, miss, have we met before?" A deep voice asked from behind me.

I rose and slowly turned. Craning my neck back due to how insanely tall he was, my gaze met with a pair of striking green eyes. I'd seen those eyes before—heard that voice. But…how?

TWO

WHEN HIS EYES LOCKED with mine, a breath hitched in his throat. There was a subtle glint in his gaze, but he was quick to mask it, flashing a pearly white smile instead.

"I don't think so. Do I look familiar to you?" I shielded my eyes with a hand from the sun.

He ran his fingers through his spiky blonde hair. "You're right. We couldn't have met. How could I forget a face like yours?"

"Does that line ever work?" I smiled and dug my toes into the sand.

He grinned again and turned his gaze away, squinting. "Once upon a time, maybe."

His eyes had me in a trance, confusing me. Where had I heard that voice before? I took notice of his bare chest—clad in only a pair of blue board shorts, the sun glowed against his tanned skin. Carved bulky muscles and one of the most prominent six-pack abs I'd ever seen in my—

"Are you picking up garbage?" He asked, snapping me from my ogling.

I jolted, and my hand tightened around the poker like a javelin. "Hm? What?"

"You've got a trash bag. Either you're picking up garbage on the beach, or you're collecting cans. Something tells me it's the former, but call it a hunch." He smirked before subtly biting his lower lip.

Clearing my throat, I thrust the handle of the poker in the sand. "Trash. Yes. I try to do it every week."

"Voluntarily?"

"Yes. I run an ocean conservation charity. While I clean up the beach, I also look for donations." Digging into my pocket, I pulled out a business card and held it out to him with my head held high.

His smile brightened once he looked at the card. Dragging a hand over his smooth chin, he lifted his eyes to mine. "I'm an athlete, you know."

I swiveled the poker in the sand and put my other hand on a hip. "Well, good for you. What do you play?"

"The waves mostly."

"The—" I frowned and looked at the vast Gulf waters behind me, then back to him. "Are you a swimmer?"

He interlaced his fingers in front of him. "Guess again."

I tapped my finger against my cheek and slowly narrowed my eyes. "No. You're not—" I let the poker stand by itself, supported in the sand, and crossed my arms. "Don't tell me you're a surfer."

He chuckled and threw his arms out at their sides, making his biceps flex. "What's wrong with surfers?"

Tread carefully here, Cory.

"Most of them seem to be conceited, grungy, and think they own the ocean."

"Most of them. So, not all, then?" His grin spread wide, further accentuating his broad jawline.

"Yet to be determined."

We went silent, staring at each other with curious intent in our gazes.

"I'm an athlete too," I blurted in a horrible attempt to end the silence.

"Oh?" He folded his burly arms. "Let me guess." Tapping his finger against his lip, he looked up as if he were thinking but snuck a peek at my expression. "Figure skater."

"No."

"Gymnast?"

I rolled my eyes. "Are you going to list every sport known for petite athletes?"

He laughed. "Why don't you tell me? You can't say you're an athlete, then leave me hangin'."

I chewed on the inside of my mouth. I'd dug the hole I was presently in. I might as well wave my hands for a rescue.

"eSports," I clipped.

He leaned forward, bringing our faces closer. "eSports?"

I lifted my chin. "Mmhmm."

"Care to explain what in the name of the Seven Seas, that is?"

"Videogames. Tournaments and such. You win money, prizes, and I have a Glitch account where I stream a couple of nights a week for a little extra cash."

Admitting this always went one of two ways—especially with men. Either they were intrigued that a "woman" played games beyond *Mario* and *The Sims*, which always made my blood boil. Or they thought I was weird.

"Videogames? Really? I never pegged you for the type." He leaned back with a snarky grin.

"You've known me an entire five minutes and think you know my type?"

He cleared his throat. "Call it a—sixth sense."

"Simon, bruh, come on. Those waves ain't gonna surf themselves," another surfer across the beach yelled at the man in front of me.

Simon. Surfer.

"Simon? Are you Simon Thalassa?" I pointed at him.

He rubbed the back of his neck. "Guilty as charged." He held up a finger at the other surfer, keeping his focus on me.

No wonder his face looked familiar. Nearly every sports channel featured him and his insane surfing abilities.

"I thought you meant you surfed for fun. You never said anything about being a legit pro." I felt even shorter somehow knowing that information.

"Does it make a difference to you?" He smirked. "Does me being a pro put me higher or lower on your mental totem pole?"

"Yet to be determined," I whispered.

His eyes sparkled, and he flipped my business card between his fingers. "Now that you know my name, care to give me yours?"

"Cory. Well. Cordelia, but everyone calls me Cory."

His smile melted into a warm, gooey upturn of his lips. Nothing snarky or coy about it. "Cordelia. Jewel of the sea."

I squinted curiously at him. "That's right."

"Well, Cory. As a professional athlete, I can stick all kinds of sponsors on my surfboard, wetsuit. You name it." He flicked my business card with two fingers. "You get me a high-res logo of your charity, and I'll add it on."

My jaw dropped. "But you don't know anything about it. How do you even know it's legit?"

"Something tells me you're good for it. And if not, well, you get to make an ass of me." He snickered. "It was nice meeting you, Cory. Hope to run into you again."

My mouth remained open, at a loss for words. He was halfway down the beach when I finally managed to blurt out, "Where do I send the file?"

He cupped his hands over his mouth. "Google me. I don't exactly have anywhere to store business cards in this suit." He gave a lopsided grin, touching over his bare chest and shoulders.

I stifled an eye roll but couldn't help the smile creeping on my lips. A mysterious man was swept into my path by ocean winds and misunderstood identity. It was a thing of fairy tales.

After ten minutes of picking up trash and trying not to let Simon catch me staring at him surfing, I wrapped it up for the day. When Meg texted asking me to come over, I was relieved. She acted far too aloof during our dive, considering she and Emma had been together so long. I knew to give her space. She'd come to me when she was ready, and that was tonight.

I stood in front of her door armed with a six-pack of Yoohoo and a family-size package of Twizzlers. She liked what she liked. I'd expected her to look like she'd been crying, hair disheveled, and a balled-up tissue in her hand. When she opened the door, what I saw was far worse. Dark bags were under her reddened eyes, and dried tears streaked her cheeks. Her nose was red and puffy, and she'd bitten down her nails to the stubs. She wore a suit with the jacket thrown in a ball on the floor.

"Meg?" I said in a hushed tone.

She grabbed my hand and yanked me inside, swiping the Twizzlers in the process. I kept quiet, waiting for her to talk.

"I came home, Cor, ready to binge-watch Wynonna Earp for the umpteenth time and fantasize about a relationship like Wayhaught, but then—" She blew out a breath, ripping the Twizzler bag open like a starving raptor. After shoving

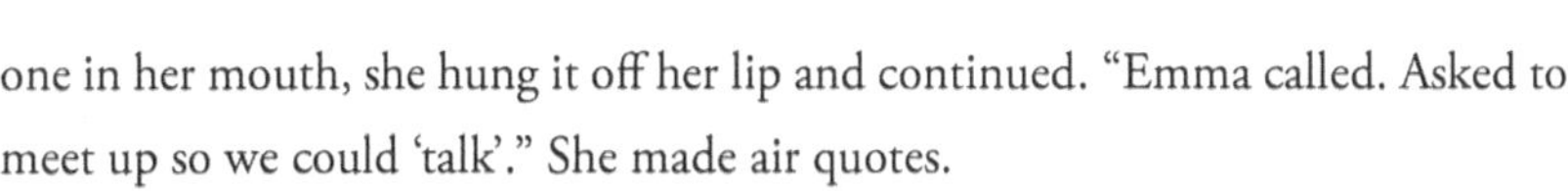

one in her mouth, she hung it off her lip and continued. "Emma called. Asked to meet up so we could 'talk'." She made air quotes.

I leaned against the back of her couch, watching my best friend pour her heart out to what had to be anything but a happy ending.

"So being the lovesick idiot that I am—"

I opened my mouth to disagree with her, but she threw her palm in the air to stop me. My mouth snapped shut.

"I thought she wanted to reconcile. Tell me she freaked out with how long we'd been dating. Not that I gave her any reason to think I needed her to put a ring on it or something. I just—" She shoved the rest of the Twizzler in her mouth and pinched the bridge of her nose.

"I got dressed like it was a date, only to get to the restaurant. She might as well have been in pajamas, Cory. *Pajamas.*"

I winced.

"Basically, she called me there to tell me we have to break all forms of contact. This dude she's seeing doesn't want us to be friends. I mean—and she said she didn't feel right telling me over the phone." She grabbed one of the Yoohoos and twisted the cap, quickly becoming frustrated when she couldn't open it.

I crossed the room and gently took the bottle from her hand, opening it on the first try with a warm smile.

"It was that quick, Cory. Two years down the drain, and now I'm supposed to not even talk to her." Tears welled in her eyes as she brought the chocolate drink to her trembling lips.

"I'm so, so, sorry, Meg." I side hugged her.

She sighed and wrapped her arms around me, resting her chin on top of my head.

"Know what the shittiest part is?" She chuckled. "Dating again. I *hate* it. Thought I was done."

I squeezed her tighter. "You're a catch. It won't take you long."

She pushed me back, narrowing her eyes at me. "Wait a minute. That tone in your voice. What happened after I left the beach?"

Was I that obvious?

I shifted my eyes. "I picked up trash."

"You're not telling me everything. Why?"

"Meg. Seriously. It's not the time to talk about it. Right now, it is about you."

Her face fell. "You know me. Do I really want to spend this entire night wallowing in self-pity? Why the hell did I call you over here?"

A nervous grin spread over my lips. "To bring you your favorite snacks, listen, and offer any and all hugs?"

"Spill." She crossed her arms.

"Do you know the surfer, Simon Thalassa?"

"Are you kidding? He's the best in the country. The way he trails his hand through the curl is like he's talking to the water itself; I swear."

"He sort of walked up to me when I was poking garbage. Asked if we've met." Those insanely green eyes haunted my memories.

"Wait. Had you? Met him before?"

"Of course not. I'd have told you."

She curled the Twizzlers and Yoohoo into her arm and pulled me to the couch. After forcing me to sit, she sat across from me, widened her legs, and leaned forward. "So, what'd you say?"

"I told him no."

She narrowed her eyes. "You're supposed to be distracting me. It doesn't help in the slightest when you're giving simplistic answers."

"I've never met him, but something about his eyes and that voice…they're familiar somehow." I sighed and slid until my butt hit the back cushion. The couch's height made my feet dangle, unable to touch the floor.

"Intriguing," Meg said, nodding.

"Anyway, it's seriously not a big deal. We talked, he offered the charity group to be a sponsor on his surfboard and—"

She flailed her hands around. "Wait, wait, wait. He offered *what*?"

"Sponsorship. Said if I send him an image file, he'll slap it on his board. What's the big deal?"

She jumped up. "Cory, it's a huge deal because *he* is a huge deal. We'll probably be swarming with donations. I mean *drowning* in them."

"You really think so?"

"I know so. And if he mentions the group on camera…" She turned on her heels, bending backward with a cackle. "We'll have to hire a PA to handle the overflow."

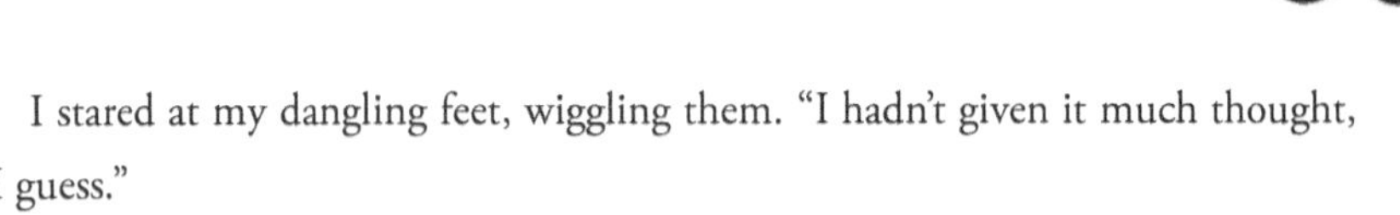

I stared at my dangling feet, wiggling them. "I hadn't given it much thought, I guess."

"You must've made quite the impression." She flopped on the couch next to me.

"I don't know what it was, but every time he looked at me, it was like he was comfortable. Like he truly knew who I was." I tucked my legs underneath me after toeing off my shoes. "Which in turn made *me* feel comfortable around a complete stranger."

"I'm sure the good looks didn't help at all, huh?" She elbowed me with half a Twizzler hanging from her mouth. "Not that I'm an expert, but from what I've seen of him on TV, he seemed the type a lot of you straight gals would dig."

I chuckled. "Yes. He's hot."

"When are you going to send him the file?"

"Tomorrow. The next day. I'm not in a rush."

Meg rolled her eyes and dramatically dropped her head on the back of the couch. "If you don't send it tomorrow, I'm doing it for you. The sooner he has it, the sooner it can get on the board, and we can be rolling in donation money."

She was right. But sending him the file meant opening another line of communication. I wouldn't say I disliked him per se based on our first encounter, but the unexplained familiarity made me uneasy.

"Fine." I yanked the remote from the end table. "Want to watch some Wynonna?"

"You're a saint, Cordelia." She held out a Yoohoo.

After cuing up one of Meg's favorite episodes, I screwed off the cap and we clanked our bottles together. We stayed up into the wee hours of the morning, watching so much of the western sci-fi show I'd be dreaming of the cast for the unforeseeable future. With my head leaning back on the cushion and Meg's head in my lap, we fell asleep.

Instead of dreaming about Doc Holliday like I imagined I would be, I woke up submerged in the ocean. But I wasn't drowning. Breaths came in and out of my lungs as naturally as they did on land. Dolphins circled me, begging me to play with them. I reached for one. White silk floated over my arm from a dress wrapped around me. One dolphin swam past my fingers, wiggling its tail from my touch.

I smiled to myself and turned, gazing up at the sun casting light rays through the water's surface. Pushing my feet, I started to swim up, but a strong hand wrapped around my wrist. I closed my eyes before opening them to gaze over my shoulder. A man with long flowing blonde hair, and a full beard, peered at me—a gaze of blazing…emerald.

THREE

UNDERWATER, A DARK TENTACLE wrapped my waist, crushing me, making it increasingly difficult to breathe. I yelled to no avail, the depths sweeping my voice away, and I clawed and punched, but the arm still didn't let go. It pulled me farther down until the cold darkness of deep-sea sunk into my pores. My lungs burned, my heartbeat slowing, movements became labored, until finally…I gave up.

I awoke sputtering, coughing, and gasping for breath. My chest ached, and I felt around my torso, expecting to see a tentacle there. Nothing. It'd felt so real. My lungs even still stung from the lack of oxygen in the dream.

Gee, subconscious, can we stick to mysterious, handsome men from now on and not dreams that try to kill me?

Rubbing my temples, I toppled out of bed and prepared to clear my mind, knowing today was a gaming day and I needed to focus. Wednesdays were always my ultimate streaming day on Glitch. Several hours of me playing through whatever game I was into at the time and entertaining my followers in the hopes of donations. Megan knew unless it was an absolute emergency, Wednesdays were off-limits. It never stopped her from trying to screw with me by hopping in and stalking the follower chatroom. I think her goal was to make me crack by screwing up in the game or doing my obnoxious snort laughing on camera. She hadn't won yet. I could've easily kicked her or let my moderators know to look out for her, but her wrath afterward wasn't worth it.

Slipping the Pelican Beach headset over my ears, I nestled into my gaming chair. Water bottle? Check. Lumbar pillow? Double check. It was time to start

this weekly party. After the loading screen for *Tides of Atlantis* finished and I logged my character into the digital sea world, I went live on Glitch. My camera spurted to life, and the Glitch chatroom blazed on my second monitor.

My head moderator for the day let me know everything was good to go via a direct text message through the system. They would help me keep an eye on chat and filter out the rotten eggs. Those who would say rude or derogatory comments, or request me to say or do inappropriate things. I was thankful for the mods. It helped me keep focused on the game. With the eSports tournament only weeks away, I needed all the practice I could get.

"Happy Hump Day, everyone," I said with a wide grin.

Dozens of comments flooded the screen. Notification of a new follower made a chiming sound.

"Seems we have a new follower." I leaned forward to squint at the small text.

New Follower: KingOfFish69.

"Welcome aboard, King of Fish," I said, avoiding relaying the immature ending of his username. He was probably some ten-year-old who snickered every time he passed by the bananas in the grocery store on sale for sixty-nine cents.

I scrolled through the menu, selecting my weapons. I'd made it a habit to start the day with PVE or player versus environment, teaming up with other random individuals to battle Atlantean monsters. However, I gained most followers from my PVP or player versus player style. Particularly in this game. Both kinds of gameplay would cycle through various maps. Some were on land, others underwater, but my favorite were the maps that encompassed both. If one knew the maps well enough, you could be the first to nab land-to-sea-vehicles with Atlantean technology.

Once my character loaded onto the screen, I did a quick scroll through any upgrades I'd earned from last week's playthrough. A new message popped into the chat.

MissTacoX: Didn't you get the last armor you needed for the Nautilus set?

I gasped. "You're right, Miss Taco, I did. I'm such a guppy."

My aquatic references had become somewhat of a gimmick as cheesy as it was. I'd been on the Glitch circuit for over a year and now even maintained an online shop filled with t-shirts and coffee mugs with my popular taglines and logo for my gamer tag: SaucySiren.

After selecting the gauntlets for the Nautilus set, I grinned, watching the gold sparkles and bubbles flash down the screen. The Nautilus gear was one of the best sets in the game. Not only did it have the highest level of protection and offer an additional experience bonus, or XP, it also looked breathtakingly awesome.

My character rotated a full three-hundred-sixty-degrees, decked in her newly equipped white and metallic gold armor complete with gauntlets, breastplate, shoulder pieces, shin guards overtop of pants, and a flapped skirt around her waist. I opted to wear a removable golden pointed tiara that served as a melee weapon versus a full-faced helmet—beauty over function, but I made up for it in gameplay. However, the pieces that glowed in radiant white when in darker areas of the map made this armor aesthetically beautiful.

FriskeeBizkit: Wow. Your character looks amazing!

HufflePufflenz: Can't wait to see you kick a$$ with this!

Smiling at all the messages scrolling through the chat came naturally, but I got distracted staring at my character. I'd given her as close a likeness to myself as I could with the long chocolate-colored hair, high cheekbones, petite nose, and brown eyes, but what pulled my attention was the way she looked in the tiara.

KingOfFish69: Can you change the colors?

FriskeeBizkit: Duh.

NinjaMod: A reminder to please respect all questions and comments from other viewers. Thank you, and surf on!

My eyes darted straight to KingOfFish's comment. "Yes…did you have a specific request, King?" My heart raced as I stared at the chat, ignoring any other comments that popped up, waiting for him to respond.

KingOfFish69: The tiara. Make the jewels teal and the metal a shimmering silver…if you can ;)

Without batting an eyelash, I did as he requested. My character, Aliandra as I named her, peered back at me, the tiara catching the fake glints of light added to the game as you turned your character to-and-fro.

"Thanks, KingOfFish. Nice suggestion." My palms clammed up, and I quickly closed the character screen, taking it back to the main menu.

"Should we—" I started, but my eyes darted to the next comment from King.

KingOfFish69: Most welcome. :-*

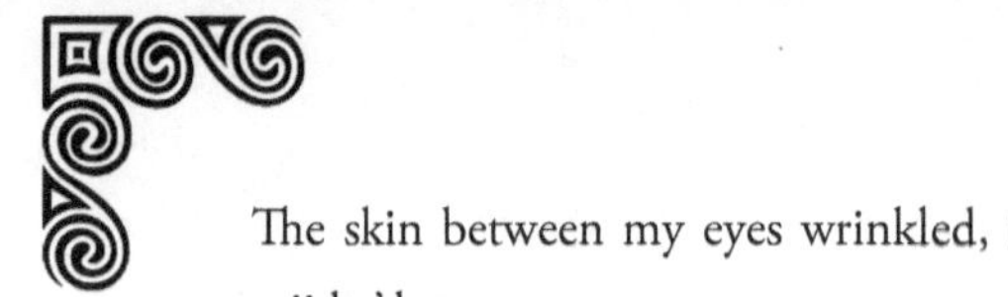

The skin between my eyes wrinkled, focusing far too long on the kissy face emoji he'd sent.

With a quick clearing of my throat, I snapped back to my monitor. "Should we start the evening with some PvE or go straight into beaching newbs?"

HufflePufflenz: With that new gear? Def PvP!

FriskeeBizkit: ^^^^ that.

I'd known the answer before asking, but it also boosted ratings to keep the viewers interactive.

"Let's start it up then." I paused for a sip of water as the game found other players to connect to. "Don't forget to send some fishy love, everyone."

Dozens of fish-themed emojis flooded the chat—clownfish, sharks, dolphins, and tidal waves.

My throat clenched, spying the image that King sent: a sea turtle.

My eyes darted to the collection of sea turtles cluttering my gaming desk—plushies, Funko POPs, carved wooden figurines.

Noticing the screen had begun to count down for the match start, I forced my attention back to the game, wiping my sweaty palms on my shorts.

The randomly selected map loaded, and I grinned to myself. Pharos Island. A land and sea map—one I knew the layout of best.

"These poor folks have no idea the plankton they're about to walk off." I equipped my character's sword as soon as it appeared on the sandy shoreline.

Several "LOLs", drums, and laughing face emojis scrolled through the chat.

Once you were in game, it was a matter of navigating the terrain, finding other players, and terminating them for points. There were several randomly sprouting spawn points with treasure chests that'd give the players temporary weapon boosts—one of which was an Atlantean canon, capable of decimating someone with one well-placed ranged shot. I'd played the map so many times, I knew each of the locations, but the order in which they appeared changed.

KingOfFish69: You're not fighting with a trident?

My face scrunched, flicking my attention back to the screen to keep watch for other players. "No one uses the trident in this game. It's one of the weakest weapons, KingOfFish."

FriskeeBizkit: Yeah. Why use a fork when you can use a canon?!

HufflePufflenz: A fork. LMAO.

KingOfFish69: Maybe no one is using "the fork" correctly.

Another player approached in *Aquaman* movie armor, sporting a computer-generated likeness to Jason Momoa's face. A purchasable skin they'd put up for grabs when the movie first released.

MissTacoX: Oh shiz, it's The King of the Seas!

KingOfFish69: Hardly.

I'd have paid more attention to King's comment were it not for morphing into full concentration mode, getting ready to act, react, and win.

NinjaMod: Please remember that when Siren is in the middle of combat, she may not see your comments! It's why you're here, after all, folks. :)

The approaching player's name appeared above their heads: **AceOfAtlantia**.

"Alright, Ace. Let's see who's 'betta'." My thumbs hovered over the joysticks on my controller, circling him.

The Aquaman armor may have looked cool and flashy, but I knew its defense stats were less than half the caliber of my Nautilus set. A few well-timed swing and I'd win. As he brought his sword crashing down over me, I raised mine, blocking his swing. Exaggerated sparks and heightened metal pangs echoed through my headset. The glowing parts of my armor pulsed in response to my character's movement.

FriskeeBizkit: Dude. That armor is SICK.

With a double-tap of the "B" button on my controller, I did a barrel roll to gain a different vantage point on him. Crouching when he swung his sword at my upper body, I rolled again and swung at the same time, landing a strike on his torso. His username flashed red, indicating severe damage. One final blow before his character had a chance to regenerate health, and…

Priscilla, my Cory Catfish, landed on my desk with a loud wet *thwap*.

With my eyes darting from the screen for that one mere moment, Ace sliced his sword at my head, terminating my character and causing me to respawn.

Priscilla flopped, trying to breathe. Not caring the viewers hadn't a clue why I suddenly dove off-screen, I scooped my fish into my hands and sprinted to the aquarium, plopping her back in. After waiting for her to breathe and swim properly, I returned to the camera.

FriskeeBizkit: What the h3ll happened?

MissTacoX: Did she rage quit?

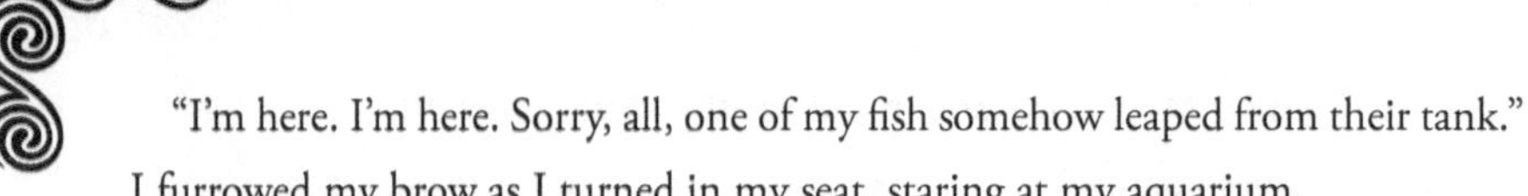

"I'm here. I'm here. Sorry, all, one of my fish somehow leaped from their tank." I furrowed my brow as I turned in my seat, staring at my aquarium.

That had never happened before, and I ensured tank security at all times to avoid accidents like that while I wasn't home.

So. Strange.

A notification chimed from Glitch.

KingOfFish69 just gave 300 shells!

My face grew hot. "Shells" was the word I chose to switch for dollars. Three. Hundred. Dollars. The most I'd ever gotten in the past was a hundred, and that only ever happened one time.

HufflePufflenz: Mr. Money Bags over here.

NinjaMod: Another friendly reminder to please be courteous to all viewers! We would hate to ban anyone for misconduct. Thank you. :)

A lump formed in my throat as I stared at the notification, watching my character on screen from the corner of my eye performing the fidgeting hops when you've gone idle for too long.

"King of Fish, what a kind donation." I plucked at the rubber overlaying on the right thumbstick of my controller. "Did you have a special request?"

KingOfFish69: I'd love to see you try the trident.

A nervous giggle fluttered from my stomach. "Oh, I don't know. I've never used it. I can't promise I won't die…repeatedly. That's not exactly fun to watch."

KingOfFish69: I think you'd be surprised. Try it. ;)

"What do you think, Sea Farers? By a show of fishy emojis, should I try the trident?" My eyes were glued to the generous donor's username, spying the flood of emojis flying through the chat.

MissTacoX: We have faith in you, chica!

After scratching my cheek, I opened my inventory and switched my primary weapon to the trident. A chorus of low-pitched male singers sounded, followed by the sound of a weapon slicing through the air.

"Here goes nothing."

I'd been standing still on the map for so long it didn't take much to find an opponent. They'd been running across the beach, hoping for an easy kill and that I was AFK (away from keyboard).

Username: **ProteinGeyser**, charged me full force, sword already aimed and

wearing matching Nautilus armor.

"Shit. Shit."

HufflePufflenz: You got this!

Please make the trident work the same as the sword.

As he got closer, a flash of an ornately patterned trident blocked my vision, turning in mid-air, reflecting rays of light like it was underwater. As if on autopilot, my fingers worked the buttons of my controller. The image rippled away, and I stared at my monitor with my character's trident skewered into ProteinGeyser's chest—long-ranged, one-shot kill.

Emojis flooded the chat, followed by so many notifications, the constant chiming made my head ache.

HufflePufflenz donated 10 shells!

MissTacoX: DUUUUUUUUDE!

KingOfFish69: :)

FriskeeBizkit resubscribed at a new tier level!

"Thank you so much, everyone. I wish I could thank you each individually, but I've lost half of the notifications it's been scrolling so fast." My cheeks flushed, and I pressed one of my constantly cold hands against my face to cool them.

Another three hours whizzed by, and I used the trident for the entire stream, wrecking in every round I played, finishing as the top player with the best kill to death ratio. King didn't type much of anything else, except the occasional smiley face when I performed an especially impressive move with my weapon. The strange vision didn't pop into my head again, and I wondered if I'd ever actually seen it. Could it have been something I ate earlier? I remembered popping a couple of Tic-Tac's I found in the abyss of my purse but didn't bother to check the expiration date?

I'd thanked King a final time for the money before signing off and sat in my gaming chair for a solid ten minutes, staring at my sea turtle collection before finally finding the will to move. My phone's screen lit up on my desk, still on silent as I always did before going live.

Meg.

"Hey," I greeted meekly.

"Hey yourself. Three hundred dollars? I'm surprised this guy didn't expect sexual favors for that kind of cash."

I moved to my aquarium, sprinkling some food on the surface and watching Priscilla swim. "For one, I would've shot that down in an instant, and two, he would've been banned from Glitch for life."

"Okay. You're taking everything literally. What's on your mind?"

"My fish jumped from its tank." I squinted, calculating the approximate distance from the aquarium to my desk. "It's a good ten feet to my desk. You know I keep this thing secure, and even if one did get out, they wouldn't make it more than a couple of feet."

"An odd mishap. Your point?"

My eyes panned up to a painting hanging over my bed. One I'd bought on vacation in Key West that called to me like a luring siren. It was a small, minute detail, but it was plain as day as I walked closer. A single, gold trident was behind the waves, drawn to blend in with the coral sprouting from all sides.

I ran my fingertips over it. "I've never used the trident in the game. Ever. And I had the best matches of my life."

"You're pulling at a fishnet here, Cory. It sounds like you need some sleep. Besides, we got a car ride tomorrow. Remember? A week in West Palm with the sea turtles and cameras?"

"I didn't forget. How could I? There's something else. I had this weird nightmare of a tentacle dragging me underwater to the point of me drowning." Remembering how real it seemed, I traced a hand over my ribs. "I woke up sputtering and choking as if it were actually happening."

"A tentacle? Like Ursula? You watched that movie a couple of nights ago, didn't you?"

The Little Mermaid. I had indeed.

"Yeah. Yeah, I guess you're right."

"Right. Well, stop overthinking things, as you always do, get to bed, and bring those three hundred bones with you. Maybe buy yourself something nice and girly."

I smiled, letting my hand fall away from the painting. "Or maybe I'll buy *you* something nice and girly."

"Was that a threat?"

"Goodnight, Meg."

"Nighty, night…Saucy Siren."

After hanging up, I focused on the trident in the painting. As my hand lifted of its own accord, fingers stretching for the weapon, a familiar voice fluttered past my ear, the feel of a beard scraping against my nape.

Eisaí i thálassa.

With a gasp, I whirled around to find my fish hovering at one side of the tank.

FOUR

WE'D ROAD-TRIPPED DOWN TO West Palm Beach, all eight hours of it, listening to a pirate fantasy novel *On These Black Sands* on audiobook for the duration of the drive. When we settled into our hotel room for the night, after lugging all equipment from my Jeep inside, I stared at myself in the mirror while Meg showered. The same face, same reflection from the past thirty-three years gazed back at me, but an unsettling notion—a feeling that I didn't recognize myself anymore made my stomach twist into knots. The reflection flashed for a split moment, and I caught a glimpse of myself in a plaid-patterned dress with rolling green hills behind me. One blink and I would've missed it.

"Should I go back into the bathroom?" Meg had walked out at some time, towel drying her cropped hair with a raised brow. "You look like you're about to…self-indulge."

My chest tightened, and I snapped my gaze to my fingers trailing between my breasts. "I—"

Meg paused and canted her head at me, brushing her bare feet across the carpet until she stood next to me.

"Do I look different to you, Meg?"

She curled her finger under one strap of her ribbed tank top, moving between me and the mirror. "You've got a glaze in your eyes lately. Like you're lost in thought more often than you're here on planet Earth. Other than that? No."

I turned for my suitcase, grabbing toiletry items and pajamas.

"In fact," Meg continued, following me. "You've been weird ever since

meeting surfer boy. A connection? Methinks so. Do your loins simply burn for him, my dear?"

"My loins, Meg?" I bit back a laugh.

"Yeah. Isn't that how all your romance novels describe it?"

Rolling my eyes, I brushed past her. "Maybe if I liked bodice rippers."

"Bodice, what now?"

"I'm taking a shower," I said, ignoring her question with a chuckle as I ducked into the bathroom.

Considering hotels never seemed to run out of hot water, I cranked it up as high as my skin could tolerate. Pressing my hands against the marble tiles, I leaned forward, dropping my head and letting the heat roll down my neck and back. Raising my lips toward the showerhead, I opened my mouth, letting the water collect, filling it. For a moment, I thought I could breathe despite the water blocking my throat and nostrils. I even tried to. Coughing, sputtering, and gasping, I pressed my back to the shower wall, dragging the water droplets from my face.

What the hell was wrong with me? Who drowns themselves in a shower standing up?

The door creaked open.

"Are you dying in here, Cor?" Meg asked.

After gulping down another helping of air, I replied, "No. Just trying to breathe water."

"Ah. As much as I know you long to be a mermaid, please remember…"

"I don't have gills." I pursed my lips.

"Good. You haven't floated completely to the clouds yet. Just scream if you slip or something because you're trying to dive into extremely shallow waters."

The door clicked closed.

After finishing up and managing not to kill myself, I headed back to the living room to find Meg sitting on the edge of her bed, staring at her phone screen.

"Meg?"

Her hand shook, and she didn't blink.

Quickly wrapping the towel around my dripping wet hair, I crossed the room and slid a hand on her shoulder. "Meg."

"She—" Meg gulped, and looked at me with bloodshot eyes. "She texted me.

She wants me back."

My chest ached and I sat on the bed next to her, forcing her to look at me as I gently grabbed her chin. "Megara, don't do this to yourself."

One of the first things we found out that we both had in common when we met was our love of Disney's Hercules after I called her Megara for the first time. It'd stuck from then on out.

"I love her, Cory." Meg's grip tightened on the phone.

I curled my fingers around the phone, prying it from her grip. "I know you do. But what she did to you is unforgivable, and I'd be willing to bet anything the only reason she's texting you is because the *man* she was dating dumped her."

After a few tugs, Meg let go with a sigh.

"You're probably right. I just can't stand the thought of starting over again. It's hard enough finding other gay women, let alone one I'm also interested in dating." Meg sighed and flopped onto her back.

I followed and rested my head on her shoulder. "It'll happen, Meg. You do you for now. Heal. Be happy. And it'll happen."

She rested her head on mine. "Not sure what I'd do without you, Hobbit."

I poked her ribs, and she let out a yelp. "Can I do you a favor?"

"What do you mean?"

I held up the phone like an Olympic torch. "By deleting her number."

"Cory…" Meg shot to her elbows, the skin between her eyes cinching. "I don't know."

"Did you want to be friends with her?"

"I—I couldn't do that." Meg bit her lip and looked away.

After pulling up her contacts list, I clicked into her ex's name and showed Meg the screen.

With one glance at the phone, she closed her eyes. "Do it."

And so, I did.

We sat on the boat the following day, sipping on our second can of Red Bull. Meg had started crying in the middle of the night, and I spent hours stroking her hair, trying to coax her back to sleep. She sat next to me on the bench seat as the

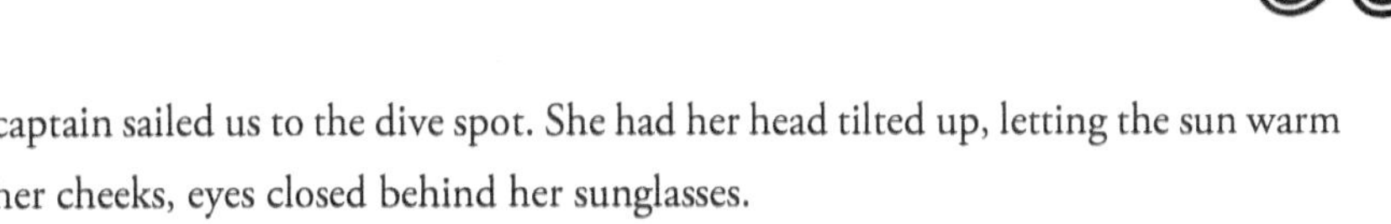

captain sailed us to the dive spot. She had her head tilted up, letting the sun warm her cheeks, eyes closed behind her sunglasses.

"How are you doing, Megara?" I bumped her arm.

She took a long, deep breath. "Better. Much better. The sun always rejuvenates me." She shoved the sunglasses to the top of her head. "I'm sorry for keeping you up last night."

"Oh, no. You're not saying any of that. Remember when I broke up with Ted?"

She exaggerated her plump bottom lip sticking out, making it press against the middle of her chin. "I'd rather not remember Ted. But man, did we binge-watch the hell out of some *Vampire Diaries*."

Sighing, I leaned back and dragged a hand down my throat. "Damon will get any girl through a breakup, I swear."

"Mm, Caroline."

We eyed each other sidelong before laughing.

"We're five minutes out, ladies," the boat captain announced to give us time to suit up.

After going through the formal process of slipping on wet suits, flippers, and masks, we hoisted the tanks onto each other's backs. I dangled my mask by its strap from my arm, double-checking I had a new SD card in my camera. We were diving in the North Double Ledges to look for prime spots for sea turtles. West Palm, in particular, had strong currents, which made for harsh swimming conditions. It called for drift diving, which would carry us over the reef with little need to swim. It also meant a negative entry, a straight descent to the bottom without stopping at the surface. It was a challenge that I loved because you had to be quick on the shutter to catch your subject matter in time.

The assistant on board yelled, "Dive, dive," once the dive entry was clear, the boat bobbed against the harsh current.

Meg and I hopped in, descending to the bottom as soon as our flippers slipped beneath the surface. A divemaster joined us because our entry and exit points were on opposite sides. Meg would serve as a spotter and backup for the dive, given the conditions. With how often I would have to slow down for photos, however, I wasn't sure how likely it'd be to stay with the divemaster. Even Meg and I would drift apart occasionally if she missed my signal that I was stopping.

I readied my camera as the drift carried me along, relaxing my limbs and letting

water curl around me like a dense fog. Fish of all colors and varieties fluttered amidst the coral reef. Snapping several photos, I didn't entirely stop for them, striving to save my energy for the sea turtles. A group of fish swam over to me, spiraling my arms and doing repeated circles around my torso.

I'd never seen fish act like this before. Especially not with a human.

A sea turtle swam directly below me, but with my new fish friends distracting me, I didn't raise the camera in time before drifting straight past it.

Dammit.

We spent the next hour taking photos of anything and everything that the magazine would pay us for, including over a dozen breathtaking shots of majestic sea turtles. During that time, more fish circled my arms and legs, an eel stared me down, and a nurse shark swam beside me for almost ten minutes straight. To say I was bewildered would've been putting it mildly. A storm had rolled in at some point during our dive, causing the current to grow more intense. Our steady drift had turned into a catapult, and we were no longer in sight of the divemaster. I tossed a hand signal to Meg, letting her know to stay within range.

Removing the delayed surface marker buoy from my utility belt, I started to unravel it, resting the camera at my side with the strap secured around my neck. I reached behind me for the alternate air source on my tank and slipped it into the underside of the buoy. I paused with a small puff of air to ensure no leaks before fully inflating it, and letting go, keeping hold of the reel. Once Meg and I were near each other, I started to tug on the buoy, signaling our new location to the boat.

No sooner had we breached the surface, the choppy waters tossed us. The boat rocked with such force the dock dipped in and out of the water. A crewman stood on the edge in a raincoat holding his hands out, instructing us to wait for a safer moment to board. The divemaster had already made it, and she too waved her hands at us.

I yanked my regulator from my mouth. "Meg, go first."

"Are you crazy?" She sputtered as our bodies bobbed in the water like matching buoys.

"I'm a stronger swimmer than you. We both know that. I'll be behind you and help you get on the boat."

The crewman frantically waved his hands for us to swim to the boat.

Meg grumbled. "Fine."

Following behind her, I treaded water with my flippers and held the camera out to her once she was safely on board. Wrapping my hands around the ladder, I pulled myself up. A massive gust of wind sent a wave over my head, tossing me from the ladder and back into the dark water. I sputtered, scrambling for my regulator as the choppy waves tossed me around like a ragdoll and carried me away from the boat.

"Cory," Meg shouted.

My breathing grew erratic, and I managed to shove the regulator in my mouth, kicking my arms and legs as fast as possible, but the current was too strong. The sight of the boat grew smaller and smaller.

A sudden force bubbled beneath me until it reached my legs and launched me forward like two dolphins were pushing the bottoms of my feet but…there was nothing but water and air. I held my arms at my sides, watching the streaks of bubbles on either side of me form straight lines as my body propelled through the water with ease *against* the current. And in the distance, I caught sight of several suckers like an octopus tentacle. It disappeared into the shadows before I could look again to confirm.

Once I neared the boat, the water lifted me to the ladder. I snapped my head over my shoulder, determined to catch a glimpse of the mysterious force. But there was nothing except the waves cutting against each other and the water turning black from torrential downpours of rain.

"Jesus Christ, Cory, are you alright?" Meg asked, yanking me onto the dock.

Water beads collected on my eyelashes, and I blinked them away, staring at the unruly surface of the ocean. "A bit shook up, yeah. But I'm fine."

Meg jolted me from my daydream when she wrapped her arms around me in a soggy embrace. "You scared the shit out of me, Hobbit."

Finally able to tear my eyes away from the water, I hugged her back and numbly patted her shoulder blades.

The rain slowed once we reached the shore as luck would have it. No matter, however, we'd gotten what we came for—sea turtle photos. I scrolled through the shots on my camera. Only two were blurry. The rest were bright, crisp, and centered.

"Isn't that the surfer guy?" Meg swatted my shoulder and pointed.

My stomach fluttered as soon as I spotted him.

Simon. He talked to a woman in a yellow string bikini, swiveling her hips and pushing her boobs together. Simon grinned, showing those sparkly white teeth, but his eyes stayed glued to her face. He rubbed the back of his neck and shrugged. The woman's arms fell at her sides, and she frowned before turning away with a flick of her wrist.

The boat lurched as we nestled against the dock and I sat still, frozen. Simon peeled the top part of his wet suit from his chest, letting it hang from his hips. My mouth dried at the sight of his bare chest despite seeing it days prior.

Meg snapped her fingers in front of my face. "The boat charges by the hour, you know?" She grinned.

"Right." I glanced at my watch. We had two minutes before they'd charge us for another hour. "Shit. Let's move."

Chuckling, I scooped my equipment into my arms and hobbled over the edge of the boat to the dock, waving at the crew with my only free hand. When I turned around, I came face-to.... abs with Simon. With a gulp I was sure was audible to everyone else on the dock, I panned my eyes up until they met his gaze.

The sun peeked through the clouds above him, framing his face with a sort of ethereal glow.

"Cordelia. Fancy seeing you here." He smiled, bright and magnificent.

"I—" I started to speak but abruptly stopped, spying our charity's logo, a circle comprised of a blue wave, on the arm of his wetsuit, as well as an even bigger one on the surfboard tucked under his arm.

I'd completely forgotten to send him the images.

"How did you—" I started again, but this time, Meg stuck her hand between us.

"I'm Meg. We spoke via e-mail?"

With the two of them being the same height—giants—I stood at sea level, trying to ignore that they towered over me.

"Oh, right." Simon shook her hand. "I slapped it on my board the same day. You like?" He held the board up, giving it a twirl.

"We love it." Meg elbowed me. "Don't we, Cory?"

I yelped, given my sides were beyond ticklish. "Yes. Thank you so much. I'm sure it will help our donations immensely."

"My pleasure. Anything I can do to help the seas and its—" He caught my gaze,

his eyes seeming to turn into two pools with gently rolling waves. "—aquatic life."

"Well, Cory." Meg slapped my back. "I'm going to stop in the gift shop. Meet me there?"

"Meet you?" I turned to face her, still holding a mountain of equipment in my arms.

"Nice to meet you in the uh—flesh, Simon." Meg gave a small wave, eyed me, and bolted down the dock.

"Did you…want some help with all of that?"

My throat tightened, and I whipped back around to face him, the bag on my shoulder slipping off and making a loud *thud* as it hit the dock.

With the same radiant grin, he picked the bag up. "Here." He reached for the other bag resting over my forearms. "Listen, do you…want to talk?"

"Talk?" My brows bobbed.

"Yeah. You know, like normal people?" He chuckled, his eyes dropping to his bare feet, pausing before looking back to me.

I snorted. "Oh, man. Not sure I've *ever* considered myself—normal."

"I know exactly what you mean." The oceans in his eyes swirled like a typhoon as he stared down at me. "What do you say?" He nudged his head at a vacant bench facing the beach.

"Sure. Okay."

As we walked to the bench, every patron we passed whispered and pointed at him. I shouldn't have been surprised, considering how famous of a surfer he was. But I'd never been one to follow "celebrities." How silly of me to have forgotten I was in the company of a "surf god."

Simon sat on the bench, resting my bags on the sand at his feet. He patted the space next to him, flashing me a smile that could have melted the bikini top I wore *underneath* my wetsuit. After running my hands over my salty wet hair, I took a seat the farthest I could from him without falling off the edge.

He glanced down at the wide gap between us. "I promise I don't bite."

"I know of you, but I don't *know* you." I offered a weak smile.

But I did feel like I knew him. As if I'd known him my entire life. That in itself jarred me more than sitting on a bench with a stranger.

"I suppose I do need to earn your trust, don't I?" He curled his hands on the edge of the bench and leaned forward.

A tickle swirled in my belly at his words. "What are you doing in West Palm?"

He casually kicked his surfboard. "I did have a competition. Small one. But they canceled it on account of the storm." He gazed skyward.

I, too, looked up, and we both laughed at the blue skies and sun shining brightly. Such was life in Florida.

"You?" He drummed his fingers on the bench.

"Sea turtles." I bit my lower lip, mimicking his position and hugging my arms against my thighs.

"I'm sorry?" He rose a brow, making his forehead wrinkle.

I chuckled at his expression. "I'm an oceanographer. A magazine hired us to take photos of sea turtles. West Palm has some of the best scenery for them."

"You took photos? Even during the storm?" He pointed at the water, almost at the precise spot I'd gotten swept away.

Bile climbed up my throat. "Yeah. It got a little dicey there toward the end." I pinched my knees together, staring at them.

"Are you okay?" He dipped his head, trying to look at my face.

"Yeah. Yes." I sat straight, rubbing both collar bones with one hand. "I'd gotten thrown into the current. But there was this weird—gust underwater. It brought me right back to the boat."

He coughed. "A gust, you say?"

"Yes." I scooted closer to him. "Have you ever experienced something like that?"

His grip tightened on the bench. "Can't say I have. Just waves and curls."

Suddenly, he couldn't look at me, and I slid closer.

He shot up like a rocket. "Listen, I have to go, but—" He rubbed the back of his neck. "I'd really like to see you again. Would you consider possibly exchanging numbers?"

It'd been so long since a man asked for my number in person, I'd forgotten how to respond in this situation properly.

"Numbers?" It came out as a squeak.

He chuckled, deep and masculine. "Yeah. Phone numbers? To contact each other? Maybe I might ask you out?"

My heart thundered in my chest. "You? Simon Thalassa. A famous surfer with abs for days…wants to see me again?"

He gave a snarky smile as he tapped his fingers against his stomach. I took

notice for a split second before forcing them back to his face.

"Are surfers with toned muscles not allowed to date?"

I pressed two fingers between my eyes and stood. "I'm sorry, I'm horrible at this whole…socializing thing in general, I suppose."

A gooey smile spread over his lips, and he said under his breath, "You always have been."

"What did you say?"

His eyes darted to mine. "I didn't say anything."

I scratched my cheek as I dug my toes in the sand, willing the grains to calm my nerves.

"We could always rely on fate throwing us in each other's path again, but I'd much rather do it the old-fashioned way." He clasped his hands in front of him.

I liked him. I did. So, what the hell was wrong with me?

"I don't have my phone on me, but I have a pen?" Crouching, I unzipped the front pocket of my camera bag and stood with pen in hand like an elegant quill.

He offered his tanned corded forearm to me, keeping his gaze locked to mine.

My fingers grazed his skin, the tautness of it—the light scattering of hair— made warmth pool in my belly. Gripping the pen tightly to keep my hand from shaking, I wrote my phone number on him. His scent floated through the air in front of me like waterfall mist—sea spray mixed with citrus and sun. I wanted to melt against him, mold to him.

"I think we're good, Cordelia," he whispered near my ear.

My eyes flew open, and I jumped back, realizing my hand still rested on his forearm, and I'd leaned toward him.

I curled the pen into my chest, clutching it with both hands. "That number is a one-time deal. Don't let it wash away."

He plucked the surfboard from the sand and folded it under his arm. "I will never let the opportunity to see you again wash away." He willed my eyes to him, and before he turned to walk away, my mind played tricks on me once more. Because I could've sworn, he whispered, "Not anymore."

FIVE

AS I WALKED INTO the gift shop to meet up with Meg after dropping off the equipment in my Jeep, I kept playing his words in my head. I squinted at nothing, moving my finger in the air as if solving an algebraic equation without pencil and paper.

The past days left me with unanswered questions I hadn't even known I wanted to ask.

"Cory," Meg shouted, grabbing my shoulders and shaking me.

I jerked within her grasp. "What? What?"

"I called your name three times. From two feet away. What the hell is wrong with you?" She raised her hand in a fin gesture and moved it from one side of my face to the other, keeping her eyes on mine.

I followed her hand before batting it away. "I don't have a concussion or whatever else you feel the need to check my motor skills on."

"Are you going to tell me about your chit-chat with Simon, or do I have to drag it out of you?" She'd thrown a plaid shirt over her swimsuit top, letting the rest of the wetsuit hang from her waist.

"He—" I fluttered past her, busying my hands and eyes with a variety of souvenirs. "Asked for my number."

"Wow. The man works fast and knows what he wants. I like it." Meg ran her fingers over the seashell keychains hanging from pegs.

"It's—I mean, I'm probably overthinking it." I snagged a water globe with a pair of sea turtles swimming between the words West Palm Beach and turned it

upside down to make it snow on them.

"Cordelia. Spit. It. Out. Since when have you been so non-forthcoming with information? Normally you'd be talking my damn ear off by now." She snatched the globe from my hand, putting it back, and tugging on my arm. "Come look at these."

"He has this sense of urgency to him. Like he's afraid if he doesn't act on the prospect of us, I'll get pulled in with the tide, never to be seen again."

Meg led me to several rows of shelves filled with miniature sculptures dipped in pearlescent sheen.

"I don't know, Cor. There's nothing wrong with a person knowing what they want and going for it. So long as he doesn't propose tomorrow, I'd ride it out." She grabbed a hammerhead shark, running her thumb over its dorsal fin. "He seems perfect for you."

"We don't know this guy, Meg." I winced, grabbing one of the sea turtles, testing its weight in my palm.

And it was true. I. Did. Not. Know. Him. But his presence was like a midnight swim—relaxing current mixed with uncertainty and eerie calm.

"That's the whole point of dating, isn't it? Getting to know him?" She kept the hammerhead shark in her grasp and reached for a bull shark figurine.

A pile of small replica tridents rested in a far corner, the overhead fluorescent light reflecting off them, making them sparkle brighter than the rest. I hovered my hand over one, and a loud buzzing pounded in my ears, dizzying me. Wincing through the bizarre interference, I snatched one, and the sound floated away, replaced by Meg's voice still going on about Simon.

"That's all I'm saying. I'm simply looking out for your best interests," Meg continued, cradling one of every shark species in her arms with a bright smile.

Holding the trident up to the light, I twirled it between two fingers. "If I text him when we get to the car, will that please you?"

"Yes. Yes, it would. At least one of us should be having a successful sex life."

"From, 'you should date him,' to, 'you should bang him' in nearly one breath. Wow." I moved past her with wide eyes to the register, slapping the trident onto the counter.

"We're both adults. And gone are the times for judgment over screwing on the first date." She shrugged and plucked a seashell keychain from a turnstile with her

name on it. "Sometimes, it's even a matter of releasing stress. And that's a-okay."

The cashier, a younger woman with ringlets of strawberry blonde hair and a small perky nose, smiled as she rang me up, her cheeks blushing.

"I mean, am I right?" Meg asked, dipping her face to try and look at the shy cashier.

The woman nodded emphatically but couldn't meet Meg's gaze.

Biting back a smile, I took my small blue bag and receipt, stepping out of Meg's way.

As the cashier rang up the dozen shark figures Meg set on the counter, I peered at the trident surrounded by blue plastic within the satchel. If the same weapon in *Tides of Atlantis* were as powerful as it had been when I wielded it in the game, why did it remain the least popular choice?

"So, you live in West Palm, huh? Ever visit Pensacola?" Meg leaned her forearms on the counter, chewing a pen she'd thrown into her haul at the last minute.

The cashier's shoulders hunched forward, but she grinned. "Sometimes, yeah. I love that Diesel Fuel drink. Not to mention the huge pile of nachos at McGuire's."

Never having been the shy type, Meg pushed the blue arrow on the cash register, making several inches of blank receipt tape appear. After tearing it off, she jotted something down and slid it toward her.

"My number. When you're in town next, you should get in touch. I'll buy you a Diesel Fuel." Meg stuck the pen back in her mouth before beating her palms on the counter in rhythmic succession.

The cashier's cheeks turned rosy, and she folded the receipt tape with a smile. "I'll be sure to do that."

Meg winked before scooping the bag full of sharky souvenirs onto her arm and joining me near the entrance.

"Back on the saddle?" I elbowed her.

She continued to chew the pen. "Trying."

Curling our arms, we tossed our bags into the back of my Jeep and crawled in, heading back to our hotel for the night. My cell phone vibrated in the glove compartment, echoing off the plastic walls until Meg popped it open and grabbed it.

"Who is it?" I bobbed my brows at her.

With a sly grin, she scrolled the screen with her thumb. "Looks like you won't

have to be the first to make a move after all. I should've guessed."

"Is it Simon?" I reached for the phone, but she leaned away.

"Uh-huh. He's asking if you want to come to his surf competition in two days."

"Surf competition? What kind of a date is that?"

She lowered the phone to her lap and gave me an exasperated stare. "Why am I having to school you on men? This is so incredibly backward, Cor."

"What are you talking about?"

"He wants to show off at the competition. Afterward, I'd bet my favorite plaid shirt he plans to take you to dinner or drinks or whatever for a nightcap." She twirled her hand in a circle, waiting for the lightbulb to go off in my brain.

"Oh." I wrung my hands on the steering wheel. "I suppose that makes sense."

Meg nodded once and rested my phone in the cupholder between us. "I already replied that you'd be there."

"What? Why would you—" I gripped the wheel tighter.

She pointed a stern finger at me, silent.

"Fine. I suppose I can pretend to be way more into surfing than I actually am for a day."

"No."

I snapped my head in her direction. "No?"

Nerves bubbled in my stomach from taking my eyes off the road, and I quickly returned them.

"You're not going to pretend anything. That's bullshit. You're going to watch Simon show his athletic prowess half-naked and hang out with him afterward. That's it." She sliced her hand through the air in front of her.

I sunk in my seat. "You're considerably fiery lately."

"A new leaf, Cor. A new leaf."

It was our last day in West Palm, and we chartered a cage dive to get some prize-winning shark close-ups, hopefully. We sat on a bench aboard the boat, and I checked for an SD card, ensured my regulator worked properly, and pulled my hair in a low ponytail.

"I've gotten so used to full-face dive masks." Meg tossed around the mouthpiece

of her regulator with a snicker. "It's going to suck not being able to talk to you."

I slipped on my flippers. "I think we'll survive for twenty minutes."

"Twenty minutes, huh? Wow. Has Cordelia Bourne grown an ego?" Meg poked my shoulder.

Flicking her in the leg with my flipper, I guffawed. "Ego? What are you talking about?"

"You've had such a lucky track record lately with your photos that you think we're going to nab a sell-worthy shark shot in twenty minutes?"

I squinted into the sun with a slight shrug. "Or under." Peeking at her reaction from the corner of my eye, she didn't disappoint. Her jaw almost touched her chest. "I'm kidding, Meg." I smiled at her, flicking her shin with my flipper again.

"Five minutes," the captain announced.

We both stood, helping the other secure the tanks on our backs. It must've been comical for anyone who watched me assist Meg, considering I had to practically make a running start to throw the straps over her shoulders. After we were suited up, we flopped to the edge of the boat, watching the cage lower into the water from an attached crane once the boat came to a complete stop.

I glared at the cage's bars and tugged on Meg's arm. "Don't those bars look a bit too far apart to you?"

She peered into the water. "Maybe an inch or two beyond what we normally see, but it'll still do its job. Keep the knife teeth away from us." After winking at me, she yanked her goggles over her face.

"Right." I forced a smile and shoved the regulator in my mouth.

The world around us quieted as we jumped into the water. The only sounds passing over my ears were the metal groans of the boat bobbing in the water, our steady breathing, and water churning around us. The cage lowered after locking ourselves inside and tugging on the cord secured by the crane operator on deck. The metal fastenings keeping the bars closed jangled when it came to a halting stop. We both lifted our cameras and began swimming circles with our backs to each other, staying toward the center.

They started to chum the water from the boat, marred bits of torn fish floated through the water, fresh blood curling around it in a spiral. My grip tightened on the camera handles as a fish head darted past my gaze. Bile crept up my throat, but I gulped it away. Vomiting in my regulator wouldn't be an ideal situation.

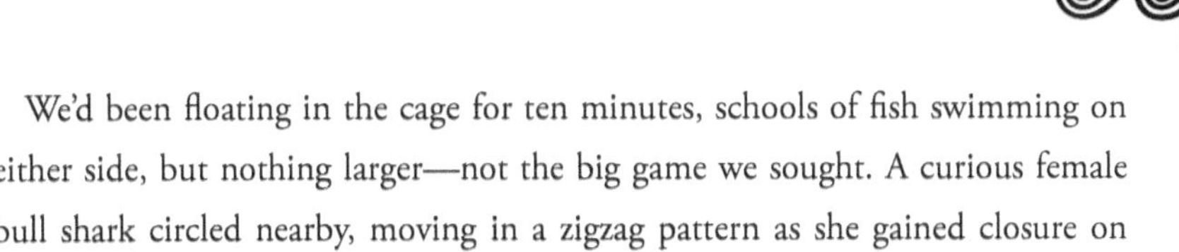

We'd been floating in the cage for ten minutes, schools of fish swimming on either side, but nothing larger—not the big game we sought. A curious female bull shark circled nearby, moving in a zigzag pattern as she gained closure on the cage. I elbowed Meg and pointed, encouraging her to frame a shot in case it graced us with its presence.

The shark swam closer and closer until suddenly it zipped away, leaving a trail of bubbles behind it. For a bull shark of that size to flee on a whim could've only meant one thing—an even bigger fish swam nearby. I whipped my head in every direction, straining to see an outline, movement, anything in the distance.

It happened with such speed, force, and pure power we didn't see it coming until a Great White shark's head plowed between the bars on the side of the cage. Bubbles surged from our mouths as we both screamed. The shark either thought we were food or a threat or possibly both and had planned a long-ranged attack.

I lifted the camera, using it as a shield once the shark started thrashing and biting—stuck. My breathing grew erratic, staring in horror at the poor creature panicking, writhing for its life to no avail. Meg swam to the farthest corner and pushed her back to it, her eyes as wide as beach balls behind her goggles.

With as deep of a breath as I could manage given a regulator, I steadied my heartbeat. Blood floated from the shark's gills, and I knew if it kept thrashing, it would make itself bleed to death.

If only I could tell it to stop so I could help push it through to spare its gills.

If only the risk of losing a hand in the process weren't astronomically high.

It. Was. Going. To. Die.

I couldn't live with myself if I stood there watching it hurt itself until going lifeless and sinking to the bottom of the ocean—forgotten.

Stop.

The shark's glossy eyes peered back at me, continuing to squirm against the cage bars.

Stop. Stop. Stop.

Swimming closer, I kept the camera between us.

The shark's writhing slowed, but the blood leaking from its gills didn't.

A spark sizzled up my spine, and I let the camera float to the cage bottom. Moving in front of the shark, a breath away, so close I could see the dozens of scars on its nose, I ripped the regulator from my mouth.

"Stop," I shouted into the water, sending a barrage of curling bubbles into the shark's face.

The shark stopped—its gills flopping helplessly against the cage, its tail idly whipping back and forth to keep it afloat. I stared at the shark's eyes, keeping its gaze as I reached a shaky hand forward. Meg's fingers brushed against my wet suit from behind me, but I ignored her, entirely focused on the shark, and locked our gazes.

The shark jerked as I neared its gills, but I fought every compulsion to snap away. Nudging my hand between the shark's gills and the cage, I grunted and pushed with all my might. The shark did a small shimmy with its head before it dislodged—free. Like the swell in the ocean, my chest soared, almost bursting, beaming at the sight of the freed shark. A film flapped over the shark's right eye before it swam away with solid strokes of its tail.

My lungs burned. The regulator. I shoved it back into my mouth and took several long gulps of air. Meg grabbed my shoulder and turned me around, frantically grabbing for my hands, checking all fingers were still intact. She shoved my shoulder before pulling on the rope, signaling the boat to make the cage ascend. I rested a hand on my throat, recalling the swirling pattern of bubbles from my underwater yell.

My head breached the surface, the sun warming my skin and calming my rattled nerves. The shouts from the boat's captain, birds flying overhead, and the water crashing against the boat faded into my ears—I felt like a stranger in my own skin.

No sooner had we climbed back on board, Meg tore off her goggles and grabbed both my shoulders. "What the ever-loving hell happened down there, Cor?"

"Miss, are you alright?" The captain asked, running a hand over his bald, sweaty head. "That shark was throwing the cage around like a damned seal. Never seen that happen before."

I furrowed my brow, dropping my focus to the laugh lines bordering Meg's mouth. "I'm fine."

"I got this handled, Captain. Can you get us back to the dock as soon as possible, please?" Meg guided me to the bench and pushed me down to sit.

"You never being threatened by sharks, Cory, is one thing. What I witnessed down there was damned shark whispering." Meg grabbed her camera and held

the digital screen on the back out to me.

I rubbed my lips together, eyes shifting to the screen. She'd taken several succession shots of me reaching my hand to the shark and even more when I pressed my hand on its gills and pushed. Closing my eyes, I turned away, my head dizzy and pulsing. "You can't publish those."

"No shit. I wanted you to see for yourself what you did." Meg rested the camera on the bench beside her and scooted closer to me, rubbing my arms. "How did you know it wouldn't bite your damn arm off, Cor?"

My body jostled as she rubbed, beads of water from my wet hair falling on my upturned hand resting on my thigh.

Drip. Drip drip.

"I didn't."

"Jesus. Why did you do it, hm? Why?" She switched to rubbing my shoulders.

"It was either do something or watch it die." Tears welled in my eyes at the mere thought. "You know I couldn't let that happen."

She side-hugged me, pulling me in tight. Given our height difference, I was able to rest my head on her shoulder comfortably. She placed her head on mine. "Please don't ever do it again. I couldn't earn enough money on my own. Kinda need you." She chuckled, making my body vibrate.

A smile pulled at my lips but faded.

There weren't any telltale signs of a shark's emotions. No gleams in their eyes. No thinned lips or reddened cheeks. But I knew with every fiber in my being— that fish not only understood me when I yelled but also *thanked* me before swimming away.

SIX

I'D BEGGED MEG TO come with me to the surf competition because I wouldn't know what to do with myself alone on the beach watching a bunch of surfers. As predicted, she refused and told me to concentrate on Simon. If he'd have been the only contestant, that wouldn't have been an issue, but I sat on a towel in the sand watching athlete after athlete catch the waves, and none of them were Simon. Stifling a yawn, I tilted my head back and closed my eyes, letting the sun kiss my skin.

"Already bored, huh?" Simon's voice spoke from nearby.

I popped my eyes open to find him standing over me with a snarky grin, his head partially blocking the light in the sky. "Full disclosure. I came here to watch one singular surfer."

"Oh, yeah?" Simon plopped on the sand next to me, propping his forearms on his knees. "And who might that be?"

Several beach-goers pointed and stared at us, whispering to each other. If Simon noticed, he didn't act like it.

"Some guy the media says is the biggest thing to hit the surfing circuit since the board leash." I pushed my sunglasses to my head, taking in the sight of him up close and at my level.

Those eyes of his never failed to make me feel antsy and calm all at once.

"Wow. Sounds talented." He winked at me before lightly nudging my elbow with his. "I appreciate you stopping by. If I'd known you were just showing up for me, I would've told you to come later." He chuckled and turned his glance to the

waves, impatiently tapping his fingers on his bronzed forearm.

"Oh? Do they always save the best for last?" I sat up straighter, causing my hip to brush his thigh.

Both of our gazes snapped to the brief contact before meeting each other's eyes.

He canted his head to one side, taking me in. "They think it's best for publicity. I don't give a damn in what order I go, so long as I get to surf."

"You really are an aqua baby, aren't you?" I wanted to drag my fingers through his hair. Instead, I dug them into the sand.

He nodded as he leaned on the elbow closest to me, the hair on his arm brushing my skin. "If I could live in the water—" His gaze lowered to my lips before returning to my eyes. "I would."

An obnoxious foghorn sounded from the other side of the beach.

Simon rolled his eyes. "That would be my sponsor. Their delightful way of letting me know there's one surfer to go before me." He leaped to his feet and dusted the sand from his butt.

"You'll stick around afterward, right? There's a great little salad bar just down the beach." He pointed with his thumb. "And the margaritas are strong." The lopsided grin that slid over his plump yet masculine lips made the insides of my thighs ache.

"I'm not going anywhere."

His expression fell, and he stared down at me, the left side of his mouth twitching. He took a step forward but retreated, giving one quick shake of his head. "At one point, I'm going to hold three fingers above my head. That signal? It's for you."

I traced a finger over my lips. "I'll look for it."

After flashing me another award-winning smile, he trotted off, waving his arm at his sponsor. Every woman he passed on his way turned their gazes on him, watching his hardened muscles tightening and flexing with each step. A knot twisted in my stomach. I barely knew the man, yet somehow, my body still figured out a way to be jealous. I yanked the camera from my bag with a grunt, setting the shutter for the appropriate lighting.

Tossing the strap over my neck, I hovered my gaze behind the viewfinder, zooming in and taking several images of the waves. Surfing photos weren't always at the top of the list of shots my clients asked for, but a few of Simon Thalassa

might be desirable.

Desire.

A lump the size of a conch shell formed in my throat, and I tightened my grip on the camera.

As the announcer's voice introduced Simon, surrounding beach-goers perked up on their beach towels. I rose to my knees with the camera perched in my grasp, spotting Simon running across the shoreline, his board nestled under one arm. The water welcomed him with every lap of the waves crashing against his calves. He flopped on his belly atop the board, swimming to where the waves broke.

He fully stood on the board as the wave curled, expertly balancing and riding the water. His right hand cut through the wave, the pipe coiling around him like an embrace. I put the camera to work, taking shot after shot one after the other to catch any subtle piece of the action. His arms flowed through the water and as I zoomed closer, the shape of a dolphin appeared, but was gone just as quickly with a furious splash.

My shoulders tensed, but I didn't drop the camera, keeping my gaze glued on Simon through the viewfinder. As he made a smooth transition from beneath the wave, he held an arm up, displaying three fingers and a wide smile.

Grinning, I took several shots of his secret message to me. Only me.

Three fingers. I blinked, my lashes fluttering against the camera—a trident.

A numbness coursed down my arms, and I sat back on my haunches. The camera would've fallen into the sand were it not for the strap keeping it hung around my neck. I rubbed the skin between my eyes, flashes of the sparkling trident beneath the water blazing through my brain as if trying to break through some mental barrier. Shaking my head, I forced my focus back through the viewfinder.

Simon surfed another four waves, not surprisingly scoring max points with the judges in every attempt. Gathering my towel and bag, I walked to the winner's circle to witness him receiving the first-place trophy. He took it with both hands, holding it above his head, the golden gleam sparkling under the sunrays. After posing for the cameras for several minutes, he turned to a young boy holding a surfboard beaming up at him.

He handed the trophy to the boy and ruffled his hair. "Something to inspire you. Never stop surfing, alright?"

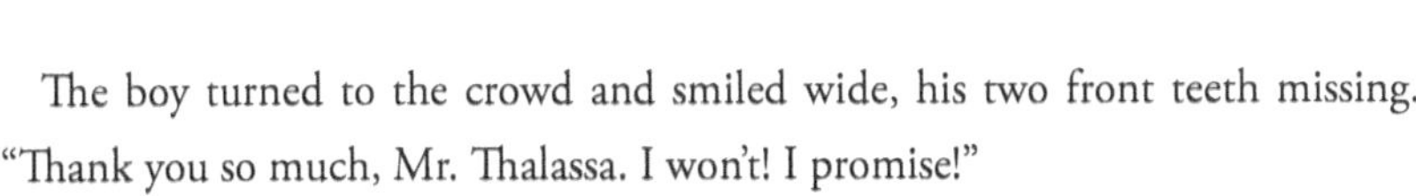

The boy turned to the crowd and smiled wide, his two front teeth missing. "Thank you so much, Mr. Thalassa. I won't! I promise!"

Simon kept the same warm smile as he gave a final wave to the crowds. I crossed my arms, grinning. His gaze fell on me, somehow finding me within the mass of a hundred people shouting his name. A group of bikini-clad women armed with sharpies and ample cleavage called to him as he passed, begging for his autograph. Making his way through the sea of people surrounding me, he didn't so much as glance at them, leaving behind frowning women in his wake. I dropped my arms at my sides, gulping.

When he reached me, he held his hand out for me to take. "Ready for that salad?"

I'd never been so excited for leafy greens.

Nodding without words, I slipped my hand into his, the calluses on his palms scraping against my skin, making my toes grip the soles of my flip-flops.

Simon led me through the crowds, each fan stepping aside as soon as we neared them. He was Moses, parting people like the sea. After a short jolt down the boardwalk, we arrived at a small restaurant with patio seating. The name "Vesta's Greenery" hung over the entrance in jagged blue and green lettering.

"You pick a spot here and go order your salad at the counter. Do you have a favorite?" Simon pulled out a seat for me at a table facing the view of the ocean.

Smiling, I sat down, curling my hands in my lap. "Surprise me."

A glint flashed in his eye, and he gave one firm nod. "You got it."

Peeking over my shoulder, I caught a glance of his board shorts hugging the muscular ass hiding beneath. My cheeks burned, and I bit my lips as a smile crept over them. Seagulls flew overhead, some landing on lamp posts, others waddling the dock hoping for humans dropping food. Though there were ambient noises of children playing, people laughing, and varying forms of low-key music from each shop or restaurant—my ears tuned to the water crashing against the sand in the distance. I took a deep breath, soaking in the smell of salt hanging in the air.

"Here we are," Simon's smooth voice announced his return. He placed a wide bowl of colorful ingredients in front of me and handed me a fork.

I took the utensil with a sparkling grin and eyed the bits of orange sprouting between the green leaves. Poking one with my fork, I held it up. "Mango. A mango salad. How did you know mango was my favorite fruit?"

Simon tousled his short hair before sliding into his seat across from me. "I'm fairly good at reading people, and you seemed like a mango kind of gal."

Saliva collected in the corner of my mouth as I eyed the rainbow salad in front of me—mangoes, romaine lettuce, cilantro, and hearty tomatoes. Gathering a variety on my fork, I slid the bite into my mouth and all but moaned.

"Did I pick well?"

I'd closed my eyes and lazily opened one. "Very well."

"Good." He smiled and cut his salad into more manageable pieces—cucumbers, tomatoes, olives, and sprinkled feta cheese.

"Greek?"

Simon had taken a bite and widened his eyes at me, shoving it against his cheek. "Me?"

Laughing, I tapped my fork against the plate. "Your salad."

"Oh, right." After a sheepish grin, he swallowed his food. "Yeah. It's the best. Less rabbit food and more beef to it without being actual beef, you know?" His gaze dropped to the heaping amount of green on my plate. "No offense."

"None taken. I love rabbit food."

Like shy teenagers, we smiled at each other, making bubbles erupt in my stomach.

"I have to ask. What got you into gaming? Especially on the professional level?" Simon leaned his arms on the table, bringing our faces closer.

It wasn't as short-winded of an answer as he'd probably thought.

"It's kind of personal." I shifted all the mango to one side of my plate in a pile, tomatoes on the other. "Are you sure you want to hear it?"

He took a sip of water, waiting for me to look at him. "Only if you want to share."

I want to tell you everything.

"I never knew who my parents were. I grew up in the foster care system and never ended up in a home with a normal family for more than months at a time. Not near long enough to feel like they were my family—even an adopted one." I traced a swirly shape onto my plate with the dressing.

"Why only ever for a few months?"

My palms clammed up. "I—" He met my gaze, not speaking but urging me to continue. "I used to talk to animals."

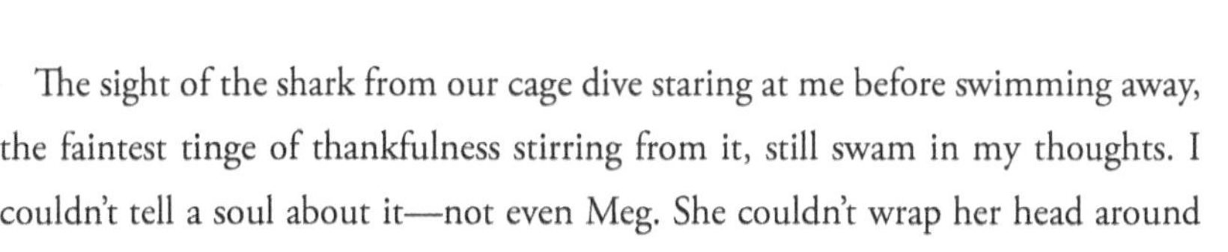

The sight of the shark from our cage dive staring at me before swimming away, the faintest tinge of thankfulness stirring from it, still swam in my thoughts. I couldn't tell a soul about it—not even Meg. She couldn't wrap her head around the shark allowing me to help it let alone say it communicated with me.

He tapped his finger on the table twice. "Don't most children at some point?"

I kept my eyes traced on him, ready to gauge his reaction. "I used to think they talked back."

And still do.

His nostrils flared, and he stared at me. He didn't lean away, didn't laugh, didn't so much as twitch.

"You're telling me no family would adopt you because you had a vivid imagination?" He frowned, forming deep creases leading from his nose to the corners of his mouth.

I shrugged, popping a mango chunk into my mouth with my fingers. "That was always my theory. Anyway, I ended up in a foster home with a dozen other kids. You can imagine how much attention we all got from the foster parents with that many kids under one roof."

His finger thudded against the table again. "You started playing video games to escape."

Heart. Squeezed.

"That's right," I whispered.

He cleared his throat as if choking on something and sipped on his water. "What uh—what games have you played?"

"You're going to laugh." I leaned back and crossed my arms.

He chuckled.

Widening my eyes, I held a hand out.

"Hey. That's not fair. You set something up like that you're asking for it." He made a "come on" gesture. "Spill."

I shoved a finger between my eyes and closed them. "I was obsessed with *Ecco The Dolphin* as a kid, and then it progressed into *Aquaria, Subnautica,* and most recently—*Tides of Atlantis.*"

He didn't laugh. Not even a snicker.

I opened my eyes to find a radiant smile playing across his lips.

"Seems I'm not the only aqua baby, hm?" He traced his middle fingertip in a

circle over the table cloth.

"I imagine my birth mother had a water birth with me." I chewed my lip, getting lost in those eyes of his like a never-ending emerald meadow.

"Very plausible."

His foot brushed mine under the table, making me gasp.

"Shit. Sorry. Long legs." He rubbed the back of his head.

"They must be to reach these stubs." I pointed down.

He rested his chin on his palm, still not letting his eyes roam away from me. "Nothing wrong with being petite."

His words made my vision hazy, and I held my breath before harshly blowing it out. "I want to ask you something, but I don't want you to think I'm weird."

"Well, you're a gamer—a professional one at that—who's obsessed with fish and picks up trash for fun. Not sure how much weirder I can think you." A dopey smile pulled at his lips.

I dropped my jaw and grabbed a tomato from my plate, throwing it at him.

His hands flew up, blocking it with a glorious laugh roaring from his chest. "I'm kidding. I'm kidding. Ask away. Some may think I'm weird too." He scratched his ribs.

"Do you—believe in past lives?"

He coughed into his fist.

Anxiety swirled my brain, and I flattened my hands on the table. "I'm sorry. I shouldn't have asked."

"No." He cleared his throat. "No. I've just never had anyone ask me that before and it threw me off guard because—" His fingertips skirted mine on the table. "Yes. I do."

Breathing air suddenly didn't seem enough, and my chest ached—not with pain but with…hope.

"Why do you ask, Cordelia?"

I slid my hand away from his, the proximity to his skin sending me through raging rapids. "I should go. This has been incredibly lovely. But the tournament is soon, and I still need to practice, and I promised Meg a vacation if I win and—"

And I was stammering.

"Sure, but tournament?" He stood, moving behind me to pull out my chair.

I stayed seated long enough to ensure the jelly my legs had turned into would

hold me up if I decided to stand.

"A *Tides of Atlantis* eSports Tournament. I've been signed up for over a year." Scooping my bag over one arm, I slipped my sunglasses on.

"Very nice. Can I walk you back to your car?"

"Sure," I squeaked.

We were silent the few minutes it took to reach the parking lot. I fished for my keys, dropped them and immediately sank to my knees to retrieve them.

He met me on the asphalt, sliding a hand over my trembling one as I grabbed the keys. "Did I say something wrong, Cory?"

Quite the opposite.

"No, not at all. You've been nothing short of amazing, Simon." I slowly rose, and his hand fell from mine.

"Then, what is it?"

Finally managing to meet his gaze, I clutched the keys, wincing at the metal impressions pushing into my skin. "I'm not good at this."

"Good at what? Dating?" A tiny smile peeked at the corner of his lips. It wasn't a mocking gesture but an endearing one.

"Dating. Socializing in general."

"Hey." He cupped my chin. "We have all the time in the world. That is—if you want to see me again."

"Yes," I blurted.

Way to sound desperate, Cor.

"Good." He dipped his lips near mine and pressed a tender kiss to my cheek, pausing there for several seconds. "I'll see you soon, Jewel of the Sea."

He walked away, and I stood by my car, trailing my fingers over my cheek. The kiss lingered on my skin, rippling like a stone disturbing calm water.

SEVEN

With the tournament the following day, I'd spent every waking moment practicing my technique in *Tides of Atlantis* until my eyes couldn't stand staring at the screen any longer. I'd been at it so long I started to see *myself* as my character within the game. It would be the third tournament I've competed in, but the first focused on this game alone. Simon continued to text me, even with a simple, "Good morning," or "Hey Beautiful," but gave me distance, knowing I needed to practice. Most of the bigger tournaments happened in central or south Florida, but Pensacola decided to put their own foot in the ring and rented space at the Pensacola Bay Center to host the event.

I streamed the last few hours of my gameplay, inviting any subscribers in the area to watch me compete at the tournament. In exchange for their support, anyone wearing a shirt with my gamertag on it would receive a free swag pack I'd leave with will call.

The morning of day one for the tournament, I packed away my game controller, charging cable, and headset. Some tournaments provided game-themed headsets for all to wear, but I wanted mine as a backup if necessary.

Pausing in front of the mirror, I smoothed out my fitted tee, staring at the SaucySiren logo—a cartoon version of me with a teal mermaid tail holding a game controller. I had yet to step foot into the convention center and could already feel the mixture of nerves and excitement swirling in my belly, competing for control. There was no telling if any other women gamers would be in attendance, but with how few we were at these events, it prickled an extra set of nerves. I didn't want

to leave fellow lady gamers down.

My phone buzzed on my nightstand. A text from Meg saying she was here. Meg offered to drive us to the tournament, so I could focus on keeping calm and not dealing with traffic anxiety. I sent her a quick reply, telling her I was on my way downstairs, and grabbed my bag.

Pausing in front of my fish tank, I blew them a kiss. "Wish me luck, guys."

Several responded with vibrant flaps of their fins.

I made my way downstairs and crawled into Meg's truck with a smile. Given how high I had to step up to get into the behemoth vehicle, it always felt like mounting a horse.

"You ready?" Meg's brow bobbed.

"I only lost one match the last three days. Not sure how much more ready I could be." Pulling the door shut, I rested my bag in my lap and focused on my breathing.

"That's my girl. Mama needs a vacation." Meg winked at me before pulling out of the parking lot and turning on the radio.

The calming sounds of Aurora singing *Under The Water* soothed my erratic heartbeat.

"Please don't remind me. It only adds to the pressure I already feel. I can't place any lower than third to win enough money for the cruise."

Meg squeezed my knee and patted my thigh. "Relax. Sure, I'd love a vacation, but don't let that give you an anxiety attack in the middle of a match. I'm going to watch you kick a bunch of young dude's asses, quite frankly."

"That—" Placing my head on the rest, I turned it toward Meg with a grin. "—I can do."

"I've never been to one of these events. Anything I should know?" Meg grabbed her Chapstick from the center console, slathering some over her lips.

"It's like any other sports event. It lasts two days. Today consists of pools and brackets as losers are weeded out, and, eventually, only the best eight remain. Tomorrow is the actual final tournament or The Big Show with the crowds cheering for their favorite players. And they live stream it. So, don't get caught picking your nose or something." I bit back a smile.

Meg stuck out her bottom lip after beating her hands on the steering wheel. "Noted."

"There's also a party tonight." I kept my face forward, waiting for her response.

"A party? What kind? Costumed?"

"Definitely. But it's an actual party. Dancing, drinking, nerding out."

She raised one brow and slowly turned her head. "Nerds party? I had no idea."

"Oh, you really should see it. We may not frequent clubs, but get us together for an event like this? You better believe we know how to throw down." I flashed a sparkling grin at her.

She shook her head. "And to think I knew you."

When we arrived at the convention center, the *Tides of Atlantis* game logo in gold and teal hung over the building. I'd managed to dry my hands and keep my nerves at bay…until now. We parted ways once we walked inside, Meg heading for the restroom, and I following the signs for "athletes." Several pairs of male eyes followed me as I briskly made my way over the orange and blue swirly-patterned carpet, focusing my gaze forward.

A woman with fifties-style flared glasses and eye make-up to match shuffled papers at a table with a sign reading, "Registration." Her black hair pulled back into two small buns atop her head and chocolate-colored eyes beamed at me as I approached the table.

"Hey there." I gave a small wave. "I pre-registered. Cordelia Bourne?"

"Bourne. Bourne." She licked the tip of her forefinger and flipped through colored tabs, yanking out a sheet marked with the letter b. "Cordelia Bourne. Here we are. We just need your registration fee, and you'll be all set."

The tournament added a portion of the fees to the overall pool for the top three players at event's end. The additional amount donated by the tournament's sponsor, Blue Ring Surfing Supply, made for a hefty winning sum despite its smaller town location. After removing the credit card from my wallet, I held it up with raised brows.

"Let me cue up the tablet. Damn thing went to sleep again," the woman said, swiping a hand over the fingerprint-covered tablet, handing it to me to swipe through the attached card reader.

After paying and horribly signing my name with my finger on the touch screen,

she held a lanyard to me.

"Lanyards too? How fancy." I grinned, slipping the teal and gold neck strap over my head.

She blew a bubble with her gum, popping it. "The first pool starts within the hour. Looks like you're in station three. Feel free to roam the showroom floor in the meantime. They'll announce it over the intercom."

"Thanks." I turned away, ignoring the steady increase in my heartbeat. "Oh, can a guest go on the floor, or is it for participants only?"

"Oh, honey, of course. The more, the merrier for those vendors. More of a chance they'll sell something." She winked at me before turning her attention to another approaching gamer.

Wrapping a hand around the lanyard, I found Meg and led her to the showroom floor. "I need you to keep me from buying everything in sight."

"You? I could barely talk you into buying fancy underwear for yourself, and you're worried about here?" Meg scanned the floor—rows of tables varying from toys, video games, authors, t-shirts, and c-list celebrities signing autographs.

"I'm nervous. And when I'm nervous, I buy things. And ninety percent of said things here make me squeal just looking at them." I gasped and darted to a table with Funko POP toys, swiping one of the Poseidon characters from the *Tides of Atlantis* game.

"Hey." Meg plucked it from my hands, gave a warm smile to the vendor, and placed it back on the table.

"But look at how cute his plastic beard looks." I conjured my best puppy dog eyes.

Meg folded her arms. "You place in the tournament, and I'll personally buy you the cute hunk of plastic."

"Bribery." I bumped my hip against hers. "I love it."

We spent the next thirty minutes perusing the tables, and I eventually shoved my hands in my jean pockets to make them behave.

"Attention, participants. The first round of pools is about to begin. All players assigned to stations one through six, please make your way and be ready to go within the next fifteen minutes. All guests, please enjoy the showroom floor as we will only grant entry to guests for finals tomorrow. Thank you," an announcer's voice boomed over the intercom.

"Oh my God." My hands instantly clammed up, and I wiped them on my pants. "What if I choke? What if I freeze? What if—"

Meg pressed a hand over my mouth, and I looked up at her pleadingly. "You are good at this game. I've watched you countless times. You play with thousands of people watching you and manage to make it entertaining. Just imagine there's a webcam and chat window. You'll be fine."

I nodded, and she dropped her hand.

"I saw a food court on the bottom level. Going to grab some grub. Text me, yeah?" She jutted behind her with her thumb, backpedaling on her heels.

"Yup," I squeaked, turning for the signs directing participants to the gaming arena.

During the pools and brackets, the setup wasn't entirely impressive—rows of monitors and swiveling gaming chairs positioned far enough apart each player couldn't see the others' screen. The final round was when they pulled out all the stops. All it was missing was a cage and it'd look like an MMA fight. I waited in the foyer for them to open the door and allow us to settle into our stations.

A younger man I didn't recognize ducked his head in front of me, scanning my shirt. "Well, well. If it isn't SaucySiren." His mop of dirty blonde hair fell over his blue-gray eyes, and he flicked his head, throwing it out of his face.

"I'm sorry. Do I know you?" I bobbed my brow.

He pointed at his lanyard, displaying the username ProteinGeyser. The player who tried to snipe me when I saved my fish from dying.

I narrowed my eyes. "Do we have a problem?"

"You got lucky, Saucy." He sniffed once, folding his hands behind his back and turning away from me. "I'm not sure what you tried to pull using the trident, but I can tell you, this is the big leagues."

Every doubt and uncontrollable bubbling of nerves I'd felt the past hours—gone.

"Absolutely. Besides, the trident takes actual skill to wield." I lifted my chin, making myself taller standing beside his six-foot self.

He bent backward, pressing a hand over his stomach. "A girl shit talker. Oh, I'm looking forward to this."

"All players move to your stations," the announcer said.

I could've continued the verbal jabs, but I needed to focus—get my head in the game.

Especially now.

A *Tides of Atlantis* headset rested at each station. After removing my gaming controller, I sat down, wiggling myself in the seat and adjusting the height until I felt comfortable. Geyser was several stations away from me, which I preferred considering I could only ignore his death stare into the side of my head for so long.

There were several gameplay styles with person versus person—team deathmatch, capture the flag, controlling zones, but what *Tides of Atlantis* focused on—was individual "Free for All." The game unleashed players on a rotating map, unaware of where the other five players spawned in. Using your wits, listening for signs of nearby players, and utilizing attack and defense, you'd play until the first player reached twenty-five terminations.

Almost an hour had gone by the time it was Geyser and me at the top, tied each with twenty-four kills. The next would win the pool and have a reserved spot in the winner's bracket. They'd purposely selected maps with a shorter range, making it quicker to find someone and not as many places to hide. I followed the shore to help track where I was on the map but hugged the tree line to conceal myself.

"Why you hiding, Saucy?" Geyser yelled from his station loud enough for me to hear *through* my headset.

A sound similar to a hundred orca whales calling out in unison blasted through my head, making me wince, but also making me hyper-focused. A twig snapped behind me, and I rotated my analog stick in time to see Geyser leaping into the air with his sword held above his head, readying to land a heavy attack. Pressing the left trigger button at the opportune moment, I blocked him, sending sparks flying. My hands tensed along with my shoulders and I took a deep breath.

I needed to focus on something to relax my mind. Tingles shot down my arm like water rippled over them. Simon's eyes. That smile. A genuine interest in everything I said during our date. My thumbs flew over the buttons, dodging at critical moments, striking when I saw a possible clearing.

Another player attacked us from the side, trying to take advantage of us distracted by the other, but I yanked my second weapon, a xiphos from my back, and pressed the "y" button, launching it into the player's chest for an insta-kill. Geyser launched another combo attack, and I timed the deflection just right for

my character to perform a move that rendered him swordless. With one push of the "x" button, I threw one light attack…and that was that.

"We have our winner. Please make your way back into the foyer and wait for instructions on stations for your assigned brackets."

Every player stopped to shake my hand once we'd left the arena with wide grins plastered on their faces and congratulating me and my skills. Geyser appeared in front of me like a looming shadow.

"You think you've seen the last of me? I'll work my way up that losers bracket to be in the final tomorrow." His thin arm lifted to point in my face.

I leaned away with a grimace. "At least you have a plan. See you tomorrow then?" Before he had time to retort, I turned with a flip of my hair.

Hopefully, it hit him in the face.

The remaining pools and brackets commenced, weeding out the weaker players, enticing anxiety and excitement packed into a singular arena with each passing hour. Geyser did as he promised, winning the top spot in the loser's bracket and gaining the last opportunity for the eight finalists. Finishing second in the winner's bracket did nothing for my nerves, but it was a guaranteed spot in the finals. I'd make up for it tomorrow.

They'd outfitted one of the many large ballrooms in the convention center to host the party for players, fans, and guests. An electronic song called *Freaks* by Timmy Trumpet blasted through the room, the bass vibrating in my chest. I'd always enjoyed the jazzy element the trumpets added to his songs. His music became a regular on my numerous gaming playlists. As I promised, there were indeed people in costume. Some were dressed as characters from the cut screen storyline of the *Tides of Atlantis* game, while others partied as generic mermaids, crabs, and pirates—which were *not* in the game.

"Mind. Blown," Meg mumbled.

I elbowed her. "Told ya."

"Do any of these players ever get so completely shit-faced they can't compete the next day?" Meg stepped aside as a giant lobster in glasses walked past, holding drinks in both hands.

"Usually not for finals, but I've heard of people missing their scheduled time for pools and getting disqualified for sure."

"I kinda dig that. Rock star lifestyle as a gamer?" Meg grinned while tapping

her hand against her hip to the beat.

"The big-time pros do live like that. The game companies will pay for their lodging, shower them with sponsor gifts. Some of the big teams even have live-in chefs." I tossed my lanyard, making it do one rotation around my neck.

Meg paused and shot her gaze to me. "No shit."

Geyser stood at the opposite side of the room, glaring at me with one eye through the sea of bouncing bodies. He lifted his fists like he held a sword and slashed the air in front of him before pointing at me.

"Who the hell is that?" Meg's shoulders rolled back.

"Apparently, my arch-nemesis. Can he be any more dramatic?"

Meg shoved her jacket sleeves to her elbows. "Need me to remind him what humility looks like?"

I grabbed her elbow and coaxed her toward the bar. "I'll remind him in-game tomorrow. Trust me."

"Have I told you how much I love this side of you?" Meg leaned on the bar top, hunching forward. "I'm totally crushing on you right now." She winked before nudging me with her boot.

"Oh, be quiet and shove a drink in your face." I slid some cash to the bartender after grabbing the two beer bottles they'd rested in front of me.

After handing her one, I turned my back to the bar only to be met with a man not much taller than me in a white toga—more like a bedsheet—a plastic trident under his arm, and a fake grey beard was partially falling off his face from failed glue.

"Are you—" He swayed as he spoke and dropped his eyes to my shirt with a gasp. "You are. Holy shit. I watch your Glitch stream every damn week. You're hellah good. And if I may say so—" He leaned in, tripping over his own feet. "Very, very cute."

Meg slid closer to me.

After discreetly waving in front of me from the stench of his beer breath hanging in the air between us, I plastered a smile. "Thank you. I appreciate the support."

"It's why I'm dressed like this. To honor your mad trident skills."

I stole a glance at Meg, who shrugged, not interfering but also not leaving me to fend for myself. "Oh? Are you one of the characters?"

"Just call me…Poseidon." He bowed, tripping again.

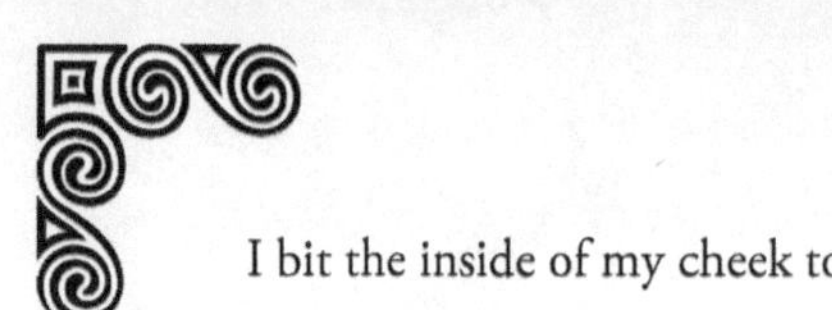

I bit the inside of my cheek to keep from laughing.

"What you need to call—is a cab," a deep voice said from behind "Poseidon."

Simon.

EIGHT

"POSEIDON" SCRUNCHED HIS NOSE and shuffled away, slurring words at a group of young men laughing and pointing at him.

"Simon?" I couldn't help the insanely wide grin pulling at my cheeks. "What are you doing here?"

Meg waved at him before hanging an arm on my shoulder and resting her chin on it. "Remember when he and I exchanged e-mails about the logo files? He asked me what tournament you were in, and so—I told him."

I let my jaw slack. "You two conspired behind my back?"

"It was for the most honorable of reasons, I assure you." His grin sparkled as he pressed a hand to his chest.

"I'm happy you came, but you didn't need to. I know this scene can't be much your deal?"

Meg playfully punched my shoulder.

"You making assumptions about hunky surfers again?" He pointed at me with his thumb and forefinger.

I crossed my arms. "Hunky?"

"Am I wrong?"

His eyes never failed to captivate. This time it was enough to make me forget how to speak, so I shook my head.

"I got us seats next to each other." Meg shoved a ticket at Simon. "Cool with you?"

"Absolutely. We can look clueless yet excited together." He curled the ticket

into his palm.

"Bruh, you're Simon Thalassa. I don't believe this," a thin, younger man with auburn hair past his shoulders wearing a *Halo* t-shirt and cargo pants said from beside us.

Not missing a beat, Simon jutted his hand for a shake. "Indeed I am. How's it hangin'?"

"Dude, an honor to meet you. Truly. Been following your surf competitions since I was a kid."

Meg and I didn't exist in this man's eyes as he remained fixed on Simon.

"Appreciate the support."

"Anyway, sorry to have bothered you."

"Have fun." Simon threw up a "hang loose" gesture with his thumb and pinky, the fan responding in kind with a wide smile.

"Even recognizable at gaming tournaments, huh?" I chewed on my thumbnail.

"Hey, I'm as surprised as you are. And do you think people realize telling them you've been into something since you were a kid is both flattering and depressing all in one sentence?" He let out a throaty chuckle, rubbing the back of his buzz-cut head.

I smiled, but it faded as soon as I caught sight of the time. "Simon, I appreciate that you came, but I need to head to bed. I'll look for you in the crowd tomorrow."

"Should I bring one of those foam fingers? An air horn, maybe?" He slid his hands in his pockets.

"Just yourself and a set of lungs to cheer me on, Big Guy."

"Can do."

Our eyes locked, swirling my stomach into a series of tidal waves and sinkholes. Grabbing Meg by her jacket, I forced her to force *me* from the ballroom.

"You didn't want to hang out with him more? I'm confused." Meg ruffled her hair.

"I need to focus. And he distracts me in the best ways possible but still… distracts me." I rubbed between my eyebrows.

"You got it bad, my friend. It's great to see you this—fluttery over someone."

I was a ravenous humpback whale with an endless appetite for Simon krill.

Finals day.

My nerves and excitement fought a deathmatch within my stomach. The arena had transformed overnight into a battleground spectacle fit for gaming. A center circular stage housed six walled stations with chairs, monitors, and headsets. Stadium seating surrounded the stage, filled to the brim with hundreds of fans. Jumbo screens hung from the ceiling, switching feeds from each of our screens or shots of our faces. Whenever they'd show me, I would more than likely be furrowing my brow with my mouth wide open the entire time.

I wrung my hands together as the game's menu theme music blared through the arena with resounding bass drums and ethereal violin and cello. As the announcer called us to our stations, I scanned the seats, spotting Meg and Simon sitting dead center, smiling at me. Simon sat up straight, and his grin melted into something else entirely as we caught each other's gazes.

Before a match, I always built myself up until I felt like I could take on the world. But that look in Simon's eyes—told me I could *own* the world.

The nerves flittered away, and I took my seat, putting on metaphorical blinders from the rest of the arena as I slid my headset on. The crowd already went wild, but I'd drown them out to concentrate. Announcers would talk strategy and segments as the game progressed, but we wouldn't hear any of it.

The game began, and hours went by of sword slashing, trident striking, mythical sea creatures we'd have to kill before returning to terminating each other. It became abundantly clear that the player to beat was PudgyPop, a male veteran pro-gamer at the ripe age of twenty—that's right, *twenty*. He led the charge with six more terminations than me and was only three away from winning it all. I'd yet to run into him in-game, and planned to avoid him at all costs. Being the last kill someone needed to win *and* causing me to lose the title? No thanks.

I'd done well not coming face-to-face with Geyser either until we neared the end. When his character stepped from behind a tree, I felt my cheeks warm. We were tied with kills, and PudgyPop only had one remaining, which meant whoever won this duel—would get second place. Processing his weak points from the several times I'd fought him, I was able to take him out within thirty seconds, with Pudgy taking first place. I finished second, but more importantly, I beat Geyser—again.

They called the three of us to a raised podium stage to announce the first

annual *Tides of Atlantis* Tournament winners. After shaking hands with Pudgy, congratulating him, I bolted from the stage to Meg's awaiting arms.

"You freaking did it. I'm so proud you wiped the floor with that Geyser prick." She playfully slapped my shoulder. "Too bad you didn't get first, though."

"Pudgy is good. Really good. He may even get a sponsorship out of that performance. But, it doesn't matter. Second place is more than enough money for a cruise."

Simon approached with his hands in his pockets and a cheeky smile. "That was incredibly hot to watch."

"Oh, yeah?" I sucked my bottom lip as I bumped my knuckle against his arm.

"I especially love your concentration face." He lifted his hands like he held a controller, furrowed his brow, and stuck his tongue to the corner of his mouth.

Laughing, I glanced at Meg before turning back to him. "I don't stick my tongue out."

"Uh, you do, Cor." Meg shrugged.

"You do. Honestly, I don't think you could make an ugly face if you tried." Simon chuckled, his green eyes twinkling as he gazed down at me.

I displayed several different expressions on my face, including going cross-eyed, making the tendons in my neck bulge, and puffing my cheeks like a blowfish.

Meg and Simon shook their heads.

"Still disgustingly adorable," Meg mumbled.

Simon lowered his lips to my ear and whispered, "Have fun on your cruise, Sea Jewel. Call me when you get back, hm?" He touched the crook of my arm, a brief brush of skin that felt like grazing the body of a stingray.

He walked past me, stealing a glance over his shoulder right before exiting the arena. The man had a presence about him that could make the ocean itself bend to his will. And I apparently would be floating right along with it.

Meg whisked through the options of onboard activities, and when neither pool volleyball nor trivia struck her fancy, we headed straight for the casino. We sat in adjacent stools, the ship having shoved off hours prior. I played with the strap of my aquamarine maxi dress, bobbing the top sandal-covered foot of my crossed

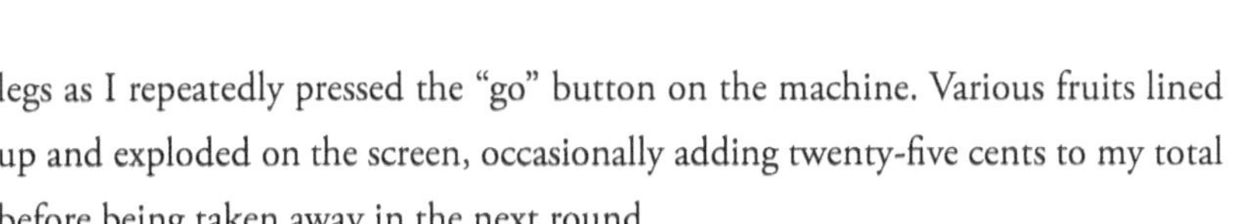

legs as I repeatedly pressed the "go" button on the machine. Various fruits lined up and exploded on the screen, occasionally adding twenty-five cents to my total before being taken away in the next round.

"Whatever happened to pulling a lever? This feels too much like a video game with none of the skill and all the luck," I mumbled, popping another quarter into the machine.

"Welcome to the twenty-first century, my friend." Meg's leather bomber jacket creaked every time she raised her arm. "We could always try our hand at roulette."

"I would have virtually no idea what I'm doing, but I'd gladly blow on dice for you and watch." I smiled at my best friend and hit the "Cash Out" button with extra enthusiasm. After ripping the exposed ticket from its slot, I shoved it into a pocket of my dress.

Meg fake cried, dabbing a knuckle at the corner of each eye. "You'd be my Lady Luck? How thoughtful."

I looped my arm with hers, and without batting an eyelash, she approached the first open spot at a roulette table. Shoving my clutch under my arm, I snagged two watered-down cocktail drinks from a tray as the waiter passed.

Meg slid the "cash out" ticket from the slot machines to the dealer, and he handed over the same amount in chips. Sipping on my rum and coke, I spied the table as if I knew how the game worked. Sure, there were black and red and numbers, but all the squares intended for player bets? No clue.

After Meg made her bet, she pushed her palms against the table's edge, idly tapping her boot. I slid my foot over hers, suggesting she tried not to show her nerves on her sleeve without using any words. Elbowing her, I held the drink out with a grin, wiggling it.

The small white ball sprung over the spinning wheel, pinging and panging as it bounced, finally landing on a black number seventeen.

Meg threw her non-drink-holding hand into a fist in the air. "I didn't lose any money that round, so it's a start."

"What's your criteria for stopping for the night? Profiting?" I sipped my drink, eyeing a man over the rim who was staring at Meg's butt in her skinny leather pants. And he wasn't trying to hide it.

"Profiting." She snorted. "That's rare. But I make a point to never walk out of a casino without at least half of what I started with, ideally as *much* as I started with."

The man licked his lips before swatting the man next to him in the stomach and starting a strut aimed at Meg.

I wrapped my arm around her lower back, resting my chin on her shoulder, hoping he'd take a hint.

Meg raised a brow at me. "Unwanted suitor?"

"Mmhm. Six o'clock and currently retreating."

"I shall do the same for you on this trip if you're fully invested in Mr. Surfer, but in the meantime, if you don't mind," Meg started before holding dice up that the dealer slid her.

I blew on them with a grin. "Yes. I'm invested."

She played for another twenty minutes, winning all of her money back plus a hundred extra dollars. After cashing in her chips, she turned to me with a wink. "I know what you want to do."

"Oh? Think you know me that well?"

"Topdeck. The view of the ocean must be crazy up there."

I played with my fingers behind my back, attempting to hide my antsy fidgeting. "I'm sure it's quite pleasant."

"Oh my God." She rolled her eyes and grabbed me by the crook of the elbow. "Come on, you."

After climbing the stairs several levels, the sight of the moon reflecting off that dark rippling water surrounding us drowned any breath before it had a chance to escape my throat.

"The views in Pensacola are amazing, but this—surrounded by water and not a shoreline insight is another matter entirely." I leaned my hips on the railing and threw my arms out to either side of me. I was Kate Winslet, and this was my Titanic moment.

"This is rather majestic. I have to admit." Meg joined me at the railing, bending forward and resting her elbows on it.

My phone buzzed in my clutch, and I jumped, snatching it.

Simon: Enjoying yourself? I'm sure the views are amazing from the top deck.

Furrowing my brow, I did a quick turn, half expecting to see him on board. He'd shown up at the tournament without a word until he was there. I wouldn't put anything past him now.

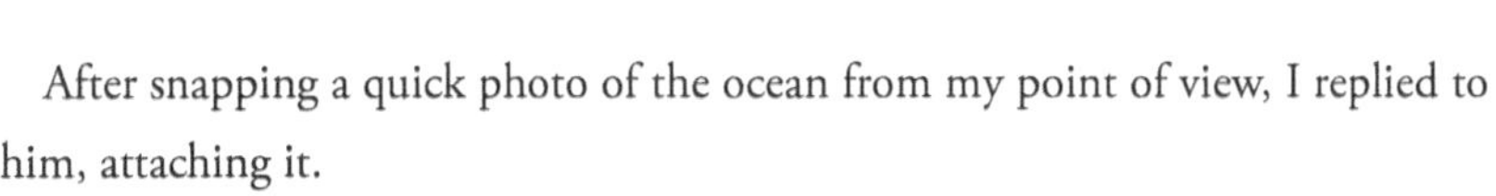

After snapping a quick photo of the ocean from my point of view, I replied to him, attaching it.

Me: You must be psychic.

Simon: :(Aw. No selfie with the ocean behind you?

Biting my lip, I quickly peeked at Meg, who was distracted by the view. Flashing a pearly grin, I held the phone out in front of me and snapped the photo, sending it to him.

Meg snorted.

I whipped my head in her direction. "What?"

"It's fun seeing you revert to what I'd imagine is a teenage version of yourself when you like someone." Meg bumped her shoulder against mine.

Heat pooled in my cheeks as I bit back another smile.

Simon: Positively gorgeous. :)

Whether he referred to the ocean or me, or both, would remain a mystery. The butterflies still performed a symphony in my belly all the same.

"Time will tell but, I do have a soft spot for this guy." Curling my hair over one ear, I slipped the phone back in my clutch and lifted my gaze in time to see dolphins leaping through the water. I slapped Meg's arm and pointed. "Look over there."

Meg gasped and slid closer to me. "How cool. I'll never get tired of seeing dolphins in the wild. They look so carefree."

I've loved all aquatic animals throughout my life, but dolphins had a special place in my heart. Meg had it right. They were carefree, jovial, and playful—everything I wanted to be and more.

"How many sharks have we cage dived with and still never swam with dolphins?" I rested my head on her shoulder, still watching the pod of four as they dove in and out of the water, communicating to each other in squeaks.

"Something we'll need to rectify when we get back."

Letting out a contented sigh, I stood and faced her. "What would you like to do tomorrow?"

"I'm not a hard woman to please, Cor. So long as it isn't something I'll embarrass myself in public, I'm game for anything." She clutched the railing and leaned back, swinging her hips to and fro.

I clicked my nails against the metal, turning my gaze away, and contemplated my next words. "Did you—happen to see the flyer in the lobby? The one for the

LGBTQ brunch?"

She raised one brow. "I did. But dismissed it considering that'd mean ditching you."

"It's not ditching me. We're still on the same boat and can meet up later. We have days on this cruise, Meg." I tugged on her jacket. "You might meet someone."

"But what the hell are you going to do then?" She hunched forward, resting her forearms on the railing and tapping her non-existent fingernails together.

"Sunbathe on this deck. I could be out here for hours and be perfectly happy."

The sun warming my cheeks, light whispers of the roiling water as the ship's engine propelled us through it, and the echoes of birds cawing as they flew overhead.

"Are you sure?" Meg squinted at me as if the sun were in her eyes.

I patted my hands against the metal to the tune of *Beyond the Sea*. "Yes. You'll have fun. I'm sure of it."

"Thanks, Cory." Meg side-hugged me, and we stood in silence, watching the ocean.

I'd been lying on the top deck for the better part of an hour, soaking the sunrays and rotating. I lay on my stomach, and a buzz vibrated my clutch. Resting my chin on my forearm, I smiled to myself. Either I'd begun to expect Simon's texts, or I recently developed a form of ESP. After swiping the screen to unlock it, my grin widened.

Simon: You can tell me to stop checking in on you every day at any point in time. You know that, right? ;)

I slid my sunglasses to my head.

Me: Would it scare you away if I said your texts are the highlight of my day?

Pinching my lips, I hovered my finger over the send button for an extra moment before pressing it.

Simon: Absolutely not. You don't have some weird taxidermy collection hidden in a closet somewhere or something, right?

I laughed out loud, noticing the empty benches surrounding me on the deck for the first time. Completely alone and free to make an ass of myself as I pleased.

Me: I'm a conservationist. What do you think?

Simon: Had to check. ;)

A loud explosion sounded from nearby, echoing off the ship's hull. I sat up with a gasp, clutching my phone to my chest to not drop it. Without thinking, I ran to the railing, searching in the direction of the disturbance.

Several motorboats bounced against the waves, speeding alongside the cruise liner. They all held large, slender devices in their hands but were too far away to make out what they were. A knot slowly coiled and tightened in my stomach.

Pirates.

I lost my footing as the ship lurched forward, picking up speed.

"Attention all passengers. If you are in your cabin, remain inside and do not leave until we give the clear. All others proceed to the lower decks immediately. This is not a drill," a voice said over the loudspeakers.

My heart raced, and I stumbled backward, fumbling with my phone.

Me: Pirates.

Simon: Pirates? Pirates, what?

Surely the cruise ship would be able to outmaneuver speed boats. The boats drifted further away, the vessel gaining distance, and I let my tense shoulders drop. The faintest sight of several large octopus-like tentacles curled beneath the boats in a barrage of sea foam and waves, launching them faster through the water. I gripped the railing, breaths escaping me.

Simon: Cory, why did you say, pirates?

I blinked away water beads forming on my eyelashes and shot my attention to my phone, dropping to my knees and crawling out of sight.

Me: We're about to be boarded.

Simon: What??? Find a place to hide, and do NOT leave for anything.

I slid my phone away and grabbed my tank top and shorts, slipping them on before crawling to the atrium.

Meg.

The anxiety roiling through me had me chilled and shaking.

They held the brunch on the opposite side of the ship, several floors down. I'd never make it to her in time.

Me: Meg, hide somewhere NOW. Don't come looking for me.

Meg: Are you out of your fucking mind? I'm already on my way up to you.

"Shit. Shit. *Shit.*"

The blast of several water cannons firing from the ship roared all around me. After finding a suitable corner, I pushed my back to it and closed my eyes, trying to calm myself enough to breathe normally. I hoped the sound of blissful silence would follow the thwart of the cannons. Gunfire rattled off the metal walls around me, and I clapped my hands over my ears.

In a language I didn't understand, various male voices spoke with urgency near the railing I'd been standing by only moments ago. I pressed my back to the wall as if it'd swallow me—shield me within its womb. The voices grew closer, and I shoved my mouth to my knees, suppressing the whimpers threatening to leak out.

A loud splash sounded, followed by one man yelling, several shots rang out, and I dropped to the floor, covering my head—thuds, screams, more gunfire, and then…silence.

The ship guards? Whoever it was, had no idea they saved me.

Slowly rising to my feet, I peered out the small circular window of the atrium door, my harsh breaths fogging it. Nothing. No men. No weapons. Simply a soaking wet deck.

"Cory?" Meg's loud whispers seeped through the door behind me.

Staying on my knees, I reached for the door handle, cracking it. Meg crouched through the atrium, turning circles, looking for me.

"Meg," I whispered back.

Meg's eyes widened once she spotted me, tears welling in her eyes—a rarity for her. She dropped to her hands and knees, crawling to me.

"Are you alright?" She gripped my shoulder, tremors lacing her voice.

"I'm glad you're here, Meg, but that was so stupid," I chastised, fear coating my heart like hardened wax.

She furrowed her brow. "You can slap my hand later. I don't know what I would've done if something happened to you and I wasn't here."

More male voices leaked through the door. I sucked in a breath and slid a hand over Meg's mouth.

The language remained indecipherable, but I picked up one word—Skylla.

My hand fell away from Meg's lips, limply landing in my lap. Why did I recognize that word?

The door flew open, and a man in a full ski mask, black jacket, pants, and

boots, holding a rifle, grabbed me by the hair, hoisting me to my feet.

Meg stood with an outstretched arm. "Take me instead."

The man babbled, waving the point of his weapon around. I winced at the pain surging through my skull from his death grip on my hair. I dug my nails into his hand in a panic, and he tugged harder.

"Please. Don't hurt her," Meg pleaded, holding her open palms up.

The man pointed down with the barrel, yelling over and over.

"Meg. Just do what he says. They're probably looking for a ransom." I'd gone beyond the point of fear. The anxiety ebbed away, replaced by numbness.

"Cory." Meg's voice cracked as she slowly sunk to her knees, her chest heaving.

"It'll be alright, Meg." Words meant to soothe us both—a hopeful declaration.

The corners of Meg's jaw bobbed as we stared at each other. The man pulled me to the deck, shoving me against the railing. My phone flew from my pocket, crashing to the wooden planks, dislodging the battery, and cracking the screen. Four men huddled in a circle, shouting, pointing, and dragging hands over their mask-covered heads.

Water sloshed over the side of the deck, a mirage following—a flash that resembled the silhouette of a human being. The men turned on their heels in a panic, aiming their weapons. One man panicked, his trigger finger twitching, sending a bullet flying—straight into my shoulder.

The pain shot down my arm, and all I could hear was my heavy breathing as I leaned back, the world circling into chaos around me. The blue sky dipped into view as my head fell back, followed by the rest of me.

A man roared the word "no" into the wind as I fell and fell, splashing into the murky waters below. Darkness overtook me, and I sank, the depths opening their watery cold embrace to me. A jolt sprung through my chest. Visions warped through my mind like a slideshow gone maniacal. Each flash was of myself—but not. Me in the Middle Ages, my dark brown hair falling in wavy tendrils to my knees. The Roman Empire. A Highlands battleground. Norway. Colonial America. The Old West. The Roaring Twenties—my hair cropped short, a fringed dress hugging my curves in a speakeasy.

My eyes flew open, and I gasped, sucking in water through my lungs like the gills of a fish.

I remember.

NINE

BREATHING UNDERWATER CAME AS easy as on land—the steady rhythm through my nose or mouth. My dark hair floated in light wisps, curling over my arms as the current washed over me—patches of bioluminescent blue scales scattered over my skin. Something stirred behind me, and I whirled around, dragging my fingers through the water and sending a swirl of bubbles. Simon floated in front of me, a cinch in his brow, staring at me with that radiant emerald gaze.

I knew him.

As I reached forward, keeping my gaze focused on his eyes, the specific part of him I recognized, his expression fell. It resembled someone who'd been punched in the gut but transgressed into shock and soon—relief.

He spun in the water, kicking up so many bubbles it impeded my vision. When he stopped, he was no longer the short-haired surfer I'd met on the beach. He appeared as I knew him with his long hair, falling past his shoulders and full beard.

"Poseidon?" I said, the water welcoming my words and not distorting them.

His brow furrowed, and he swam toward me, letting me touch the side of his face. No sooner had my skin brushed his, he closed his eyes with a contented sigh. "Amphitrite."

"I don't understand what's going on." I tangled my fingers through his wet beard. This was the man I knew. The god. My husband. My king.

I snapped my hand away and turned my gaze down. *Was* my husband. The suppressed emotions punched at my skull—hurt, abandonment, guilt.

"Amph, look at me." His large hand cupped my chin as he lifted my eyes to his.

"We have a lot to talk about, but right now, I need to stop the rest of those pirates from taking over the ship."

That first group of pirates. The mysterious force that made them all disappear.

"You've been here since I texted you. Haven't you?" I stared into his eyes, welcoming the safety they had always exuded like our hideaway grotto.

He nodded and took my hand in his. "All things we can talk about later."

Before I could say any more, he catapulted us through the water like a great white shark readying to breach the surface. We landed on the deck. With ill-practiced sea legs, I fell to my knees, sputtering water.

A memory sizzled over my brain, my knees crashing against the wet wooden planks of a classic tall ship. Night had overtaken the sky—a storm making thunder boom overhead, the rain pouring over the boat in droves. My soaked linen dress clung to my legs as I scrambled, my long dark hair stuck to my face. A burly man with a shaved head, his bronze skin caked with oil and tar despite the rain, barreled toward me, a toothless grin pulling at his lips. My chest pumped with erratic breaths as I backpedaled on my heels, colliding with the wooden mast, my neck brushing against the coiled rope around it. He snatched my wrists, and I screamed, pinching my eyes closed.

"Amph, it's me," Poseidon's voice soothed.

Refusing to look, I shook my head, trying to force the memory away.

"Amphitrite," Poseidon yelled.

My eyes flew open, and I stared up at him, my wrists held within Poseidon's delicate grasp, concern furrowed in his brow.

"This is all too much, Seid. So many years of memories. How am I going to filter through them all without it driving me mad?" My limbs went limp as I slumped to the deck as if defeated.

"Look at me." He tugged one wrist and slipped his fingers under my chin.

Doing as he asked, I lifted my eyes to his, my gaze blurring with tears.

"You *can* do this because you have to. You need to find Meg."

"Meg," I breathed out, wincing at my buzzing brain.

"Amphitrite. You *will* get through this. And I know because you are the strongest woman I've ever met. Even twice." His callused thumb circled my cheek.

I slipped my hand over his and a weak smile quirked my lip.

"But right now, sweetheart, I need you to *move*."

Meg. I couldn't lose her. It was enough to force me to my feet, holding onto Poseidon's arms as leverage.

"Meg is right around the corner. You'll have to go on your own. I can't have anyone noticing me." He pinched my chin with two fingers. "You're going to be alright. They won't get that close to you again. I promise you." His last words rolled off his tongue in a snarl.

"Go stop those assholes."

Poseidon backed away with the grace of the sea god I knew him to be and pointed at my arm. "You'll need to make those disappear."

"I—I don't know how to do that. I don't remember." I held my arms up and stared at the glowing scales, shaking my limbs as if that were the answer.

He delicately pinned my arms at my sides, the calluses on his palms making my toes curl. "Close your eyes and think about them disappearing. Will them back to the sea."

Doing as instructed, I let my lids shut and thought of nothing but the vast empty ocean. Calling to it, I beseeched it to hide my scales—my true self—until I beckoned for it again.

Poseidon's lips brushed my cheek, his beard tickling my skin. "They're gone. We *will* talk about all of it."

With a shaky breath, I blinked my eyes back open. "When?"

He was gone.

I bolted around the corner, finding Meg curled against the same wall I'd been. "Meg, it's me," I whispered, trying not to startle her.

"Cory?" Meg stared at me wide-eyed before launching at me, pulling me down, and hugging me.

"I'm okay. Everything's going to be fine. We just need to stay put." The anxiety I'd felt melted away with the knowledge of who was on board, ridding the decks of pond scum.

She peeled away and touched my face, my shoulders. "I don't understand. You're soaking wet, and I *heard* that gunshot. It took everything in me not to scream."

"They did shoot but missed. It startled me, and I fell overboard."

It felt so wrong to lie to Meg. What's worse—it was the first in a forthcoming string of hidden truths. How did someone tell their best friend they were a sea goddess in a past life? A queen? The instances she couldn't explain my connection

to sea life were because I could speak to them and control them.

"How the hell did you get back on deck, Cor?" Her eyes frantically searched my face, her lips thinning.

"You know I'm a strong swimmer. Besides, I knew I needed to get back for you." A weak smile tugged at my lips.

Lies. Lies. *Lies.*

Meg was an intelligent human being. The situation warranted her questioning expression, and I braced for the impact of her fiery interrogation techniques.

"Ladies and gentleman, the situation has been contained. We are turning course for the nearest port, and as a safety precaution, we ask all guests to migrate to the bottom deck for the duration of the trip. Upon arrival in San Juan, you will be given complimentary flight service back to Orlando and a full refund. We hope you'll still consider a future cruise with Calypso Cruises, and we deeply apologize for today's occurrence," an announcer voiced across the deck over the intercom.

"Let's get below decks." I helped Meg to her feet.

As we walked, Meg stayed deathly quiet, switching between rubbing the back of her neck and running a finger over her eyebrow.

"You okay?" I risked more questions asking this, but I couldn't in good conscience pretend I wasn't concerned. We'd gone through a life-threatening ordeal. It could rattle anyone.

"All things considered? Yeah. But I can't get past something." Meg shook her fist as if she played roulette again.

"Oh?" A barnacle formed in my throat.

I wasn't ready for this conversation. I'd yet to figure out things for myself, let alone explain it to someone who had no idea our world existed.

"There is no feasible way that boat could've caught up with the speed of this cruise ship. Not to mention the water cannons. It barely phased them. How?" She snapped her gaze to mine, her jaw tightening.

All valid questions. And the answers I knew lay with Poseidon.

"I don't know, Meg." I frowned and hugged her to my side.

When we reached the lower decks, hundreds of people scattered the tables they'd spaced throughout, including a dozen buffet counters with various foods and bottled water. It took several hours to travel back to San Juan and another couple of hours to fly to Orlando. With our vacation cut short, I accepted a job

offer to fill in for a tour guide who called in sick at an aquarium in Orlando. Meg hadn't complained much, considering she planned to spend the day with Mickey in the Magic Kingdom. I told her to grab me a pair of Little Mermaid mouse ears.

Donning my striking oversized blue polo with the Brizo Aquarium logo over my left boob, I led a small group of attendees. Two parents carted their twin toddlers in a conjoined stroller, an elderly couple who couldn't stop making googly eyes at each other, and two young women who spent more time taking selfies for social media than looking at the fish.

We approached the jellyfish tank, and my heart wrenched. Their anxiety pulsed through me in waves. They wanted to be in the open ocean. Their appreciation for being in the tank and out of harm's way was evident, but it couldn't compare to freedom. Gulping down the anger and irritation storming in my core, I drowned them out as best I could before I suddenly started Operation: Free the Fish in the middle of a public aquarium.

"A little known fact, but jellyfish are one of the oldest multi-organ animals, having been around for at least six hundred million years." I referenced the floating, gracefully flapping jellyfish with a hand, beaming at my tour group.

"Wow. Before the dinosaurs?" The older man asked, wrapping his arms around his wife from behind her.

"Yup. Even before the dinosaurs, before plants or fungi in fact, as well."

One of the young women finally lifted her nose with a sneer. "I still think they're aliens. They don't have brains or any other real guts for that matter."

"Fair point. But they do have an advanced nervous system. Does anyone know what all their receptors can detect?" I lifted my brows, waiting for an answer.

"Vibrations?" The mother of the family of four chimed in.

I pointed at her with a smile. "That's one thing."

When silence fell over them, I folded my hands behind my back. "They also help detect light and chemicals in the water. With these extra senses and their gravity navigation abilities, it's how they chart themselves through their environment."

"Have you heard of the immortal jellyfish found in the Mediterranean Sea?" A deep husky voice asked from behind the crowd.

Every nerve in my body sparked like tridents clashing.

Poseidon.

The small group of tourists stepped aside as Poseidon made his way forward.

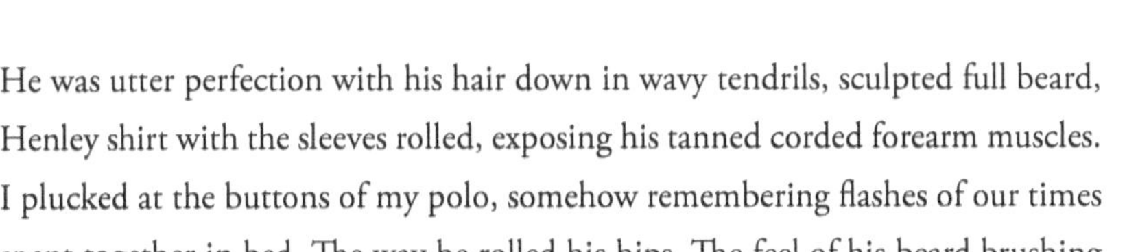

He was utter perfection with his hair down in wavy tendrils, sculpted full beard, Henley shirt with the sleeves rolled, exposing his tanned corded forearm muscles. I plucked at the buttons of my polo, somehow remembering flashes of our times spent together in bed. The way he rolled his hips. The feel of his beard brushing my inner thighs when he—

"Miss?" The older woman asked, making me jolt from my daydream.

"Yes. Sorry. I'm sorry. That concludes the tour. If there aren't any questions, please enjoy the rest of your stay here at Brizo Aquarium." With a quick, bland smile to reassure the tourists, I curled my hand with Poseidon's arm and dragged him to an alcove where few attendees walked.

Poseidon smiled wide, his bright white teeth shining in stark contrast to his darker beard. "You look adorable in that polo, but they didn't have a smaller size?" He chuckled, pointing at the length draped to my knees like a dress.

I pulled at the hem, feeling my cheeks warm. "How did you find me?"

His brows bobbed as he stared at me, waiting for me to answer my own question.

I palmed my forehead. "Right. I don't remember how to use my—" Lowering my voice, I leaned into him. "I don't remember how to use my powers."

"Amph, you're not going to have them all anyway. You're mortal." He rubbed my shoulder, a sympathetic pout melting over his lips.

Turning away from him, I flopped onto the bench facing the Mediterranean Sea tank. "You can't call me that in public, *Simon*."

Poseidon winced before sitting in the space beside me. "You finally realize who you are, and we still have to pretend. The irony."

"And why are you still in your true form? How is Simon Thalassa going to explain growing long hair and a beard overnight?" I ran my fingers through his blonde tendrils and gulped.

By Olympus, he was beautiful.

"I'll tell them magic. They'll think I'm being a smart ass and forget about it in a week. Guaranteed." He smirked and gripped the bench's edge, moving his gaze to watch the fish—a blue tint flowing over his features from the tank lights. "Besides, I don't ever want to lose that look on your face when you saw the real me and *knew* who I was."

As pleased as I was to see him and as grateful as I was to no longer be stuck in the sky as a constellation, we had such a rocky past, he and I.

"I don't know where to start with this," I whispered, my nose stinging, threatening tears.

"Yeah. Not sure there's a written protocol for a situation like this, Starfish."

The nickname made my heart swan dive, and I snapped my gaze to his, tears clouding my vision.

He gave a sheepish smile, cocking his head to one side, causing his hair to fall in glorious shambles over one eye. Reaching a hand, he swiped a rolling tear from my cheek with his thumb. "We both did some things. Some—horrible things. But it was a lifetime ago. I'd like to think we're—" He bent forward, dropping his hands between his knees.

"Getting a second chance," I finished for him.

He nodded, lifting his eyes back to the colorful fish in front of us. "If we want it."

Why would anyone not want a second chance at anything? But could we honestly work through what we'd done? And more importantly, what we'd done to each other?

"What's the last thing you can vividly remember?" He played with one of several hemp bracelets on his wrist, twirling a small shell attached to one between two fingers.

"Of which life?" I huffed a breath, disorientation roiling in my brain as soon as I tried to recall all the lives I'd led.

His jade eyes found mine. "Ours."

Pinching my knees together, I folded my hands in my lap. "Zeus exiling me to the stars. Pure darkness with the occasional glimpse of Olympus until one day I just—" I paused, glancing around us to ensure no one was within earshot. "I was a child in the Middle Ages."

"Shit. Reincarnation. Is that what happened on the boat? Did you have a memory? Thought I was someone else?" He sat up straight.

I raised my shoulders to my ears before letting them flop back down. "Yes." It came out stilted. "And I keep having these random flashes like a real-time slideshow in my mind."

He slid his hand on my knee, and I zoomed to a memory of us on our thrones in Atlantis, his hand sliding over that same knee, smiling at me. When I tensed under his touch and looked away, he slid his hand to the bench.

The skin between his eyes formed a deep groove—his expression when deep in thought. "We'll figure it out, but I think this—" He paused to point between us. "Is the more immediate hurdle to overcome."

"We're a hurdle now?"

He bumped his shoulder against me. "That's not what I meant, and you know it."

"What have you been doing all this time?" I scooted backward, making my toes barely touch the ground.

He blew out a harsh breath, making his lips vibrate. "Oh, man. Well, once mortals stopped believing in us, we all had to start disguising ourselves if we wished to stay amongst them. I've donned many hats. Military diver. Dockworker. Ship captain. Even worked as an actor for a spell."

"An actor?" I pinched my lips together, attempting to hide my smile. "You?"

He playfully nudged my chin with his knuckle. "Yeah? How's that so unbelievable, miss pro gamer?"

I gasped, feigning offense with a dramatic hand over my chest, and then…I narrowed my eyes. "You're KingofFish69."

A gooey smile played over Poseidon's lips, and he lifted a palm. "Guilty."

I rolled my eyes and leaned on the carpeted pole behind us. "You knew who I was this entire time and have been so—" My gaze fell to the horse tattoo covering the inside of his forearm. "—patient."

He nodded, beating his fist against one knee. "A lot of things have changed about me, Amph." He quirked one brow and scanned the area.

"Yeah. I can tell." Feeling bold, I brushed my pinky against the hand he rested on the bench between us.

"You have as well." Poseidon eyed our skin touching, and he curled a single finger with mine. "Maybe that's what it took. Eons apart."

"Rebirth," I said on a breathy exhale.

"Go on a date with me." His green eyes sparkled.

"A date?" A fluttery laugh escaped my throat.

"If we're starting over, we might as well go all out. Besides, we never even had a first date. I sort of—" His cheek twitched.

"Claimed me?" I raised a brow.

"I'm not proud of it."

"As long as you pick me up in a car and not a dolphin, then yes." I tightened

my one-finger grip on him.

He chuckled—deep and godly. "Deal."

The aquarium boss tossed me a glare as he pointed at the last tour group for the day waiting.

"Damn. I have to give a final tour." Standing, I turned to Poseidon towering over me.

"Tomorrow at seven work for you?" He slipped his hands in his front pockets.

I played a finger over the tip of my nose. "Perfect."

"Cool. I'll uh—I'll see you then." He dragged a hand through his long hair before turning on a heel and walking away, stealing a final glance at me over his shoulder.

Two gods torn apart for past selfishness brought together again in search of hope and serenity. Ages ago, the idea of it would've brought me comfort, but despite our history, it was as if we were meeting for the first time. I wasn't the same person as I was back then, and it was clear—neither was he. Still, the Fates gave us another opportunity to find the happiness we'd lost. Could we work through it? Could I deal with the onslaught of past life memories? Would they stop? All of it aside, I owed it to myself to *try*.

TEN

MEG AND I DROVE HOME the following day, and she regaled me with her time spent at the Magic Kingdom. I didn't tell her about Poseidon er—Simon showing up at the aquarium because it would've led to more lies about our conversation. A kept mistruth versus lying seemed a better alternative at this stage. When she dropped me off at my apartment, I walked up the stairs on autopilot, scarcely remembering how I'd reached my front door. Unlocking it, I shuffled my way inside in a daze, removing the mermaid mouse ears Meg had bought me, and resting it on the counter but missed. My bag ended up in a slump near my coffee table, missing that surface as well.

I was Michelle Pfeiffer after being brought back to life by a dozen cats in an alleyway, spiraling her way into becoming Catwoman. Only instead of cats—it was fish.

My gaze snapped to my tank, where all seven fish huddled together in a group at the frontmost glass. Squinting, I pressed a finger against the tank on the opposite side, making them all scurry to greet me.

"I'm so sorry I've kept you all in there." I scratched the glass, simulating a petting gesture.

Unlike the jellyfish at the aquarium, my fish were content in the tank—happy even. Less room than an entire enclosure at an aquarium but somehow, their presence with me this whole time mattered the most. I glanced at the analog clock with a seashell border hanging in my kitchen. Thirty minutes until Poseidon would pick me up. Nodding to myself, I snapped to attention. Thirty minutes

until my ex-husband showed up for us to start the first day of our reconciliation…
or not. My palms clammed up, heart racing, beads of sweat rolling down my neck.

Sprinting to my bedroom, I whipped open the closet doors and stared at the
array of clothing. As I shoved hanger after hanger aside, panic latched onto me
like a snapping turtle. I was still Cordelia but didn't feel like myself. A mind stuck
between two worlds, many lives, and a being once reliant on magic now rendered
almost powerless. Mortal.

Giving up on finding anything suitable for a former queen, I slammed the door
shut and stormed into my living room, plopping onto my blue sofa. Dropping my
face in my hands, I concentrated on slow, steady breathing, mentally announcing
to the tears which threatened a visit, they weren't welcome here.

My mind fizzled, and my knee pressed into the dirt, crouched behind a round
wooden shield—scents of blood, sweat, and dirt floating around me. I shouted
something in a language I couldn't translate to the woman beside me, her hair
pulled into knotted sections on the top of her head, middle, and at the nape of
her neck. Black paint smeared over her eyes,

Knock. Knock. Knock.

With a strangled gasp, I sat up, cutting my eyes to the clock. Five minutes early.
Punctual now? Poseidon was *never* punctual. Now of all times.

I headed for the front door with a grimace while rubbing my temples. The
distance, in actuality, was several feet from my sofa, but the walls appeared to
expand, creating a narrow path that seemed miles away. Peering through the
peephole to ensure it was my fish god on the other side, I whisked open the door,
hiding behind it, and peeking over the side at him.

A sparkly grin played over his lips. "Uh, hi. This a bad time?" He pressed a
forearm above my head on the doorframe, waiting for an invitation.

Remaining silent, I shook my head.

He shifted his eyes left-to-right, still waiting and still grinning.

Oh, to Tartarus with it.

I pushed the door open, revealing the same v-neck t-shirt and jersey shorts I'd
worn all day traveling. "I couldn't figure out what to wear. The last I remember
about the true me? Well, there's nothing in my closet that even comes close." It
came out far more whiny than I'd have preferred.

The smile on his face had yet to fade. "May I come in, Amph?"

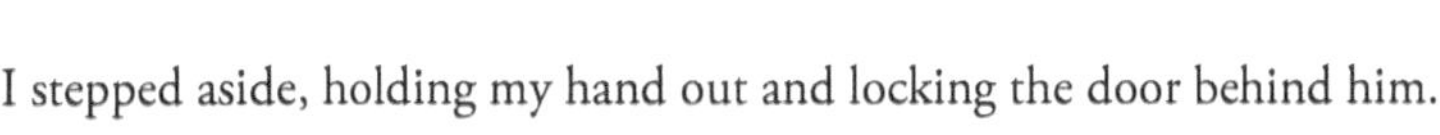

I stepped aside, holding my hand out and locking the door behind him.

"There's a reason you're not going to find togas or wispy see-through dresses." He plucked the bit of hair below his bottom lip, roaming his eyes over my body before forcing them away.

Crossing my arms in a huff, I leaned against my kitchen counter. "I know I'm in the twenty-first century. I haven't forgotten Cordelia. I'm just having a—I don't know. An identity crisis?"

"You've changed, Starfish. Cordelia is more you than the oldest version of Amphitrite." He folded his hands in front of him as if he wasn't sure what to do with them.

"That name doesn't even feel like me anymore." I frowned, moving my gaze to my fish floating in the corner of the tank near me, flapping their tiny fins.

"What? Starfish?"

I cut my eyes to his. "No. That name makes me feel bubbly as it always has."

"Well, maybe Amphitrite doesn't suit you any longer." He cocked his head to the side. From the way his right knee bounced on occasion, I could tell he was antsy. He more than likely wanted to take me in his arms and pick up where we left off—when we were happy together.

Maybe I left the name Amphitrite up in the stars.

"So, where are you taking me on this date? It'll help me decide what random piece of clothing to grab from my exploding closet."

With a swagger that'd been impossible to forget, he walked in front of me. Holding up his fingertips, they turned into water, and he bobbed his brow. "May I?"

Despite the ability to breathe underwater, staring up at him with his power surging in his palms, I forgot how to breathe land air and managed a nod.

With his hands on my shoulders, a dress materialized over my chest in splashes of water and sparkles. It traveled over my hips and didn't stop until it reached my ankles, forming a flowy train. Poseidon released a raspy breath before taking a step away, urging me with a flick of his wrist to look at his handiwork.

I traced my fingers over the radiant white and silver sparkles adorning my body. A slit ran up my left leg, stopping just below my hip, and a drape of fabric hung over my chest. "This looks like—" I gasped. "Ariel's sparkly dress from *The Little Mermaid*?"

Poseidon rubbed the back of his neck. "I figured you'd be a fan of that movie—

especially in modern times."

"You would be right." I grinned at him before twirling several times, making the train swish around me and the light catch the sparkles in the dress, bringing them to life.

"By Olympus, you're beautiful," he murmured, gawking at me. "No longer a constellation, but the stars are forever with you."

I gazed at him from across the room, picturing him with his golden crown, the matching trident with Atlantean symbols carved into its hilt, clutched in his grasp.

"You ready to talk?" He held out a hand.

It was a simple gesture, but in truth, his palm held the universe within it—a possibility to find the happily ever after I've always strived for but lost sight of so long ago. But it also held the potential for heartbreak.

Clutching one arm to my chest, I slid the other hand into his. "Are you porting us there? We're not going to drive?"

"What would you prefer, Starfish?" His grip tightened on my hand as if now that he had me, he never planned to let go.

I stepped closer to him, a breath between us. Closing my eyes to let the scents of sea spray and sun spark dozens of memories—magical midnight swims, stolen kisses on Olympus, lights glinting from his majestic gold crown. "I want to feel the magic again."

He slipped an arm around my lower back, pulling me flush against him. I fluttered my eyes open, gazing up at him.

His beard tickled the tip of my ear as he whispered, "Hold on."

My dress's train circled me as a surge of water erupted around us but didn't make us wet. The water swirled in overlapping spirals, and in a shimmer of light, we appeared on a rooftop with a single table, two chairs positioned beside each other, and a dozen candles with flickering flames.

"Where are we?" My arms were still around his waist, and I left them there as I scoped the beautiful setting.

"A restaurant." He hugged me and delicately rested his chin on my head. "I wanted it to be as normal as possible but still have the freedom to talk about *everything*, so I rented the entire building for the night."

I peeled back, squinting at him with one eye. "Mighty romantic of you, but

how are we getting food?"

His eyes turned to the stars. "That was the only part I hoped you'd be fine with not being normal?"

"Suits me fine. Both of us are lousy cooks."

We laughed in unison, only letting the chuckles dissolve when our eyes met, and a flame flickered within them. I stood barefoot in my sparkly Ariel dress on a rooftop with the King of the Seas in my arms. He splayed his hand at our feet, making his shoes disappear, and skirted a sheet of lukewarm water across the concrete.

I smiled, letting my toes splash.

"Figured it'd make it feel more like home without flooding the building." He grinned, gave a quick peck to the corner of my brow, and led us to the table.

Like two teenagers with first date jitters, we fumbled to our seats. I'd been halfway to sitting before realizing he pulled the chair out for me and had to readjust with a blushed smile. He waved his hand over the table, producing bountiful plates of leafy greens with colorful splashes of tomatoes, cucumbers, and a variety of other fruits and vegetables.

"I can see you were in the kitchen all day with a meal like this." I winked at him, unfolding the white cloth napkin and placing it over my lap.

Poseidon brushed each of his shoulders. "A lot of blood and sweat went into this meal. I certainly hope you enjoy it."

I paused the fork midway to my mouth, scrunching my nose at the mention of blood and sweat.

He chuckled, never taking his eyes off me as he took a bite. After listening to the melodic crunching with each rotation of his jaw, I followed suit. We had countless moments like this at the beginning of our marriage—so enamored with each other we couldn't get enough. How had we let ourselves grow apart?

I wanted to ask something but feared killing the moment before we had a chance to develop one. Letting my gaze fall to my plate, scraping my fork across it, I derailed—for now.

"How did those pirates get on the cruise ship? I got Bloodhound Meg off the scent, but she was right to find it suspicious."

Poseidon swiped his napkin over his mouth. "Skylla."

"Skylla?" My fork clanked as I dropped it. "I thought most of the creatures

were dead."

"Atlantis has been off the charts for decades. With it lacking the security it once had, it brought unwanted attention. I wanted to keep busy, but I never thought it'd be playing gatekeeper to creatures of the deep and the modern world." He smirked, bumping a tomato from one side of his plate to the other.

"I don't understand what was in it for Skylla, though. Aiding a group of sea thugs to rob or ransom off passengers on a cruise ship?"

Or surely, she hadn't been after me all this time? My dream of plummeting into the depths, tentacles wrapped around me—the sight of those same tentacles making the pirate boats move faster…

"You've got me there. If I had to guess, she probably made a deal. She's always wanted control of the seas, but she forgets a tiny detail." He leaned his chest on the table, sliding his hand across it to rest on top of mine. "She has to get through me."

Memories of us battling under the seas, protecting them, protecting our *family*—a pain twisted in my chest, and I yanked my hand away, pressing my back to the chair.

"Amph?" He frowned. "What is it?"

"How are our—" The words stuck in my throat, clinging to it like saltwater taffy. "—children?"

I snapped my eyes to him, a trident twisting in my gut at the sight of his solemn face.

Poseidon blew out a breath before rolling a tomato between two fingers. "Triton is doing very well for himself. He's captain of a fishing boat and loves it. I'm guessing he'll stay there until him not aging becomes alarmingly obvious."

Triton. My sweet boy. Now a grown man. A god in his own right.

"*Fishing* boat?"

Poseidon threw his hands up. "Not what you think. He goes after whalers, stops them using any means necessary that won't get them flagged by the Coast Guard."

"Why use a human boat? Couldn't he use his powers?" I ran my finger over the hem of the slit in my dress.

Poseidon tapped the table with his forefinger. "He prefers working for it. Says it means more at the end of the day. Wonder where he got that from, hm?"

Tears threatened, but I forced them back.

We had another child—a daughter. Nerves coiled my lungs, squeezing the breath out of me. "And Rhode?" She was so small the last time I'd seen her, so young.

Poseidon licked his lips, casting his gaze away from me before sliding his chair closer.

"Oh my—" I clapped my hands over my mouth. "—she's not…"

"No." He peeled my fingers from my face, holding my hands in his large grasp. "No, she's not. As I told you, anomalies have been occurring in Atlantis. She'd gone to try and fix it, despite me firmly telling her no, that it was too dangerous."

"I wonder where she got that from," I said weakly, a crackle in my voice.

Poseidon didn't smile. He didn't even look at me, his grip tightening around my hands. "Atlantis took her. She disappeared."

"What?" I shouted, pushing out of my chair, toppling it over. "What do you *mean* she disappeared?"

Poseidon stood, dragging a hand over his beard. "Atlantis is the heart of altering dimensions. It has portals. One opened and…took her."

Pacing the roof's perimeter, I slapped a hand on my forehead. "And you haven't tried to find her?"

"Of course, I have. I tore apart half the universe looking for her." His voice dropped an octave, no doubt insulted by my accusation.

Panic. Pain. Fury. Anger at *myself*. It all engulfed my senses, tore at my insides.

"And you just gave up?" I stopped and glared at him from across the space. "You should've tried harder."

He rolled his shoulders back, his nostrils flaring. "And *you* should've been there. It's one of the reasons she went. To look for you."

A tear rolled down my cheek, and I swiped it away.

"As if you were always there for them. Don't you dare put this all on me." My bottom lip trembled, and I turned my back on him.

"They were children when you disappeared, Amphitrite. I *raised* them."

The stern expression on his face brought back memories of one of our past arguments. He'd been away for days performing his aquatic duties without so much as a word to me—to us. The loneliness I'd felt far too many times to count made my gut wrench.

"I knew this wasn't going to work," I whispered.

The heat radiated from his chest, pulsing against my back as he stood behind me. "What are you saying?"

"We've done too much. I'm not even sure it's repairable. And for you, this all happened a lifetime ago, a lifetime to get past it—to accept it." I turned to face him with a scowl. "For me? It was like it all happened days ago."

The memories were all so fresh, rushing through my mind, making the present mix with the future. The last argument I remembered us having pinched my brain—both accusing the other of putting the job before family.

His jaw tightened, and he sneered at the ground.

"I know about Medusa." Further torture inflicted by Zeus during my constellation prison. Glimpses of Earth and Olympus, to witness those I loved thinking I was gone.

His eyes snapped to mine, and he shook his head. "I thought you were dead. That was years after you disappeared. It was a fling, at most."

"I know. I'm not mad because you slept with other women after I was gone. It's what Athena did to her as a result." The skin between my eyes wrinkled as I imagined what agony she must've gone through, realizing she couldn't look at anyone without them turning to stone—not to mention the head of snakes for hair.

Poseidon pursed his lips. "I'm not proud of it."

"Is she still alive?"

"Yes. Though, I haven't seen her since. She's become a recluse."

I nodded, hugging myself. "You should rectify that."

"Maybe I will," he said softly, barely audible against the harsh winds that'd picked up.

"I need you to take me home, please." A sea urchin poked at the backs of my eyelids, trying to force tears out.

"We can work through this, Amph. You just need to give us another shot." He wrung his hands together, a deep furrow forming in his brow.

"I'm not saying no, but I'm not saying yes either. I need some time, Seid. I need to process this, to—"

Before I could finish my sentence, he wrapped his arms around me, and we appeared in my apartment.

"Thank you." My throat betrayed me, making my words quiver.

He stepped back, running the back of his hand over his nose. "I'll recruit a few

more gods to help search for Rhode. I never stopped, Amph. You need to realize she can be in virtually any dimension or time period. It's like looking for a black speck of sand in a dune of tan."

"Thank you." I turned my attention to the fish tank.

"Take all the time you need. I've been waiting this long. I can wait an eternity if it comes to it."

By Olympus, how much my king had changed.

He stood in front of me, delicately placing a finger under my chin and turning my face to him. "Hey. Regardless if you come back to me or not, we *will* find Rhode."

He made it so damn difficult to be mad at him. To not simply throw the neglect I'd felt in the middle of our marriage, the loneliness, straight out the window. But no—as sweet and attractive as he was, he'd have to own up to it. I needed to be in the right headspace for that conversation. Otherwise, he'd be talking to idle ears.

"Text me when you're ready to talk." He slowly backed away, fighting the disappointed look on his face with tightened lips.

And with a blazing white flash and sea spray, the King of the Seas disappeared into the night, leaving only the sparkling dress clinging to my body as a pale reminder he was ever here.

ELEVEN

I'D BARRICADED MYSELF IN my apartment, missed my usual streaming night on Glitch, fed my fish but barely fed myself, and answered with vague one-word answers whenever Meg texted me. The knock on my door came as no surprise because it could only be one of two people. Considering Poseidon told me to let him know when, and if, I was ready to talk. Considering we were on thin ice prepared to crack—it could only be one other.

Sighing, I paused the movie *Fool's Gold* playing on Fox and slumped to the door.

"Open the hell up, Cor. You have some serious explaining to do," Meg's voice boomed from the other side of the door.

Bracing for impact, I said a silent prayer to my fish before greeting her with a forced smile. "Hey, Meg."

"Hey, Meg? Oh, can it, sister." She pushed past me, turning circles and all but sniffing the air of my apartment. Snapping her fingers, she pointed at the TV. "Uh-huh. Kate Hudson movies."

As she stormed past me for the kitchen, I was too weak to protest and leaned on the doorframe with crossed arms.

She yanked the fridge open. "You've been surviving on expired milk and olives for the past few days."

I canted my head to the side, noting how cute she looked in only her jeans, boots, and brown vest. I'd never say the word "cute" to her, though.

"Your hair is greasy, and your clothes have more wrinkles than a shar-pei

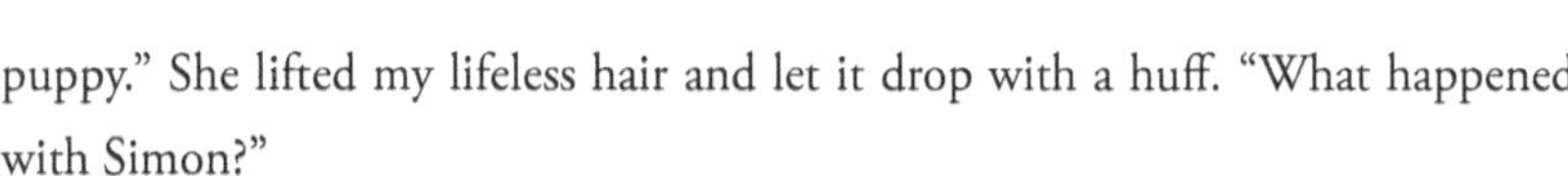

puppy." She lifted my lifeless hair and let it drop with a huff. "What happened with Simon?"

I groaned and walked past her. Without turning, she reached behind her, grabbed my shirt, and dragged me back in front of her.

"Sit." She pointed at my lounge chair. After I obliged, she sat across from me. "Talk."

"It's tough to explain." I slouched until my chin met my chest.

"Try me." She spread her legs and leaned forward, resting her arms on her knees. "You know I've been through the seven dating circles of hell."

She had. I could attest to it.

I flicked the air and let my hand drop at my side. How the Tartarus did you explain to your best friend a godly past that not only she didn't know existed but would make you sound two seas short of a horse? "We—both have things we've done in our past that we're not sure we can accept."

"You? What have *you* done he has such an issue with? Your one unpaid parking ticket? Running a yellow light?"

Or feeling neglected millennia ago, and rather than talking to my husband, I consumed myself with aquatic life?

"You know how much I love the ocean and fish, right?" I sat up, wiping my hair from my face.

"I have a vague idea, yes."

"In some of my past—relationships—I cared more about the seas more than humans, i.e., the men I dated." I squinted, knowing the odds were slim she'd feed into this.

She steepled her fingers between her knees and glared at me.

Dammit. She was *not* buying it.

"And Simon kind of has the same deal, I mean, he's been extremely consumed with his career." I shot to my feet. "If we were to date—we wouldn't be each other's number one."

Meg clucked her tongue against her cheek, stormed from her seat, and yanked me back to the lounger, sitting on the armrest. "Do you remember Cassandra?"

"Yes."

Meg hiked one knee on the armrest and moved her gaze to stare at the carpet. "Do you remember how she had a gambling problem in her past? We're talking,

she was still in debt when I met her, kind of problem?"

This relationship ended in heartbreak, so I wasn't entirely sure where she was trying to go with it.

"I do."

"It bothered me in the beginning. Really bothered me. At any moment, she could've fed into temptation, asked me for money I would've had a hard time refusing. There was also the thought of: What else could she get addicted to?" Meg wrung her hands in her lap.

"But she didn't." I nudged her hip with my shoulder. "You broke up with her because she didn't want to commit."

"That's exactly my point, Cor." She turned and smiled down at me. "That relationship lasted for three years. And it was a happy one until it wasn't, but it had nothing to do with her past."

"You're slick, Megara. Very slick." I beamed up at her.

She slapped her hands on her thighs and stood, swiveling on her booted heel. "So. What is the moral of this story?"

"Uh, something about not letting the past ruin the possibilities of a future?" I bobbed my brow.

She blinked once. "Damn. That's better than what I had brewing in my head, but yeah."

"I get what you're trying to say, I do, but—it's more complicated than simply looking beyond it." I pushed to my feet, images of Poseidon's smile swirling in my brain. He'd changed so much, but the crippling anxiety I'd felt of all those times spent alone night after night, not even knowing where he'd gone, dug into my skin.

"It's really not." She grabbed each of my shoulders, squeezing them. "Do you *want* to give him a shot? A real chance?"

The first year after our arranged marriage had been the happiest. We couldn't get enough of each other—kissing, making love, swimming together. I wanted those exact moments forever.

"Yes," I answered, my voice garbled.

"Then text him right now. Ask him to come over and to his face, ask him on another date. If he fucks up, he fucks up, but at least you gave it a *chance*, Cor."

Slipping my phone from my pocket, I puckered my lips at her. "Have I told

you lately I love you?"

"I believe you just did." She slapped my shoulder.

I opened Poseidon's text window and paused with my thumb over the screen. "Wait. This is just as much his decision as it is mine. Even if I convince myself I can deal with his baggage, who's to say he wants or *can* deal with mine?"

Meg rolled her eyes and walked to my fish tank. "Was he still giving you that dopey but handsome smile last night?"

"Maybe." I clutched the phone to my chest.

"Something tells me he'll be willing to give it a try." Meg waved at one fish, but unlike me, they only responded by opening and closing their mouths. "I don't hear those thumbs flying on your phone screen."

We could be a family again. Poseidon, Triton—Rhode. They were children when I disappeared. How did they look full grown? Would they recognize me?

I tapped the phone against my forehead, forcing the tears down, knowing there was no possible way to explain *that* to Meg. Not right now. But both she and Poseidon were right. This could be the Fates willing us another chance. There had to be a reason for my continuous reincarnations. Had to be a reason we inexplicably ran into each other on the same beach at precisely the right moment.

I started typing.

Me: Can you come over ASAP?

Simon: On my way.

"Good. I'm gonna use the head, and then I'll be out of your hair before he gets here." As Meg walked down the hallway to the restroom, she backpedaled and pointed at me. "Proud of you."

My damn palms clammed up again, and I peered into the fish tank with a deep sigh. "Think we can do this, guys?"

Their fins waved in unison.

"Always so supportive." A small smile tugged at my lips.

Ding dong.

I stood straight with widened eyes before bolting across the room and whipping open the door.

"Hey, Starfish." Poseidon stood there in a white shirt hugging at all the right places of his arms and chest, distressed jeans, and that long wavy hair hanging over one eye.

"What are you doing here already?" I whispered, snapping my head over my shoulder to check for Meg.

His eyes narrowed. "You said ASAP. I figured I'd port over." He pushed past me, lazily pointing a finger around the apartment. "Is someone here?"

His tone sounded borderline jealous.

"Don't even go there." I raised onto my toes to poke him in the chest. "It's Meg. Care to tell me how you're going to—"

"You sure got here fast." Meg stood in the hallway with her hands on her hips.

"I was at the gas station across the street when she texted. Came right over." Poseidon turned at me and winked.

"Convenient." Meg squinted at us before moving forward.

"They are, indeed. Gas stations, I mean." Poseidon clasped his hands behind his back.

I rubbed the skin between my eyes with an exasperated sigh.

"Right. Well, I'll go so you two can talk but first, Cor, can I borrow a book? I have lifeguard duty tomorrow." She stuck her tongue out.

"Of course. You know where my shelf is in the bedroom. Pick whatever you like." I gave as warm a grin as I could. "Just don't bend the spine or so help me—"

"I know, I know." Meg held her palms up in defense before disappearing into my room.

"How are you doing, Cordelia?" Poseidon folded his arms like he didn't know what to do with them.

Hearing him call me Cordelia instead of Amphitrite gave almost as many bubbles in my stomach as Starfish.

"Better. Open-minded. You?"

"Apologetic. I thought back on it. And I was a dick to you. I honestly have no idea how I could let a 'job' take me away from someone like you." He ruffled his hair, making it bunch on the crown of his head before falling in seaweed-like tendrils.

"All things we can talk over. But not right now." I shifted my eyes toward my room.

"Right. After she leaves?"

"I was kind of hoping we could go on another date?" I one-arm shrugged.

"You know I can't turn you down." His eyes brightened. "Have somewhere in mind?"

"The Quarter? They have dueling pianos on Wednesday nights and quarter beers. Between the loud music and cheap alcohol, I figured we'd be pretty free to talk but also be on a real date?"

He chuckled and bowed his head. "Clever. I like it."

The door whooshed open. "I finally left him."

A tall, slender woman with waves of dark brown hair down to her hips, full lips, sharp jawline, and pale, perfectly almond-shaped eyes stood at the doorway. Her peacock feather necklace swung as she stopped short, looking between Poseidon and me.

"Hera?" I whispered.

"Amphitrite?" She whispered back.

"I ended up with something called *Then a Hero Comes Along*? I assume it's a—" Meg stopped short with the paperback held in mid-air, shifting her gaze from us to Hera. Her throat bobbed at the sight of her, lips parting before she licked them and forced her eyes away.

"Meg, hey. Yeah, that's a great choice."

Please, Hera, do not call me by my godly name.

"Okay, but what's going on?" Meg used the book to point at each of us, avoiding eye contact with Hera.

Poseidon wrapped his arm around Hera's shoulder, wrinkling the jacket of her black and white pinstriped pantsuit.

"My sister decided to make a surprise visit. Isn't that right, sis?" He squeezed her with a wide grin.

Hera's mouth opened, not saying anything at first, staring at Meg before finally blurting, "That's right."

Meg scanned Hera from head to toe before turning her gaze on me. "Do you know her?"

The hole grew deeper and deeper with each passing lie.

"I tracked him," Hera said.

"My phone, she means," Poseidon added.

"I've got to go, but, Cory, everything alright here?" Meg raised her brows at me, staring me down.

I nodded emphatically. "Absolutely. Thanks for everything, Meg. I'll call you

tomorrow?"

She shimmied past us, but Hera broke away from Poseidon, turning to face Meg with grace only a goddess could exude. She extended her thin hand, the gold chain hanging from it catching the glint from the sun peeking through the curtains.

"I'm Hera."

Meg stiffened before shaking her hand. "Her-Hera? Like Queen of the Greek Gods?" A shaky laugh floated from Meg's belly.

She was nervous. I'd *never* seen her nervous around anyone.

Hera held onto her hand for another beat longer before tracing her thumb over a knuckle and letting go. "That's right. But also…a goddess to the life of womankind." Hera smiled, bright and sultry, revealing her perfect snow-white teeth.

A breath pushed from Meg's nose as she traced the spot on her hand Hera had caressed. "Sorry. Guess I've forgotten a lot of mythology since high school."

"No need to apologize, my dear." Hera stepped forward, her black stiletto heel clicking against the hardwood floor. "You, yourself—" She ran a finger over her bottom lip with a sultry smile. "Are a goddess."

Meg's chest heaved, extenuating her bosom beneath the vest. "Th-thank you. I really do need to get going, but Hera, it was genuinely nice to meet you." She smiled and scanned Hera's face one last time before leaving.

Hera bit her knuckle, smiling as she watched Meg leave and shut the door behind her. She pressed her back to the door, still grinning. "She is an absolute treasure. Mentally. Physically. Who is she?"

"Meg. My best friend."

"Meg," Hera whispered, running a fingernail over her collarbone.

"Care to explain what the Tartarus you're doing here?" Poseidon's voice boomed.

Hera shook her head as if awoken from a daydream. "As I said, I left Zeus."

Poseidon and I exchanged perplexed glances.

"You just—" I flicked my wrist. "Left?"

"I at least wrote him a note, if that's what you mean." Hera pushed off the door and sauntered past us, moving to the fish tank.

"I'd love to say, 'About damn time,' but he let you? Just like that?" Poseidon threw his arms out at his sides.

Hera eyed me. "Didn't Zeus banish you to the stars?"

Tunnel-vision took over my sight, warping me to that pivotal moment in time with Zeus looming over me, shouting at me, announcing my punishment. I'd not only slacked on my duties but ignored *both* warnings Zeus had given me before finally drawing the line. How could I have been such a fool? The King of the Gods had given me chances, and I hadn't taken them.

Closing my eyes to will the memory away, I gave a curt nod. "Yes. And now I'm back—" I crossed my arms in a huff. "And don't know how, but let's not change the subject from the fact you left the King of the Gods Queenless?"

Hera bent forward, waving one finger at my fish, who followed it back and forth. "Not my problem anymore. I'm sure he will have no issue finding another. The man can be rather convincing, as we all know."

"You were willing to give up the throne? A portion of your power?" Poseidon sat on the armrest of my lounger.

Hera sighed and stood straight, facing us. "You both know we were an arranged marriage—"

"So were we," I interrupted with a frown.

Hera held a hand up at me. "But, unlike you two, we never loved each other. We tried. But in the end, we led different lives, had countless lovers, and upheld our duties."

I spied Poseidon over my shoulder. He'd been staring at my hair and gave me one of his warmest smiles—like light rays pulsing beneath the surface of the water.

We had loved each other. So how did we drift so far apart?

"You asked if I was willing to give up my crown and part of my power? The answer is yes. I'd rather be completely powerless than unloved. I'm tired of it. I want something real." Hera dragged a finger under her chin.

"Wow." I rested a reassuring hand on her forearm. "I fully support it. But Zeus isn't going to have some outlandish backlash over this, is he? I remember how well he took it the last time you betrayed him."

"It's not like that this time. I told him it was happening, he called my bullshit as he usually did, but this time—I really did it." She patted my hand. "It's been three days. I've been laying low, and he hasn't tried to stop me. Believe what you all want, but he and I have both changed since we met. I think we *both* would be

happier with other people. I just hope he isn't so pigheaded to not simply settle for the first pretty mortal who bats her eyelashes at him but truly finds someone suited for him."

"He has changed. But I'd lie if I said he still wasn't pigheaded." Poseidon snorted.

"Besides, I can finally be the goddess of women and marriage alone. It's grown tiring being known only for the goddess married to Zeus and people thinking I repeatedly let him fool around on me." She rolled her shoulders back. "It's time I make a name for *myself*."

It'd been so long since I'd seen my sister-in-law. As queens to kingly brothers, we had always gotten along, vented to each other.

I raised to the balls of my feet to hug her. "This is amazing."

She returned the embrace. "I'm happy you're back."

"Do you need a place to say?" I peeled away, dabbing the tears collecting on my lashes.

"I do still have most of my power, Amphitrite." She smiled and bumped her knuckle on my shoulder. "But you—" Her lips tilted downward. "Don't? You're mortal. I don't understand."

"In all her lives, she's been a mortal. She has to accept queenhood again with Zeus's approval." Poseidon patted the tops of his thighs. "If she desires it."

I peered at him from across the room. The memories we shared, both good and bad, had my heart swelling like a tidal wave. We'd be fools not to explore it. Not only had we been a strong alliance in both love and power, but we were an unstoppable force protecting the oceans—defending Atlantis. And now creatures of the deep threatened Atlantis.

"Ah," Hera said, slowly making her way to the door. "Sounds like you two have a lot to talk about. I shared my news, so I'll be on my way, but Amphitrite—"

I turned to look at her with raised brows.

"Would you mind telling me a bit more about Meg at some point? I'd like to get to know more about her."

"If you like her, then why not ask her yourself?"

Hera pressed a hand to her chest. "I don't—I mean, how would that work?"

It tickled me to no end to see my sister and best friend show vulnerability at the thought of each other.

"Why not?" Poseidon added, catching my gaze.

Hera grinned, chewing on her thumbnail. "I'll—think about it. You two makeup and pay my ex-husband a visit." With a swoosh of her arm around herself, she disappeared in swirls of dark purple haze.

"Well, this has been an eventful day." Poseidon chuckled as he slid from the lounger, crossing the room to stand in front of me.

"I still can't believe Hera isn't Queen anymore. It's been eons."

"I know. And I'm insanely curious to see how my little bro handles this. Twenty bucks says he demands her back after day five."

My fish danced in circles through the water, making me grin. "No deal."

"Really?"

"If my return has proved anything to me, it's that we live in an entirely different universe than before. And here—anything is possible." I turned to him, running my hands down his muscular forearm. "Even Zeus listening to something else besides his dick."

Poseidon barked with laughter, cupping a hand over his mouth. "I don't think I've ever heard you say 'dick' before, Amph."

"We've *all* changed."

"Wait a minute. You said Wednesdays are dueling pianos. That's today." He pointed at the floor with a quirked brow.

"Yes. I want to go tonight. It's been long enough, Seid. Time to clear the air. *Tonight.*

TWELVE

I'D THROWN ON MY little white dress with cap sleeves to wear to The Quarter with Poseidon. He picked me up in his navy-blue Chevy Silverado truck, holding the door open for me both in and out, and yet again as we entered the bar.

"You're laying the charm on thick tonight, Simon. Hoping to get lucky?" I elbowed him in the side.

He slipped a hand over my lower back, making a breath catch in my throat. "I'd like to think I already have, but I'd be lying if the thought of you underneath me again doesn't entice me." His beard brushed against my nape as he whispered into my ear.

I'd be lying too if I said the thought didn't ignite every possible nerve in my body.

The sight of the shoreline in the distance caused me to freeze. A pale mirage of my children playing in the tide shimmered over my mind, my daughter barely old enough to walk, her older brother helping her up whenever she'd fall on her butt. A whimper fluttered from my throat.

"Cory?" Poseidon's hand pressed between my shoulder blades, kneading my muscles.

Sniffling, I gave him a warm smile and squeezed his arm. "I'm fine. Let's get inside, hm?"

As we stepped through the doorway, the loud sounds of two pianos playing, accompanied by men singing and the murmuring crowds, pulsed in my ears.

"You want a drink?" Poseidon pointed at the bar extending the room's length

except for the dance floor in the corner.

"Absolutely." I slipped my hand into his, letting him lead me through the droves of people standing near the stage, others leaning on hi-top tables with varying colors of plastic cups filled with watered-down beer.

The Quarter's décor made it feel like stepping back in time—stained glass domed lights, ornate patterns carved in the wood ceiling, framed advertisements circa eighteen hundred. Even the bar itself had old-fashioned brass fixtures for the beer taps.

"Here we go. I do believe someone mentioned cheap beer." Poseidon grinned, making his bicep peeking from the aquamarine v-neck shirt he wore bulge as he handed a blue plastic cup with a handle to me. "They had a bunch of colors, but I got us both blue."

"Thanks." I smiled, taking the cup with both hands.

All tables were occupied, so we found a vacant spot near a pole to lean against, watching the show. Two white pianos faced each other while two men sang *The Joker* by the Steve Miller Band. Each piano had a glass jar filled with cash and request cards rested at each table. Poseidon's burly arm wrapped around me from behind, pulling me against him. He let his hand rest on my hip.

"I truly am sorry for neglecting you," his low voice rumbled in my ear.

I shook my head, trailing my fingers over the masculine scattering of hair on his arm. "I'm the one who should be sorry. I should've come to you. Talked things out. Instead—"

He took my words away by pressing a kiss to my temple and gripping me tighter.

"Daddy Poseidon." I simpered. "I'll never forget the mesmerizing look on your face when Triton was born. Or the way you held tiny Rhode as if she'd wither in your arms. You looked like a Titan holding a glass statue."

Every time I brought up Rhode, it carved another piece of my heart away. But I knew there was little I could do in my mortal form. If I wanted any hope of helping to find my daughter, I *knew* what I would have to do.

"Do you remember teaching Triton how to swim?" He rested his chin on my shoulder.

I chuckled, making a strand of hair fall over my gaze. "How could I forget? He wanted to use the full course of his power before he learned to swim normally and

almost took out an orca."

It was one of the last memories I had of my son, years shy of being a godly version of a teenager. And Rhode had been *half* his age.

Poseidon curled the loose hair over my ear and kissed the tip of it.

"Thank you."

"I figured your hands were tied up, and you wanted to see the show." He shrugged, gesturing toward the stage with his cup.

"Not for the hair."

"Then what, Amph?" He lowered his voice when saying my name, pressing the bridge of his nose against the side of my head.

"For raising them. I really wish I could've seen them grow up. Mature into gods." I sniffled back tears.

"You don't have to thank me for that. In all honesty, it made me more involved in their lives than I may have been otherwise." He turned my head to look at him. "And don't think they won't be ecstatic to see you. *Both* of them."

See them again—my children. A family I hadn't remembered having until only days ago. The thought excited me as much as it terrified me to my core.

A group of women at a nearby table gawked, giggled, and whispered over the man standing behind me. Poseidon hadn't seemed to notice the attention—but I did. One woman bit her lower lip, idly licking the corner of her mouth and standing as if she were coming over to pounce on him.

I wanted to kiss him—to show all he was mine. My king. My children's father. My—.

"Holy shit. When did you get back?" A man slid in front of us, blocking the woman's path. His long, dark wavy hair with blonde streaks fell past his collar bone.

Dionysos.

"You expected me back?" I raised a brow.

His dark eyes squinted at me as his lips curled into a mischievous smile. "Nothing, and I do say nothing, Pops cooks up is ever final." He winked before slapping Poseidon's shoulder. "Look at you rocking your true self. I have to say, man, the beard is where it's at." Dionysos ran a hand over his own dark facial hair.

Poseidon shifted behind me, his crotch pressing against my ass before disappearing again. "Not as if I have to ask, but what are you doing here, Dion?"

"The Quarter on a Wednesday night? Debauchery and delights to be had 'o

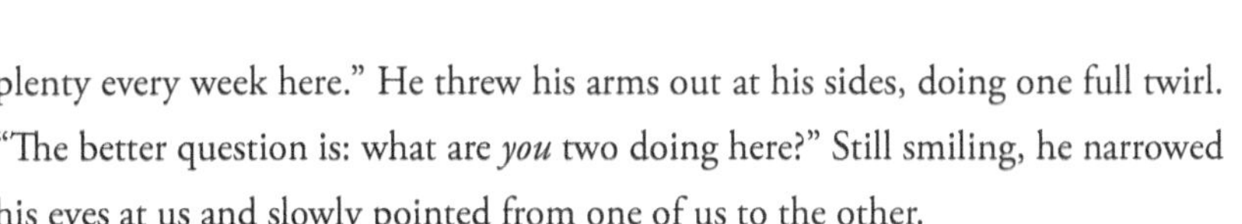

plenty every week here." He threw his arms out at his sides, doing one full twirl. "The better question is: what are *you* two doing here?" Still smiling, he narrowed his eyes at us and slowly pointed from one of us to the other.

"I didn't remember who I was until recently. We're—working things out."

Poseidon gave me a reassuring squeeze.

"Fuck. You didn't *remember*? That's heavy." Dion scratched his chin with the tip of his thumb.

"And she's mortal," Poseidon added.

Dion bobbed his brows. "Double fuck."

"But I remember everything now. Even when I was in the stars."

"The stars. What the shit was that like?" Dion took a swig from his beer bottle.

A chill shot down my spine as I conjured those moments trapped in space and time.

"You're aware but the most relaxed you've ever felt in your entire life. Content yet—distant." My grip tightened on my cup, making the plastic squeak.

Poseidon rubbed my lower back.

Dion tapped his finger against his lips before raising his cup, gesturing at Poseidon. "Yamás."

Poseidon glared at him before tapping his cup against Dion's. "Yam—ás. What are we toasting to?"

"Your cup is now enchanted to turn any liquid into ambrosia wine. How can you two let loose and air out dirty laundry if only one can get tipsy, eh?"

Poseidon stared into his cup and sniffed it. "Yup. Ambrosia wine."

"How is getting drunk going to solve anything?" I asked.

"You two have a wicked past. Trust me. You'd be surprised what a little shield lowering will do for the soul." Pressing a hand to his chest, Dion gave a mock bow. "Now, if you'll excuse me, I have a red-head to show how to have a good time." He turned away.

"Hey, Dion. Your horns are showing." Poseidon pointed to his head.

Dion froze and felt each side of his forehead before glaring at the sea god and pointing. "Trying to pull a fast one on me, are ya?"

"It worked." Poseidon chuckled, making the rumble from his chest vibrate at my back.

"You two kids have fun." Dion scooted past us and waved his arm above his

head. "Chels, over here."

We stayed silent for several moments before Poseidon cleared his throat. "We don't have to drink."

"I don't often say this, but I think Dion's right this time. Maybe it'll help us relax and bring us back to our old selves." I held the cup in the air to toast.

"Except for the neglecting, ignoring, and refusing to talk parts," Poseidon added, raising his drink.

"Except for those."

We tapped our cups together and, in unison, pronounced, "Yamás."

An hour later…

My cheeks warmed, and my head fuzzed just enough to make me giggly. "Do you still have that pet dolphin?"

Poseidon sat on the stool next to me, slurping on his fifth ambrosia wine. "Delphinus?" He snorted. "He was never my 'pet.' I specifically created him because I knew you couldn't resist that face."

I squeezed his cheeks with one hand. "I resisted yours."

"You gave in eventually." He smiled and pretended to bite one of my fingers.

I stroked the hair on his chin. "I should've thanked Delphinus when I was up there."

"As if he could've strolled on by." Poseidon snickered as he kneaded my hip.

Making an exaggerated pout, I added, "I'm serious."

"Thank him for what, Starfish?"

"I always thought when he told me marrying you would bring peace and harmony to the seas was simply a ploy but now—" I locked gazes with him. "I realize he told the truth."

"Hm. You're right. I should've thanked him more too." Poseidon beamed with a mischievous sparkle in his eyes. "I know you said you started playing video games to escape, but if I'm being honest—it still surprises the hell out of me."

"Why is it so surprising?" I tugged his beard.

He narrowed his eyes at me, playfully poking me in the ribs, making me yip. "I know you're not the same woman I married, but I never knew you to be into games of any variety."

Letting out a rolling sigh, I rested my head on his shoulder, watching the dueling pianists. "And this is the part where I need to remind you of your continuous absence back in the day."

"Shit," Poseidon grumbled, adjusting himself on the stool, making me bounce.

Raising my head, I flicked my hair at him and poked between his pecs.

So. Much. Muscle.

"Uh-uh. You made this bed, and now you're going to listen to it." I looked skyward. "Or something like that."

He chuckled, beating his fingers against the side of my ass. "Let's hear it."

"When the kids were little, I made up all sorts of games to keep them entertained. Seashell puzzles, catch the seahorse, guess the fish. But one they particularly enjoyed—" My brow pinched, just now remembering what I'd called the game. "—was Heroes of Atlantis."

"What?" Poseidon bumped his knuckle under my chin. "You called it that?"

I nodded, absently staring at his collar bone. "I conjured play weapons for them and water monsters, and we'd fight for Atlantis." Laughing, I pressed a hand to my chest. "Usually, they'd wind up fighting each other, but those are some of my best memories with them."

"Olympus, Amph. I'm an asshole." Poseidon made a clicking sound with his teeth, his gaze dropping to my hand resting on his shoulder.

"I wouldn't have called you a full-blown asshole, Seid. More like—a work in progress. And one that I loved."

He squeezed my thigh. "I'd give anything to have had even one of those moments with the kids and you."

"I'm an adult, and I still play games. Who's to say they don't still, too?" I kissed the tip of his nose.

"You, Jewel of the Sea, are something else." His hand trailed over my lower back.

My skin burned for him, but my brain kept telling me to wait—take this slow.

Playfully swatting him in the shoulder, I slid from my stool. "Be right back. I have to use the little girl's room."

"Want me to walk you?" Poseidon turned on his stool, interlacing his hands between his legs.

"I think I can handle it, Big Guy, but thanks." I flashed him a grin over my shoulder before ascending the stairs.

The line was out the bathroom door along a railing that overlooked the bar

floor. Poseidon remained on his stool and smiled to himself, tapping his fingertips against his thighs.

What are you thinking about?

A grin tugged at my lips and faded as a group of women walked up to him.

A gal leaves her guy alone for thirty seconds, and the circling lady sharks go in for the kill.

Poseidon waved his hands before pointing up, saying something to them I couldn't make out. He grabbed two cocktail napkins and scribbled his signature before handing them to the women. One pouted, another shrugged, and the third hadn't stopped smiling so wide it made her eyes form slits. Once they left, Poseidon looked up, spotting me and waving.

I wiggled my fingers at him, feeling my cheeks turn rosy. After waiting another ten minutes, forcing me to pinch my knees together and waddle like a penguin I had to go so badly, I was finally able to do my business and return to my awaiting sea god.

"There you are. I was beginning to think you fell in." Poseidon snorted, turning his back to the bar and resting his elbows on it.

"Wow. You even make dad jokes now." Grinning, I tugged on his shirt's hem.

"The next song is a requested dedication to an exceptional lady named Cordelia," one of the piano players announced.

I snapped my attention to Poseidon, who held a finger over his lips in a shoosh gesture. As soon as the first few notes played, tears filled my eyes, and my chest tightened.

Beyond the Sea.

"How could you possibly know that's my favorite song?" I propped myself on one of his knees, sitting on his lap and curling my arms behind his neck.

He slid an arm around me. "I heard you hum it. Couldn't think of a more suiting song."

As the piano players sang, I closed my eyes, swaying to the soothing melody.

"Beyond the stars. Beyond the moon. The sea really did lead us together, Starfish." His warm palm pressed against my cheek, making me flutter my eyes open.

"And it will never tear us apart again." Pressing my hands to each side of his face, I slid my lips over his.

The kiss ignited endless memories blazing through my mind, but the one which stuck out the most was the first time we'd kissed—truly kissed. Our wedding hadn't counted. It was the time Poseidon strolled on the beach with me, swam with me—made the entire day fully about me alone. The moment we realized our marriage had blossomed into something unexpected—a love for each other.

He pulled me tighter against him, snaking his free hand through my hair, massaging my scalp. The kiss began as subtle and sweet but now turned carnal and ravenous. Flutters exploded in my stomach, my skin, my body, remembering him, craving for him again. I peeled away, pressing my forehead against his. His green eyes stared lazily at me, his tongue skirting his lower lip.

"Swim with me, Seid," I whispered.

He traced my jawline with a single finger. "It's nearly midnight."

"I seem to recall midnight being the *perfect* time for a swim." I combed my fingers through his ash-blonde waves. "And the ocean has no choice but to behave as you see fit."

His fingers trailed up my spine, his hand wrapping the back of my neck. "Do you want me to give you fins?"

"I'd be disappointed if you didn't."

"Then what are we waiting for?"

Biting my lip, I hopped from his lap. He slapped cash on the bar top to cover our tab, and as the piano players brought *Beyond the Sea* to a close, it served as exit music while we whisked out the door hand-in-hand. As soon as we rounded the corner to a deserted alley, Poseidon ported us to the shore.

The bright moonlight bounced over the lapping waves hitting against the sand. Without care or thought or worry, I slipped the dress over my head and opened my hand, letting it drop. Standing in only my bra and underwear, I raised a brow at Poseidon's stunned expression.

"Not what you remember, Seid?" I crossed my arms over my stomach.

His callused fingers took a gentle hold of my arms, and he slowly parted them, staring at my bared tanned midriff with a heat building in his gaze. "No. You're exactly how I remember, Amph. I'd forgotten how much I missed you." His throat bobbed as he let his eyes roam.

"I missed you too, Seid." I stepped forward, playing my fingers over his arms. "Now, take your shirt off."

He grinned—bemused and satisfied. "I like this new commanding side to you." He reached over one shoulder, bunching the fabric in his large hand before yanking it over his head and throwing it in the same pile as my dress.

Pure. Tanned. Male perfection.

Whether it'd been the alcohol fueling my boldness or the memory of how attracted I'd been to him when we were together, for either reason, I traced my hands over his beefy sculpted arms, the ridges of each abdominal muscle.

"I love when you do that," he said through a growl. Walking behind him, I dragged a finger over his skin. "Touch me like I'm Poseidon the man, not the god king."

I paused at his words, flashing a warm smile at him. A black trident tattoo started between his shoulder blades, its hilt traveling the length of his spine. "That's new."

"Oh, yeah. I couldn't be the only brother without tattoos. And I made sure to outdo them both." He winked at me over his shoulder, extending his hand to me.

"Of course, you did." As I slipped my palm against his, the moon brightened at our touch.

"You ready?" Poseidon nudged his chin toward the awaiting ocean.

"More than ever," I whispered, longing for the feel of salt and silk against my skin.

We walked to the water's edge and didn't look away from each other as the water enveloped us with each step taken. When the water reached my chest, I let go of his hand and dived in, welcoming the scales I'd commanded away to appear again. They'd glowed before but now shone with a radiance stemming from the moonbeams and my own gradual acceptance.

Poseidon joined me, smiling as his hair floated in wisps behind him. He touched my hip, turning my legs into a teal mermaid's tail. In my past life as a sea goddess, I'd often give myself a tail to swim alongside the dolphins, to keep their pace. There was something especially tantalizing about him *gifting* it to me.

Dragging my arms through the water, I flapped my fins, turning several times in a full circle, kicking up bubbles. Poseidon chuckled before wrapping a single arm around my bared stomach, twirling with me, kneading the middle of my back with his strong fingers.

"I'll race you," I flicked my tail at him.

His smile spread wide. "A mortal demi-goddess with a tail versus the King of the Seas? That's almost fair."

"You're on, KingofFish69." I flapped my tail again, sending a shockwave through the water at him.

It pushed him back, and he tightened his muscles to stop, raising a brow at me. "You're never going to let me live that down, are you?"

"Probably not. Three, two, one," I quickly counted down before darting through the water, my arms pinned at my sides, and letting the tail work its magic.

It didn't take long for Poseidon to catch up. He swam on his back beneath me, his hands interlaced behind his head, a smug grin on his lips.

"Hey there." He waved at me.

I glared at him before banking to the right, kicking the tail into overdrive.

He appeared at my side, his muscular arms cutting through the water like pushing aside clouds. With his arms wrapped around me, he tackled me. In a bout of laughter and a pretend struggle on my part, he catapulted us into a grotto. We landed on the sea bed, him on top of me, straddling me, his arms caging me in on each side of my head. I flicked my tail between his legs and gleamed up at him.

"I've missed you, Amph. Truly missed you."

I slid a hand over one of his forearms. "I mi—"

"Well, well. It must be my lucky day," a woman's voice echoed off the stone surrounding us.

Poseidon's face morphed into a predator—cold and angry. He shot to his feet, making his golden trident appear in his grasp.

Several curling dark tentacles like an octopus emerged from the shadows, followed by six limbs with snapping dragon heads on the end of each one. Attached to the tentacles was the torso of a topless woman, her long black hair shielding her breasts when it grazed over them.

"Skylla," I gasped, pushing off the seafloor and floating near Poseidon.

"Imagine my surprise when the word on the waves was that Cordelia Bourne was more than some petty mortal. Amphitrite. Queen of the Seas." Skylla's blood-red eyes glowed, her pointy fingernails clacking together as she petted one of the dragon heads. "You've somehow avoided my wrath."

Poseidon ushered me behind him with one arm. "I'd watch your tone, sea witch."

"Ah, yes. You don't know. Your lovely former goddess is the reason *why* I'm a witch, as you so graciously describe me."

It'd been an accident. I never meant for her to turn into—this.

"What the Tartarus are you barking about?" Poseidon slammed the trident's hilt against the stone floor.

"I have a chance to be something in these seas with only one sea god to contend with. And now that I know the Queen is back? I will end her while she's vulnerable before she decides to do something stupid."

Skylla let out a howl like a canine before the dragon heads snapped in our direction. Poseidon turned to me with a growl and wrapped us in a dome of water. We splashed onto the floor of my apartment, my elbows smacking against the wood. My feet slid as I stood, the mermaid tail a distant memory.

"I don't know if I can do this," I stammered, wiping away the water collected on my brows.

Flashes of war on land, on the water—swords clashing, people screaming in agony—it all punched at my mind, making me collapse to the floor.

"Amphitrite, what's wrong?" Poseidon was at my side, but the sporadic memories continued.

Each memory, each life led, scorching my brain with bright flashes of white in between. I clutched my head, screaming, trying to make it stop.

Stop. Stop. *Stop.*

"Amphitrite," Poseidon roared, shaking my shoulders.

The memories faded away, and I blinked my eyes open, staring up at Poseidon. His jaw tightened, and he rubbed my arms. Something wet collected on my lower lip, and I touched it—warm and red. Blood. My blood.

"Fucking Olympus." He held me firm, and I was glad for it. Otherwise, I may have slunk to the floor in a heap. "Are you alright?"

The question confused me. I shook my head. "I've lived so long as a mortal, Seid. Through so many lives. Battling sea creatures—real battling—dealing with the other gods, Olympus, the politics and procedure, and I—" My chest heaved, and I stared in horror at the puddles collected on my rented apartment floor.

It took several attempts to stand before Poseidon relented, letting his hands fall with a sigh. Sprinting to the linen closet, I returned with every towel I owned, dropping them on the floor and hurriedly mopping up what I could.

"Amphitrite," Poseidon beckoned, his half-naked form moving to stand beside me.

Ignoring him and the tears welling my eyes, I continued to dry the floor.

"Cordelia." He snatched my arm, halting me.

I looked up at him, numbly holding a soaked towel in my grasp.

"If you decided to take the title back, no one is saying you'd need to battle sea creatures…unless you want to."

Whimpering, I tossed the towel to the floor and turned away from him. "It's so confusing. At one moment, I want it all back. You. The seas. Our family. Queendom. But then I remember how settled I've become in leading a semi-normal life."

"I can't sympathize. But I am jealous you've gotten to experience the beauty that's mortality." He wiped his hand over his chest, ridding it of water beads.

"I need to get some rest."

His jeans clung to his legs, making a puddle collect at his feet. Scampering for another towel, I batted his feet until he lifted them. "Let me stay here, Amph. I can sleep on the couch."

"Stay? Here? Oh, I don't know…," I trailed off, clutching a wet towel under my chin.

"Skylla threatened you. And until you work through these memories, it's better if I'm here to snap you out of them. Your nose bled this time. *Bled*, Amph."

"What is Skylla going to do? Climb up the apartment building with her tentacles in open view?"

He rested his hands on my shoulders. "If she knows, others might too. You know as well as I do, there are far more spiteful gods than not. The chance to take out a Queen before she's Queen again?" He furrowed his brow.

"This is what I'm saying. I didn't even think about that. I haven't *had* to."

"Let me stay."

I gulped, staring up at him as his fingers brushed my skin. "Fine. But we're both adults here. Just sleep in the bed with me."

"Are you sure?" He cleared his throat and rubbed the back of his head.

"Can I trust you?"

He frowned. "Yes."

"Then get in the bed, Seid."

After drying off our hair and clothes, we each took opposite sides of my bed. I turned my back to him, pinching my knees together once I felt the bed dip from his heavy frame.

"I did have one question before we go to sleep," his voice rumbled next to me.

I turned on my side, resting my head on my hand. "Yes?"

"Skylla said you're the reason she is what she is. That true?" He slipped one hand behind his head, making his bicep twitch before turning to look at me.

"It was an accident."

There was no hiding the surprised look on his face. He turned on his side to face me. "Mind giving the quick version?"

"It's silly, but—I thought you were having an affair with her. When she, you know, was just a nymph?"

"I was a lot of things, but a cheater wasn't one of them."

I patted his arm. "I know. I know. But I was so upset you were never around, and I didn't know where you were. Rumors flew. I actually believed them and got jealous." My cheeks flapped as I blew out a breath.

"It's okay." He caressed my cheek with his thumb.

"It's not okay. I slipped these herbs into one of her drinks. They were supposed to give her bad acne or gas or huge bags under her eyes." I shook my head. "And worse, it wasn't supposed to be permanent."

"Well, you're right. That's pretty messed up, but it was a long time ago. Leave it to a mythical being to hold a thousand-year-old grudge."

"Did you *see* her?"

"Then take your own advice. Apologize."

I flopped to my back. "You think that'd make her stop? She wants us *both* gone. I'm just the easy target right now."

"You don't have to be."

I turned my head with softened eyes.

"Just promise me you'll think about it more?"

"Of course, I will."

He nodded once and kissed my forehead. "Goodnight."

"Goodnight," I whispered back, numbly turning off the lamp on my nightstand.

I lay in the dark with my hands folded atop my stomach, watching the steady rise and fall of the sea god beside me. A man who could conjure typhoons and

hurricanes, crash aircraft carriers, or summon any sea monster of his choosing—wanted me back. He wanted me ruling at his side. But most of all—he wanted to be a family.

THIRTEEN

I AWOKE THE FOLLOWING day with my butt nestled against Poseidon's hips, his large arms wrapped around me, and his breath scaling the back of my neck. During the happy years, there were so many mornings like this. Only the golden pillars of Atlantis would greet me versus a humble apartment bedroom. Could I go back to it? It sounded absurd, but was I still made for the life of royalty? Of a goddess?

"Is this okay?" Poseidon's gruff voice mumbled near my earlobe.

I smiled to myself, nuzzling closer and pulling his arms tighter around me. "More than okay."

"Survived the night without any more sea hags threatening your life. That's a plus." He grinned into my hair, inhaling me.

"Oh, good. You two are already sleeping together. Progress," a woman's fluttery voice filled the room.

We sat up, and I clung the sheets to my chest like I was naked. Poseidon conjured his trident, darting all three prongs at the throat of the blonde woman standing at the foot of the bed.

Her hands splayed and waved in front of her, producing a red wall of swirling glitter like a shield. "Woah there, spinach chin. It's Aphrodite."

"Aphrodite?" I kicked the covers away and rustled to standing, smoothing my hair out. "What the hell are you doing here? And in the middle of my bedroom, for that matter?"

Poseidon narrowed his eyes, keeping the weapon aimed at the love goddess.

"Seriously, P?" Aphrodite pointed at the prongs.

"Answer her question," Poseidon barked.

Aphrodite fluttered her fingers, making the glittering shield disappear, and crossed her arms in a huff. "Yeesh. You do the family a favor and get a trident at your throat."

"What favor?" I cocked a brow.

"I'm sure you've been wondering how you got out of the stars where my dear dad so graciously banished you?"

I stole a glance at Poseidon, who didn't take his gaze from Aphrodite, his grip tightening on the trident's hilt. "The thought crossed my mind."

Aphrodite pointed at her chest. "You're lookin' at her."

"You? But why?" I tapped a finger against my lips.

"Why? I had to have a reason? I *am* the goddess of love. Give me a little cred?" She hung her thumbs from the belt loops of her pale pink skinny pants.

Poseidon grumbled, making the trident disappear in shimmering sea spray. He stood and crossed the room to stand next to me.

Aphrodite pressed her palms together, curling her hands under her chin with a sparkling grin. "I can't tell you how happy I am to see this."

"Don't get too excited. We're not *together*." Poseidon ran his fingers through his hair, followed by his beard, quickly grooming himself.

Ouch. He'd spoken the truth, and I gave him no clue to the contrary, but the words still stung like the wrath of a man o' war.

"You're right. I suppose you'd have been naked when I popped in. Poo." Aphrodite stuck her bottom lip out as she tapped her white heel against the hardwood floor.

"Are you going to explain how you did it?" I scooted closer to Poseidon, aching to feel his warmth against my skin.

"I'm rather proud of myself." She ruffled her wheat-colored locks and clapped her hands together. "With my dad's power, there are always loopholes. It keeps him from being all-powerful. He turned you into a constellation, right? Which made your organic form non-existent. To pull you straight from the stars as you were was impossible, especially the goddess part." The golden heart pendant hanging around her neck swayed on its chain as she paced.

"Go on," I encouraged, fishing for Poseidon's finger and curling mine around

it once I'd found it. I caught a quick smile on him from the corner of my eye.

"It was a simple reincarnation spell. You'd be reborn as a mortal. A demi-god. And all you'd have to do is find Poseidon, agree to become Queen again, schlep on over to Zeus, and *boom*, done deal." She made explosion gestures on each side of her head. "Nifty, right?"

"As much as I appreciate what you did, did you honestly think it'd have been that easy to find Poseidon in one lifetime?" I pressed my cheek against Poseidon's arm. "I couldn't remember who I was, and he didn't know I was alive."

Aphrodite snapped her fingers. "A small oversight on my part, but with continual reincarnations, it gave you all the time you needed to come together. However, I didn't know the opposing curse annoying Athena invoked at the time." She rolled her eyes and stared at her fingernail, flicking something from it.

"What curse?" Poseidon stepped forward.

"On you, surfer boy."

Poseidon chuckled, looking at me and pointing to himself. "Me? She put a curse on one of the kings?"

"Yes. That whole Medusa business? My sister is a rather smart cookie. Medusa wasn't the only one punished for your little frolic in Athena's temple."

It hadn't bothered me. We weren't together. He didn't know I was alive. It still didn't make the green-eyed monster any less ferocious.

"Out with it, Aphrodite," Poseidon snarled.

"Okay, okay." Aphrodite held her hands up and flicked her hair. "She knew she couldn't punish you to the lengths she did Medusa, but when she heard about my spell—she cursed you. As many times as Amphitrite would be reincarnated, if you saw her, you wouldn't recognize her. Until you became a changed man— selfless, humble, loving." She shifted her weight to one hip, tapping a fingernail against her cheek. "She never did specify if it was one or all of those things."

"Are you fucking kidding me?" Poseidon clenched his fists. "I could've found Amph hundreds or thousands of years ago? We could've already been together?"

"Fraid so, P. But hey, you finally found each other, right? Though, why the Tartarus aren't you Queen again yet?" Aphrodite raised her thin, sculpted brows.

"It's complicated," I mumbled.

"I can't believe her. You better believe I'm giving Athena a piece of my mind." Poseidon started pacing, dragging his hands over his face and beard.

"Seid." I touched his forearm, willing him to stop moving and look at me. "You said it yourself. My banishment to the stars had a positive spin to it. It made you a loving father and a changed man. If we would've met before we *both* had changed—this may have never worked."

The skin between Poseidon's eyes cinched, and he took my face in his hands. "You're right."

"Okay, so what exactly is complicated about this? Do you two realize how much love is coursing through this room? It's almost strangling me."

Poseidon winced and shook his head, pressing a palm to his temple. His hands fell away from my skin with a grimace. "You've got to be kidding me. Elani has the worst timing."

"Elani? She talked to you too?" Aphrodite leaned against my bed frame.

"Yeah. She wants me to turn her. I just didn't think it'd be that quick." Poseidon rubbed the back of his head.

"If Elani's anything like my son, once she knows what she wants, she goes for it." Shooting her gaze to me, Aphrodite grinned.

"You're leaving? Right now?" I asked, trying to hide the disappointment in my voice.

"Five minutes, Starfish." He kissed my forehead. "I promise I'll be back. It's a favor for Eros." He backpedaled, holding five fingers up before he disappeared.

"Eros? What's going on, Dite?"

She played with the heart charm, working it back and forth on the chain. "My son found true love."

"Found? What about Psyche?"

Aphrodite coughed and scratched the back of her head. "Mistakes were made, obstacles overcome, but the important thing is he found Elani. She's a gem."

"And she's mortal…" I trailed off, turning away and walking into my living room.

"Listen. I'm not exactly the best to give relationship advice, but—" Aphrodite followed me, making exaggerated steps by planting her heel first.

"Shouldn't you be *the* best, goddess of love?" I bit back a smile as I trickled fish food into the tank.

"You would think, but most people find the lack of my own relationship distrusting. Go figure." She snorted. "But all I wanted to ask was why you're so

afraid. You were born for this, Amphitrite."

"I know. And everything about it feels like home but—" Bunching my shirt at my stomach, I stared at the fish. "I don't want to revert to that old version of myself."

"Phi." Aphrodite tapped my shoulder, causing me to turn on my heel to face her. "You've lived over a dozen full lives. Have experienced virtually everything a mortal can. What makes you think for a moment you haven't learned from all these lifetimes? You won't do it again. And neither will Poseidon. As flawed as he was, he missed you like Tartarus."

A weak smile pulled at my lips. I *did* want to calm the seas once more with him at my side.

"And despite Zeus hounding him every other year to marry another Queen, he refused. Got pretty ugly up there on Olympus a time or two. Those two can fight like bulldogs, I swear." Aphrodite blew out a breath.

He never married again. Not even for politics's sake.

"About these other lives—" I turned to face her with folded arms. "I get flashes of memories so vivid it's as if I'm reliving them. It's damn near debilitating. I couldn't risk it happening in the middle of a fight, or when I'm addressing the council, or—what kind of Queen would I be?"

Aphrodite fluttered her lashes with widened eyes. "You remember all of them? All of your lives?"

"Yes."

"Well, shit." Aphrodite frowned and scratched her cheek. "I didn't see that one coming."

Flopping to the edge of the bed, I sulked. "I've tried to suppress the flashes, but the power behind them is too strong."

"Maybe—" Aphrodite sat next to me. "—it'd be different when you're a goddess again. You'll have the strength to fight them?"

"I don't think I should take that chance. There have been mortal lives at stake with some of the battles Seid and I have fought. I'd never forgive myself if someone died because I froze during a flashback." Balling my hands into fists, I beat them against my thighs.

"What a bummer," Aphrodite whispered, clicking her nails together before snapping her fingers. "I got it. Mnemosyne."

"The Titan?"

Shaking her head with a fluttery cackle, Aphrodite slapped my shoulder. "Olympus, no. When Dad imprisoned them, she transferred her powers to a river in the Underworld."

Gripping the mattress, I turned to her with a raised brow. "What kind of powers?"

"Memory." She grinned with her chin lifted.

I sucked in a breath, holding it until my lungs burned.

"Phi, you don't have to make a decision now, but promise me you'll think about it?" Aphrodite rested a hand on my knee, making me jump.

"Of course, I'll think about it."

"That's my girl." Aphrodite squeezed my thigh.

My mind dove into the possibilities of what life would've been like if we were to have lived mortal lives as a family. An animated image of my children surrounding the tank and feeding the fish swam through my brain. Rhode stood on her tiptoes, trying to reach it, and Triton picked her up. Closing my eyes, I pushed off the bed to stand. "I abandoned my family once. I'm not doing it again."

Aphrodite followed and gave me a side hug. "We've all done things in our formative years we regret, even if some of us would never admit it. Olympus knows I could be a real harpy back then, but I'd like to think we still all had our moments."

Chuckling, I nudged her in the side with my elbow. "Careful. You're starting to sound like Athena."

Aphrodite gagged before giggling.

The swirls in the carpet came to life as I stared at them, transgressing into a paintbrush in my hand swirling in water. An emerald green dress clung to my legs as I raised the brush to the canvas, painting a landscape of rolling green hills and a perfectly formed stone castle against a brightly lit horizon.

"Phi?" Aphrodite's voice echoed through my mind.

The feel of the brush's handle became less and less concrete as I pulled myself away from the memory. Aphrodite tugged on my shirt sleeve, and I snapped my gaze to hers.

"It just happened, didn't it?" Aphrodite's brow furrowed as she stroked my hair.

"How long was I staring into space?"

She continued to soothe me. "A few minutes. Please, please consider the river, Amphitrite."

"I need to talk to Poseidon," I whispered, gulping.

Aphrodite nodded and stepped back after giving my arm one last reassuring squeeze. "The hardest part is over. You found each other. You'll figure it out."

"Thank you, Dite."

She smiled, sparkly and radiant. "Anytime, toots." And she was gone in a blast of glitter and rose petals.

I stepped to my fish tank, swirling my fingertips through the surface, preening as the fins occasionally brushed my skin. Closing my eyes, I whispered, "Poseidon."

In a breath, he appeared behind me, his arms enveloping my waist.

He kissed my nape and splayed his hands over my stomach. "You rang, Starfish?"

"Everything good with Eros and—what was her name?" I sank into him, tracing my hands over his arms, still keeping my eyes closed.

"Elani. And mmhm. She's a goddess of love, and they're bonded. I did my part. Rest is up to them." He pulled me tighter against him, trailing his lips over my ear, moistening it.

"Any other interruptions I should be expecting in the next twenty-four hours?"

"By Olympus, I hope not."

Turning to face him, I cupped his cheek. "I spoke with Aphrodite about my constant flashing memories."

"Oh? Did she have an idea how to stop them?"

I let my gaze fall to the hemp bracelet on his wrist, running my fingertips over one of the shells. "The Mnemosyne River."

"I forgot it even existed." He grinned and tightened his grip on my waist. "What are we waiting for?"

"Seid, I don't know how it works. There is no way in Tartarus I'm losing my memories of the kids, of us, of my life as Cordelia? I won't let it happen." Slipping away from him, I turned my back and cupped my hands over my mouth to stifle a whimper.

His hand slipped over my elbow. "Then we'll talk to Laurel."

"Laurel?" Sniffling, I gazed at him over my shoulder.

"Apollo's wife. He made her leader of the Muses."

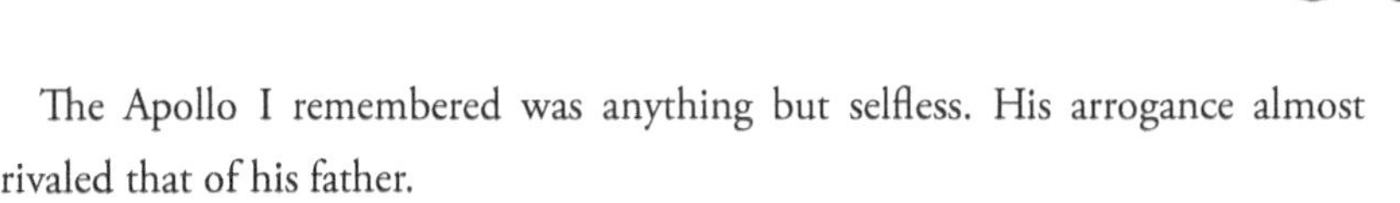

The Apollo I remembered was anything but selfless. His arrogance almost rivaled that of his father.

"No shit."

Poseidon let out a hearty chuckle. "I know, I thought that too, but Laurel can get us in touch with a Muse, and maybe they can give us more information. Their mother *was* Mnemosyne after all."

A newfound hope erupted in my chest like a geyser. "Yes. Let's do it."

"Your chariot awaits." He held his hands out to me with a wry grin.

Slipping my palms over his, I slid into his arms, and he ported us away. We stood in a studio with ballet barres on three walls, mirrors on the fourth, and speakers aligned in each corner. A blonde woman with her hair in a bun stretched on one barre, gasping when she spied us over her shoulder.

"Poseidon," she breathed out, clapping a hand over her chest. "Muses, you startled me."

Poseidon pressed a hand to my lower back, urging me to step forward. "Laurel, this is Cordelia or as she used to be known, Amphitrite."

Laurel's sky-blue eyes widened as she fluttered toward us, her pointe shoes clonking against the floor. "*The* Amphitrite?"

"Yes, it's—complicated." I shook her hand.

Laurel smiled and cocked her head to the side. "You're mortal."

"As she said—complicated," Poseidon added with a smirk.

"Well to what do I owe the visit from the King and Queen of the Seas?" She folded her arms, making the black leotard on her torso tighten across her chest.

"We hoped you could call one of the Muses for us. Any of them would do. We have some questions only they can answer." Poseidon wrapped an arm around my shoulders.

Laurel closed her eyes for several moments before blinking them open. "Absolutely. Euterpe is the only available one, but she's already been summoned. Should be here momentarily."

"Thank you." I distracted myself by scanning the studio. "Is this place yours?"

Laurel nodded with a broad smile, displaying her arms at her sides. "Yes. Apollo and I bought it to have our own place to practice."

"And Apollo? How's that going?" Poseidon asked gruffly.

Laurel batted a stray piece of blonde hair from her eyes. "I couldn't ask for a

better partner in virtually every aspect of life."

My emotions seemed to be on overdrive lately as the serene look on her face brought tears to my eyes. Forcing them back, I pressed a hand to my chest with a warm smile. People—even gods—*could* change.

A *whoosh* sounded behind us.

"Apologies for the delay," Euterpe started, dusting off her robes as she moved to stand beside Laurel. "I had to finish scribing the notes for a new piece before I forgot them."

"No matter." Laurel smiled and rested a hand on Euterpe's shoulder. "Poseidon and Amphitrite have a question for you."

Euterpe's eyes widened at me, and she bowed her head. "Amphitrite, I had no idea you were back."

With vigor, I shook my head and held up a palm. "No need for bowing. I'm not Queen."

"Yet," Poseidon added.

My cheeks warmed, and I smiled.

"The Mnemosyne River. How does it work exactly?" Poseidon folded his arms, his jaw tightening.

Euterpe cut a glance to Laurel before looking back at us. "You wish to have memories erased?"

"Me. Yes." The words came out as a whispered squeak.

"If you decide to drink from my mother's river, you must know this—only the memories you hold dear will remain. Be certain you know what those are, or you will lose even the happiest of memories—" She paused, making sure I looked her in the eyes before concluding. "—forever."

I stumbled backward, and Poseidon caught me, pressing his muscular chest to my back.

"Are you certain? There's no way to pinpoint the memories?" Poseidon traced his fingers over my biceps.

Euterpe shook her head with a frown. "I'm afraid it's not that simple."

"If you don't mind me asking, what memories are you trying to get rid of?" Laurel played with the string of her ballet skirt.

Did I want to lose the memories of my past lives altogether? No, not really. They were as much a part of me as Amphitrite and Cordelia, but my family—this

life was far more important.

"Memories I don't need anymore." I looked up at Poseidon and slipped my hand into his.

"Do you need me for anything else, my liege?" Euterpe turned to Laurel.

Laurel bowed her head. "No, Euterpe, thank you. Go finish your symphony."

Euterpe turned to face us. "I hope you get the answers you seek, Amphitrite." After a swirl of her arm, she disappeared.

My heart thumped against my chest. "Seid, let's go to the Underworld before I lose my nerve."

"Are you sure?"

I nodded instead of answering him, unsure if I could say the words.

"It was a pleasure meeting you, Amphitrite. I hope the river works in your favor." Laurel gave a warm smile, followed by a graceful curtsy.

"Thank you, Laurel." I squeezed Poseidon's hand, urging him to port us.

Poseidon hugged me to him. "Tell Apollo it's his turn to host poker night."

Laurel laughed and tapped the wooden block of her pointe shoe against the floor. "I'll be sure to do that."

My hair flew behind me as Poseidon took us to the Underworld. It'd been so long since I was here. The chill in the air and the smell of sulfur surrounding us sent a shiver through my bones.

"It's right in front of you, sweetheart." Poseidon kissed the top of my head. "All you have to do is drink if this is what you want."

I had my forehead pressed to his chest; my eyes closed so tightly it made the skin above my nose ache. After taking a deep, calming breath, I slipped away from him and turned to the dark river water, the sconces hanging above us in the dank cave reflecting orange shimmers over the surface. Dropping to my knees, I scooped the water into my palms and held them in front of me, hovering near my lips.

FOURTEEN

All that was left to do was sip the water cupped in my hands. One sip to stop the sporadic images flashing through my brain. One sip to bring me closer to my family. Closing my eyes, I lowered my mouth.

"Stop," Hades's voice boomed from behind me.

Gasping, I let the water in my hands splash to the sandy shoreline. Turning on my heels, I stared up at the imposing god of the Underworld. My previous brother-in-law, who I'd remembered never failing to come across powerful while remaining the most levelheaded of the brothers. I cared for Poseidon, but I'd be the first to admit he could be frivolous.

"Hades, it's what she wants." Poseidon slipped a hand over his brother's shoulder.

Hades didn't tear his glowing white gaze from mine and brushed Poseidon's hand away. "Amphitrite, I'm equally delighted and shocked to see you back. But tell me, why do you wish to terminate memories?"

Wringing my hands together, I glanced at Poseidon for backup. He gave me a curt nod, and I blew out a breath before speaking. "Aphrodite created a reincarnation spell. And it worked countless times leading me into dozens of lifetimes before being born into this current one."

Hades nodded, not appearing as surprised as the others. His floating white hair brushed against his dark robes. "And the memories?"

"At any given moment, flashes from all my past lives consume my mind. It's brought me to my knees more than once." I rubbed my stomach as nausea

bubbled, remembering how it felt when my nose bled.

Hades nodded again, the flame crown surrounding his head flickering. "Living through the ages, living these multiple lives—it seems like something one wouldn't wish to forget."

"I'd rather have the chance to be with my family again." I squared off my shoulders, staring at Hades unblinking.

"Drinking that water is too risky, Amphitrite. Allow me to offer an alternative." Hades nudged his chin to the right, his pointed ears sticking out from his long hair.

"Alternative? What else is there?" Poseidon followed beside me as Hades led us along the shore.

"Thanatos's twin brother, Hypnos." Hades's voice sounded like a dozen whispers in varying pitches.

"Hypnos? The guy who helped Hera try and betray Zeus?" Poseidon quirked a brow at me.

"That would be the one. Though most only use him for his sleep abilities, he also has powers of the mind and forgetfulness. I believe he can help you."

I quickened my steps to walk alongside Hades. "Do you know where he is?"

"Here."

Poseidon pointed down. "Here?"

"Yes. When he woke up to an angry Zeus looming over him, Hypnos asked for refuge in the Underworld. He's been here ever since."

We rounded a rocky corner to a smaller cave, its entrance glowing a welcoming orange from a lit fire within.

"He lives there. I will not be accompanying you as I have to feed Cerberus, however, explain to him the situation, and I'm certain he'll be more than happy to help."

Hades feeding Cerberus. The thought of it made a smile creep over my lips.

"Thank you, bro." Poseidon extended a hand to him with a firm nod.

Hades shook it before patting Poseidon's shoulder. "I'm glad you get to be happy, Poseidon. And Amphitrite, welcome back."

"Thanks, Hades."

After nodding a goodbye, Hades disappeared in ash and fog.

"Let me go first, Starfish." Poseidon coaxed me behind him with a burly arm.

He didn't have to tell me twice. Hypnos was a primordial god. I couldn't

remember the last time I'd been around one.

We edged closer to the cave entrance, and once we were at the threshold, a voice rang out, "Who's there?"

"Poseidon and Amphitrite. Hades sent us." Poseidon spoke to the entrance.

When silence fell across the cave walls too long for comfort, I gripped Poseidon's arm.

"Come in," Hypnos finally answered.

We moved forward, our feet scraping against the stone floor. The inside didn't look like what I imagined a cave home. It was cozy, warm, and inviting with a roaring hearth, a quaint wooden table with a bowl of fruit in the center. A modest bed with red and gold blankets rested in a far corner, while a chess set resided in the other.

Hypnos stepped from the shadows, tugging at his maroon robes as if not knowing what to do with his hands. His dark brown hair fell in waves to his hip bones, and the small black wings on either side of his head perked when he laid eyes on us.

"You'll have to excuse me as I've never had—visitors down here." Hypnos gulped and sprinted to the table, splaying his hands to make an array of meats, cheeses, and a pitcher with mugs appear. "Please, sit."

The desire to get this done and over with took a backseat to how grateful Hypnos looked to have company.

Tugging on Poseidon's shirt to let him know I was alright with staying a little while, I took a seat at the table with a smile. "You have a lovely home, Hypnos. You've made a dreary and dank cave look like a cottage on the inside."

After grumbling something under his breath, Poseidon sat next to me.

"Thank you, Amphitrite. Being alone for so long, I wanted to feel as comfortable as I could." Hypnos grinned and urged us to eat by gesturing at the wooden plates in front of us. The wings folded back, circling his head.

After scooping some fruit onto my plate, I poured from the pitcher—ambrosia wine. "I'm sure Zeus wouldn't smite you were you to join everyone on the surface again."

Poseidon coughed and discreetly shook his head at me.

"You weren't there." Hypnos frowned and plopped in the seat across from us. "His rage at what Hera and I had tried to do rattled the mountains surrounding

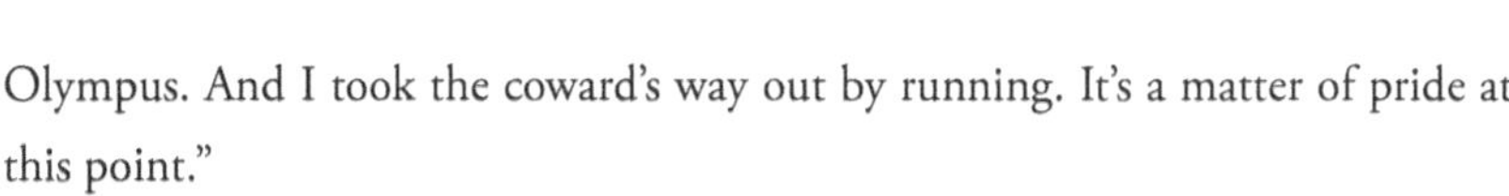

Olympus. And I took the coward's way out by running. It's a matter of pride at this point."

"Hera left Zeus." Poseidon popped a grape in his mouth. "Pretty sure he wouldn't give a shit about you returning, Hyp."

The wings fluttered as Hypnos's eyes widened. "I'll…consider it."

I tapped my finger against my mug before scooting to the edge of my seat. "Listen, Hypnos. I need a favor if you're able and willing to do it."

"Unless you're asking me to murder someone or assist in betraying a king god, I'm all ears." He grinned as he folded his hands on the table and leaned forward.

"I've been reincarnated multiple times through the ages, not remembering who I truly was. Now that I know who I am—all those memories come pouring in like lifting a floodgate." I gripped the mug, frowning. "It's too much."

Hypnos nodded, the warm smile he'd given moments prior still present. "Ah, yes. I do believe I can help, Amphitrite."

I leaned back, flattening my palms on the table. "You can? That easy?"

"Yes. I simply need your permission to touch you as I need direct access to your mind." Hypnos's grin faded as he cut his gaze to Poseidon as if looking for his permission moreover mine.

Poseidon glared at him.

I stood and leaned in front of Poseidon, blocking him. "You have my permission."

Hypnos cleared his throat as he stood and walked toward me, raising his hands to press all fingers on each side of my head. "All I need you to do is relax and try to keep your mind as clear as possible."

The inability to clear my mind of all thought was the precise reason I'd never been able to meditate successfully. I'd have to dig deep.

Closing my eyes, I forced my concentration on my breathing—the sound of it as it left my nostrils, the feel of my chest rising and falling, the air filling my lungs.

"Done."

My eyes flew open. Hypnos steepled his fingers and took a step back.

"Done? That's it?" I felt my forehead, checking for fever or some leftover residue or—something?

"I've had these powers for a very long time. It doesn't take much to accomplish a wanted task. I've suppressed only your alternate life memories, but they're not

lost forever. If you wish to recall them, then and only then will they surface."

I'd never met Hypnos and only knew him for the several minutes we'd been here, but as tears filled my eyes, I threw my arms around him and hugged him.

"Thank you, Hypnos. You have no idea how much this means to me."

Hypnos stiffened from my touch at first before he hugged me back, the rustling of his feathers as they bristled echoing in my ears. "You're most welcome."

After I stepped back, wiping tears from my eyes, Poseidon jutted his hand. "Thanks, Hyp. You should really consider visiting the new world. You'd be quite the asset up there."

"Thank you. I will. If I can get over the shock of how much has changed, perhaps I'll pay you both a visit."

"We'd be glad to show you around. Anytime at all. I owe you a favor." I curled my hands under my chin and smiled.

Hypnos bowed his head and pressed a hand over his chest. "My dear Queen, you don't owe me a thing. I appreciate the company, but being as she's mortal Poseidon, you'll need to get her back to the surface." He frowned but urged us with a flick of his hand.

Poseidon pressed a hand to my back before pulling me against him. I rested my head on his chest, listening to his heart as I smiled at Hypnos before Poseidon ported us away.

Poseidon's nose nuzzled my cheek. "It's been a whole twenty-four hours, and you haven't had one flashback, right?"

Not in the slightest. It was a form of bliss I didn't know I missed.

"Not a one," I whispered, nestling against him with my eyes closed as we lounged on my couch.

"Good." He kissed the side of my head and lazily stroked my arms.

Fluttering my eyes open, I pulled his arms tighter around me. "When I'm Queen again, I will pull rank on any god or goddess to find one who can help us find Rhode."

"I'm with you, but—" His body stiffened, and he pushed me forward before gently grabbing my chin to turn my face to his. "Are you saying what I think

you are?"

I nodded as tears filled my eyes, and I combed my fingers through his wavy hair. "Now that I remember who I am, I don't think I'd ever feel complete without accepting what I was born to do. So, yes. I'll become Queen of the Seas again, *your* Queen, and reunite this family."

"Amph," he said through a loosed breath. His chin dipped to kiss me, but I pressed a finger over his lips.

"I have but one request."

He kissed my finger. "Anything."

"The name Amphitrite belonged to a failed Queen. I want to be called Cordelia from here on out—the name in the lifetime where things fell into place. Fate." I smiled up at him, holding back tears.

This was happening. Even a goddess could be starstruck.

"Cordelia suits you." He pressed his palm to my cheek. "I've thought it since the first moment I re-met you. But I'd never say you were a failed Queen. More like…a work in progress."

I burst a single laugh, a tear rolling down my cheek before I tackled him and kissed the ever-loving shit out of the love of my life—the love of *all* my lives.

Meg.

Pulling away from the kiss with a sigh, I pressed our foreheads together. "There's someone I need to talk to first before I do this. She deserves to know the truth."

"Meg?" He secured my hair over one of my ears. "Are you sure you're ready for that? It'll be a lot for her to take in."

"Did I tell you how we met?" I grinned at him.

He shook his head, tracing one of his fingers over my cheek.

"We met years ago on a dive. Well, we were on separate dives, but she was photographing barracudas, and I was after reef sharks." I sat up, straddling him and trailing my fingers over the horse tattoo on his arm.

He grabbed my hips and pulled me tighter against him.

"Meg was so caught up in her shot she didn't see one of the sharks in her peripheral."

Poseidon smiled. "Did you beat it up?"

"Oh my—" I swatted him with a laugh. "Of course not. I did, however, bump its nose with my camera rig. When we both surfaced, she thanked me a dozen

times and offered to buy me lunch for saving her life."

The memory pulled a wide grin over my lips, and I was thankful for Hypnos's help even more now because I wouldn't know what to do if I'd lost memories like this.

"I told her it wasn't that big of a deal, but she insisted, and we spent the next three hours talking about diving, camera rigs, and Disney's *Hercules*, of all things." I flicked my fingernail over the buttons of Poseidon's Henley shirt. "A month later, we agreed to be partners, and the rest, as they say, is history."

He massaged my lower back. "Sounds like you two are pretty close."

"We're like sisters, Seid. So, believe me, when I say it may take some convincing, but Meg will come around."

Poseidon kissed the tip of my nose. "You know your friend better than I do, and I can tell this is something you need to get off your chest, so, go." He bucked his hips. "Get."

Laughing as he continued to bump me off of him, I crawled from his lap. "Okay, okay. I'm going." I dove in for another kiss with a grin. "I'll be right back."

"And I'll be here waiting. Always and forever." He smiled back at me before slapping my ass. "Now. Go."

Backpedaling, I blew him a kiss and exited to the hallway.

Once in front of her door, I knocked three times. Anxious, I followed it up with repeated light taps until finally, the door swung open.

"For crying out loud, Cor. What the hell's going on?" Meg asked with wide eyes before squinting into the sun.

I hugged her tight, sending us fumbling into her apartment. She laughed and patted my back before shutting the door behind us.

"Okay, I'm all about the hugs, but seriously, what's going on?" She folded her arms, making the ribbed lines of her white tank top stretch.

"I've got something to tell you. Something—huge." I waved my arms in large circles.

She puckered her lips. "Do we need whiskey for this conversation?"

"Probably?" An anguished smile tugged at my lips, and I let out a nervous laugh.

"Alrighty. Follow me to the kitchen."

Watching Meg grab two tumblers and a bottle of Jim Beam, I drummed my fingers on the counter.

What was the best way to do this? Lay it all out in one swoop? Use analogies?

She set one glass in front of me and held hers up in a cheers gesture before taking a swig. "Let's have it, Cor." Leaning one hip against the counter, she draped an arm over her stomach and looked at me expectantly.

"Okay. So, you know how animals seem to react differently to me? For instance, you naming me a shark whisperer?" I tapped my fingernail against the tumbler, feverishly chewing on my lip.

"Uh-huh. You told me it was your experience and presence. You called my bullshit, remember?" She pointed at me with her glass-holding hand.

"I did. Scratch that because—you're right." I snapped my gaze to hers, nerves somersaulting in my belly.

She squinted at me, shifting her stance. "So…you *are* a shark whisperer?"

"More than that." I guzzled half of my drink and winced from the burn coursing down my throat.

"You know I'm not a beat around the bush type of person, Cordelia. You got something to say, say it." Meg sipped her drink.

I placed a hand under her glass and tilted it up, encouraging her to drink much more than a tiny sip. With a cock of her brow, she obliged.

"Do you believe in reincarnation?" I was tip-toeing around it again, but I couldn't—I just could not come right out and say I'm the former Queen of the flipping seas.

"To a point, sure." She narrowed her eyes, and after scanning my face, she finished her drink.

"Meg—" I slid forward and pressed my palms against the marble top. "I'm Amphitrite reincarnated."

An invisible whale lifted from my shoulders, only to be replaced by uncertainty and fear.

"Who's Amphitrite?" She casually slipped her phone from her back pocket, averting her gaze.

This is what happened when a Greek goddess turned into a constellation— they're forgotten.

Gently taking her phone away, I placed it on the counter. "Greek mythology. Queen of the Seas."

She blinked. Her lips quivered, and she pursed them together, laughter following.

I should've seen it coming. Sighing, I turned on my heel and pressed my back against the fridge.

"Holy shit. You're not laughing. Cory, I'm more open-minded than even you are, but you're trying to tell me you're a Greek goddess?"

I didn't say anything, just locked our eyes and shrugged.

"Fuck me." She grabbed the whiskey bottle and poured more into her glass. "You mean that someone, a real person existed back then, and she was known as Amphitrite, right? That's who you're a descendant of?"

"No, Meg." I crossed the room to stand in front of her. "I am Amphitrite. I used to be a goddess, Queen of the Seas, and married to Poseidon. *Simon* is Poseidon."

She sputtered her whiskey and wiped the back of her hand over her mouth. "Wait, what?"

"It's why I kept telling you I felt like I knew him, that he already knew me. It's because we had dozens of years together before meeting again centuries later."

This was far worse than I imagined. If the roles were reversed, I'd be interrogating my friend about what narcotic I was on.

"Okay, okay, okay." Meg closed her eyes and held the tumbler up. "Let's say I'm tracking you so far. And you and Simon are star-crossed lovers reunited in modern times. Is he reincarnated too?"

"No."

Far. Worse. Then I imagined.

"I'm officially lost." Meg downed the rest of her drink.

"Let's sit down. I'll explain everything from beginning to end, and you can make it what you will. Deal?" I gestured toward the living room.

"Sitting. Yeah," she murmured, shuffling against the area rug before claiming a seat on the sofa.

"We had an arranged marriage, and it took us a while to love each other, but once we did, we were an unstoppable force. And crazy over each other." I looked at my palms resting in my lap and smiled. When I lifted my gaze, Meg had a

warm grin displayed.

"But over time, Poseidon became consumed by his job, and I saw him less and less. I started to feel neglected, depressed. And I turned to the one being I knew would never let me down—the sea." I wrung my hands, sniffling. "I should've talked to him about it. But instead, I distracted myself in the sea, ignoring my duties, my responsibilities, and also…my family."

"Family?" Meg propped her head on her hand.

Oh, boy.

"I have two children. Triton and Rhode."

"Jesus," Meg whispered, pushing a breath from her lungs. "Continue."

"Because I wasn't upholding my responsibilities and had made no move to change it, Zeus banished me to the stars. I was to live the rest of my days as a constellation, looking down on those that I loved but no longer existing."

If I concentrated enough, I could dig up memories of Poseidon's face when he realized I was gone. He'd destroyed an entire atrium in Atlantis out of fury. And despite his best efforts, he couldn't make Zeus budge on his decision. They didn't talk for a decade. Aphrodite was right—he did miss me.

"That seems a tad harsh. Why didn't Poseidon get punished?" Meg leaned forward, resting her arms on her knees.

Questions and curiosity meant progress. Good.

"Zeus always knows what he's doing. He couldn't formally punish another king, but banishing me, taking me from him—was punishment enough." I rubbed my thumbs together. "Aphrodite created a spell to start my reincarnations."

"Time out." She made the time-out gesture. "Reincarnation plural?"

I nodded. "Countless times."

She tugged on her bottom lip and stared at the floor before giving a firm nod. "Continue."

"It was a matter of Poseidon and me finding each other again. But Athena put a curse on him that if he ever found me, he wouldn't recognize me unless he'd changed as a man."

And he had in so many ways. I was proud of him.

"That's. Horrible." Meg frowned, her eyes glassy.

"It is, but we found each other. We're reunited, and that's the most important thing." I canted my head to the side, spying her erratic bouncing knee. "Meg?

You okay?"

"Not really. I'm trying to believe you here, Cory. I really am. But this is all crazy to me." She shot to her feet. "But the way you talked about all of this was as if it was *your* life to tell."

She needed more, and I didn't blame her.

My scales.

Rising, I held my palms out for her to take or ignore. "Can I show you something?"

Her eyes panned to my palms before landing back on my face, and she took my hands. "Alright."

Closing my eyes, I willed the scales to show themselves—the blue radiant patches shimmering in the dimly lit room.

She gasped and tightened her grasp on my hands, making me wince.

"You're not joking." She stared wide-eyed before poking the scales on my arm with a single finger. After rubbing her fingers together and seeing no signs of paint, she shook her head. "Greek mythology is—real?"

"Yeah, Meg." I made the scales disappear before her eyes, making them widen again. "And I think you knew deep down that something was different about Simon. I could see the cogs turning in your brain from a mile away."

"Sure, but I would've never come to the conclusion he was Poseidon. I wouldn't have even believed myself." She beat her hands against her cheeks like a drum. "This is surreal."

"I wanted to tell you the truth because I've decided to become Queen again."

Meg grabbed my shoulders, a scowl forming in her brow. "What does that mean? What does it entail?"

"When I married Poseidon and took shared responsibility of all waters, it brought a sort of harmony. In my absence, my home has become catastrophic." I squeezed her shoulders back. "I prove to Zeus I'm worthy of the title again, and I get my home, the love of my life, and my family back."

"Wow, Cory." She pulled me to her, hugging me tightly. "Just wow."

Given her newfound information about the Greek gods, should I tell her about Hera? No. It wasn't my truth to tell. That was Hera's choice when and where if she truly wanted to confess.

"Have you heard from Hera?" I peeled back, keeping one hand on her shoulder.

Meg laughed, dragging two hands through her short dark hair. "You throw me that curveball and then want to revert to peon conversation about my love life?"

"This doesn't mean we'll stop being friends. It doesn't change us as photography partners or picking up trash on the beach to promote our conservation group either. I *do* need a cover after all." I jostled her.

"We could still be friends?"

My lips parted beside myself. "Meg, of course. You're as much family to me as all the gods in Olympus."

She hugged me again, sniffling, before leaning back. "Hera and I have had multiple phone conversations, and we're supposed to be going on a date tomorrow."

"What?" I grinned and swatted her in the arm. "That's amazing. Why do you not look excited?"

"Because I don't know how to act in front of her, Cor." She brushed past me, rubbing her eyes with her palms.

"What do you mean?"

"She makes me feel different. Flustered. Vibrant." Meg turned to face me, pressing her fingertips together. "I don't even know how to categorize it."

"Flustered?" I bobbed my brows, trying to hold back the gooey grin yanking at my lips.

"No one. Not a soul has ever made me feel like this." She ran a hand through her hair, bunching it atop her head.

I beamed up at her, letting her sort out her thoughts.

"I don't even know what to wear." Meg stared down at me like a baby seal looking for its mother. "She's incredible, Cory."

"Do you want my help?" I rubbed her arm.

She forced out a breath and looked skyward. "For the love of God, yes."

We both chuckled and spent the rest of the night digging through clothes in her closet, sipping more whiskey, and talking about my previous life. With each passing hour, she sounded more accepting and open to my being a goddess. It was the reassurance I needed for myself and her to go through with it entirely. I spent the night at her place, knowing it was my last chance to be Cordelia, her mortal friend. Poseidon and I would go to Zeus and announce that the Queen had returned and wanted her crown back.

FIFTEEN

I'D PORTED BACK TO my apartment from Meg's living room, hearing Meg gasp as I disappeared. Poseidon lay on the couch, precisely where he said he'd be waiting on me.

He stood with a grin, tossing the photography magazine he'd been flipping through to the coffee table. "How'd it go?"

"Better than I expected." I interlaced my fingers behind my back, grinning and swiveling my hips.

He stood in front of me, gazing down at me with hooded lids. "And you still want to go through with this?"

"There isn't a doubt in my mind, Seid." I leaped into his arms and kissed him.

He coaxed my legs around him, wrapping one arm under my butt while the other kneaded the back of my head. With every caress of our lips, every lap of our tongues, the familiarity settled into our veins—our bones.

Pulling away from him with a whimper, I said, "I lied. I have one more request."

"What do you need?" He adjusted me in his arms, causing my pelvis to rub against his stomach.

I bit my lip, moaning. "Be with me like this—before I'm a goddess. I want to *feel* your magic before I have my own again."

With an accepting snarl, he crashed his mouth against mine, diving us into a carnal exchange of kissing, nipping, groaning.

"No other woman could've ever lived up to you, Cordelia. I was ready to spend eternity alone." He tapped his forehead with mine, moving us into my bedroom.

"Shh," I whispered against his lips. "I'm here, Seid. I'm right here."

He searched my face, memorizing every freckle, every groove before kissing me again and pushing us to the bed. Instead of landing on a mattress, he ported us to an underwater grotto, keeping us dry within a created air bubble filling the space. I broke away from his lips long enough to grin at our atmosphere. Water walls surrounded us, giving a prime view of the aquatic life swimming around it—fish of all shapes and colors, sea turtles, and dolphins. It was as if they came to pay their respects to our reunion.

"Shouldn't we be worried about Skylla here?" I lay beneath him, gleaming up at his emerald gaze.

"She won't be able to sense us through my protection spell. And I'd pity anyone foolish enough who tried to interrupt what's about to happen." He dragged a hand through his hair, parting it from his face with a smolder capable of boiling the water around us.

"What's about to happen?" A sultry grin melted over my lips.

He rolled his hips, pressing himself against me, making me gasp. "I'm going to remind you how the Seven Seas themselves couldn't compare to how wet you always got around me."

His words alone had me soaked, and I pinched his sides with my knees. "Remind me, Seid."

With a devious curl of his lip, he pulled spirals of water from the ocean, disguising us, and circled them over my body. Every pass over my clothes made them disappear, each brush of the silky moist tendrils making me writhe beneath him. His arm turned into water, joining the spirals as they tantalized my skin in tandem. He skirted his hands up my inner thighs, yanking my knees apart to display myself for him.

His tongue lapped at the corner of his mouth as he gazed down at me, and with one flick of his head, water splashed, and he was fully naked. I sat up, reaching for him, ready to greedily roam my hands over every toned piece of him, but he snatched my wrists.

As he coaxed me to lay back, his length brushed my folds. He leaned over me, grinning like a tiger shark. "Not yet, Cory. I've got so much reminding to do first." His brow bobbed.

Hearing my new name on his lips with him between my legs was almost

enough to send me over the edge right then and there.

His beard tickled my skin as he kissed my neck, traveling to my breasts, sucking on each nipple before trailing his tongue the length of my stomach, stopping right above my clit. Grinning against my hip bone, he gave my folds one slow, torturous lap of his tongue. My back arched from the sea bed, fingers tangling in his hair, holding him captive. He used the tip of his tongue to flick, switching to nibbling, sucking, lapping, and all forms in between. He pressed a firm hand on my stomach, keeping me still as I squirmed with pleasure.

He paused, hovering over me, evidence of my appreciation for his efforts laced in his beard. I propped on my elbows, panting, gazing back at him. The first time we slept together, I'd been a virgin sea nymph—nervous, afraid, apprehensive. I hadn't expected him to take the care he had, the patience. And the sex became a wildfire even fathoms below the surface through time.

Keeping our eyes locked, he lowered his lips between my legs, covering me with his mouth. His cheeks filled with warm water, rolling against my folds in partnership with his swirling tongue. I gripped the cushioned floor beneath me, my nails digging into the spongey surface. An earth-shattering cry poured from my lungs as I climaxed, shaking, bucking, and writhing.

Poseidon had no plans to let me come up for air, splashed water over his chin, crawled over me, and thrust. I gasped, throwing open my eyes and wrapping my arms around his neck.

Poseidon peered down, rocking in and out of me. He kissed the tip of my nose, my cheek, my lips. "Gods, I've missed you. I've *fucking* missed you."

Digging my fingers into his strong shoulders, I lifted my hips, making him go deeper. "I've missed you too, Poseidon."

A satisfied masculine grin played over his lips and a sparkling water surge coiled through my hair, surrounding us like a halo. As a soft satiated moan escaped my throat, I reached behind me, plunging my hand through the water wall and letting the outside salty ocean wet my fingertips. One of his hands curled under my ass as he pounded harder into me.

Sitting up, grinding myself against him, I pressed my lips to his ear. "I thálassa eínai to spíti mou allá esý eísai to katafýgió mou." After sucking on his ear lobe, I leaned back, peering at him with ravenous eyes.

The sea is my home, but you're my sanctuary.

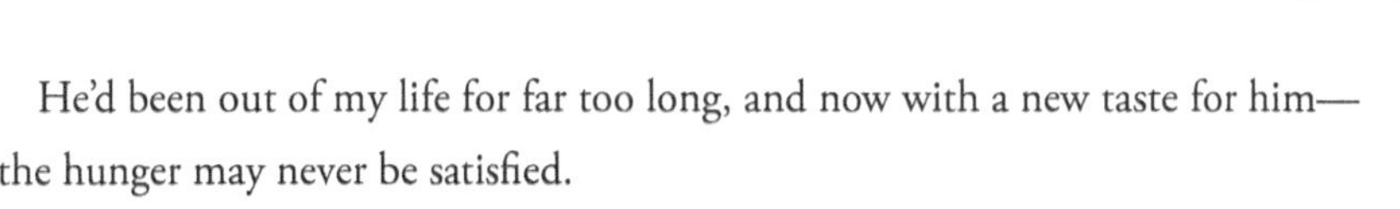

He'd been out of my life for far too long, and now with a new taste for him—the hunger may never be satisfied.

His eyes twinkled, his hand cupping the side of my face, before he pushed off the seafloor, launching us skyward. We plunged through the top wall, circling into open water, sending fish darting in all directions. Bubbles ebbed and swirled, floating through our hair in sinewy wisps. In the water, it was akin to being near weightless. Holding onto his shoulders for leverage, I moved up and down over him, the chilled ocean water flowing over my nipples plummeting me into euphoria.

My scales appeared—vibrant and shimmering. Poseidon smiled against my lips before opening his mouth and curling his tongue with mine. He grabbed my hips, halting me, and I opened my eyes, blinking, a flash of the golden crown on his head sparking in my brain.

"Kósmima tis thálassas," Poseidon said, his strong hands guiding my hips up and down his length, those jade eyes holding our entire past and future gleaming within them.

Jewel of the Sea.

As Poseidon held me close, angelfish swam circles around us, swirling our bodies in a descending typhoon. Our feet emerged through the water wall, back to the dryness and protection of the grotto. Water bubbled under my feet, floating us down to the sea bed, our hair soaked and wavy, sticking to our foreheads—our chests.

"I chose you that day when I saw you dancing on the bank, not only because I thought you were the most beautiful creature I'd ever seen, but—" He pulled out of me, pressing his hand to my chest and backing me to the nearest water wall. "I chose you because I could see my life with you with every sway of your hips. Saw our bond with every swirl of your arms. And envisioned our children in every breath you took."

This was what I'd always wanted. This. Right. Here.

"Oh, Seid," I sighed out.

He lifted one of my legs, curling it over his hip, pressing my back against the liquid wall. He made the wall solid but alive, the ocean tickling against my skin as I rested against it. He pushed into me inch by inch, slow and delicious. "I love you. I've always loved you." Before I could say it back, he covered my mouth with

his and filled me to the hilt.

At that moment, he didn't need to hear me say it back but knew *I* wanted to hear it more than anything. Words scarcely exchanged between us so long ago.

He pressed a hand above my head and made the water supporting us glow and pulse with each bonding thrust. The sweet ache pooled between my hips, building and building until it reached its peak. After several more thrusts, Poseidon reached his own euphoria, spilling inside me and growling into my nape.

I nuzzled my nose against his cheek. "I don't want to leave this place. Not yet. I haven't felt this comfortable in my surroundings in such a long time."

"We can stay here as *long* as you want," he said, the satisfaction in his tone making his voice extra raspy.

I ran my big toe up his lower back before pulling him tight against me. "You most certainly haven't lost your touch, sea god." I grinned and walked my fingers up his abs.

A deep chuckle rumbled from his chest. "Crisis averted." He slowly pulled out of me, standing and moving to the center of the grotto. "Come here."

I bit my thumbnail as I sauntered to him.

His arms turned into water as he waved them at the floor, turning it even spongier than before. He lay on his side and opened his arms wide and inviting. I lay down with my back to him, all but cooing once he wrapped his arms around me.

"Can you still do the water horse trick?" I nestled my ass against him, grinning to myself at the hardness still there.

"You insatiable nymph." He playfully nipped my earlobe, shoving himself harder against me. Without answering me, he lifted his hand, making it form the clear liquid. Gradually it took shape, morphing into a horse and galloping around the grotto. Its water mane left a sparkling trail in its wake.

I laughed, kissing his shoulder as he obliged me with the water show.

"Olympus, that laugh." He kissed my cheek, dropping his hand, the horse fading away in a wave of bubbles.

"Do you remember that shimmering negligee I conjured on special occasions?" A wicked grin fluttered over my lips.

His cock bounced against me. "You're kidding, right? How in Tartarus could I forget *that?*"

"I hope I can remember how to do it. I hope I can remember how to do *any* of it." I frowned, curling his arm around me again. Playing with his fingers, I pushed our hands together, noting how small mine was by comparison.

"It's like riding a chariot, Cor. Once you have the power again, it *will* come back to you."

"What if he doesn't accept me?" I traced the grooves in his palm, scraping my nail against the calluses.

"Who? Zeus? I'll *make* him if he doesn't." His arm tightened, and I trailed my finger over the scattering of blonde hair on his tanned arm, calming him.

"You know that's not how it works. We have to prepare ourselves for the worst-case scenario."

"No. I won't let him fuck us over a second time." He rested his chin on my shoulder. "You've changed. He can be a prick, but he *is* a smart man. He'll see it."

"So, what other sea monsters have returned since I've been gone? Please tell me the Kraken is still dormant."

Silence.

"Seid?"

Bubbled water collected at his fingertips, and he massaged one of my breasts, making my stomach tingle and flip.

"Hm?" He lazily asked as if not hearing my question.

I moaned as his silk water touch traveled to my stomach. "Are you distracting me to avoid my question?"

"Because you absolutely hate it, huh?" He slipped a finger inside me, stirring the bubbles.

I arched against him, groaning.

"All the more reason for you to become Queen again, Cordelia." He slid another finger in me, warming the water, sending a surge straight to my toes. "We can fight them together and send them all back to their holes."

I cried out, reaching for the back of his head to hold onto something.

"Restore Atlantis to its prior glory." He flicked the water with the tip of his finger, grinding against my spot.

Moaning his name, I grabbed his hair, pulling him to me for a kiss.

After briefly kissing me he said, "And put fear into anyone or anything who tries to *fuck* with our home."

Yes. Yes. All of it. *Yes.*

After one final flick, I came undone, quivering in his arms, kissing him again. I pushed his shoulder, forcing him to his back, and straddled him.

He grinned, letting me hold him down.

"Promise me one thing. We will always be equal rulers. Where you go, I go. The seas are *ours*."

He grabbed my hips and narrowed his eyes. "I promise on Rhea's life what happened before will not repeat itself. You'll be my Queen. I'll be your King. Our thrones touching side-by-side."

A grin tugged at my mouth, wide and brimming with life. I kissed him with the soul of the sea coursing through my veins.

"Now, let me remind you of a skill of mine I remembered you *never* complaining about." My scales shimmered.

A wicked smile slid over his lips, and we made love throughout the night, re-introducing ourselves and bonding, surrounded by what we swore to protect, to control, and improve—the mysterious depths of the sea.

SIXTEEN

"HEY." POSEIDON REACHED FORWARD, tapping my knee. "We don't have to do this right now. The seas have waited for a long time. They can wait for more."

We sat in my living room, Poseidon on my couch, and I in my lounger. I'd sworn up and down when we left the grotto, I was ready to go to Zeus. To ask him to be Queen again.

"Only the seas have been waiting?" I nudged his foot with mine.

He sighed and wrapped his arms around my shoulders. "I have too, yes. But seriously, take the time you need."

"The sooner I get my powers back—my reign, the sooner we can find Rhode." I pressed my palms together, slipping them between my knees.

"It *would* help, yes." He scooted to the edge of his seat and grabbed my knees. "But I can tell you with the utmost certainty our daughter is alive and well wherever she is, and you'd be doing her no favors rushing into this."

"How can you be so sure?"

"Because she has the strength and wit of her mother coupled with the courage and fighting sense of her father. She's going to be fine until we get to her. Tartarus—" He rubbed the back of his neck. "Who knows? She may not want to come back."

My throat tightened because I knew he was right. If she were anything like me and found someone she cared about in all the time she'd been gone, she wouldn't leave it for anything.

"Way to kill my hope before the box is even opened, Seid." I frowned with a partial smile.

"I didn't mean it like that. We'll—cross that bridge when we get to it." He kissed my temple and squeezed my thigh.

"I haven't seen Zeus since he banished me." I wrung my hands together, a crinkle forming in my brow.

Poseidon rubbed my shoulders. "Zeus does *not* have full power over me. I do have veto rights. And you think Hades would vote against it? It'll be fine, Cor."

I sighed and looked to Olympus above. "I know you and Hades would have my back. That isn't the point."

"What is it?" He rubbed between my shoulder blades.

"Is it crazy I want Zeus to accept me? To *want* to give me my Queendom back?" I couldn't look at him as I squeezed my hands together in my lap.

"You really give a shit what he thinks?"

"Under normal circumstances? No. But this is different, Seid. You were right when you said he'd be able to sense if I'd changed. So, if he disagrees…" I let my voice flutter away, turning my attention to my gaming setup. I'd neglected it for days. My Glitch viewers probably wondered why I'd suddenly disappeared.

"Take twenty-four hours. Let it settle. I'm asking you. Please."

I pressed a palm to his cheek. "Alright, Seid. But would you do me a favor?"

"Anything I do for you at this point, sweetheart, isn't a favor. It's a given." He kissed my hand. "Out with it."

"Would you—make an appearance on my Glitch channel as Simon Thalassa?" I squinted one eye. "It'd shoot my ratings through the roof."

A deep chuckle roared from his belly. "That's it? Let's do this." Slapping his hands on his thighs, he stood, walking to my gaming desk.

With a grin as wide as my face, I flopped into my rolling chair, pushing the power buttons of my console, monitor, and webcam.

"Did you—want them to know we're together, or will that ruin your image?" He asked in a strained voice.

My heart sank, and I swiveled to face him. "Is a gal supposed to be ashamed of a guy like you?"

"I'd certainly hope not, but I figured ninety percent of your following are dudes, most of which undoubtedly have a crush on you." He raised a thick brow.

"Oh? You think they only watch my stream because I'm a woman and not because of my gaming prowess?" I folded my arms.

He glared at me and grabbed the back of my chair, rotating it. "You're purposely being difficult, aren't you?"

I curled my fingers around the leather strap hanging from his neck, the pewter trident pendant cool against my palm. "Maybe. But I have an idea. I can tell them I've been away getting—" My eyes lifted to meet his, and I flashed my scales at him. "—engaged."

A moan escaped his throat and he curled a hand behind my back. "And it wouldn't be a lie, would it?"

"Nope." I grinned and shook my head, leaning forward to give his lips a quick peck.

"If that's the case. You're going to need proof." He held his fist between us.

I sat back, pressing a hand to my chest.

His hand morphed into water and returned to normal after a bright shimmer. A ring rested in his palm when he turned his hand over. "I know we've technically skipped ahead and already consummated the marriage—" A wicked glint flashed in his gaze. "—three times, but what do you say we do things properly this time, hm?"

My vision blurred with tears, sinuses stinging, and I cupped my hands over my nose. Smiling at me, he dropped to one knee and held the ring between two fingers.

"Cordelia—mother of my children, my forever Queen, and caregiver to the seas—will you marry me?"

"Poseidon, for the love of Olympus," I cried out, leaping from my chair and wrapping my arms around him, sobbing.

He softly laughed into my hair and wrapped one arm around me. "Love, you didn't say yes."

"Yes," I yelled, pushing against his shoulders to stand straight. "Times every year we've spent apart, *yes*."

Grinning, he slid the ring on my finger and remained on his knee as I lifted my hand to gaze at it. A silver mermaid made up the band, her scaled tail circling it, her hair made of intricate looped metal coiling around the prongs, which held a vibrant aquamarine stone.

"Seid, it's beautiful."

He pulled me closer, his head in line with my hips. With a deep sigh, he pressed his forehead against my stomach and held me. I rested my hands on the back of his neck and lowered my lips, pressing a kiss to his head and freezing there in blissful silence.

"I should probably wait to go on camera now. My eyes are puffy and red." I sniffled and laughed.

He tilted his head back and wiggled his fingers over my face. "It's going to be fun when you have your powers back reminding you of everything you can do with them."

"Shut up." I swatted him in the shoulder, my new ring sparkling from a nearby lamplight.

"Do you like it?" He rose to his feet, pulling me to his side.

Resting my head against his bicep, I turned the ring left to right, smiling at its glitter. "It's so me it makes my heart ache."

"You ready?" His eyes lifted to my awaiting powered-up gaming system.

"Yeah. It'll be quick, promise. Just a check-in so they know I'm alive."

Nestling in my chair, I grabbed my Pelican Beach headset and the generic standard set that comes with every console, handing it to him. "You get the dorky pair."

"Aw, you're so sweet." He plucked the headset from my fingers and poked me in the side, making me yelp. After he slipped it over his head, a strand of hair falling over his gaze, he turned to me with a raised brow. "How do I look?"

The man was physically incapable of being unattractive.

"Like the world's sexiest telemarketer."

He pumped his fist. "Nailed it."

Chuckling, I started my webcam and went live on Glitch. No need for a moderator with how long we'd be on. I tapped my fingernails against my desk, waiting for viewers to realize I'd randomly gone live.

"Oh, I should appear from out of frame, right? Make an entrance?" He bobbed his brows with such a charming ass grin I couldn't help but kiss him.

"I'm surprised you didn't think of that sooner, King of the Seas." I flashed him a sly grin.

He glared at me, pointing, and wheeled himself out of camera.

It took several minutes, but soon, the list of attendees grew by the dozens leading into the hundreds.

"Oh, wow. Hey Sea Farers." I waved at the camera with a beaming smile. "Thank you all so much for joining me on this random stream."

I paused to watch the chat feed.

MissTacoX: OMG! I thought you quit.

HufflePufflenz: You've literally been the highlight of my week. SO glad to see you back.

"Told you," Poseidon mumbled at my side.

I swatted him on the knee. "Sorry I've been absent, everyone. I've just been busy…well—" Holding the back of my hand at the camera, I shoved the ring into frame. "Getting engaged."

MissTacoX: WHAAAA Congrats!!!

FriskeeBizkit: Who's the lucky S.O.B.?!

"Some of you may have heard of him. Simon Thalassa."

Poseidon dipped his head into frame, holding his hand in the hang loose gesture. "What up, fishies?"

MissTacoX: AHHHH

HufflePufflenz: I'm legit about to lose my s* right now.**

Poseidon pointed at the comments and laughed—the jade in his eyes intensified from the camera. "And you're right Friskee, I am a lucky, lucky dude." He planted a kiss on my cheek, making me blush.

MissTacoX: Staaaahp you two are adorbs!

HufflePufflenz: If you tell me he's going to start showing up as a guest gamer on your channel, I'm going to completely lose my s*.**

Poseidon dragged a hand through his wavy locks, squinting at the camera.

MissTacoX: Oh. Dear. Gawd.

"Well, it just so happens I am. You better believe all should fear us when we team up in *Tides of Atlantis*." Poseidon pointed into the camera. "And I'm mostly talking to you—ProteinGeyser."

FriskeeBizkit: Daaaaaayuuuum!

MissTacoX: LMAO

I bit my lip, attempting to hide the shit-eating grin that so very much wanted to show.

"Yes, indeed. Stay tuned, everyone. Anyway, I just wanted to pop on really

quick to let you all know. And I promise I'll be back to my regular streaming within the next few weeks." I blew air kisses. "Keep swimming."

FriskeeBizkit: Congrats!

Dozens of other comments flew through the chat, but I didn't bother to read anymore as I cut the feed, turned off the camera, and took Poseidon's face in my hands. "Soon, the whole world will know about our alter egos."

"Why stop at the world? There's a whole galaxy out there."

Removing his headset, followed by mine, I spied him from the corner of my eye. "Let's go to Atlantis."

He coughed into his fist. "*Atlantis*, Atlantis?"

"No, *Tides of Atlantis*." I referenced the poster hanging above my desk. "Of course, I mean the real Atlantis."

"Uh—not sure that's such a great idea, Cor." He scratched the back of his head.

Folding my arms, I leaned back in my chair, swiveling. "And why not?"

"For starters, I told you it's a mess. And secondly, Skylla *will* be able to find you there." He grabbed my armrests and rolled my chair in front of him.

"I don't care how messy it is. I want to see it. And wouldn't my apology to Skylla mean more as a mortal?"

He puckered his lips. "Probably, but why risk it? You're too vulnerable right now."

"You wouldn't let anything happen to me. Besides, give me a trident, and I'll make sure I use it *if* she shows up." I tapped my fingers on my bicep.

"Oof," Poseidon responded, adjusting himself. "The thought of you with a trident in your hand again..."

"Will you take me home, Poseidon? I think seeing it, especially if it's in the state you say it's in, will be the final push to stand in front of Zeus and ask he reinstate me."

He slowly nodded. "Alright."

I jumped in my seat, my phone vibrating in my back pocket. "It's a text from Meg."

A selfie photo of her and Hera, their arms draped around each other. I hadn't seen Meg that happy in such a long time, and Hera—possibly never. Showing the screen to Poseidon, I grinned.

"Cute. Did Hera tell her yet?"

"Give her some time. I wasn't as hard of a sell because I already knew all this existed, remember?" Moving behind him, I held the ring up between our faces and took a selfie to send back to her.

Me: I'm so happy for you, Meg.

Meg: Is that a ring?!

Me: It's happening tomorrow.

I'd made up my mind, but Atlantis was the final piece I needed to face the King of the Gods.

Meg: You're going to be amazing.

Me: You two have fun. ;)

Slipping my phone away, I lifted my gaze to an awaiting Poseidon in front of me with his burly arms folded.

"I still don't think this is a good idea," he grumbled.

"But a favor is a given?"

"I'm going to regret ever saying that, aren't I?" His beard hid the smile on his lips, but his eyes sparkled, giving him away.

"Time will tell." I took his arms and wrapped them around my hips. "Whisk me away."

He ported us underwater in the middle of the ocean. If I'd been a full-fledged goddess, the sight of Atlantis would've shown immediately. After he waved his hand in front of us in an arch, the familiar pillars and spires nestled fathoms below any unknowing human eyes or mind appeared. Kicking my feet behind me, I swam forward, gasping at the rubble of the once powerful city. The blue beacon that shone from the center tower, beaming skyward, had gotten so dim you could scarcely make it out through the murky waters surrounding our home. It didn't even have enough power for the dome shield it produced, keeping out all unwanted guests.

"You weren't kidding. How did this happen?" I gulped, swimming to a building with a giant hole in the side.

"The creatures have battled for control of it. I've stopped them every time, but without harmony, chaos is bound to ensue."

Without...me.

"I knew you wouldn't be able to resist coming back here," Skylla screeched from behind us. Her tentacles lashed out.

"Cordelia," Poseidon yelled, making a silver trident, the twin to his own but

more petite, appear in my hand.

My old trident. He'd kept it.

Twirling the trident in my palm, I held it above my head in a stabbing motion. "I don't want to fight you, Skylla. Simply talk."

"Talk is so very cheap, Amphitrite. I've been waiting a long time to get my revenge. Have been ever so patient." She let out a shrill scream and launched two tentacles at me.

Using the prongs of my trident, I deflected one. Poseidon darted in front of me, stabbing his trident through the second.

Skylla let out a blood-curdling cry, yanking her tentacle from the sharp prongs, sending a spray of blood.

"Skylla, I want to apologize. I was a completely different person back then. I was jealous. Confused." I held the trident's staff above my head as one of the dragon heads on her tentacles snapped at me, making it bite the indestructible metal—Atlantean metal.

"Jealous? Over something I didn't do? And so you turned me into—into this?" She roared, throwing her large arms out at her sides.

"I didn't know the herbs would do this to you, Skylla." My brow pinched, and I tightened my grip on the staff. "If I could drop the curse, I would."

Skylla's chest heaved before all dragon heads snapped and snarled. "It isn't good enough. Nothing you say or do will *ever* be good enough."

"That is enough," Poseidon's voice boomed as he sent a sonic wave through the water with his hand, forcing Skylla back. "If you won't accept her apology, then you best make yourself scarce and *pray* she doesn't want to hunt you down when she's Queen again."

I kept the prongs pointed in her direction, furrowing my brow.

Had I thought it'd be that simple? She'd accept my apology, we'd hug it out, and the dragon heads would let me scratch them all under the chin?

Skylla's fists clenched and vibrated at her sides before she disappeared in the dark depths, a fading shriek following her. The trident fell limp in my hands, and my shoulders slumped forward. Poseidon floated in front of me, gently taking the weapon from me.

"You alright?" Despite the very recent threat on my life, his gruff voice still made my skin tingle.

"I feel terrible. How could I have done that to her?"

He scoffed. "I've done far worse. Trust me."

I cut him an exasperated glare.

"Not helping. Right." He snapped his fingers, floating tiny bubbles in front of him. "When you're Queen—you can lift her curse. At the very least, manipulate it."

"I can? But how? The herbs came from—" I bit my knuckle. "I don't remember who I got them from."

"Doesn't matter. She's a creature of the sea now, which will give you the means to control. Not to mention she was a previous nymph, like you."

I curled my hands under my chin. "I'm so ready, Seid. I am." Turning to look at a once vibrant, brightly shining city's ruins and rubble, I sighed. "And I *must* fix this."

"You will." He slipped his hand into mine, making circles against my palm with a thumb.

Lifting my head high, I nodded. "Set up a meeting with Zeus. First thing tomorrow, I'll stand before him and ask—no—*demand* my reign back."

"You're going to *demand?*" A sly grin curved his upper lip.

"Don't think I can?"

He turned to me, tugging my hand to bring me flush against him. "I *dare* you."

"Challenge accepted." I preened up at him, snaking my arms around his neck. "Spiral us."

"You better hold on tighter, soon-to-be Queen." He brushed his lips against mine, waiting for me to tighten my grip around him.

Making his trident disappear, he held onto me with one hand, turning his other into the same ocean water we floated in. After several twirls, we slowly spun in a circle, his power creating streams and helixes of bubbles around us. The momentum built and built until we spun in unending spirals toward the surface. Laughing, I'd grazed over the thought of the consistent circling making me dizzy as a mortal, but pressed my cheek to his to ground me.

We breached the surface and bobbed, wrapped in each other's arms. The setting sun cast purple, pink, and orange hues in streaks across the sky, reflecting in the sparkling ocean waters.

"I love you," I whispered, and we watched the rest of the sunset with the best seats in the house.

SEVENTEEN

We stood in front of the Crane, Crane, and Wallace Law building in New York City. I donned the one dress jacket and pencil skirt I owned, styled my hair, and fished my black stilettos from a black hole in my closet.

"I cannot believe Zeus, King of the Gods, is practicing law," I mumbled, folding my arms.

Poseidon put on a dress shirt and slacks but refused to tie his hair back, stating his brother would have to get over it. He opened the door for me, ushering me inside. "You don't want to hear other cover jobs he's had through the years. Trust me."

"You're right. I don't. Is he at least a good lawyer?" I held my clutch in one hand and grabbed Poseidon's hand with the other.

"Unfortunately, he's the best this side of the country."

"Why, unfortunately?"

"Because he's a damn criminal defense lawyer," Poseidon grumbled, pressing a hand to my lower back and guiding me to the front desk.

"What?" I snapped, prepared to spout unending questions when a woman my height with cropped brown hair approached us.

"Are you Mr. Vronti's three o'clock?" The woman twirled her hair as she scanned Poseidon's arms and chest.

Sliding in front of my soon-to-be-again husband, I flashed a charming grin. "We are."

"So, you're his brother, huh? The apple most certainly does not fall far from the tree. I can see the resemblance." Ruth bit her lip, leaning to the side to peer around me.

"Just what I love to hear," Poseidon mumbled.

I took one of his arms and wrapped it around my shoulders.

The woman cleared her throat and adjusted her wire-rimmed glasses. "Right this way, please.

Poseidon's mouth pressed against my ear. "Defending your territory there, Starfish?" He grinned into my hair.

"You bet your ass I am." I playfully elbowed him in the ribs.

Chuckling, he curled a hand over my hip as we followed the woman.

"I'm Ruth, Mr. Vronti's assistant. He said he's been looking forward to this meeting all day." Ruth offered a warm smile over her shoulder.

"I bet he has," Poseidon said through a cough.

I bit the inside of my cheek. "You always get so feisty when you know we're going to be around your brother," I whispered.

"He brings it out of me."

"Here we are." Ruth opened her hand to an awaiting meeting room. "Do either of you need any refreshments while you wait? He should only be another minute or two."

"Water?" I hovered by one of the rolling chairs nestled against the long glass table.

"Of course. Bottled okay?" Ruth's perky nose perked even more when she smiled.

"Perfect," I answered before taking a seat.

Ruth scurried away, letting the glass door click shut behind her.

I sat straight, folding my hands in front of me first on the table, dropped them to my lap, and then back to the table.

Poseidon slid his large hand over both of mine and raised a brow. "Relax. It's going to be fine."

Nodding, I flattened my palms on the table. "I'm actually looking forward to the look on his face."

Poseidon snorted, and we both stiffened as the door swung open.

Ruth trotted in, setting two bottles of water in front of us. "I swear he should only be a few more minutes. He's in a meeting with the prosecution over his latest big case, and it's gone over the scheduled time. This happens often." She gave a reassuring smile before bouncing on her heels and exiting.

I blew out an exasperated breath and slumped in my chair, resting my head on the back. "He hasn't changed a bit."

"I highly doubt his punctuality ever will. He likes to make people sweat." Poseidon leaned his forearms on the table, swiping one of the bottles into his grasp.

"Oh, that has already started." I plucked my jacket's collar. "Thank Olympus, I'm wearing a jacket over this blouse."

"How many times did you practice your speech in the mirror when I dropped you off last night?" Poseidon's eyes gleamed at me as he sipped from the bottle.

"Only twice." I crossed my arms in a huff. "Okay fine. Four times."

"Want to practice? I can pretend I'm him."

I scrunched my nose. "Thanks, but no thanks. I don't want you even pretending you're him."

Chuckling, he tilted his head back and finished the water.

I stood, moving to a corner of the room, pinching the bridge of my nose, and going over in my head what I planned to say to him.

The door cracked open, and I froze with my back to it.

"I'd say I'm sorry I'm late, but then I remember the company," Zeus said as he entered, smirking and closing the door.

"How's it going, asshole?" Poseidon said.

Why hadn't I turned around yet? My heels were clearly glued to the floor.

"Eh. Things are bound to turn around eventually. Who's the babe?"

I clutched my hands at my chest.

Poseidon cleared his throat.

Rolling my shoulders back and wiping any evidence on my face that my nerves were on overdrive, I turned on one heel.

Zeus had a smug grin on his face, but it morphed into shock and anger when he locked eyes with me. "What. The fuck?"

"Surprised to see me?" I raised my brows.

"You're damn right I am." He cut his glare to Poseidon, pointing at me. "What is this all about, Don?"

"What the Tartarus does it look like? She's back. We're together again." Poseidon pushed off the table, standing and tensing his arms.

Zeus rolled his eyes and turned away from us. "Oh, for fuck's sake. Can a King god catch a break?"

Mustering every ounce of courage surging through me, I crossed the room, standing directly behind Zeus. "I want my Queendom back. My immortality. All of it."

"Oh, do you?" Zeus whirled to face me, looming over me like the rain clouds he commanded. "Tough. Shit."

His words jarred me, making my brain fuzzy. Shaking it off, I stood my ground. "Yes. I know I failed on my responsibilities thousands of years ago. But banishing me to the stars? Making me watch my family gradually forget about me? Don't you think it was a tad, I don't know, harsh?"

Zeus's left nostril bounced. "You got off easy, Amphitrite because you were my brother's wife. Would you like to know what happened to other gods who failed me?"

"Zeus," Poseidon growled, stepping toward us.

"Don." Zeus pointed at him, lightning sparking from his fingertips and flashing in his eyes. "Don't even think about it." He cut his glare back to me. "I gave you chances. Twice, in fact. You didn't heed my warnings."

"Zeus, please." Resorting to begging made me nauseous. "We've both changed. I won't turn away from my true duties again. He showed me Atlantis—the state our oceans are in. I can *fix* all of it. And I want to more than anything."

The lightning fizzled away, and he lowered his hand, his gaze faltering to the floor.

"You know there's no one more fit for this than her. Stop being so godsdamned prideful." Poseidon's chest heaved.

Zeus clucked his tongue against his teeth. "It has nothing to do with pride. The decisions I make are for the betterment of the universe. It has nothing to do with *me*."

"I will not fail this time, Zeus. I won't." My throat bobbed, thinking of Rhode. "I can't."

A scowl distorted Zeus's features as he shifted his gaze from me to Poseidon and back again. He played with one of the "Z" cufflinks on his shirt, his jaw tightening.

"Amphitrite. If I do this, and you fail again, I will make certain there is absolutely *no* way you can come back. Do you understand?" Zeus's cheek twitched, a hint

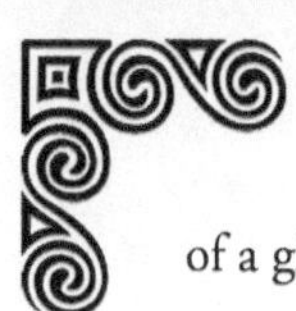

of a gleam in his eyes.

"I understand."

Zeus turned his head at Poseidon. "This is on you if she fucks up."

"She won't." Poseidon shook his head.

My heart soared at Poseidon's words while at the same time raced with the intimidating god king standing toe-to-toe with me, holding my fate in his palm.

Without asking if I was ready, Zeus gripped my shoulder and closed his eyes. My back arched as the familiar power surged through me, intertwining with my bones and pulsing into my veins. Ocean waves crashed against my mind, the rough texture of shark skin brushed my fingertips, and the salty scent of the sea settled around me. Once Zeus's hand fell away, reality trickled in like raindrops on a boat deck—collecting little by little until I stood in the meeting room as myself, as Cordelia, but so much more. My very pores coursed with power, begging to be free after being suppressed for such a long time.

Zeus's glance turned toward the window behind us, where New Yorkers scurried on the sidewalk. "Are we done here?" He cracked his knuckles, tossing a piece of ambrosia to Poseidon, the glowing orange crystalline substance landing in his palm.

"I wouldn't dream of asking anything else of you, brother." Poseidon clenched the ambrosia in his fist, glaring at Zeus.

"Good. Take her to Atlantis, I want that situation fixed *today*." Zeus headed for the door.

I ported in front of him in a shimmering sea spray that matched Poseidon's. "Wait."

Zeus thinned his lips. "Oh, is there something else I can do for you, your highness?"

"Rhode. You can help us find her." I pressed my fingertips against the glass behind me.

"What makes you think that?"

"You're King of the Gods. Surely you could—"

Zeus bent forward, bringing his face closer to mine. "I'm not all-powerful. Gaea sure as Tartarus made sure of that. I can't help you. Now move."

I gulped, pushing my hands so fiercely against the door the glass cracked. "No. I *must* find her."

Zeus's eyes dropped to his damaged door, and he sighed, dragging a hand through his dark, neatly trimmed short hair. "Talk to Kairos. He won't be able to take you to her but may be able to tell *when* she is."

I blinked, half expecting him to put up more of a fight. Zeus was…different. An older version of him would've made me grovel at his feet to gain my Queenhood back—and he would've toyed with me, possibly for days, before eventually doing it as a favor in exchange for something else. But now, he only hesitated because he was concerned I wouldn't do my job.

Had Hera leaving him rocked his world more than he let on?

"Thank you." I squinted at him as I stepped aside.

He snarled under his breath, whisking open the door. "Uh-huh."

"Zeus, are you—" I reached forward but curled my fingers back. "Are you alright?"

He paused with a stiff arm on the door. "Nothing Hermes can't look into for me." His jaw tightened. "I will expect double the work from you."

And with that, the King of the Gods prowled to his den as the mortal lawyer.

"Are you ready to finish this, Starfish?" Poseidon stepped to my side, dragging his finger over my cheek.

As a mortal, his touch electrified my skin, but as a goddess, it positively melted it.

"She's calling to me, Seid." I beamed up at him, wrapping my arms around his waist, and after ensuring the blinds were closed, I ported us to the shore.

The waves lapped against my bare feet, whispering to me, beckoning me, asking me to heal it.

"Do you remember what to say, my love?" Poseidon pressed a hand to my cheek.

Even though it'd been eons ago, I remembered saying the words to him for the first time like it happened yesterday.

"I claim the Seas and its King, as he claims me."

He kissed me, making circles on my cheeks with each of his thumbs. Water launched around us, shooting geysers toward the skies. A watery swirl encompassed me, returning my original white robes, my trident, and finally…my silver seashell crown with three petite points. Poseidon slipped the ambrosia in my mouth and kissed my brow. A spark of light blasted through me, traveling to each neuron, tearing them apart before fusing together, binding them for eternity.

Immortality. I'd forgotten how bittersweet it felt—forever finality.

"My Queen," Poseidon whispered against my skin, taking my hand with the ring he'd given me in his and stepping back.

He appeared in his golden armor in a gusting wave—shoulder pieces, gauntlets, grieves, bare chest. His golden pointed crown gleamed atop his dirty blonde hair, and he kissed my ring.

"Let's go restore our home, Cordelia." He held his hand out, encouraging me to walk to the water's edge.

Closing my eyes, breathing the life that vapored around me from the depths of the ocean, I took my first step home. A sonic wave blasted over the surface, pulsing into the sky. Poseidon stood at my side but didn't touch me. Not yet. He let me re-familiarize myself on my own terms. With each step I took into the water, my trail glittered and glowed, warming to my touch. Once the ocean reached my hips, I twirled my hands, casting dew from my fingertips. Inch-by-inch my legs disappeared, replaced by a teal mermaid's tail. I dove in, turning to wait for Poseidon to follow me.

He grinned, circling his hand around himself, producing a golden tail. "As I told you. Like riding a chariot."

I flipped my tail, out-stretching my hands for him to take them. "I don't remember the way to Atlantis, Seid. Show me?"

Interlacing our fingers, he made us barrel roll around one another, our tails brushing.

"We'll take the scenic route. The sea, the animals, all of it—can you feel how much it missed you?"

With every swipe of my arm through the water, it pushed back like an embrace.

"Yes," I breathed out.

He tugged my hand, and swimming side by side, led me through the ocean, our crowns gleaming and glowing bright like a beacon for all aquatic life—an announcement that both the King and Queen had returned. Fish of all varieties circled our arms and tails, sea turtles brushing our arms as they passed. A pod of dolphins appeared from below us, squeaking their excitement, begging me to play with them.

Poseidon squeezed my hand and jutted his chin. "Go on. Keep following me, and they will too." He smiled at me, urging me to swim with them again with a nudge of his elbow.

With a jovial laugh, I swam between the six dolphins, matching every stroke of their tails by flapping mine. Two moved on either side of me, urging me to hold onto their dorsal fins. Grinning, I wrapped my hands around them and with the brute force of two of them together, they catapulted me toward the surface, causing me to breach. The moon above beamed down at me, making my scales shimmer before I flipped backward and dove, re-joining Poseidon at his side.

"It's amazing seeing you like this again." He trailed his fingers over my tail at the flare of my hips.

I shivered against his touch. "It's amazing *feeling* like this again."

"We're almost there. Can you sense it?" Poseidon produced his golden trident, readying to battle off any creatures that could be lurking.

Producing my silver trident, I curled it against my arm, closing my eyes to feel Atlantis's pulse. At first, it was weak, but after pouring all of my power into it, the steady rhythm like a mighty bass drum vibrated in my chest. I flew my eyes open and there in front of us, with no need to reveal this time, was Atlantis.

I wasted no time, reaching for the first pile of debris. The shambles glowed and pulled back together, sealing with a beam of blue light.

"Keep going. I'll keep a lookout and alert you if I see anything." Poseidon curled an arm around my waist and kissed my forehead before swimming up to gain an aerial view of our surroundings.

I continued to work my way around the ruins of our city, pulling it back together, rejuvenating it, giving it life and purpose again. With every completed structure, the building would sigh as if in relief at my healing touch. It'd been so long since I used my powers to this magnitude, the effort was exhausting to the point of almost falling limp to the ocean floor.

A loud growl vibrated off surrounding buildings, followed by several giant black tentacles wrapping around structures and crushing them. A pair of large glowing red eyes appeared from the shadows, its bulbous head sleek with slime.

The Kraken.

"Fucking Tartarus. Keep going, Cordelia. I'll fend it off. We need to get that beacon working," Poseidon yelled, twirling his trident and cradling it in the crook of his arm.

The sight of the monstrous squid may have jarred me—terrified me as a mortal.

As a Queen, I sneered at its presence and readied my trident at my side. Lifting my hands, I continued to heal my fallen city, fighting the urge to collapse. Using the trident's hilt, I pressed it against the ground—leaning on it, touching, and stroking each piece of rubble.

Poseidon roared, swinging his trident and stabbing one tentacle before yanking it out to impale another. Tendrils of black blood clouded surrounding waters, and the Kraken's wails shook the sea bed like an underwater earthquake. The glow of the creature's red eyes pulsed, and it launched two tentacles into Poseidon's stomach, throwing him into the building I'd been mending, destroying it again.

"Honey, I'm trying to repair Atlantis?" I yelled out to him, swirling my hands to bring the fallen pieces back together once more.

Poseidon grunted, the Kraken's tentacles wrapped around him, squeezing him. "I'm so sorry sweetie, I'll be sure to ask the Kraken if it wouldn't mind tossing me in the other direction." With a snarl, Poseidon stabbed through the underside of the tentacle and the creature let go.

Zooming horizontally through the water, Poseidon aimed for the Kraken's neck, using the trident and his arms to choke it. All of the creature's tentacles wiggled, writhed, and swung in frantic movements. Poseidon leveraged his feet on the creature's shoulders, pushing away and leaning back. With gritted teeth, he growled, pulling harder and harder before yelling.

With the last building healed, I used the ounce of strength I had left, flicking my tail to meet with the Kraken face to face, my silver trident gleaming in my palms. The creature glared at me, darting its tentacles, trying to wrap around my waist. I sliced to the left, cutting off one tentacle, stabbed to the right, skewering another. Rolling my neck, I pulled energy from the ocean, replacing only a fraction of what I'd used up repairing Atlantis. Throwing my arms out at my sides, trident in my grasp, I pulsed an echo through the water as soon as Poseidon let go of it. The pulse traveled in ringlets until catapulting into the Kraken, flying it fathoms away, the darkness consuming it and swallowing it whole. My shoulders slumped, the trident falling limp in my hands as I leaned against a pillar, out of breath and woozy.

"Are you alright?" Poseidon's hand caressed my arm.

"I'm fine." A weak smile fluttered over my lips. "Just not used to exerting that much power anymore."

Poseidon smiled, curling one of my arms over his shoulders while one of his

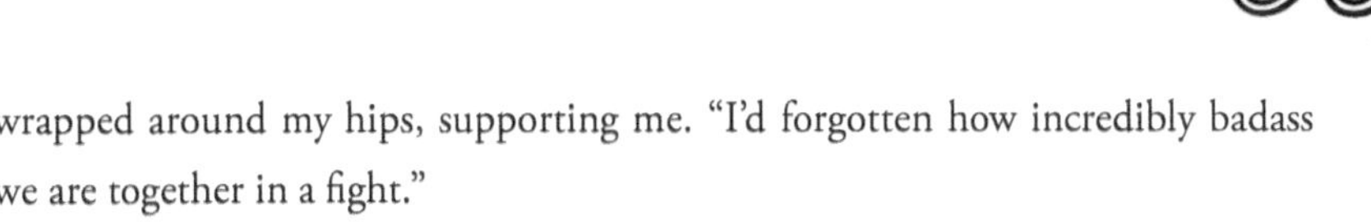

wrapped around my hips, supporting me. "I'd forgotten how incredibly badass we are together in a fight."

"Shame on you." I smirked.

"It looks better than it ever has, Cor." Poseidon swam us in circles, marveling at what I'd created.

"There's one final piece, Seid. But I'll need your help." I held my hand out to him.

Grasping it, he kissed my knuckles, and swam us to the highest point of the tallest building. We each took a side, and holding our tridents with two hands, we slammed the hilts down in unison. A bright beam of blue light flew high, serving as a road map for any worthy of its glory to find Atlantis. A blue holographic dome of hexagons formed over the city, sealing it tight.

Poseidon hugged me to his side and we beamed at the light shining at the city center again.

"Well, well. Look who got her power back," Skylla's slithery voice echoed off the stone buildings around us.

Poseidon and I turned in unison, readying our tridents at our sides.

She'd already been inside before we sealed it off.

"Skylla, wait. I can help you now." I held one palm up, spreading my hand wide.

I hadn't a clue *how* I would help her, but Poseidon said I could…

"No one can help me. You're lying in an attempt to save your own skin." Skylla's dragon head tentacles flapped and snapped.

"You should be worried about *your* skin, Skylla. You're lucky she hasn't already skewered you where you float." Poseidon spun the hilt of his trident in his grasp.

Closing my eyes, I called to my power, keeping my hand outstretched in Skylla's direction. What could I do for her? How? As if answering my unspoken pleas, my magic settled an answer over my mind like water droplets.

"Skylla, I can't make you a sea nymph again, but I can make you a different creature. Though I can't promise you still won't crave flesh. Perhaps it won't be purely of the human variety." I kept my hand up, ready to use my power on her the moment she agreed.

"Another creature? What would be the point? All creatures of the deep are monstrous and vile." She snarled, curling two of the dragon heads to her chest.

"I can make you a mermaid." I felt Poseidon's eyes tracing over me.

Skylla scoffed. "A mermaid that craves flesh. Absurd."

"I'm giving you one opportunity to be transformed, Skylla. After today, the offer no longer stands. Would you rather be a mermaid or a half-woman, half-octopus with dragon head tentacles who sounds like a dying sea lion whenever she speaks?" I glared at her.

Take the deal.

The dragon heads hissed, rotating and gyrating as if they understood they might soon not exist.

Skylla frowned, petting one of the heads with the delicacy of touching a house pet. She lifted her chin and slowly shook her head. "No."

I blinked, dropping my hand at my side before raising it again. "No?"

"Your offer isn't for me. It's for you. No doubt, to make yourself feel better. You want to help me?" She urged the dragon heads forward, their mouths billowing fire. "Fight me."

Fighting wouldn't solve anything even if I did have the strength in me.

"I won't. Let me help you, Skylla. It's not only about relieving my conscience. It's about undoing a wrong. What can I do?" I made my trident disappear, holding my palms up at her.

"Cordelia, what the Tartarus are you doing?" Poseidon growled and swam to my side, pointing the golden prongs of his weapon at Skylla.

"There's only one thing you can do to make me happy, sea queen." She threw her hands to her sides, unleashing the ten black claws. "Die."

Welcome back, Cordelia. Welcome back, indeed.

Skylla screeched and darted forward, Poseidon darting in front of me to block her first blow. I closed my eyes, splaying my hand to pull some of the water's energy into myself—temporarily revitalizing me. Refusing to stab her with my trident accidentally, I clapped my hands together, causing a shockwave to travel through the water and catapult into Skylla. She flew into a nearby building, crumbling it again, making me grimace.

"Seid, whatever you do, please don't kill her." I grasped Poseidon's elbow, looking at him pleadingly.

His jaw tightened before he gave a curt nod.

Skylla let out a blood-curdling scream, her dragons hissing and baring their

teeth. She swam toward us, and I swirled my arms, kicking up a water tornado that made her freeze in place, spinning. Every time she tried to escape, I'd push my hands forward, creating an invisible water wall.

Poseidon smirked at my side, his grip tightening on the trident's hilt.

"You're trying to best a pair of sea gods who can hold their own against the Kraken even, Skylla. Do you really think you can win?" I frowned, ignoring the exhaustion pulling at my brain.

Skylla growled, snarled, and screamed as she continued to try and escape from my swirling water.

"Either let me help you or leave, Skylla. I can't let you destroy Atlantis again." I clenched one fist, making the spinning stop, but holding her in place.

"Just kill me." The words came out of Skylla's throat—strangled.

Witnessing her anguished expression made a lump form in my throat. "I can't do that. It's not the kind of goddess I am."

The dragon heads pulled back, their mouths clamped shut and Skylla's shoulders slumped. "Put me down."

Doing as she asked, I lowered her to the ground and gently pulled my hand away, allowing her free movement. "I am truly sorry for what I did to you. We can't allow you to stay in Atlantis, but you can have whatever place you wish to make a sanctuary under the seas. And you *will* be safe."

"I'm unsure if I'll ever be able to forgive you, Queen, but I do accept your offer of sanctuary."

I nodded to her, a knot forming in my gut. "Then pick the place, and we'll do it. Poseidon will put a shielding spell over it."

Skylla cut her gaze to my king.

Poseidon went silent for a beat before he slammed the trident's hilt against the seafloor. "It will be done. You have my word."

Skylla bowed her head with a scowl, her tentacles curling through the water, pushing her through the dome shield into darkness before disappearing.

"I'm sorry." Poseidon placed a hand on my back. "I can't imagine that's the kind of closure you hoped for, sweetheart."

"It's not, but I shouldn't have expected she'd forgive me. I'm at least happy to know she'll be safe, wherever she ends up."

He kissed my temple. "We've done the illustrious Zeus's bidding. What do you

wish to do now?"

I rested my head on his shoulder and sighed. "There's someone I need to see. And I hope…he wants to see me."

EIGHTEEN

THE PORT OF SAN DIEGO, California. Home to the ship Sea Urchin when it wasn't defending the seas from the surface, stopping whalers. According to Poseidon, the ship my son Triton manned disguised as a mortal for the past decade. I stood on the dock, watching crew members exit the massive ship after roping off. Despite the weather reaching a balmy eighty-five degrees, I shivered from bubbling nerves.

What if he was still angry with me? What if he wanted nothing to do with me? And I couldn't blame him for feeling any of it.

A tall man with ash blonde hair to his collar bone and a light beard hopped to the dock, swinging a duffel bag over his shoulder.

"See you next week, Tim," another man called out to him.

Tim was Triton. He had to be.

When we locked eyes from across the dock...I was sure of it. He was the spitting image of Poseidon with his blonde hair and eyes the same color as the stone on my ring. And he had my nose and sharp jawline. My. Son.

Triton froze, staring at me, a wrinkle in his brow. I'd gone over this scenario a dozen times, weighing out all the possibilities. Hope fluttered in my stomach, but the scowl on his face had me reeling.

"Triton," I whispered, knowing he could hear me despite the distance between us.

The scowl disappeared, and he dropped the bag on the dock with a thud. He power-walked toward me, and I met him halfway, clapping my hands over my nose to keep from crying.

"Mom?" He searched my eyes as if trying to remember my look—trying to remember a face from when he was a child.

"Hey Turtle," I choked out his nickname I'd given him as a boy, making my scales flash on my skin so quickly the human eye would miss them. But he wouldn't.

And now I knew why my entire mortal life as Cordelia I was always so drawn to sea turtles. My subconscious had been throwing me hints at every turn. The only life I led that it ever had. Did fate know I'd finally meet Poseidon?

His black T-shirt hugged his muscular, tanned arms. Not bulky like Poseidon but lean like the body of a swimmer. "I don't understand. How is this—how is this possible?" Without warning, he hugged me, sniffling.

Tears rolled down my cheeks as I wrapped my arms tightly around him. "I can explain everything, but not out in the open like this."

"Right. Yeah. Um. I know somewhere we can go." He peeled back, quickly turning his face away from me and wiping his cheek.

After trotting to his abandoned bag on the dock, he ran back to me, curling his arm around my shoulders with a wide grin and leading me away.

"So, let me see if I have this straight. You've been reincarnated an insurmountable number of times thanks to Aphrodite's spell, but you never remembered who you were? And even if Dad saw you, he wouldn't have recognized you if he hadn't changed because of Athena's curse?" Triton sat across from me with that same quizzical squint Poseidon did when confused.

He'd taken us to the boathouse he stayed in when docked in San Diego. It was quaint, masculine, and surprisingly well kept.

I tapped my fingers on the tackle table between us. "I gave you the short version, but yeah. Once your dad recognized me, little by little, I started to remember."

"And you two are back together? Happy? And I mean *genuinely* happy, not just pretending to save face?" Triton cocked his head to the side, staring at my expression.

No doubt trying to catch me in a lie.

"We've both changed. And yes. What we are now is all I've ever wanted." I sucked in a breath. "Him…and my family."

Triton licked his lips, smiling only with his eyes before he sulked in his chair. "Did he tell you about Rhode?"

I pressed my elbows against the table. "Yes. We're going after her."

Triton's bright eyes snapped to mine. "You know where she is?"

"Not yet. But Zeus, of all people, gave us a lead."

"I'm going with you once you figure it out." His jaw tightened.

"Triton, I—"

He held his hand up, halting my words. "And I'm not taking 'no' for an answer. She's my little sister, and I want to help. I'm not a guppy anymore, Mom." A small smile crept over his lips.

Tears filled my eyes, and I sighed, leaning back in my chair. "No, you're certainly not." I bent forward, sliding my hand over his that rested on the table. "I'm so, so sorry I wasn't there to watch you grow up."

He placed his other hand over mine. "I know you are. Honestly, it's been so long I'm not even mad about it anymore. During my teenage years? Oh, I was so angry, I'd make mini typhoons in the middle of the ocean, but—I eventually accepted it. And Dad. He really stepped up."

"I'm so glad to hear it." I squeezed his hand with a warm smile before sitting back.

"Besides, the memories I had of you when I was a kid—Mom, you were the best. I cherished those times the three of us spent together. The games. The laughing. The swimming. It was enough because I never thought you were coming back." He scratched the back of his head, revealing the small trident tattoo on the inside of his bicep. "I'm sorry. Did you want anything to drink or eat or—I don't have much, but I could conjure us something?"

I waved my hand. "I'm fine. But I do want to hear more about the Sea Urchin. How did that all start?"

"It actually started from me almost getting caught." He smirked, beating his fist against the table. "These whalers, Mom. They're horrible news. They disguise themselves as 'Science Vessels,' but all they're doing is slaughtering thousands of whales. I attacked a ship using my powers, and one of the crew took a photo with his cell phone."

"Olympus. What did you do?"

"Made a wave crash on deck, swept the damn thing into the depths." Triton

shook his head, folding his arms with a sigh.

"Quick thinking." Pride swelled in my chest over the man my son had become. "And that's why you started the Sea Urchin as a mortal."

"Yeah. I mean, don't get me wrong, I still use my powers, but not to the full extent I'd like to. Hopefully, now that you're Queen again, some of the whaling will stop."

"I'll do what I can."

"So, tell me, *Cordelia*—what have you been doing all this time in this life? Marine biology? Surfing like dad?" Triton chuckled, crinkling the skin at the corners of his eyes.

"Marine biology? Yeah, I don't think in any of my lifetimes I could've lasted through that amount of schooling." I laughed, interlacing my fingers in front of me. "I'm an oceanographer and run an ocean conservation charity with my friend, Meg."

"Not surprising in the least." He bumped my hand with a knuckle and a grin.

"I'm also a pro gamer who streams on Glitch every week." I moved my gaze to my palms, squinting.

"Did you just say you're a *pro* gamer? What game?" Triton pressed his forearms on the table, his eyes brightening.

"*Tides of Atlantis.*"

Triton slapped the table. "Holy shit. Mom, that's amazing. Not to mention *incredibly* cool."

"Yeah? I thought you'd think I was a dork or something."

"Are you kidding? It makes total sense, too, with how much I remember you loving games. It's great you found something to make you happy besides the ocean."

"Oh, you mean the video game *about* the ocean?" I laughed, resting my chin in my hand.

"Hey." Triton threw his hands up. "It doesn't involve getting wet."

I sighed, staring at my handsome son, putting his face to memory. "I'm so proud of you, Triton."

His cheeks turned crimson, and he scratched the back of his head—another gesture he inherited from his dad. "Wow. I never thought I'd hear that from my mother again."

"Well, get used to it. I have a lot of lost time to make up for."

"As long as it doesn't involve spankings or embarrassing me in front of my friends, I'm game." He winked at me with a wide grin.

"Ah, I see. So, you're saying the next time I make a surprise visit to the docks, I should give you a big fat wet kiss on your cheek in front of your crew?" I wiggled my eyebrows.

"Hey now." He pointed at me. "The jokes on you. They'd be jealous their own hot moms aren't there."

My cheeks warmed, and I shook my head, snickering. "Oh, stop, Triton."

"I'm glad you're back, Mom. I really am. And once we find Rhode…we'll all be together again."

I sighed, closing my eyes and envisioning it. "It's all I dreamed about since the moment I remembered who I was, honestly."

"We'll find her. You don't back down on anything once you set your mind to it."

"You remember that do you?" I grinned.

A laugh swelled from his chest. "Dad certainly does."

I joined in the laughter, and it continued for a solid minute until we both dabbed tears from the corners of her eyes as it died down. "This has been nice, but I should get out of your hair. I know I showed up out of the blue and—" I stood but cut my sentence short once Triton appeared in front of me.

"Out of my hair? Mom, I haven't seen you in *hundreds* of years. The only place I want to be right now is right here with you getting reacquainted." He squeezed my shoulders before pulling me in for another hug. "And probably at least a dozen more of these."

Laughing, I hugged him back, positively beaming inside. "Alright. Deal."

We spent hours talking, reminiscing, laughing, and the reunion was everything I could hope for. We were in the middle of a game of Red Hands, trying to out-slap the other, when Poseidon appeared, sending a sea spray throughout the cabin.

"I had a lot of things in mind that I'd walk in the middle of, but my wife trying to slap the top of my son's hands was *not* one of them." Poseidon quirked a brow.

Grinning, I leaped from the table, wrapped my arms around his neck, and kissed him.

"It's been ages since I've seen it, and it's still as gross as I remember," Triton

teased.

Poseidon chuckled. "How you doing, son?"

Triton threw his hand out for a shake, and the two manly gods proceeded to do what I'd dubbed the "bro hug."

"I was doing great before, but now—" Triton flashed me a smile. "Even better."

My word. He was so much like his father.

"Glad to see the reunion is going well." Poseidon wrapped one arm around Triton's shoulders and the other around my hips, pulling us both to his sides. "I have some news."

"Oh?" I peered up at him.

"I tracked down Kairos."

Gasping, I turned to look at him. "You have?"

"Yeah. We can go whenever you're ready, but I don't want to rush you both."

Triton gave a hearty slap on Poseidon's back. "If this is about Rhode, you two should go. Mom and I have plenty of time to catch up."

I squeezed Triton's hand.

"You ready then, Starfish?" Poseidon trailed his fingers down my arm.

"I'm going to tell you the same thing I told Mom. When you go after Rhode, I *am* going with you. I don't care where or when. I'm going to be there." Triton rolled his shoulders back, standing the same height as Poseidon.

"I wouldn't expect anything less, my boy." Poseidon clapped his hand against Triton's shoulder before holding his hand out to me.

I pressed my hands together and fluttered to Triton, raising on the balls of my feet to kiss his cheek. "I'll see you soon."

"I know, Mom. Now go." He gave a reassuring smile.

I didn't take my eyes off my son as Poseidon wrapped his arms around me and ported us away.

We appeared in a front tiled courtyard of a white-washed building with green roofing. Iron lamp fixtures hung from the walls between every rounded archway opening leading inside.

"Where are we?" I asked as Poseidon led me inside.

"Morocco."

Inside, the archways continued, and a stone fountain stood in the center of the next room, surrounded by rounded pillars and benches. Further in, the tiled

walking path turned into a vibrant red carpet with intricate mosaic designs. Rounding a corner, I gasped at the floor-to-ceiling shelves of books—rows and rows of them.

"A library?" I whispered, even though there wasn't another soul in sight.

"The oldest in the modern world." Poseidon squeezed my hand, leading us into a room filled with wooden tables and chairs.

"And Kairos is here?"

We moved into a room with a singular large desk at the front of the room. "He's the curator." Poseidon spun in circles, searching, and still holding my hand, bringing me with him. "Kairos?"

A man appeared with a withered red book in his hands from the shadows. There was very little hair on his head, but what remained was stark white along with the long beard that hung to his stomach. He squinted at us through his monocle.

"How do you know that name?" The man asked, slamming the book shut, sending dust flying.

"Are we alone?" Poseidon twirled his finger in the air.

The man rested his fists on his hips. "Yes."

"I'm Poseidon."

"Uncle Poseidon. Not sure we've ever met." The man smiled, and in a swirl of torn paper and glowing numbers, he transformed into a young man with a single lock of hair draping from his forehead to his hips.

Poseidon looked down at me with a smirk before moving his gaze back to Kairos. "You'll have to excuse me if I've lost track of my brother's children."

"No offense taken in the slightest." Kairos waved his hand. "How can I help you?"

"We were hoping—" I stepped forward and paused. "Sorry, that was rude. I'm Cordelia. Formerly known as…Amphitrite."

Kairos grinned wide and pressed his fingertips together. "The King and Queen of the Seas reunited at last. How delicious. I tracked you through all your lifetimes, you know. My, my, did you have some *lives*."

I rubbed the back of my neck. "You're telling me. But we were hoping you could help us find our daughter. She got pulled through a portal in Atlantis, and we think it may have been to another time."

"It is Rhode you speak of, I presume?"

"Yes," Poseidon replied with a frown.

Kairos nodded, steepling his fingers. "I can see what the universe says to me, but I'd need something of hers."

"Something—but how could we possibly—" I started, feeling my body as if I actually had an item from her possession.

"Here," Poseidon's voice boomed, removing one of the bracelets from his wrist. A simple one made of twine with a singular cowrie shell in the center.

I touched the crook of his arm with a crinkled brow.

"When she was eight, she made us friendship bracelets, and she gave me this one saying it was hers. We've never taken them off." He smiled, but forlornness muddied it.

"Oh, Poseidon." I gulped and shoved my face against his shoulder.

"This will work nicely. Thank you," Kairos said, curling the bracelet into his palm and closing his eyes.

A circular band of glowing sparks curled around him, forming a helix before settling as a halo circling his chest. Shooting stars arched over his head followed by flaming rocks, geysers of volcanic lava, and descending numbers—they spun and spun until abruptly, they stopped.

Kairos's eyes flew open, glowing red. "1719. The Caribbean."

"That's still the golden age of piracy," Poseidon mumbled.

Fear burned down my spine. "By Olympus."

"And she's alive," Kairos added before he exhaled and his eyes returned to normal.

"I've told you all I can. And unfortunately, I have no means of transporting you there, nor do I know of any such god with the power to do so." Kairos steepled his fingers again after handing the bracelet to Poseidon.

"There has to be someone." I slapped a hand on my forehead.

"I do know of one person, but I'm not too keen on the risk we'd take releasing the raging asshole." Poseidon tied the bracelet back to his wrist, nestling it in with the others.

"Kronos? Tartarus no. I just found you again. Last thing I need is you getting eaten."

Poseidon grabbed one of my belt loops and pulled me to him. "We'll figure it out. Now that we know where she is, it'll make things that much easier."

"Can I help you two with anything else?" Kairos clasped his hands behind his back.

"You've been a great help, Kairos. Thank you." I slipped my hand into Poseidon's.

"Any time." Kairos bowed, morphing into the older man before walking away.

"Do you think she's mixed herself in with pirates?" Poseidon rubbed his chin, glaring daggers into the red carpet.

"Nah. There's far more in the Caribbean in that time other than piracy. Surely she's a merchant or scholar or…"

Poseidon locked gazes with me, and we both knew, given her powers, the likelihood of what would make an ideal cover for herself, but neither of us wanted to say it out loud.

Piracy.

NINETEEN

WE'D RACKED OUR BRAINS for days, asking dozens of fellow gods who might have the power to time travel, and continually came up empty. It was an odd feeling possessing so much power as the Queen of the Seas, yet powerless to find my daughter. I'd promised Meg my transition wouldn't affect our friendship and had already gone radio silent on her since getting wrapped up in finding Rhode.

I knocked on her front door, smoothing out my shirt as I waited for her to answer. Laughter floated from the other side—from two people. Smiling, I sucked on my lips as the door whipped open. Meg had been grinning, and it widened when she spotted me.

"Cory, holy hell. I haven't heard from you in days." Meg yanked me to her for a hug.

I hugged her back, spying the fridge door open in the kitchen with a pale hand wrapped around the handle. "I'm sorry about that. I've been—."

Wait. Meg knew I was a goddess but didn't know Hera not only knew too but was one herself. When did my life become this complicated?

"Occupied with something very important." I gave an exaggerated wink to Meg.

She leaned back until the realization slowly dawned on her, and she nodded. "Right. Yeah. Muy importante."

"Hey, Hera," I said toward the kitchen with a grin.

Hera's head popped over the top of the fridge door. "Amp—er, Cordelia."

"I see you two are getting well acquainted." Clasping my hands in front of me, I nudged Meg in the ribs.

"I guess we have been spending almost every waking moment together these past few days, haven't we?" Meg ran a finger down the bridge of her nose, looking at Hera sidelong.

Hera rested her forearms on the still open fridge door, and with her chin resting on an arm, smiling, she replied, "And I'm not complaining one bit."

Meg's cheeks turned pale pink.

I bit the inside of my mouth so as not to squeal like a teenage girl. "I hoped, if it's alright with you, Hera, I might borrow my friend for a couple of hours?"

"Of course. You *did* see her first." Hera winked, tapping her red nails on the door with a grin.

Meg choked out a laugh before bobbing her brows at me. "What'd you have in mind?"

"It's a surprise. I'll meet you out by the Jeep?"

"Sure. Okay?" Meg scrunched her nose before moving for the door. "Feel free to stay here. Oh, and snoop around if ya want. I ain't got anything to hide." Chuckling, Meg beat her hand on the doorframe before exiting.

That would make *one* of them.

After hearing Meg's footsteps fade away, I bolted for the kitchen. "Have you told her yet?"

"Told her? Told her what?"

The fridge door creaked from her leaning on it, her bare feet shuffling on the tiled floor.

"You know exactly what I'm talking about." I squinted at her feet and panned up to her arms.

"Of course, I haven't," Hera spat in a loud whisper.

"Why are you still *in* the fridge?"

Hera clucked her tongue at the inside of her cheek. "I'm naked."

"Oh." I widened my eyes. "*Oh.* Oh, shit. Did I interrupt something?"

"No. You didn't. I'm just me, and I walked out of the bathroom like this to surprise her."

I folded my arms. "Why don't you conjure clothes on yourself?"

"Because—" She sighed and beat her forehead against her arm. "My powers aren't acting normal. Ever since I cut ties with Zeus, one day I could be overpowerful and the next practically mortal."

"That's strange. Maybe your powers are readjusting? Reverting to the way they were before becoming Queen?"

"I hope you're right." She bit her thumbnail.

"You should tell her. She knows about our world already, which gives you a huge advantage."

Hera slapped a hand on the door. "You told her?"

"She's my best friend. I couldn't keep that from her. And she took it surprisingly well, all things considered."

"Wow." Hera's gaze fell to her knuckles. "We've had a good thing going. I didn't want to risk screwing it up."

"Tell her. Air everything out, let her process it, and I promise you, it won't change anything. What it *will* change is you one hundred percent being able to be yourself around her and most importantly—no lies." I patted her arm.

"I'll think about, Amph." She patted my hand back. "Thank you.

I snapped my fingers. "Oh, and I know it's a little thing but, it's Cordelia now. Amphitrite is a name locked in a corked bottle at sea."

Hera grinned and nodded. "Cordelia it is. I like it."

"I better go before she gets suspicious. She's incredibly intuitive." Giving her arm one last squeeze, I turned away.

"I know." Hera smiled, her eyes trailing off into who knows where. A dress materialized over her body, and she gasped. "Well, look at that."

Grinning, I left Meg's apartment and met her in the parking lot. She leaned against my Jeep, her feet crossed at the ankle, chewing on a toothpick and staring at the asphalt.

"The real reason I've been MIA for a few days is that I've been finding information about where my daughter is, Meg."

"Jesus. You have kids. I already forgot." Meg grabbed my shoulder. "Wait. You said she's missing?"

"An accident in Atlantis and a story I swear I'll explain in its entirety someday." I tugged at her jacket with a warm smile.

Considering Meg just recently learned Greek mythology was anything but myth, trying to describe Atlantis and the way it operates seemed like begging for her head to explode.

"Atlantis," Meg mumbled, staring at the ground.

"It, too, is real." After patting her arm, I climbed into the Jeep, whistling at her to get her attention.

"Before we head out, I have something for you." She shoved a pink plastic bag at me with a stiff arm.

Frowning, I took the bag, but didn't look in it. "It's not my birthday."

"Just. Open it, Cordelia."

As I peered inside, I recognized the Funko logo and gasped before yanking the box out. The Poseidon toy from *Tides of Atlantis*. It looked nothing like the real Poseidon—my Poseidon—but it was the version I knew of him in my mortal life as Cordelia Bourne. He had long white hair past his chest with an equally as long beard, blending in. Green octopus tentacles replaced his legs, making me frown at the thought of Skylla, but the usual radiant three-pronged trident would remain synonymous with the King of the Seas.

"I promised if you placed in the tournament, I'd buy it for you, remember?" She nudged my knee.

"I do." I squeezed her thigh with a grin. "Thank you."

"So, you're a goddess now? A full-fledged goddess?" Meg asked me with wide eyes as she crawled into the passenger seat on autopilot.

"I am. Queen of the Seas and all." After giving her a warm smile, I slipped my sunglasses on and pulled out of the lot.

"You don't seem any different."

"Well, good. It'd be a real drag if mortals could tell I wasn't one of them."

Meg held her hand out the window, letting the wind caress through her fingers. "Where are we going, Cor? You know I hate surprises. Especially if this is of the godly variety."

"We're going swimming."

"Swimming?"

I beat my hands against the steering wheel to the tune of *Beyond the Sea*. "Yup. With sharks. And all you need—is a tank." Cutting my gaze, I caught her expression bordering on excitement and terror.

"They don't like me. Who's to say they'll listen to you?"

"Oh, they'll listen. Sharks fear humans more than the other way around. Fear is just as potent as blood in the water." Pulling into the beach's parking lot, I moved to the back, grabbing the scuba tank and gear.

Meg shut the car door and shuffled toward me. "We're seriously doing this? What if people see?"

"They won't." I handed her the gear. "I'm going to port us away from the tourist traps and directly underwater, so check your regulator and suit up, my dear."

She took the tank and let her arms flop. "I retract my statement. You're definitely not the same."

I frowned as I turned to walk along the shoreline. "Is that a bad thing?"

"No. You're more confident. Comfortable. Like you've settled into your own skin." Meg bumped me with her shoulder.

"I have. And Poseidon he—" I clutched my hands to my chest, missing him already. "We're a force to be reckoned with now."

"A power couple. I dig it." Meg slung the tank over her shoulders after sliding into her wetsuit.

Far enough away from any crowds, I stopped, letting the water's surf lap against my toes, waiting for Meg to finish gearing up.

"Just talk like we normally do. I'll be able to hear you." I smiled up at her, going on my tippy toes to pull a piece of hair out of her mask. "Ready?"

She gave a thumbs up.

After curling our arms together, I ported us to the depths where several circling hammerhead sharks swam. Meg gasped, and I gripped her tight to keep her from fleeing on the spot.

"Trust me," I said, floating to the sharks and outstretching my hands to them.

They both swam under my touch, letting my fingertips trail over their hands and down their bodies and tail. They repeated the motion, turning around once they'd reached the end, only to get pettings all over again.

"Come here, Meg. I promise they won't bite you."

After a few deep breaths on her part, she appeared beside me with shaky hands. Gently, I took one and held it out. One shark continued to circle under my touch while the other switched to Meg.

Meg gasped and laughed. "This—this is amazing."

Closing my eyes, I willed my scales to appear, feeling more at home with them radiating from my skin. Meg smiled at me from behind her mask, her eyes beaming at the shark.

"Follow my lead." I turned on my belly, swimming in the style of a dolphin without my mermaid tail.

The sharks changed course, settling on either side of me. Kicking her flippers, Meg caught up, and we swam in tandem, each with a shark on our right.

"Woo! This. Is. Amazing," Meg screamed, shoving her fists sky high and laughing.

Grinning, I stopped swimming, tuning my ear to the familiar sound waves pulsing through the sea. A great white shark emerged from the dark shadows below us, making Meg shriek and swim behind me. The hammerheads darted away.

I curled an arm behind me, giving Meg a reassuring pat on the arm. "I promise you, you're fine. She's curious."

The great white floated up until we were face to face. She was one of the largest I'd ever seen at roughly six meters. She had multiple scars over her gills and toward her neck—some from mating, others from Olympus knows what. She had an exhausted glaze in her eyes that choked my heart.

Reaching for each side of the massive shark's head, I pressed our foreheads together and closed my eyes. Siphoning every ounce of pain and every tendril of sadness from her into myself, I passed on a fraction of the true happiness blossoming within me. My scales buzzed against my skin. Little by little, the brightness in the shark's gaze returned. I opened my eyes, smiling at her change in demeanor. After kissing the tip of her nose, she flicked her tail and swam off. When I turned to Meg, she floated motionless with eyes as wide as buoys.

"If somehow I wasn't fully convinced you were who you say you are, there's no denying it now," she said, her eyes still wide.

I tugged on the straps of her tank. "You alright? Want to call it a day?"

"Are you kidding? Let's do this until my air supply is out."

We laughed and swam with sharks, whales, dolphins, and every other variety of animal Meg requested for the next hour. The pure delight radiating from her in unending waves gave me all the reassurance I needed that not only was Meg adjusting to the true me but accepting it.

I sat at my desk, scrolling through hundreds of photos from a recent dive, marking the first round of candidates for editing and eventually selling to magazines.

Cocking my head to the side, I noticed a familiar blob in the background of one shot and zoomed in. These were taken before the cruise—before I remembered who I was, and there was Poseidon as a mirage, barely caught in the lens. He may have looked like driftwood and seaweed to the human eye, but I recognized my husband from the way his hair floated in the water alone.

"Seems I've been caught," Poseidon's voice rumbled near my ear.

Grinning, I swiveled in my chair to face him, receiving the kiss he immediately swooped in to give. "I can't believe you were there the entire time, and I had no idea."

"It was your less advanced demi-god brain." He tapped the top of my head.

I swatted him away with a laugh.

"What in the Seven Seas is—that?" Poseidon pointed at the Funko Pop Meg bought me displayed on my gaming desk.

Biting back a smile, I held the figure out to him. "Poseidon. Don't you recognize yourself?"

"This looks nothing like me. And why the Tartarus do I have sea witch legs?" The size of his hand made the modest-sized figure look microscopic.

"Just another depiction of you, hun. How would mortals know what you look like? They had to come up with something for the game."

He grunted and shoved the figure back at me. "Remind me to write the video game company a letter."

Chuckling, I snatched the figure and set it back on my desk. "I took Meg swimming with the sharks today without a cage. You should've seen her face, babe." My chest hummed.

"No kidding. It must've been some experience for a mortal. Perks to having a Queen goddess as a best friend, huh?" He bumped a knuckle against my cheek.

"I should be done here pretty soon." Lazily, I pointed at the computer monitor.

"Can it wait? There's something I need to do, and I'm afraid if I don't do it while I have the nerve built up, I'm going to back out." He cracked his knuckles.

Standing, I wrapped a hand over his wrist. "What is it, Seid?"

"Medusa. I'm going to apologize."

My jaw dropped, and he stuck a finger under my chin to close it. "But you want me to come with you? Wouldn't that only piss her off more?"

"Doubtful. You didn't do anything. I need her to see there's no foul play. I'll do

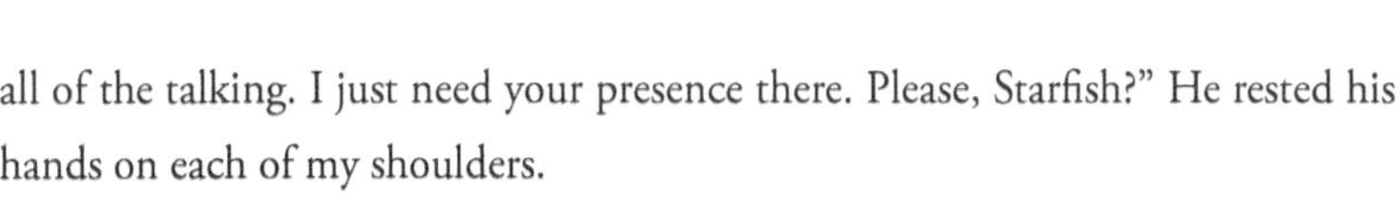

all of the talking. I just need your presence there. Please, Starfish?" He rested his hands on each of my shoulders.

"Yes. Of course." I slipped my hand into his, waiting for him to take us to wherever Medusa hid.

We appeared in front of a dark cave and a chill coursed through my bones. I tightened my grip on Poseidon's hand, and he pulled me closer.

"Does Medusa's power work on gods?" I whispered, my bottom lip quivering from the damp chill inside the cave as we entered.

"Not kings or queens," he answered simply, his jaw tightening.

I curled against his side once the smoke skirted the ground from a nearby cavern. Hissing sounds reverberated off the walls as we drew near. As we rounded the corner, Medusa sat on a single wooden chair at a simple wooden table in the center of a stone room, rock formations hanging from the ceiling—jagged and deadly.

"What in the seven hells are you doing here?" Medusa roared, slapping her palms on the table and standing.

The snakeheads all snapped in our direction, hissing and baring their fangs. Medusa's face remained beautiful with deep brown eyes glowing yellow at certain angles from her power, full lips, and high cheekbones—but centuries worth of pain and suffering settled in her gaze.

"Medusa—" Poseidon started, holding up his palms. "I swear on pain of death I've come to make amends."

"Death? What would you have to fear from such a thing? You, King god, are never punished due to your status, let alone killed." She dug her long black nails into the wood, the tail from her snake body coiling around one of the legs.

"What he says is true, Medusa." I made the scales appear to prove who I was. "I can attest to it. If you'd only listen to him."

Her face softened for a fraction of a second before hardening into the same stone she turned everything else.

"Amphitrite. You were banished to the stars by Zeus." Medusa scoffed, flicking her wrist at Poseidon. "Even your own Queen was punished while you remained unscathed."

"Not true." Poseidon clenched his free hand into a fist.

"I'm listening." Medusa clicked her fingernails together, her snake body moving

from behind the table.

"Athena cursed me as well after our—encounter. Aphrodite created a reincarnation spell to bring Amphitrite back, but she wouldn't remember who she was without me."

Medusa yawned, flicking a finger against the small skull at the center of the belt hanging around her hips. "This doesn't sound nearly as cruel as what she did to me."

"Until I changed as a man, as a god—I could see Amphitrite but wouldn't know who she was. She reincarnated countless times, and we kept missing each other."

Medusa paused and then let out a villainous bout of laughter, the golden metal pieces positioned over her breasts reflecting the fire from the hanging sconces as her chest bounced.

Poseidon and I remained silent. Despite how much it hurt hearing someone laugh at our lifetime of misfortune, she had to contend with her own mishaps.

"I'll admit, knowing this does help a tad, but—" She zoomed in front of us, all snakeheads rearing back and hissing at Poseidon. "You still were not turned into a fucking gorgon. You weren't forced to live a life of seclusion because you fear turning innocent children into stone—fear *killing* them."

"And that's the reason I stopped Perseus from killing *you*." Poseidon glared at one of the snakes, and it whimpered away.

He did what?

"What?" Medusa's face fell, and so did the snakeheads, relaxing.

"Hermes can be a blabbermouth when he's drunk. He told me all about Perseus' plan. The sandals he'd given him, Hades' helmet, a shield from Athena. He planned to protect himself from your sight with the shield and behead you in your godsdamned sleep." Poseidon folded his arms. "I offered to rescue his mother from King Seriphus in exchange for leaving you alone."

"I—" Medusa pressed a hand to her bosom, gliding backward until she bumped into the table, leaning against it.

As if I couldn't love this man anymore.

"That day in front of the temple, I was furious with Athena. You were there, and I knew you desired me as soon as our gazes met. I asked. You agreed. But I should've known Athena would've been a spiteful harpy that it happened in her temple. And for that, I'm sorry. She cursed us both, and I apologize for all of it."

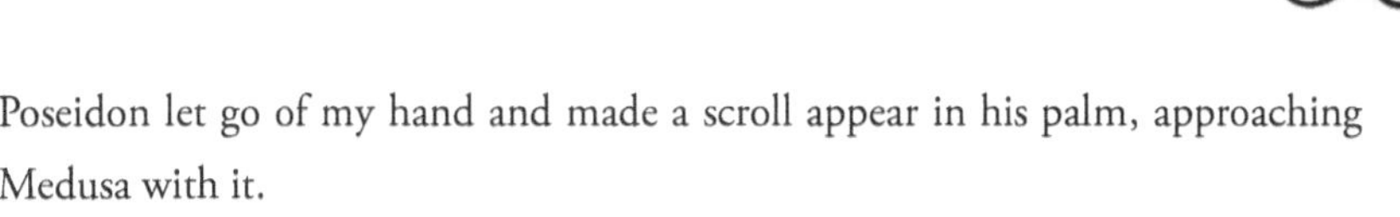

Poseidon let go of my hand and made a scroll appear in his palm, approaching Medusa with it.

Medusa leaned away as if Poseidon would hit her, shielding her face with a forearm. "What is that?"

"A peace offering. A cursed man exists. Anything he touches turns into gold. To further the curse, he was made immortal, so he has to live with it for the rest of his unnatural life."

"So?" Medusa shrugged.

"He can't turn you into gold, and you won't turn him into stone when he looks at you."

The snakeheads of Medusa fell limp, framing her face and simply dangled, shifting against one another. She traced a finger over her lips, staring up at one of the sconces.

"If you decide you want to meet him, this scroll will tell you where he is at all times, whenever you desire." Poseidon held the scroll out to her. "Take it. Please."

Locking gazes with Poseidon, she slowly slid the scroll from his grasp, holding it out in front of her as if it'd catch flame.

"I hope you can find happiness and companionship. You don't deserve living like this." Poseidon bowed his head and turned away, returning to my side and ready to port us away.

"Poseidon—" Medusa called out.

We froze.

"Thank you," she whispered.

Poseidon nodded once and whisked us away.

We were back in my apartment, and I jumped into his arms, kissing him deeply, trailing my fingers through his blonde hair. He held me against him even when we pulled away.

"I knew you changed, but Seid, you have *changed*."

"A man gets a lot of time to think when he loses the love of his life and doesn't know he'll have the chance to make her fall for him all over again."

A tear fell down my cheek, and I hugged him. "We could be torn apart and thrown in each other's paths a thousand different times, and I'd fall for you each and *every* instance."

"But thank Olympus—we don't have to. This is it right here, Cor. This is it."

TWENTY

"YOUR THREATS ARE AS empty as your hands. Because I keep taking the sword from them." Poseidon roared with laughter.

I peeked over my shoulder at my husband. We'd outfitted him with a corner of my apartment to situate his own gaming setup, complete with a monitor, console, controller, chair, and better headset.

"You're really getting into this, aren't you?" I spoke through my headset's mic since we were in a party chat through the game.

"It's crazy, Cor. I *live* this life and yet playing it through the game gives it a whole other angle. Does that make sense?" His controller's triggers made clacking sounds as he feverishly worked the buttons.

"I'm sure your prowess against the AI players and consistently high scores has nothing to do with it, hm?" In the game, I swung my trident around my head before stabbing it into the next approaching enemy.

"You know me so well." Poseidon chuckled as his character, whom he created to look as close to himself as possible, threw the trident across the map like a javelin, skewering the enemy into a nearby stone wall.

"Think you've had enough practice? Ready to take this live and play against other gamers?" Pausing the game, I turned in my seat, letting one arm dangle off the back of the chair.

"We did promise your audience. I'd hate to disappoint them. But first—" Poseidon hooked his foot under my chair and pulled me toward him as he took his headset off.

The armrests of our chairs bumped together, and Poseidon widened his legs, encouraging me to shimmy between them. Pressing my palms on the seat, my fingertips a breath away from his crotch, I bent forward to kiss him.

"I appreciate you doing this, Seid."

When I leaned, it made my shirt billow open. Smiling, he slid a finger inside and trailed his touch between both breasts. "How appreciative?" A growl laced his words.

"You're bad." I slapped him in the shoulder with a grin. "Very appreciative, but we do that now, and I'll be all forms of distracted. I need complete focus."

He frowned, still lazily running his finger over my chest. "I'd hate to be the reason you lose subscribers. You'd never let me live it down."

"And eternity is a long time, Seid." Combing my fingers through his hair, I smiled wide.

He jutted his head at the monitor. "Let's spin this up. The sooner we own enemy players, the sooner we can get to the 'appreciation' portion of the evening." After kissing the tip of my nose, he spun in his chair, scooting himself closer to the desk and sliding the headset back on.

After pulling everything up, I drummed my fingers on my desk, waiting for the moderator to start the chat. It didn't take long for several familiar names to join, and after taking a deep breath, I started the webcam.

"Hey, Sea Farers! I know I primarily stick to free for all mode in *Tides of Atlantis*, but tonight I thought we'd switch it up for a bit of Team Deathmatch." I grinned, waiting for comments to flood the screen.

FriskeeBizkit: Does this mean what I think it means?

"If you haven't guessed, this Wednesday, as will be every third Wednesday of the month, I will have a guest gamer. Everyone, please flap your fins for Simon Thalassa." Clicking into the webcam situated on Simon's monitor, I brought our faces side by side in the corner of the screen.

Poseidon waved, his green eyes popping like gleaming emeralds. "Hey there."

MissTacoX: Sultry, I know he's your soon-to-be husband but pardon me for saying...he's HAWT.

Poseidon chuckled, and my cheeks warmed.

"I couldn't agree with you more, MissTaco. You all ready to see double trident team action?"

HufflePufflenz: This is going to be epic!

My heart raced as a surprising bout of nerves fluttered in my stomach. I'd always played alone. This would be the first time live with a partner—in more ways than one. When the first map loaded, I grinned. I knew it well.

"Simon, head right, and I'll take left. There's a wall some players always climb on top and try to snipe with arrows. We'll beat them to the punch."

Poseidon smiled at me through the camera. "I like your style."

MissTacoX: I can't even with these two.

Just as predicted, another player waited at the top, bow aimed, waiting for the first sap to run below.

"On my count, charge your trident, so it makes a sound and gets their attention, then crouch." I had my character waiting around a corner, careful not to show myself too early.

Still grinning, Poseidon did as I asked, his gold trident bursting with white light as it charged. The opposing player's character turned its back on me, launching an arrow at Poseidon, but he crouched in time, avoiding it.

Holding down the right trigger button, I charged the trident for a heavy attack knowing it'd take several seconds for their bow to reload. As the opposing player turned around, I hurled the prongs of my trident into their chest, and they dematerialized to respawn elsewhere in the map.

FriskeeBizkit: You say epic, I say legendary.

We'd spent the next hour double-teaming other players and dominating the scoreboard with every passing match. We worked like a well-oiled machine, the cogs aligning with every strategy and fighting combination we tried. It made me miss the days we battled together in real-time, but I appreciated the safety which accompanied the silence of the seas.

After saying goodbye and signing off, my arms were around Poseidon's neck before his headset hit the desk, my mouth covering his. He chuckled against my lips as he pulled me against him.

"I truly didn't believe you could get any more attractive," I said through heavy breaths.

"I strive to keep you guessing, Starfish."

In a swirl of shimmering spray, I ported us to Atlantis. A massive bed outfitted with gold embossed sheets rested in the center of a room surrounded by windows

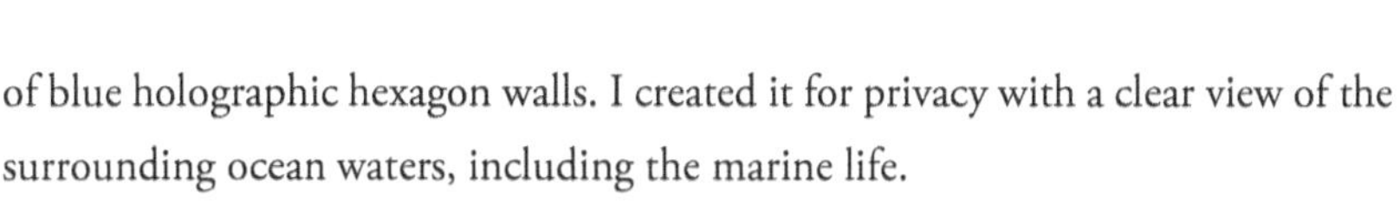

of blue holographic hexagon walls. I created it for privacy with a clear view of the surrounding ocean waters, including the marine life.

"This is new," Poseidon mumbled as he scanned the room.

"I thought I'd do a little redecorating." I held my palm up, wiggling my fingers, creating interlacing tendrils of water. They spiraled around Poseidon, coiling around his arms, his neck, and through his hair.

"Mm. I'd forgotten how good this feels." He closed his eyes, his muscles tensing with each swipe I made with the water.

"The water?"

He returned his heavy-lidded gaze to me. "Your magic."

"Intertwine with me, Seid," I whispered in his ear.

His nose brushed my cheekbone, a low purr vibrating in the back of his throat. As he trailed his fingers down my arm, his magic bubbled from his palm, turning our limbs into water. I kept swirling my power around us, the spray misting against our cheeks. Our bodies continuously morphed from water to flesh when we kissed, causing my insides to writhe. Like falling back into an awaiting pool, I pulled him toward me, porting us to the bed and landing on my back naked.

He landed on top of me, caging my head with his arms, his blonde tendrils skirting my forehead. "Welcome home, Queen."

As if cementing the declaration through action after his words, he plunged into me, rocking his hips against mine. Our water powers had their own reunion, making patterns in the air—figure eights, helixes, sunbeams. Light spilling from the ocean waters around us cast blue shadows through the holographic windows, a manta ray darkening the room for the few moments it took to pass with each flap.

Pinching my knees against his sides, I arched into the sheets, turning the bed beneath me into water, cushioning me, and tantalizing my skin. I flashed my eyes open, staring up at the King of the Seas—my equal. Morphing my fingertips into water, I traced over his lips, leaving a sparkly trail that disappeared with one lap of his tongue. I dragged my fingers down his chest, making goosebumps sprout with each passing touch.

He furrowed his brow with a grunt. "You keep doing that, and I'm going to come undone, Cory."

"Come undone with me then." Sucking his earlobe, I continued my torturous liquid touch, circling right at the base of his shaft.

His lips became a liquid stream as he dipped to kiss my neck, shooting vibrations through my skin and straight to my core. Gasping, I willed my fingernails to return, digging them into his back as I cried out, tensing around him. As I'd asked, he joined me, shaking and rattling through his release. After trailing a feather-like kiss over my lips, he slid behind me to his side, pulling my ass against him.

Smiling, I watched a family of sea turtles swim past and cooed within Poseidon's arms. "Do you think the shield will hold now against the sea monsters?"

"One could only hope. Though I wouldn't mind battling off one or two with you again." He nibbled my shoulder.

"I'd be lying if I said I didn't wish the same." I laughed and trailed my finger over the hair on the back of his hand.

His nose rubbed behind my ear. "Now that Hypnos has allowed you to control your past memories, is there one that sticks out the most to you?"

"The Viking Age." It took only a passing thought to recall it—the smells of blood and sweat, the weight of my shield in my grasp, longhouses in the distance with moss growing on the roofs.

"Shit, really?" Poseidon sat up on one elbow. "Tell me."

I turned on my back, peering up at my husband with a small smile. "I was a shieldmaiden."

"Not surprised by that in the least."

"The memory that keeps rolling through my head is us leaving our village to conquer land. I had a husband—a blacksmith. He'd spend the entire time I was gone forging weapons and would be the first on the shoreline when our boats docked, ready to greet me." Cutting my glance to Poseidon's eyes, the glare I'd expected cut through his gaze.

"I hope we do find someone who can port us to different times so I can kick this guy's ass." Poseidon hugged me to him tighter.

Laughing, I nudged him with my shoulder. "Very long time ago. We didn't know each other existed. Remember?"

"I know, I know. Still." Poseidon kissed the side of my head. "Did you die in battle in that life?"

My heart grew heavy, remembering the distance I'd felt on my deathbed. "No. I got sick. My husband put a sword in my hands, but I remember shoving it back at

him because I didn't want to go to Valhalla without him. And he wasn't a fighter."

"That's—wow," Poseidon mumbled.

"I'd do the same for you, Seid. If there were such a place gods would go—Chaos, perhaps? I'd want to make sure we ended up there together. I married you for eternity." I cupped his cheek in my palm.

He kissed me—delicate and sweet before brushing our noses together. "I'd follow you to the stars now, Cor."

A blue portal appeared at the foot of the bed, making us both jolt to attention. A dark-haired man with a full beard sporting a duster jacket toppled out of it. We both sat up straight, Poseidon snapping his fingers to make a white flowing dress appear over my body.

The man's arms flew up in an "X." "Bloody hell. Were you two—?"

"Take a wild guess, Heph," Poseidon grumbled, not bothering to clothe himself as he moved from the bed.

"Hephaistos?" My brow shot up. "I haven't seen you in ages. Even before I was banished."

Heph clicked his teeth. "Can't say I've been around the 'ol stomping grounds enough to socialize with the pantheon elite. So, no offense taken."

"I wasn't—" Poseidon shot me a look that suggested I'd be wasting my breath if I continued that sentence.

"What are you doing here?" Poseidon folded his arms.

Heph took one step forward and dropped his gaze to Poseidon's bare lower half. "You know, this is the second time I've been in this situation in less than a year. I severely question my life choices." Wiggling his fingers, Heph produced a square device from a jacket pocket.

Sliding from the bed, I clutched my hands to my chest, hope tingling my skin, giving me goosebumps.

"Word on the waves is—" Heph spun the device in his palm, making another portal appear behind him. "—you two need to do a tick of time travel."

Poseidon and I exchanged glances, a glint sparking in our gazes.

"We better grab Triton." Poseidon took my hand.

Hang on, Rhode. Your family is on their way.

WANT TO DONATE TO A REAL OCEAN CONSERVATION GROUP?

I'm currently partnered with Blue Ring, Inc. and ALL proceeds made from my contemporary shark romance (with a hero based on Shark Week's Paul de Gelder): THE OTHER TIDE are donated to them. Please consider checking out the book (Kindle Unlimited counts as well) or going directly to their website to make a donation!

CHECK OUT THE OTHER TIDE:
mybook.to/TheOtherTide

BLUE RING'S WEBSITE:
bluering.blue

BONUS SCENE

POSEIDON

AMPHITRITE. I'D THOUGHT THE name but it stumbled past my lips in a bewildered whisper. I stood at one end of the beach staring at a brunette woman collecting trash from the sand and stopping on occasion to hand something to beach-goers.

It couldn't have been her. My Queen. My Wife. She'd been banished to the stars eons ago with no hope of escape and yet, every neuron in me rippled at the sight of her. A coincidence, maybe? A mortal born who looked similar?

I had to get a closer look—hear her, smell her—from *afar* just incase this wasn't her. Strangers didn't take blatant sniffing lightly, so I've heard.

A blonde woman sunbathing on a towel leaned back on her elbows and shielded her eyes from the sun, looking up at my questionable Queen. "Do you have a flyer or a business card for the charity you work for?"

Charity? Huh.

With so much discreetness I bumped into a young guy's shoulder, making him yell some form of "Watch it," I shuffled behind my mystery woman for her not to see me, but close enough to still hear their conversation.

"We're localized to the Gulf coast." Her voice echoed in my ears, making my heart beat throttle into a Clydesdale's-sized gallop. She had the same lilt, the same breathy cheeriness in her tone, and an alike melodic pitch.

"Donated money helps rid the Gulf of garbage, and every year, we donate to an animal rescue and rehabilitation center." The brunette handed the blonde a business card from her front shirt pocket.

Disregarding her duties to take care of the aquatic life living in our home—the seas and Atlantis—had been the main reason for Amph's punishment.

This. Could. Be. Her.

My palms grew sweaty. Me. A godsdamned sea god with perspiring hands like a prepubescent boy trying to ask his crush to prom.

Poseidon. You're getting ahead of yourself.

"Wow. That's amazing. I'll look it up when I get home," the blonde woman said, slipping the card into her beach bag.

The brunette turned head with a smile, showing me her profile. "Well, thank you very much, ma'am."

That smile. Those dimples. The same dimples our son Triton has.

I slid closer, my toes curling in the sand, hesitation holding me back, a bewildering surge of fear mixed with anxiety pinning me in place.

Let's say this *was* her. We hadn't seen each other in hundreds of years. I'd changed. And I'd be a damned fool to think she would be the same. We had a lot of fond memories together, a family even, but for every treasured moment, there were plenty of horrible ones too. Could I forgive her for abandoning her children? For ignoring me?

In the distance, she grabbed a green plastic bottle from the sand and held it in the air yelling, "You're welcome," to a young man who'd thrown it there by the trash can.

And I hadn't been a saint as a young King. I'd ignored her just as much, didn't give our children as much attention as I could and *should* have. I'd let the seas consume me. So, for that matter, could she forgive *me*?

She squatted to pick up the remaining garbage and after sucking in a sharp, deep breath, I took the plunge, whipping off my sunglasses to ensure she could see my eyes.

"Excuse me, miss, have we met before?" I asked, blocking the sun with my head so it wouldn't blind her when she looked up.

She slowly rose, craning her neck back to look at me. Our eyes locked, silence following.

Despite the sunglasses, there was no mistaking those chestnut eyes. Amphitrite. It was her. By Olympus it was *her*. I didn't even know what to do with myself.

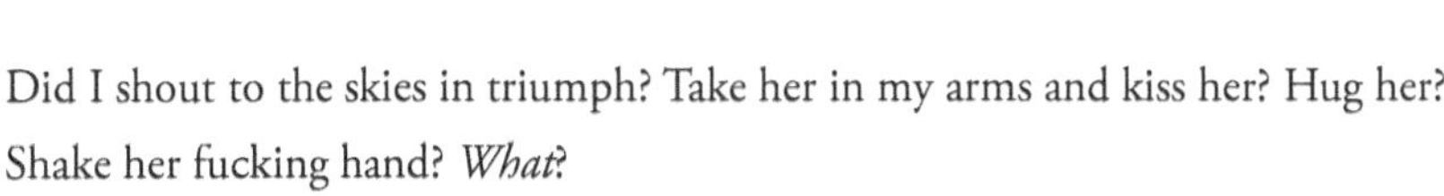

Did I shout to the skies in triumph? Take her in my arms and kiss her? Hug her? Shake her fucking hand? *What?*

I flashed a smile in an attempt to hide the barrage of emotions whirlpooling through me.

"I don't think so. Do I look familiar to you?"

My heart sank to my feet. She didn't recognize me. Sure, I donned my mortal form with short hair and smooth chin versus my usual beard, but surely she'd see past it. In fact, the way she looked at me initially I could've sworn—had it really been that long?

"You're right. We couldn't have met. How could I forget a face like yours?"

She dug her toes in the sand, still smiling. "Does that line ever work?"

Those lines *had* worked countless times in our youth. If for anything but eliciting a chuckle from her on how "corny" they'd always sounded. "Once upon a time, maybe."

The skin beneath her eyes crinkled and her gaze searched my face, the confusion washing over her features as clear as the Gulf waters to our right. She continued to peruse me, pausing when her eyes landed on my stomach. The way her lips parted—it was as if she were seeing my body for the first time—mesmerized by it.

I'll be damned. She had *no* fucking idea who I was. What in the Tartarus?

Desperate for more information, I cleared my throat and pointed to her hand. "Are you picking up garbage?"

She snapped to attention, her eyes darting back to my face, hand tightening on the trash poker. "Hm? What?"

Call me crazy, but it was almost as if she *did* recognize me, or my voice, or something about me but couldn't understand how or why.

"You've got a trash bag. Either you're picking up garbage on the beach, or you're collecting cans. Something tells me it's the former. Call it a hunch." Smirking, I bit my lower lip, forcing the rest of what I wanted to say into a hollow pit in my stomach.

Was there an ethereal rule book on how to handle this situation? Did I come right out and say it? Did I change forms here in front of her? Maybe if she saw me, the *real* me, she'd remember, maybe—

Seid. There are easily a hundred people on this beach. Going to cause a scene, blow your cover, and traumatize all of these mortals for the mere hope she'd recognize you?

This woman always had the ability to turn me into a bumbling pile of goo and scattered thoughts. A feeling I'd grown to associate with being *home*.

She thrust the handle of the poker in the sand. "Trash. Yes. I try to do it every week."

"Voluntarily?"

"Yes. I run an ocean conservation charity. While I clean up the beach, I also look for donations." Digging into her pocket, she pulled out a business card and held it out to me, her chin raised with pride.

Of course, she ran an ocean charity. It made all the sense in the world.

Alright. She didn't know who I was, didn't know who *she* was, there had to be an explanation. But firstly, I had to act like we truly were meeting for the first time.

I brightened my smile once the card slid between my fingers. Dragging a hand over my chin, I lifted my gaze to hers. "I'm an athlete, you know."

She swiveled the poker, fidgeting with it as if she were nervous. "Well, good for you. What do you play?"

Was I wrong to think this whole thing was, I don't know, a bit—fun?

"The waves mostly."

"The—" She frowned and looked at the water before returning her gaze to me. "Are you a swimmer?"

Fun but also pure. Torture.

"Guess again."

She slowly narrowed her eyes like she always had done when reaching a revelation.

My heart thudded against my chest. Did she finally remember something?

"No. You're not—" She let the poker stand by itself, supported in the sand, and crossed her arms. "Don't tell me you're a surfer."

Damn it all to Hades. And since when did she have a thing against surfers?

Feigning my disappointment, I forced a laugh and threw my arms out at my sides. "What's wrong with surfers?"

"Most of them seem to be conceited, grungy, and think they own the ocean."

But my Queen, I *do* own the ocean. If only you'd remember that.

"Most of them. So, not all, then?" I spread my grin wider.

"Yet to be determined."

Just as I had all those years ago when she was a delicate sea nymph, I seemed to

be reeling her in with each passing moment.

"I'm an athlete too," she blurted after a beat of silence between us.

That I hadn't expected to hear.

"Oh?" I folded my arms. "Let me guess." Tapping a finger against my lip, I looked up, pretending to mull it over, and snuck a peek at her expression.

She glared at me with her hands gripping her hips.

"Figure skater."

"No." Her glare deepened.

"Gymnast?"

As much as I did it to fuck with her, I couldn't imagine Amph doing any form of professional sport save for Olympic swimming but then, how unfair would *that* be?

She rolled her eyes. "Are you going to list every sport known for petite athletes?"

"Why don't you tell me? You can't say you're an athlete, then leave me hangin'." Chuckling, I canted my head to the side, genuinely curious.

She didn't answer at first, her finger absently twirling her chocolate hair. "eSports," she clipped.

What in the Tartarus did the "e" stand for?

Leaning forward, I brought our faces closer. Scents of cherry blossom, citrus, salt and sun wafting from her forced me to focus on beach bums behind her to keep my wits about me. "eSports?"

She lifted her chin, her fingers fumbling with the hem of her shorts. "Mmhmm."

"Care to explain what in the name of the Seven Seas, that is?"

"Videogames. Tournaments and such. You win money, prizes, and I have a Glitch account where I stream a couple of nights a week for a little extra cash."

There'd be no hiding the delightfully surprised look on my face. Amphitrite. Professional gamer. But then again, she'd always loved playing games with our kids.

"Videogames? Really? I never pegged you for the type."

If I could've palmed my face and warp back in time by a mere five seconds I would have after letting that little gem slip. But she made it so damn easy to sink back into our old dynamic. Gods, I missed her.

"You've known me for an entire five minutes and think you know my type?"

Fucking Tartarus.

Wincing, I cleared my throat. "Call it a—sixth sense."

"Simon, bruh, come on. Those waves ain't gonna surf themselves," another surfer across the beach yelled to me, unknowingly saving my ass.

"Simon? Are you Simon Thalassa?" She pointed at me, a new glint in her eyes.

She recognized my mortal pro surfer name. Color me continually surprised.

"Guilty as charged." I held a finger up at the other surfer, signaling for him to wait, but not once moving my eyes from *her*.

"I thought you meant you surfed for fun. You never said anything about being a legit pro." Her shoulders slumped.

"Does it make a difference to you?" I smirked, wanting nothing more than to lift her chin with my knuckle. "Does me being a pro put me higher or lower on your mental totem pole?"

Please say higher.

"Yet to be determined," she whispered, carving a deeper hole in my gut.

If she didn't even remember *who* she was, what did she call herself, I wonder?

Flicking the business card between my fingers, I dipped my face closer to hers. "Now that you know my name, care to give me yours?"

"Cory. Well. Cordelia, but everyone calls me Cory."

Olympus above. Cordelia. A name that not only suited her but that I loved as much as Amphitrite, if not more.

"Cordelia. Jewel of the sea."

She squinted at me. "That's right."

Time to work into her favor. Now or never, King of the Seas. Do or die.

"Well, Cory. As a professional athlete, I can stick all kinds of sponsors on my surfboard, wetsuit. You name it." I pointed at her with the business card. "You get me a high-res logo of your charity, and I'll add it on."

Her jaw dropped, making my chest swell. "But you don't know anything about it. How do you even know it's legit?"

My gorgeous sea Queen. How badly I wanted to take her face in my hands, swirl my thumbs over her cheeks, and *kiss* her.

"Something tells me you're good for it. And if not, well, you get to make an ass of me." I chuckled. "It was nice meeting you, Cory. Hope to run into you again." As much as it killed me, I turned away from her and walked.

We *will* run into each other again. I'd make damn sure of it.

Finally, she yelled out, "Where do I send the file?"

Grinning to myself like a lovesick fool, I turned on my heel and cupped my hands over my mouth. "Google me. I don't exactly have anywhere to store business cards in this suit." Touching my bare chest and shoulders, I gave her a lopsided grin—that same gooey smile I *knew* always made her feel all bubbly inside as she'd once told me.

Turning back to face the water, I let my grin fade to a thin line. I'd lost her once and now that I found her by some cosmic twist of the Fates, there was no way in Tartarus I would let her out of my sights. Even if it meant winning her affection all over again from square one. She's worth it. And I should've told her that—eons ago.

BOOK SIX

ZEUS

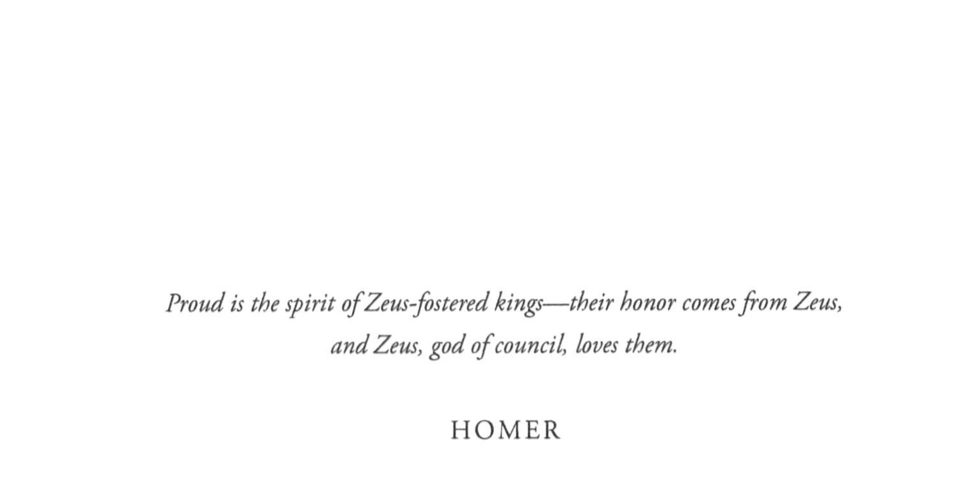

*Proud is the spirit of Zeus-fostered kings—their honor comes from Zeus,
and Zeus, god of council, loves them.*

HOMER

Heavy is the head that wears the crown.

WILLIAM SHAKESPEARE

ONE

ZEUS

SHE DIDN'T THINK I heard her slip out of bed in the middle of the night. Didn't think I saw her nab a twenty from my wallet before ducking out with a light click of the door. At least she had the decency to look at my ass peeking from the sheets before leaving. It *was* a nice ass.

She also probably didn't think I remembered her name. Elena.

I didn't bother locking the door behind her. In fact, it'd be entertaining for someone to barge in and try to kill me. The King of the fucking Gods. It'd been far too long since I'd seen the terrified look on a mortal's face when they realized who I was. Any attempt to announce it in the modern age…they'd look at me like I was insane. Fucking mockery.

And I know what you're thinking. This scenario isn't surprising. Dickhead Zeus sleeps with yet another woman, cheating on his wife. Shocking. There *is* more to that story, but I digress.

This time…I'm not the asshole. This time, I fucked her fair and square. Hera left me. Gave up her Queendom, sneered at me, and left.

And I let her.

Despite the humiliation. Despite the absolute fury. It hadn't been the first time she rebelled against me, only this time I didn't care. Because in a bizarrely fucked up way…I admired it. It grew old and tiresome pretending things were as they'd been all those ages ago. She changed. The world changed. And most importantly, hold onto your asses, *I* changed.

I shook my head at the notion, rattling away whatever fog clouded my brain.

Besides, I couldn't remember the last time I was single—a bachelor. She may have unleashed a monster. A short-lived one anyway.

I crawled out of bed, slipping on the boxers I'd haphazardly tossed to the floor earlier, making my way to a back room. Lightly touching the knob, I cracked the door open, greeted by a large wet black nose.

"Come on, boy," I said to my white Labrador, Levin.

Yes, I did name him after an archaic word for lightning. Shouldn't be surprising. What *may* surprise you, however, is that he's a rescue. I "stole" him from an abusive home and gave him a better one. Think of me what you wish, but beating up innocent beings simply because you *can*? Not on my fucking watch.

He forced his shoulders into the door, sprinting down the hall, slipping and sliding with each passing step. I smiled to myself, patiently following him. No woman I'd ever brought here deserved to meet Levin. He was the only being in the universe who'd ever seen past all the bullshit, didn't give a fuck about my past, and loved me unconditionally. When I rounded the corner, he was already making circles on the bed, finding a suitable spot to curl up and sleep for the night.

Before crawling in myself, I paused at the edge, taking his large head in both of my hands, scratching behind his ears. His wide pink tongue flopped to the side of his mouth, panting.

"Good boy." After turning off the light, I climbed into bed and felt Levin's furry warm body shoving against my back after only thirty seconds.

Morning seeped through the cracks of the black curtains in my sleek downtown New York apartment, making me grumble. As much sleep as I got, and it never seemed to be enough. Ironic considering I'm a god, right? It's what happens when you partially hold the entire cosmos on your shoulders—always on your mind. The important thing was to *never* show it on my face in front of my people. And I hadn't for millennia.

Ruffling my hair, I shoved my face into the pillow, ignoring the scent of Elena's shampoo, or fragrance, or whatever the fuck it was she'd left behind. The metal eagle statue in mid-attack protruded from the wall, staring down at me from above my headboard. Levin was sprawled on his back, curled to the side with his legs spread, sleeping away. Slipping out of bed, I paused to stretch my arms to Olympus, gazing at my reflection in the mirror—cut, toned, tanned, and immaculate. A physique that never changed, and I had to do absolutely nothing

to maintain—perks of being a Greek god.

My face. The closest semblance I could replicate to the true me. Unless, of course, I enjoyed the sight of each mortal I passed on the streets catching flame. A younger, more ruthless me might have grinned at the thought. But no, I've learned to admire the poor bastards. My mortal guise was a version of me that existed before fighting for and *earning* the right of chief deity. But my eyes... those would never change.

Where was I? Ah yes. My small window of bachelorhood. Thanks to the overpowerful bitch of a grandmother of mine, Gaea...there's a stipulation to my Kingdom. At all times—there must be a Queen. If the expiration date lapses, I not only lose my title but part of my power to go with it. We couldn't have that, now, could we? And to be honest, I'd never given the clause much thought. There'd only ever been Hera. I didn't think she'd give up her crown. At any rate, I'd take the next few nights to "live it up," so to speak, and then pick the nearest mortal woman who was pleasing to the eyes to be my Queen. Done deal.

Any and all of them would pine over the idea of it. And why wouldn't they? To become not only a goddess but an immortal Queen? Not to mention I could walk down the street and have any one of them if I so desired. Fuck—if I had a thing for man-ass, I could have that too. The world was my oyster, and I'd shucked my share. But I'd be lying if I said the ease of the conquest on the rarest of occasions never felt...hollow.

Sneering, I turned for my walk-in closet, the light automatically illuminating as I entered. Hundreds of pristinely hung suits lined the walls, dozens of glossed dress shoes resting on matching shelves. Displays held a different Rolex for each day of the week and several shined and glinting pairs of silver and gold cufflinks.

I could conjure clothes with a snap of my fingers, but for as long as I'd roamed the Earth one starts to appreciate the smaller things—things mortals take for granted. A uniquely tailored suit created to fit you like a glove. The feel of it as you slip it on like liquid sex. Even the scent of the fabric calmed me far quicker than any steaming hot shower. And I never wore the same suit twice. Ever.

I donned a light grey ensemble with a white shirt and dark blue tie. And, yes, I did up the tie as well every time. Peering into the full-length mirror, I did the necessary overlapping and pull- through to secure the perfect knot in the silk tie, smoothing it down. I turned my face to the side, running a hand over the light

beard on my chin. My godly King form was far less…clean. Ironic that between my brothers and I, Hades' true self was the only beardless one.

Upon securing the gold Rolex on my left wrist, I attached the gold "Z" cufflink to one sleeve, a lightning bolt on the other, and paused to stare at the New York City skyline through the wall of windows near my king-sized bed. Mortals of all varieties busied the streets, appearing as ants in a structured maze. Chins tilted down, eyes glued to their phone screens, missing half the world around them. It was no wonder they didn't believe in us anymore. They were far too busy worshipping technology and the media. Eons ago, I may have asked Poseidon to wipe the slate clean by making Earth's oceans swallow it whole, but I no longer interfered that deep. There was an entire universe to oversee, and if you think the Greek gods are the only deities from "mythology" in existence—you'd be sorely mistaken.

I turned to Levin, who was still snoring, fast asleep on the bed. With a smirk, I snapped my fingers, making raw meat chunks appear in his dog bowl in the kitchen. Levin's body writhed, and his head shot up, nose sniffing the air. He jumped off the bed and scurried over to me, sitting but shaking, waiting for permission to eat. Crouching, I scratched under his chin and gave a quick kiss to the top of his head.

"Be good. Go on." I motioned with my head at the kitchen, and with an excited yip, he trotted off to eat.

New York. I've lived in many, many places. Aside from Olympus, aside from Greece, New York felt like a kingdom to be ruled—even if they had no idea who walked amongst them. Slipping my hands into my pockets, I made for the elevator and began my daily stroll to the firm's building. I could've had a chauffeur, *me* knows I could afford it. Could've even simply ported there. But there was something about feeding on the energy of mortals—their expressions. Their reactions as pure raw power waltzed right past them. A pity they didn't believe in the old gods anymore. We could all have *so* much more fun.

It was time to don the mask. A façade forged through the ages that mortals molded and adapted to fit their own needs. Their own agenda. Same old song and dance. It'd become as much a part of me as the warmth of a perfectly aged scotch settling in my stomach. Could I have taken the time to convince a world there was more to me than the endless parade of women? More than the meddling god-king who cared for nothing or no one else but himself? Sure. But I had an entire

fucking kingdom to oversee. Hundreds of gods beneath me and seemingly more even within the last few months. We'll get to that tiny detail later. There were far more pressing matters to deal with over a reputation I've grown to accept. If it gave them comfort to hate me, I'd be their sounding board because I'm a leader. The alpha. A godsdamned admiral.

The Jupiter Bistro. A coffee shop directly below my penthouse apartment. The fucking irony, right? I breezed past the line leading out the door, and they all let me—because they wouldn't dare otherwise.

The barista, Claire, grinned as she set a steamy paper cup on the counter, slipping a cover on. "Dark roast, black, Z. All ready for you."

Taking the cup from her hand, making sure to drag my finger over her knuckle, I winked. "Thank you, as always, my dear."

She bit her lip after letting out a shaky breath. Immediate putty in my hands. Not uncommon in the slightest. But anymore? Almost too easy.

After tapping my card on the reader, I turned with the cup in hand, spying a buxom red-head giving me a sultry smile. Her emerald gaze dropped to the impression of my cock through my pants. Making a piece of paper with my address appear between two of my fingers, I slipped it into her palm as I passed, sending a light current of electric shock against her skin. She gasped, and I exited with a broad smile.

Storm clouds rolled in, and with a quirk of my brow, they froze. I couldn't walk into the firm looking like a soaked rat. As soon as my feet hit the foyer carpet of the thirty-story building owned by Crane, Crane, and Wallace Law, rain poured down in buckets with another raise of my brow. A satisfying crackle of lightning streaked the sky.

Why is the King of the Gods practicing law, you ask? A part of me might say the power and irony in controlling mortals in such a way intrigues me. Another part of me might say it's a genius way of keeping badly-behaved mortals in my sights. And an even smaller part of me might say—because I'm fucking bored. Not to mention how much it annoys my brother, Hades. Sure. I keep his ass happy so he does his job, but at the end of the day…I'm going to have a little fun in the process.

Let us not forget that besides my kingly status, I also oversee law and justice. Defending a known criminal may not exactly be viewed as justifiable. Still, my status as chief deity of the Greeks not only meant sovereignty over the gods but

a responsibility to humankind as well. Such is the role of *any* chief deity—Greek or otherwise. And I'd learned through time, the best way to help mortals is to witness them at their absolute worst.

Removing the lid from the coffee cup, I tossed it into the trash, blowing on the hot liquid as I made my way through the bullpen.

"I swear this piece of shit gives me a blue screen every other month. Can't the firm spring for new computers?" An intern, Larry, with far more humility to learn and a set of balls to grow, spat from a nearby cubicle.

With an idle sway of my hand, I sent an electric pulse into the device, rejuvenating its life for precisely another two months. At some point, he'd finally break down and humbly ask one of the partners' assistants to request a new computer. Until then, I entertained myself watching him prolong his own misery.

My assistant, Ruth, came trotting from around the corner, sporting her usual attire of a modest skirt that went to her mid-shins, flats, and a cardigan sweater. Her cropped brown hair bounced as she ran, a pen resting on her ear, notepad clutched to her chest. She adjusted her squared glasses as she stopped in front of me. When she smiled, it extenuated the mole above her lip. At a petite five-foot even, she had to crane her neck back to look me in the face.

"Mr. Vrontí, there's a new case file for you to review," she said, her hazel eyes beaming.

I caught her gaze over the rim of my cup as I sipped. "Ruth, you can call me Zane or Z. We've been over this, sweetheart."

"Yes. Of course, Mr. Vron—I mean—" A nervous, shrilled bout of laughter poured from her throat.

Smirking, I pointed toward my office. After a tiny jump, she turned on her heel and power-walked.

I'd never slept with my assistant. Not because I didn't want to—Tartarus, no. I always did love the small ones you could toss around in the bedroom. No. It was due to us seeing each other several days a week for hours. I couldn't risk her becoming…attached. And it's not as if she never tried with her varying moments of brushing her tits against my arm or undoing several buttons on her blouse to give me a view as she bent over to place paperwork on my desk.

I sat in my leather-back rolling chair, resting the coffee on a mahogany coaster. I'd kept my workspace simple and clutter-free. Aside from my gold nameplate, a

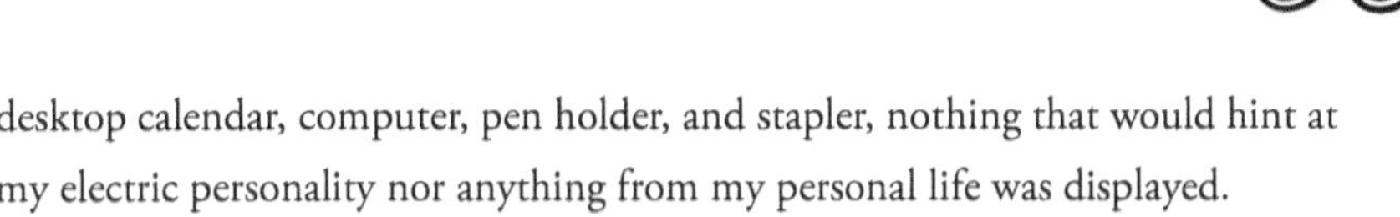

desktop calendar, computer, pen holder, and stapler, nothing that would hint at my electric personality nor anything from my personal life was displayed.

Whose photo would I put on my desk anyway? Apollo? Sure, if I wanted every other client to start probing about my son being the rockstar "Ace." Athena? A woman in ancient Greek armor could look strange. She was one of the few who didn't bother to show herself to mortals. No. I preferred keeping that part of my life completely separate from the mortal lawyer. It made things far easier to deal with—to pretend for several hours a day I didn't carry an invisible boulder on my back like fucking Atlas himself.

Without disappointing, Ruth "discreetly" adjusted the collar of her shirt before trotting over to me with a folder. She leaned forward, squeezing her tits together, and dropped the papers in front of me with a flourish. Obliging her, I stole a glance at her cleavage before scooping the folder into my hand.

She smiled, chewing on the end of her pen before standing straight. "Murder case."

"Oh?" I flipped through the papers, eyeballing mugshots, receipts, internet history printouts.

"Killed her husband."

Ah, the ancient tale of a wife murdering her husband for one of a dozen reasons. And this one didn't look much different.

"Shoved him in a tub of acid."

Without looking up, I continued to shuffle through more digital evidence paperwork in the folder. "To dispose of the body?"

Ruth cleared her throat and squeaked before saying, "Alive."

I paused, shooting my gaze to hers. "Fuck."

"Right?" Ruth lifted her hand and dropped it, slapping her thigh.

Well, now things just got far more interesting.

I picked up the paper with the accused woman's mugshot. A portly woman with curly hair and a glare that could curl the paint from a fence. "Have they announced the lead prosecutor yet?"

"Yes. Keira Bazin." Looking away, Ruth scratched the back of her head with the pen.

A woman. This would be a first.

I tossed the paper to the stack. "Why have I heard that name before?"

Ruth snorted. "You should have. She's *never* lost a case. I've heard some other lawyers call her 'The Bulldog.'"

After a quick Google search, I pulled up several full-body photos taken by the media. Starting at her tanned, toned legs peeking from her skirt, I panned up to her perfectly rounded ass, and landed on a gorgeous face with bright blue eyes, plump red lips and a head of *very* light blonde hair.

A conquest if I ever saw one.

After raising my coffee in a cheers gesture to Ruth, I said, "This'll be far too easy."

TWO

KEIRA

"THIS ISN'T GOING TO be easy. Did you say who I think you said is on the defense?" I asked my paralegal and best friend, Olivia, through the phone as I paced back and forth in my apartment.

"Eric Carter, yes. But you shouldn't be so bloody nervous, Keira. You've never lost a case. Why would who's on the defense change that?" Olivia murmured something, sounding like she held the phone away from her face.

I narrowed my eyes. "Are you with someone right now?"

It *was* three in the morning, but given Olivia and I were both night owls, her calling in the middle of the night to relay the news wasn't surprising.

"No…" Her answer sounded more like a question.

I knew she was lying, not only because of the lilt in her voice but because I had what some would refer to as—empathic powers. Anyone I was near, I knew all the emotions they were feeling, the emotions they projected versus bottling up, and when only hearing them versus seeing—the truth fluttered through my ear like static raindrops. It was the main reason I stayed at the office late and arrived super early. The fewer people I encountered on my walk to work, the better. Ironically, I'd ended up in one of the continent's most populated, bustling cities.

"Ollie, you know you can't lie to me." I zig-zagged through the boxes strewn about my living room floor. Boxes I hadn't unpacked since I moved in after my divorce. I was rarely in my apartment except to sleep anyhow. Work was my significant other—which was undoubtedly the main reason Tyler left me.

"How is that exactly, hm? Do you have ESP?" Olivia's "you" sounded more like

"ya" given her Australian accent. She'd been in the country for over seven years, but her accent remained thick as molasses.

With a deep sigh, I moved to my window that faced the luxury apartments across the street. The apartment building that Zane Vronti, a slimy criminal defense lawyer, lived in. The universe's idea of a cruel joke. "Go hang with your man of the hour. We'll talk about this in the office tomorrow."

"Aye, aye, ma'am," Olivia said with an American drawl. She giggled and told someone to "stop it" before hanging up.

I rested my chin on top of my phone, watching a woman with long black hair walk from the apartment building's lobby barefoot, letting her heels dangle by the strap from her finger. The woman hailed a cab at three in the morning, and there wasn't a doubt in my mind she was one of Zane's regular fuck toys. On many late nights, I'd see him with a variety of women on his arm, waltzing them up to his penthouse apartment. And every morning, they'd leave, never staying long enough for breakfast.

Typical New York playboy—always dressed in a pristine suit, hair slicked back with gel and a swagger that suggested he owned the world. I'd only ever seen him from afar and the occasional blips on the news that I mostly ignored. I loathed defense lawyers. I'd be lying if I said what I *had* seen wasn't attractive, but honestly…how could any self-respecting person be perfectly sound with a revolving door of partners?

I couldn't even remember the last time I'd had sex. It wasn't because I didn't enjoy it, nor because I wasn't capable of seducing someone. Not only was my brain far too wrapped in casework up to my ears to care, but sensing every passing emotion from your partner during the act could be overwhelming and borderline exhausting.

Scooping the Melissa Daniels case folder into my hand, I slipped off my heels, scrunching my toes into the carpet as I paced and read. As a criminal prosecutor, especially in New York, it took every bit of cunning and finesse a lawyer had in their arsenal to win cases like this. Wife kills husband. Jury, making preconceived judgments that the husband had to do something to drive her to such a state, sympathizes with woman. And maybe the husband *did* do something. But it also took a special kind of evil to shove a human being, living or not, in acid and shove the barrel in a storage locker.

Not looking down, I stepped over the box I knew rested between where the carpet ended, and the tile began, leading to my kitchenette. I set the stack of papers on the counter as I grabbed a bottle of water. My eyes felt heavy, and sleep tugged at my brain. Half-past three in the morning. An hour of sleep and then straight to the office.

The obnoxious alarm sound chimed from my phone at four-thirty in the morning, and I rolled out of bed, showered, styled my hair, slapped on some make-up, and slid into my work uniform—pencil skirt, heels, an eggplant-colored button-down shirt, and jacket. With my briefcase strap tossed over one shoulder, pea coat draped on my back, I made for the street, walking the four blocks to the courthouse. The subway or bus was almost always out of the question. No matter what time of day or night, public transportation seemed to be perpetually packed with people. Walking allowed me to pick alternative routes if the current one suddenly grew too busy for comfort.

As I stopped at a crosswalk, the emotions started flowing like a ruptured dam. The man on my left talking a mile a minute on his cell phone was anxious, panicky, and confused, making momentary jitters flutter over my skin. I shrugged the feelings away and an overwhelming sadness seeped into me from a woman behind me. Her eyes were dark and sunken, hair greasy and disheveled, pieces sticking straight out from her low ponytail. A deep depression nestled into my bones, weighing on my brain like cement.

I turned around to face her. "Ma'am, are you alright?"

"Excuse me?" The woman's chin lifted along with her eyebrows, and a tiny spring of hope bubbled in her chest.

"I asked if you were alright?"

"I—" The woman pulled her shirt sleeves over her hands. "No one's ever asked me that before."

Oh, dear.

Quickly glancing at my analog watch, I canted my head at her. "Would you like a cup of coffee? Maybe a chat? I have some time before I need to be at work."

It would mean walking the remaining two blocks during peak hours, but the

heavy cloud hanging over this woman frightened me.

"You'd do that? For a complete stranger?" The woman's eyes glazed over as if she were about to cry.

The gratitude and sheer surprise beaming from her made my chest tighten.

"Absolutely, come on. There's an outside café right on the other side of the street."

Part of my abilities allowed me to inherently know what a person needed—how they wanted to feel but may not have been able to get there on their own. Some closed themselves off with a mental shield, and although I could still sense their emotions, it was challenging to help them. I don't know how or why I'd received this gift, but I'd make the most of it in any way I could.

Choosing a corner table outside nestled under the dimly lit sky, I motioned for the waiter as we took seats across from each other. The woman ordered a plain black coffee, the same as I.

She wasn't used to someone caring and simply needed someone to listen. I couldn't read minds, so I never fully knew why they felt the way they did, but I gave them every opportunity to explain—if they wished.

"Do you always randomly buy coffee for strangers at crosswalks?" The woman folded her hands atop the table after smoothing the disarray of her hair with a palm.

I extended my hand. "My name is Keira."

"Beth." A warm smile slid over her lips as we shook.

"There. Now we're not strangers."

The waiter returned with our coffee, and Beth curled her hands around it, relishing the warmth.

"Life hasn't exactly dealt me the best hand lately." Beth lifted the cup to her nose, letting the steam collect on her cheeks.

I sipped my coffee, keeping quiet, not pressuring her to elaborate.

"I lost my job last month, and I'm weeks away from losing my apartment. I'd moved here for a now ex-boyfriend. Left everything and everyone I knew in Nebraska."

This story sounded familiar. I'd given up my life in Canada to move to New York for my now ex-husband. The only saving grace has been taking the bar to practice law in New York and building an image that would last me a lifetime. It didn't mean I didn't miss a steaming pile of delicious poutine now and again.

She sipped her coffee, wincing when the heat passed her lips. "It took me

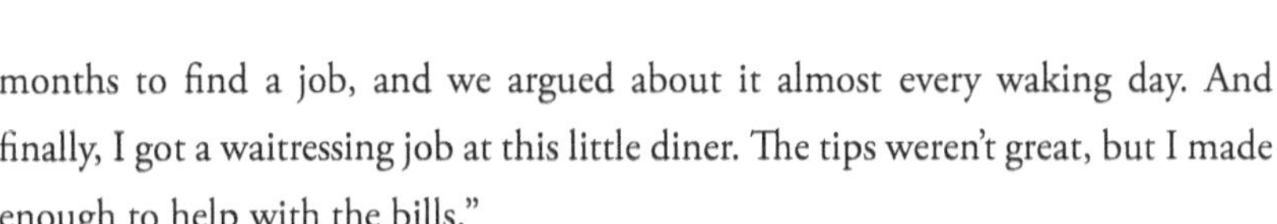

months to find a job, and we argued about it almost every waking day. And finally, I got a waitressing job at this little diner. The tips weren't great, but I made enough to help with the bills."

With each moment, her demeanor calmed and brightened. I could never be sure if I could pass emotions from myself to another. It was always a fine line to tell someone about my abilities, let alone ask if I could use them as a guinea pig. Still, it never stopped me from trying. With Beth, I dug into every vibrant memory I could bring to the surface—showering her with positivity and warmth.

"One day, I came home from an overtime shift. Two o'clock in the friggin' morning and there was George, packing a suitcase." Beth's eyes glazed over.

I reached a hand across the table, lightly touching her forearm but still saying nothing.

A small smile crept at the corner of her lips, and she patted my hand before leaning back. "He said he needed more out of life, and neither this state nor I was going to be part of it."

A knot formed in my stomach, and I wanted nothing more than to sucker punch this "George" in the gut. As a wrinkle formed between Beth's eyes, I pushed the thought away, concentrating on the moon still looming in the sky above us instead.

"He left me with a rent I couldn't afford on my own, in a place where I knew no one, and with a broken heart." She scraped her thumbnail over the side of the ceramic mug. "I tried to explain it to my work, to get more hours, and they informed me the diner was losing business and shutting down. I also tried to talk to my landlord to work out some kind of payment plan until I could find another job and all he could do was make snarky comments about other ways I could 'pay' him."

A hope fluttered from her, settling over my skin like warm fleece.

"Will you let me help you, Beth?" I peered at her over the rim of my mug.

Beth shifted in her seat before her spine straightened. "I—you'd do that?"

"We all need a lifeline now and again. I have the means to help, so I will if you let me."

Most would never come right out and ask for it, but the decision to allow help still needed to be theirs.

"I honestly don't know what I did to deserve such kindness, but I will gladly take whatever help you're willing to give." Her eyes glistened from built-up tears.

Resting my mug on the table, I slipped a business card from my pocket and slid it to her. "I work for the state. A prosecutor. There are several jobs open, and I'd be happy to give you a reference if you're interested."

I'd sensed enough of her good character to vouch for her. The poor woman just needed a break.

"I—" Beth started, but the words caught in her throat. She launched from her chair and hugged me, sobbing. "I can't thank you enough."

I wasn't what you'd call a "hugger." But for those I'd helped through the years, embracing seemed to be the only form of gratitude they could muster. It still was enough to make my body stiffen at their touch and triggered a mental game of suppressing the discomfort leaking from my pores.

"Everyone deserves a chance to be happy, Beth. Especially when life puts us through trials, attempting to derail us." After throwing several bills on the table, covering both her coffee and mine, I stood. "When you apply, be sure to add my name. I guarantee with my recommendation, they'll hire you so long as you show the bright side of you in the interview."

"Yes. Absolutely. I'll do you proud, Miss Keira."

I slipped my briefcase on my shoulder and offered her a warm smile, and after pocketing several sugar packets from the dispenser on the table to consume later, I left.

The walk to the office was borderline nauseating. There was so much anxiety seeping from everyone I passed, I felt antsy and dizzy by the time I'd made it to the foyer. I needed to make it to my office to decompress. Everyone and their mothers greeted me when I entered, and I offered small waves and meager smiles in return.

I breezed into my office, whisking the door behind me. Instead of the gratifying clicking sound it should've made upon closing, it muted against a fleshy palm.

"There you are. I was about ready to send out a search party, and then I thought—" Olivia gasped with a hand over her mouth. "Maybe she got laid last night and needed to sleep in from hours of nastiness."

After tossing my briefcase on the desk, I flopped into my chair with a roll of my eyes. Olivia considered my sex life, or lack thereof, a side mission to *her* everyday life. Why she cared so much about the fate of my vagina was beyond me.

"Only one of us got lucky last night, and that one of us wasn't me." I shuffled

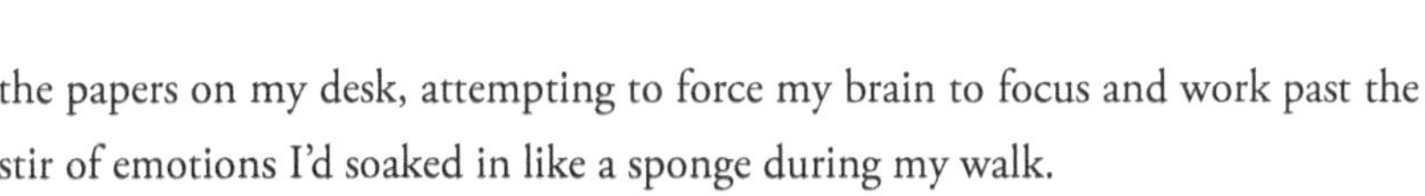

the papers on my desk, attempting to force my brain to focus and work past the stir of emotions I'd soaked in like a sponge during my walk.

Not bothering to shut the door, Olivia strode in with a manila folder pressed to her chest and her face glued to an e-reader. Olivia had accentuated curves in all the perfect places with a confidence about her that could make any woman envious. My admiration for her never failed, and I'd hired her on the spot the day she applied for the position. I'd have called it a done deal within five minutes but prolonged the interview to checkmark all the necessary boxes. Not to mention, having her around with the glowing positivity she gave off, always refreshed me.

"What are you so intently reading?" I pointed at the tablet.

Without even cutting her eyes to me, she replied, "A book."

"A book? I thought you were reading a paperback. *The Hating Game* or something?"

"Yeah. That's my subway literature because it's got the cute illustrated cover. My e-reader now that is where all the filthy, dirty smut lives." She popped her glance to me long enough to give a sidelong grin.

"Alright, I'll bite. What are you reading?" Tapping my pen against the desk, I rested my chin in my hand.

She bit down on her plump bottom lip, smiling. "It's a cyberpunk romance called *Rescued by Her Enemy*. Action, intrigue, and the best part? Sex. Lots and lots of sex."

"You? Reading such explicit content? Shocking."

She flipped the cover shut on the tablet and rested it on my desk. "I know, right? Speaking of lucky, it's one thing not to want to deal with the peskiness of getting a man involved, but it's another to ignore *her* completely." She pointed below her belly button. Slipping the folder under her arm, she gave one toss of her light blonde bangs and removed her phone from her dress pocket.

Raising a brow at her, I paused mid-flip through a stack of papers.

"Look. This one has a Fifty Shades theme, vibrates, and has this little rabbit deal-y that stimulates your—" She'd held her phone screen out to me, showing a picture of said sex toy, but paused when I nudged my chin behind her at a group of men leaning in their chairs, straining to listen.

"I appreciate your concern, Ollie." I lowered the phone from view. "I really do, but the last thing we need is one of them filing a complaint about us talking—

devices—in the workplace."

Ollie pursed her full lips together, those bright green eyes narrowing before tipping her chin over her shoulder. "They should be taking notes. Maybe you blokes will learn a thing or two."

"I'm going to assume that the folder shoved in your armpit is the acid case?" I pointed with a grin.

She jumped to attention and removed the folder, fanning her palms over the crease down the middle. "Rest assured. I *did* put on deodorant this morning."

"How fortunate for the entire building." I smirked and snatched it from her.

Olivia's jaw dropped as she slid into the seat across from me. "Someone's fiery this morning."

"If you say it's because I'm horny, I'm kicking you out of my office." I offered a small smile but kept my gaze on the case files.

"ESP. I told you. I bloody told you." She snapped her fingers before taking out her cell phone again. "Don't forget you have your client's wedding soon."

I groaned. "I did forget about that. Who invites their lawyer to a wedding? Honestly."

"Keira, you kept him from falsely going to prison. I'd say he's, I don't know, grateful?" Olivia stuck her bottom lip out.

"Where is it again?"

"Argentina."

"Jesus. They couldn't keep it more local?"

Her face fell, deadpan. "Only you, of all people, would complain about having to go to Argentina for a wedding."

"I'm in the middle of a case."

"That won't go to trial for at least lord knows how long. We both know this."

I grabbed a pen from the holder at the corner of my desk and tapped it. "Did you already book the flights?"

"You'll leave the morning of and fly back the day after. In and out."

I twirled the pen between my fingers. "See if you can reschedule for the red-eye flight the same day. That way, I'm only wasting twenty-four hours."

She stared at me wide-eyed, her jaw dropping. "Are you human? I swear sometimes you're an actual robot."

Chewing on the tip of the pen, I ignored her question and raised my brows.

"Ollie."

"Red-eye. You got it." She nudged me with her elbow. "Who knows? Maybe some hot Argentinian guy will tango with you."

"Tango?"

"Yeah. Didn't you say you took ballroom dancing classes at university?

Sighing, I shook my head. "One course. One. It was an elective, and it was required. Trust me. I would've taken something English-y or science-y if they'd have let me."

"Alright there, Buzz Killington." Olivia folded her arms in a huff.

"I still can't believe the defense hired Eric Carter." I bit my thumbnail, stopping on the paperwork that outlined preliminary evidence.

"You're telling me. If I can manage not to drool a lazy river and happily float down it in his presence *and* actually get some work done, it'll be a miracle."

The lust wafting from her like vapors made the small space of my office suddenly cave in.

"I'm sorry, what?" I snapped my gaze to hers.

She leaned forward, slapping her palms on my desk, making her six Alex and Ani bracelets jingle together. "Don't play coy with me, Keira. Any woman in her right mind knows that man is attractive. Gross defense lawyer? Sure. But still wouldn't stop me from riding him like an ostrich."

I scrunched my nose and let the papers fall to the stack. "Oh, come on. I haven't even had breakfast yet."

Olivia's phone chimed from the desk outside of my office, and she leaped for the door. She talked, but I was far too busy rummaging through the case file paperwork to concentrate on what she said.

Her head poked out from the doorframe. "Um, apparently, the defense wants to have a pre-pre-trial conference to discuss their client and any evidence currently held."

"We can have a pre-trial conference with the judge same as any other trial as soon as I've had the time to look through the damn case."

"They want to meet within the hour." Olivia scratched the side of her deeply slanted nose with a nervous smile.

Sighing, I slammed the folder shut. "It never fails. It's always the prosecution that has to bend over and take it in the ass."

"Until The Blonde Bulldogs wipe the floor with them in the trial itself," Olivia added with a brightened grin.

"And this is why you're my wing woman, Ollie." We fist-bumped as we made our way through the cubicles.

On the cab ride over, I'd pored through as many of the files as I could. It wouldn't be the first time I'd had to come prepared on a whim. My heart thundered against my ribcage as we neared the conference room. These conferences were never easy and most often a struggle to maintain professionalism. I'd never cracked under pressure or lost my cool with a defense lawyer, but I'd be lying if I said there hadn't been numerous points of temptation. They were the enemy in that courtroom, and it all started here—the pre-trial conference.

The room was empty when we entered, and I took a brief moment of reprieve to calm my nerves, regain composure, and browse through the evidence folder one last time.

"You're bloody adorable," Olivia said, taking the seat next to me.

Concentrating on the list of audio recordings, I dragged my finger down it. "Why do you say that?"

"You've gone over the evidence a dozen times. You know it. You're fine." She closed the folder with my hand still on the paper.

"How long have you been my assistant?" I didn't move my finger, saving my spot on the list.

Olivia puckered her plump, glossy lips. "Years? I've lost track. Time flies when you're havin' fun, right?"

"Two years, six months, and eleven days."

Olivia sat up straight and counted on her fingers, mouthing numbers to herself with a perplexed brow.

"My point is, we've known each other a long time. This is my system. It works, and—"

A deep, masculine voice from the hallway seeped through the window. It sounded familiar, but I couldn't place where I'd heard it.

The door opened, and a man entered the meeting room—a man who was *not* the assigned defense lawyer. This man was infamous. One of the best. The nerves I'd fought to calm ramped into overdrive at the thought of going up against him.

I locked gazes with a pair of deep-sea blue eyes, luring me in to hurl me to the

depths and crush me.

Zane Vronti.

What was worse?

The man. Was. Gorgeous.

Shit.

THREE

ZEUS

THE JAIL SET ME up in a private room and I sat at the table, mindlessly scrolling through dozens of images of my opposing counselor, waiting for my client's arrival. It was no wonder the media had a field day with her. She was practically a supermodel practicing law. But one thing I noted, despite over a hundred images, in not one of them did she smile. And she was always alone. Was she depressed at all times? Angry? Putting on a serious demeanor for the sake of the cameras?

And why the fuck did I care?

The door burst open, and I immediately turned the phone screen black, resting it on the table in front of me. Adjusting in my seat, I smoothed down my tie and waited.

Melissa Daniels. Late forties. Dark hair with exposed grey roots in wiry disarrays of frizzy curls. Double chin. And that same scowl from her mugshot.

I nudged my chin at the officer, signaling he could leave. As Melissa maneuvered into the chair across from me, the cuffs on her wrists jangled. Removing the folder from my briefcase, I slapped it down between us, locking eyes with her.

"They say you're the best," she said, her voice gruff and lifeless.

"They say a lot. But on that, they'd be correct. It's a wonder you didn't hire me in the first place." I flipped open the folder, shuffling the papers like the professional I was.

Melissa snorted, sucking snot back into her throat through one nostril like she was getting ready to spit a godsdamned loogie. "You've cost nearly every penny I have."

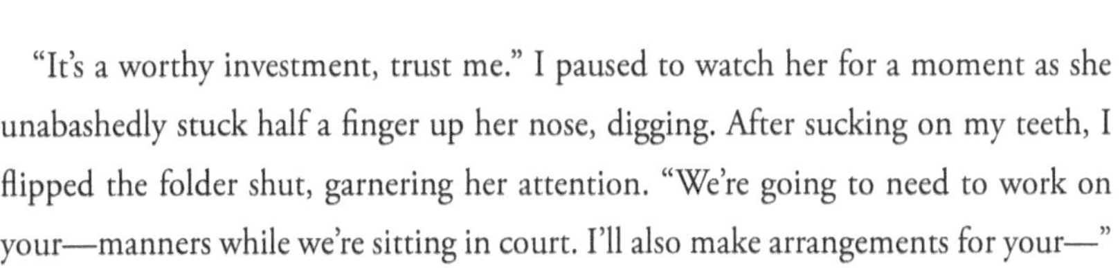

"It's a worthy investment, trust me." I paused to watch her for a moment as she unabashedly stuck half a finger up her nose, digging. After sucking on my teeth, I flipped the folder shut, garnering her attention. "We're going to need to work on your—manners while we're sitting in court. I'll also make arrangements for your—" I flicked my wrist at her head. "—hair."

She frowned and dragged a hand over the bird nest atop her skull. "What's wrong with my hair?"

"Everything. You want sympathy from the jury? They need to see you at least give one out of two shits." I held my phone up, acting as if its presence in my hand had a correlation to our conversation.

In reality, I worked up an e-mail asking for a meeting with the lovely prosecution. Considering I'd already lost time given the last-minute change of attorneys, the prosecution would have no means to deny the request—not that they *ever* had the means. Not to mention, the sooner I had Keira within my sights, the sooner I could have her—underneath me, on top of me, in front of me…

I grimaced at the amount of evidence already piling up against her as I flicked through the folder. "Did you tell your hairstylist you could kill your husband and get away with it?"

She tapped her pudgy fingers against the table. "People say a lot of things."

"That they do." Grabbing a pen, I jotted notes. "It's not recorded, so we have that going for us. The dozen answering machine recordings however, are a little harder to skirt around."

She rolled her eyes as if her time spent here was an inconvenience.

"Was your husband abusive? Physically? Emotionally? Was he a bad father?" I tapped the pen on the paper, making dozens of dots.

I'd briefly skimmed family and friend testimonials, all stating that he was, in fact, a good father. But I needed to understand her angle. If she even had one. The serpent-like glint in her gaze—the hollowness I could sense through her mind suggested she may have simply "snapped."

"Being a dad to our kids was about the only damn thing he was good for. He'd watch them while I worked and made all the money." She rolled her shoulders with a sneer. "I'd be lucky if half the time I came home to a cooked meal. Not even sure what the bastard did all day."

Rubbing my chin, I kept my gaze fixed on her, noting the aloofness when she spoke about him. No guilt. No remorse. I'd venture to guess she couldn't remember most of what she and her accomplice carried out that day—acting and reacting on pure rage.

"Is that the reason you left the voicemails? Angry at him for not upholding his stay-at-home-dad duties?"

The words sounded fucking ridiculous out loud, and it was the part of the job I hated most. As a defense lawyer, it wasn't my job to judge or cast blame. All were innocent until proven otherwise, right? Fuck me. At least I knew what waited for her at the end of the river Styx when she arrived in the Underworld.

"It says here, months before the incident, you landed a rather large contract with one of the largest pharmaceutical companies in the country. That true?" I leaned back, pinning my gaze to hers, studying her.

She glared at me. "Yeah. So?"

Tossing the pen on the table, I held back an exasperated sigh begging to escape from my chest.

The selfish harpy wanted all of her newly hard-earned cash for herself—especially with a looming divorce started by her dearly departed husband. She couldn't give me a legitimate means to defend her even if she wanted to, which meant it would rely heavily on the dismissal of evidence. A notification blipped on my phone, and I stole a glance at the reply e-mail from the prosecution agreeing to meet.

"Let's cut straight to the chase, Daniels." Staring at her, I lowered my phone. "Did you do it?"

She blinked. Silent.

"Mrs. Daniels. Did you murder your husband?" I purposely emphasized the 'Mrs.' part of her name, knowing full well I'd hit a nerve. The divorce was never finalized before his death. Therefore, she still legally bore the name of a man she hated enough to kill.

Am I already accusing her? Yes. Ninety-five percent of the criminals I represented were guilty of their crimes. In all honesty, it made winning a case easier than if they were innocent.

Melissa's face distorted into a grimace, her hands balling into fists on the table, making the metal cinched against her skin squeak.

"Nothing leaves this room, but it makes it easier for me to formulate an argument on your behalf if I know the truth." My electric powers sizzled over my skin, desiring nothing more than to force the confession out of her.

Her dark eyes panned to mine, an unspoken evil floating within them. "Yes. You're damn right I killed him, the fucking asshole."

And there we have it.

I nodded once, sliding the folder off the table and back into my briefcase with one swift motion. "There should be no need for you to testify, but now under no circumstance are we letting you get on that stand." Standing, I pulled my jacket sleeves down, realigning them with my cufflinks.

"Are we done? That's it?" Melissa looked around the small room.

"That's it. Now I get to work. If I need any clarification on the evidence presented, I'll arrange for another meeting." I pressed a button, alerting the officer to retrieve Melissa.

Melissa Daniels was evil incarnate. One had to be to do what she did over the simple fact of "not liking someone." But again, it wasn't my job to judge them. And I certainly didn't condone murder. It didn't matter what my personal scruples were. She was a human being, and with that came certain rights. Rights that needed protecting. Guilty or not, someone has to be willing to say, "I'll defend you." And it might as well be me. A certain strength was needed to take the burden from others onto your shoulders. I'd been doing it for eons.

I stood in the men's restroom of the courthouse, only several rooms, and across the hallway from the assigned meeting room. I'd arrived early but purposely waited three minutes over the agreed time—an excuse to make an entrance. Peering at myself in the mirror, I traced my hand over my beard and adjusted my sleeves. A snap of my fingers put every hair back into place atop my head, the cufflinks and watch sparkled with radiance, and not one hair within my beard was left untrimmed. As easy as I had it with the mortals I set my sights on, certain women took extra care—extra steps to ensnare. Given Keira's reputation, I fully expected a pacing lioness. With a glance at the clock hanging on the wall, I'd become fashionably late and smiled to myself before exiting.

Slipping my hands in my pants pockets, I made my way down the hall, halting by the meeting room's window. A man walked past, and I greeted him, not knowing who the fuck he was but needing an excuse to say something. She'd hear the boom in my voice through the wall—the power lacing every word. And within a few seconds, the daunting realization would crawl through her. That deep voice—*my* voice, didn't belong to the previously hired defense lawyer.

Adjusting the knot of my tie with one hand, I opened the door with the other, focusing my gaze on my glossed shoes as I entered. "Apologies for being late. I had some…catching up to do on the case."

It was subtle, but the smallest of feminine gasps escaped her throat.

Finally lifting my eyes to hers—was like being punched in the gut. The media hadn't done this woman one ounce of justice. She was fucking gorgeous. The buxom and curvy blonde woman next to her widened her green eyes at me and squeezed Keira's knee below the table.

"Keira. That's Zane Vronti," she loud-whispered, staring at me.

Keira slapped her hand, her nostrils flaring, heat flushing her light skin. "I can see that, Olivia," she spat through gritted teeth, trying desperately not to glare at me.

Oh, the fire exuding from her like a backdraft.

Keira stood, smoothing her hands over the faux designer suit jacket hugging her tits. "I'm sorry, you failed to mention a counsel change in your e-mail request."

"I figured this meeting would serve both purposes. Is there an issue, counselor?" I leaned a hip on the table.

Keira rolled her shoulders back, making herself taller before jutting her hand out. "Not at all. Keira—"

"—Bazin," I finished for her. "Trust me. I've researched you." Slipping my hand into hers, I sent enough electricity over her skin to elicit a reaction but not enough to hurt her.

Her face stayed neutral save for the slightest twitch of her upper lip.

Huh. Peculiar and incredibly…irritating.

Keira recoiled her hand and wiped it on the front of her pin-stripe skirt as if my palm was covered in shit. A grin tugged at my lips as I took a step back.

A femme fatale disguised in imitation Versace.

"My paralegal, Olivia." She referenced the eager shorter woman to her left.

Olivia threw out her hand, a radiant smile plastering her face. "An absolute honor—" Her eyes cut to Keira and back to me. "—er, a pleasure to meet you."

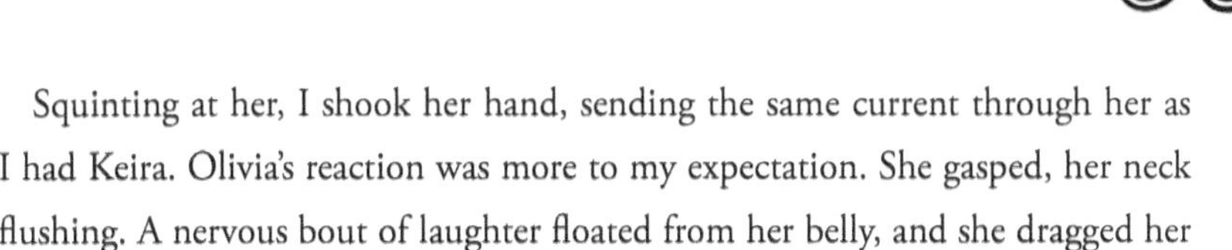

Squinting at her, I shook her hand, sending the same current through her as I had Keira. Olivia's reaction was more to my expectation. She gasped, her neck flushing. A nervous bout of laughter floated from her belly, and she dragged her fingers through her wheat-colored waves of hair.

"Love the accent." I pointed at her and winked, inciting another trail of bubbly giggling.

"Cheers," she responded before plopping in her chair and fanning herself.

Keira sat down and folded her hands on the table, not sitting back.

All the more curious about her.

Moving to the opposing side of the table, I sat on the edge, gaining the high ground over Miss Bazin.

The suit jacket shifted as her shoulders tensed beneath the fabric. "You don't want to have a seat, Mr. Vronti?"

"I'm fine right here." I patted the glass table. "And please. It's Zane." Flashing as charming of a grin as I could manage without spraining something, I gauged her reaction.

She undid the top button of her purple blouse and re-buttoned it. "I assume you have evidence you propose to dismiss, Mr. Vronti?"

This. Woman.

"That confident, hm? No plea deal?" I plucked a pen from the holder in the center of the table and twirled it between my fingers.

Olivia's gaze fell to my hand, and her palms flattened on the table.

"Not a chance." Keira flipped the folder open. "Evidence you wish to challenge?"

For the love of me, give me something.

Pushing from the table with a smug grin, I rocked back on my heels before pacing the length of the room. Olivia's eyes trailed me like a bouncing shiny red ball. Keira glanced only long enough to stifle an eye roll before removing a pen from her jacket and slapping it to the awaiting paper.

"The answering machine recordings," I challenged.

Keira started to write but paused, furrowing her brow. "All of them?"

"All of them." I tapped my fingertips to the table as I passed.

Keira rested the pen on the table. "There are several recordings of her threatening to kill her husband. Why would it be agreed to withhold those?"

"Fine. Keep those, but dismiss any where she goes into a name-calling barrage."

Keira's chest lifted as she sighed but kept it inaudible. "They're still threatening."

"Oh, come now, Keira." I jiggled the keys in my pocket as I turned on my heel. "You're telling me you've never dropped a curse word or two while arguing or—" Her gaze met mine. "—in the *throes* of passion?"

"Dear God," Olivia whispered.

Not quite.

Keira undid two buttons on her shirt, taking several more seconds this time around before doing them up again.

I may not have broken through yet, but perhaps…*cracked* her invisible shield.

FOUR

KEIRA

HIS EMOTIONS WERE A tidal wave repeatedly hurling me against other incoming waves. It took everything in me not to show the turmoil surging through me on my face. Since I was a child, I'd had my empath ability and experienced all levels of emotion from hundreds of people. His were the most intense I'd ever felt—burdened, arrogant, powerful. *Very* powerful, but most of all? Insatiable lust. In the passing minutes, it'd become so overwhelming I couldn't sift through his emotions versus my own.

The bastard refused to sit down—no doubt a power play against me. I undid the top button of my blouse, touching my fingertip against my skin before doing it up again—a habit I'd formed to calm myself. It pissed me off to no end that the man was undoubtedly attractive as well. I'd done my best to avoid lingering on news stations talking about him. It was bad enough spying him across the street from the safety of my apartment window. But now those sapphire eyes I'd glimpsed only on a TV screen lingered in front of me—probing me, seducing me.

Slapping my palms on the table, I shot to my feet. "Mr. Vronti, I'm not entirely certain where you get off talking to me in such a manner. It's entirely unprofessional, but furthermore, you want *half* of the recordings dismissed?" I tightened my jaw, not letting my eyes tear away despite the lust pouring out of him in droves. The devious glint in his gaze had my insides twisting. "Fine. We have plenty of other ammunition."

In truth, I did not want him to request *anything* dismissed. His requesting dismissal of evidence would have to be brought up before a judge, further

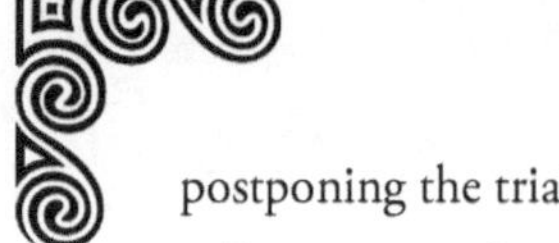

postponing the trial.

Irritation and confusion bubbled over him but were soon overshadowed by determination, which dissolved them in the thick air hanging between us.

A jackal's grin pulled at the corner of his lips. He crossed the room with deliberate steps, his serpentine gaze fixed on me. "You know how this works, Keira." He stood in front of me, scents of sandalwood and cologne permeating the air. "You're required to reveal *all* the dirty laundry at your disposal." He bit on his lower lip, eyes squinting.

Standing this close to him had my brain whirling while simultaneously making the hairs on my arms stand on end. Rather than peel my eyes away, suggesting he had some form of power over me, I distanced us by taking a step back.

Olivia tugged the hem of my jacket.

Thankful for the reprieve, I bent at the waist, lowering my ear to her mouth.

"I think my undies melted," she whispered…very loudly.

I loved Olivia. Really, I did. But her filter was Swiss cheese on the best of days. My eyes snapped to Zane's satisfied smile.

"I have that effect on *most* women, Olivia." His gaze roamed my body before lazily lifting back to my face. "Don't hate yourself for it."

Squaring off my shoulders, refusing to let him see the effect he *could* have on me, I slid the folder across the table. "And you know how this works, counselor. You can review with prosecution present."

His eyes dropped to the folder, a challenging smirk creasing his mouth. As he slid a large tanned hand over the manila, his pinky brushed the tip of my finger. The same mild static shock I'd felt when he shook my hand earlier shot through my skin. My right nostril bounced, and I ignored the tingling sensation his touch left behind as he scooped the folder into his grasp and started to flip through the papers.

He waltzed around the room with a pinched brow, squinting here and there as he sifted through the evidence files. Hiding my hand beneath the table, I tapped it on my knee, suppressing an annoyed sigh. Zane started to hum a song, his tone deep—baritone. It sounded familiar, but I didn't want to focus on his voice enough to decipher it.

Olivia leaned over. "Is he singing Acca Dacca?" She poked my ribs, her large green eyes even larger as she stared at the criminal defense lawyer circling us.

We really needed to discuss proper whispering decibels.

"Why, yes, I am. *Thunderstruck* by AC/DC for some reason always helps me concentrate." He paused and shot his gaze to mine, impaling me with it. "You know?"

"Whatever speeds this up. I'll even play it on my phone if it means spending less time in a six-by-six room with you." I slipped my phone from my jacket pocket and rested it on the table with a smug grin.

"Not a fan of my serenading?" He leaned on the table across from me.

Pulling up a streaming service, I queued up the song. "Why settle for second best?" I pressed the play button, keeping a challenging stare fixed on him.

The opening guitar riff to *Thunderstruck* blared from my phone's speaker. Olivia scrunched her face and threw up rock horns on both hands.

A wicked glint flashed in his eyes, a hint of a smile hiding over his lips. His emotions shifted—intrigued, more irritated. But the lust? Amplified.

I just. Didn't. Get it.

Leaning back in my chair, I folded my arms and held my hand out to him. "Please continue."

The tip of his tongue skirted his bottom lip before he finally lowered his gaze back to the papers and began his proximity march again. At my side, Olivia switched from the air guitar to drums, her blonde bangs falling over her eyes.

Slowly turning my head, I cocked an eyebrow at her.

Out of breath, she froze mid drumstick twirl and tousled her hair. "Too much?"

"Maybe a tad." I gestured my hand up high and lowered it, asking her to bring it down a notch.

"Right." She cleared her throat and tugged on the hem of her jacket. "Serious mode."

Despite her best efforts, she sat still for the most part, but her foot kept tapping. She'd fist pump under the table during specific lyrics and attempt to subtly lip sync.

I bit back a smile. Olivia could be such a goofball, but I wouldn't have had it any other way. Her presence alone helped me cope every day.

There was a knock at the door, and I quickly shut the music off. Zane glared at the door with one hand rubbing his chin.

"Mr. Vronti? Sorry to bother you, but your three o'clock appointment is here,"

Ruth said, pausing with her hand on the door handle and adjusting her glasses.

"I still have work to do here." Zane's tone was abrupt. Turning his back to her, he returned to the paperwork.

"But sir, it's your br—"

Zane snapped her a look over his shoulder, and flipped the folder shut with a loud *thwap*.

"Right. I'll let them know you'll be late," Ruth squeaked before closing the door behind her.

Impatience. Ever-growing irritation.

"There isn't any reason to drag this out, Zane. Everything is there for you in black and white. Either request a hearing on the evidence with a judge or let me get back to work." Scooting to the edge of my seat, I folded my hands on the table.

Zane opened the folder and dropped his gaze to the papers. "Such impatience for a woman's life hanging in the balance."

"Don't try to act as if you care about the client. You care about winning." I narrowed my eyes at him, and crossed my legs under the table to ignore the throbbing happening between them.

Lust. Anger. Desire.

"Regardless of your preconceived notions, for once, it isn't about me, Keira." He tossed the folder on the table and shoved his hands in his pockets.

"Are you trying to imply you inexplicably grew a conscience?" I panned my gaze to the awaiting folder.

"Fine. I'm formally requesting a hearing on the evidence before a judge."

Heat surged up the back of my neck, molars cracking as I gritted my teeth. Olivia sighed beside me, jotting down notes on a legal pad.

He jiggled keys in his pocket, his jaw tightening. "Are we done here?" Glancing at his watch, he started for the door. "I have more important things to do."

My jaw wanted to drop, but I forced it to stay put and, instead, squeezed the life out of the pen in my hand. "But you—" I cut myself short once his brow raised to the heavens.

This guy was one colossal mind fuck. And he *knew* it.

Standing, I shoved the folder under my arm and stormed at the exit with my chin held high.

"Looks like I'll be seeing you soon for the evidence trial—" His gaze lowered,

lingering over my chest. "Counselor."

Impatience. Smugness. Attraction.

He made no move to shake my hand, so I gave a simple nod. "May the best man win."

A chuckle—low and smooth—flowed from his chest. The sound vibrated to my toes, making my lips part as if they had a mind of their own.

His eyes dropped to my mouth before turning away, not muttering another word.

The further he got away from me, the more relaxed my mind, my nerves, my *everything* became. Rubbing my forehead, I leaned against the doorframe, exhausted as if I'd just run a marathon—twice.

"You okay?" Olivia nudged me.

"Yeah. Tired is all. I think I'm going to head home." I caught sight of Zane disappearing into another meeting room down the hall and sighed with relief.

"Woah. Home? And at half-past three in the arvo?" Olivia slapped a hand on my forehead.

Used to Ollie's antics by now, I let her palm my face. "Ollie. What are you doing?"

"Checking for a fever. Pretty sure this hasn't happened since the Fueller case."

She wasn't wrong. On any given day, I'd barricade myself in my office and pour myself into my work until the wee hours of the night. Sometimes even well into the early morning. After the overwhelming emotions exuding from Zane like a damn geyser, however, the only thing my mind would excel at currently would be absolutely nothing.

"I'm tired." Removing her hand, I pushed past her, heading down the hall. "I want my bed, a fluffy blanket, and Barns Courtney music. Tomorrow, I'll be good as new."

"Holy shit. Does this mean I have an early day?" Clapping, Olivia bounced on her heels.

"Knock yourself out. You've earned it." I whisked through the foyer to the sidewalk outside, grimacing at the flood of emotions hammering my brain from every corner.

"Catch you later, Keir-Keir." Olivia held her fist up.

With a weak smile, I bumped mine against hers. "Blonde Bulldogs, out," she shouted, fanning her hand out before turning away and almost barreling into a

businessman briskly walking.

He sneered at her, and Olivia threw her arms at her sides.

"What? It's a thing we do, alright?" Olivia said to the man's back, who made an active effort to ignore her.

My smile faded into a wince as bouts of anxiety, anger, fear, and worry flooded me from New York's inhabitants.

Was no one happy anymore?

Yanking earbuds from my briefcase, I slipped them in to cue up music. With any luck, it'd drown out most if not all of the emotions running rampant in the streets. *Tonight (I'm Lovin' You)* by Enrique Iglesias blasted into my ears. Concentrating on the beat, the feel of the concrete beneath my heels, and the bitter cold crispness in the air, dulled the floating feelings around me.

Stopping for a red light at the next crosswalk, I patted my hand against my hip, continuing the rhythmic distraction. I swiveled my hips ever so slightly, unable to control them. Lust washed over me in waves—a faint whimper collecting at the back of my throat. I opted for the explicit version of the song where "fuck" replaced the word "love." Because let's be honest, everyone knew what was *really* going down in that song. Pure. Carnal. Fu—

"*Come* here often?" A deep voice rumbled by my ear.

Jumping, I ripped out an earbud and whirled around.

Zane towered over me, sporting a long tan Burberry jacket with the collar popped. "Nice moves, by the way." He pointed at my hips.

"Are you stalking me?" In a huff, I shoved my earbuds into my jacket pocket.

"Someone thinks rather highly of themselves." He bobbed his brows at the illuminated walk sign.

With quick steps, I crossed the street.

Hopefully, he changed directions.

One glance over my shoulder made it abundantly clear. He still followed me.

"For your information—" Zane started, falling in stride beside me. "I live three blocks down."

You knew that, Keira.

"And you're *walking* there?" I slipped my gloves on.

"Why is that so hard for you to believe? You're doing the exact same thing *right* now."

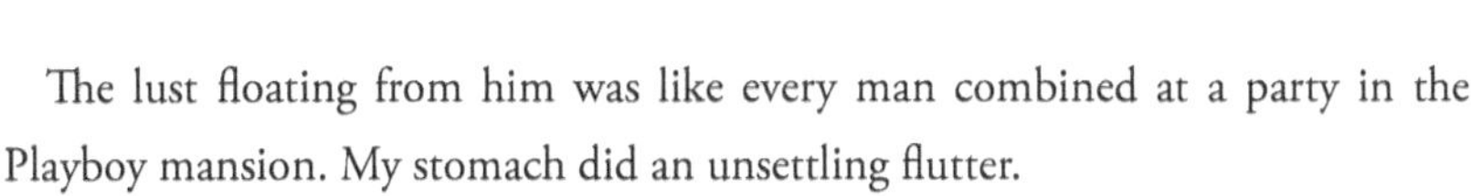

The lust floating from him was like every man combined at a party in the Playboy mansion. My stomach did an unsettling flutter.

Biting the inside of my cheek, I ignored it, slipped the strap of my briefcase over one shoulder, and wrapped my arms around myself. "I have my reasons."

A woman with bouncing waves of auburn hair walked past us, plastering a sultry grin at Zane. She waved at him, and I caught a glimpse of him grinning like a fool at her. Rolling my eyes, I shoved my gloved hands into my pockets as we reached another stop light.

"I'm dying to know said reasons." Zane took a step closer to me.

Heat radiated from him like magma, and I fought every compulsion to wrap him around me like a blanket.

"I said I have them. Not that I was going to tell you what they were." My hot breath curled in the cool air like an angered dragon.

"Keira, Keira, Keira. Just because we're opposing counsel doesn't mean we can't be—" He bent forward, lowering his face to my level. "Friends." A spark ignited in his gaze.

The walk signal blazed, and I bolted forward. "No, Zane. That's precisely what it means. We'll say our arguments in the courtroom, I'll win, and after it's all over, hopefully, we'll *never* see each other again."

We neared our apartment buildings and Zane came to a pause, shaking his head at me but grinning. "Your confidence is astounding."

"And your ego is nauseating."

We locked gazes, and an electric current sizzled down my spine. I held back a breath that longed to escape my throat, my chest tightening.

"Okay, then. See you around." Peeling my eyes away from him, I turned to my building.

"Wait a minute. You live *here*?" He pointed a leather-covered hand and tipped his head to one side.

"Uh-huh. Have a good day." I wrapped my hand around the door's handle.

"Wait." He slapped a hand near mine but made no move to touch me. "There is absolutely no way I wouldn't have noticed you lived across from me for—how long have you been here?"

Grinding my teeth, I took a step back. "It's none of your business how long I've lived here, but if you must know, it's because I'm rarely home."

"You're a workaholic, aren't you?" He crossed his arms, a gleam in his sapphire eyes.

"Don't lawyers have to be?" I tightened my grip on the briefcase.

"Good ones, sure. But even dedicated lawyers have to come up for air, don't they?" He squinted at me.

Uncertainty. Longing. Frustration. It all fluttered from him, settling over my skin like static cling.

"Well, you don't have to worry about bumping into me. I practically live in my office." I scratched the back of my head, averting my gaze to a woman sitting at her window three floors up, reading a book.

"Do you do *everything* in your office?"

Gone were the real emotions—and back was the insatiable lust.

Snapping my gaze to his, I moved past him for the door handle. "Goodbye, Zane."

Stepping away from the door with a chuckle, he flew his palms up. "I'll be sure to leave my blinds open for you."

My insides clenched at the implication, my gloves creaking against the door as I gripped it. "Why the hell would you do that?"

He backed away with his hands in his pockets, his jacket flapping as he shrugged. "Guess you'll have to wait and find out." Smiling, he winked at me, that same spark flashing in his gaze.

I bolted inside without another word, another passing thought, or another betraying flip of my stomach. Zane played a game, unaware that I had an ace up my sleeve. There he was grinning at me from across the poker table with the four of a kind in his hands, waiting to lay the cards out and win. He didn't know being an empath gave me a royal fucking flush.

FIVE

ZEUS

WHAT WAS *WRONG* WITH this woman? Not only did she not so much as bat a fucking eyelash over my godly mojo, which, by the way, I'd been pumping out like a damn fire hose, but she also felt compelled to *challenge* me.

She couldn't have been mortal. A faerie, maybe? Nymph?

Rubbing my chin, I poured another scotch and leaned against the bar in my loft, absently scratching Levin's head as I stared into oblivion.

Hermes appeared in my living room in a flash of light and feathers, rubbing the back of his head and doing that Clint Eastwood squint of his. I'm sure women found it attractive. I, however, always felt compelled to ask him if he needed glasses.

"What did you find out?" I stood straight, resting the tumbler on the bar.

After the debacle that was the evidence meeting, I needed to know more about her. Any bit of dirt or information that could possibly explain why I didn't wake up with her in bed next to me *this* morning.

"Gee. Great to see you too, Dad. Can't you at least pour me a drink first?" Hermes smirked as he scratched the stubble on his chin and slid onto a stool.

Levin trotted over to him, and Hermes smiled as he scratched the dog behind both ears.

Tightening my jaw, I grabbed another glass and obliged him—this one time. I eyed the "flyboy" aviation jacket hanging over his frame as I slid the scotch toward him. "Still working the pilot cover, I see?"

"I like flying too much, and considering winged shoes aren't exactly discreet, modern technology is my calling." He grinned, forming those same creases in his cheeks as mine before taking a long swig of whiskey.

I tapped my pinky ring against the glass several times.

Hermes's gaze dropped to my hand before he lowered his tumbler. "Before I tell you what I found out, Pops, level with me here. Why the sudden keen interest in a mortal? I can count on one hand the number of times you asked me about one in the past century."

"So, she *is* mortal?" I pressed my fingertips into the marble.

Hermes blinked rapidly. "What else would she be without you knowing?"

Fuck. Me. Could any of this have been easy?

Pinching the bridge of my nose, I snarled. "Hera is no longer Queen."

"What? How? Is that—" Hermes slid from the stool and leaned his forearms on the bar. "That's possible?"

"Yes. And I let her leave." Staring at the swirling smoke patterns in the bar top, I curled my lip back before downing the rest of my drink.

"Wow, but—"

I cut a glare at my son. "Be careful with your next words, boy. I have a matter of days. *Days* to find a new Queen or risk losing not only the crown but part of my power as well."

Hermes nodded, taking a step back. "And this woman is a candidate? Why go through the trouble? You're King of the Gods, just force her to—"

Slamming the glass down, I pressed my palms against the bar. "What did you find out?"

"Alright, alright. Calm down. Last thing we need is a random lightning strike in New York City in the middle of winter." He snapped his brown leather jacket. "This'll probably make you feel better. She's a divorcée."

I balled my hands into fists. "How is her being previously married supposed to make me *feel* better?"

"Because that marriage was the only thing keeping her legal in the US." Hermes folded his arms.

Hope sprung eternal.

"Come again?"

"She's about to be an illegal alien. Canadian citizen, living in the US, practicing law. She passed the bar in New York while she was still married, but without the proper immigration status again, and fast, not only will she be kicked out but won't be able to practice here."

A grin tugged at my lips. "And with how wrapped up in her work she is, why would she remember a little thing like a deadline?"

"Sure. Clearly, you've been…investigating her on your own." A sly grin pulled at my son's lips, his fingers drumming on the bar.

Aggravation tugged at my spine. "Not as *thoroughly* as I would prefer."

Hermes's expression fell flat. "You mean you two haven't—"

"No," I growled.

He blinked once. "I don't know what to say to that."

"You say nothing. That's what."

Hermes whistled and drummed his fingers on the flat surface. "Man, this chick has done a number on you, hasn't she?"

The question made my blood boil. How *had* she worked under my skin? And *why* did I feel the need to pursue it?

"It's not anything I can't handle. She thinks she has some form of power over me." I dragged my knuckle under my bottom lip, electricity sparking in my palms. "She's sorely mistaken."

Hermes held his hands up, eyeing the lightning still circling my arms. "Ever stop to think *feeling* powerless with someone doesn't have to be the same as *being* powerless?"

Cutting my gaze to his, I shot a bolt at his tumbler, shattering it.

Hermes slapped the bar top. "Right. I know when I've overstayed my welcome."

Levin touched my leg with his paw, panting.

"Take Levin for a walk," I barked at Hermes.

He glared at me and scoffed. "I'm not your godsdamned errand boy."

I returned the glare. Only mine would've rattled Olympus's foundation.

He gulped and hopped from his stool, whistling for Levin. "Right away, sir."

I had far more pressing matters to deal with…

I paused outside the courtroom. No doubt my presence would cause a stir, especially considering I hadn't done the "courteous" action of announcing my

arrival via phone call. No. I needed to swoop in, discreetly work my magic, and get the Tartarus out of Dodge. I'd donned my dark blue suit with a matching necktie, knowing it made my eyes pop, slathered in extra hair gel, and as I entered, flashed a radiant-as-fuck grin.

The whispering and murmurs started as soon as my shoe touched the tan carpet leading into a barrage of cubicles. With one hand in my pants pocket, I used the other to give idle waves to those who chose to stare at me.

A random man walked up to me, puffing his chest, trying to make himself look taller. "Mr. Vronti, we uh—we weren't expecting you."

"Yes." I squinted, panning the heads peeking over cubicle walls, looking for one blonde in particular. "I was in the area and thought of something last minute to discuss with—I'm looking for Miss Bazin's paralegal, Olivia. Is she in?"

"Fuck me," an Aussie woman whispered nearby.

Smiling at the random man, I nudged my head in the voice's direction and swiveled on my heel. Resting my forearm on the cubicle wall, I leaned over. Olivia had her head crouched near her computer monitor, hands pressed against the desk and splayed open.

"Hello there," I said, dropping my voice an octave.

Olivia shot up, the phone headset nestled atop her head yanking off from lack of cord length. "Zane. Mr. Vronti." She cleared her throat and batted her bangs from her eyes before grabbing a tissue and dabbing between her tits with it. "Zane."

"Olivia." Stroking the wall with a single finger, I subtly chewed on my bottom lip.

Her eyes snapped to my finger, and she gulped before letting out a nervous laugh. "Is there uh—something I can help you with? Keira isn't uh—isn't here. She went to lunch."

"Perfect. Because I hoped to speak with *you*." I bent forward, finally managing to catch her gaze.

It was so much easier when they looked at me.

Her plump lips parted, and she absently dropped the tissue as she stuck out her chest. "Me?"

"Mmhm. Mind if I...*come* around?" I did a circle gesture with my hand, making my lightning power spark in my eyes.

"Come? Around?" She pushed her rolling desk chair back and opened her

arms. "Have at it."

Keeping her gaze without blinking, I curved my lips into a grin, and walked around the corner of the cubicle with powerful, calculated steps. I stood in front of her, widening my stance.

Her chest heaved as she stared up at me, her hands gripping the seat of her chair on each side of her wide hips. "Hi."

"Hi," I whispered, sitting on the edge of her desk and crossing one ankle over the opposite knee. "Olivia, I need you to do me a favor."

Olivia halfway stood from her chair, glancing around the office with her fingers grazing her chest. "Here? In the middle of the office?"

"Olivia," I beckoned, making her look me in the eye again.

She slowly sat back down, rubbing her lips together as she devoured me with her gaze.

"Under other circumstances, I may have taken you up on such an enticing offer." I leaned forward, tilting my head, relishing in the whimper that escaped her throat. "But the favor I need involves your calendar."

"My—calendar?" She scrunched her nose.

Sitting back, I interlaced my fingers, letting them hang between my legs. "Particularly the one you keep for Keira?"

"Oh. Sure. What about it?" Olivia's gaze moved to her computer monitor as she rolled her chair to the desk and pulled up a digital calendar.

I was next to her in a swift move undetectable to the mortal eye, leaning on the desk.

Dipping my chin and lowering my voice, I laced every word with power only a god-king possessed. "Her paperwork deadline. The divorce. Her residency status situation. Erase it."

She stared up at me, sticking out her chest before letting out a moaning sigh.

Leaning forward, I moved close enough to let her smell the scent wafting from me that I'd explicitly conjured for her—eucalyptus, barbeque and...Vegemite. I would've chosen Aqua di Gio or even fucking vanilla and laundry, but no—this woman liked what she liked. "Olivia."

"Yup. Right. On it." Her hand worked the mouse, eyes wide as she clicked onto the calendar, pulled up the instance...and hit the delete button with a single finger.

"Good girl." I rested my hands in my lap.

She let out a sensual groan, rolling her chair closer to me, puckering her lips, and closing her eyes. Scooping a folder from her desk into my hand, I lifted it between us, making her lips meet with it rather than my mouth. She fluttered her eyes open with an exaggerated pout.

"The entry never existed. In fact, blame it on a glitch if she asks. And I—" As I leaned forward, her chest swelled, and her eyes grew heavy. I bopped her on the nose with the folder. "—was never here."

Olivia's eyes closed again, and she moaned, gripping the armrests of her chair as her head fell back.

I stood, pulling on my shirt sleeves and scanning the other cubicles. Not a soul peeked. Just the way I'd willed it. Buttoning my suit jacket, I strolled from Olivia's cubicle and started to walk away.

Olivia gasped behind me. "I think—I just came and have no idea how."

Peeking a glance at her over my shoulder, I grinned at her fists thrusting into the air as she leapt from her chair.

"But I am *all* about phantom orgasms," she exclaimed.

Remember when I said it was far too easy?

I smirked to myself before exiting the building.

The first step was complete. The damsel would soon be in distress, and I could swoop in to save the day and make her an offer she couldn't refuse. Still, I needed more information. I'd only known Keira for a matter of days and she'd already managed to surprise me far too many times for comfort. A meddling god could not meddle properly without ammunition. And I knew precisely who to call on to provide me with an arsenal on our darling spitfire prosecutor.

I stood in my living room, waiting for the arrival of my enforcers, throwing a tennis ball for Levin. His ears flopped as he returned with it in the corner of his mouth. After dropping the ball at my feet, he bent forward with his butt in the air, tail wagging excitedly. Scooping the drool-covered ball into my palm, I threw it down the hall for the fourteenth time.

A side window flew open, the sound of feathers rustling echoing in my ears as

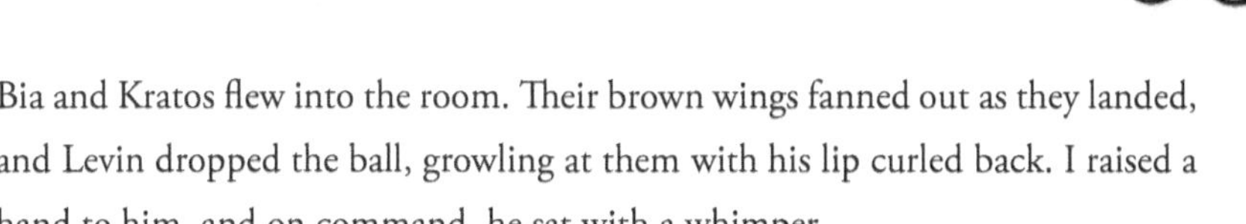

Bia and Kratos flew into the room. Their brown wings fanned out as they landed, and Levin dropped the ball, growling at them with his lip curled back. I raised a hand to him, and on command, he sat with a whimper.

"Please tell me you both disguised yourselves before *flying* into my apartment on a bustling street in New York?" I flicked my wrist to shut the window behind them.

"We may not be on Earth often, but we do know the protocol, sir," Kratos said, his voice as deep as the Titans themselves. His tanned leather vest stood out in contrast to his umber skin, his bald head reflecting the overhead lights.

Bia bowed her head, her black hair shifting over the loose tunic top she wore. "*My liege.*"

Bia never spoke. Any communication she did was telepathically and only other gods could hear her.

"I have a task for you both." Spying Levin vibrating from the corner of my eye, I whistled at him, and he ran to my enforcers, circling them.

Bia lifted her hands, and folded her wings behind her as if Levin would chew on them.

"Interesting choice in enforcers, sir." Kratos crossed his massive arms, lowering one for the moment it took to pat Levin on the head.

"The last time you two worked together was Prometheus. I'd say you're due." Moving behind the bar, I poured myself a scotch, raising my brow at them as an offering.

They both shook their heads, and I shrugged.

"What would you have us do? A heist? Robbery, perhaps?" Kratos snapped his fingers. "Infiltration."

I sniggered at him over the rim of my tumbler. "You've been watching far too many movies, old friend."

Kratos's full lips tilted down in a deep frown.

"*What do you wish of us, my lord?*" Bia steepled her terracotta fingers, piercing me with hazel eyes. Her voice traveled over my brain like scattered whispers.

"I want you to follow someone. A mortal. I need to know absolutely everything about her." My grip tightened on the glass, making it squeak.

"A mortal? But wh—" Kratos started.

I pointed at him. "If one more god asks me *why*, one more time, I'm sincerely

going to lose my shit. Since when am I questioned at every turn?"

"I meant no disrespect. We just need to know what we're looking for." Kratos interlaced his fingers behind his back and bowed his head.

"She's—different. I need to know why. What makes her tick, what makes her happy, how she spends her days. Be on her ass like a fly on shit. Get my drift?" I downed the whiskey.

"Yes, my lord," Kratos answered, flaring out his wings.

Levin yelped, his claws slipping against the floor as he scurried away.

"*Do you wish me to read her mind?*" Bia twisted her wrists as she canted her head to the side.

Bia's ability to read minds only extended to the mortal variety…thank Olympus.

"Yes. All of it. Any of it. Whatever it takes. You'll report in within twenty-four hours." Blowing out a breath, I leaned on the bar.

"A day? My liege, that's not a lot of time." The feathers in Kratos's wings rustled.

Tightening my jaw, I shook my head. "I don't *have* time. Currently, there is no queen." I cut my gaze to them. "Understand?"

Bia and Kratos exchanged bewildered glances before nodding.

"Good. Off you go." I jutted my head toward the window and waited for them to exit before slumping against the bar.

Holding my head in my hands, I let out a deep sigh. Levin's paw touched my thigh, and I smiled down at him, his pink tongue sprouting from the corner of his mouth, his brown eyes gleaming with happiness.

I patted him on the head and rubbed my temple. "I'm fine, boy. Just exhausted."

So. Incredibly. Spent.

SIX

KEIRA

"KEIRA," OLIVIA'S VOICE CALLED out.

My body jostled and I shot up, sucking in drool collecting at the corner of my mouth.

"What?" I grumbled, dragging my sleeve over my lips, wincing through a pair of dried eyes.

Olivia crossed her arms and tapped her foot. "You fell asleep at your desk again. Why don't you just go bloody home, Keir?"

My right cheek felt numb from lying on the hardwood, and I rubbed it. "I can't. I've got to go over this case file with a fine-toothed comb before the evidence hearing tomorrow."

"What would be the point of that? You don't want to bank on evidence we may not get to use. Go home." She moved behind me and jiggled the chair until I stood. "Take a hot shower, maybe flick the bean, and go to sleep in an actual bed, yeah?"

Moving hair stuck to my forehead out of my eyes, I squinted at her. "Flick the bean? Are you talking about masturbating?"

"What else would I be talking about?" She grabbed my pea coat and held it open, waiting for me to slip my arms through.

I frowned and let her dress me.

She shoved my briefcase into my chest and pointed at the door. "Go. I'll wrap things up here."

"Thank you, Ol—" I started, but she turned away from me, turning circles with a confused expression.

"What's that? Would that be the distant voice of a woman who should be halfway home by now with a hand in her undies?" She cupped a hand over her ear.

Rolling my eyes, I waved at her. "I'm gone. I'm gone."

"Love you, Keir Keir," she yelled to my back.

I made the same quizzical face she had while turning circles. "What's that? It sounds like a didgeridoo in the distance?"

Olivia burst out laughing and pointed at me.

"Love you too, Ollie." I blew her an air kiss before exiting to the sidewalk.

I'd taken the long way home, avoiding more people scurrying around holiday shopping and having lunch. Christmastime in New York City never failed to be magical, but it always left a pit in my stomach, knowing it also meant more tourists, more people, more crowds—more emotions. At times, it was enough to make me want to scream.

Once I reached the reprieve of my apartment building, I tripped over something resting on the ground in front of my door.

"What the hell?" Squatting, I scooped a box into my palms.

We had designated compartments for packages to pick up via assigned keys. This…was odd.

After walking into my apartment and locking the door behind me, I rested the mysterious parcel on my kitchen counter and stared at it. It wouldn't be the first time I'd received a nasty-gram from a disgruntled suspect's family that I'd put behind bars. I'd even been threatened in the past.

Would someone go so far as to send me a bomb that'd explode upon opening it?

I lowered my ear to the box. Silence.

"To hell with it." I ripped away the brown wrapping, opened the white box, and staring back at me were a pair of pink binoculars.

What. The actual. Fuck.

As I lifted the binoculars with two fingers, a folded piece of paper fell. Glaring at it, hoping it'd spontaneously combust from my stare, I opened it.

So you can get a better view. -Z

I turned my glare out the window, eyeing the penthouse suite in the adjacent building I knew belonged to Zane. Before yesterday, the blinds had always been

drawn. And now, as he promised, a singular window was wide open.

Growling, I shoved the binoculars back into the box and pushed it away. "What a grade-A asshole, I swear."

A woman left his apartment building, adjusting her skintight dress once she reached the sidewalk. She flicked her dark brown hair, twisted on her heel, and gave his window the middle finger before hailing a cab. After rolling my eyes, I crossed the room and yanked on the cord to close my blinds.

I needed precisely what Olivia prescribed—a steaming hot shower.

I pressed my hands against the tiles, letting the hot water roll down the back of my head, my neck, my spine. It was absolute bliss when my mind had the chance to relax—to know the emotions I felt were entirely my own.

Zane's face shimmered through my mind. The electric blue eyes, the way they squinted when he smiled. His knuckle grazing his bottom lip. The way he moved around a room as if every crack in the floor, every pane of glass was his to own—to control. The man was a walking powerhouse, and I had no idea how he managed to make it leak from his very pores.

I traced my finger over my hip, trailing my stomach and dipping between my thighs. Zane Vronti was everything I hated in a man—a human being. Biting my lip, I fingered my folds. He was arrogant, boastful, overly confident…charismatic, powerful, and far too fucking attractive for his own good.

Sputtering water, I pressed my forearm against the wall, holding myself up and massaging my clit with two fingers.

I couldn't stand defense lawyers. Combining all of what Zane represented with the one job I despised most of all should make him my arch-nemesis. And yet, here I was, getting off at the thought of him—the idea of him, picturing his face as I did it.

There were fleeting emotions I'd gotten glimpses of from him. Feelings that didn't match up to the ones he brought to the surface. Was that what I held onto? The possibility that the first man to ever infiltrate my every thought, to make my insides twist simply from the smell of him, may be something more than an arrogant prick?

Because…he'd have to be. Or it'd make me all forms of backward. Deranged. Out of my right mind.

Whimpering, I cried out through my release, the euphoria circling through my

stomach, making my spine tingle. I should've felt dirty—that of all the people I could have pictured, I chose to think of Zane. But I didn't feel dirty. He was merely a tool for my own pleasure—a plaything who would never get the satisfaction of giving me a climax himself. I *used* him the same way he used all of those women night after night.

After drying off and throwing on a camisole and shorts, I walked to my kitchen with the sole intention of making a bag of popcorn and watching something on Netflix. What possessed me to eyeball the box sitting on the counter with the binoculars—I couldn't say. What further possessed me to go to my window and part the blinds—eluded me. But what would eat at my brain for the unforeseeable future was the curiosity overcoming me to the point I raised the binoculars…and took a peek.

My throat dried, spying a fully nude Zane parading his apartment. His back was to me, giving me a clear view of his perfectly rounded, tanned, and muscular ass. The man was a Greek god statue in human form. He slowly turned—meticulously even, as if he knew I were watching. When he fully faced me, there it was. His. Dick. Before I could do the appropriate calculations in my mind, taking into account my distance from him and how far it fell against his thigh, I fumbled with and dropped the binoculars.

Probably for the better. I shouldn't have looked. What if he had seen me? He could hold the fact I spied on him over me. Possibly even use it against me in court. Slapping a hand over my face, I shoved the binoculars back in the box, stomped to my bedroom, and kicked it under my bed. Let it die there with the dust bunnies, lost pens, and paperclips.

Making my way back to the living room, I flopped onto my couch, sans popcorn, and clicked on the first movie that caught my eye. *Immortals*. Yes. Henry Cavill could cure anything. Nestling against the cushions, I rested my head on my hand and forced my concentration on a tale of Mount Olympus, Theseus, and the ruthless tyrant Hyperion. To say I hadn't thought of Zane's ass or other areas of him several times throughout the rest of the night—would've been a complete lie. And I hated myself for it.

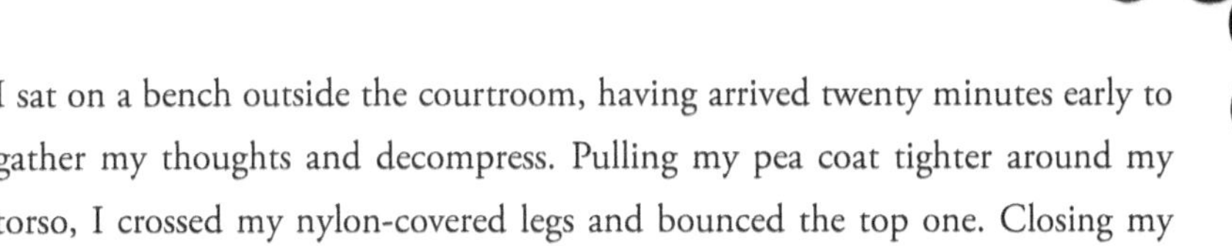

I sat on a bench outside the courtroom, having arrived twenty minutes early to gather my thoughts and decompress. Pulling my pea coat tighter around my torso, I crossed my nylon-covered legs and bounced the top one. Closing my eyes, I concentrated on the steady hum of the fluorescent lights above me.

"Good morning," Zane's deep as sin voice sounded near me.

Opening one eye, followed by the other, I hugged myself tighter. He stood in front of me clothed in his usual suit attire and Burberry coat, but all I could see was what I had seen last night. It was as if I'd gained the ability of x-ray vision. A heavy lump formed in my throat, and I fought back the urge to gulp.

He squinted at me and cocked his head, pointing at me with his hand still in his coat pocket. "You alright there, counselor? You look a bit flushed."

My cheeks *did* feel warm. Shit.

"Perfectly fine. It's stuffy in here." I sat up straight, focusing all of my attention on his face to avoid the temptation to travel my gaze lower.

"And yet you still have your coat on." He rubbed his chin.

Grinding my molars, I glared at him. "I like stuffy."

"You don't say." After smirking, he sat next to me, leaving only a foot of space between us.

"I can't believe you're not only on time but early." Heat coiled from his leg, caressing my thigh. The usual lust and power flowed from him, but I also caught an overwhelming sense of exhaustion—so much it made me yawn.

"I have no issue making feisty prosecutors wait on me, but judges? I need them in my corner." His gaze dropped to my crossed legs, eyes roaming over my calves.

Part of my heel slipped, revealing half of my foot. His glance snapped to it, and I secured it back on, holding my breath. "And I'm sure you never fail to charm the pants off them."

Perhaps literally if it were a female judge.

"Level with me here—" He leaned his forearms on his knees, turning his face to look at me. "What is your beef with defense lawyers?"

I guffawed. "I should think that's fairly obvious, Zane."

"Maybe it is, maybe it isn't. But I want to hear from *your* lips." His gaze dropped to my mouth, the tip of his tongue skirting his bottom lip.

Did he imagine what I'd taste like?

Moving my attention to the light snow flurries stirring outside from the foyer

windows, I took a deep breath. "You represent people who have done despicable deeds and fight to win their case despite knowing it."

"That hardly seems fair."

I snapped my focus back to him. "Fair? What isn't fair is when known murderers go free. Doesn't it bother you to know they'll more than likely do it again?"

"No, it doesn't. Justice was served, and they'll have something far worse to answer to at the end of it all." He circled his finger at the ground, pointing to hell itself.

He had a point, but it still didn't negate the fact that instead of rotting in a prison cell waiting to meet their maker, they were on the streets.

"I don't even know why I'm trying to debate this with a defense lawyer."

Confidence surged from him as he shifted on the bench, stretching his arms over the back of it. I stiffened when his jacket sleeve brushed my shoulder. "You better get used to it. You're about to debate with this lawyer on something far larger."

"You could've taken your skills elsewhere and done virtually anything else with them. Why a defense lawyer? Why?" I slapped my hand on my knee.

His eyes shot to my leg, acutely aware of every move they made. "Aren't there worse occupations out there? Pimps? Mafia bosses? I went to college for this career, built a legitimate and lawful reputation for myself."

Fuck. We weren't even in the courtroom yet, and this guy was already debating me straight into a hole. And *why* was it so damn hot?

"The same could be said for heart surgeons." Turning my hips toward him by an inch, I tilted my head back.

His eyes roamed down again before panning to stare in front of him. "Are you trying to tell me prosecutors have never put innocent people in jail?"

I dug my nails into my ribs through the jacket with my arms still tightly wrapped around myself. "That's rare."

He leaned forward, his sandalwood scent dizzying me. "It still happens."

"Run out of arguments to plead your case, Zane?" I brought our faces closer, masking my expression from every neuron that sparked beneath my skin.

"I find it borderline amusing you think I have to explain myself at all to you, honestly." He stared at my lips, canting his head to one side.

We were a breath away from each other. He could've kissed me so easily—and I couldn't say that I would've stopped him.

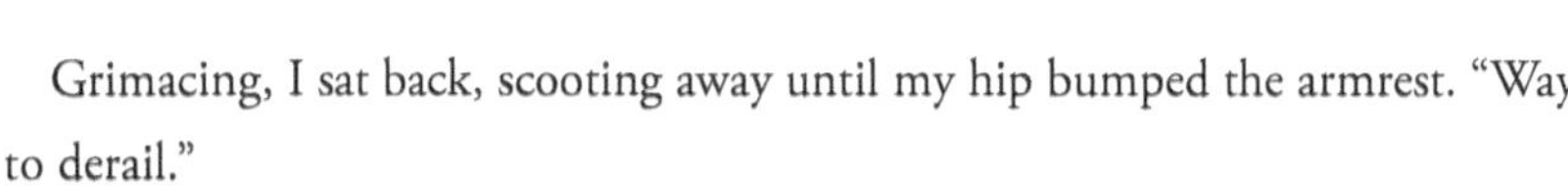

Grimacing, I sat back, scooting away until my hip bumped the armrest. "Way to derail."

"Look, Keira. At the end of the day, remember that she, most of all, would disagree with your sentiments toward defense lawyers." Zane pointed to a painting hanging on the adjacent wall. A depiction of Lady Justice holding a scale and sporting her usual blindfold.

Justice is blind.

Satisfaction oozed from his pores, contrasting with the fury that shot down my spine.

"Fuck you," I whispered to him.

Zane drummed his fingers on the bench behind me as he looked around. "Well, we only have a few minutes, but I'm sure we could find a closet somewhere."

Heat rushed to my stomach, and I bit the inside of my cheek to keep from smiling at his somewhat humorous joke.

"Good morning, counselors," a woman's voice announced as she breezed through the foyer, shaking out her graying hair, ridding it of snowflakes.

A lady judge. Just. Perfect.

Under normal circumstances, I would've hoped to have an edge given the woman-to-woman stance I could take without even implying it. But with Zane, he could turn one notch of his charmgasms on, and she'd be putty in his hands.

"Sylvia, a pleasure to be working with you again." Zane stood with a handsome smile, bowing his head at her.

The woman grinned as she fixed her hair, smoothing it over her ears. "Mr. Vronti."

Zane held his hand out once the judge entered the courtroom, edging me to follow her.

I paused as I passed, glaring up at him. "Did you sleep with her?"

"Not relevant to the case, Miss Bazin." His hot breath curled over my skin as his lips hovered by my ear.

Sucking in a shaky breath, I stormed into the courtroom, regaining my composure once I'd taken off my coat and organized my paperwork, notepad, and pens.

Zane coolly took the seat at the table next to me, folding his coat over the back of his chair and buttoning all buttons on his suit jacket. He sat down and leaned

back with such casualness you'd think we were about to discuss the weather and not the evidence leading toward a murder conviction.

The judge shuffled papers on her podium, and slid the squared reading glasses attached to a chain on her nose. "Confirming this is in regards to audio recording evidence in the Melissa Daniels case?"

"Yes, your honor," I answered, trying not to let the sight of nothing on the table in front of Zane bother me.

"Prosecution, please present your argument first as to why they should be included." The judge folded her hands, giving me her undivided attention.

I stood, feeling Zane's scorching eyes roaming over me. "Your honor, the recordings are relevant for establishing motive. It was clear from the defendant's tone she had immense hatred for her husband. She even stated it more than once."

"I object, your honor," Zane started before standing, towering over me. "Hatred toward a spouse isn't motive for murder. It could've easily been temporary feelings after a heated argument."

The judge turned her attention back to me. "Sustained. Counselor, was there anything more *specific* that you could directly relate to motive?"

"Yes. She said verbatim that she was going to kill him." I tapped my fingernails against the manila folder resting in front of me, keeping my gaze away from Zane.

"Your honor, with the number of voicemails there are, including *all* of them would only survive to unjustly bias the jury in favor of the prosecution. They were voicemails left in the heat of moments leading after an argument. It would be an unfair trial in direct violation of the tenets of which this country was founded upon."

My insides fluttered. Here I was, defending my argument for a case I wanted to win—to wipe the floor with the lawyer standing next to me, and yet the way he presented himself, the way he phrased things—he *was* good. Powerful. Commanding. I pinched my knees together.

"Counselor, do you argue for the inclusion of *all* voicemails?" The judge tapped her pen against her desk.

"Yes, your honor. All of them *are* relevant."

"The only reason to include all recordings as evidence is if the prosecution is unsure of my client's guilt and needs them to support a completely circumstantial case." His voice boomed like thunder right after a lightning strike.

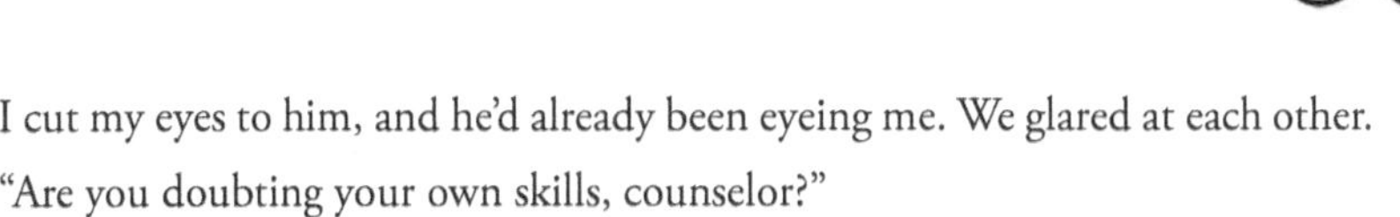

I cut my eyes to him, and he'd already been eyeing me. We glared at each other.

"Are you doubting your own skills, counselor?"

Confidence. Lust. Satisfaction.

Emotions both from him—from me, mixing, swirling, and striking against my stomach.

"This has nothing to do with the uncertainty surrounding guilt, only the prosecution's desire to have every available piece of evidence pointing toward Mrs. Daniels' immense hatred for her husband, which could've been a direct factor in his death." I beat my fist against the table once, solidifying my final argument.

The judge nodded and peered at Zane over the rim of her glasses. "Anything else left to say for the defense?"

"No, your honor."

"Given the nature of the voicemails, I'm ruling that the only recording to be presented and used in court as evidence for the prosecution's case is the one stating she was going to kill him. All others will be dismissed." The judge slammed her gavel. "Adjourned."

My chest heaved as I turned to look at him. A sensuous, victorious smile pulled at his lips. I wanted to gouge his eyes out while also craving to ride his face. A battle of hate versus lust, despising versus respecting that had me whirling.

"No hard feelings?" He extended his hand.

I stared at it, struggling to keep my breaths even—to not outright pant in front of him. "Would you meet me outside?"

His cerulean eyes pierced me as he lowered his hand. No smirk. No frown. But a heat sparked in his gaze before I turned away, and he followed me out of the courtroom. All sensible rationalization had left my brain. I needed a release, a place for the swirling emotions—the overpowering feelings coursing through me to settle and hopefully…disappear.

Spotting a janitor's closet door cracked, I yanked it open and paused. Was I about to do this? When his sandalwood scent hit my nostrils, and I gazed at him over my shoulder, standing coolly with his hands folded in front of him, a challenging glint in his gaze—I'd made up my mind. Grabbing his arm, I pulled him into the closet and he let me, a newfound warmth radiating from him.

Shutting the door behind us and locking it, I slowly turned on my heel, coming

face-to-face with Zane Vronti. Shelves of toilet paper, cleaning supplies, and a mop bucket surrounded us, leaving barely enough room to shift our stances. My heart raced, pounding in my ears. The lust coiling in the air between us, trapped in such a small space, had me quivering.

"You have me at your mercy, counselor." He held his palms up. "What are you going to do with me?"

He *wanted* to be controlled as much as he desired to *do* the controlling.

We locked eyes, and an urgency tugging at my brain had my fingers trailing up his jacket's lapels, not stopping until I reached his neck. I pressed my mouth to his lips, immediately slipping my tongue in, circling with his. Whimpering at the swirls, dips, and flips exploding in my stomach, I bunched my hands in his hair. Once his hands traced my lower back, I pushed off him, only so far away to make the tips of our noses brush.

"This is so fucked up," I whispered, keeping my gaze on his, drowning in the deep blue.

He chewed on his lip, chest heaving, his hands now raised at his sides. "It's only fucked up if you call it that. I've often lived under the principle of…if you want it—*take* it."

His eyes flashed with a beam of light I chalked up to my body and mind battling for control to the point of hallucination. I tightened my grip on his hair.

"I'm right here. Do you want it?"

One drop of my gaze to his tongue licking his bottom lip, my mouth covered that same lip, kissing him. No sooner had Zane been given the green light for the second time, his arm wrapped around my waist, and he turned us, shoving my back against one of the shelves, knocking a roll of toilet paper to the ground. I skirted my knee up his side, kissing him, devouring him, taking everything he'd give me. He pulled away, licking down my neck, biting it hard enough to make me gasp but not break the skin. His hand grabbed my ass, squeezing it, using it to pull me tighter against him—make me feel that cock I'd gotten a glimpse of last night.

Moaning, I grabbed his jacket and switched our positions, pushing him against the same shelves, crashing a sealed bottle of soap to the ground. Electric current pulsed over my skin, tantalizing it.

Surprise. Attraction.

A wicked grin pressed against my lips as I kissed him, sliding my hands into his

jacket, feeling the hard muscle that made me whimper. Walking my fingers over the carved abs hiding beneath his shirt, I flicked his belt and cupped him. *All* of him. Hard as a fucking rock.

Jesus. Christ. What the hell was I doing?

I pushed away as far as the small room would let me and wiped the back of my hand over my mouth. "I—I got that out of my system. It's never happening again, Vronti. It can't."

He dragged a thumb over his bottom lip, smiling at me.

Frustration. Longing. But not surprised. Like he'd been expecting me to bail out.

"You made one small mistake, counselor." He took the singular step needed to bring us toe-to-toe, pressing his hands above my head on the door behind me, caging me. "Now you've had a taste." He pressed his lips to my ear. "You must've liked what you saw through my window last night, hm?"

"But how did you—" I stared up at him, trying to be angry about it but felt more like laughing.

Pushing away, he adjusted his tie, did up the button of his jacket, and dragged his hand through hair that I'd ruffled. "You may want to wait five minutes before leaving after me. I can't imagine the scandalous rumors that'd fly if word got out of two opposing counselors exiting a broom closet in the courthouse together." That same flash blazed in his eyes.

I gripped the shelf behind me to keep myself upright, pressing my head against the cool metal.

He flicked the lock and placed his hand on the doorknob before resting his other hand on my hip. "Think about me tonight when you finish what you started, Miss Bazin." After slipping my earlobe between his teeth for a fraction of a second, he was gone.

Slapping my hands over my face, I slid down the shelves until my butt met with the ground. Glaring at the mop bucket in the corner, I kicked it with a growl. I'd been so unable to control myself, I resorted to pulling Zane into a fucking musty broom closet. Worst of all, I couldn't promise myself I wouldn't do it again. He was complicated, exuberant, and laced with so much sexual energy. That inner part of me I'd buried deep from past partners for fear they wouldn't understand poked at the surface, begging to be set free.

SEVEN

ZEUS

ON THE OUTSIDE, KEIRA was professional, orderly, put together. On the inside, she was broken, intriguing, and kept an absolute freak buried deep. And I fucking *dug* it. All of it. Yesterday convinced me of my worst fears—no other woman would do. It *had* to be her. Keira. My history spoke for itself—when the King of the Gods desired something or someone, it was rare it didn't come to fruition.

"Are we just going to sit here, or are we going to fuck? Is this really what you brought me up here for?" the raven-haired woman with topaz eyes asked, sitting in a frump in the chair across from me.

I sat with my forearms resting on my knees, hands steepled as I eyed my deluxe rotating Scrabble board, the faux ivory letters staring back at me, waiting for me to spell a damn word.

Did I think having Keira see a parade of women waltz from my apartment building every night would make her jealous? I hadn't a fucking clue what made that woman tick, but I'd pull every damn card I could.

Grabbing several letters, I placed them on the board without looking at her. "I told you I'd entertain you. If you misinterpreted my intentions, that's your business. PS – you don't spell penis with a 'z,' but nice try at triple points."

"I'm so out of here." She scoffed and rolled her eyes as she pushed from the chair and made for the door.

Glancing at my watch, I dug into my back pocket and slapped a hundred-dollar bill on the table. A woman like her would undoubtedly recognize the sound of cash, possibly even smell it from across the room. "Sit down. Finish the game.

And you leave with a consolation prize."

She folded her arms and smacked her pink glossed lips together. "Make it two hundred, and I won't tell anyone that Zane Vronti invited me up here to play Scrabble." She did air quotes.

I ground my teeth together, narrowing my eyes at her from across the room. If only this woman knew who she was talking to—if only I could make a lightning strike singe the carpet between us. No.

Plucking another hundred from my pocket, I slapped it atop the other bill. "Only if when you walk out the door, you look—happy."

"Fine." She shrugged and moved back to her seat across from me, adjusting her faux fur jacket. "Oh, I'll be happy. Been eyeing these new Christian Louboutins, and you're about to give me the rest of what I need."

"Sure. Whatever," I grumbled.

Turning the board to face her, I bobbed a brow, insinuating it was her turn. The woman tapped her shoe against the hardwood floor, absently scratching her neck as she looked at the ceiling. She did everything except make an effort at spelling another word.

Sighing, I pinched the bridge of my nose. "You can go," I snapped, standing and shoving my hands in my pants pockets, jingling my keys as I waited for her to bounce her way out.

She clapped her hands before scooping the cash into her palm. After blowing me a kiss she said, "Well, at least you were nice to look at the past forty-five minutes." Winking, she swept out the door, not bothering to shut it behind her.

"You're welcome," I scoffed. With a flick of my wrist, I *whooshed* the door shut and let Levin out to run around the apartment. He'd spend the next ten minutes sniffing every inch the woman had touched, wagging his tail all the while.

Rubbing my temple, I walked to the window facing Keira's to see if she reacted to the woman leaving. Keira always seemed stone cold, but I knew she held back, especially after she shoved me in a closet and devoured me like a lioness in heat. Her taking control like that, having no idea she held a Greek god in her petite hands—fuck. Keira glanced out the window, but if she had any emotion, she didn't show it. Still, she took the time to look. That spoke volumes.

"*Are you alone, my liege?*" Bia's voice shuttered over my brain.

"Yes."

Kratos and Bia materialized into the room versus *flying* through an unopened window as they had before.

Still spying Keira through her window in a dress shirt and pencil skirt, but pacing barefoot with a folder in her hand, a tumbler of scotch in the other, I asked, "What did you find out?"

"This mortal is extremely job-oriented. From the moment she wakes up, she walks to work avoiding people at all costs—" Kratos started.

I snapped a gaze at him over my shoulder, finally looking away once Keira was out of view. "Avoiding people? Interesting."

"—yes. When she arrives at work, she breezes past everyone and sits in her office alone for an hour or more as if she's decompressing." Kratos folded his brown wings behind him, clasping his hands behind his back.

"I wonder why?" Rubbing my chin, I squatted as Levin approached me, scratching his head. "What else?"

"The only person she confides in is her paralegal, Olivia. She spends her day at work, most of the night and then walks home. Again, avoiding people even if it means taking a longer route home."

Work. Work. Work. It hit far too close to home.

"Bia, my dear. I'm *very* interested to hear your take."

"*Firstly, you know how I cannot read the minds of the gods?*" She took a seat on my leather lounge chair, adjusting her wings as not to sit on them.

I squinted at her, rising to my feet, despite Levin's groan. "Yes?"

"*It took extra effort on my part to get through to her. It was borderline exhausting.*"

"What does that mean? She's not a goddess. She's not even immortal." I pressed my palms against the bar top, glaring at it.

Levin forced himself between Kratos's legs, wiggling his ass to be scratched. "A demigod, perhaps?" Kratos obliged my dog, petting him with a wince.

"No. I would sense that. Anyway, go on, Bia."

"*She may not realize the lengths she's pulled toward it, but the woman is immensely drawn to power. Control.*"

"Her power? Her control?" Standing upright, I stepped closer to my lady enforcer.

Bia shook her head slowly.

A wicked grin tugged at my lips. "I *am* power."

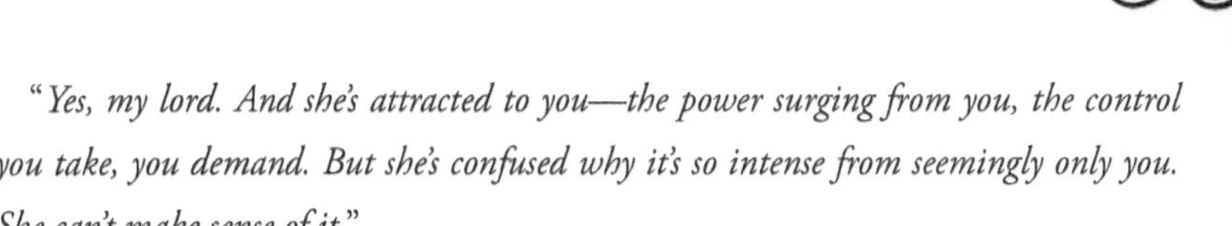

"Yes, my lord. And she's attracted to you—the power surging from you, the control you take, you demand. But she's confused why it's so intense from seemingly only you. She can't make sense of it."

And she says she hates me. Hardly.

"You could always tell her the truth. Imagine her reaction to power knowing who you really are." Kratos lifted his chin.

"It isn't that simple, Kratos. You both don't have interactions with mortals daily anymore. They think we don't exist. To flat out tell her would result in marriage proposal suicide. No. I have to work my way under her skin." I rubbed my neck, already feeling tension from the effort.

Bia stood, floating over to me, hovering at eye level. *"Out of all mortal women, you've chosen to pursue this one."* She canted her head to the side. *"You're intrigued by her. Her work ethic. The ravenous desire she keeps hidden."*

"I thought you couldn't read my mind." Rolling my shoulders back, I made myself taller despite her floating at my height.

"I don't have to when female intuition plays a part."

Grimacing, I turned away from her and rubbed the back of my hand over my mouth. "Anything else I should know?"

"Her birthday falls on the winter solstice. I saw it on her calendar. It's as if she has to write it down to remember it." Kratos ruffled his wings, plucking a feather that had started to break off.

Or other vital deadlines…

Nodding, I glanced at Bia over my shoulder. "Bia?"

"If you truly wish to pursue this woman as your future queen, I've felt her inner self, sir. She's a passionate woman who shifts it all to her job. She wishes to be the best at what she does but longs for more. Past mortals she's been with had issues occasionally being second best to the job."

I turned to face her, squinting. "Are you talking about her or me?"

Bia smiled. A rarity for her.

Kratos's lip twitched before he flared his wings. "Are we dismissed?"

I continued to stare at Bia, but she stayed quiet and sprung her wings. "Keep your eyes and ears open with her and inform me immediately of anything important. Dismissed."

As they both disappeared, I moved to the window and almost did a double-

take. Keira stood with her back turned, her blonde waves falling over fully exposed skin. Her perky bare ass was in clear view, and as she squinted over her shoulder, showing only a hint of her nose and mouth, she gave a peek at the side of her breast, the nipple in shadow.

Fuck. Me.

Arousal dipped into possessive irritation, knowing anyone else in this building could see the same show. She could lie through her teeth any which way from Sunday, but I knew this display was for *me*. The rest of them be damned. I dragged a hand down my face, staring at how sexy she looked, the table lamp near her accentuating her curves, giving her hair a golden hue. She reached for the lamp, and with one last smirk over her shoulder, she wrapped her gorgeous body in a cloak of darkness.

I'd waited until I knew Keira would be exiting her apartment to walk to the courthouse, meeting her on the sidewalk with a smug grin.

"You've got to be kidding me. You *never* walk to work this early," she spat, the chilled air making her breath fog the space between us.

"Not sure if you heard, but I'm working on this high-profile case. Figured I'd get a few early mornings in." I winked at her, rubbing my leather gloves together and flipping the lapel of my jacket around my neck.

She pointed at me, squinting those bright blue eyes. "I'm onto you, Vronti."

"I wish you would be." I dropped my tone an octave and leaned toward her, making my power hover like an invisible shield.

My gaze dropped to her throat, watching it bob.

She bit her lips, no doubt holding back a smile. "You're a pig."

"Well, if you'd only give me a chance—I'm certain I could make you squeal."

She dropped her jaw, suppressing a grin again, and swatted my arm.

Her touch ignited a spark over my skin, even through layers of cloth.

Clearing my throat, I shoved my hands in my pockets and walked beside her. "Nice weather last night, wouldn't you say? Extra…nippy?"

She slipped her briefcase over one shoulder and tugged the coat tight around her chest. "I *knew* you could see me."

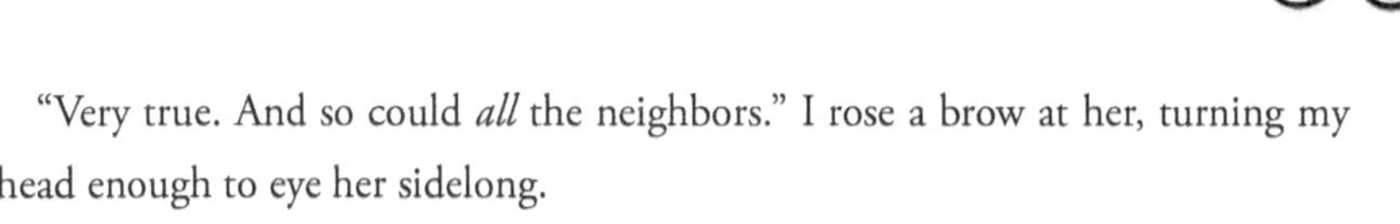

"Very true. And so could *all* the neighbors." I rose a brow at her, turning my head enough to eye her sidelong.

She clucked her tongue against her teeth. "They couldn't see my face."

"That's what you're concerned about?" I asked, chuckling through my words.

"If you got it, flaunt it?" She shrugged, still not looking at me.

There went that irritating jealous pang in my gut again, making my lip bounce.

"Was that your idea of torturing me? Punishment, perhaps?" Discreetly, I got close enough to her our elbows *almost* brushed.

"Absolutely. Showing you something you'll never have." She lifted her chin, the tip of her nose rosy red, and she sniffled.

I side-stepped in front of her, walking backward. "Well, I've been a naughty, *naughty* boy. You should punish me further but maybe in a bedroom this time instead of a closet? Hell, I'll even settle for one of our offices." Flashing a confident grin, I watched her neck flush.

She stopped walking, stomping her foot for extra emphasis. "I've already told you that was a momentary lapse in judgment. You're attractive. So, sue me."

I morphed the most panty-melting smolder I could muster. "Bold words to say to the best lawyer in New York City."

She idly sucked on her bottom lip before snapping it out of her mouth and bouncing on her heels. "*One* of the best. I've earned that title too."

And why would she want to give it away for some petty thing like being deported when she had options?

"Did you do what I asked last night?" I dropped my gaze to her hips before lifting my eyes back to hers. "Finish what you started?"

"Why yes, I did. I had company last night." She sniffled again, rubbing her wool glove under her nose.

"No, you didn't."

She guffawed, the skin between her eyes creasing. "You don't see everything that goes on in my apartment. And besides, I'm not like you with a new bang every other night."

Bingo. It *did* bother her.

"I wouldn't have to see a thing."

"What the hell does that mean?" She blinked her baby blues, the gray hues in the sky from an impending snowfall making them brighter.

"I could smell him on you."

She scrunched her nose and leaned back. "What are you? A wolf or something?"

"Much better. I don't have fleas."

She let out a single laugh and brushed past me, continuing to walk.

"Is there a reason you insist on walking to work over public transportation? Especially in a skirt? Even Jack Frost's balls would freeze out here." I pretended to shiver.

"It's a good thing I don't have balls then, huh?" She stopped at the crosswalk, bouncing on her heels.

"Prove it," I whispered in her ear from behind her.

She loosed a breath and peered at me over her shoulder, our lips almost brushing. "You never give up, do you?"

"And you won't ever admit you *like* being chased, will you?"

She remained silent, simply staring up at me with doe-like eyes.

Yanking one of my gloves off with my teeth, I touched her cheek. Ice cold. "For fuck's sake, Keira. You feel like death. Let me call you a damn cab. Stop being so stubborn." I walked to the sidewalk's edge, holding an arm up.

She grabbed it and yanked it down. "No. I don't want a cab."

"*Why?*"

"Because."

Getting more pissed off by the minute, I deepened my tone. "Because. Why?"

"I don't like being around people, alright? Cabs give me the creeps being trapped with a stranger in a small space—and a bus or train?" She sighed. "Claustrophobic."

She was only telling half the truth, and it boiled my irritation even more.

Snapping her eyes to mine, staring at me for a beat, she made a tsking sound with her teeth. "Goddammit. Do you want to—grab a coffee to drink on the way? It'll warm me up." She couldn't make eye contact with me, her eyes falling to the concrete beneath us.

And so it began.

I half-grinned and pointed to a cart across the street. "I'll even buy."

"Wow. The fancy lawyer man wearing the Burberry jacket will spring for a whole four bucks worth of coffee. I'm a lucky gal."

Shaking my head, I dug in my pocket, producing a money clip. "Smartass.

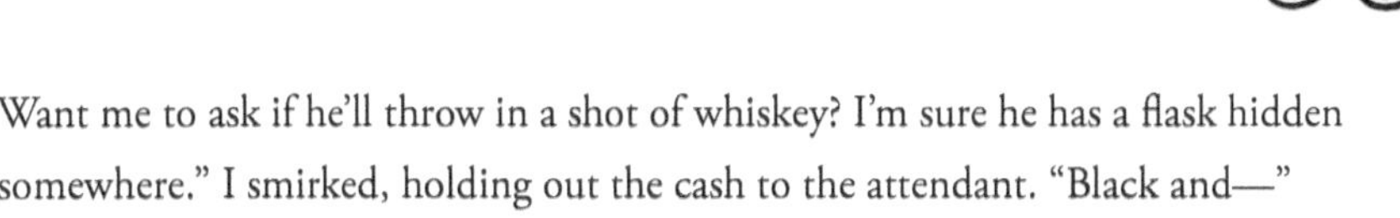

Want me to ask if he'll throw in a shot of whiskey? I'm sure he has a flask hidden somewhere." I smirked, holding out the cash to the attendant. "Black and—"

Keira cleared her throat. "Black."

"Two blacks."

The attendant adjusted the New York Yankees beanie on his head before grumbling and pouring the coffee. Sliding them toward us with his fingerless gloves, he mumbled some form of having a good day as I handed Keira the second cup. I moved to the nearest trashcan to remove my lid and toss it. Keira stepped beside me, performing the same action, and we both locked eyes.

"I uh—" She wrapped her hands tightly around the cup and dipped her face over it. "I like to feel the steam on my nose." Discreetly, she shoved several sugar packets into her jacket pocket, but didn't put any in her coffee.

She continued to pleasantly surprise me at each and every turn.

Fucking Olympus. I really was in trouble.

"I, on the other hand, find the covers to be for pussies. If I'm going to burn my mouth, well, that's my own damn fault, isn't it?" I squinted at her as I took a tiny sip, pretending to burn my lip and sputter. "Shit. See?"

She laughed and grabbed a creamer from the vendor, tossing it at my chest. "You know these street vendors make it hot enough to melt a tire."

"You're right. I should sue them like McDonald's." I winked at her, sipping on the small container of creamer.

"Hey. She had a case. They had a corporate policy to serve it at a temperature that could cause serious burns in seconds. She wasn't the only one who got injured, just the first one to take it to the next level." Her eyes beamed at me as she sipped on her coffee, lifting her shoulders as the warmth coursed down her throat.

"I agree, but I would've gotten her triple the settlement. Easily." Smiling, I tossed the empty container in the trash and we continued walking.

"What are we doing, Zane?" She looked straight ahead, drinking her coffee.

"We're walking, I believe."

She rolled her eyes, and for the first time, when she smiled, I noticed the small dimple that formed in her left cheek. "We can't be friends. At some point we're going to be at each other's throats on this Daniels case in front of a jury. That can't end anywhere but uglytown."

"Have you ever had a relationship with another lawyer, sexual or otherwise?" I

raised my brow at her, leaning forward in an attempt to catch her gaze.

"No." She frowned.

"Then how would you know?"

Her jaw tightened, and she stared into her cup before briskly shaking her head. "I can't. I just can't. Look, I appreciate you walking with me and buying me coffee, but I need you to let me walk on my own from here on out, alright?"

Tartarus. This woman was wound tighter than the Fates' spindle.

"Sure, but Keira—" I bumped her elbow.

She paused and tossed me a glare over her shoulder.

"You look good smiling. You should try it more often." I shrugged before backpedaling away with a lopsided grin, heading in the opposite direction.

Again, she bit back a smile and shook her head before walking.

I'd laid the foundation. *Knew* she was into me. And next...I'd offer her a solution to the problem she didn't think she had.

EIGHT

KEIRA

AS SOON AS I passed Olivia's desk, I motioned for her to follow me, making her smile turn into a frown. "My office. Now."

Tossing my briefcase onto my chair, I dragged my hands over my face, pacing and not bothering to take my coat off.

"Am I in trouble? Because I do feel like I was supposed to remind you about something, and I can't for the bloody life of me remember what it is." Gazing skyward, she tapped her finger against her plump lip.

"What? No. And isn't that client wedding soon?"

She pointed at me with a broad smile. "That's it. Yes. The wedding. Whew." She slapped a hand on her chest. "And I'm so proud you remembered that."

"Can you please close the door?" I flicked my hand at the entrance.

Olivia's eyebrows rose before she slowly closed the door and locked it. "Okay. Something is clearly up. What's going on, boss?"

I sat on the corner of my desk with a groan. "You never call me boss. Why are you calling me that now?"

"It felt appropriate at the moment?" She steepled her fingers before tugging my coat down my arms.

"First, you dressed me the other day. Now you're undressing me," I mumbled, staring numbly at the floor.

"Well, I'm stopping at your coat." She dipped her face into mine. "Unless you're into that kind of thing, then I'm probably game to try."

I tossed her an exasperated glare.

"Right. I was kidding. Mostly." She tossed my coat over my chair.

"It's probably a good thing I'll be leaving the country for a bit. Will be good to…get away, you know?" I chewed on my thumbnail.

"Woah. Seriously, what is going on?" She grabbed my shoulders. "You've never been game for even leaving the state in the middle of a case, let alone the country."

"I kissed him, Ollie."

She gasped and grinned, punching me in the shoulder. "Who? That cute intern bloke in cubicle B?"

I looked from left to right. "Milo? *You* kissed that guy."

She snorted. "Oh, right."

"Zane, Ollie." I pushed to my feet and paced. "Zane fucking Vronti."

"What?" She yelled.

I widened my eyes at her, twirling my finger above my head in a circle, referencing the entire office could hear us.

She crouched, holding her hands at her sides. "What?" She repeated in a loud whisper.

"I seriously don't know what gotten into me." I stared at my hands, remembering how they felt wrapped in Zane's hair.

"Well, that's easy. You're—the 'h' word. Rhymes with corny?" She raised her brows. "How'd it happen anyway? Where? Did you use tongue?"

I cupped my hands on my forehead, circling through events that led to the incident on a loop in my brain as if it were a case I prepared to argue in court. "We were in the midst of the evidence trial, and the way he talked, the way he presented himself—he's good, Ollie." Unbuttoning my top two shirt buttons, I shot my gaze to hers. "Real good."

"No bloody shit. He's Zane Vronti. What were you expecting? Mediocre?"

No. But I wasn't expecting to be pulled in by his prowess like he was a black hole.

"I became so swept up in his skill, Ollie, that I actually dragged him into the first broom closet I saw, shoved him against the shelves, and *kissed* him." Between my legs pulsed, and I sat down, pinching my knees together.

Olivia grinned and bounced. "Holy hell. That's *hot*."

It was. It really, really was.

I undid another button on my blouse. "It was stupid, is what it was. What if someone had seen us go in there? What if someone had snapped a photo with their phone when we left?"

"It was you acting on impulse because you wanted something. It's bloody hot. End of story." She stomped her foot.

"I don't understand why I wanted it at all. I hate everything that man represents. Do you have any idea how many women's tongues have been in that man's mouth? I see women parading out of his apartment building practically every night." I grimaced. "And I stuck my tongue in there."

"Bugger me. You know how to take the fun out of a situation." Olivia sighed and sat beside me. "Hate and love are blurred lines, for one. For two, most blokes who are stallions in the sack, have, and this is shocking, slept with a few women."

Hate and love are blurred lines.

"That isn't the point. I have absolutely no intention of screwing him." Standing in a huff, I turned to face her.

"Whatever you say, Starshine. But I can tell you exactly why you're so into Mr. Hotshot Lawyer Man." She drummed her fingers on the desk's edge, stretching her legs out in front of her and crossing them at the ankle.

Folding my arms, I glared at her. "And why would that be?"

"Much like your job entails, you like a challenge. Tyler was an incredibly nice bloke, but he was simple and to the point."

A lump sprouted in my throat. "Do you have to bring up Tyler?"

"Yes. Because it's how I intend on proving my point. You and Tyler were smitten from what, the first two dates? All batty-eyed and puppy love. He had a good job, worshipped the ground you walked on, and at the end of the day came home and did you in the missionary position." She bounced her top foot, making the ballet flat fall from her heel.

Ugh. Her bringing up Tyler only brought back the depressing memories of what happened between us. He *was* a nice guy.

"But he wasn't what you, Keira Bazin, needed." Olivia stood and interlaced her fingers behind her back.

"And how the hell would you—"

Olivia raised a finger to silence me. "You are a strong woman with arguing skills that rival a master debater." She snorted, cleared her throat, and waved a hand over her face, morphing it back to neutral. "You need someone who can match

you point for point, challenge you. Someone who is as passionate about their career as you—to *understand*. And maybe at the end of the day…fuck you from behind against a wall."

My brain betrayed me, dipping into thoughts of Zane behind me, my palms pressed against my office door, sweat beading my forehead.

I shook my head and moved away from the door, closing my eyes with a wince. "I get what you're saying, Ollie. But I can find that elsewhere. Zane isn't the only man in existence who has those traits."

"Yeah? You're in your mid-thirties, Keir. You find him yet?" She threw her arms out at her sides and let them flop back down.

Ouch.

"Maybe I was meant to go it alone. Ever think about that?" I crossed my arms again in a huff.

"I don't buy it. You wouldn't have ever gotten married in the first place if you were okay with being alone." Olivia frowned, crossing the room to rest a hand on my shoulder. "How did you feel during that kiss, huh?"

Alive. Reborn. Ravenous.

"It doesn't matter. It's not happening again, and that's final."

I'd also not felt overwhelmed by his emotions as I normally did in sexual situations. It was as if everything equalized between us the moment our skin touched.

"I'm going to say one last thing, and then I'm done playing the role of the best friend who makes you see through the bullshit…for now." Olivia took a dramatic deep breath. "You can be into something else besides your job and still be good at it. It's part of being human, mate." She patted my arm.

"I'll keep it in mind," I mumbled.

The day wore on, and I spent most of it daydreaming about the swirl of emotions passed between Zane and me during that walk to the office. Flirtatious. Lust. Happiness. The occasional bout of irritation. And I could *not* get him out of my mind. Sighing, I pinched the bridge of my nose, forcing my brain back into work mode.

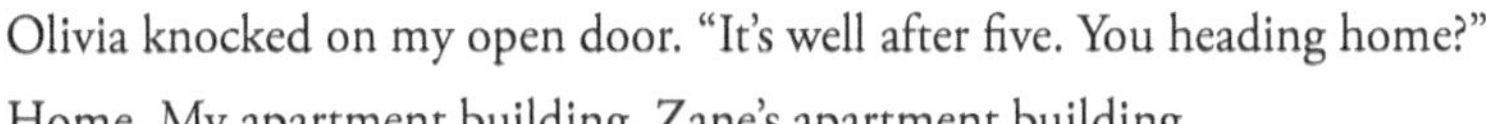

Olivia knocked on my open door. "It's well after five. You heading home?"

Home. My apartment building. Zane's apartment building.

"No. I'll probably stay the night here going over paperwork." I moved behind my desk, shifting papers from left to right as if I were organizing them.

"You're going to avoid him now, aren't you?"

After that kiss? After the alarmingly normal moment walking to work this morning? Bet your ass I was.

"No. I just want to go over the files more." I kept my gaze down, avoiding eye contact.

"You're an amazing liar when you want to be, Keira, but I know you well enough to know that is precisely what you're doing." Olivia grabbed my coat and threw it at me. "Come on. I'll sleep at your place tonight. He won't try to sweep you off your feet if I'm there to cockblock him."

"I think you underestimate him," I muttered, slipping the coat over my arms and grabbing my briefcase.

She paused, blinking. "*That* good, huh?"

Pulling my hair from the jacket collar, I fished for my gloves. "Broom closet, Ollie. Broom. Closet."

Olivia grinned and stared at the ceiling as if trying to conjure the image of Zane and me making out. "Still so hot."

Olivia came over as promised, grimacing at my boxes littering the living room floor. "You seriously haven't finished unpacking?"

"Essentials, sure. Those boxes are just full of junk mostly. Haven't had time." I shrugged, playing with the seam of my pajama bottoms.

"And you also didn't have time to at least stack them against a wall?"

I narrowed my eyes at her. "Did you come over to chastise me about cleanliness or to distract me?"

"It's only—how are we to have a dance party with these boxes strewn about? Hm?" Olivia kicked a box with her foot, making whatever was inside clank.

"Dance party?" My stomach gurgled.

"Uh, yeah. Didn't you do that in college? Dance parties and drinking?" She

rushed past me to the kitchen, rummaging through my cabinets.

"I think you know the answer to your own question, Ollie. College for me was pulling all-nighters studying law until my eyes bulged from my skull."

"Right." She ducked and returned with a bottle in her hand. "Maybe we should invite Johnnie Walker to the party. Is this really all you have? Should've stopped at the bottle-o on the way over."

"Yes. It's all I have. It's all I ever drink, and it's only to help clear my head at times."

She grabbed two glass tumblers from the cabinet in front of her, sliding them across the counter. "It'll have to do then. Even though I think it tastes like arse."

Stealing a peek over my shoulder, I squinted through the slit in the blinds to see if Zane's light was on. It wasn't. I frowned.

"What you lookin' at?" Olivia asked, appearing at my side with a scotch in hand.

I jumped and snatched the glass from her grasp. "The moon."

"You're quick, Bazin. And good too because you're not technically lying, are you?" She grinned and took a sip of her drink, scrunching her face like she drank gasoline.

"What? It *is* a full moon." I gulped the scotch, sighing as the delicious smoky taste coated my tongue. A full moon always revitalized me.

"You want to catch a glimpse at a full moon, alright, but *not* the one in the sky." She snorted before bolting toward the windows.

"What are you doing?" I sipped more scotch, fighting the urge to down it.

She parted the blinds with about as much covert ability as a wolverine. "Which apartment is his?"

In an attempt to change the subject, I asked, "How was your date with uh— what was his name? Blake?"

"Eh. He was good for a night."

"You sound bummed about that. Doesn't sound like your usual self. What's up?"

Sighing, she let the blinds close with a loud *fwap*. "I just—I guess I need someone more…adventurous?"

"Adventurous? You? No offense, but I never took you for the type."

She blew her bangs from her eyes. "I haven't done much since moving to New

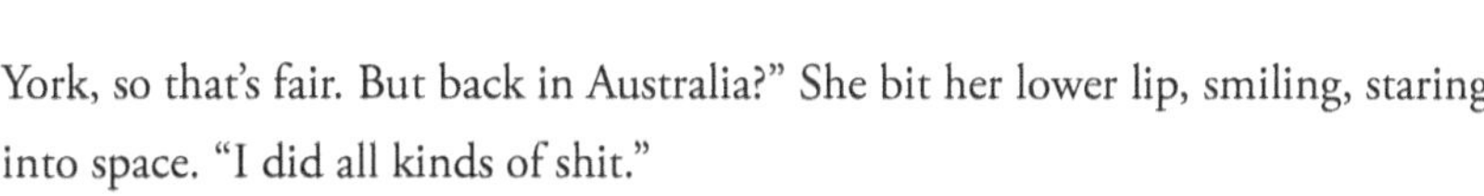

York, so that's fair. But back in Australia?" She bit her lower lip, smiling, staring into space. "I did all kinds of shit."

"Seriously?" I grinned and nudged her arm.

"Yeah. Even scuba diving."

I cocked my head to the side, attempting to imagine her in a snorkel. "No kidding. Huh."

Olivia sighed and moved her gaze to the swig of alcohol left in her drink. "I miss it sometimes. The motherland."

Melancholy. Homesickness.

"Do you ever think about going back, Ollie?" I rubbed her shoulder.

"Hell no. My family and friends are here, and I *love* it here. Mum passed away when I was a kid, I followed dad when he moved here for a job, and then—there's you." She smiled and bumped my shoulder with hers. "You're like a sister to me."

The momentary sadness swarming through her floated away as quickly as it arrived.

"You know what? You and I should go on vacation sometime—to Australia. I've never been."

Olivia's eyes widened, and she squished each of my cheeks. "Woah. Are you a doppelganger? Keira Bazin speaking of *vacations*?"

"Maybe I've seen the light. Maybe it's the alcohol. Either way, I want you to hold me to it. Deal?" I lifted my glass.

"That—" We clanked our tumblers. "I can do." Olivia tilted her head back and finished the drink.

"Did I tell you he gave me binoculars?" I dipped my pinky in the scotch and traced it over my bottom lip—the image of that muscular ass of his etched into my brain.

She sputtered and wiped the back of her hand over her mouth. "Um, no?"

"The bastard left them in a box on my doorstep with a note saying, 'So you can get a better view.'" Rolling my eyes, I stuck my nose back in the glass, slurping more elixir.

She squeezed her glass with both hands, beaming. "You looked. Didn't you?"

"Maybe." I tapped my fingernail against the tumbler.

"Good *on* ya, mate. What'd you see? Tell me." She made a hurry-up gesture with her free hand as she made her way to the kitchen, pouring herself another drink.

"His ass." I couldn't think about his dick. I just couldn't.

She squealed and did a spin before grabbing onto the countertop to steady herself.

Smiling at her extra enthusiasm and mixed with the speed I sipped my scotch over usual, I added, "There's more."

She leaned on her elbow, resting her chin on her hand, staring at me from the kitchen unblinking. With every sip of scotch, she'd wince and gag.

"I may have teased him back with—" I dragged my hand over my body.

Gasping, she ran back to me and playfully shoved my shoulder. "You did not. Who *are* you?"

"It was completely inappropriate and out of line, wasn't it?" I downed the rest of my scotch.

"Who cares if it was? What is life if not occasionally being inappropriate? Boring. That's what." She threw her arm around my shoulders, pulling me to her side. "I like this side of you."

"More Johnnie?" I pointed to the bottle with a grin.

After finishing what she'd just poured, making less of a disgusted face this time, she held her glass out. "Definitely. The bloke's warming up to me."

Pouring doubles this time, I hopped onto a stool near the counter.

Despite the company and the drinking, I still couldn't help thinking about the case. The nerves that bubbled every time it crossed my mind—going up against Zane. For the first time in my career, I actually *feared* losing.

"Do you remember the Johnson, Ekols, and Mirand case? The one where we convicted those three young guys for the drowning of the little girl?"

Olivia did one slow-motion blink. "Well, that was out of absolutely nowhere, but, yes. Why the bloody hell are you bringing that up *now* while we're trying to get our buzz on?"

"I can't help it." I rubbed my glass, making it squeak. "It always eats away at my brain the investigators couldn't find DNA that matched later on, and they were released from prison on an Adams plea. They served thirteen years in prison and may have never even done it."

Olivia gave an exaggerated head roll, and bumped her finger under my tumbler, encouraging me to drink more. "And they very well could have. It's all speculation. The prosecution had plenty of evidence to convict them."

"I haven't lost a case, and yet, technically, I won that one, but they were released."

Olivia gasped. "A light just went on in the apartment on the top floor. Is that his? He seems like the type to live in a penthouse."

Excited jitters fluttered in my stomach. "Yes."

"Where are those binos?" Olivia spun around, flicking her head left to right, making her bangs fall into her eyes.

"I threw them away." Sipping on my drink, I kept my back to the windows.

Don't look, Keira. Do. Not. Look.

"Yeah, right." She whizzed past me, heading straight for my bedroom.

I chased after her, holding the glass above my head, trying to keep it level as I ran. "Ollie, don't."

Her ass was in the air on her hands and knees, bent forward, and rummaging under my bed. She sat up with the box in her hand, holding it above her head like the Holy Grail. Ignoring my continued protests, she scurried past me, removing the binoculars as she went, and tossing the box to the floor.

Rubbing my thumb between my eyes and sipping on my scotch, I shuffled down the hall, groaning at her as she peered out the window through the blinds.

"Bugger, I don't see anything." She frowned at me over her shoulder.

Shaking my head, I sat on the sofa, and curled my feet underneath me. "I highly doubt he'll do it twice."

I gulped more scotch, my cheeks warming.

"Fuck me dead," Olivia said.

The warmth in my cheeks traveled down my neck, settling in my chest. "What?"

"I just—" Olivia walked over, the binoculars limp in her hands. "I just saw his donga."

"You did?" I leaped up, snatching the binoculars from her. As I neared the window, giggles followed me.

Zane was nowhere to be found in the lit room across the street.

"I knew it." Olivia pointed at me.

"You didn't actually see it did you?" I rolled my eyes at her before shoving the binoculars into her chest.

"Nope. But you sure as hell want to." She chuckled and did a little dance.

Oh, I had. And *felt* it against me.

Sitting back down, I leaned forward and absently traced my finger around the rim of my glass. "The kiss *was* hot, Ollie. So fucking hot."

"You should tell him that." She flopped next to me, giggling as she fell sideways against the cushions.

"Please. As if the man needs any more of an ego boost." I sipped more of my drink.

"Who cares? Besides, you've got an ego too." She elbowed me.

I snapped my gaze to her. "I do not."

"Yes. You do. It's part of the reason you're a confident, good lawyer." She crawled to the nightstand, grabbed my phone, and shoved it at me. "Text him. Tell him."

"Do you really think I have the defense lawyer in our case's personal phone number?"

She stuck her bottom lip out to the middle of her chin. "True. But you *do* have his e-mail." She wiggled the phone until I snatched it.

With the alcohol bubbling in my brain, lulling me into a wistful intoxication, I shrugged. "Why the hell not. It'll torture him even more."

"That's the spirit," Olivia shouted, spinning until she lay on her back with her head in my lap.

Pulling up a new e-mail, I worked my thumb across the touch screen.

To: Zane Vronti

From: Keira Bazin

Subject: Expletive Content

Now that I have your attention, I just wanted to say…I really, really really, REALLY enjoyed that kiss.

All the best,

Keira

Send.

If I'd stayed awake long enough, my mortification may have been a distant memory by the time I woke up the following day. But at three in the morning, still on the couch, and squinting into the darkness, the blinking blue notification

light caught my attention.

A work e-mail? This early?

Groggily pulling it up, all my limbs froze, seeing it was an e-mail *reply* from Zane.

Oh my god. Had I actually sent that? *Why* would I send that?

With a shaky thumb, I selected it.

To: Keira Bazin

From: Zane Vronti

Subject: RE: Expletive Content

You did, did you? Maybe you should try me again sometime. ;)

Always ready for more,

Zane

Dropping the phone in my lap, I slapped my hands over my eyes. I'd been avoiding him for a reason, and now there was no way in hell I could face him after this. Jumping to my feet, I sprinted to my bedroom to change. If I hurried, I could start my walk to work before Zane conveniently met me on the sidewalk.

"Why are you making so much noise?" Olivia whined from the couch.

"I'm getting ready to go in for work." After getting dressed, I quickly pulled a brush through my hair.

"At three in the bloody morning?"

Trotting back to the living room, hopping on one foot while I slipped on a heel, I handed her my spare key. "I know it's early, but if I go now, I'll avoid Zane. Here's my extra key so you can lock up after you leave."

She groaned and snatched it from me, slamming it on the coffee table in front of the sofa. "You realize doing this is only delaying the inevitable, right?"

I thinned my lips and grabbed my coat. "I'll see you later, Ollie."

Maybe it would, or maybe it wouldn't, but I knew whatever may have been bound to happen between Zane and me—I wasn't ready for it. But would I ever be?

NINE

ZEUS

THIS WOMAN WAS GOING to be the divine death of me. I was sure of it. Hot and cold. Back and forth. She shoves me into a broom closet to have her way with me. Then basically tells me to fuck off. And now? This damn e-mail. *What* was her angle?

I sat on a bench in Central Park, letting Levin run freely with the other canines left off-leash. Glancing at the calendar on my phone, I growled at the time I had left to wrap up this arrangement. One of three scenarios was bound to happen with Keira. The most likely being she'd ask for some time to think it over. Least likely? Saying yes without a passing thought. Wouldn't *that* be delightful?

One thing was certain—I needed to bring it up, and I needed to do it now. I managed to make an impression on her, but now using her deportation as leverage? It was bound to piss her the fuck off, and I needed time for her to cool her jets about it and realize…it was a solid deal.

"Oh, my God," a woman screeched. "Is this your lab?" She knelt by the bench where Levin sat next to me, moving her hands toward his head.

"Don't touch him." I snapped my gaze to the curly-haired woman sporting bright purple spandex pants and a matching long-sleeved shirt.

She froze and looked up at me, confused. "I'm sorry?"

"Don't touch him. I don't know where you've been."

She snapped her hands away and shot to her feet with a glare. "Jesus. I just wanted to pet your dog. You don't have to be a prick about it."

I flashed a spark of lightning in my eyes, waiting for the fear to pour over her

face before continuing her jog.

A little over the top? Maybe. But Keira Bazin had me so fucking on edge I wanted to roast every tree in the damn park.

Scratching behind Levin's ears, I rose and shortened his leash. "Come on, boy. We've got a Queen to nab."

I stood outside of Keira's apartment, leaning casually on the doorframe, waiting for her to answer the door. Her feet brushed the carpet, and a faint "shit" fluttered into my godly ears. I'd bet my left nut she was going to pretend she wasn't home. And judging by the fact I'd been standing here for a solid thirty seconds, knowing she already spied me through the peephole, it's precisely what she was doing.

"I know you're home, Keira. Come on. Being an ass isn't your jurisdiction. That's mine." I patted my hand on the doorframe and grinned once I heard the chain lock being removed.

She whipped open the door with such force it sent her hair flying. "What do you want, Zane?"

"You—" I bopped her nose with a single finger. "Have been avoiding me."

"Wow. Did you deduce that all by yourself, counselor?"

Smirking, I pushed off the door, standing straight and gleaming down at her. "Why?"

"The usual reason someone avoids someone else. I don't want to see you." She crossed her arms over her grey t-shirt, a pair of jeans clinging to her legs.

I rubbed a hand over my chin. "Even though you really, really, really, *really* enjoyed it?"

Her cheeks turned rosy. "People say a lot of things when they're tipsy."

"It's been proven that alcohol brings out your true self."

She dug her bare feet into the carpet. "And what sources do you have to support this claim?"

Damn, I loved when she talked like that.

Chuckling, I shook my head. "I've got to talk with you. Mind going for a walk?"

"It's about to get dark."

I slid forward, my toes inches over the threshold. "I could always come inside?"

She pressed her hand on my chest. Just as before, despite layers of clothing, the touch still managed to ignite my nerves. She gulped and took in a quick breath in an attempt to hide the reaction I could sense from her a mile away.

"Stay *right* there. I'll grab my coat."

I went to take a step forward to wait in her apartment, but the door slammed in my face.

Such a minx.

Grinning, I leaned on the opposite wall, watching the darkness starting to overtake the sky.

"This better be about the case," Keira said as she locked her door behind her and slipped a bright red wool hat over her head.

"Oh, it is."

Considering her distaste for crowds and the conversation we were about to have, I led us away from downtown. Sounds of tires screeching, people whistling for cabs, and random shouts from food vendors drifted away—replaced with the faint hum of traffic lights and melting snow emptying into storm drains.

"I enjoyed it too, by the way. In case your declaration was founded, and you're too embarrassed to admit it." I grinned down at her, giving her a sidelong glance as we walked side-by-side.

"I'm not embarrassed. I just didn't want to ignite your ego." She huffed, focusing her attention forward.

"If we men aren't complimented, though, how else can we please you?" My power surged through my veins, and I choked it back.

The lack of Keira's heat near my arm gave me pause, realizing I was several feet ahead of her. Turning on my heel with my hands in my pockets, I spied her standing motionless like a statue.

"Keira?" I closed the distance between us with steady steps.

She closed her eyes so tightly it pinched her entire face. "Do it again."

My power swelled, striking through my fingertips. I balled my hands into fists within my jacket, squelching it. "Do what again, Keira?" I whispered the words, and stepped closer.

"Kiss me," she breathed out, tilting her chin to gaze up at me, her chest rising and falling.

Hot and cold.

I'd take the hot whenever she offered it.

Removing one glove, I grasped her chin, lowered my lips to hers, and kissed her. Thrusting my tongue between her lips, not bothering with an invitation, I swirled it into her mouth and curled my other arm around her waist. Grabbing her ass, kneading it, I backed her up until she bumped into a nearby pole, pinning her against it and grinding into her stomach.

Testing the limits on what she'd let me do, what she *wanted* me to do, I traced my gloveless hand over her chest, grabbing one breast through the thickness of her coat, making her whimper. Continuing my test, I trailed my hand down her stomach and continued until I reached that convenient seam in her jeans, using it to rub her clit.

She whimpered and I drowned it by deepening the kiss, hiding her body with mine from anyone who might pass by. I sent a tantalizing sizzle of electricity through our joined lips, coursing it through her chest and down to the spot I sensually tortured with my fingers. It didn't take long for her to shudder in my arms, her knees buckling as she moaned into my mouth. Holding an arm around her to keep her standing, I slowly peeled away and grinned wickedly at her.

"What the *fuck* just happened?" She whispered, gazing up at me with a mixture of ecstasy and confusion.

Pressing my cock bulging through my pants against her hip, I lowered my lips to her ear. "I believe I made you come in public with all your clothes on."

"Jesus, Zane. I just wanted you to kiss me." She gulped and let out a sensual sigh, her gaze as she looked up at me suggesting she was almost ready to let me take her right here on the street corner.

"Well, things escalated. And you didn't stop me." I brushed our lips.

She breathed against me, sweet smells I couldn't decipher floating from her neck—her hair. "No, I didn't."

"We really need to talk, Keira." Adjusting myself with a tug at my belt, I stepped back, slipping my glove back on.

Getting a complete look at her made my gut twist. She was gorgeous before, but fuck, if she didn't look even better satiated. A radiant glow and color in her cheeks, her eyes slightly groggy—and that tiny smile tugging at her reddened lips. I held my hand out to her, and to my surprise, she took it after only one moment of hesitation.

We continued to walk, and after a moment to psych up, don the mask of the mighty god-king, I took the plunge.

"I know something about you that you don't think I know." I tightened my grip on her hand.

"Alright, Riddler. Care to speak English to me now?"

Licking my lips, I cut my gaze to her. "You're Canadian."

She gasped, pressing a hand to her chest. "A Canadian in New York? That's shocking."

Do or die.

"And about to be deported." Cut and dry.

She stopped walking and yanked her hand away.

Here we go.

"What did you just say?" Her cheeks were still rosy from when she came but now, they flamed.

I interlaced my fingers in front of me and widened my stance. "You're about to be an illegal resident of the US because your resident status was through your American husband. Your ex-husband. And you forgot to file the necessary paperwork on time."

"I—what? This can't be. How the hell do you even know this?" She fumed, pacing a small square on the sidewalk in front of me.

"I told you, Keira." I tightened my jaw, keeping my strong demeanor firm. "I always research my opponents."

Her lips slowly parted, her chest rising as she took a deep breath. "You're going to use this against me, aren't you? To get me off the case." She let out a feminine growl and turned away from me. "I should've known all of this—everything you've been doing was to distract me."

Standing firm, I watched her pace. "I don't plan to use it against you. I plan to offer you a solution."

"A solution? Oh, you're just going to help me out of the goodness of your black heart?" She clenched her fists at her sides.

"No."

She stormed forward, tapping her toes against mine and glaring up at me. "Why don't you just come out and fucking say it, Vronti?"

How the woman managed to make me hard despite the conversation was

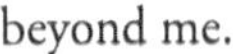

beyond me.

"The solution would also benefit—me." I pointed to myself and leaned forward, bringing our lips closer.

She sneered at me and turned away. "Of course, it would."

"Marry me."

She whirled around, her eyes cutting into me, tearing at my flesh. "Excuse me?"

Even having been proposed to before, I didn't imagine this is how she pictured future ones.

"Marrying an American citizen is your fastest and only way to become legal and still work the Daniels case."

"And what would *you* be getting out of this?" The scowl forming on her brow could make Cerberus whimper away.

Think fast here, King of the Gods. You can't tell her the truth, but it also has to make sense.

"I recently came upon an inheritance. To receive it, the will clearly states I need to be married." I chewed on my lip, still cementing my feet to the sidewalk.

Her eyes blinked with the speed of a jackhammer. "You have *got* to be fucking kidding me." She stormed up to me again, poking me in the chest. "I'd be doing this to save my livelihood, and you are doing it for goddamned money?"

More like eternal power and maintaining the kingdom and only livelihood I know.

"That about sums it up, yes."

She turned away in a huff, the fury building in her so strongly it was almost as if I could *feel* it carving into my bones. It was enough to make me roll my shoulders, attempting to shrug it away.

"How exactly did you picture this going, Zane? You'd ask me, I'd give you a big hug, thanking you for saving my career, and we'd be off to a justice of the peace?" Her top lip curled in a snarl.

"No. But I at least expected you to say you'd think about it. You don't have a lot of choices here. And you could do a lot worse for a husband." I held my arms out at my sides, displaying myself like a prized stallion.

"I do have another choice. Suck it up and march my ass back to Canada with my head held high."

I lowered my hands. "You hate me that much, you'd be willing to give up the

career you built for yourself here?"

"I can still practice law in Canada." She gulped, and by the way her eyes glistened it looked like she was about to cry.

Fuck.

"Yeah? How many high-profile cases are there for you in Saskatchewan? Hm?" I slid forward.

She stepped back and pointed at me. "It's not about the high-profile cases. Law is the law. I'd still be helping people."

"High profile cases *made* you into the lawyer you are now." Cautiously, I moved closer again. This time, she let me. "Take some time and think about this, Keira. You're not going to find a better offer anywhere else."

Her knee bounced, and she rubbed her forehead. "I wasn't sure if what I felt toward you was hate or just resentment over defense lawyers as a whole, but it is crystal clear to me now, Zane."

We were arguing—fuming at each other. I'd just dropped a bomb, and yet the arousal in her stare was plain as day.

We're both officially fucked in the head.

"Tell me you'll think about it."

Her lips were still slightly red from our kiss, and she pursed them. "Fine. But you need to stay away from me."

"Why's that?" I breached her invisible shield again, looming over her, igniting my scent tenfold into the air around us—sandalwood and cologne.

Lust flashed in her gaze as she stared up at me, anger still tightening her jaw. "You could have asked any woman to do this. Why me?"

"You—intrigue me." I trailed the tip of my nose over her cheek.

She pushed me back. "I *intrigue* you? And that's enough to be roped into this with me for the rest of your life?"

It was so much more than that, and I couldn't even explain it to myself.

"Also, I mean—look at you." I referenced her face, her body.

She rolled her eyes. "Stay. Away. Zane. I'll reach out when I've made up my mind."

Squinting at her, I took a step back and watched her make her way down the street until she disappeared around the corner.

I sure as hell had no plans to stay away. The need to *show* her what could be

hers ran far too deep to ignore.

"Trouble in paradise, Pops?" Hermes slunk from the shadows with a snarky grin.

Pointing a stern finger, I took one last glance in the direction Keira had stormed off, hoping like some damned fool she'd have come running back. "I'm not in the mood, Herm."

"I have some information on your darling girlfriend you might like to hear." He peered at his cuticles before rubbing them against the collar of his aviation jacket.

"Out with it," I growled.

"I saw her name on the flight passenger list for tomorrow. She's going to Argentina."

My mind raced with possibilities. "In the middle of the case? What the hell for?"

"I did some more digging, and apparently, it's for a former client's wedding."

A feral grin played over my lips.

"Make sure you're a pilot on that flight. Keep an eye on her. Let me know when you land and where she is so I can port there."

Hermes snapped his fingers, slipping his Aviator sunglasses on despite it being nighttime. "One step ahead of you. Consider it done."

A wedding in a romantic setting like Argentina. I planned to charm the ever-loving shit out of her and leave her begging for more.

TEN

KEIRA

THE TRIP TO ARGENTINA could not have come at a better time. I was still fuming over Zane backing me into a corner like that. A corner I demanded to be backed into, but I just couldn't get over how I felt around him. Whenever we touched, all the swirling emotions settled over my skin, comforted me. It was surreal to simply *feel* something I *wanted* to feel instead of trying to wade through it and organize.

"Miss, would you please mind grabbing your belongings?" A male TSA agent said to me, pointing at the bin of items I'd put through the scanner.

I jolted to attention and grabbed it. "Sorry, I was day-dreaming."

"Must've been some dream." He raised one brow and turned his attention to the next person.

Sulking on the nearest bench to put my shoes and watch back on, I scowled at the floor. How could I have possibly forgotten about my residence paperwork? And I couldn't blame Olivia. It wasn't her responsibility. She was my paralegal. My friend. Not a damn servant.

In fact, I should be giving her the benefit of the doubt.

Fishing my phone from the front pocket of my briefcase, I called Olivia as I rolled my carry-on suitcase through the terminal.

"G'day?"

She never failed to make me smile. "G'day? Really?"

"I bet it put a grin on that pretty face of yours, though, didn't it?"

"Guilty. Hey, I had a quick question for you, and if you didn't, I'm *not* mad at

you. I just need to know."

She went silent for a beat.

"Ollie?"

"I'm here. Just sweating my tits off, wondering what you're about to ask."

I licked my lips as I stopped in front of my gate. "My residence permit paperwork. Did you have a reminder in your calendar or anything?"

"I—" Typing on a keyboard and frantic clicks of the mouse sounded from the other line. "Keira, I know I put it on the calendar. I have no idea what happened. Shit. Fuck. Shit. Did it lapse?"

I closed my eyes and sighed. A small part of me hoped she'd tell me I still had time, but I knew around my birthday was when we'd gotten divorced, however long ago it was. And here we were in December already. "Yes. But I'll figure it out. No worries."

"No bloody worries? Keir, you're going to be kicked out of the country. You're my lawyer. I can't be one half of the Blonde Bulldogs by myself." She sniffled.

"It's going to be fine. Worst case scenario, I go back to Canada, get it straightened out, and come back."

"Oh, yeah? How many years later?"

I pinched the bridge of my nose. "I know, I know. Like I said, I'll figure it out. This quick trip should be a good time to clear my head."

"Enjoy the hell out of yourself, alright? No thoughts of dudes in acid, evidence trials, or defense lawyers. Or *do* think about defense lawyers." I could tell she smiled at that last part from the inflection in her voice.

I pinched my thighs together, recalling the exploding orgasm I had on a damn street corner simply from Zane rubbing me *through* my jeans.

"I'm not going to think about anything except how beautiful Argentina looks this time of year."

"Good on ya, Keir. Have a safe flight. Kisses."

"Bye, Ollie."

The boarding process started not too soon after I hung up with Olivia. I stood in line, waiting in the terminal tunnel leading to the airplane door, still marveling how many passengers were on the red-eye flight. As we neared the cockpit, one of the pilots stood near the entrance, casually leaning against the doorframe and greeting passengers.

When his blue eyes fell on me, his smile brightened, creasing his cheeks and giving his gaze a sort of Eastwood-like squint to them. He was pretty damn sexy.

"Good morning, miss. Enjoy your flight." He winked at me, a sparkle in his gaze as he kept me in his sights.

"Well, that's entirely up to you, isn't it?" I smiled, feeling confidence floating from him and the same plain arrogance Zane exuded.

"I suppose you're right. I'll be sure to take real good care of you." With a dimpled grin, he nodded at me.

Finally getting to my row, I couldn't stuff my bags in the overhead compartments fast enough. As soon as my butt hit the seat and I put on the buckle, slipped the sleeping mask over my eyes, popped in my earbuds, and readied to sleep for the longest number of hours I had in *years*.

"Sit on my face, Keira," Zane whispered in my ear.

I let out a harsh breath. "What?"

"Sit. On. My. Face," he commanded, pulling my hips to straddle him, both of us naked.

Doing as he asked, I slid forward on my knees until my pussy hovered over his lips, my breathing going erratic.

"Now ride me like I'm your damn pony." Zane's sapphire stare gleamed at me from between my legs, his tongue lapping over my folds…

"Miss. Miss." A woman's voice said, shaking my shoulder.

I jumped awake, the song *Pony* by Ginuwine blasting through my earbuds. Groggily slipping the mask off, I squinted up at her.

"Sorry, miss, but I need you to put your seat in the upright position for landing?"

Smacking my lips together, I sat up, wiping the back of my hand over my mouth. "Sorry. Of course."

After I pushed the button, raising my seat, the flight attendant gave a kind smile and continued her routine through the aisle.

The dream came back to me as the song played, and I rubbed between my eyes. Ride me like a damn pony. Jesus. I couldn't even *not* think about him if I tried.

I took a taxi from the Ezeiza International Airport in Buenos Aires to the closest hotel I could find to Rivadavia Park, where the wedding ceremony and reception would take place. I had no intention of spending the night and planned

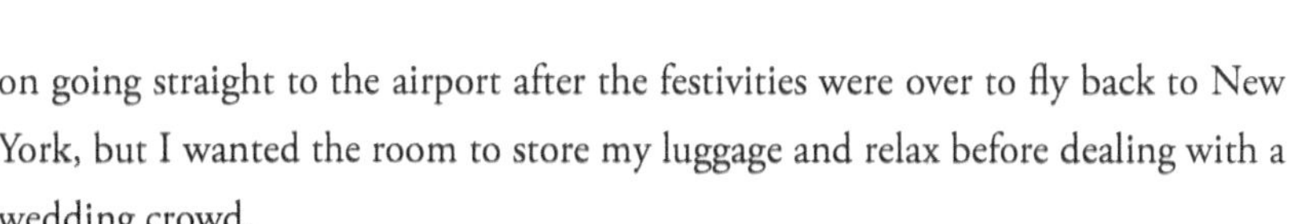

on going straight to the airport after the festivities were over to fly back to New York, but I wanted the room to store my luggage and relax before dealing with a wedding crowd.

Once in the comfort of my room for the next several hours, I slipped into my silver sparkly dress, sticking my leg out to the side from the slit gliding up my right thigh. The design exposed most of my back, and it had a swooping neckline. I'd owned this dress for years, having bought it on a whim when I saw it in a shop window, but never had an excuse to wear it. After styling my hair into loose, long waves, I slipped into a pair of silver heels and breezed out the door with a deep inhale.

As my heels met the concrete sidewalk outside the hotel, an onslaught of murmured conversations in Spanish, children laughing, car horns blaring, and every emotion possible flooded me like a monsoon. I winced, curling my arms around myself as I walked, concentrating on the sounds of my heels clicking on the hard surface beneath me. It didn't take long to reach one of nine entrances into the park, and I took a hard turn, letting out a roiling sigh once I found an area flourishing with palm trees.

The sight of the wedding was evident given the lights hanging in a circle around a central space in the park near the Simon Bolivar monument. A concrete walkway widened at the center, leading to the statue while several smaller paths darted in all directions, park benches every few feet and trees of varying width and height. Magnolia arrangements, as well as a flowered arch, stood at the end of the walkway. Dozens of white folding chairs were intricately placed in parallel rows, facing the arch and they'd hung lit lanterns from some of the lower hanging tree branches.

"Holy shit. Keira?" A man's voice said behind me.

Whirling on my heel, I spied Todd, my former client, standing on the other side of the walkway with his jaw dropped.

"Todd, long time no see." I walked close enough to outstretch my hand. "Congratulations, by the way."

He wore black tuxedo pants, a white jacket, and a pastel pink bow tie. "I honestly didn't think you'd show up." His eyes glistened like he was about to cry as he eagerly shook my hand, making my whole body rattle.

Fear. Anxiety. Suffocation.

Not exactly the best emotions to be exuding on one's wedding day.

"I wouldn't have missed it for the world." Offering a warm smile, I cocked my head to the side. "Are you alright? You seem nervous. More than the usual jitters."

A knife twisted in my gut, remembering how I'd felt the day I married Tyler. I hadn't been nervous per se, but it was as if I had an out-of-body experience, watching myself marry one of the nicest men in the world. Any woman would've killed to be in my position, and I was happy, I was—but that whole saying of the love of your life feeling like your other half? I'd still felt like a lone half.

"I—" He lightly touched my elbow and led me off the path near a large tree. "I don't think Cynthia wants to actually marry me." Frowning, he wrung his hands together.

"Why would you say that?"

Fear. Mortification. Self-Consciousness.

"She's been extremely distant the past month leading up to the wedding, and when we have talked, she's been *so* spiteful."

Poor guy.

"Think it could just be wedding nerves? They made an entire show about Bridezillas, you know?"

A flutter of amusement.

"I don't know. I do know I have this deep-rooted fear of being ditched at the altar, though."

Oof.

"Todd, I'm sure you're getting in your own head about this. Look at this beautiful setting you're in. And dozens of people have flown from all over the globe for it." I squeezed his shoulder.

When I decided to come to Argentina for this and…relax, the last thing I expected was to play therapist to my former client.

"Would you talk to her?" His brown eyes widened, his palms pressing together in prayer.

I pressed a finger on the bridge of my nose. "Oh, I don't know. I don't want to get in the middle of—"

"Please. You can read people so well with your profession. It'd really ease my mind." He pushed his hands together so tightly they turned white.

Desperation.

"Fine. Where is she?"

He hopped, and before I could stop him, hugged me. With the five inches I had on him in heels, his ear pressed near my cleavage. "Thank you. She's in the bridal suite in that hotel there on the corner."

I patted his back with a sigh. "Does she remember me?"

"Are you kidding? It's hard to forget the woman who proved someone you love's innocence."

After giving his shoulder a last squeeze and shoving every thought away about this being a bad idea, I ventured to the bridal suite.

I shouldn't be here. The bridal suite was a place for the mothers, the bridesmaids, friends. Not former prosecutors who represented the groom-to-be.

Crying—no, sobbing, flowed from the other side of the door.

Fear. Anxiety. The *same* emotions as Todd.

I raised my fist and grimaced before lightly knocking. "Cynthia?"

Through several sniffles, she replied, "Who's there?"

"It's Keira Bazin. I'm not sure if you—"

The door flew open and the same fiery red-head I'd remembered sitting in the courtroom during Todd's trial threw her arms around me, dressed in an ivory mermaid wedding gown.

These people acted like we were all best friends. I'd seen them for half a year on and off and said goodbye over a year ago when the trial was over.

Shh, Keira. Since when were you so impatient? Zane must be rubbing off on you.

Rubbing.

"You're crying on your wedding day?" I patted the part of her back covered by cloth.

She pushed back, a wad of tissues in her hand, her mascara partially running down her face. "I don't think Todd wants to marry me."

For fuck's sake.

I loved helping people with my gift. I did. But sometimes, it was a matter of two people simply *talking* to each other to clear the air.

"Funny. He said the exact same thing about you." I grabbed a fresh tissue and started to dab the mascara away from her pretty bridal face.

Had the make-up artist not heard of waterproof mascara?

"What? How could he possibly think that?" The curled ringlets of her up-do hairstyle bobbed as she shook her head.

"Have you been distant? Maybe a little…snappy?"

She sniffled again, turning to look at herself in the mirror. "Maybe? I've been so busy with the last-minute plans for the wedding. If I ever did this again—which I hope I never have to—I'm *not* doing a destination wedding. It's been a logistical nightmare."

Ugh. I hoped I'd never had to do it again either. And my second husband could very well end up being an arrogant asshole lawyer with a killer ass.

"Plain and simple. You took out your stress on him, and he backed off because he didn't want to stress you out more, which made you both distant." I tugged on the tulle veil falling down her back. "It's your wedding day. You have a man who loves you, waiting to marry you. Smile. Be happy. And most of all, stop worrying."

There weren't many positive things happening in my life lately, but I tried nonetheless to push as much positivity out of me, offering it to her.

"You're right, Keira. Thank you, sincerely. You've always been so good with people. I know lawyers sort of need to be, but you—you have a gift." She took both my hands and squeezed them.

If she only knew the half of it..

"It's really no problem at all. And you look beautiful."

She guffawed. "Me? Look at *you*, you smokeshow."

My cheeks blushed, and I ran a finger under the hem hanging over my chest. "Well, thank you. I'll see you after the ceremony."

She bounced as she turned back to the mirror, smiling wide and giggling as several bridesmaids barged into the room.

Jealousy. Excitement. Resentment.

Yet each of them smiled radiantly as if they had no other thought other than the bride's happiness.

Slipping past them, I made my way back to a nervously waiting Todd. I held the train of my dress as I passed and waved. "It's a go, lover boy. Everything's fine. Go get hitched."

"Oh my—really? Keira, you're a goddess. A living, breathing goddess." He blew several kisses at me before jogging off.

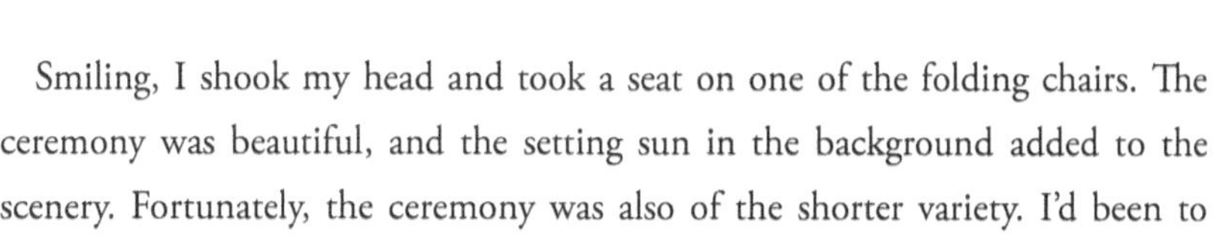

Smiling, I shook my head and took a seat on one of the folding chairs. The ceremony was beautiful, and the setting sun in the background added to the scenery. Fortunately, the ceremony was also of the shorter variety. I'd been to some that lasted damn near an hour.

I now sat at one of several rounded tables under a canopy in the park, trying desperately not to glance at the time every five minutes. Sipping on champagne, I poked at my wedding cake, not feeling up to consuming sugar. A live band played in the corner, and there were two dance floors. The one that called to me the most was the one outside underneath the moon and stars. Not to mention, it had far fewer people crowding it. A small smile tugged at my lips as I watched Cynthia and Todd dancing on the floor beneath the canopy, the happiness swelling from them so pronounced, I could feel it from this distance.

"Excuse me, miss?" A deep voice laced with an Argentinian accent said.

I looked up at a tall man with a thin face and chocolate-brown hair. "Yes?"

When he smiled, it was lopsided, curving higher on the left side of his face, and tiny creases formed under his pale blue eyes. "I was hoping I could ask you to dance?"

My throat tightened as I stared up at him and his chiseled jawline with a scattering of dark stubble. After downing my drink, I stood. "Sure."

He held his hand out, keeping the drool-worthy smile plastered over his thin lips. I took it, and he led me out of the canopy and to the stone dance floor. Wrapping an arm around my lower back, he pulled me closer.

Lust. Lust. And more lust.

There was no doubt in my mind this man's number one objective tonight was to feed off the romantic vibe women felt from weddings. I'd dance with him because I was bored, but he'd better think again if he thought there'd be more.

"The name's Rodrigo, by the way," he whispered, his Argentinian accent making my toes curl. I'd give him that much.

"Keira."

His hand explored further, dipping near the lowest exposed part of my back. "Do you know how to tango, Keira?"

The callused bumps on his palms slid across my skin, giving me goosebumps. Unlike someone else I knew, Rodrigo's touch failed to suppress the emotions floating around us from other couples dancing. It was so fucking distracting.

"I'm a bit rusty, but I think I can manage."

He pulled me tighter with a sultry grin.

"Move," a baritone voice barked.

Rodrigo glared over my shoulder, not dropping his arm from my waist. "I believe the lady and I are dancing."

Zane appeared beside us, his eyes feral. "Move. Now." A flash in his gaze was followed by a random crackle of lightning streaking the sky.

Rodrigo threw his palms up and backed away. "Me chupa un huevo. She's all yours."

Fury shot down my spine as I turned to face Zane. The sight of him made my mouth dry. Tall. Imposing. His white linen shirt flapped in the breeze, while enough buttons were undone to show his tanned, muscular chest. And those blue eyes I'd repeatedly drowned in countless times trailed over my body before he pulled me against him.

"What the hell are you doing here, Zane? How did you even know I was here?" I pushed against him, but he held firm.

"I'm on vacation," he said through a snarl.

"Bull. Shit." I tried to pull away again, but he took my other hand in his.

Staring up at him made my chest pulse—our emotions swirling together like paints in water until eventually blending. "I'll make a scene."

"No. You won't." He dipped his nose near my neck, inhaling me.

"You're so sure of yourself." I forced myself not to close my eyes as his lips traced over my jawline.

"At least one of us is." He lifted his gaze back to mine, probing me with it. "If you don't want my hands all over you right now, push me away again. I'll let you."

My heart pounded against my chest, the exposed leg from the slit in my dress pressing to his thigh. "Bastard." I kneed him in the stomach, making him grunt.

He snapped me to attention, moving the hand on my back to my ass, squeezing it. A light shock zapped through it, causing me to yelp. "Tease."

What the hell? I'd have thought it static shock—if we were on carpet.

The band played a tango, the fluttering of the guitar melody matching the swirls in my stomach. We started circling each other with my hand pressed against his chest, his fingers grazing my forearm. He spun me, and I slid one leg behind me, dipping into a lunge. He pulled me to him, and I raised that same knee to his hip, staring at him. My feet moved of their own accord, my mind focused on the movements and the man in front of me.

"You drive me batshit crazy. I'm jealous over a woman who isn't even *mine*," he said, ending his last word with a conquering growl.

He spun us with my leg wrapped around his waist and paused, dipping me backward with his arm curled against my lower back.

When he pulled me up, I pressed our foreheads together. "Aw. Is the criminal defense lawyer mad he's not getting his way?"

We crisscrossed our feet, moving in a circle with our foreheads still connected, glaring at each other.

"How much longer are we going to play this game? Hm?" Zane pulled me against him, my breasts pushing against his chest.

I turned my back to him, and with one of his hands on my hip, the other holding our arms out, we danced to the side, my ass bumping against his already hard impression. "I haven't the foggiest idea what you're talking about."

He spun me out and away from him and at the last moment, grabbed my hand, stopping me. Turning his back to me, he peered over his shoulder, waiting for me to approach. With the sultry grin of a tigress, I stepped forward, wrapping my arms around him from behind, but instead of pressing my palms to his chest, I dug my nails into his exposed skin, smooshing my breasts against his back and grinding my hips against his ass. He growled but let me claw him. I traced my leg up his side, and as soon as his hand landed on my thigh, I pushed away, backpedaling.

He stormed forward and in pure tango fashion, I dropped to one knee, gazing up at him with an arousal dancing in my eyes. He pulled me up to him, spinning me around and shoving his chest against my back.

His hands dragged over my stomach as we swayed. "You know exactly what I'm talking about." He kissed my neck. "The mind games. The fleeting touches, stares, the verbal fucking we've been doing." He squeezed one breast, kneading my hip with his other hand, his teeth nipping my earlobe.

I took several steps forward, and he grabbed onto both my forearms, halting me, urging me to come back to him. Spinning back into his arms, I grew dizzy, not from twirling but from that look in his gaze.

Need. Lust. Possession—the glow of the moon and stars above us blanketing me like night-lit velvet.

I kissed him, still swaying my hips to the rhythm of the tango music. He dipped his fingers into the hem at the back of my dress, drumming them against one ass cheek before grabbing it, kissing me back with nips, licks, and raw energy.

He pulled away, pressing his cheek to mine, turning us in circles. "This could be yours *every* night, Keira."

Letting out a moaning sigh, I wrapped my arm around the back of his neck, and he dipped me backward. Thunder boomed, followed by a sudden torrential downpour that sent the other dancers scurrying for the canopy. I moved to stand, to follow them to shelter, but Zane held me tight, dragging his hand between my breasts as the rain soaked us. When he pulled me up, lightning flashed across the darkened sky, reflecting in his eyes.

"Why do you have to be so stubborn about this?" He searched my face, his jaw tightening.

Impatience. Confusion.

"You like when I'm stubborn. Why do *you* need to be an asshole?"

His white shirt clung to his body, reminding me of what lay beneath the shield of his clothes. Even drenched with rain, his hair still looked sexy as hell, falling in tendrils over his forehead.

"No, I'm a dick. Assholes and pussies get fucked." He pulled me tight against him again, making the water spray from our soaked clothes. "Besides, you get *wet* whenever I'm a dick." He trailed a hand down the side of my face, running his thumb over my bottom lip and slipping it into my mouth.

With a grin, I bit it.

He smiled back and hoisted my knee up, encouraging me to wrap it around him. With one hand on my ass, the other curled under my knee, he trailed his touch down my thigh, torturously slow.

"I play games because—" I dipped a hand into his soaked shirt, scraping my nails against one of his pecs. "I don't know what else to do with you."

Lightning sizzled across the sky, and a tingle coursed through my inner thigh. I fell against him with a gasp, holding onto him with my arms curved around his neck.

"There's *so* much you can do with me." His fingers inched closer, skirting up the inside of my thigh.

A haggard breath escaped my lungs, fluttering over his lips, water beads collecting on my eyelashes. Lightning crackled behind him and a surge pulsed down my leg, circling my clit and making me cry out. He crashed his mouth over mine and hoisted me up, wrapping both of my legs around his waist. I flicked my hair back, sending a spray of water, and gazed down at him, panting. He walked with me curled around him, his hands on my ass, my fingers grabbing his hair.

My back hit against a tree trunk in the shadows away from the crowds at the reception. He ground against me, dry humping me with his hard-as-sin cock bulging against his soaked pants. He lifted me, throwing my legs over his shoulders and burying his face between my thighs. His nose brushed my folds through the fabric of my panties and he smiled against my leg before lowering me to the ground.

I was aroused, confused, and ready to throw him to the ground and reenact my dream from the plane. I parted wet hair from my face and stared up at him.

He snapped his head back, flicking water from his hair and face, and pushed against me. With a thumb teasing one nipple through my dress, circling it, he whispered, "I'm going to be the one to walk away this time, Keira. And it's going to drive you *mad*."

I shuddered a breath, blinking away water as he slowly backed away. "Zane. Zane, wait." Pushing off the tree, I trotted forward, reaching.

He grinned at me as he walked and a flash of lightning crashed above us, blinding me. When I opened my eyes…he was gone.

ELEVEN

ZEUS

"I DON'T KNOW WHAT else to throw at this woman. She was ready to fuck against a tree trunk, but has she called? Texted? E-mailed saying 'marry me now, you bastard'? The answer is no, Levin." I sighed, looking over at my dog, who cocked his head back and forth at me.

Levin yipped and scurried away as Kratos appeared with his wings splayed wide, Bia following him.

"We have some interesting news that you'll definitely want to hear, my liege." Kratos stood tall with his hands folded in front of him.

Bia had a conniving grin on her face, and she flicked her fingernails together.

"Let's hear it." I leaned on the bar.

"Your hopeful bride-to-be is, in fact…a demigod." Kratos's jaw tightened.

Shaking my head, I worked my pinky finger in and out of my ear as if Kratos had just told me Aphrodite was celibate. "That isn't possible. I would've smelled it from miles away."

"*It* is *possible if her mother put a spell on her*," Bia chimed in.

I gripped the edge of the bar, lightning sparking down my arms. "A spell? Who the Tartarus is her mother?"

"Oizys."

I stood straight. "Oizys? She's still active? Haven't heard about her in eons."

"*She is not on Earth anymore. But for a time, she fell in love with a mortal man, thus producing Keira*." Bia floated to stand in front of me, canting her head to one side.

"I kind of gathered that, Bia. It *is* how pregnancy works. I should know." I ground my teeth together.

"She spends her time in Tartarus now, assisting Hades and using her powers of misery to torture the condemned."

I scratched the back of my head, growing more impatient by the minute. "Oh, good, I'm glad she's keeping busy—would you two get to the point?"

"We 'coerced' the information out of her, sir. She did not wish Keira to grow up dealing with the gods and politics of Olympus. She left her with a mortal couple and put a shielding spell so that no other god could detect her blood. Not even you." Kratos clenched his fists as if preparing for my backlash.

How much more complicated could this possibly get?

Kratos shifted his stance. "Oizys also told us that her father had a message for you."

"Erebus? What does that 'ray of sunshine' want?"

"He said you should stop by to his new 'operation' in Chicago." The skin above Kratos's eyes wrinkled as he lifted a brow.

"Operation?"

"Apparently, he's running a highly organized crime ring."

A chuckle escaped my lips after pausing mid-sip. "He *must* be joking. I can't show this face mixed into that bullshit."

"He always *has* had a bit of dark humor, sir." A gleam formed in Kratos's eyes, which was the closest one would get to witness him smile.

Downing the rest of my drink, I shook my head. "He knows the deal. I don't fuck with them, and they don't fuck with us."

When I became king, I struck a bargain with the primordials. There'd be no interference both on their part or the Olympian gods so long as they played nice. And it would stay that way, otherwise, I'd need to banish them the same way I did another group of rather large bullies.

"Is there anything else about *Keira* I should know?" I looked between my two enforcers.

"*We also believe she's your—fated bond.*" Bia brought our faces closer and grinned.

I glared at her. "That's impossible. What are you trying to say? The Fates made me wait for thousands of years?"

"*Do you think, sir, it is a coincidence that Hera, after thousands of years of marriage,*

left you right before you and Keira crossed paths?"

"Fuck," I said under my breath.

Kratos crossed the room, standing beside Bia as if they were about to have a united front. "Forgive the insubordination, sir, but you really need to tell her who and what you are."

"Fuck if I will." I shoved away from the bar, turning my back on them and raking my hands through my hair. "I'm *this* close to snaring her."

"If you want any chance of a relationship beyond what you and Hera had, a partnership, she needs to know what she's getting into so she can make that choice for herself. Meddling won't solve this one—my liege." Kratos pounded his fist against his chest and bowed.

"What makes you think I care if I have anything beyond what I had with Hera?" I spoke to the mirror behind the bar, my reflection partially skewed from hanging wine glasses.

"*You do care.*" Bia leaned to the side, peering at me through the mirror, still grinning.

The lightning pulsed over my skin, swirling over my arms and sparking in my eyes. "Out. Both of you. Now," I roared.

A fated bond? Me? Not. Possible.

And she's a demigod?

I leaned against the wall, my head heavy, tiredness pulling at my bones, begging for rest. Maybe just for a moment. Moving to my leather chaise lounge, I slowly sat with a deep sigh, closing my eyes.

My phone buzzed on the counter.

"You've got to be fucking kidding me." Groaning, I pushed to my feet and swiped the phone screen.

Melissa Daniels wished to speak to me. With the first day of the trial tomorrow, it didn't surprise me in the slightest, but the last thing I wanted to deal with was her acid husband-dunking ass. Not to mention the irritation of the hope that'd idiotically bubbled in my stomach that the message would've been from Keira. Rage shot down my spine, and a blast of lightning shot through my arm, shattering the scotch decanter resting on the corner of the bar.

Levin had creeped his way out from his hiding spot after Kratos and Bia left, only to yelp and scamper away again.

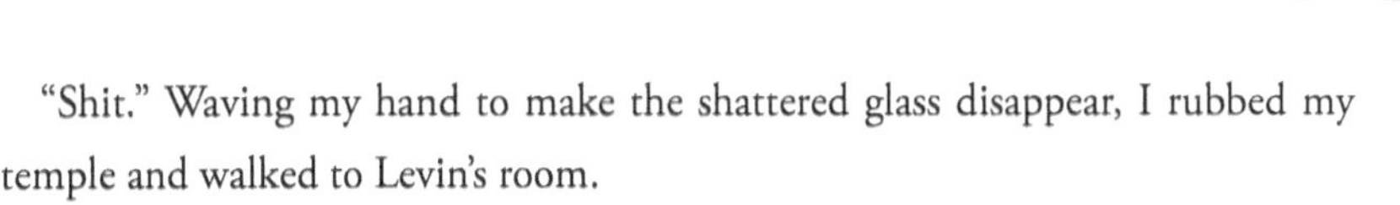

"Shit." Waving my hand to make the shattered glass disappear, I rubbed my temple and walked to Levin's room.

He cowered in a corner, shaking.

And now I *was* an asshole.

Sinking to my knees, I patted my leg and spoke softly. "Come here, boy. I'm sorry."

Levin didn't budge at first, and I sat on my ass with a sigh, holding my head between my knees. Eventually, a tongue lapped my knuckles and a furry head pushed against my palm. I lifted my chin, and petted Levin's head with heavy eyes.

"Sorry, boy." I opened my arms to him, and he scooted closer, resting his head on my chest. I hugged him and rested my cheek against the fur on his back.

It would've been so easy to fall asleep like this—listening to the dog's steady heartbeat, the softness against my skin. So. Fucking. Tired.

My phone buzzed again—another notification about the meeting with Daniels.

"Fucking Olympus. Fine, fine." I scratched Levin's chest before forcing myself to my feet.

I sat across from a more well-presented Melissa Daniels, having had her hair cut and styled. Twirling a pen on the table, I eyed her hands wringing in her lap.

"You seem nervous, Mrs. Daniels. Something you want to tell me?" I pointed at her busy hands.

"The trial starts tomorrow."

"Yes, it does."

She shifted forward, slamming her shackled arms on the table. "I covered my tracks, I'm sure of it, but—what if—what if they find the check written to the storage facility?"

Clicking the pen, I pressed it to the notepad. "The storage facility where they found the barrel?"

"Yes. I had to fucking pay for it somehow, didn't I?" She yelled, her top lip bouncing.

"When you say you covered your tracks, how exactly?" I scribbled, but it had

nothing to do with what she was saying. I just wanted to look busy.

What? A Greek god keeping notes? Please.

"It'd been processed through Quickbooks, and I changed them all around, shredded the original check, so it never showed."

"Smart thinking. So, what's the issue?"

Her light eyes widened. "The issue? What if they discover it? They search computers and junk, don't they?"

"Mrs. Daniels, there's always the possibility of them finding anything. We can argue that it's the only storage facility in the immediate area. Doesn't mean you stored a decomposing body."

She rubbed her upper lip, sweat collecting on it. "Okay. Okay. But what about the barrel? I *did* purchase it, and they know that."

"You're a biochemist. Why wouldn't you need barrels for the lab?" Drawing circles now on the notepad, I rose a brow at her.

She blinked once. "Damn. You are good."

"If I had a dinar for every woman who told me that…"

"What?" She scrunched her broad nose.

"Nothing."

She thinks of you, sir. Thinks of how she…needs you.

Bia's voice trickled over my brain.

A feral grin tugged at my lips, and I snapped my gaze to the killer across from me who was keeping me away from my horny future Queen.

"If you have no further concerns, Mrs. Daniels, I'll see you in court tomorrow." I stood and shoved the notepad under my arm.

"Wait, I—" Melissa held her hands up, stammering.

I slipped a hand over her shoulder. "You look tired."

She slumped in her chair, sleeping and snoring.

"Where is she, Bia?" I adjusted my tie, waiting.

Her office.

My grin turned downright villainous.

Once I was near the courthouse, I made myself invisible so no one would see me walk into her office. I could be an outright bastard, but she'd never forgive me if I sullied her reputation. Still hidden from everyone else's view but Keira's, I slowly opened her office door, only to find her sitting on the front of her desk,

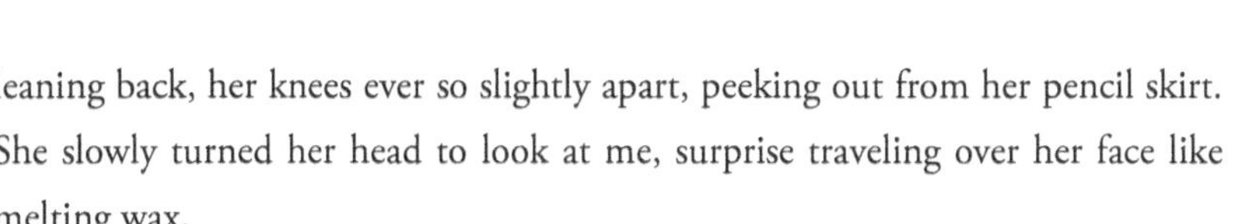

leaning back, her knees ever so slightly apart, peeking out from her pencil skirt. She slowly turned her head to look at me, surprise traveling over her face like melting wax.

"I got this peculiar feeling that you—" I closed the door with an audible click but didn't lock it, showing her she was free to go at any point. "—needed something from me." I'd made my voice extra husky.

"How could you possibly know that?" She unbuttoned two buttons of her dress shirt and pinched her knees together, sliding her heels back.

She didn't deny she needed me. Mm.

"Intuition? Magic?" I took several steps forward, testing if she'd stop me or run away. "Does it matter?"

She shook her head, her chest rising and falling with quickened breaths the closer I got.

"So, what do you need then, Keira? Hm?" A step forward. "Sustenance? Legal advice?"

She kept quiet, simply shaking her head, and as I stood a breath away from her, her bottom lip quivered.

I cocked my head to the side, standing in front of her but careful not to touch—not even a brush. "That dance in Argentina? I'd go so far as to say if you didn't 'hate' me, we might've fucked in the nearest stone alley."

She gripped the desk with both hands, but I kept my gaze focused on her. "After the stunt you pulled regarding my deportation, you're lucky it even got that far. Look. You're attractive, you know it. That doesn't mean I'll spread my legs for you."

Mm. Or was that precisely the reason why.

I let my gaze drop to her lap before slowly panning it back to her face.

"Not to mention we're opposing counselors, as I've said many, many times." Her grip tightened on the wood, knees pressing so hard together they turned red.

Mm. Mm.

The rabbit was wound so tightly in my snare.

"True. True. Doesn't mean we have to—" I took a small step forward, enough to brush my pant leg against her bare knees. "—go full tilt. So many other options."

A breath caught in her throat, and goosebumps littered her skin.

I nudged my knee between hers, testing her again, seeing if she'd deny me.

"You say, 'stop,' and I will." I willed her gaze to mine, further clarifying I meant what I said. "But something tells me—this is precisely what you need."

Her throat bobbed as she yet again remained silent.

I traced a hand over her knee, traveling to the top of her thigh, waiting, waiting for her to say, "no," or, "don't." But to my fucking sheer delight…she kept quiet, only making enough noise to let out a shaky breath. Her knees spread an inch, inviting me.

Moving my fingers to her inner thigh, I coaxed her legs wider, trailing my hand until I felt the lace of her panties against my fingertips. Flicking at them with a single finger, I raised my brows, waiting for the signal to retreat.

Instead, she didn't say a word and leaned back with a moan.

I parted the cloth with one quick swipe and plunged a finger into her.

Fuck. Me. Already so wet.

She gasped, and her neck craned back.

Pumping in and out of her, I watched her every reaction and wanted to make damn sure she knew what she'd been missing the entire time we've played games—what more she could *have*.

"I *crave* consent because it gives us both power to devour each other." I thrust a second finger in, and her thighs tightened on my waist. "And you repeatedly keep giving it to me without so much as a whispered word. The way your thighs pull me closer, the whimper escaping your throat." Dropping my face near her neck, I dragged my lips over her skin and paused at her ear. "The fact you're so wet right now you'd damn well slip off the desk if I weren't grabbing your ass."

She moaned, not caring if it was loud enough for surrounding offices to hear. Not that they could, I made sure of it.

"I could bend you over the desk right now, and you'd let me, wouldn't you?" I whispered, coating it with gravel.

She thinned her lips and craned her neck back. "Currently, I'm physically incapable of saying I wouldn't." A sigh escaped her lungs as her eyes panned down to watch what I was doing to her.

"But I won't."

Her gaze snapped to mine, distance and arousal playing in her stare.

"I want you to be able to scream without fear of someone hearing. To become unbridled. Because that's what you truly *need*, isn't it, Keira? No burdens.

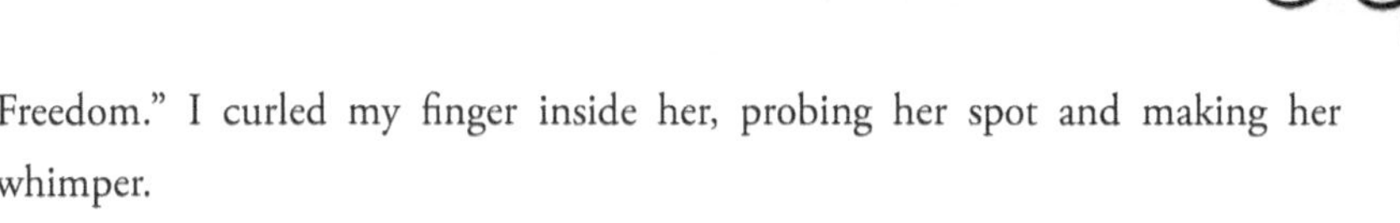

Freedom." I curled my finger inside her, probing her spot and making her whimper.

"I didn't know I needed it until I met you, Zane." She wrapped a hand around my tie, pulling me closer. "Why is that?"

Slipping out of her, I dragged the juices collected on my fingers over her lips, locking our gazes again.

My dick had gotten hard the moment I knew she wasn't going to stop me and it fucking throbbed at the sight of her licking herself from her lips.

I leaned in. "See you in court tomorrow—counselor." And I left her with nothing but the memory of me inside her.

I'd be the first to say this method would be bound to have me exploding, but that's what I needed her to be…a volcanic eruption of need and want for the King of the Gods. Mainly because I knew Kratos and Bia were right. I *did* have to tell her, or I'd surely lose her. We'd get through the first day of the trial, she would get to see me at work, *really* at work, not some damn trivial evidence trial, and when she was coiling with admiration—I'd strike. Still, there was the unsettling notion how I knew what she needed. And it's because…I needed the same damn thing.

TWELVE

KEIRA

NOT ONLY WAS THE trial weighing heavy on my mind, but the possibility of being deported and the only two solutions I had were as well. One would destroy the career I'd built for myself in New York. The other might destroy my dignity. Possibly. I didn't even really know this guy, minus what I could feel from him and what he shared about himself thus far, which wasn't a lot. Not to mention how *he* made me feel. It wasn't as if my first marriage ended all that well—maybe love wasn't the key. Part of me wanted to tell him no, simply so he didn't get his way. Petty? Childish? Maybe.

I wanted to be angry at him, not only for using my misfortune as leverage but the repeated confusing moments of sexual encounters. But try as I might, the fury would dissipate, and I'd be ravenously curious and hungry for him all over again. What held me there? What kept me coming back for more? Like freshly wiped glass, I could see straight through to his true nature. Something ate at him, made him leak desperation from his pores, made him smell hopeful, and I wanted to know why. I'd kept opening myself to him, but he did the exact same thing for me. *Why?*

Olivia snapped in front of my face. "Thinking about Argentina still?"

Argentina. The broom closet kiss. Yesterday in my office…

"That one couple I caught watching is certainly still thinking about Argentina," I grumbled, sulking in the back seat of the cab as it whisked us to the courthouse.

When Zane had stranded me in the middle of pouring rain after nearly driving me to orgasm, an older couple under a nearby canopy had gasped, staring at me

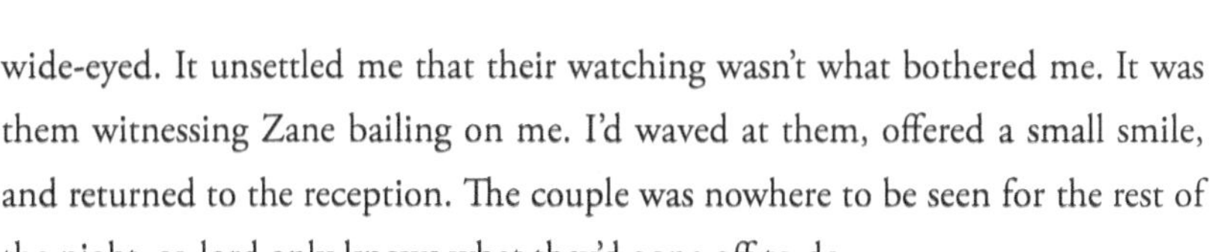

wide-eyed. It unsettled me that their watching wasn't what bothered me. It was them witnessing Zane bailing on me. I'd waved at them, offered a small smile, and returned to the reception. The couple was nowhere to be seen for the rest of the night, so lord only knows what they'd gone off to do.

Olivia scrolled through her phone, frowning. "You would think with all the phones in existence, one person would've recorded it."

"Did you seriously Google that? To see me grinding on Zane?"

Glancing up from her screen for a millisecond, she shrugged. "So, what? You're both hot. I did, however find this smoking dance number from Magic Mike Live." She shoved the phone in my face. "Lookie, here."

It was a video recorded by a screaming group of women audience members—a tall man with long dark hair danced provocatively with a blonde woman on an elevated clear stage, rain pouring over them throughout the dance.

Gently, I pushed the phone back to her. "Last thing I need right now is my mojo going into overdrive. I need my head clear."

After watching the video for several more seconds, Olivia tossed her phone in her pocket. "So you almost had sex in public, big bloody deal. Do you have any idea how many times I have?"

"Seriously?"

"The beach, in the back of a car in a Macy's parking garage, the bottle-o," she counted on her fingers as she recalled.

"Wait. You had sex in a liquor store?" I bit back a smile.

"Yeah. It *was* out of the view of security cameras." Her tone suggested she'd been mildly insulted I was surprised.

"Oh, then that makes all the difference." Grinning, I shook my head, and turned my face toward the window, groaning at the standstill traffic.

"Here's what I don't understand. Why haven't you two fucked already?" Olivia leaned toward me, her arms slapping on my lap.

I shot a look at the driver in the rear-view mirror, hoping he'd pretend he couldn't hear our conversation. The arousal ebbing from him suggested otherwise.

"It's some sincerely screwed up game we're playing. A tug for power, if you ask me." My groin pulsed, thinking about Zane's fingers inside it. I pinched my thigh.

Focus on the case.

"It sounds like you're losing this battle, Keir Keir. You may as well lower the wall and get something good out of it."

A man with dark hair and a tan Burberry jacket whizzed past the cab, hurriedly talking on his cell phone and running to a coffee vendor on the corner. My stomach fluttered and then deflated when the man turned around, showing his face. Not Zane.

"Maybe." But I needed to know more about him. And after the trial today, he was going to tell me whether he liked it or not.

When we walked into the courthouse, Zane paced the foyer, talking to someone on his cell phone. As if sensing my presence or something, his gaze snapped over his shoulder when I entered his proximity, and he grinned.

"Just get it done," he said before hitting his thumb on the screen and slipping it into his pocket. "Well, you look spry this morning." His eyes panned to my lips before snapping back up.

One look from this goddamned man and everything he did to me in my office yesterday flooded my brain, making a small whimper in the back of my throat.

"I'll uh—I'm going to meet you in the courtroom, Keir. Yeah?" Olivia patted my arm before walking away.

I'd absently nodded at her, only half hearing what she said.

"What the hell were you even doing at the courthouse yesterday, Zane? How many people saw you walk in and out of there?" A sudden panic twisted my gut.

After scanning the area, he pressed a hand between my shoulder blades and led me to a vacant corner. "No one saw me. I assure you."

"How is that possible? Did you crawl through a damn window or something?" I crossed my arms in a huff, glaring up at him, ignoring the continued pulse between my legs.

He shook his head as he narrowed his eyes. "Why don't you save all the questions for the trial, hm?"

"You aggravate me to no end."

He bit his lip. "You keep telling yourself that, counselor." His mouth lowered to my ear. "Because you didn't seem mad in the slightest with my fingers inside you."

His scent. How close he was. The sizzle that tantalized my skin. All of it was enough to have me moaning in the hallway.

I put a hand on his chest, which was—a horrible idea. Instead of pushing him

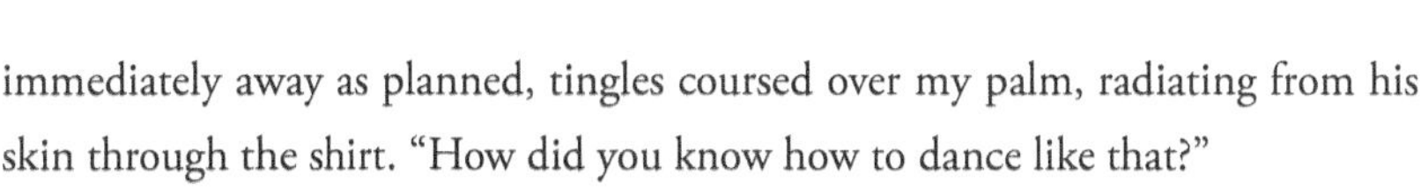

immediately away as planned, tingles coursed over my palm, radiating from his skin through the shirt. "How did you know how to dance like that?"

"Been around. Learned a thing or two." He didn't step away from my touch.

And I didn't pull my hand back. "I've never danced like that before."

"Well—" He slid forward, pressing my hand between our almost touching chests. "—when given the opportunity, I can be an *amazing* lead."

I gulped. There was no hiding it.

"Don't let dirty thoughts distract you too much, Miss Bazin. I expect the 'Bulldog' to challenge me in there." He stepped away, catching my hand in his when it fell from his chest.

Anger. Lust. Determination.

With a final smirk, he let go of my hand and whisked into the courtroom.

After composing myself and slapping my face several times to float back down to planet Earth, I readied for the fight of my life.

The trial ran smoothly at first, with Zane not throwing any curveballs or surprises as I'd expected. The usual questioning and presenting of evidence— receipts, digital evidence captured from computers, things of that nature. It was when we started to call in witnesses that he began his usual Zane bullshit.

I'd just finished questioning the accused's hairdresser, confirming they talked about how much Melissa wanted to kill her husband and that she could get away with it. When I passed the table, allowing Zane to rise for his turn with the witness, he slid a piece of paper to the corner and bobbed his brow.

Too curious to ignore, I bit the bait and read to myself:

Tell me the truth. Are you thinking about it right now?

He drew two boxes: One with a yes next to it, the other—also a yes.

Grinding my teeth, I snatched the pen as he brushed past me. He adjusted his tie with a smug grin. I drew my own "no" box and circled it several times, adding: Because I'm a professional.

"Miss Nichols, how well did you know my client?" Zane asked the hairdresser witness, slipping one hand in his pants pocket.

"Pretty well, I'd say. We talked a lot, and she came in for her hair every six weeks."

Where was Zane going with this?

"Right. So, you're saying gossip and rumors never *ever* happen in a hair salon?"

He flashed a charming grin to the women sitting on the jury stand.

They all wanted to smile, everyone could see it, but they held back by either adjusting in their seats or covering their mouths with a hand.

"I mean, it's possible?" Miss Nichols answered, shrugging.

Zane walked toward the jury, his debonair swagger plain as day. "So, it *is* possible my client was simply venting about trouble at home and not actually planning her husband's demise, as you so eloquently put it?"

Fuck.

Miss Nichols gulped and looked first at me, then the judge, as if hoping I'd object to the question. How could I?

"Please answer the question, Miss Nichols," the judge said, nodding.

"Yes, it's possible."

Zane smiled and patted the corner of the stand before turning on his heel. "No further questions, your honor." He sauntered back to the table, sliding the paper I'd written on with two fingers toward him, a light chuckle fluttering from his chest.

I folded my arms and crossed my legs, forcing my attention in front of me. Out of the corner of my eye, I spied him writing again and risked craning my neck to look. Like a third grader guarding anyone copying his work, he lowered his shoulder to block the paper.

"Miss Bazin," the judge's voice boomed.

Jolting in my chair, I snapped my attention to her. "Yes, your honor?"

"I asked if you have any further witnesses to present?"

Olivia snickered at my side and nudged me under the table.

"Yes, your honor. I do have one final witness." Rising, I flattened my jacket. "The prosecution calls Miguel Huarez to the stand."

Surprise. Anger. Fear.

The emotions swirling through the courtroom often had my head spinning, which made for complete exhaustion at the end of every day of trial. Between squelching the feelings in the air and the mental mind game of being a good lawyer, it took every ounce of gasoline in me, including reserves. But I couldn't see myself doing anything else.

As I shimmied past the table, Miguel made his way to the witness stand, and I caught Zane's intrigued grin. Miguel was a family friend who'd known Mr.

and Mrs. Daniels for over a decade, which I had him confirm from my first few questions. I then had him confirm Melissa's sudden change in behavior leading up to the time of the incident, how good of a dad her late husband was to their children, and how her husband was the type to avoid confrontation at any cost. Once satisfied I'd pulled at the jury's heartstrings, making them sympathize for the unsuspecting *dead* husband, I concluded.

Zane slid a paper to me again as I passed, and I yanked it toward me with more force than last time.

It read: *Do you like me?* With two boxes again, yes and no.

His gaze caught mine, making my stomach clench, my throat drying as I thought back to that kiss, the feral look in his eyes as he walked toward me in my office. Grinding my molars, I wrote "hell" above "no" and checked the box several times.

Chuckling, he balled the paper as he stood and re-did his top jacket button. After tossing the paper into the closest wire wastebasket he spun to face Miguel.

"Mr. Huarez, you were very close with the Daniels. And it sounds like you were at their house often, is that correct?"

Miguel squinted at Zane. "Yeah. That's right. Me and Larry were tight. Watched sports, talked politics, sometimes smoked cigars."

I caught Melissa rolling her eyes from the table next to ours.

"So, you would know about Larry and Melissa's sex life, correct?"

Slapping my palms on the table, I stood. "Objection, your honor. Their sex life has no relevance to the motive."

Sex. Sex. Sex. That's all this man ever thought about.

"Sustained. Mr. Vronti, please reword your question or specifically address the relevance?" The judge adjusted her glasses.

"Absolutely, your honor. I'm merely attempting to have the jury consider the possibility of the emotions that can stir when a marriage is unsatisfactory in the bedroom."

Fucking. Fuck. Who *was* this guy?

The judge tapped her finger on her podium before nodding. "Overruled. Mr. Huarez, please answer the question."

Fuming, I slowly sat back down.

Olivia leaned over, gulping. "Holy balls. He *is* good."

Zane flashed me a villainous grin over his shoulder before he continued his questioning. I knew from the moment he breezed into the meeting room that first day this wouldn't be easy. But what I hadn't realized was not only would it be difficult to fight him in the courtroom, it proved increasingly difficult to fight my growing attraction for him.

The trial lasted for several hours before the judge dismissed us for the day. Zane hadn't slid me any further notes, but the smugness and arrogance never ceased. What irritated me to no end, however was his arrogance was somewhat warranted. The man knew what he was doing and could work the courtroom like a surgeon with precise, unwavering movements.

Once everyone filed out, I shoved my paperwork into my briefcase before turning to Olivia. "I'm going to grab some dinner and head home. Meet up with you tomorrow?"

"Yup. Probably going to grab some gyros myself. That cucumber sauce is calling my name." She rubbed her tummy before frolicking away.

My elbow brushed with Zane's as we turned for the walkway at the same time, glaring at each other as we walked pace for pace to the doors exiting the courtroom.

"Zane, we need to talk. And we need to talk now," I barked once we were alone in the hallway.

Zane did a quick glance at our surroundings and gently grabbed me by the crook of the arm. "I couldn't agree more."

"What?"

He pulled me into a nearby holding cell and locked the door behind us.

THIRTEEN

ZEUS

I'D TAKEN A RISK locking her in the cell with me, but I knew she'd protest about it at first only to give in to the idea, maybe even enjoy it. It was as if I *knew* her without knowing her. Knew what she needed versus wanted. Knew how to hand her Olympus itself but not knowing—if she wanted it.

Without dampening the power as I'd been doing since we met, I flashed lightning in my palm, frying the surrounding cameras and blanketing us in darkness. Red washed over our skin as the single emergency light sprung to life in the corner of the room.

She slammed her palm on the door, the only lock available from the other side. "Zane, what the hell are you doing?"

I stepped forward, pressing my forearms to the door on each side of her head, smiling down at her. "We really need to stop meeting like this."

"Zane." She pressed a hand on my chest, sending a surge down my arms that had nothing to do with my lightning power.

Any other woman would've flown into a panic being locked in a room with a man she claimed to hate. Any other woman may have even slapped me. But not Keira. No. Because this was yet another segment in our game, and she was ever the willing participant. And it's what kept me coming back time and time again.

"You're right. We need to talk. And what I need to tell you can't be seen or heard by anyone else." I rolled my bottom lip past my teeth.

Keira ducked under my arm and walked to the opposite side of the room—standing her ground, open to what I had to say, but showing me, she wasn't going

to make it easy.

I'd be disappointed if she did.

"Well? It's not as if I'm going anywhere. What do you have to tell me?" She folded her arms.

Might as well come right out and say it.

Clasping my hands in front of me, I locked gazes with her, the emergency light giving her cheeks crimson shadows. "My name isn't Zane Vronti. It's a name I use as a cover along with the lawyer job." I took a step forward. "My real name is Zeus. And I'm King of the Greek gods." Another step.

She didn't say anything at first, pressing her ass against the wall behind her, her eyes searching my face…and then she burst out laughing.

"Fuck, Zane. I've heard a lot of ego complexes, but this has to take the cake." She flicked her wrist. "You think you're a *god*, now? And not just any god but a god-*king*?"

"I am, Keira." The lightning sparked over my arms, circling them.

Just believe so we can move on from this.

I'd never been so close to begging in my immortal life as I was at this very moment.

She gasped and shook her head, her gaze falling to the electricity coiling around me. "No. No, this must be some kind of trick. Zane, how dare you—"

We *don't* have time for this.

Growling, I ported across the room, appearing in front of her. Taking her face in my hand, I gently forced her gaze to mine, sending a series of tingles from the lightning rolling over my knuckles into her cheek. "I. Am." The lightning took over my eyes, pulsing in them, making me see in black and white. "I could port us to Mount Olympus, right *now*, if I wanted, and *fuck* you on my throne."

Her bottom lip trembled as she looked up at me, a mixture of fear and lust washing over her features. "But you won't."

My power fizzled, and I blinked, recoiling an inch. "Excuse me?"

"You're so used to getting your way, to everyone and everything around you doing your bidding without hardly flinching. You *want* me to ask." She tightened her jaw.

The lightning pulsed again, reacting from the sheer confidence and balls this woman had.

"Where is this coming from?" I narrowed my glowing eyes at her.

Most importantly, I needed to know because…she was right.

"No. You finish explaining this first." She rested her hand on my forearm, my power reflecting in her light eyes as she stared at me. "How?"

Scraping my callused fingertip over her skin, I kept her gaze. "You're having a hard time *not* believing it, aren't you? There's a reason for that too, Keira."

Silence.

She licked her lips as her gaze dropped to my mouth. It was one thing to feel my power when she thought I was a mere mortal, but now to see it? Feel it? Have it standing right in front of her?

"You're part goddess." I hovered my mouth near hers but made no move to kiss her.

"What?" She spat, her forehead crinkling.

"Did your parents ever tell you, you were adopted?"

She gripped the sleeve of my jacket, wrinkling it, pulling it taut over my arm. "Yes, but—they were older. They've been gone for years now." She frowned, letting herself slump against the wall.

"Your birth mother is a goddess." I cupped her chin, lifting her bewildered gaze to meet mine.

She balled her hands into fists and beat them against my shoulders. "This doesn't make any sense."

Her expression suggested otherwise. It was as if my words were the most sense she'd heard in some time but couldn't process why.

"Her name is Oizys. She's a goddess of specific emotions—misery, depression, anxiety." I kept my hand on her face, caressing her cheeks with my thumbs.

Her gaze dropped, and she palmed her forehead. "Please step back, I need to—this is all too much."

As she requested, I slid away, willing my power to dissipate.

Anger suddenly flushed her face. "Wait a minute. How long were you going to wait to tell me this? You were just going to let me marry you without knowing it meant signing up to be a Queen or a goddess or whatever the hell this entails?" Her chest pumped, her breaths increasing.

"I figured telling you too soon would have you running for the hills. Doesn't this make your decision easier?"

Frustration twisted at my gut.

"What?" She growled, dragging her hands through her hair and shaking her head. "You cannot be this dense, Zane."

"I'm not sure what the hell you have to be angry about. You thought you were marrying into an inheritance when it's more than that. A queendom. Godhood." I ran a hand over my beard, trying to hide the irritation and confusion punching through my veins, the lightning sizzling under my skin. "*Immortality*, Keira."

Her eyes widened, lips parting ever so slightly. "I honestly can't believe you. I just found out you're Zeus. *The* Zeus. And I'm part goddess, and you expect me to what—say hell yeah, let's do this?"

I scratched the back of my head, wincing like I'd been mentally slapped. "It would be preferable?"

"Oh my—" She turned her back on me, pressing her forehead against the door with a stifled scream.

"I don't know what you expect from me. This—I'm not used to this." King of the Gods—reduced to a stammering fool. Bile would've worked up my throat if my body were capable.

This is what I got for having mortals eating out of the palm of my hand for nearly my entire life. Especially. Women.

She whirled around. "Doing what? Holding a civil conversation? One that doesn't involve innuendo and jabs?"

Ouch. I adjusted myself, feeling like I'd been kicked in the nuts with her foot never leaving the ground.

"Trying to convince a woman to be with me. To not only explain what I could offer but show her." I clenched my fists, reining in my power. It wanted to light up the whole fucking room.

She dropped her hands at her sides. "And there we have it. It always circles back to you."

I opened my mouth, and for the first time in my unnatural life…nothing came out.

"Open the door," she huffed, pointing behind her and keeping her gaze fixed on the floor.

"Keira, we don't have a lot of ti—" I started, crossing the room to her, the anger scraping my spine, puncturing it.

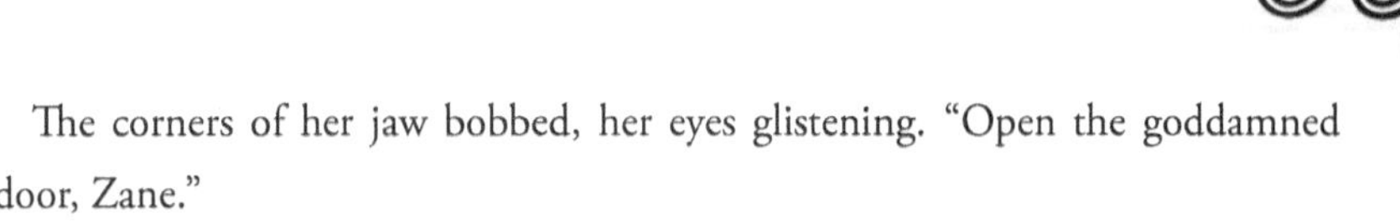

The corners of her jaw bobbed, her eyes glistening. "Open the goddamned door, Zane."

"Fine," I growled, waving my hand at the door, making the metal slab slide.

Without another word from either of us, she stormed to the hallway.

What the actual fuck just happened? The polar opposite of what I thought would, that's for damn sure. I offered the woman a kingdom, the chance to be an immortal goddess and she says it's about more than that? What the Tartarus else is there?

Sitting on the edge of the metal table, I dropped my face in my hands. Tiredness tugged at my brain again, and I glanced at my watch, sighing at the time left until my kingly demise. Rounds. I hadn't done rounds in weeks. Sparking life back into the room—the lights and cameras—I ported to a live concert being held in Buffalo, New York. Walking amidst the crowds of people in stadium seating, I remained invisible to all mortals and immortals alike.

My son, Apollo, blazed onto the stage, fronting himself as the lead singer of the band Apollo's Suns. He definitely inherited his cunning and ego from me. In all the years he'd been performing, I'd only watched him once. He did exactly what I expected him to—danced shirtless, focused on the women, and used his Fates-given gifts to inspire the masses. At least he was doing his job.

He strutted out on stage with his guitar strapped to his back, asking the audience how they were doing, referring them all to the city name itself. But unlike the last time I'd watched him, he stretched his hand behind him and welcomed someone else on stage. A blonde woman in ballet attire with one of the most radiant smiles I'd ever seen. His goddess and newly appointed leader of the muses, Laurel.

Observing the two of them, I rubbed my chin. Overseeing the muses had always been Apollo's favorite part of his duties. He'd been focused on himself since he was a teenager and the little ass drove me mad. And one run-in with this woman... changed everything. They didn't even have a fated bond—plopped into each other's paths, both missing a part of themselves they hadn't known they'd lost.

Huh.

Apollo curled Laurel against him, kissing first the side of her head, followed by a practical make out session for all eyes to see. Grimacing, I snapped my gaze away, peeking now and again to ensure they weren't licking each other's faces

any longer before I continued to watch. I'd seen my son happy, but never like this—slaying the Python, the victory at Troy, after Eros lifted that idiotic spell, so Apollo was no longer in love with a damn tree. He had countless women he pursued, but all ended in tragedy. If I had to take a step back and look at the bigger picture—his experiences could've been entirely my fault. Who else did he have to emulate? Who else did he have to admire? Rubbing the back of my neck, I tore my eyes away from the stage.

The crowd roared with applause as Laurel spun in circles on her toes, and Apollo danced around her, playing guitar. Something told me I'd never need to worry about these two slacking on their godly jobs. There was so much inspiration floating in the air, it almost had *me* spinning damn circles. But my son performed one of the most selfless acts for this once mortal woman, gave up his leadership for her to make it her own.

I wasn't my son. And my leadership wasn't one I could give up. It had to be supported. Understood.

Snarling, I ported to the next location. Los Angeles, California. My daughter, Aphrodite, sat in front of a vanity, staring at herself in the mirror. She lifted her hands, conjuring her powers in her palms, but it resulted in crackles and pops versus its full force.

"I don't understand it," she snapped, throwing a hairbrush into the mirror, cracking it.

Shit. I'd *never* seen her this angry.

A woman swept through the door with wide eyes once she spotted Aphrodite's chest heaving at the broken mirror. "Ma'am. Sorry to disturb you, but you have a visitor?"

"Who?" A scowl morphed over Aphrodite's face, an anguished one.

The woman remained in the doorway, using the door as a makeshift shield. "All he said was to tell you it's Heph."

My daughter's face softened, brightened even, before she wiped an invisible slate over it, ridding it of all emotion.

"Tell him I'll be right out."

"Yes, ma'am." The woman quickly retreated.

Aphrodite swirled an arm around her, appearing in a tight light pink dress. After fanning her hand at the mirror, repairing it, she leaned forward and primped

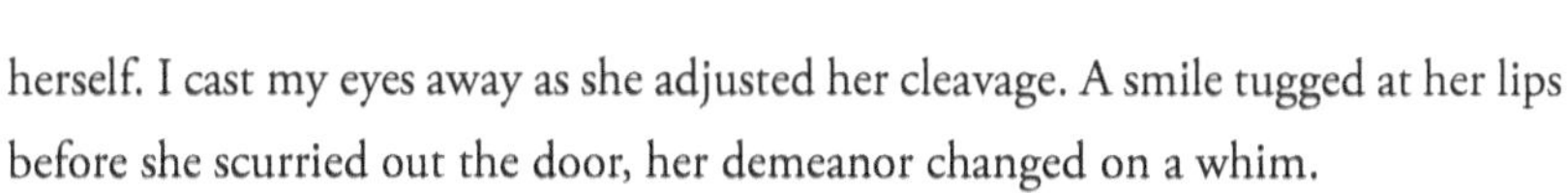

herself. I cast my eyes away as she adjusted her cleavage. A smile tugged at her lips before she scurried out the door, her demeanor changed on a whim.

Heph as in Hephaistos? Seriously? That dopey oaf? Did not. See. That coming.

I hesitated at first before snapping my fingers, and porting to Pensacola, Florida. Hera whisked through an apartment living room, walking back and forth from the bedroom to the kitchen and back again as if flustered. Observing her, I folded my arms.

She suddenly halted near me, squinting, her finger aimlessly searching the air. "Do you think after all this time I couldn't sense you and your little invisibility trick?"

Fuck.

Making myself visible to her, I kept leaning on the counter with crossed arms. "Hi, Hera."

"Zeus." She lifted her chin, standing regal and posh as ever. "If you came here to—"

I lifted a hand and shook my head. "No. You deserve to be happy. And clearly, that wasn't with me."

Her jaw fell open, and she slow-blinked like I'd blindsided her. "I—I mean, we could have been. You realize that, right?"

"I honestly don't think so, my dear." Rubbing my chin, my eyes heavy, I lifted my gaze to hers. "We were never right for each other. Just convenient at the time."

"Olympus. You look like shit, Zeus."

"I've got a lot on my mind. You kind of left me in a situation." I smirked and adjusted my cufflinks.

"Situation? You haven't picked a new Qu—" She stopped short and placed a hand over her opened mouth. "Did you *meet* someone?"

The last thing I wanted to do was talk about Keira. I decided to go on rounds to distract myself from the entire fucking thing.

"Take care of yourself, Hera. And if you need anything, all you have to do is ask." I pushed off the counter and slid a hand in my pocket. "You'll always have a spot on the Olympian Council. Whatever the shit good it does in the modern age, but it's still yours."

"I—" Hera pressed a hand to her chest. "Thank you."

Grimacing, I ported outside. I didn't know where I intended to go next, but I

couldn't stay there anymore. This whole new dynamic I suddenly decided to try on myself already had my asshole hurting.

Sighing, I ported to Denver, Colorado. The Bulldog gym, to be exact. My son Ares sparred with his also newly formed goddess wife, Harmony. I was still bitter he didn't ask me to turn her and went behind my back to Hades instead. But could I really blame him? And even still, when I first met Harmony, I had to lay down the law. I was her leader, and she had to realize there were consequences for pussy-footing around. She wasn't only good for my son, she was good amongst the war gods, period.

Ares leaped from the mat with a snarl. "I still can't believe what that maláka said to you. He's lucky I didn't bash his teeth in on the spot."

And he hadn't?

"Ares," Harmony started, curling her hand over his bicep. "Breathe. We've talked about this, remember?"

Ares's lip bounced, and he wrapped a hand around the back of her neck, pulling her to him. "You're right. What would I fucking do without you, gatáki?"

"We're in this together, war god." She cupped his face and kissed him.

The kiss soon turned ravenous, and they dropped to the mats. Smirking to myself, I let my gaze fall to my feet.

My one legitimate child was the only god who could ever overthrow me if they tried and also…the most like me.

Against my better judgment, I appeared in Keira's apartment. The room was pitch black save for the light beaming from a computer monitor. Keira sat at the desk with her nose inches from the screen, chin resting on her hand.

I could've done this at any moment—appeared invisible and watched her. So, why did I send my enforcers to do it?

Bia could read minds. Yes. That was the obvious reason. Yeah.

Peeking over her shoulder, I spotted several windows and tabs open in her browser, her hand feverishly working the mouse as she bookmarked websites, jotted notes, and scanned endless text.

And what had she typed repeatedly into her Google search bar?

Zeus.

She…was Googling me. It was ego-boosting yet altogether nauseating at the same time. The internet was an absolute rabbit hole of hell when it came to

information about me.

Grimacing, I turned away from her. This was wrong—spying on her, invading her privacy because I *could*. It was as if I were cheating in this elaborate game we'd created between the two of us. I winced, the realization hitting me like a thunderclap.

Fuck. Me.

I held my head low as a slight grin pulled at the corner of my lips.

All this time, and she was the one who ensnared *me*. And I hadn't a fucking clue how she did it.

After placing a single kiss against her head, one that'd feel only like a passing breeze to her, I whispered, "This is it, Keira. It's either you or no one. And it's completely your choice."

And with that mind-boggling revelation…I disappeared.

FOURTEEN

KEIRA

"HE TRANSFORMED HIMSELF INTO a shower of gold?" Staring at my computer screen with a scrunched face, I slapped my hand over my forehead. "How does one even fuck a shower of gold?"

I'd been researching myths about Zeus for the past several hours and grabbed my third can of Red Bull, swigging more of the energy elixir down my throat. Adjusting my clear framed blue screen glasses, I eyed the open internet tab I'd yet to have the guts to look at: Oizys. He said she was my biological mother. A goddess. Which made me—no. It just couldn't be real. But not one ounce of deceit flooded from his emotions. He'd spoken with the same conviction as when he declared himself Zeus.

It sparked so many more questions. What was my birth mother like? Why didn't she want me? Who was the mortal man she spent her time with? Did he know I existed? Was she still alive? *Could* gods die in some specific way, like vampires or werewolves? Is she the reason for my empathic abilities?

A phantom breeze blew through my hair, making me shiver. Furrowing my brow, I glanced at the windows behind me, knowing full well I'd never leave them open in the dead of winter, but where else would a draft come from?

With a groan, I snatched the can again, tilting my head back to take a swig and frowning when I realized it was empty. Resting the glasses on top of my keyboard and rubbing my eyes, I pushed from the desk, heading for the kitchen for another energy drink. My phone buzzed on the counter, and I swiped it into my hand as I popped the can.

"Hey, Olivia."

"I'm coming over."

I made a slurping sound, nearly choking on my drink. "Now? Why? It's two in the morning."

"When has the dead of the night ever stopped me? And what do you bloody mean *why*? I'm bored."

Throwing a silent temper tantrum by kicking my feet and beating my phone against my forehead, I held back a sigh. I'd planned to spend the better part of the night into the wee hours of the morning inundating myself with information on a would-be suitor. The King of the Gods. It seemed crazy, outrageous, positively bonkers, but he wasn't lying. The lightning—the sight of it, the feel of it—was undeniable. And the desperation steaming from him as he almost begged me to believe him…that did me in.

"I'm kind of in the middle of something, Ollie. Can we hang out tomorrow?"

"Nope. I'm outside your door. Answer it, hoe bag." She knocked on my door.

Groaning, I flopped the cell phone back to the counter and shuffled to the door. Olivia waved at me from the other side of it and whisked past before I had a chance to close it.

"What in the hell are you doing? It's pitch black in here except for the computer—" She gasped and turned on her heel with a wide grin. "Were you watching porn?"

I rolled my eyes and took a swig of my drink before moving back to my desk. "No. I wasn't. I'm doing research."

Before I could minimize the window, Olivia darted in front of me. "Research? On Greek mythology?" She clicked through the thirty-two tabs I had open, her eyes widening with each passing website. "And these are all on Zeus. What does this have to do with the case?"

Nothing. Absolutely nothing.

"Ollie, it's tough to explain." The can crinkled in my hand as my grip tightened on it.

Olivia stood straight as she raised a thin brow and circled me. "What are you hiding, Miss Bazin?"

"Are you seriously trying to lawyer me?"

She tapped a finger over her lips. "And now you're sidestepping the question."

I didn't have time for this.

"For fuck's sake. Come here." I motioned with my head toward the couch, sitting with one leg propped. Zane's penthouse light came on across the street, and like a moth to a flame, my eyes darted straight to it.

"You're acting far stranger than normal, Keir." Olivia slowly sat down with her palms pressed against her thighs.

"Zane isn't really Zane. He's Zeus, King of the Gods. And I'm apparently the daughter of a goddess, making me a demigod."

Could I have done that more eloquently? Definitely, but not only was it two in the morning I was also downing my fourth Red Bull.

Olivia squinted at me before snatching the can from my grasp with lightning speed. She sniffed the mouthpiece, still eyeing me. "Hm. I don't smell vodka."

"You would barely smell it anyway."

Not tearing her gaze from mine, she took a sip and gagged. "Nope. No vodka. Just arse."

I yanked it back. "Do you think everything tastes like ass?"

"If it doesn't taste any bloody good? Yeah."

Repeatedly flicking the tab of the can, I spied Zane's shadow waltzing back and forth in his apartment. One singular shadow. A peculiar wave of relief washed over me.

"Keira, are you being serious?" Olivia threw her hands at her sides, shrugging.

"Yes," I said, the word barely escaping my throat, my gaze still drawn to Zane's window.

Olivia's palms slapped her thighs as she dropped them. "Huh. I would never under any circumstance call you crazy, but this is all a bit wonky sounding, don't you think?"

How had I expected this conversation to go?

The only reason I somehow managed to believe it so quickly was because I had ties to their world—my mind, my body, my very bones all sang to me that it was all real. Not to mention my ability to know whether he lied or not.

My ability.

I turned to her, dropping my foot to the floor and resting the can on the coffee table between us. "I've never told you this—well, I've never told anyone this, but I have special abilities. And until yesterday, I thought it a weird quirk, but

apparently…it's because of my lineage."

She leaned forward. "What abilities?"

"I'm an empath. A heightened, specialized, empath." I steepled my fingers. "It's why I walk to work. Why you always see me in my office alone after I get there. It's to give myself a break from the surge of emotions that flood this city."

Olivia's eyes shifted from left to right. "So, at any point in time, you can tell how I feel, even if I'm saying otherwise?"

"Yes. But I'm around you so often I've been able to drown most of yours out. It feels intrusive otherwise."

She thinned her lips and lifted her chin. "What am I feeling right now, then?"

I rolled my shoulders back, opening my mind to her emotions again—a feat I hadn't done in years. With her vibrant personality, her emotions tickled over my skin. Holding back a smile, I answered, "Skeptical. And horny. Very very horny."

How shocking.

She gasped and pointed at me. "You're good."

With her emotions open to me like a floodgate again, I let out a roiling sigh and sulked into the couch cushions. "You don't believe a lick of what I'm saying, do you?"

She gave a half chuckle. "Come on, Keir. I'm trying here. I really am. But—Greek gods? We all know they were mythology made up by 'Thosecles' and 'Homeboy,' or whatever their names were."

I could've corrected her, but what would've been the point?

Grinding my teeth, I pushed off the couch and grabbed my coat.

"Where are you going?" Olivia leaped to her feet.

"For a walk. I need to clear my head." It came out far more gruffly than I'd intended.

Olivia crossed the room, grabbing my elbow as I slipped the coat over my arms. "Keira, come on. Be reasonable. It's three in the bloody morning in New York City."

"It's not as if I've never walked around here this early before." I plucked her fingers from my arm and slipped the jacket on the rest of the way. "This apartment suddenly feels suffocating, and I need fresh, cold air."

"Keir, I'm sorry, I—" Her large green eyes blinked.

Remorse. Guilt. Sadness.

I patted her shoulder. "I know you are. And I don't blame you a bit. I'll be right

back, okay? You have my key if you want to leave. Lock yourself in, alright?"

As she stared at me wide-eyed, I gave her one last pat and exited, heading down the stairs and to the quiet sidewalk outside.

Popping my earbuds in, I cued up a random Spotify playlist and hit shuffle. I started walking in the direction toward work, shoving my hands in my pockets and ignoring the loud chatter my teeth made.

Fuck the cold. I needed its harshness to ground me—to numb me.

The song *Hail to the King* by Avenged Sevenfold blasted in my ears, making me pause. I gazed up at the sky, the moon peeking through the dark wispy clouds that'd rolled in. Zane was a king. And not just any king…a godly, immortal one that could control lightning. The realization struck fear and lust, mixing, molding together until an ache pooled between my legs. Snarling, I started walking again, this time faster. The song continued to play, and I timed my steps with the rhythm, my gaze glued to the sidewalk.

What would it even mean to be Queen? What would it entail?

I stopped at a crosswalk and shook my head, diving through my mental bank of factoids I'd researched the past several hours. "And wait a fucking minute. Why would Zeus be looking for a wife? Whatever happened to Hera?"

Thank Christ it was early morning, or my out loud thinking may have turned a few heads, even if it *was* New York City. The walk sign illuminated, and I continued my brisk pace, paying no mind to my knees shaking beneath my thin yoga pants.

No. It all made absolutely no sense.

Maybe he was good at hiding when he lied. He was a damn good lawyer, and I'd heard about people who could fool lie detector tests by controlling their heartbeats. It was as reasonable an explanation as any. And yet—every other emotion I felt from him wasn't fabricated.

A car door from a parked car suddenly swung open. Someone dressed in all black, sporting a ski mask, grabbed my shoulders and shoved me into the nearby alley with such force it jostled the earbuds from my ears. Fear wrenched down my spine with such ferocity my throat forgot how to scream.

Fear. Anger. Confusion.

The masked person faced me, and I lifted my knee, ready to strike them in the gut, but they grabbed my shoulders and shoved my chest against the stone wall. Cool metal pressed against the back of my head, and my breaths grew shaky, knees

numbing—the wall my fingernails clawed was the only thing keeping me upright.

"Don't scream. Don't move, or I *will* shoot you," the man growled near my ear, the heat from his breath leaking through the mask.

"Alright. Alright," I managed to blurt out.

I'd gotten several threats since practicing in New York, and one had been severe enough I started to carry pepper spray with me everywhere. Not once had I ever needed to use it. I picked a bad day to forget.

"You put my little brother behind bars, you prosecuting bitch," the man snarled, shoving the point of the gun harder against my skull, making it ache.

Wincing, I sucked in a breath to keep my voice from sounding as petrified as I felt. "Who's your brother?"

"Mark Valesco. You remember him? Or do you just ruin lives and dust them under a rug?" He pushed between my shoulder blades, causing my cheek to scrape against the bricks.

Valesco. Murdered three innocent people. One of them was a ten-year-old boy. And all because they happened to be in the wrong place at the wrong time when he was fleeing the scene of a bank robbery. I *never* forgot a case.

"Yeah, I remember Mark. He *murdered* three innocents." I gritted my teeth. Stupid. Stupid. Don't bait this guy.

The gun dug further into the back of my head, and I bit the inside of my cheek to keep from whimpering.

"The judge could've given him twenty, thirty years. But no. Because of you, he got life without parole. We'll never see him outside that damn place anymore, and neither will his baby girl."

A knot formed in my throat. "I'm sorry."

I wasn't sorry for putting a murderer behind bars for the rest of his life, but I *was* sorry a girl had to grow up without her father because he chose poorly.

"Yeah. You're going to be." He shoved his mouth near my ear again. "Hope you've made peace with your maker."

The sound of the gun cocking flashed through my head.

Fear. Indecision.

This guy was just as terrified as I was. I pushed as much of my own fear as I could toward him, hoping it would overwhelm him and make him stop.

"You shoot me in an alley in the middle of downtown, and you don't think

anyone will hear?" I controlled my breathing, slowing my erratic heartbeat.

Hesitation. Questioning.

He blew out two harsh breaths and ran the back of his hand under his nose. "Makes no difference to me. Cops can kill me for all I care. At least I'll die knowing *you're* dead."

Shit. He was too far gone to allow my ability to seep through. I closed my eyes, wincing, saying a silent prayer to whatever deities existed in the world to do something—anything to stop what was about to happen.

A sizzle of lightning blazed through the alleyway in a blinding flash, sparks flying. The pressure from the man's hand and gun disappeared. Darkness spilled over the alley, not one single street lamp lit. Slowly, I turned.

Zane stood at the opposite wall, the man in his grasp, booted feet scraping the asphalt as his hands clawed at the one Zane had wrapped around his throat. Lightning curled around Zane's chest and arms. I side stepped until I stood next to Zane laser-focused on the man in his grasp. Zane's eyes glowed bright white, the lightning crackling within them. His expression was cold, predatory—deadly.

Anger. Distaste. Absolute fury.

"Zane, don't." I lifted a hand to touch his arm but snapped it back when the lightning hissed, swirling around his body faster.

"He was going to *kill* you."

The man gagged and gurgled within his grip, what little pale skin that showed through the mask, reddening.

Licking my lips, I stepped closer. "But he didn't. You stopped him. You can't do this."

"Watch me," he snarled.

"I know you *can*, but you shouldn't. There are security cameras everywhere." My chest heaved, and I moved so close, I could feel the heat from the lightning coursing over him—feel the hairs on my arms standing on end.

"I fried them upon arrival." Zane's lip bounced, and he gripped harder around the man's neck.

The man's feet kicked harder, and his arms fell limp at his sides.

"Zane, stop," I yelled.

Silence.

I stared at the man dying with each passing second.

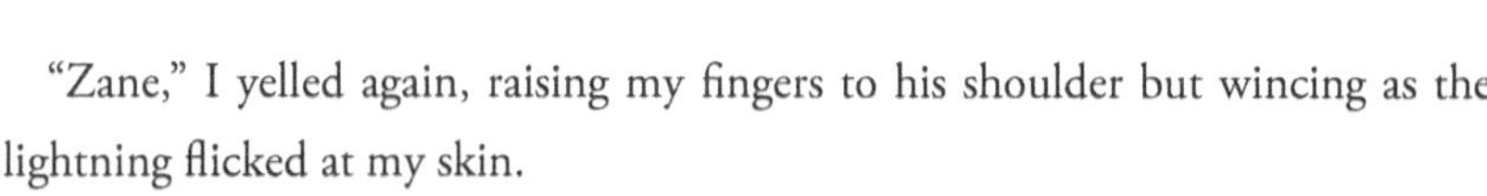

"Zane," I yelled again, raising my fingers to his shoulder but wincing as the lightning flicked at my skin.

Still such utter silence.

"Zeus," I said quietly, ignoring the sting from the lightning as I slid a hand over his shoulder. "Please. Stop."

He rapidly blinked, those brightened lightning eyes turning to look down at me. The lightning curling around his arms fizzled away, and all that remained was the bit ignited in his gaze.

Confused. Shocked. Still angry, though.

Zane lowered the man and loosened his grip but didn't fully let go. Dipping his face closer, he said, "The only reason you're still breathing is that I'm trying to get in this woman's good graces. Remember that the next time you're seeking petty revenge against a woman who was just doing her job." He let go of the man's neck, moving his hand to his shoulder, and making him slump to the ground unconscious.

Anger. Fear. Lust.

I stared up at him as he turned to face me, his blue eyes back to normal. A deep crease formed in his brow, his eyes heavy and sullen as if he were exhausted. He wiped it away as he lifted his chin, not tearing his gaze away from me—waiting to see what I'd do, what I'd say.

I leaped against his chest, curling my arms around his neck and kissing him. He wrapped his arms around my waist, kissing me back, his hands roaming up and down.

That was so fucking hot but so, so fucking *stupid* on his part.

Angrily I pushed away, beating one fist against his chest before I stepped back. "Why do I always want to punch you and fuck you all at the same time?"

His lazy gaze took me in, his tongue licking his bottom lip, tasting me. "You—" He pointed at me with a wicked glint in his eye. "Called me Zeus."

I picked at flecks of wood in the doorframe, focusing on it. "You wouldn't answer to Zane. You were about to kill him. What else was I supposed to do?"

After what I'd just seen, the display he'd given…there was no denying he was who he said.

"How did it feel? Saying my real name? Feeling the lightning sizzle against your skin when you touched me?"

Powerful.

I poked his chest and tightened my jaw. "We need to talk. Now. And you're going to answer every damn question I have."

He batted my finger away with a smirk before pulling me against him. The world whizzed past us in a vibrant blur, and within seconds, we stood in the middle of…his penthouse apartment.

FIFTEEN

ZEUS

DON'T GET ME WRONG. I was ecstatic she was curious enough to ask questions. It meant she was actually considering my proposal, but fuck me if it wasn't going to be as painful as an ass full of razor blades. Since the age of mortals worshipping and believing in the gods, let's just say the modern era had never painted me in the best light? I may as well have been the poster boy for everything everyone should hate.

Keira stood in the middle of the living room, her coat still on, hands wrapped around herself. Creases formed in her forehead as she turned circles, almost as if she were afraid the place was booby-trapped and one false move would cause a door in the floor to open.

"I promise you nothing will happen beyond talking—" I flashed her a grin. "—unless you want it to." Moving behind the bar, I grabbed the decanter and two tumblers. "I brought us here because it's soundproof."

"If it's soundproof, then why didn't you bring us here before instead of yanking me into a damn holding cell?" Her shoulders relaxed, and she shrugged off her coat, making sure to fold it before draping it delicately over the chaise lounge in the corner.

"Ah, yes." I poured scotch into one glass. "Bringing you to my lair would've made the 'Greek gods are real' conversation far easier." Offering her a small smile, I lifted the bottle.

She scratched the back of her head. "Point taken."

I shook the bottle. "Scotch? Could help. Trust me. This is going to be a strange

conversation."

"You're right. Make it a double. No ice." She leaned against the bar, tapping her fingernails on the marble as she scanned my place.

Levin came barreling around the corner, his tongue flopped out the side of his mouth.

I stopped mid-pour, slamming the bottle to the bar top. "Shit. I forgot I hadn't put him up. Sort of well, left in a—" Stopping short as I rounded the corner, I paused at the sight of Keira squatting with my dog between her knees. He licked every dry spot on her face as she laughed and scratched behind his ears.

"You have a dog?"

A warm smile pulled at my lips, and I folded my arms, watching them. "You sound surprised."

"I guess I am. You didn't seem the dog type. How come I've never seen you walk him?" She cooed at Levin, scrunching his face within her hands. He repeatedly lifted his paw to her knee every time she dared to stop.

"I don't tend to walk him at four o'clock in the morning usually." Canting my head to the side, I marveled at Levin's behavior. He never acted like that around anyone else but me. "He…likes you."

"Now *you* sound surprised." She cut her gaze to me as she sucked her lips into her mouth to avoid Levin's slobber getting on them as he licked under her chin.

Scratching the back of my head, annoyed at the continuing confusion plaguing my every damn thought as of late, I said, "I suppose I shouldn't be. I just don't normally like too many people touching him on account of his past, but with you—" I trailed off and shook my head, returning to the scotch.

She stood and moved in front of me with the bar top between us. "I, what? Finish your sentence."

"It's nothing, Keira." After pouring her scotch, I slid it across the bar to her.

"Every. Damn. Question." The corner of one of her thin brows quirked.

I ran my teeth over my bottom lip, eyeing the way her chest swelled whenever she challenged me. She pushed past my lightning in that alleyway, despite the fear of death prickling her skin, despite the fear that I was about to kill that man—and I would have. She stopped me. It was enough to make me want to bend her over a barstool and fuck her brains out, but—a promise is a promise.

"I don't mind seeing him with you. In fact, I enjoy watching you with him." I

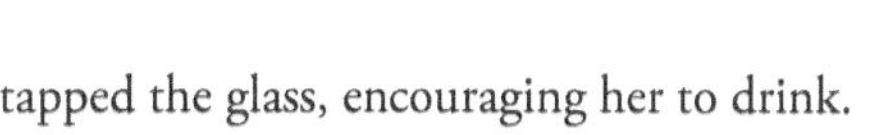

tapped the glass, encouraging her to drink.

She took a sip, not moving her gaze from my face. "You're a peculiar man."

"That's because I'm not one, my dear."

We both drank, taking each other in, undressing one another with our eyes alone.

Levin rested his head on her lap, giving her his best puppy dog stare, begging for attention. She obliged him and scratched his head with a small smile.

"You have questions, Keira." My shoulders tensed, mentally preparing for what I knew she would ask.

She took a deep breath and curled both hands around her glass. "The women."

Here we fucking go.

It took every bit of strength in me not to roll my eyes. She couldn't know the truth. How could she? Cool it.

"What about them?" I downed the rest of my drink and poured another, highly considering switching to ambrosia wine to obtain an actual buzz.

"I read some pretty crazy shit, Zane. Animals? A fucking cloud?"

I ground my teeth together and leaned on the bar top to bring our faces closer. She didn't back away. "Alright, look. Let me make something perfectly clear. The myths were written by a bunch of horny old men who lived vicariously through the stories they created."

"Uh-huh. So, you didn't sleep with a bunch of women?" She raised a thin brow before finishing her drink.

"I never said that. I love women. I love sex. But I never had to turn myself into something other than what I am to seduce them. Give me a little credit here." I poured her another double, and she immediately scooped it into her hand. "And before you ask…I don't force myself on *anyone*. Besides the fact I find it wrong, it's far sexier when they want it—ask for it."

"Alright. So, a lot of it was made up. But why? What good did that do for them?" She shrugged, her bright blue eyes searching my face.

"A lot more than you think. It gave them excuses for their misdeeds, their taboos. It gave rhyme and reason for everything." Holding back a grimace, I rubbed my beard. "If the King of the Gods did it himself, surely it's okay. Right?"

"Shit. I never even thought about it that way." Her gaze bored into me.

I hadn't seen that look in a very long time—understanding. It damn near made

my chest tighten.

"Most don't. You see, as more and more towns throughout Greece began to worship me, they molded me into the version of myself that best suited their needs."

She scooted forward on her stool, bringing our hands a breath apart. "And you just let them?"

"Of course, I did. And still do." I chuckled, closing the distance between our skin, brushing our knuckles. She didn't budge. "What am I supposed to do? Smite them?"

"No, but it doesn't bother you? The way people think about you if it's not accurate?" She canted her head to the side, a slight frown pulling at her lips.

"You have to understand something about a divine leader, Keira. It's not my job to be liked. It's to give the people what they need to thrive—to survive. And if putting me in a certain light is what does it? So be it." I clenched my jaw as I traced my pinky finger over her skin.

She gulped, her gaze falling to our hands touching. "But you still cheated on your wife countless times."

Fuck me sideways.

"In the eyes of the sanctity of marriage, yes. But with our agreement we made? No."

Look at me, Keira. Please look at me.

Her eyes lifted, and she blinked. "Agreement?"

"Hera and I were an arranged marriage of convenience. For politics' sake. We tried to make it work. We really did. Had Ares together. But at the end of the day, it just didn't work out between us." I leaned back and took a large gulp of my drink. "We decided to stay together and perform our duties, but anything outside of that? We'd seek elsewhere. She too had lovers."

Keira's head snapped back. "And that didn't bother you? Your wife sleeping with other people?"

I traced my fingers over the hair above my upper lip, mulling it over. "No. It didn't."

"But the possibility of anyone in your apartment building seeing me naked when you didn't even know if they had…that bothered you?" She narrowed her eyes at me, rechallenging me with a heated stare.

The sight of her naked ass from her apartment window sparked in my mind, the thought of another man, any of my neighbors seeing it, infuriating me. "Yes," I answered simply.

"You sound like a werewolf with its mate in a paranormal romance novel right now. You know that, right?" A fluttery laugh bubbled from her chest.

I didn't smile. It jarred me how spot on the nose the statement was.

"Zane. What?" Her grin faded, and she flattened her palms on the bar.

Not like this. I did not want to tell her like this.

"Nothing, Keira. Ask another question. I know you have to have more."

She stood on the rung of her stool, gaining height on me. "I do. What the hell was that look on your face after I made the werewolf comment?"

She had one thing right. I *did* like her stubbornness. And it was so ass-backward.

Glaring up at her, I leaned forward, my chin in line with her collarbone. "I don't want to tell you like this. Not right now. I don't want it influencing your decision one way or the other."

"Tough. Shit. Tell me." She dug her nails into the marble, her neck turning pink.

"We have what's called a fated bond."

Her entire demeanor changed, the expression on her face resembling someone who'd been punched in the gut. She slowly lowered herself back to sitting, silent and staring behind me.

"It's rare amongst our kind, but I confirmed it. I didn't fucking believe it myself at first." I pressed my palms to the bar's edge, turning my gaze away from her.

"What does it mean?" She whispered in a voice that sounded like a little girl.

Sucking air through my nose, I played with my lightning bolt cufflink. "It means—our destinies are intertwined. No matter if we part ways and never see each other again, they always will be."

The thought pained me more than I was ready to admit. I sucked on my teeth to keep my expression neutral.

"So—" She slouched as she looked at her palms, studying the lines in her skin as if they held the answers. "I don't have a choice. It *has* to be you."

"No, Keira. You do have a choice." I hunched forward, dipping my face to look at her, to urge her to look at me. "I told you I won't force anyone into doing anything. Coerce. Meddle. Perhaps. But at the end of the day, it boils down to *them*."

Her eyes finally lifted back to mine, exhaustion settling into them. "Is there a grain of truth to anything I read? Are you as ruthless as some of the myths describe?"

Rubbing the back of my neck, I came around from the bar, sat next to her, and turned her to face me. She didn't fight me on it.

I'd trade places with Prometheus if it meant I could avoid having this conversation, but—she deserved the truth.

"There is some truth to it. Yes, Keira." Resting one elbow on the bar top, I leaned the other on my thigh, dangling my scotch glass with two fingers.

She folded her hands in her lap, piercing me again with her gaze, carving me a new asshole. "Then speak some truths."

"Before I do, tell me—are you the same woman you were at age ten? Seventeen? Twenty-five?"

"Of course not."

"Keep that in mind with what I'm about to tell you, and remember that I am *thousands* of years old." I guzzled some of my scotch, focusing on her throat bobbing when I mentioned my age.

"I keep forgetting somehow, despite you sitting right in front of me." She forced a small laugh.

With one swift thought, I pulsed my power over my arms, lightning swirling and crackling. "Does that help?"

Her fingers wiggled on the bar as if she wanted to touch the electricity again, and she nodded.

"When I initially became king, I was hungry for power. I couldn't get enough of it. I was young. Naïve. And well, pig-headed."

Half of her lips grinned. "You? Never."

I squeezed her knee with a smirk, retreating my hand back to the bar.

Her eyes snapped to the spot on her skin I'd touched before lazily rising back to my face.

"I *did* rescue my brothers from our beloved dad's stomach, trapped the Titans, bestowed my brothers their kingdoms, and took the Olympus throne for myself. I'd earned it." I shrugged, still believing I was the best of us for the job to this day.

She dragged a finger over the exposed flesh on her chest, listening to me intently.

"Did I order some ruthless punishments? Yes. Did they all deserve it? Some of

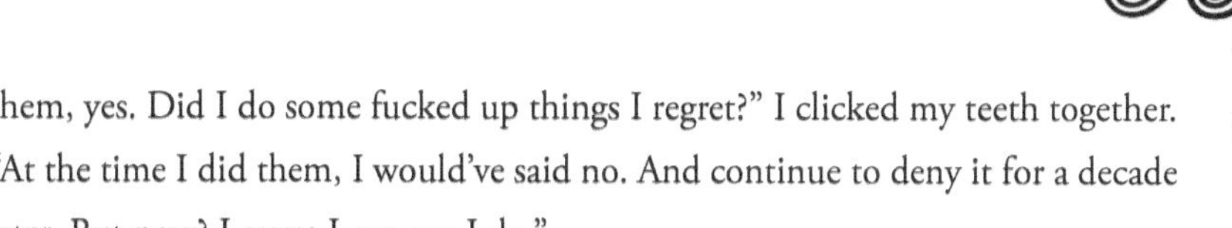

them, yes. Did I do some fucked up things I regret?" I clicked my teeth together. "At the time I did them, I would've said no. And continue to deny it for a decade later. But now? I guess I can say I do."

"And is that what you most regret?"

The question jarred me, making the back of my head throb. Rubbing my skull, I tapped my finger on the glass. "No."

"Then what do you regret most, King of the Gods?" She slid forward on her stool, resting a hand on my knee and staring at me with those sky-blue eyes I wanted looking at me while taking her from every angle and on every surface of this apartment.

"Ares," I said gruffly.

She leaned back. "Having him?"

"Olympus, no. He's the only legitimate child I have." I drained my scotch and tossed it to the bar with a sigh. "I regret being so harsh with him. He needed it, and it shaped him the way he was meant to be, but I ruined any possibility of ever having a relationship with him."

"Are you joking?" Keira snickered, slipping her hand to my thigh.

I frowned. "No. You asked me the question, and I gave you a damn answer. And now you're mocking me?"

"I'm not mocking you. You just make it sound like all hope is lost. It's called an apology."

I shook my head and turned my gaze to the eagle statue above my bed. "No. I can't do that."

"It's easy." She grabbed my chin and turned my face to look at her. "Ares, I'm sorry. See how easy that was?"

Gently taking her hand, I moved it back to my knee. "It's not that simple, Keira. You don't understand what position a role like mine puts me in."

"Fine. Explain it to me. You're asking me to put everything aside to be Queen, and now you make it sound like a burden."

It partially was. It really was.

I placed a hand on each of her shoulders and pushed down with enough pressure to make it uncomfortable but not hurt her. "Imagine this is a portion of the universe resting on your shoulders. It never lessens, never disappears, and if anything, backing down for a moment could make it even heavier."

Keira winced and rolled her shoulders after I removed my grip. "Don't you ever take breaks?"

"Do you?"

She slipped her hands under her ass. "I mean, I—"

"You don't. Because you want to be the best, as do I—the best leader I can be. This means there is no backing down, no breaks, constantly on at a hundred plus at all times. Such are the sacrifices we make, right?" I tightened my jaw, clenching my hand into a fist on the bar.

"You're right, but there are too many times to count I've done this and it makes me the opposite of what I seek to be." Her eyes grew heavy.

Olympus. We were so much alike.

"You have a hard time sleeping, don't you?" I pressed a knuckle under her chin, lifting it.

She nodded. "Half the time, I feel guilty when I'm sleeping. Isn't that the craziest thing you've ever heard?"

Not in the slightest.

"What my people don't see, Keira, is that I'm exhausted. My tank has been running on vapors for quite some time, but not only can't I afford to rest, I also can't let them see me tired." My entire body tensed. I'd never told a soul what I just told this woman. Not a soul.

Her eyes lifted to mine and she slid from her stool, slipping between my legs and taking my face in her hands. With a tenderness only a woman could give, she kissed me—sweet and light.

After she pulled away, I rested my hands on her hips. "I reveal a weakness, and you kiss me?"

"It's precisely why I kissed you—" She brushed her lips against mine again. "—Zeus."

It was only the second damn time she said my real name, and just as the first, the sound of it made my dick hard.

I rubbed the back of my neck. "There's also—Eris."

"Eris?" She canted her head to the side and touched my forearm.

Dropping my gaze to the floorboards, I sighed. "Goddess of discord. My daughter I created in the hopes of balancing chaos. I should've learned with Athena. I'd created her with the intention of balancing war, to balance Ares, but

all those two did was argue."

Her grip tightened on my arm, but she remained silent.

"At least Athena turned out to be a righteous war goddess. Instead of balancing chaos, Eris *caused* it." I beat my fist against my knee.

"Couldn't you, I don't know how it works, but simply tell her *not* to do it?"

Tracing a finger between her knuckles, I let out a roiling sigh. "I can't stop a god from performing their purpose. There was no way to predict that's what hers would've become." I lifted my gaze to Keira's. "Evil exists in the universe to shed light on the good. I only regret that I lent a small piece to it."

Keira frowned and wrapped her arms around me. She rested her head on my shoulder and hugged me tight.

An embrace from a woman that had nothing to do with sex. I never knew how much I wanted it—needed it. Until Keira gave it to me.

Zeus. King of the Gods liked *hugs* now. Fucking Olympus.

"Wait." She slapped a hand over her forehead as she pushed back. "If Greek mythology is real, does that mean Celtic is? Egyptian?" She gasped, and her eyes widened as she dropped her hands at her sides. "Holy shit. Is *Thor* real?"

If I could get through one more lifetime without hearing that asshole's name once, I'd be a delighted god-king.

"Fuck Thor. He can do his little lightning tricks, but at the end of the day, *I'm* the one with the true power." I pointed at myself and stood.

She blinked, and her lips slowly parted. "So, it *is* all real." Her eyes panned to the floor as she went silent before snapping her gaze back to me and crossing her arms. "You sound jealous."

"Of Thunder Nuts? Please." I bent forward, lowering my face to hers and brushing our lips. "I'll gladly compare *bolts* with him any day of the week. You can even set up the meeting."

Keira gulped as she trailed my tie through her petite fingers and stared up at me. "The uh—trial is in two hours. I should go home and try to get *some* sleep."

Clearing my throat, I squeezed her hip. "You're right. I need you to be in top form. Give me a challenge tomorrow." Winking at her, I took a step back.

"Oh, don't you worry, Vronti. I've won plenty of cases on zero sleep, let alone an hour." She winked back.

Walking her to the door, my hand on the small of her back, Levin trotted

behind us, waiting for his goodbye pettings.

Keira chuckled and scratched behind Levin's ears, his chest, and under his chin. "Thank you for being honest with me."

"You're welcome." I opened the door and stared down at her.

Every fiber in my being told me to pull her toward me, kiss her, and slam the door shut as we tore each other's clothes off during our trek to the bed. But no. She would be the one to make this happen. And when it did…

She bit her lip, baiting me, enticing me. "See you tomorrow." With one last smile and a pat to Levin's head, she whisked out the door.

After she was down the hallway, I let the door shut and pressed my forehead against it with a deep sigh.

Two more days, and I could very well be crownless.

SIXTEEN

KEIRA

I SAT OUTSIDE THE courtroom, my legs crossed, the nylons brushing against each other causing static. My mind should've been focused on nothing else but the trial ahead. The trial I was only minutes away from walking into and fighting against Zeus, the King of the fucking Gods. And he is precisely who I couldn't get out of my head long enough to concentrate on my standing arguments. The conversation we had earlier this morning. The conviction in his voice with each passing word. His confession to me. Me. I'd gotten the sinking feeling he hadn't told anyone else before either, so why me?

"You ready for this, bulldog?" Olivia asked, looming over me with several folders cradled in her arm.

Gulping, I rose and smoothed out my suit jacket, tugging the hem of it. "Always."

Zeus was already there when we entered the courtroom, sitting at the table with Daniels at his side. He leaned over, whispering something to her, and she remained stone cold and expressionless as usual. We reached our table, and Zeus slowly turned his head to catch my gaze over his shoulder.

When our eyes locked, a twinge rocketed through my stomach. After the trial—I was going to fuck him. I knew it from the moment I'd left his apartment this morning when I wanted to do it right then and there. If it weren't for this trial today…I probably would have. Even with dozens of people surrounding us in the busy courtroom—media, audience, the jury, security guards. His lust, his power, his growing need, stood out, settling over my skin like warm silken drops.

Those deep blue eyes gave a subtle squint. He knew it too. Tonight would be the night I fucked a Greek god. The thought should've terrified me—or at the very least bubbled my nerves, but instead, I felt determined and antsy.

The trial started, and we each did the usual song and dance—bringing in witnesses, questioning them. Presenting evidence, correlating it to the case whether it proved her guilt or innocence. We'd locked gazes several times and sent so many secret signals to each other, I'd already gotten wet.

It was when I pulled my wildcard, signaling to the custodian to bring in the large blue barrel into the courtroom, that I'd gotten the stare from Zeus I'd been craving all day. As the custodian wheeled the barrel down the middle aisle on a dolly, Zeus slowly turned his head toward me, the lust and admiration pulsing from him so profusely it almost knocked me out of my chair. The custodian displayed the barrel—a replica to what Daniels used when filling it with both acid and her husband—in the corner I'd instructed him to in clear view of the jury. It would serve as a constant reminder every remaining day of the trial of the gruesome act this woman carried out.

A small smile tugged at Zeus's lips, one he only let me see before hiding it with his hand, his other hand drumming fingers on the table. Daniels whispered something to him, and he shook his head, flicking his wrist at the barrel and cutting his gaze to me sidelong as he spoke to her.

The trial went on for another three hours, and by that point, I was ready to tear the clothes from Zeus's body and throw him to the hallway floor as soon as we exited the goddamned courtroom.

No sooner had the judge thrown the gavel down, dismissing everyone, I stood. "I'm out of here, Ollie. See you tomorrow?"

"You—" Olivia looked around her, palming the table, the folders, her chest. "Already? Where the hell are you going?"

"I uh—out. On a date." Wincing, I shoved the paperwork in my briefcase, and stole several glances at Zeus, who looked just as hurried, waiting for them to retrieve his client and cart her back to her holding hole.

"A date? Seriously?" Olivia tugged my jacket sleeve. "With who?"

I wanted to tell her. I did. But we were in a courtroom with dozens of ears. Any one of them catching the mention of Zane from my lips could turn the situation sour. "I promise I'll fill you in tomorrow, okay?" After squeezing her hand, leaving

her standing there slack-jawed, I made a beeline for the aisle.

Once in the foyer, I rounded a vacant corner, holding my briefcase by its handle with two hands. The crowd filed out, soon fading into only several stragglers.

"Call me crazy, but I have the feeling you need something from me again." Zeus's voice sent tremors of warmth and ecstasy vibrating through my chest and down to my toes.

Closing my eyes, I took a deep inhale, dizzying myself with his masculine scent. His body hovered behind me, his crotch inches from my ass.

"What do you *need*, Miss Bazin?" He whispered.

I whirled around, my heart racing, pounding, punching at my chest. "Take us somewhere. Anywhere but here."

A knowing, wicked grin curled over his lips, and he pulled me to him, into the shadows and away from prying eyes. We appeared a blink later in his penthouse apartment—his lair, as he called it. I splayed my hand, dropping my briefcase without caring where it landed. We stared at each other before letting our eyes wander over one another's lips, our chests…

His mouth crashed against mine, and he pushed me against the nearest wall, his hands slamming on each side of my head. I bunched my hands on the lapels of his jacket, yanking it off his shoulders.

He pulled away, dragging his thumb over my bottom lip, waiting for me to open my eyes. "You didn't answer my question."

"What?" The question pushed from my throat like a moaning whisper.

He pressed his cock still hidden within his pants against my stomach. "What. Do you. Want, Vasílissa?"

He wanted me to ask for it. To crave it. And he wanted to hear me say it.

"I want you to fuck me." With a firm grip, I took his face in one hand. "Zeus."

Lightning flashed in his eyes, and he snarled, kissing me again, hoisting me up with the wall as leverage behind me. I wrapped my arms around his shoulders, my back arching as he shoved the pencil skirt up my legs, bunching it at my hips.

His fingers brushed the nylons between my legs and panties, and he paused, his gaze lingering downward. "I don't recall a shield before?" He turned his head to one side.

"I only wear them for trials," I said, breathy. "Get rid of them."

He met my gaze and, with a harsh tug, ripped a hole. He could've used his

powers, I was sure of it, but instead, he chose the feral route.

I gasped and grinned at him, my hands greedily fishing for his belt and zipper, undoing them until his pants fell to his ankles. After tugging his black boxers, they too fell to the ground, and the thick, long cock I'd spied that night made another appearance. Binoculars could do it no justice in the slightest.

I felt my panties disappear, and before I could even process another thought, he plunged into me—filling me, shoving me hard against the wall. Stifling a scream, I dug my nails into his shoulders, every muscle in my body tightening.

"Remember, the walls are soundproof." He sucked on my earlobe, biting it. "Absolute. Freedom."

As he pumped inside of me, swelling with each stroke, I cried out loud. "Holy fuck."

We were both still in our lawyer attire save for the lower half, not bothering with the pesky tasks of removing all clothes before having each other. It made it all the more erotic, and with my legs wrapped around his waist, I dug one of my spiked heels into his ass cheek.

He growled and kept one hand on my ass, holding me, while the other hand bunched in my hair, yanking my head back. He kissed me as he fucked me—deep and rough, his beard scraping my chin, reddening it.

"How long have you wanted to do this, Keira?" He rolled his hips, shoving into me with such rhythmic timing it had my eyes rolling back in my head. "And don't you dare fucking lie to me."

I gulped, gyrating my hips in time with his now, meeting him stroke for stroke. Locking his gaze, I bit my lower lip. "Since the moment I heard that deep voice on the other side of the door. Before I ever even saw your sexy as hell face."

His nostrils flared, and his eyes glowed bright white. "Fuck," he breathed out before covering my mouth with his, his fist punching against the wall near my head.

He brushed the spot inside me with every thrust and pump, the swirls and familiar tightening in my stomach soaring. Gripping his hair, whimpering into his mouth, he pulled away, letting me scream through my release, shuddering around him.

When I opened my eyes, we took each other in, both panting, and he slowly lowered me to the ground. He waved his hand in front of him with a wry grin,

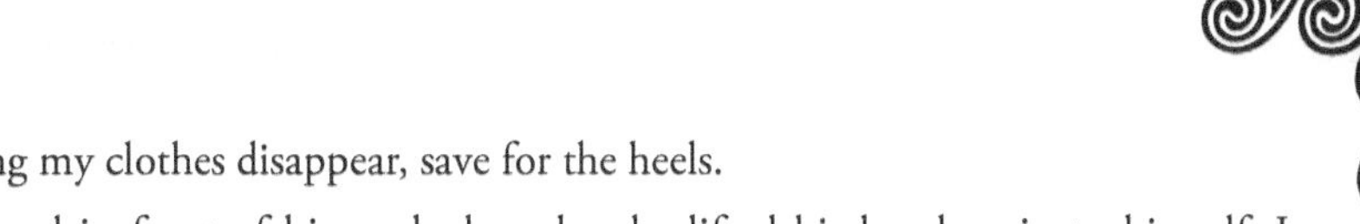

making my clothes disappear, save for the heels.

I stood in front of him naked, and as he lifted his hand again to himself, I snatched his wrist. "Wait. Not this." Loosening his tie, I slipped it over his head.

He raised a brow, that wry grin sliding into a villainous one. Once the tie was safely in my hands, he stood nude, tanned, and muscular in front of me. Fucking immaculate. The mere sight of him made me soaking wet all over again. Letting my bottom lip roll past my teeth, I guided his arms behind him, testing to see if he'd let me. I knew at any moment he could overpower me if he desired. Obliging, he didn't fight against me, that same smile plastered on his lips.

Holding his gaze with mine, I slid the tie over his wrists, pulling it tight. I kept the tie in my hand, forbidding him from touching me as I sank to my knees. Not taking my eyes away from him, I licked the tip of his cock, teasing it with short wet flicks of my tongue. It pulsed from my touch, and Zeus's head fell back with a moan before returning to watch me. Licking my lips, I slid my mouth over him, inch by inch, taking him all in until I could feel it hitting the back of my throat.

He groaned, his arms twitching within the confines of the tie. I held it tighter, pulling his arms against the back of his legs. Working in tandem with my hand, I stroked, sucked, licked, my stomach fluttering from the groans, moans, and growls pouring from the god-king's throat.

He blew out a breath. "Come here, Keira."

Dabbing the corners of my mouth with my thumb, I rose, letting go of the tie with a grin.

He snapped the tie away and, with a carnal gaze, lifted me into his arms. "Let me remind you who you're fucking."

My heart raced at his words as he crossed the room to his bed, the eagle statue above it bearing the same feral look in its eyes as Zeus. He tossed me to the bed, and I landed on my back, propping myself on both elbows. Tracing his fingers down my calf, he kept his gaze locked with mine as he removed my heels, tossing them aside.

"Don't want me digging my heels into your ass anymore?" I raised a wicked brow.

He leaned over me, grinning and trailing his touch over my knees, stopping at my thighs. "If you want to show appreciation for what I'm about to do to you, Keira—use your claws."

My throat became sandpaper as I gazed up at him, the sound of my beating heart pounding in my chest rivaling a bass drum.

He clenched his fists, and lightning began to crackle and swirl his arms, curling over his chest, his neck, and sparking in his eyes. "Lie back," he ordered.

I did as commanded, resting my hands on my stomach. He moved near me beside the bed and took hold of my wrists, forcing them at my sides. He hovered his hand over my chest, and the lightning brightened until a small current struck from his palm, settling into my skin. It didn't hurt, didn't shock me—it was a feeling of warmth and shivers and a passing caress. His hand traveled over my ribs, making my back arch from the bed. The sensations continued to entice my body as he moved over my stomach and settled at my pussy, sending tiny warm strikes one after the other, making me convulse.

I pinned my knees together to keep them from shaking. He walked to the foot of the bed, still holding his lightning power on me before he paused long enough to slide his hands to the insides of my thighs and yanked my legs apart. My breaths quickened, diving into a sensual frenzy of panting as he lowered his face to my folds, the glow of his eyes staring back at me. The lightning coursed over his lips as he lapped his tongue over me, sparking against my clit. As he worked his tongue, darting in and out of me, licking, and surging the lightning power through every nerve with expert intricacy, I gripped the sheets.

"Oh my—" I started before crying out in pure fucking ecstasy, my entire body becoming one tense muscle.

He stood, a confident grin playing over his mouth as he dragged a hand across his lips. The lightning didn't fade away as he crawled onto the bed—want playing in his gaze as he neared me—the wolf coming to claim, to possess. I lay with my legs still sprawled, my chest pumping, the swirling euphoria from coming only moments ago still swelling. He curled his hands on my hips and, in one swift motion, flipped me to my stomach and hoisted my ass into the air. I bent forward, pressing my forearms into the bed, waiting, anticipating, craving it.

Kneading my ass with his palms, he plunged into me from behind. I clenched around his cock as he thrusted, making him grunt with every other stroke. He slapped my ass first with one hand then both, leaving behind a pleasuring sting. I rocked my hips back every time he pushed forward, our bodies making the satisfying *clap* every time they met with each hard motion we made together.

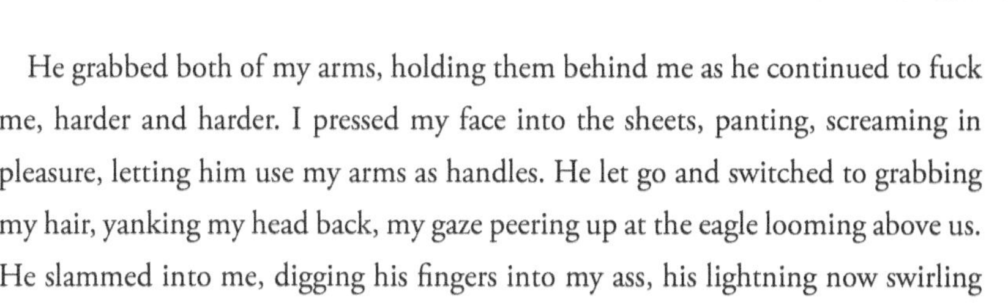

He grabbed both of my arms, holding them behind me as he continued to fuck me, harder and harder. I pressed my face into the sheets, panting, screaming in pleasure, letting him use my arms as handles. He let go and switched to grabbing my hair, yanking my head back, my gaze peering up at the eagle looming above us. He slammed into me, digging his fingers into my ass, his lightning now swirling over *my* body. It sizzled and hissed, circling my arms and legs, skirting over my chest. A sort of tingle prickled the back of my neck before whizzing down my spine, and heat flushed in my chest, making me gasp.

Zeus paused behind me, panting. He let go of my hair and pulled me up by the crooks of my elbows, rocking in and out of me, slower this time, deliberate. "Did you feel that?"

"Yes," I whispered, moaning. "What was it?"

He traced a hand over my stomach, trailing down to my clit and circling it with a finger. "The bond." He massaged one breast, pinching my nipple between two fingers. "We're officially connected for as long as we both live, Keira." His hand moved over my collarbone, lightly wrapping around my neck for a moment before cupping my chin, turning my face to look up at him. "Even if you don't choose me, I'll always be a part of you. When you make yourself come at night, it'll be *me* who invades your every thought."

My body ached for him, even with him already inside me. With a whimper, I grabbed the back of his head, pulling his mouth down to mine, kissing him, raking my nails over his skull. With his fingers between my legs and his languid thrusts pulsing in and out of me, I came undone for the third time that night, moaning and groaning into his mouth.

He pulled out of me and guided me to lay on my back, his body crawling over me as soon as my head hit the pillows. Grabbing both of my wrists in one hand, he shoved them above my head, pressing some of his weight to hold them there. The lightning fizzled away, his blue eyes returning as he took all of me in—lingering over my breasts and stomach before returning to my face.

"Fuck. You'd make such a Queen." He kept my gaze as the tip of his cock teased my entrance, rubbing against it.

"Shut up, Zeus," I said, breathy and lustful.

He glared at me, his hand gripping my wrists tighter.

"Tonight, you fuck me. Keep showing me what I'd be missing." I bucked my

hips, forcing part of him inside me. "Tomorrow, we can talk."

He grinned, a deep chuckle resonating from his chest before he thrust forward, filling me to the hilt. As he pumped in and out, rolling his hips, the motion turned from feral overtaking to—something else. He let go of my arms, fingers tracing the side of my breast, my ribs, and to my hip. I stared up at him, trailing my hands over his back muscles, before finding my way to the muscular ass I'd been drooling over, digging my nails into it.

His blue eyes became two rushing currents, pulling me through the rapids with nothing to grip. And I welcomed the chaos, opened my heart and soul to it. Another tingle, but more intense than the last, jabbed at the base of my neck, trickling down each vertebra until it reached my tailbone, sizzling. I arched from the bed, burying Zeus's head into my breasts, encouraging him to lick them. His tongue lapped over one nipple and bit it, the cool air in the room making it harden.

Pinching my knees at his sides, I shivered, quaked, and screamed so loud it hurt my ears as the euphoria erupted in my core. He trailed his nose over my chin and to my neck, taking a long-drawn breath, smelling me. His thrusts quickened, pounding into me, pushing my body toward the headboard. With a ferocious snarl, he gave one final thrust and spilled himself inside me, biting the side of my neck but not breaking the skin. He slowly pulled back, staring down at me with a wicked glint in his eye.

"What?" I smiled, my skin flushed and beading with sweat.

"You felt it a second time, didn't you?" Still inside me, his cock pulsed.

I locked my ankles together behind his back, holding him captive. "Maybe."

"You want it, Keira. You want me. You want all of it." He traced his thumb across my bottom lip.

I pressed a finger over his mouth. "I said tomorrow."

He nipped at my finger.

"You called me something earlier. Started with a 'v.'"

He stiffened. "You heard that, huh?"

Using my legs still locked around him, I pulled him closer. "What was it?"

"Vasílissa," he whispered against my cheek, the way the word rolled off his tongue making my stomach clench.

"Is that Greek?"

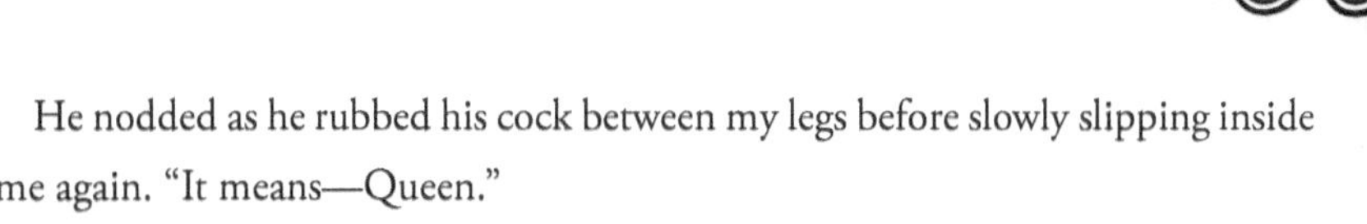

He nodded as he rubbed his cock between my legs before slowly slipping inside me again. "It means—Queen."

As I took a sharp inhale, I snapped my gaze to his, my grip tightening around his neck.

The faint sound of nails scraping against hardwood sounded from the side of the bed. A pair of big brown eyes peeked around the corner.

"I'm honestly surprised he stayed in his room," Zeus said with a smirk.

I turned my head to look at Levin. "Let him sleep with us."

"I—I mean, shit, what a cockblock you are, Levin."

Playfully swatting him in the shoulder, I trailed my fingers over his chest, and traced each abdominal muscle. "Nothing's stopping us from exploring every other room in this place when we can't sleep in the middle of the night. The kitchen. The floor. The balcony."

"Is that a promise?" His cock twitched.

I gave a soft kiss to his lips. "A promise."

He groaned, kissing me one last time before pulling out of me and slipping us both under the sheets. "Come here, Levin," he grumbled.

The dog came trotting to the bed, his large pink tongue flopped from his mouth as he jumped up. After working a corner of the bed in a circle several times, he curled up, satisfied, and closed his eyes. I nestled my ass against Zeus's hips, moaning as his large arms wrapped around me from behind.

"You're such a tease," he whispered, his breath coating my ear.

"And you love it," I whispered back, feeling his smile against my cheek.

With a fizzle of lightning striking from his palm, the lights went out. We didn't wind up fucking in the middle of the night as I promised because, for the first time since I was a kid, I slept to morning, wrapped in the god-king's embrace.

SEVENTEEN

KEIRA

I'D EXPECTED TO WAKE up to a room filled with darkness, but instead, a faint light peeked through the blinds from the rising sun. The scent of sandalwood surrounded the air around me and a strong tanned arm curled over my body, his hand cupping one breast. His beard tickled the back of my neck as his nose trailed my skin.

"Good morning," he whispered, kissing my ear.

I ran my fingers down the dark hair scattered on his muscular forearm. "Good morning. I can't remember the last time I slept like that. I don't think I woke up once."

He moaned, pulling me against him tighter. "Mm, I don't think I did either." His cock hardened as he rolled his hips against my ass.

I smiled as I bit my knuckle, recalling what happened last night with vivid, visceral detail. Closing my eyes, I lifted my leg, welcoming him. He grinned into my hair, moving one hand to my stomach while the other held up my leg from my inner thigh. The tip of him pushed at my entrance and I moaned.

A whimper sounded from the side of the bed and I flew my eyes open. Levin's head rested on the sheets, his body sitting on the floor.

Zeus sighed behind me, his forehead pressing into the back of my shoulder. "He needs to go out. I'll take him for a quick walk and be *right* back."

Biting back a smile, I scratched Levin's head, feeling the bed dip as Zeus crawled out.

"Who'd have ever thought the King of the Gods would be thwarted by a mortal

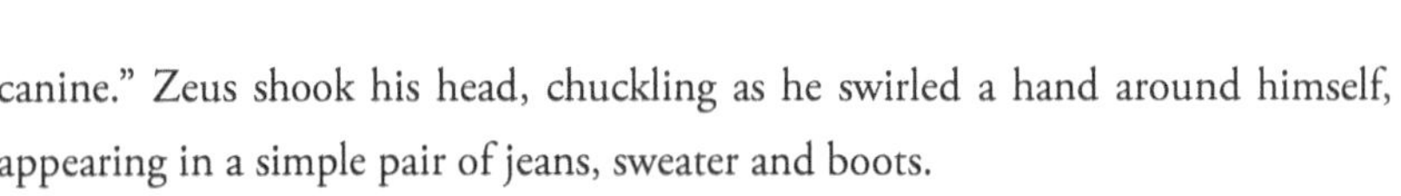

canine." Zeus shook his head, chuckling as he swirled a hand around himself, appearing in a simple pair of jeans, sweater and boots.

Biting my lip at the sight of him, I curled the sheets to my chin. He was beyond sexy in a suit, fucking sin naked, but in this get up? He looked so normal and so at ease I wanted to eat every inch of him up.

Zane grabbed a leash hanging on a peg by the door and whistled at Levin. "Come on, boy."

Levin ran so excitedly to Zeus he slipped several times on the way over.

"If I come back and you're still here plus all of my valuables, I'll take that as a sign you like me." Zane flashed a charming grin.

I guffawed, grabbed a pillow and hurled it at him, laughing.

Zeus winced and ducked out the door with a chuckle, the pillow colliding into it.

He could've created a companion for himself, I was sure of it. Some divine animal that would live forever and possibly even fly or something, but he decided to own a mortal pet. One that came with the same responsibilities as any human being—food, water, all the necessities. He *chose* to care for him. He showed me a vulnerable side to him, and I believed there was more buried deep but he feared bringing it to the surface. Yes. Feared. I refused to think even divine entities didn't fear something, didn't have weaknesses. It's what made the world turn. The balance.

I sat up, letting the sheet fall away and hanging my legs off one corner of the bed. His apartment left no clue a Greek god dwelled within. It wasn't simple by any means, but I suppose I shouldn't have thought a King would settle for any less. Every piece of furniture, every fixture, even the selections of alcohol in the bar were all top of the line. Did he fabricate the money himself? Earn it? Make it appear in his pocket whenever he needed it? So many questions and barely enough time to ask them all before the inevitable. Immigration would be knocking on my door soon, throwing my illegal alien status in my face. And the worst part of it? I didn't know when.

The door swung open and I turned my frown into a smile, sitting up straight, and pressing my palms to the bed between my legs. Levin ran past me, heading straight for his room to chew on a toy. Zeus paused at the doorway, his eyes turning carnal once he spotted me naked and waiting.

"This is certainly a sight to come home to." He chewed on his bottom lip, not tearing his gaze away from me as he hung the leash up and locked the door.

My nipples hardened as I watched him cross the room to me, pushing his sweater sleeves up, and sinking to his knees. He placed his hand on my ankle, delicately dragging his touch up my shin, circling my knee with a single finger, and tantalizing my thigh. I let my head fall back with a moan. He grabbed my left ass cheek before giving it a light slap. Grazing his lips up my ribs, he kissed, nipped, and sucked. His hand cupped one breast, massaging it as he playfully bit my ass with a growl.

As he traced his callused palms over the tops of my thighs, he gave a quick subtle lick to his lips. "Would you believe me if I told you, you are the most gorgeous woman I've ever seen?"

My heart missed a beat as I gazed down at him.

Lust. Admiration. Respect.

"Considering how old you are, I'd say it was hard to believe." But his emotions didn't lie. It had me reeling.

"Believe it." A devious grin tugged at his lips. "You're positively filthy, however. You could use a shower."

Shoving his shoulder, I laughed and pushed to my feet. "Well, I guess I'll head in there alone then if I'm so filthy."

"Oh, no." He stood and snapped his fingers, making his clothes disappear. "Who else is going to show you how to properly scrub behind your ears?"

My eyes unabashedly dropped straight to his already hard as granite cock asking for attention. I trailed my gaze over the body I wanted pressed against me now, tonight, tomorrow, possibly forever. "Lead the way."

He took my hand in his and led us down the hall to a massive marbled bathroom complete with hot tub and a shower wide enough to fit eight people. I dragged my fingers over the smooth countertops—swirls of black, grey, and white. He slid a hand to my lower back, leading me into the shower, his hand waving above us. The squared chrome showerhead sprung to life, sending a high-pressured downpour of simulated rain.

"If I would've stayed in Argentina—" He lightly shoved me against the tiled wall in the same motion as when I'd been sensually pinned to the tree. "—how do you think this moment, *right* here, would've played out?"

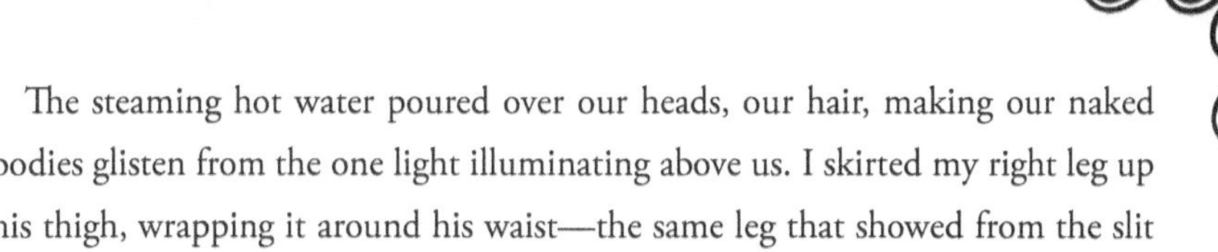

The steaming hot water poured over our heads, our hair, making our naked bodies glisten from the one light illuminating above us. I skirted my right leg up his thigh, wrapping it around his waist—the same leg that showed from the slit in my dress.

"I would've let you have me right there against that tree. Fuck everything else." Gazing up at him, I roughly tangled my fingers in his soaked hair.

Groaning, he gripped my chin, tracing his thumb over my bottom lip, catching on it. His hand slipped to my ass and unlike last night where he would've claimed me with one thrust, he pushed himself in inch-by-inch, grinning as he made me whimper. He pressed the other hand on the tiles by my head, starting slow rolls of his hips.

"And it wouldn't have bothered you if someone saw you getting railed in a public park? At a wedding reception no less?" Pumping, rolling, writhing inside me, he brushed his lips over my cheek.

"No. Just because I take what I want, doesn't make me a whore. It makes me empowered." I pressed my head against the wall behind me, groaning as he rubbed that spot inside me so feather-like it caused tremors and tiny quakes within my belly.

His thrusts grew in intensity, urgency at my words, the hand on my ass pulling me onto him further. "I'd never call you a whore. Unless of course, you wanted me to behind closed doors." He smiled against my neck, before licking and kissing it.

Dirty, filthy, talk.

"Use it," I breathed out, digging my nails into his shoulders.

As if being able to read my thoughts or sense my need, the lightning pulsed over his skin, traveling to mine, entwining us in an electric embrace. The water from the shower made it hiss and smoke, filling the shower with an ethereal lit fog. I bit my lip, waiting for the sensations to titillate my skin, my nerves, my insides. It started at my lips as he kissed me, sparking against my skin before traveling over my breasts, through my stomach and finally—a pulsing radiation intensified by his thumb circling my clit, crackling the lightning directly over it.

I cried out and not just a cry—I fucking screamed in pleasure, digging my nails into his back, scratching him. If he'd have been mortal, I would've scarred him. He growled and pumped inside me harder, firmer, sliding my body up the wall, the water splashing around us. The lightning didn't stop, still cracking and

surging around us—our union. As he pumped his final thrusts, he settled his hand around my neck. Not gripping it, simply rested it there, taking my gaze with his lightning blazed one as he came undone inside me.

We spent the next several minutes taking an actual shower, his hands still roaming my body as he sudsed me up, bathing me. When we finished, he made himself instantly dry, but I still stood on the mat, dripping wet.

"Are you not going to dry me off too?" I asked, snickering.

He canted his head to one side, taking me in with those sensual sapphires he called eyes. Producing a fluffy grey towel, he handed it to me with a grin. "I would but you look so fucking sexy right now."

Smiling, I yanked the towel from his grasp. It was perfectly warmed. Hugging it to my chest to relish in the heat wafting from it, I dragged it over my skin, drying myself as he watched me.

He folded his arms and leaned on the doorway, letting out a deep sigh. "Have you made a decision yet, Keira?"

My smiled faded and I crinkled my brow, tying the towel around me, suddenly feeling exposed. "What?"

"You know what I'm talking about. You've heard my offer. I've answered your questions. You've experienced what *else* I can offer, multiple, multiple times—" He cut his gaze to mine. It wasn't ruthless or conniving, but serious. "—it's time to cut a deal…or not."

Fury exploded in my chest and I pushed past him, back to the living room and away from the steam and heat of the bathroom. He followed behind me, directly on my heels.

"I can't believe you. You're making this sound like some sort of business transaction," I snapped, leaning on the bar top with my back to him.

He shoved his hands in his pockets, the skin between his eyes wrinkling with no hint of a smile. "It is."

Impatient. Nervous. Irritated.

Taking a quick inhale, I turned to face him, still leaning on the bar. "How could you possibly say that?"

"It's more than that, yes, but at the end of the day it's an arrangement to help us *both*." He shook his head, holding one hand at his side.

Arrangement.

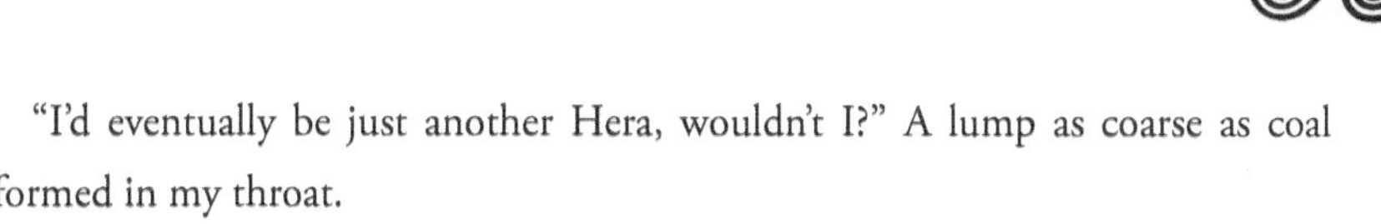

"I'd eventually be just another Hera, wouldn't I?" A lump as coarse as coal formed in my throat.

He rested his arms at his sides, and grabbed a fistful of his hair, tugging it once as he took a step forward. "No. This is different."

"Is it?" My sinuses stung. "This is arranged. We'd be jumping into it sooner than we'd have ever done in a real situation—so what's to stop this from fizzling out a year from now? Ten? A thousand?"

He furiously rubbed his chin, his eyes dropping to his feet before cutting back to me. "That won't happen. This. Is. Different."

Storming forward, I fumed up at him. "How?"

His mouth opened and closed several times, but nothing came out.

Confusion. Rage. Slightly frantic.

"I—" He paused to loosen his tie, his jaw tightening. "I don't know what you expect from me. This is who I am, Keira. You either take it—" Sucking in a deep breath, he lifted his chin. "—or leave it."

Hurt. Anger. ...sadness.

My eyes blurred with tears as I stumbled backward. "That's it then, huh?"

With a discomfort that flowed from him like a waterfall, he rubbed the back of his neck, dragged a hand down his face and after locking eyes with me, raised his hand, fingers ready to snap.

He was going to port away. "Don't you dare, you son of a bitch." I jolted forward.

He snapped his fingers, drying me off, clothing me, and...disappearing.

Growling, I circled the room as if he were still here. "You fucking coward," I screamed into the void, panting and on the verge of sobbing.

I dropped to the floor in a slump, curling my knees against my chest, letting the tears roll down my cheeks. Levin approached with his ears drooping, tail between his legs.

Coaxing him over, I wrapped my arms around him and stroked his soft white fur. "It's okay, boy. How do you deal with him every day, hm?" I smirked. "That part's obvious I suppose. Non-verbal communication is the key to your relationship with him, huh?"

Whereas with us? Talking was the *only* solution.

And like that, it was crystal clear to me. I couldn't do this. Who in their right mind would agree to this? The possibility of leading a lonely, loveless marriage

was too great to risk—right? But he kept repeating it was different for us. All I want him to do is tell me why.

Why?

Having no idea when or if Zeus would come back, I had to head to work, but couldn't in good conscience leave Levin in the apartment without food. After rummaging through the kitchen cabinets and drawers, I couldn't find any dog food nor even any real food in the fridge. What was I expecting? He was Zeus. He could create anything his heart or canine desired in a blink of an eye.

I ran to the convenience store down the street, bought some kibble, and gave Levin a heaping bowl of it. My hand was on the door knob, ready to leave, when I realized—the door would be unlocked. Anyone could waltz in and rob him blind, or worse yet…steal Levin. Frowning and against every cardinal rule I imposed on myself, I moved into Zane's bedroom to search for a spare key.

Hovering my hand over the first drawer in his armoire, I held my breath. Would it be so much to ask I'd only find socks, boxers, and condoms? Maybe a bottle of lube or two? Hell, I'd even be okay with butt plugs, but what exactly did the King of the Gods store in his drawers?

Biting the bullet, I yanked the drawer open.

Nothing.

Not even a lining of any kind, just bare wood with nothing inside it.

The rest of the drawers were the same. And so was the nightstand.

The entrance to his walk-in closet stared back at me like a luring web of darkness. Gulping, I flipped the light switch, revealing immaculately organized rows of suits, shoes, watches, and cufflinks. I traced my fingers over the suit jackets, sighing at the feel of the fabric against my skin. Designer brands always had the softest materials but I could never afford them, having to settle for the scratchy imitation varieties.

Licking my lips, I reached to the shelf above the clothes, feeling around for a key. My fingers brushed something rounded and rough, and I grabbed it. It was a large black rock with letters carved on the back. The symbols resembled the letters a, p, n, and c. There was only one god whose name started with an A and had four letters I could recall.

"Ares," I whispered, running my finger over the haphazard carving that resembled a child's handiwork.

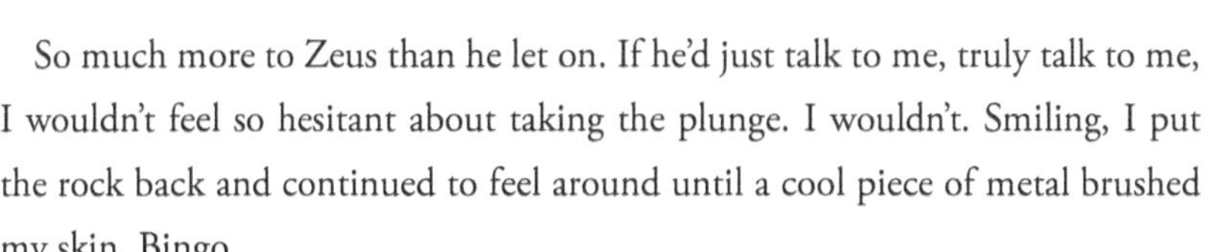

So much more to Zeus than he let on. If he'd just talk to me, truly talk to me, I wouldn't feel so hesitant about taking the plunge. I wouldn't. Smiling, I put the rock back and continued to feel around until a cool piece of metal brushed my skin. Bingo.

With key in hand, I turned off the light, gave Levin a quick kiss to his head, and whisked out the door to distract myself with piles of paperwork.

I'd been sifting through case files for the Daniels case when a light knock sounded at my office door.

"Come in," I said flatly, squinting at a storage facility invoice.

"Are you still not talking to me? Because I'm not sure how much longer I can take this torture," Olivia said, grinning at me from the crack of the door.

Sighing, I waved her in. "I'm sorry, Ollie."

"Uh-oh. You don't look like a woman who's been sufficiently screwed. What happened?" She shut the door behind her.

Oh, I'd been screwed, in far more ways than one.

"It was Zane. I slept with Zane and I thoroughly regret it."

Her jaw dropped and she sprinted to my desk. "There is no way in hell I believe you regret sleeping with the King of the Gods for one bloody second."

"You—" I narrowed my eyes at her, dropping the papers to my desk. "You said you didn't believe me."

She snapped her hands to her hips. "I never said that. Can you blame me for needing some time to let it process? To do—research?"

"So, you believe he's Zeus and I'm a demigod?"

She folded her hands in her lap. "Yes. Read me if you must."

I searched her face, her body language, and a small smile managed to work its way over my lips. "No need."

"Now that that's out of the way, what's really going on, Keira?" She nudged my shoulder.

Who else would I talk to about this?

"He offered to marry me to keep me from being deported and damaging the career I've built here in New York." I couldn't look at her when I said it.

"I'm sorry, hold it, hold it, hold it." She moved around the desk and leaned into my face, pressing her hands on the armrests of my chair. "He offered to make you *Queen?*"

"Yes."

She blew out a breath, laughing. "Leave it to you to not only stew this long over an amazing offer but also look depressed about it."

"Ollie, it's not that simple. He's only doing it to save his own ass in the process. Hera left him. Their marriage never ended in love. It ended with them living separate sexual lives while staying married for politics' sake." I couldn't help the worry and fear displaying on my face as my forehead cinched and my throat bobbed.

Pouting, Olivia shook her head. "I see what's going on here. You're scared the same thing will happen to you."

"Yes, but—" I stood and dragged my hands through my hair. "It's not only that. This whole thing started out of a selfish act for him to save his own goddamned ass. A lot of the myths about him may have been warped and fabricated but his arrogance and self-centeredness? That's all there."

"I don't know. He may have spun it as selfish, but if you look at it from a different perspective it's an arrangement that benefits you both. You need a husband to stay here, he needs a Queen to keep his power and title." Olivia shrugged and leaned her hip on the desk. "He could've married anyone, Keir. Hell, he could've asked *me*. But he's asking to marry *you* because I'm going to guess one: he likes you and two…it's more than marriage, it's *helping* you."

Here I was, the powerful prosecutor who could solve some of the craziest cases, and I couldn't even navigate a relationship. But Olivia? She's always been so good at thinking outside the box.

"Wait. How do you know he needs a Queen to keep his power and title? He never even told me that." I stood in front of her, folding my arms.

"I told you. I researched. Gaea made a clause when he became King. There always has to be a Queen. If there's not, he has a certain timeframe to find another. If he doesn't…he loses part of his power *and* his crown." She leaned back on her palms, crossing her legs, and bouncing one foot. "Textbook fantasy irony, really."

My heart raced. How long did he have? The Greek gods without Zeus as their King? It seemed absurd.

"Ollie, what timeframe? How long does he have?" I grabbed her shoulders.

"It didn't say. I looked. I couldn't find it. Why? Do you think it's soon?"

Numbly, I let my hands fall away, the rawness traveling to my toes. "It has to be. This morning he sounded so—urgent."

"Keira, sweetie." Olivia appeared at my side, grabbing my elbow to turn me toward her. "The fact you're concerned about this, tells you all you need to know. He's not just doing this for himself. Remember that."

And maybe he wasn't. But was it so much to want to hear *him* say that?

EIGHTEEN

ZEUS

SHE HAD ONE THING right. I was a son of a downright bitch. And not my mother—my father. Now there was a *real* dickwad. We gods aren't unlike mortals—spending the better part of our lives finding ourselves. How much of our parents will reflect in us? Can we stop it? Do we want to? About the only thing I ever wanted that Kronos possessed was his sheer fucking determination. Too bad I'd inherited more than that.

Groaning, I beat my head against the stone behind me, swigging down my third bottle of ambrosia wine. Like an absolute pussy, I'd ported away in the middle of Keira's argument. Disappeared to the one place I knew I could go to be alone and—call a meeting of The Brothers. And instead of telling them precisely where I was, I took the opportunity to get piss-assed drunk while waiting for them.

I couldn't remember the last time I'd drunk this much. It dulled your senses— made you make extraordinary decisions or horribly bad ones, hardly ever in between. The job came first. It always had.

"Tartarus. You look like shit," Hades said, appearing in front of me in a swirl of black fog. His glowing white eyes radiated from the darkness, and he wiped a hand through his fiery crown, making it fizzle away.

I sat on the ground, not caring that the moist cold from the cave soaked through the ass of my pants. Holding the bottle up to him, I belched. "And I *feel* like shit. How ironic."

"How many of those have you had, brother?" Hades swiped some of his long white hair over one pointed ear.

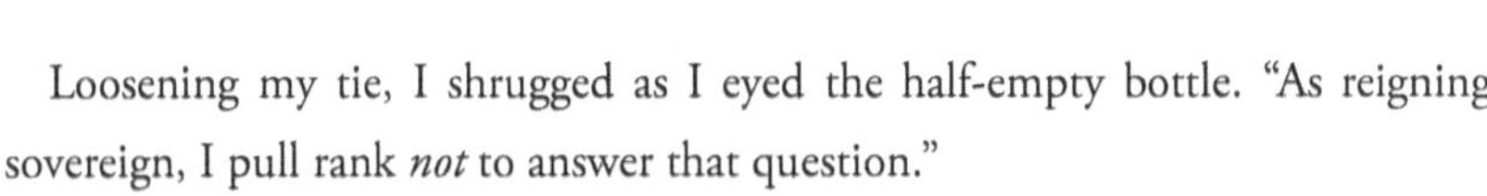

Loosening my tie, I shrugged as I eyed the half-empty bottle. "As reigning sovereign, I pull rank *not* to answer that question."

"Of course, you do." Hades all but rolled his eyes and turned his gaze to the hanging sconces harboring blue flames.

"What the shit?" Poseidon's voice boomed as he appeared in a flash of sea spray. "I thought you called us because the Titans escaped or something, but I get here to find you wallowing in a corner?"

Groaning, I pressed my skull to the cave wall again and sipped more wine, not bothering to greet the sea god.

"What's going on, Zeus? We have better things to do than to stand here and watch you look miserable." Hades folded his arms as both of my brothers loomed over me, their expressions unenthused, borderline agitated.

Closing my eyes, I pressed the bottle against my forehead with a deep sigh. In all the years I'd been my brothers' king—it took a half-mortal woman for it to come to this. "I need—" A razor tore at my throat, and I gripped the bottle tighter. "—your…help."

"What the fuck?" Poseidon blurted.

I flew my eyes open to see them both eyeing each other sidelong with raised brows. "You really don't need to make this into something more than it is."

"Like Tartarus we don't." Poseidon smirked as he leaned against a stone pillar. "Not once have we gotten to be actual big brothers to you since you took the crown. Not that you ever even wanted us to be."

Nausea coiled in my stomach. I wasn't sure what was worse—trying to sort out feelings with Keira or getting these asshats to help me with it.

"And say we find it in our good hearts to help you despite your years of mistreatment. What exactly is the problem?" Hades's brow bobbed, and his black robes shifted as he folded his arms.

"Mistreatment?" I glared at my brother before rising to my feet, the bottle still in hand. "Where do you get off saying I mistreated you? Do you have any idea what I go through on a daily basis? The decisions that fall on my shoulders and mine alone?" Scoffing, I took a sip, standing so close to the Underworld King, our toes touched.

"How could we? All we have to go from are your actions. You never *talk* about anything." Hades's eyes flashed brighter.

My lightning power coursed over my hands as I subdued a snarl, making Hades's gaze pull into a glare. Forcing it back, I pointed at him with the same hand that held the bottle. "I gave you this kingdom knowing out of all three of us, *you* had the strongest mind for it. Did you know that, *bro?*"

Hades stood firm. "How generous of you."

"Yes, you can't leave on a fucking whim, but you take the job to heart. It would've crumbled within days if either of us would've taken the helm." Nudging my head at Poseidon, I swayed on my heel, gulping more wine and enjoying the liberating feeling of not giving a shit.

"Hey, speak for yourself," Poseidon grumbled.

"Oh, can it, Flipper. You know as well as I do. Are you telling me you could imagine yourself away from the seas except for two weeks out of the year?" I stuck my chest out, challenging him.

He slow-blinked. "I hate you."

"There's the family spirit we've been missing." I threw my hands out at my sides, sending lightning crackling. "Your sacrifice never went unnoticed, Hades. I discreetly did all I could to make you happy. You wanted Persephone?" I snapped my fingers. "I made it happen. She left you, and you were prepared to spend eternity alone. But that's not *you*, brother." I poked him in the chest before lightly beating my fist against it. "You asked for opportunities to surface with your new Queen? To take breaks? I gave you that too. Something I don't even take for *myself.*"

His eyes panned to my hand before returning to my face, curiosity, and astonishment flooding his expression.

"I didn't force Stephanie into anything. I disguised what I did as meddling but what you both need to realize—" I caught Poseidon's gaze as I held up a single finger and looked between the two of them. "—none of them can see me as soft. Do you understand?"

Hades clenched his jaw. "I—appreciate you saying all of this, brother."

Nodding, I turned my attention to Poseidon. "And you, Fishsticks—" I rubbed my chin, thinking, contemplating. "—nah. You're still a prick."

Poseidon chuckled and punched me in the shoulder. "Love you too, Bolt."

"What? You fight with a giant fork. It's hard to take you seriously at times." I bit back a smile and hid my mouth with the bottle.

"Spar with me some day and I'll show you what that giant fork can do, little

bro." Poseidon shook his head with a smirk.

"You're on." Sighing, I let the bottle fall limp in my hand. "Considering word travels so swiftly through Olympus, I'm sure you both know of Hera's departure?" I finished the bottle of wine before chucking it over my shoulder, making it disappear before shattering to the ground.

"Wait. Have you not elected a new Queen yet?" Poseidon's eyes widened as he took a step forward, the three of us now standing in a triangle.

Shock morphed over Hades's features, his lips parting. "Brother, the expiration is—"

"Tomorrow. I know." I held my head low, rubbing furiously at my temples.

Poseidon gripped my shoulder. "You've fallen for someone, haven't you?"

Was that what it was? Had I somehow fallen for a woman I'd only known for a matter of weeks?

"Shit." Poseidon laughed before slapping me on the back. "Another thousand years could've passed, and I still would've never thought I'd see the day."

Exhaustion pulled at my brain like melting caramel. "Not helping."

"Cutting it kind of close, aren't you? Why not select any mortal? Why not—" Hades started, but I cut him off with a flick of my hand, silencing him.

"We're fated." Unable to meet their gazes at first, I kept mine focused on the ground.

"Olympus," Poseidon breathed out.

"It has to be her. And even if I could find some way to coerce her beyond her own thinking, I wouldn't." I lifted my eyes to my brothers. "Because I *want* her to want this. *Want* her to want me. All of it."

Poseidon gripped Hades's shoulders, and they both stared at me as if I were a younger version of myself and just told them I'd lost my virginity. Jostling my shoulders, I waited for one of them to respond. Anything would do. Even laughing in my godsdamned face would've been better than this torturous silence.

"There's something else." I cracked my knuckles. "She's a demigod."

A single brow rose on Poseidon's face.

"Who's the god?" Hades asked.

"The goddess is Oizys." I cut my gaze to the god of the Underworld.

"Oizys? I barely even see her. When would she have had time to—"

I cut him off. "It was before she secluded herself to the Underworld. Is she

accessible? I'd imagine Keira might wish to meet her at some point."

Hades rubbed his chin. "I couldn't say. She hardly has connections with people—deity or otherwise—except those souls she tortures in Tartarus."

"What a lovely woman." I quirked a brow.

Hades smirked. "Who are you telling?"

Pinching my lips, I let my gaze drop to my feet with a sigh.

"You wish to know how to win her favor," Hades whispered.

Rubbing the back of my neck, I let out a deep sigh. "I suppose that's what I'm asking, yes."

"And you're willing to potentially lose your crown if she doesn't decide in time?" Hades canted his head to the side while Poseidon shook his shoulders with a wide shit-eating grin.

It didn't register in me until Hades said the words aloud. What had this woman done to me? Was she an enchantress?

"Yes," I pushed out, my voice gravelly.

"This is serious," Hades mumbled before swirling his arm, making us all appear in his fire-lit Gothic-themed living room.

I sat alone in a black lounge chair and instantly slumped in it, resting my head on my hand as my brothers loomed over me like investigators ready to interrogate.

"Why do you like this woman?" Hades asked, clasping his hands behind his back.

I'd never had a mortal headache, but somehow, I felt this conversation was bound to give me one. "What do you mean why? She…intrigues me."

Fucking Tartarus. The same damn answer I'd given her, and it went *so* well the first time.

Poseidon made an obnoxious buzzer sound. "Wrong. Clearly, she intrigues you if you're into her; you need to answer the true 'why.'"

Sighing, I leaned forward, pressing my steepled fingers to my lips. "I don't know. She—" I gripped my hair, ruffling it before falling against the back of the seat with a snarl. "She's a damn good lawyer. Better than me if you take the fact she's doing it with a half-godly brain. She's stubborn. Quick-witted. Bold. Works herself to the bone." I paused as flashes of her mouth around my cock as she held my hands captive in my own damn tie coursed through my brain. "And fucking hot as Olympus forges."

"Have you told her any of this? Any at all?" Hades raised a brow.

Grumbling, I folded my arms. "Whatever happened to actions speak louder than words?"

"For shit's sake, Z. You think a woman doesn't want to *hear* things every once in a while?" Poseidon interlaced his fingers behind his head, shaking it.

Tension built in my shoulders. "Fine. I'll craft a speech. What else do I need to do?"

"You said she's a lawyer. Are you both working on the same case?" Hades paced in front of me, rubbing his chin.

"Opposing counsel."

Poseidon snatched a silver unlit candlestick holder from the mantle and tossed it in his palms. "Is your client guilty?"

"As sin." I ground my molars, knowing full well exactly where they were going with this.

"You say she's good. I assume she knows who and what you are now. Can't imagine she'd take it too lightly if you still used your powers of persuasion to work the trial in your favor." Hades took the candlestick from Poseidon and placed it back on the mantel.

I gripped the armrests. "Yes, but—"

"She wins the case fair and square, brother," Hades interrupted.

Growling, I replied, "Fine. What else?"

"It's going to take more than a speech. You need what's called a 'grand gesture,'" Poseidon muttered, scratching the full beard on his chin.

I furiously rubbed my face. "And just what the shit would that be?"

"That has to come entirely from you. Sweep her off her feet. And we don't mean into bed. You're a natural seducer—a charmer. Use it for something else besides sex for once. You might surprise yourself." Hades opened his palm toward the fireplace, making the flames roar.

A grand gesture. Her birthday. New York City. Huh.

"You obviously had a blowup to drive you to come down here of all places. To seek our help. What happened, Z?" Poseidon dragged a hand through his long hair, genuine concern for my well-being playing in his gaze.

It made my neck stiffen.

"She thinks she'll be another Hera. That the passion will fizzle, and we'll end up married but not together as she and I had. She also said I was treating the whole arrangement like a business transaction." I beat my knuckles against my knee, recalling the fury coiling from her—but most of all…the hurt.

"And what did you say to that?" Hades winced.

"The truth. It *is* a business transaction. Offers and reasons for both parties to form an alliance. What the fuck else was I supposed to say?" Pushing to my feet, I raked a hand through my hair and moved to the fire.

Poseidon groaned and patted my shoulders from behind before leaning on one, staring at the fire with me. "Not that, bro. Not that."

"I think…" Hades started as he moved beside us, all three of us gazing at the flickering flames like they were the sparks of life itself. "You need to realize what you want before you can recognize what *she* wants. So, Zeus, King of the Gods, our brother, what do *you* want?"

Extending my hand, I struck lightning within the fire, making a mesmerizing fire-lit show within the hearth. "A partner. A friend. Someone who's going to understand the job at times must come first. We'd fuck like damn rabbits, and maybe, just maybe, she'd occasionally let me fall asleep using her tits as a pillow while she scratches my scalp with her nails."

"Perhaps not put quite as elegantly, but something tells me, brother—" Hades squeezed my shoulder. "She seeks the same things."

Poseidon stood on one side of me, Hades on the other, and for the first time since I dragged them out of our father's stomach, I felt truly part of a brotherhood again.

"I know what I need to do," I muttered, closing my hand, dousing the lightning with it.

"I feel like hugging you right now. You know that, right?" Poseidon nudged me.

"Please don't."

"Nope. It's happening, little bro. Hades, you too, come on." Poseidon pulled us both in for a hug.

Stiffly, Hades and I landed reluctant pats on Poseidon's back.

"The first group hug in almost a thousand years. Unreal. I definitely need to meet this chick soon." Poseidon pulled away with a wide grin.

I adjusted my jacket, redoing the buttons, tightening my tie, and fixing my

ruffled hair. "With any luck, it'll happen sooner rather than later. But if not—
there's someone I need to talk to."

Bowing my head to my king brothers, I took a step back. "Brothers."

"Good luck, shithead," Poseidon scoffed before I disappeared.

My son Ares seemed to spend more time in his gym than anywhere else.
Undoubtedly, the sparring which inevitably led to other activities with his warrior
goddess played a huge part. I waited in a darkened corner near the lockers, only
emerging from the shadows when he neared.

"Ares." I lifted my chin, fully prepared for a verbal slapping.

Ares threw his gloves to the floor, his bare chest heaving as he walked up to me.
"What do you want, maláka?"

"Honestly, I thought you'd calmed down since bonding with Harmony. No?"

Harmony approached us with her arms folded, clad in only a sports bra and
skin-tight shorts. It took everything in my power not to scan her body. "He has
calmed down. Funny how any mention of you or your presence gets him riled up."

Cracking my neck, I shot my gaze to Harmony's. "You're a good woman,
Harmony. An amazing war goddess. But I need a moment alone with my son. I
can assure you it won't involve punches and clashes of lightning."

Harm stole a glance with her war god, who gave her a curt nod before slicing a
glare aimed at me. "It better not."

Such fire that one. Huh.

"What is this all about, old man? You need me to do your bidding? Came to
blow smoke up my ass again?" Ares clenched his fists at his sides.

"I always thought kicking you from Olympus was the best thing for you. The
best way for you to channel your anger and use it in other ways." I jingled the
keys in my pocket, shocked he hadn't interrupted me already or told me to go to
Tartarus. "I still believe it to be partially true but I wasn't entirely honest with you
about the *largest* reason I did it."

"This ought to be good." Ares crossed his arms after freeing his hair from the
rubber band holding it in a bun.

"I'd like to think I inherited nothing from my father, but it simply wouldn't

be true. Much like he cowardly tried to destroy his children for fear of them overtaking his throne…I did the same thing." Sneering at the ground, I clenched my jaw.

"What are you trying to say?"

Forcing myself to meet his gaze, I took a quick breath. "I kicked you from Olympus because you had and still have the power to overthrow me. But I realized recently, you would've never done it—out of respect."

Ares's nose twitched, and he scratched it with a thumb. "You're right. I wouldn't have. Not to mention I want nothing to do with fucking Olympus."

"You've become a better god than I could've ever predicted, Ares." I smirked, playing with the hair below my lip. "And Olympus is precisely what I've come to talk to you about."

"You don't sound like yourself. What the hell is going on?"

"This first bit should amuse you. Your mother left me."

Ares half-smiled, snorted and then frowned. "Wait, what? How's that possible?"

"It's not as if I held her captive, Ares. She's always had the choice, and she made it. Which has left Olympus without a Queen and with a clause to be upheld… by tomorrow." I'd never been nervous about one godsdamned thing in my divine existence but this—fuck.

"So you find another Queen. What does this have to do with me?" Ares poked himself in the chest, the armor full sleeve tattoo tightening.

"As we continue to have more things in common than I'm sure you'd like to admit, I also have what you share with Harmony." Scratching the back of my neck, I waited for my words to sink into my son's thick head.

"You—have a fated bond with someone?"

"Her name is Keira. I believe you, of all people, will understand when I say, it can't be anyone but her. If I settled for someone else, it'd be like removing two of my limbs and giving them to Keira to keep for all of eternity." My lightning crackled in my eyes, my palms. The thought alone made me want to destroy mountains.

Ares took a step closer. "I *do* understand."

"I'm going to try everything in my power to win her over, but son, if this goes south—" Taking a deep breath, I closed the distance between us and squeezed his shoulder. "Olympus is yours."

He shook his head and batted my arm away. "No. Why would she refuse you?"

The irony of that statement. Laughing, I tilted my head to the side. "Moments ago, you were ready to tear my head off with your teeth as your only blade. And now you compliment me by saying there's no way she wouldn't want me?"

"Maláka, no. I figured you'd have used your powers or—"

"They don't work on her, son. And even if they did, she's different. Would take all of the fun away." A weak smile pulled at my lips. "I need you to agree to this. I don't trust anyone else with the reins. No one. Else."

Ares growled and turned away, dragging a hand over his beard and shaking his head. Returning to stand in front of me, he held out his hand. "Alright. But you better have a hell of a plan, old man. Because—" He paused, his teeth grinding together. "I can't see anyone else ruling Olympus besides you."

If that were the one good thing my son ever said to me for the rest of eternity, I'd store it in a fucking mason jar with the date labeled on it.

"I'm going to deploy everything in my godly arsenal." We locked forearms, my white lightning sparking against his red sparks, sealing the deal. "I hope we can spend more time together."

Ares sniffed once, nodding as he backpedaled. "Yeah. We'll uh—we'll see."

Nodding, I stepped away, making myself reappear outside the courthouse, staring up at the office light I knew belonged to Keira.

Time to perform the seduction of a lifetime.

NINETEEN

KEIRA

SO. FUCKING. TIRED. DESPITE several cups of coffee and a Red Bull, sleep still pulled at my brain, and I rested my forehead on my arm in my office. A five-minute power nap wouldn't hurt anyone.

Ice clanking against a glass sounded in my ear.

"Keira," Zeus whispered, resting the glass on my desk near my head.

Groggily, I lifted my head to see the insanely gorgeous King of the Gods looming over me with a tumbler of scotch in hand that matched the one resting next to me.

"A peace offering." He lifted the glass in a cheers gesture and nudged his chin at mine.

Eyeing the alcohol, I shifted my gaze to his face, glaring at him. "I fed and took care of your dog, by the way."

He rubbed the back of his neck as he stared at his shoes. "Yeah. I uh—I appreciate that."

Embarrassed. Regretful.

With a sigh, I lifted the glass, and we clanked them together. I remained sitting, sipping on my scotch and waiting to see what wondrous words he came up with after how swimmingly our last encounter went.

"I'm a dick. I'm an asshole. I'm a bastard. Whatever name you want to call me, I'm all of them." He crouched in front of me, resting one forearm on the top of my thigh, his blue eyes pulling me to him. "I didn't expect any of this to happen. Not Hera leaving. Not running into you. And especially not…having my entire

world turned fucking upside down—by you."

Sincerity. Hope. Admiration.

My grip tightened on the glass as I pushed down the burning sensation in my sinuses.

"I've spent my entire life living a certain way, having that life ruled by Olympus, contrary to what most think is the other way around. You catapulting into that life made me realize it's possible to have both Olympus and—" He squeezed my knee. "—more."

"Is this an apology?" I squinted at him, biting back a grin.

He smirked. "Definitely not." A hint of a smile played at the corner of his lips before he patted my leg and stood. "Come with me." He held out his hand, the light from my desk lamp glinting from his silver pinky ring.

"I don't know, Zeus."

His hand lowered. "That was the first time you called me Zeus without us fucking each other or your life being threatened."

Hope. Flutters. *Actual* flutters.

As I stood, my chest tightened. I hadn't even realized I'd said it. "I—"

Shaking his head, he brushed his thumb over my lips to silence me, his palm pressing against my cheek. "You don't need to rationalize it. Just come with me. A little birdie told me it was your birthday. You shouldn't be spending it in your office."

"I've spent every birthday since living in New York in my office." I shrugged, nuzzling against his hand still stroking my face.

"That doesn't surprise me and all the more reason you should come with me." He stepped back and tugged my hand. "Now."

Smiling, I grabbed my coat. "So bossy."

"You love it." He helped me with my coat, even going so far as to do up the buttons.

I did love it. Damn it all to hell. I loved it all.

Canting my head, I saw a new side to him—as if he'd opened a hidden passage to let me in, one he hadn't even opened to himself in a long time.

He wrapped an arm around my waist and, with the blinds closed in my office, ported us to an alley near Rockefeller Center. We were blocks away from where I knew the gigantic tree and ice-skating rink were, but even from this distance, the

emotions pouring from the crowds of tourists punched at my mind.

"Keira? What's wrong?" He cupped my elbows, keeping me upright.

I hadn't even told him yet. Here I was expecting every bit of truth from him, and I'd left out that tiny detail?

"I can't handle the city right now. I just can't." I shoved my face against his shoulder, trying to drown out the overwhelming feelings of joy and whimsy—emotions that individually caused euphoria but combined in droves made for hysteria.

"Keira." He pushed me back, tilting my head up to look at him. "Talk to me."

"I'm—" Squeezing his biceps through his jacket, I gulped. "I'm an empath. I guess I got it from my mother because it's—intense. So intense all the time when I'm around a lot of people. I can sense emotions, fleeting feelings, and can even tell when someone is lying."

What started as a light chuckle transformed into a glorious masculine laugh—deep and throaty.

I wanted to laugh, but tears threatened to push their way through. "Why in the hell are you laughing?"

"It just all makes so much sense now. Who better to be at my side than someone who can always see straight through my bullshit? For fuck's sake—the Fates are such conniving, intuitive pieces of work." He chuckled a little more and pulled me to him, hugging me, his nose grazing my hair.

"And now knowing you're a Greek god, it makes sense why emotions were so intense from you." I pressed my ear to his chest, listening to his divine heartbeat thrumming like a giant's steps.

"Try something with me," he whispered, slipping off his glove and shoving it in his pocket. He lifted one of my hands, and with a seductive curve of his lip, he removed my glove finger-by-finger.

"What are you doing?"

"I have a theory because of our formed bond." He took my hand, our skin touching.

I closed my eyes, the copious amounts of emotions around me dissipating with each passing second. Joy melted into my joy—his joy. Wonder morphed into my own. Hope settled into Zeus's hope alone.

His lips pressed to my ear, the warmth from his breath making heat pool in my

stomach. "Did it work?"

"Yes," I breathed out.

"Good." He tugged my hand, causing my eyes to fly open. "We have ice skating to do."

"Ice skating? Zeus, I've never skated in my life." I laughed, scanning the busy sidewalks filled with people dressed in wintry attire with their arms loaded with shopping bags. Familiar smells of roasted nuts, baked goods, and hot dogs pervaded the air.

"I'll just get to laugh at you falling on your ass every other minute then, huh?" His face beamed at me as he flashed a grin.

I pointed at him. "You will do no such thing."

He pretended to bite my finger. "No promises. Besides, you might drag me down with you considering I can't let go." He lifted our joined hands—the only thing keeping the emotions from hundreds of people infiltrating my brain.

And he wouldn't let go. Not for anything. I knew it with every breath escaping my lungs. It made my heart swell.

Lit angel sculptures bordered the ice rink with dozens of people skating in circles—some hugged the wall, others skated like pros, and some shuffled rather than gliding. But what stood out most of all was the majestic sight of the glittering tree at the heart of Rockefeller Center, piercing the sky like a towering Titan.

My eyes blurred with tears staring up at it, the chill in the air making my cheeks numb, but I only gripped Zeus's hand tighter.

"All the time I've been here, and I've never seen this. I've been so caught up with my life and work I never stop to breathe—to enjoy the little things." I sniffled, fighting back the tears that threatened.

His thumb kneaded between my knuckles. "If anyone can relate to you, it is me on the grandest of scales, Keira."

"My mother. Is she alive?" I continued to stare up at the tree, trying to keep my voice steady when I asked.

He circled my palm with his thumb. "Yes."

"Do you—" I turned my gaze to him, taking a deep inhale before my next question. "Do you know where she is?"

"Yes." His face softened.

"Do you think she'd want to see me?" I tightened my grip on his hand, terrified

of the response.

"If you ever want to meet her, all you need to do is speak with Hades."

My shoulders tensed. "She's in the Underworld?"

"Tartarus."

An overwhelming sadness tugged at my brain. "By her choice?"

"I think, my dear, that's something you'd need to ask her." He offered a small smile as he tugged my hand.

Pursing my lips, I turned my attention back to the tree. "Tell me something. If we do this—tell me it'd be different. The job will have to come first at times, but the times that it doesn't—we make it for *us*. About us."

He pulled me tight against him, yanking off his other glove to cup my face in his hands. "Those words are the biggest part of the reason no one else can be at my side. I physically couldn't stand it."

He only had so long to get this done. What the hell was he talking about?

"What?" It came out like a squeak.

"You take as long as you need. Because I'm not asking anyone else." His jaw tightened as he stared down at me, the sparkling lights hanging from street lamps framing him, paling in comparison to his lightning.

Was he willing to let the time lapse? To give up the crown? It was so…selfless.

"And to answer your question, you'd have to be willing to share my time with the universe, but when duty doesn't call—" He dipped his lips to mine, kissing me, his tongue skirting the tip of mine before pulling away. "—I'm all yours."

All *mine*. Heart. Pulverized.

I smiled against his lips, and brushed my nose against his to warm it. "Care to watch me look like a penguin in a pair of ice skates?"

"Nothing would give me greater pleasure." He chuckled, and after donning our skates, we circled the ice over a dozen times, hand in hand.

Despite his jabs, he never let me fall and only laughed when I let out an infectious bout of giggles from slipping. He used every opportunity and excuse to touch my ass and cop a feel at my boobs through my jacket, grinning like a jackal each time. We also stole kisses too many times for me to count—the faint sound of holiday music fluttering in the background from outdoor speakers.

We'd retreated to a corner, and he stood behind me with his arms wrapped around me, our bare hands still touching. His beard tickled my cheek as he kissed it. "Have you ever seen thundersnow?"

"What the hell is that?"

He chuckled. "I'm going to take that as a no. It's a rare occurrence, but the people of New York City should thank you that it's your birthday because today—they're going to witness it."

His grip tightened on my arms, and with a cue only a god could give, snowflakes fell on my lashes. Grey clouds filled the sky as blankets of white fell from above like static, making the view of the New York skyline with the giant tree in the forefront look like something from a Norman Rockwell painting. Static flowed from him behind me, followed by a subtle electric current.

A crisp, clean, and wondrous bolt of lightning flashed across the sky, its radiance bouncing off the white snow, illuminating a several block radius of the city in shimmering vibrance. The crowds around us gasped, yelped, and wooed at the rare show in the sky—cheers roaring once the boom of thunder followed.

"That's remarkable," I whispered, sticking my tongue out to catch flakes on it.

"Hey now, I need that tongue. Don't get it electrocuted." He bumped his hips at my back, and grinned against my ear.

"This is the best birthday I've had in a very, very long time."

He continued the thundersnow show as people whipped out their cell phones to record the strange occurrence, children laughing and weather nerds shouting about how rare it was.

"Good, because you realize how off-theme a Hallmark moment like this is for me, right?"

I nuzzled against him. "Yes. And it delights me to know you're screaming inside but still doing this all for me."

"Mmhm." He nibbled the side of my face.

"Was I destined to lose the Daniels case the moment you signed on?"

He grabbed my shoulders and turned me to face him. "What?"

"You're not human. You can spin a case in your favor, I'd imagine?" I frowned.

His eyes shut, and he shook his head before flashing his gaze at me. "You said you can tell when I'm lying, correct?"

I nodded.

"You are the best damn lawyer I've ever seen, Keira Bazin. Even with only half a godly brain, you surpass any power I'd have in that courtroom." He massaged

my shoulders before cupping my chin with a gooey smile.

Sincerity. Admiration. Lust.

I grinned at him and took both his hands in mine. "I asked you this once before, and I'm going to ask you again. But I want a real answer this time. Newsflash: Saying I'm hot is not part of the answer."

He lifted a finger. "Let the record show, however, that you *are*."

"Fine. Thank you." I rolled my eyes with a smile before meeting his gaze. "Why me, Zeus?"

He licked his lips, the static still sizzling over my skin as he continued to produce lightning in the clouds. "You challenge me. Ground me. Drive me fucking crazy—"

I playfully nudged him in the stomach.

He grunted with a grin. "*And* I love it. But mostly because—you understand me. See me. Really see me. I can be myself around you."

Sincerity. Hope. Pure happiness.

"And that, counselor, was a solid argument." Smiling, I raised as high as I could on skates and slid my arms around his neck. "Let's do this."

He squinted at me, tensing beneath my touch. "To clarify, by 'this,' you do mean getting hitched, right?"

"Yes."

His gaze turned predatory. "Fuck, Keira." He kissed me—deeply, longingly, his arms wrapping around me and lifting me from the ice.

The lightning show intensified in the sky, crackling, hissing, striking, and booming. All surrounding lights went out, coating the entirety of Rockefeller Center in darkness. He pressed his forehead to mine, and I couldn't see my hand in front of my face, it was so dark.

"What the hell are you doing?" I whispered.

His eyes glowed with lightning. "I need to show you something before we do this and it can't be here." He grinned as he ported us away from the middle of downtown.

We reappeared in his penthouse, minus the ice skates, and he snapped his fingers.

"Please tell me that snap was returning those beloved lights to full glory, right?"

He kissed my temple. "Yes, it was."

Pulling away from him, I greeted Levin as he trotted over to me with his tongue out. "So what could you possibly need to show me? I've seen every square inch of you." I smiled mischievously over my shoulder at him as I scratched Levin's head.

"Not quite." He played with his jacket sleeve. "If you were full mortal, I wouldn't be able to show my true form to you. Mortals—well, sort of spontaneously combust if they were to lay eyes on my divine form."

My throat tightened, and I slowly rose. "Spontaneously combust? Like—" I made an explosion gesture with widened eyes.

"Yes." Zeus's cheek twitched.

"And you're positive my demigod self is safe from this? That'd be quite a damper on the entire situation, don't you think?" I let out a high-pitched laugh.

"You'll be fine. Are you ready?"

I chewed on my lip, shook out my hands, and stood upright before vigorously nodding.

A massive bolt of lightning struck over him from an invisible pocket above him, the brightness almost blinding me, making me wince. I held a hand above my eyes like one would do to shield from the sun. When my vision acclimated to the light, my lips parted.

It was still him, the same face, the same eyes, but—older. No, not older. Distinguished. Ancient. His dark hair turned silver and longer, reaching to his collarbone. His beard matched in color and hung to just above his chest. He was bare-chested and positively majestic, his muscles far more significant than in his mortal form and cut so pristinely like they were carved from marble. A gold metal crown circled his head, the middle rising to a sharpened point. Golden shin guards covered his knees and legs, his feet in sandals. On one knee bore an eagle's head, the other a crown. His muscular, tanned thighs were exposed from beneath the blue tunic circling his waist, golden chains and adornments hanging from his hips.

With my hands cupped over my mouth, I moved closer. He stood still and tall, gripping a sunburst shield in one hand, the pulsing thunderbolt spear in the other. Once I stood toe-to-toe with him, I gazed up at the familiar eyes and placed a single finger on his cheek, followed by my whole hand. Golden beads with carved ancient Greek lettering were woven into his beard and parts of his wavy hair.

"Hey," he said with a grin, the lightning flashing in his eyes more vibrant than when he was in his mortal guise.

I let my eyes roam over his face up close, and my hands, of their own volition, dragged over the bulging hard muscles that made up his chest, his arms, abdominal muscles over abdominal muscles I didn't even know existed.

Dipping my fingers into the front part of his tunic, I slid closer. "Damn. I never knew I could be so attracted to a silver fox."

He groaned. "Like my godly form, do you? You can fuck this form whenever you please. Except if we're in mortal public. That could—kill the mood rather quickly."

I sputter-laughed, slapping a hand over my mouth as soon as it happened. He smiled at me, and I kissed him—hard.

After kissing me back for far less time than I'd have liked, he gently coaxed me back. "As much as I love where your head's at right now. We really do need to get this show on the road." His gaze lifted to the clock hanging on the wall behind me. "I only have a matter of hours, and we still have someone we need to talk to about this."

"Hours?" I swatted him hard in the chest. "You're cutting it *that* close? Why didn't you tell me?"

"I needed to know that you truly wanted this. No outside interference. I'm a master meddler, Keira." He twirled the thunderbolt in his palm. "I figured you'd appreciate knowing it came down to you and *only* you as well."

This was the man I sensed bubbling under the surface from the day I met him but couldn't pinpoint what it was. This. Right. Here.

"Who do we need to talk to? Hera?"

"No. I've already spoken to her. Trust me, she's fine."

I bit the inside of my cheek to keep from smiling. "You checked in on her?"

"Yeah. I had to make sure she wasn't going to try and come back around and bite me in the ass."

There was no stopping the grin now. "Uh-huh. I'm sure that's all it was. You know, King of the Gods, you can be rather sweet when you want to be."

He scratched the back of his neck with a pointed part of his sunburst shield. "In the right company, maybe. But don't tell anyone."

After making the gesture of zipping my mouth shut, I asked, "Then who do

we have to see?”

Zeus sighed, his gaze lifting to the ceiling with a disgruntled groan. “My godsdamned grandmother—Gaea.”

TWENTY

ZEUS

AFTER TRANSFORMING MYSELF BACK to my mortal form, because dear old grandma didn't need yet another reason to be a wise-ass commenting on the godly form I hardly donned anymore, I ported Keira and me to the celestial gardens. A cottage surrounded by all forms of plant life, flowers, fountains, and lawn ornaments appeared in the distance—a steady smokestack puffing from the chimney. Keira gasped and walked toward the cozy-looking abode, but I hooked her by the elbow and pointed up.

What started as a cloud began to morph into overlapping green leaves, floating from the sky in sea waves—flowers bloomed, a deer trotted, sunbursts blazed. The earthy craziness spooled in front of us until finally, Gaea appeared in her human form—long white hair down to her ankles with vines and scattered flowers, and a dress made entirely of willow branches, moss, and far too sheer to my liking.

The woman always had to make a damn entrance.

"Hey, Yia-Yia." A wicked grin pulled at my lips, knowing full well she hated being called any form of grandmother.

Smirking, Gaea played with the petunia flower charm of her necklace. "You've changed so much and yet the smart ass remains."

"Not sure even I could make that stop," Keira said, smiling at me. "Or that I want it to."

Gaea propped her hands on her hips. "A fated bond for the ages, I'd say."

"What do you know? A third attempt at dethroning me—" I stepped forward, sinking my face into my dear primordial grandmother's. "—and you failed. Again."

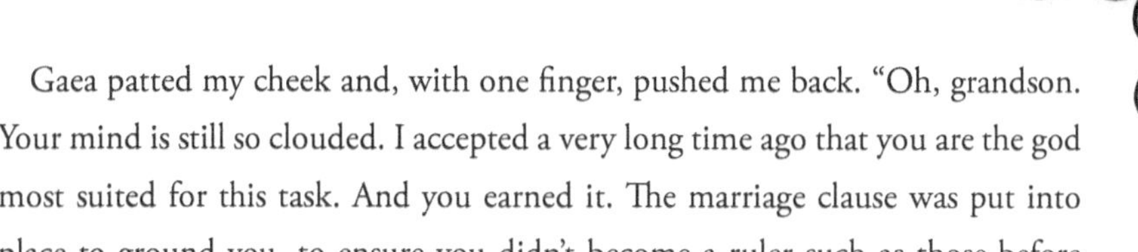

Gaea patted my cheek and, with one finger, pushed me back. "Oh, grandson. Your mind is still so clouded. I accepted a very long time ago that you are the god most suited for this task. And you earned it. The marriage clause was put into place to ground you, to ensure you didn't become a ruler such as those before you. Also—to make you put your ass in gear when this opportunity presented itself to you."

What was this harpy going on about?

Scowling at her, I moved closer to Keira, making our arms brush.

"Judging from that look on your face, you need me to spell it out for you." A coy grin pulled at her lips as she steepled her long pale fingers.

Keira slipped her hand in mine, sending an electric pulse through my arm into my chest that did *not* come from my power.

"It has been far too long since our kind has driven into a new era. The moment has come for a change. As time changes through the ages, so must we. This is the dawning of a *new* age, and it starts with progression." Her hands fanned above her, projecting images of aligning planets floating above us. "I ensured all mortals were born and paths intertwined through this very cycle with their gods."

"There's been more than just us?" Keira's grip tightened on my hand.

"Oh, yes. And far more to come. But this past cycle has been vital." She slapped her hands together, making the images disappear, and cutting her rainbow-colored eyes to me.

I looked from left to right. "Are you waiting for me to ask you why? Get on with it."

Keira elbowed me in the ribs, causing a satisfying smile to appear on Gaea's face.

"You, Zeus, King of Kings, witnessed sons, brothers, a grandson, a wife—all find the happiness they'd long since given up on, and little by little, it chipped at the metal that's been weighing you down for far too long."

The lightning hissed in my palms, flashing in my eyes as I ground my teeth.

"As we must progress in this modern age, so must our king." Gaea leaned forward with a gleam in her eye. "And Keira was the final piece. Do you both know the purpose behind a fated bond?"

Keira vigorously shook her head.

"Oh, I'm sure you're going to tell us." I rolled my eyes and added, "Always one to ramble," in a mumble.

Gaea made a tree branch slap me in the face, enticing a growl from the pit of my stomach. I'd defeated the Giants this woman threw at me, *and* a fire-breathing dragon, but still could never predict her conniving little outbursts.

"A fated bond is meant as comfort in a union—a completion of one half to a whole. With both of you accepting it, I suspect you've already begun to experience its effects. And once you are married—it will be tenfold." She clasped her hands together with a brightened smile.

Keira leaned toward my ear. "What does that mean?"

"Only pay attention to half of what this woman says, trust me," I whispered back.

"When Zeus was a little boy growing up in Crete—"

Stepping forward, I opened my mouth to stop her from talking, and another branch slapped me in the face, sticking to me this time.

"—he used to pretend he was a baby goat. Made the noises, hopped around on all fours with sticks on either side of his head to serve as horns, but the best part? He even suckled from one of the real goat's teats." Gaea cut me a wicked grin.

Keira bit her lip, trying to subdue her smile and no doubt holding back a laugh.

Snarling, I sizzled the tree branch away from my mouth with one flash of lightning. "Uh-huh. We're kind of on a time crunch here, as you fully know, *Granny*. You have an eternity to embarrass me."

"For once, you're right." She snapped her fingers, appearing in front of us, and slipping her hands over our shoulders. "Keira Bazin, do you agree to marry Zeus, King of the Greek gods, and thereby becoming Queen and the goddess of healed emotion?"

Keira paused, a warm subtle smile edging over her lips before her gaze lifted to mine. "I do."

My heart boomed in my chest, the thunderous echo pounding in my ears.

"Do you Zeus, King of the Gods, ruler of the skies and wielder of lightning, accept Keira as your new Queen to rule at your side as an equal?"

Without a breath of hesitation, I answered, "I do."

Gaea's grip tightened on our shoulders, making Keira wince. A bright light burst from Keira's chest, blasting through her mouth and eyes before an explosion of golden shimmers trickled over us, and Keira disappeared.

Fury. Anger. Fear.

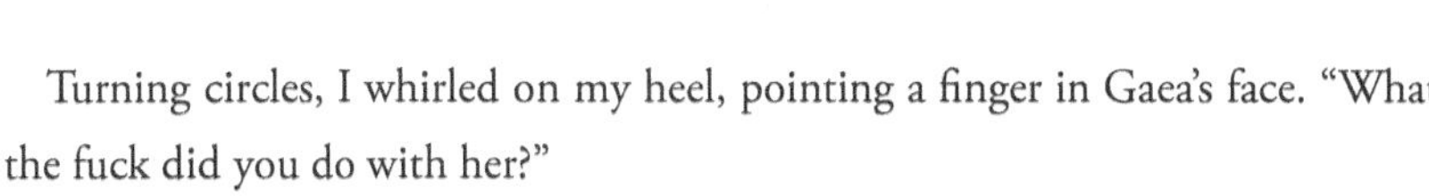

Turning circles, I whirled on my heel, pointing a finger in Gaea's face. "What the fuck did you do with her?"

Gaea placed one palm on my chest. "Your mother says hello, by the way."

My foster mother, Amalthea, was long gone, so there was only one other she could've been talking about.

The anger trickled away, and my face fell. "Rhea? But you—"

Unlike my brothers, I couldn't remember my birth Titan mother. She handed me off as soon as she gave birth to me to be raised without her, to save me from the fates of my brothers.

"She still lives but is one with Chaos now where she has a purpose."

A peculiar tightening pulled in my chest at the mention of my mother. The realization settling in that she'd been alive this entire time.

"In Chaos, is she able to see everything?" I cast my gaze downward, clenching my fists at my sides.

"Yes. Despite the little shit you've been, Zeus, she is still proud of you and bore witness to this union."

I lifted my eyes to meet Gaea's, and puffed my chest. "Where's Keira?"

"Where else would Zeus's Queen be for a royal—consummation?" Gaea raised a thin brow, eliciting a sly smile from me.

Gaea had a naughty side. And here I thought I'd always gotten it from dear 'ol dad.

"She waits for you, grandson." Gaea pushed my chest.

Nodding, I backpedaled away. Right before porting, I kicked over one of several garden gnomes bordering the cottage and could hear the faint whisper of the word "brat" as I disappeared.

The perfectly formed white clouds and skies of purple and orange welcomed me as I set foot on Olympus marble for the first time in a decade. It had little purpose now, with most of our duties being upheld elsewhere. Perhaps now with this "new age" Gaea spoke of, Olympus could have its uses again. Pillars lined the path leading to the thrones, spires of white and gold towering from the mountains in the distance.

One singular look at her—my new Queen and I transformed into my godly form. My body would accept no other form for the first time I'd be with her. The first time I'd *fuck* her as a goddess, my wife—my. Queen.

She sat on the throne next to mine with her legs crossed and exposed beneath a long white dress. A golden brooch held the strap of white fabric coiled around her neck right above her left breast, and a matching gold belt cinched at her waist. She brought an apple to her lips, her eyes glowing with an orange hue as she bit into it, watching me walk toward her. Golden armbands hugged each of her biceps, and ornately-designed sandals with crisscrossing leather ties traveled up to her knees. As she shifted her waves of blonde hair over one shoulder, my dick got hard.

"Mighty bold of you making your new Queen wait so long alone on her throne." She tossed the apple in her palm, fingernails tapping the gold armrests.

My greaves clanked as I took step after step, not tearing my eyes away from her for anything. "I couldn't agree more. You should allow me to make it up to you." I plastered a devious smile across my lips.

She grinned back, tossing the apple over her shoulder, making it disappear.

Producing ambrosia in my palm, I stood in front of her, outstretching my hand. "Eat this so we can consummate this marriage properly."

She dragged a finger over her lips, still smiling at me as she slowly opened her mouth.

Leaning over her, I slipped the ambrosia in, her tongue licking the length of my finger. My dick twitched, and I groaned. Once she swallowed it, immortality seeping into her bones from the ambrosia's power, she gasped. Her hands gripped the armrests, legs uncrossing and widening as the light and shimmer swirled around her, delivering my wife goddess in only a matter of seconds.

She'd closed her eyes, and once the transformation settled, they flew open, the glowing radiance intensified in her stare. She pushed from the throne, leaping into my arms, curling her own around my neck, kissing me with such force it made me stagger back. Her fingers tangled in my long hair, tugging it. I cupped her ass with both hands, the wide belt hanging over my hips grinding against her.

She pulled away from the kiss, my hair still wrapped in her grip. "I recall an arrogant god telling me he could at any moment port me to Olympus and fuck me on his throne."

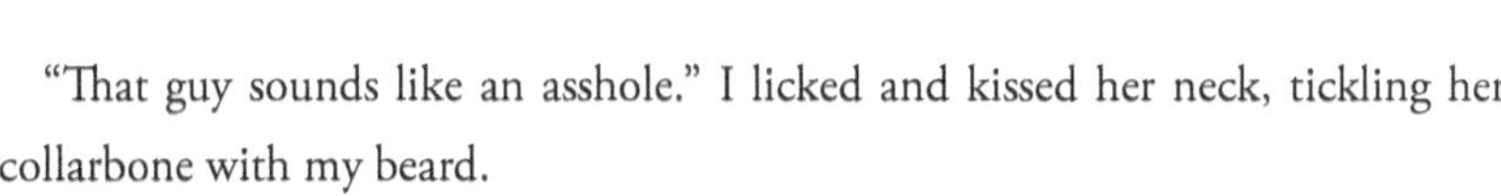

"That guy sounds like an asshole." I licked and kissed her neck, tickling her collarbone with my beard.

"He's no asshole."

I lifted my godly gaze to hers.

"He's a dick." She grinned as she slid down my body. Once her sandaled feet touched the marble floor, her finger dipped into my tunic, making my cock throb for her as she pulled me to the thrones. "I want to hold him to his claim—but fuck him on *my* throne."

This. Godsdamned. Woman.

She pushed me to her throne, forcing me to sit on it, more strength behind her movements than her demigod self. Spreading my legs wide, I shifted the tunic to free my cock, stroking it as I watched her saunter over to me, pulling the dress up to her hips. The sight of her bare pussy had me growling, and I dug my fingers into the armrest as she straddled my lap. As I moved my hands to her ass, guiding her, she slapped them away.

"This is my show, god-king," she whispered, nipping at my ear.

Fuck. Me.

Moving her hands to my shoulders, she slowly began to lower herself. As the tight warmth passed over the tip, it sent a tingle down my shaft, straight to the fucking base of my spine, and I groaned. Once our hips met, she stilled, my cock pulsing inside her. She moaned and began to rock, grinding her clit against my stomach as she damn near milked me.

She was so tight and so fucking wet it had my spine stiffening. With a snarl, I let my head fall back, fighting everything in me not to touch her—to squeeze her tits, her ass. The bond pounded through my chest, settling over my brain like the static aftershock from thrown thunderbolts in a heated battle. Keira gasped and pressed her face against the side of my neck, breathing me in.

"Touch me," she whispered.

Seeing as this woman never had to command me to do *anything* twice, I took her face in one hand, our glowing eyes sparking at each other before I kissed her. My other hand grabbed her ass, pulling and pushing her on and off me, deepening her thrusts. Traveling my touch up her back, I yanked the top of the dress down, exposing one breast, and broke away from the kiss to suck on it, flicking my tongue over the nipple before biting it.

Pressing a hand to the back of my head, she rocked back and forth, whimpering and gasping. White lightning crackled in the sky, brought on by my powers going into overdrive from the bond—the connection—my fucking gorgeous Queen writhing on top of me. Her nails dug into the back of my head, her pussy clenching around me as she cried out, coming on me. A small streak of orange lightning blasted through the sky directly above us—silent with no thunder to accompany it.

That…didn't come from me.

The familiar pressure built at the base of my cock, and I grabbed her hips, taking over the thrusts, bucking against her as it built and built. The glorious torture churned until an uncontrollable roar burst from my lungs, and I came inside her, my hips locking. Waves passed over me until finally, I sunk into the throne, holding my new Queen in my arms and keeping her from falling backward with that glowing satiation in her eyes.

"I felt something I've never felt before." She combed my beard with her fingers.

I traced her exposed breast. "The bond?"

"That was far more intense, yes, but this was as if I had an electric pulse radiating from my chest and not settling *over* it like when you use your lightning on me." She caressed my chest.

"The summer lightning. That was you," I whispered.

I'll be damned. I'd given her some of my power through the bond and didn't even realize it.

She sat up straight, my cock still inside her hardening again as she tightened. "I have lightning powers? How?"

Shifting beneath her, I pulled her closer. "Transference, I'd guess. Suppose we should add Wielder of Silent Lightning to that ever-growing list of titles you have, hm? Though I believe *heat* lightning would be more appropriate considering how it happened." I grinned and traced her jawline with a single finger.

She smiled and kissed my lips, starting to rock on me again. "I never got to thank you for saving my career properly."

Moaning, I massaged the back of her neck. "Nor I, you."

We fucked each other senseless for hours amidst the silent halls of Olympus— the marbled floor, the thrones, the atrium, even on the damn mountain's edge. And when we were finally spent, we slept for even longer. And yes, she *did* let me use her tits as a pillow. With our royal consummation duties solidly upheld, tomorrow would lead to other concerns. Our alter-egos had to get married as well. I've heard the weather in Vegas this time of year is perfect for a quickie wedding.

TWENTY-ONE

KEIRA

THE FIRST MOMENTS TOGETHER with my new god-king husband were what could only be described as legendary. We transgressed from fucking to making love and fucking again in all forms and locations across the wonders of Mount Olympus. At one point, I asked him simply to *sit* there. To sit on his throne as the king, legs spread wide, spear in hand. He did as I asked and stared me down with a feral gaze as I danced in front of him, slowly removing my new Queenly attire with every other sway of my hips. He looked *glorious* on his golden throne. Powerful. Commanding. And he was all *mine*.

Tingles. It was the best way to describe how my skin felt whenever I read emotions with my new powers. Static water beads trickling over my skin. But one single touch from him—my husband, my king—would make the world go silent. Blissfully quiet. I'd thought my empathic abilities would somehow work differently as a goddess, but instead, they became amplified. And sex with Zeus? The sensations were tenfold and made me ravenous for him at any given moment.

Two Greek gods sitting on a curb in Las Vegas, waiting for our turn to have a man dressed as Elvis Presley marry our mortal guises. Weeks ago, the notion of it would've had me laughing hysterically, and though it still enticed a snicker, I couldn't imagine a better way, nor could I imagine it happening with anyone else.

Zeus sat between my legs with his back to me, his arms wrapped around my thighs.

I trailed my fingers through his hair, pausing here and there to scrape his scalp with my nails. "The media is going to have a field day with this, you know?"

"Fuck the media," he grumbled, kissing my knee.

"How are we going to explain this? The next court date is tomorrow, and we show up inexplicably married?" I tensed, resting my hands on his shoulders, and staring at the slew of hardened gum littering the sidewalk.

"Hey." He tugged my arm, bringing my gaze to his. "Come here."

I lowered my face, and he brushed a kiss over my lips, his hand cupping my cheek.

"Master meddler, remember? I got it covered." He grinned, jiggling my chin between two fingers.

"Vronti and Bazin?" A man from inside the chapel called out.

Zeus stood first, holding his hand out to me, helping me stand. I brushed dirt away from my ass as we made our way inside. It was gaudy and quaint with only several rows of bright white pews, dozens of heart decorations, and a rounded arch with fake flowers where our minister, Elvis, stood waiting.

Elvis walked up to us, clad in a black jumpsuit decorated with ornate patterns and red rhinestones. He adjusted the oversized gold sunglasses on his nose, and as he bobbed his head, the black wig shifted. "Thank you all for choosing our chapel. Thank you very much."

I bit my lip to keep from laughing at his horrible impersonation of Elvis's iconic voice.

Zeus hugged me to his side, curling one hand over my hip. I opted to wear a simple floral dress, and he donned one of his many suits.

"Before we begin, do you both have rings?" Elvis pointed between us with a curl of his lip, his one large golden ring glinting from the overhead fluorescent lights.

Shit.

I slipped my hand behind my back, Zeus mimicking me, and we both used our powers to make rings for the other appear in our closed fists.

"Yes, we do," my husband responded with a charming grin.

Elvis leaned to one side, glancing behind us. "No guests?"

"We're kind of in a hurry," Zeus replied with a wink.

Considering the magical ceremony I'd already had on Olympus, I had no scruples in the slightest with making our mortal ceremony as quick as humanly possible.

"I like your dedication. Let's get on with it then, yeah?" Elvis snapped his fingers and shimmied to his spot under the altar, motioning for us to follow.

I was a living, breathing goddess now, a Queen, married to one of the most powerful men in the known universe, and—I'd *already* married him—but yet my stomach fluttered with anticipation.

"If you two would hold hands and face each other?" Elvis made a circling gesture with his hand.

With a sensuous curl of his lips, making my stomach twist even more, Zeus took my hands, running his thumbs over my knuckles. Elvis sang *Love Me Tender* offkey as the accompanying music played over the speakers.

"You ready to do this, counselor?" Zeus winked at me, dragging his middle finger over my palm with languid strokes.

For the second time, for the hundredth time, I'd say yes to marrying him countless times.

"This is the easy part." I smiled at him, squeezing his hands.

"Groom, if you would put the ring on her left hand, ring finger," Elvis said.

Zeus dug into his back pocket and slid a silver band over my finger. Several shimmering stones shined in a zigzag pattern when the light caught it —like lightning.

Zeus pressed his lips to my ear. "Those aren't diamonds. It's captured lightning." He kissed the corner of my jaw before leaning back.

I wiggled my fingers with a grin, making the lightning dance from the assistance of the fake lighting in the room. "It's beautiful."

"Sir, as you look into your bride's eyes, do you promise to love her, respect her, and honor her for the rest of your life?"

Zeus's grip tightened on my hands.

The rest of our lives…eons—eternity.

"Abso-fucking-lutely," Zeus answered with a warm smile.

"Wow. Great answer. Bride, if you wouldn't mind placing the ring on his finger," Elvis replied before turning to me.

I slipped the ring I'd conjured from lava rocks, its dark grey coloring a stark contrast to my brighter ring, onto his finger.

"Miss, do you promise to love him, respect him, and honor him for the rest of *your* life?"

"For eternity," I whispered, tears starting to cloud my vision.

Zeus stole a tear that'd escaped from my cheek with one quick swipe of his thumb. We'd said our vows to each other, promising to take the other through good times and bad, sickness and health, richer or poorer for as long as we both lived. Despite the ethereal nature of our first ceremony, saying the words I'd said before to my first husband made everything so much more real. As the final step, we lit a unity candle together, using our smaller candles to light the larger one in the center in unison. It'd been my missing link all this time. I'd never felt like someone else's crucial half. With Zeus, we were powerful as individuals, but we could conquer galaxies *together*.

"Congratulations to you both. After hearing the vows spoken by both of you, I can now officially pronounce you husband and wife. Sir, you can kiss your wife now."

Zeus flashed a sultry grin before dipping me and planting his lips to mine. I wrapped my arms around his neck, kissing him back, his lightning power coursing through my veins. Elvis sang *Viva Las Vegas* to us as we walked down the aisle toward the exit hand-in-hand. Zeus had fabricated a wedding certificate for us as further proof to immigration once they'd gotten wind of my illegal residency.

Once we were standing outside of the chapel, he slipped his ring off and squinted at the inside of it. "I think your powers need a little more work, sweetheart. Shouldn't that say 'KZ' not 'KB'?" He pointed at the engraving I'd done on the inside of his band.

Smiling, I shook my head. "Nope. I got it right. Keira's Bitch."

He glared at me with a wicked glint in his eye before he let out a roar of masculine chuckles, and slipped the ring back on. He grabbed me by the waist, tickling me, making me cackle before pulling my back to his chest, hugging me from behind.

"Honestly, don't worry about any of it. The media. The trial. Immigration. Big Daddy Z will handle *all* of it." He kissed my cheek and hugged me tighter.

"Big Daddy Z?" I smiled while biting my lip. "I'm not calling you that."

He shrugged, giving my nape a nibble, smiling against it. "Time will tell."

We shared a cab the next day to the courthouse, our hands intertwined, only parting ways once we walked inside. He was off to prep his client, and I was getting used to my new skin—how different it would feel standing in front of a judge and jury knowing I was now a celestial being amongst unknowing mortals.

"Keira fucking Bazin," Olivia shouted, power-walking through the lobby until she stood in front of me.

"Olivia—" I raised a hand, but she batted it away.

"I came into your office with a cake and a gift ready to celebrate your birthday the usual way you bloody prefer, and do you know what I found?"

I opened my mouth to reply, but Olivia cut me a glare.

"Nothing. That's what. And then I don't hear from you?"

Not bothering to speak anymore, I lifted my left hand and wiggled my fingers.

Her eyes widened before snatching my wrist and bringing my hand so close to her face I could feel her breath on my knuckles. "Did you or Zane or you and—" She rolled her neck, her eyes still wide.

"Both." My stomach clenched as an image of my god-king sitting on my throne in his full Zeus form flashed through my mind.

She tugged me closer. "Wait. So you're—"

Taking a quick scan of the area, I leaned forward, making my eyes spark with orange lightning.

Her grip tightened on my wrist as she stared up at me. "Holy shit, Keira."

"It's all happened so fast it's enough to make my head spin." I waved my fingers, making the lightning in my ring glisten.

"Wait. You all eloped, and I didn't get invited? Where'd you get married?" She threw my hand away as if she were disgusted by it.

"Vegas. We were in a hurry, Ollie. You know I would've asked you to come if it were possible." I rubbed the back of my neck with a frown.

"Vegas?" She slapped her hands on her head, laughing and twirling circles. "That couldn't be more perfect. Please tell me you at least took pictures?"

My frown deepened. Fuck. I hadn't thought about that. "I guess we forgot."

"Keir, what if immigration showed up *today*? They're going to ask to see photos of you both." Olivia grabbed my shoulders, concern cinching in her brow.

Nervousness. Anxiety. Regret.

"I—" My phone buzzed in my briefcase, and I grabbed it.

Several texts from Zeus. Photos of our Vegas Elvis wedding. Smiling to myself, I scrolled through them. Us holding hands, facing each other, both smiling. Zeus in mid-answer of his vows with me glassy-eyed. Him dipping me as he kissed me.

Zane: I told you. Don't Worry. ;) – BDZ

Laughing, I shoved the phone at Olivia. "Apparently, my darling husband snuck in photos I wasn't aware of."

She snatched it from me, giggling. "Oh my—you did an Elvis one? Keira, this is too rich." Pressing a hand to her chest, she sniffled. "You look so, so happy. Legitimately. Look at the way you are absolutely swooning over him."

She wasn't wrong. From the first day I'd laid eyes on him, even when he was just a crummy defense lawyer with a pretty face—I was smitten. At the time, I couldn't make sense of the emotions, the carnal power radiating from his skin, the spark in his gaze that had nothing to do with his lightning. It'd been a destined meeting preconceived in the universe, and who were we to deny its pull?

"Before the trial starts, here." Olivia shoved a small box wrapped in snowflake paper into my hands. "Happy belated birthday."

My chest tightened. I'd gained a husband, godhood, and immortality for my last birthday as a mortal. The thought brought a warm smile to my lips, and my fingernails dug into the paper surrounding the box.

"What is it?" I flashed her a devious grin, knowing she hated whenever I asked that.

"I'm not sure you'll have much use for it now, but—I mean, the thought was there at the time." Olivia folded her hands in front of her and averted her gaze skyward.

Squinting one eye at her, I tore off the paper and flipped open the brown box hidden within. I pulled out a small white ceramic elephant holding a marker with its trunk and folded cloth with its tail.

Grinning, I held it up. "It's adorable. What's the marker for, though?"

Olivia held her hand out, and I rested it on her palm. She removed the marker and wrote something on the elephant's side before showing me.

"File your damn paperwork," I read aloud, laughing.

"It's a dry erase elephant. I figured it'd look cute on your desk *and* serve a

purpose. Multi-functional." She rubbed the words away with the cloth and handed it back to me.

"It's perfect, Ollie. And I'll still use it, but maybe more for naughty encrypted messages or something." I winked at her, slipping the elephant into my case.

"I like where your head's at. Ready for what I hope to be one of the final days of this damn trial?" She curled her arm with mine.

After taking a deep breath, knowing Zeus and I's marriage changed the dynamic, I let my godly intuition calm me as I breezed into the courtroom. Zeus already sat at the table with his client, immediately moving his gaze over his shoulder to grin at me.

What were you up to?

Giving a subtle smile back, I took my seat at the table only to rise seconds later as the judge entered the courtroom.

"You may be seated," she announced, adjusting her glasses and shuffling papers.

Zeus cleared his throat, remaining standing. My heart boomed in my chest. What was he doing?

"Mr. Vronti, is there something you need to address before we proceed?" The judge eyed him over the rim of her glasses.

Zeus adjusted his tie. "I'm sorry, your honor, but I've briefed my client, and with her consent, another partner will be taking over this case as—" His eyes cut to me, fully smiling before turning back to the judge. "—I'm now married to opposing counsel."

My cheeks flushed and I sunk into my chair. I'd wanted to make an announcement, knew we had to tell them, but did *not* plan to make it a spectacle. Considering I knew who I married, it shouldn't have surprised me.

Melissa Daniels' face scrunched, and she shook her head. "We never—"

Zeus waved his fingers behind his back at Melissa, making her face neutral, followed by a firm nod.

"Well, in the thirty years I've been doing this, I can honestly say this has never happened before. Thank you for bringing this to our attention. In light of the change in defense, we'll adjourn the proceedings until tomorrow." She slammed her gavel.

Olivia smacked me in the shoulder with a grin. "He's *so* good."

Oh. I know—the charming, gorgeous asshole.

Zeus approached me as I stood, his hands jiggling the keys in his pants pocket. "I know that's probably not how you wanted to announce this, but I wanted them to know I'm stepping down." He leaned in, unabashedly sliding an arm around my waist now that everyone knew. "Win the case, my Queen."

A sensual shiver shot up my spine, fluttering over my skin.

"And now, to handle the slew of media I know lurks behind that door." Zeus smirked before holding his hand out for me to take.

"Olivia—" I started, flicking my gaze over my shoulder to her.

She held up a hand as she gathered papers into her briefcase. "I'll catch up with you. Trust me. I'm elated your first instinct isn't to go straight to the office to over-prepare." She tugged one of my jacket lapels as she passed and grinned up at Zeus before pointing a finger in his face. "I don't care who you are. If you hurt my best friend, I'll do bad things to you."

"Careful, Ollie. Don't threaten my husband with a good time, or I may get jealous." I smiled at her, offering a tiny wink.

Zeus squeezed my hand.

After Olivia guffawed, she slapped my shoulder. "Yup. I like this version of you. Call me later."

I elbowed Zeus. "Quick work with those photos."

"Mmhmm." He bumped his knuckle under my chin. "What did I say?"

"That you had everything under control." I bit back a smile.

He held up a single finger. "That *who* had everything under control?"

Glaring at him but still smiling, I said, "Big Daddy Z."

"That's right." He kissed my brow.

No sooner did we step outside of the courtroom cameras and reporters swarmed us.

"Miss Bazin, did you ever imagine yourself with a defense lawyer?"

"Mr. Vronti, what does this mean for your career?"

I stepped closer to Zeus, squinting from the flashes going off in waves.

"I'm sure you all have a lot of questions, and we'll answer all of them in due time. Considering this is so new, however, you'll respect us if we wish to enjoy this momentous occasion—alone." Zeus's voice commanded attention, everyone falling silent as soon as he opened his mouth and nodding in agreement without asking anything else.

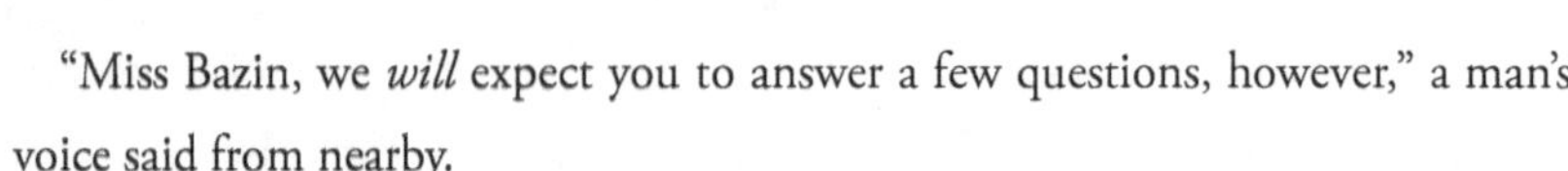

"Miss Bazin, we *will* expect you to answer a few questions, however," a man's voice said from nearby.

When I turned to face him, he flipped his wallet open, revealing a USCIS badge, making my throat tighten.

It was only a matter of time.

"Miss Bazin, is Mrs. Bazin-Vronti now. She's legally in the country with her marriage-based green card." Zeus said, holding up our joined left hands.

"Be that as it may. We'll need to take you both in for questioning due to the urgency and convenience of your marriage to ensure its legitimacy." The man stepped aside and held out his hand. "If you'd both follow us to the immigration office."

Zeus dropped his lips to my ear. "You're a Queen goddess now. Use that charm for questions we'll undoubtedly be unable to answer. Unless the person interviewing us is a man, then maybe tone it back a tad." He grinned against my cheek.

Let the interrogation commence...

The officers led us to the same room with a single desk, overhead light, and three chairs. I cleared my throat as I adjusted in my seat, purposely playing with the new band on my finger to show my immediate familiarity with it. Zeus sat next to me, but they'd made us far enough apart we couldn't hint answers to the other.

"It may have taken us longer to catch wind of you were it not for going through customs after your quick trip to Argentina," Officer Miles said as he twirled a pen on the desk.

I folded my hands and calmly placed them in front of me. "I wasn't worried about it because I knew I was already marrying Zane."

Zeus grinned and bobbed his brows at the officer.

"You seemed to have a short engagement. Care to explain?" Miles cut his gaze to Zeus.

Zeus casually leaned back in his chair and bent forward, resting his forearms on the table. "Do you believe in love at first sight, Officer Miles?"

"No."

"Well, then how could you possibly understand why we were ravenous to make it official?" Zeus spied me out of the corner of his eye, smiling at me.

Ravenous.

I bit my lip and crossed my legs with a flick of my hair.

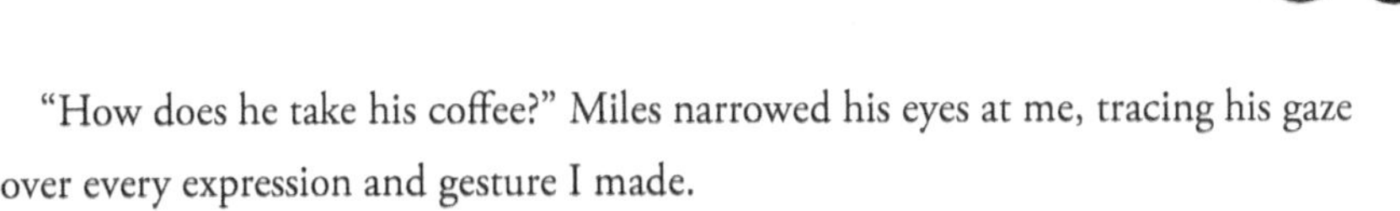

"How does he take his coffee?" Miles narrowed his eyes at me, tracing his gaze over every expression and gesture I made.

"Black. No lid," I answered quickly.

Seemingly satisfied, Miles nodded and turned his attention on Zeus. "And hers?"

"Black, but I've also seen her sneaking a packet of sugar in now and again. When she wants to be hyper-focused."

He noticed that?

I didn't want the officer to catch the surprised expression on my face, so I hid it behind a smile.

"What side of the bed does she sleep on?"

"That all depends on which position we finished in." A glint flashed in Zeus's eyes.

My stomach flipped several times.

"Any children from past marriages?"

Zeus stared at the officer before squinting. "Can you repeat the question?"

I slid a hand over my mouth, grinning behind the guise of my palm.

"How long has he been in his current state of employment?" Miles tapped the pen against the table as he shifted his gaze between us.

I shrugged. "Years, but honestly, sometimes it feels like—forever."

"And the wedding, where did it take place?"

Zeus slid his phone from his back pocket, pulling up the gallery of photos he'd fabricated from his memories. "A chapel in Vegas." He pointed at his phone. "They streamed it on Facebook, too, if you need further proof."

"Have you planned the honeymoon?"

I frowned and traced my thumb over my lightning ring. "We haven't talked about it." Stealing a glance at my new husband, I caught his gaze, and he too frowned.

"Have you met each other's parents?"

We both turned our attention back to the officer and responded in unison, "They're dead."

The officer clucked his tongue against his teeth and tapped the pen faster. "What about your spouse's best friend's name?"

Frustration. Annoyance.

Zeus shifted forward. "Olivia."

"Levin," I said, grinning at the god-king when he raised a brow at me over his shoulder.

"Do you live together or plan to live together?"

Live in my tiny apartment with painful memories of my divorce? Fuck that. Besides, I still had half my shit packed anyway. "I'm moving into his penthouse."

Zeus nodded. "Mostly because it's soundproofed."

I choked on my spit, holding back a laugh, and coughed into my fist.

The interrogation continued for another fifteen minutes, and we newlyweds answered each question with ease and precision. The officers informed me I could maintain my green card, which would expire ten years from the current date. We strolled out of the USCIS office holding hands.

"So, you're moving into the penthouse with me, huh?" Zeus tugged my arm.

"Damn right I am. Hope you're prepared for that—hubs." I kissed his cheek.

"So bossy." Zeus flashed me a grin as he slid his sunglasses on.

"You love it."

"Speaking of bosses, we need to introduce you as everyone's new 'co-boss' formally." He brought my hand to his lips, giving a quick peck to my palm.

"How do you propose getting everyone in one place?"

"It's been a very long time since I called everyone home—to Olympus."

TWENTY-TWO

ZEUS

I SAT ON MY golden throne comprised of two eagles, their wings making up its back. My gorgeous Queen sat next to me, casually crossing her legs, wrists dangling off the edge of her armrests. The jewels hanging from her hair shimmered and jangled when she turned to look at me, smiling that she caught me staring at her.

"What is it?" Her glowing orange eyes pulsed.

I leaned toward her, resting the thunderbolt I had clutched in my hand on the ground, perching it against my throne. "It's only been a matter of days, and already this role suits you."

"My foster mother always used to say, 'It might take a day. It might take a year, but what's meant to be will always find its way.'" She smiled at me, fucking radiant and ethereal.

"Sounds like a well-spoken woman."

Foster mothers. Workaholics. Passionate. A fated bond made more and more sense with each passing day.

"She was." Keira kept smiling as she turned her head to the other gods as they began to appear in the great hall.

I knew not all of them would or could come, but even a handful of gods to bear witness to me placing the new crown on the new Queen would suffice. It almost seemed bizarre having an official ritualistic ceremony after so long. Gaea said the changes were far from over—that our fated union would pave the way for progression. Whatever the fuck that meant. I think my grandmother delighted in knowing more than any other deity. It continuously gave her leverage over every

one of us.

After a dozen arrived, including Apollo, Artemis, Athena, Demeter, Poseidon, Hermes, my enforcers, and even Ares—I couldn't wait any longer.

Standing, I picked up the thunderbolt and waited for the murmurs of conversation to die down. "Those of you who heeded my call know it's appreciated. We could have upheld this tradition with only the Queen and I and my brothers as witnesses, but I propose we make use of Olympus more often again." Displaying my arms wide, I swiveled. "For how could we continue to call it a Great Hall when it remains silent?"

More murmurs and nods floated amongst the gods.

"As you all know, Hera has stepped down as Queen, which led me in the search for another." I paused to look at Keira, who lifted her chin, grinning. "Little did I know when I set my eyes on her, she would not only be my future Queen but that I had found my fated bond. A bond I never knew existed."

Several of the gods gasped, but I kept my gaze on my goddess.

"She has accepted the role of Queen, goddess of healed emotion, and agreed to be my wife, but she has yet to be properly crowned." Resting the bolt and shield on the seat of my throne, I produced the baroque crown I'd created for her in my palms. Golden metal curved into ornate patterns from Hephaistos' forge, blackened gems and lava stones matching the wedding ring she'd given me.

Keira pressed a hand to her chest, a small whimper fluttering from her throat. She hadn't expected this, and her sincere reaction had my heart singing. Moving behind her, I held the crown above her head and looked to the other gods, most of them my family, now *her* family as well.

"Bear witness to your new Queen, gods of the Greek pantheon. May you respect her, honor her, and obey her not only as Queen but as my equal and my wife." I sparked lightning in my eyes as proof I'd smite any of them for any misdeeds toward her.

They all raised their fists to their chests, pounding in unison. With a slight nod, I lowered the crown to Keira's head, sending a shimmer of gold dust and coils of lightning encircling us both, white and orange hissing vibrant and strong. Keira took a deep breath, her chest rising, before settling into her throne once more.

"May I speak, Zeus?" Keira's thin brows raised.

I cupped her chin with a warm smile. "You never need permission for that."

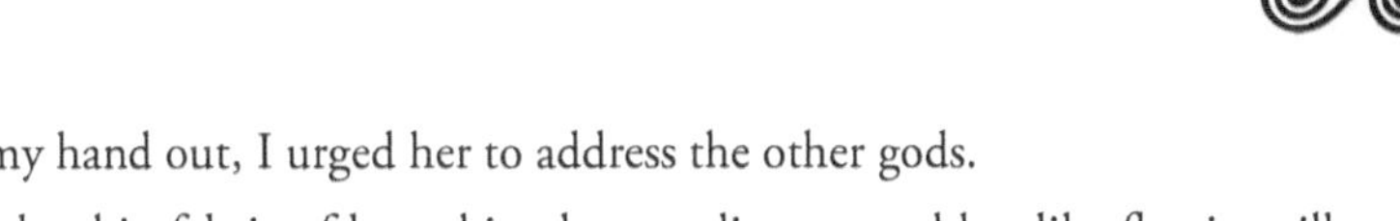

Holding my hand out, I urged her to address the other gods.

Rising, the thin fabric of her white dress curling around her like floating silk, she stepped to the front of the raised platform holding our thrones. "Gods. Family. I know I must seem like a stranger—a stranger taking over the second most powerful standing amongst the Greek gods, but I can assure you it doesn't come without rhyme or reason." She glanced at Apollo and Ares, knowing full well they'd brought other mortal women into our world.

She held her arms out. "Gaea told us that this is to be a time of progression, and I plan to be the stepping stone for that new age. I come from the modern world while having a piece of this world unknowingly inside me, and I believe with every fiber of my being—" She turned to look at me, crossing the way to take my hand. "—combined with Zeus's immense power, the dawning of this day…is today."

Fucking Tartarus. I thought the way she carried herself in a courtroom was a sight to behold but her as a Queen? Nothing compared.

"Now that we're done being all formal—" She waved her hand, making a table littered with food and ambrosia wine appear near the other gods. "—what's a celebration without food and drink?"

Once the other gods began to attack the table, I pulled her against me, kissing her, trailing my hands up her back and into her hair.

She pulled away, curling her fingers through my long silver hair. "Did I do alright?"

"Alright? You fucking showed *me* up." I chuckled and kissed her.

A chill settled in the air, followed by trickling embers and ash in the center of the atrium. Eris. Godsdammit.

"You have one thing right. You *are* a stranger on the throne," Eris spat as she glared at Keira.

My shoulders tensed from her bone-chilling voice. Growling, I turned on my heel, coaxing Keira behind me on basic instinct alone. "What the Tartarus are you doing here, Eris? I made it explicitly clear you're not welcome in these halls."

She flicked her long black hair, the red streaks in it igniting a newfound fury in my gut like a bull readying to charge. "I'm offended I wasn't invited to this little soiree. The invitation must've gotten lost in the mail." With a crooked grin, she narrowed her eyes at Hermes and waved.

Hermes cut his gaze to me, eyebrows raised, and cheeks full of food.

"Leave. Now," I made my voice boom, echoing off the stone pillars surrounding us.

As she stepped from behind me, Keira's fingers grazed my elbow and she stood at my side with her chin held high.

Eris appeared in front of me in a flash of embers, hissing and pointing a black claw in my face. "All of these new goddesses and none of us had a say in any of them. Particularly—" She cut her gaze to Keira. "—the Queens."

You ever regretted something so profusely it makes your balls ache, knowing it's where it came from? I care for all my children. But Eris? She's always been a fucking *challenge*.

"You don't need a say." I dipped my face into hers. "I'm your King. And if you think I'm incapable of putting someone worthy on the throne to rule beside me, I dare you to say it." Lightning flashed in my gaze.

She sneered at me, making her lip curl. "It was bad enough when a previous mortal joined the ranks of war gods, but to make *this* harpy, Queen? You've grown *soft*, old man."

Ares stepped forward with clenched fists, baring his teeth like a snarling grizzly.

I held my palm up to him, keeping my focus on Eris. "I got this handled, son."

After several nostril flares, Ares gave a curt nod and stalked away.

Fury shot down my spine, and I lashed lightning around Eris, pinning her arms at her sides. "Talk about my wife like that again, and I'll banish you to the furthest nebula to be forgotten. Do you understand me? She is your Queen. Get the fuck over it or get out."

"Banish me?" She cackled and stared at me with those lifeless midnight eyes. "Do it."

Keira's hand slid over my forearm—her calming touch soothing me. She gave one light bob of her thin brows, and I released Eris from my electric grip. After nodding to Keira, I stepped aside.

My Queen took charge as she stood tall in front of Eris with her head cocked to one side. "When Zeus mentioned you before, I hoped we'd meet Eris."

"Why?" Eris scoffed.

Keira stepped closer to her. "So I can help you."

"Help me?" Eris snickered and flicked her hair. "I don't *need* helping."

"Pain. Resentment. You're imbalanced, Eris." Keira's gaze roamed Eris's face.

"How did you—" Backing away, Eris shielded her cheek with a hand as if one of us were going to slap her.

Keira followed her. "Chaos, too, needs balance. And it's up to you to do it—to find it."

"Oh? And how do you propose I do that, my *liege*?" The words dripped from her tongue like snake venom.

My nostril bounced, and I coursed lightning down my arms as I glared at Eris and her wise-ass little mouth.

"The same way as Ares and Zeus. They opened their hearts to two mortal women and in turn balanced themselves the same way they balanced us." Smiling, Keira glanced at me over her shoulder.

Still letting the lighting coil around me, I grinned back.

"You've got to be kidding me. You're telling me to go find 'love.'" Eris rolled her eyes after making air quotes.

Keira stuck out her chest. "I'm not telling you. I'm ordering you. It may not even be love for another person but yourself. That's for you to figure out. Uphold your duties, Eris. Zeus doesn't make empty threats, and neither do I."

Damn. That's my wife, folks. *Mine.*

The surrounding gods widened their eyes as whispers and light chatter amongst them followed. Eris narrowed her eyes at my Queen before scanning the other gods around her. She dragged a hand down the front of her leather corset before lifting her chin. "Consider it done—" Eris took a deep breath before ever so slightly bowing her head. "—my Queen."

Before we could reply, Eris disappeared with a grimace, leaving floating bits of embers and ash spiraling in the air.

Keira let out a breath, and I stepped behind her, pressing my bulge against her ass, and grabbing her hip. "If we were alone right now—" I growled against her neck.

"I wasn't too harsh on her?" Keira snaked her hand behind my head.

"I think you're incapable of being too harsh." I drummed my fingers on her waist. "Except with me. Something tells me you'd hand me my own balls if I did something to incur your wrath."

She pulled my lips to hers. "And don't you forget it."

Ares cleared his throat as he approached us. He bowed his head and pressed a fist to his chest. "I wanted to welcome you personally to the family, my Queen."

"Ares, I know it's been a long time since you've been back here. I appreciate you making an appearance. It means the world to me." Keira bent forward and pressed a kiss to my son's forehead.

"To us," I corrected, holding out my hand for Ares to shake. "Thank you, son."

Ares glared at my hand at first, clenching his jaw before slapping his hand against my forearm, shaking it. "Don't expect me to call her stepmom or anything." He pointed at each of us with a hint of a smile.

"Noted." I chuckled but let it fall away, only to be replaced by a stoic expression. "But you *will* call her that if she one day wishes it."

Keira squeezed my arm and laughed. "Ares, I wouldn't expect that. I'm not taking over anything of your mother's. I think of it more as picking up where she left off in a new era."

"Much like me with my goddess, I can see the bond at work." Ares looked between us before bowing his head. "And speaking of which, I should get back to her."

Keira leaned against me, running her fingers along my bared skin. "You two are so much alike it's almost uncanny."

Grumbling, I responded, "I know. I think it's why we've butted heads for eons."

The day went by with each of the gods introducing themselves to Keira, Apollo playing music on his lyre—an actual lyre—versus his modern-day guitar. As they disappeared one-by-one, Poseidon finally approached us with a wide grin.

"Well, well, hello, *sis*." He stood with his hands folded behind his back and winked at me. "You did good, little bro."

Keira smiled and extended her hand. "Poseidon. I assume you're one of two reasons for Zeus's grand gesture?"

Poseidon chuckled, covering his mouth with a hand as his green eyes brightened.

"Hey. I was more than capable of thinking of that on my own." Feeling my nose twitch, I cut Poseidon a glare.

Keira curled her arm with mine. "Maybe now you are, but at that precise moment? You needed the push, hun." She rose on the balls of her feet to kiss my cheek.

"I'm going to push something alright," I mumbled, narrowing my eyes at Poseidon over Keira's head and out of view.

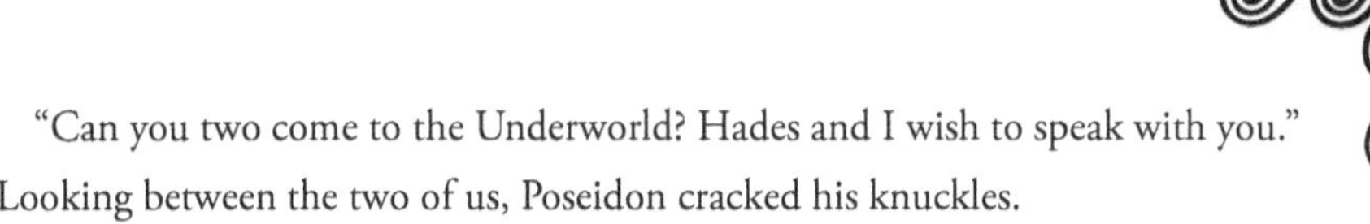

"Can you two come to the Underworld? Hades and I wish to speak with you." Looking between the two of us, Poseidon cracked his knuckles.

Nodding, I slipped a hand to Keira's lower back and ported us to Hades's throne room. He sat on his throne, talking with his own Queen, Stephanie, seated upon her throne. Stephanie smiled and trotted across the black sand to greet us, taking Keira's hands into hers.

"It is an absolute pleasure to meet you, Keira." Stephanie bowed her head and did a small curtsy. "My Queen."

Squeezing her hands, Keira replied, "I appreciate you saying it out of respect, but please call me Keira."

Beaming, Stephanie stood tall and stepped to Hades as he approached us.

"Keira has a similar power as you, darling." Hades squeezed Stephanie's shoulders.

Stephanie gasped. "You see auras too?"

"I guess emotions can also be associated with auras, but no, I'm an empath. I can sense emotions from anyone mortal and immortal alike. And since becoming a goddess, I can project any emotion I wish on mortals." Keira ran the skirt of her dress through her fingers.

"She's selling herself short. She was a powerful empath before becoming Queen and now, well—" I paused, at a loss for words. No form of verbal description could possibly do this woman justice.

"Little bro, we were thinking." Stepping beside me, Poseidon wrapped a hand over my shoulder.

"Here we go." I pinched the bridge of my nose.

"You raised a valid point when you said you granted me the means to take breaks but not yourself." Hades lifted his chin.

The idea of leaving Olympus in anyone else's hands made my neck tense.

"It's because I can't afford to take breaks. Those moments are for you and your Queen to make you happy, Hades. It doesn't have to be fair on all fronts."

"Bullshit, Z," Poseidon barked.

I tossed him a glare over my shoulder, the lightning swirling in my eyes.

"Do you not think you're deserving of happiness, brother?" Hades rose a single brow, and Stephanie rested her head on his shoulder.

Keira's hand slipped over my arm. She was beautiful, there wasn't a doubt in my mind about it, but the tiredness I could feel floating from her was too

distinct to ignore. Combined with my own exhaustion—it was enough to make me audibly sigh.

"What are you proposing?" I lifted my gaze to Hades.

"Take a week. Go on a honeymoon. Go wherever you wish, but leave knowing Olympus is taken care of and in good hands. Relax. Rejuvenate." Hades stepped forward, curling his hand over my shoulder. "Between the three of us, Olympus will be *fine*."

"I don't know. It's not only Olympus. It's all of the gods, the universe, mortals. How will you handle any of that from down here, Hades? Hm?" I held my arms out, swiveling my hips as I referenced the Underworld.

"You'd be surprised at all of what I can do from here. We have it handled."

Licking my lips, I scratched my chin. "What about Levin?"

"Cordelia is already at your apartment taking care of him as we speak. You know how my wife is with animals. He's in good hands." Poseidon crossed his arms and leaned into my face. "Stop making excuses and go."

My gaze shifted to Keira's eyes—the hope swirling in them. If I felt any ounce of being undeserving of happiness with all I've done in my past, she *did* deserve to be happy.

Holding my hand out to her, I smiled. "Bali?"

Stephanie clapped her hands and hugged Hades to her side.

"Anywhere, Zeus. Anywhere." Keira interlaced her fingers and beamed up at me.

"If Olympus is in ruins when I return, I'm making you live in a desert for a week." I pointed at Poseidon, followed by Hades. "And you'll be forced to smile for twenty-four hours."

"Oops," Hades said right before waving his hand at us and making us disappear.

No sooner had we landed in the lobby, it took Keira an entire five minutes before finding an unhappy couple arguing at the front desk. She'd tried to be discreet, casually waltzing past them, but she forgot who she married. And judging by their sudden change in demeanor, going from fighting to googly eyes the moment my wife passed them, it was fairly obvious.

"By Olympus, you're worse than me." I pulled her to me, wrapping my arms around her. "We're supposed to be *relaxing*, love. Not working."

"I know. I promise that was it. Besides, I couldn't let them feel like that in paradise. It didn't seem right." She poked me in the ribs. "And you think I couldn't sense you checking on your brothers moments after arriving?"

Busted.

"They're asshats. One last little check calmed my growing anxiety." I shrugged.

"First time your children are being babysat jitters, huh?" She grinned up at me as she elbowed my side.

I kissed the top of her head. "Something like that."

When we appeared in our room in Bali, it was in such seclusion Keira could scream her lungs out, and only the birds would hear it. I planned to make the most of it during our stay here—the most of the unburdening of our work, the most of the open floor plan, and definitely the most out of the tub I'd coaxed her into within minutes of our arrival.

"I've seen Olympus itself, and yet this place still looks like a thing from fairytales to me," she whispered as she twirled her finger in the steaming water filled with rose petals, her blonde hair pulled in a bunch on top of her head.

The tub was situated underneath a gazebo on the deck outside of our room, giving us full view of the valley of palm trees and fog collecting in the air. Two lounge chairs and a private pool also faced the trees. A king-sized canopy bed rested in the bedroom behind us inside, the pale purple comforter littered with the same rose petals in our tub water.

I curled an arm around her from behind, pressing beneath her breasts and pulling her back tighter to my chest. "Never lose that sense of wonder, Vasílissa."

Queen.

Smiling, she reached for her flute of champagne resting on the nearby table. "Were you close to your foster mom?"

"Very." I grabbed a bottle of oil, pooling some in my palm before massaging her shoulders, her neck. "It angered me to no end when she died."

She closed her eyes and let out a contented sigh from my touch. "Do you think that's why you were so ruthless in your youth? Lashing out?"

"Possibly." I kneaded a tight spot in her neck—the same place I always seemed to form a knot. "But I wouldn't want to blame my choices on someone else. At

the end of the day, *we* make the choices. No one else."

"And that is why I wish you'd somehow make the world know about the true Zeus." She rubbed my calf beneath the water.

"It's not my place, sweetheart." I kissed her cheek and brushed my nose over her jawline. "Mortals have been the ones to depict us. If someone wants to envision me differently someday, I'd be fucking ecstatic, I truly would, but I've accepted it." Pinching one nipple, I kissed her neck, lightly biting it. "You know me. That's all I need."

"I haven't been able to make lightning since the day on Olympus. How do you conjure it? Especially with such precision?"

Grinning against her cheek, I trailed my fingers down her stomach until I reached her clit. "You mean when I do this?" Calling to my power, I flickered it over her, making her cry out.

She laughed. "Yes. Exactly."

"The precision has taken hundreds of years of practicing, but this—" The lightning swirled over my arms before crackling across the grey sky above us. "—is easy to master."

"Show me," she whispered, rubbing her cheek against a knee I'd poked from the water.

"Everything starts here." I traced my finger between her breasts. "You can feel it building up, sizzling, waiting for you to release it and direct it where to go."

She closed her eyes, and I could hear the hissing emanating from her chest.

"I can feel it."

"Good. Now pull it out of you, guide it, using this." I dragged my fingertips over her forehead. "It'll start at your arms, but if you want it in the sky, *tell* it to go there. Command it."

Her forehead wrinkled as she concentrated, her nails digging into my leg as she fought to control the bit of lightning I'd passed onto her. Slowly, the orange electricity pulsed over her shoulders and after several moments of grunting and further nail digging into my flesh, a silent flash of heat lightning overtook the clouds.

"I love the way that feels," she murmured, her eyelids heavy.

"Oh, yeah?" My white lightning bubbled in my palms, fanning over her skin in short languid bursts of electricity. Goosebumps covered her arms, and she bit

her lip, her eyes closing, back arching. Chuckling, I doused the power and kissed the corner of her brow.

She moaned and sunk further into the water. "Tell me to sit on your face."

My cock twitched against her ass, and I couldn't help but chuckle. "I'm sorry?"

"Just say it. Please."

Pressing my lips to her ear, moistening it, I whispered, "Sit on my face, Keira."

Her hand found my cock under the water, idly stroking it as she kept her eyes closed. "Now repeat it, but command it."

This. Godsdamned. *Woman.*

"Sit. On. My. Face," I growled against her neck.

"Mm, that's so much sexier than my dream."

Chuckling again, I groaned at the feel of her hand still stroking me. "You dreamed about me? When?"

"On my way to Argentina. And don't sound so surprised. You probably commanded Morpheus to do it."

I nipped at her ear lobe. "As much as I would love to take the credit for that little gem, I really would. That was all you, sweetheart."

She turned in the water, pressing her tits to my chest with a brightened smile. "I guess I couldn't help myself."

"You know what would be far sexier than me saying it, Keira?" I scooted down in the water, encouraging her to stand over me.

We continued to act out her salacious dream in vivid detail, taking it a step further by fucking both on the pool deck and in it. We spent the week showing our appreciation for the other in every held conversation, every position imaginable, and slept more than either of us had in several lifetimes. I'd have to thank my brothers for this, which annoyed the shit out of me, but these days...I had *a lot* to be grateful for.

EPILOGUE

KEIRA

THREE MONTHS LATER...

IT TOOK ME MONTHS to work up the courage to ask my brother-in-law to escort me to Tartarus. The looming question of whether my mother would even want to speak with me hung over me like a raincloud—not to mention the emotion in this place.

Agony. Pain. Suffering. Remorse. Regret.

Gripping my head, I paused, causing Hades to turn and squeeze my shoulder. "Keira?"

"It's too much. Can you drown them out somehow?"

I could've asked Zeus to come with me, and none of this would've bothered me, but this was something I needed to do by myself. *For* myself.

"For a time, but you won't have long. These souls are too strong for me to dampen it permanently." Hades waved his hand.

Like the deafening aftermath of a nearby explosion, the emotions overwhelming me fizzled away.

Sighing, I stood straight. "Thank you."

"If she wishes to see you, she'll be through this door." Hades displayed a doorway leading into nothing but darkness.

Nodding, I stepped through, never being one that feared the dark or the creatures that lurked within it. Flames flickered around me, creating enough

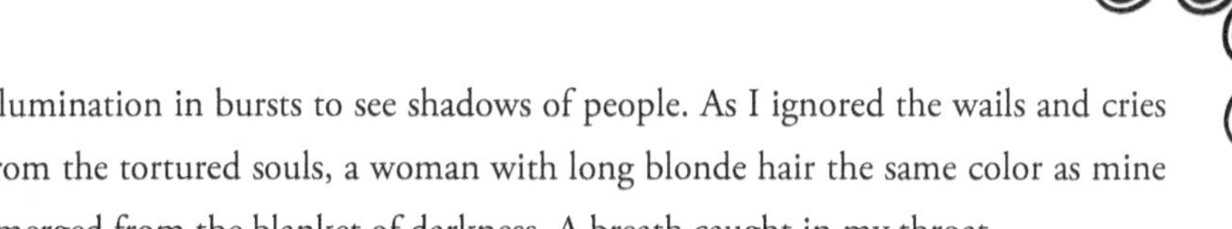

illumination in bursts to see shadows of people. As I ignored the wails and cries from the tortured souls, a woman with long blonde hair the same color as mine emerged from the blanket of darkness. A breath caught in my throat.

"Why are you here, Keira?" Her long flowing black dress made her float above the ground. Two black orbs served as eyes, and her teeth were jagged and deadly.

"You really have to ask me that?"

No regret. No remorse. Only sadness.

A tiny smile pulled at her lips. "You inherited the gift of emotion reading."

"You didn't know?" I wanted to be mad at her for abandoning me, but how could you resent someone you never knew?

"I suspected it. But I imagine there are two questions you seek answers for. Why I didn't raise you and who your father is." She cocked her head to the side, floating in front of me, and raising one pale hand to my face.

I recoiled at her touch, stepping back. "Yes."

"I wasn't supposed to be able to have children, but the Fates had other plans. A destiny that I could've only given with the gifts I possess. I was in no place to raise you and wished only to protect you from the meddling of Olympus. The mortal couple I left you with, they treated you well, yes?" She folded her hands in front of her.

"Yes. They did." Tears stung my eyes.

Did Gaea plan for my birth from the very beginning?

"Your father. You have his eyes, his nose—" She traced her fingers over her face with a small smile. "I loved him. He never knew you existed as he died before you were born. Cancer." Her glistening black gaze fell to her feet. "It was another reason that drove me here. The pain of loss."

"Did you know I had a fated bond to Zeus?" I clenched my fists at my sides.

At first, she didn't speak, and her inward gaze lifted to mine. "Yes."

"Yes?" I yelled. "You knew and you kept him from me? With the spell you put on me to keep my lineage a secret, what if—what if we had never found each other?"

"In one way or another, no matter what—you would've found each other, Keira. Fate always figures out a way. Always." She floated closer. "You must understand I did that to protect you as a child. You were able to grow up as a mortal and have a carefree childhood."

"Carefree? You think it was carefree? I didn't have anyone around to explain to me the tidal wave of emotions I felt whenever I was in public. No one to explain a way to control it. I had to figure it all out on my own." I pointed to the ground, my tone turning more infuriated with each passing word.

"And for that, I can only offer you an apology, but it shaped you into the woman you are today. A goddess. My Queen." She bowed her head.

Shaking my head, I stepped away, the agonizing emotions from the surrounding souls starting to seep their way back into my bones. "And you wish to stay here, Oizys? As an enforcer to Hades?"

"Yes, my Queen. My powers are most suited here." She bowed her head further. "One last thing before you leave. You may find yourself connected to the moon and darkness given your family ties. It may even increase your power versus the daylight."

Being the ultimate night owl made a lot more sense.

"Then so be it. If you ever wish to see me again, to get to know anything about me besides what you knew to be prophesied, inform Hades, and I'll come."

She didn't answer me one way or the other, lifted her head, and stared at me with those lifeless eyes.

Frowning, I called to Hades with my mind and instantly appeared on the banks of the river Styx.

"I'm gathering the visit didn't go as well as you hoped?" Hades squeezed my arm.

"I'm not sure how I expected it to go, honestly. I'm just thankful for some answers."

He nodded, and I glanced at my wristwatch. "Shit. The mortal job calls."

"Say something derogatory to my brother for me, would you?" A hint of smile pulled at Hades's lips before fading away.

Grinning, I made myself appear in my office at the courthouse. Already feeling his presence behind me, I pushed my fingertips against my desk, the office door creaking shut. Zeus stood behind it, casually leaning against the wall with his feet crossed at the ankles.

"Why, your honor, have I misbehaved again?" Raising a brow, I turned to face him, sitting on the edge of the desk.

When Zeus had stepped away from the Daniels case, it wasn't too difficult for

the prosecution to establish a win. The evidence had only continued to pile up against Melissa, including a testimony I managed to get from her accomplice, Jimmy, under the agreement his own sentencing would be less severe than hers. That combined with computer evidence showing her searches for "acid to digest animal tissue" when her shop only worked on soil-based items. The proof of her ordering over a year's supply of sulfuric *and* hydrochloric acid, and proof of purchase of the blue chemical barrel right before the incident—it was a shoo-in. She received life without any hope of parole, and I kept my winning streak.

Not soon after the trial ended, Zeus announced that Zane Vronti would no longer serve as a defense lawyer. He ran for a judgeship and won by a landslide. Zeus, King of the Gods, and god of justice seemed so much more fitting as a judge at any rate. Not to mention it allowed us to work in the same building and have lots and lots of scandalous office sex.

"Very. I may have to resort to drastic measures this time around." He peeled back his jacket, tapping the metal clasp on his belt.

Biting my lip and smiling, I outstretched my arms for him to hug me. Obliging, he wrapped his burly arms around me, his beard tickling my cheek as he nuzzled it.

"How'd it go, sweetheart?" He asked, his nose brushing my ear.

"I could've misinterpreted it, but it almost sounded as if Gaea made sure Oizys would get pregnant with me. She wasn't supposed to be able to have kids," I mumbled against his chest.

He pushed back, holding onto my shoulders with a scrunched nose. "You don't have a father?"

"She didn't pluck me from her head or anything, Zeus." Poking him in the chest, I gave a tiny smile. "I did have a father. He died before I was born."

He rubbed my arms. "I'm sorry. I know you hoped to meet him."

"Shit happens. I've got enough family to last me an eternity now, I suppose." Smiling, I dipped my fingers into his belt, pulling him between my legs. "Now about that punishment."

He lowered his lips to mine as he grabbed my ass, pulling me forward. I dipped my hands into his shirt, making the top two buttons pluck away as I greedily groped his chest.

"Sorry for interrupting, Keir. Sorry," Olivia said, ducking her head through

the cracked door, her hand firmly over her eyes but peeking through her fingers.

Zeus held his head low with a gruff sigh. A warranted reaction considering this was the fourth time this week we'd been "disturbed." After patting his chest, I stood and adjusted my skirt.

"Why do you have your hand on your face, Ollie?"

"Not taking any chances anymore, Keir. Not doing it. You walk in on your best friend making out with her husband one time, and that's quite bloody enough." She waved a folder of papers at me. "Just take it, and I'll be on my merry way."

Grinning, I snatched the folder, and she slipped away, shutting the door behind her. I threw the folder to my desk, knowing there were other matters to attend to before my mortal job duties.

"My turn to make the rounds, right?" I slid between Zeus's legs who'd changed positions with me. He was sitting on the desk now.

"If you're up for it. I can always do it again." He kneaded my hips with his strong fingers.

"We talked about this. Shared responsibility so neither of us burn out. Remember?" I bopped him on the nose.

He chuckled and drummed his fingers on my ass. "Then off you go."

Leaning forward, I placed my lips to his, kissing him tenderly. "Promise we'll pick up where we left off at our place later tonight?"

Our place. The penthouse I'd sneered at for months and now considered my sanctuary from the world.

"You know I'm always good for anything you ask. Especially if it involves fucking you." He slapped my ass. "Now go so you can get back."

Stepping away and blowing him a kiss that he caught and placed on his dick, I ported away laughing.

I enjoyed making rounds the most of all as part of my Queenly duties. Not only checking on all the other gods to ensure they were doing their jobs but also tuning into their well-being. Tap into their true emotions and aid if necessary. Everyone needed to be their best selves if what Gaea said was true—that the paving of progression started with Zeus. We'd all need to be ready for our world to go *beyond* anything we knew.

THE END

Well, not exactly.
Us Greek gods do love the attention
Especially. Me.

Sincerely Big Daddy Z.

ALSO BY
CARLY SPADE

Be sure to check out the first in Carly's paranormal romance series: *After Midnight*. Vampires, shifters, Aztec mythology, and enemies to lovers.

IRRESISTIBLE DEMISE

Be sure to check out Carly's Celtic urban fantasy romance with Celtic mythical heroes, creatures, and a run-in with The Dullahan, a headless death god.

POWER OF ETERNITY
(DRUID DUO, #1)

Both Available on Amazon

ABOUT THE AUTHOR

CARLY SPADE is an adult romance writer who has been writing since she could pick up a pencil. After the insanity of obtaining a bachelor's and master's degree in cybersecurity, creating worlds to escape to still ate at her very soul. She started writing FanFiction (which can still be found if you scour the internet), and soon felt the need to get her original ideas on paper. And so the adventure began.

She lives in Colorado with her husband and two fur babies, and revels in an enemies to lovers trope with a slow burn.

Find her online:

WWW.CARLYSPADE.COM